Strapped

by Al-Saadiq Banks

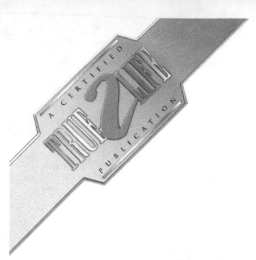

Strapped

by Al-Saadiq Banks

For information contact:
True 2 Life Publications
P.O. Box 8722
Newark, N.J. 07108

Website: www.True2LifeProductions.com
Author's E-mail: Alsaadiqbanks@aol.com

ISBN: 0-974-0610-6-9

"How do you expect
to soar with the eagles
when you're riding with turkeys."

–Anonymous

///// CHAPTER 1 /////

January 20, 1999

14 year old Amber Jones sits on the edge of the park bench inside of Weequaich Park. This would be quite normal if only it was ten hours and two seasons earlier. Instead it's the middle of the winter at 1:00 A.M.

Amber blows into her hands with hope of temporarily warming up her frostbitten fingers. They are numb to the bone. She leans over as her body shivers uncontrollably. The cold steel bench sends a body tingling chill from her rear all the way up her spine. The sensation is quite painful causing her to cry harder. The tears that leak from her eyes freeze up as soon as the air hits them, making her face even colder.

"God, why me?" she asks as she looks up into the dark sky. A sudden noise sounds off from behind her, startling her to death. Her heart pumps vigorously. She turns her head only to find a black cat cutting across her path. "Owww," she screams as she attempts to lift her feet from the ground onto the bench. Her legs are so stiff and numb that she can barely lift them. The cat's tail drags across her shin, giving her the chills. She's always heard of what would happen if a black cat crosses your path. Believing that, she can only imagine what could happen if the black cat actually ran over your feet. More bad luck, she thinks to herself. "Impossible," she utters. She truly doubts that her life can get any worse. She hopes that her bad luck results in her death because at this point she believes death would be better than living. At least she couldn't hurt anymore.

She's sure no one in the world has had a less fortunate life than she's lived in just fourteen years. Here it is the coldest day of the year and she's out here sitting in the middle of a pitch black park, cold, hungry and scared for her life. She's homeless with no one to turn to for help. "How did I get here?" she asks God as she looks up to the sky with tears leaking from the corners of her eyes.

Her empty stomach growls like a vicious pit-bull. The school lunch she ate this afternoon has evaporated in her tiny stomach. She slides her cold hands down her waist band tucking them into her cotton panties with hope of obtaining some warmth and to thaw her fingers out.

As she sits here she wonders how her life will end. Will she die from starvation? Will she be raped and murdered here in this park by some sick perverted individual or will she just die here on this bench from freezing to death? She can't imagine how her situation can get any worse off than it already is.

She peeks around nervously as she spots a man walking through the park slowly. His dark colored clothing has him camouflaged in the darkness, making it slightly difficult to see him. The closer he gets to her, the more frightened she becomes. She hopes and prays that he doesn't notice her sitting here. She sits still while barely breathing.

To her relief he passes by her without taking one peek in her direction. She watches him closely as he struts along his path until he disappears into the darkness. "Thank God," she manages to whisper through her dry, chapped lips.

Her lips are so cold, tight and blistered that they're bleeding. They're so numb that she doesn't even realize that the cold air has busted them in the seams. "Thank God for what?" she asks herself sarcastically as she thinks of the terrible hand that she's been dealt. She speaks of God every now and then but to her it's only a figure of speech. She's actually given up on God a few years ago. How can she believe that there's such a thing as God with all the terrible events that have taken place in her life? She believes that if God exists he would be here to protect her from all of this madness.

Her mind begins to wander. Suddenly her entire life plays clearly in her mind like a horror movie. She sits back and watches all the horrific events that she's seen first hand through her young eyes. Watching her life is worse than actually living it. She realizes that while living through it, she didn't have the time to sit back and evaluate the situations. Now while here on this park bench, she has no choice but to sit back and watch the Merry-Go Round that Little Amber calls her life.

///// CHAPTER 2 /////

June 10, 1991

The heavy thumping noise sounds off loudly before the sharp, ear piercing scream of terror echoes throughout the shabby apartment. Amber lies in her bed quietly, awaiting the next phase of the dilemma. Amber's mother screams at the top of her lungs, causing goose bumps to pop up all over Amber's body. Each scream sends another chill up her spine.

Amber has gotten quite accustomed to this drama due to the fact that this is how most nights end in this house. You would think that she would be used to it by now but it's just way too much for a six year old to get accustomed to.

"No more, Craig, please," the woman pleads in a hoarse voice. "Please?" she begs before the gasping begins. Her circulation is cut off by the huge hands of her boyfriend who happens to be drunk out of his mind. He chokes her abusively as if he's actually trying to strangle her to death. She gasps loudly, trying to get some air. He loosens his grip long enough for her to utter a few words. "Craig, you gonna kill me," she says as her body flops lifelessly. All the fighting has taken toll on her. She has very little energy left. "Please," she begs before the gasping begins once again.

Her words instill even more fear into Little Amber as she imagines the sight of what's happening in the back of the apartment. "Craig, please? Think about the kids in the room. Please don't do this to them," she begs.

"Fuck the kids!" he growls angrily before a loud clapping noise sounds off consecutively. He slaps her violently as she cries silently. She bites on her top lip to keep from crying aloud.

Amber's face sinks into the wet pillow which is drenched from her own tears. She reaches over and pulls her one year old sister closer to her. Her sister is sleeping like the baby that she is. Amber loves her sister dearly but at times she despises her due to the fact that she's the offspring of the man who is making her life a living nightmare. She shakes her head from side to side as she nestles her body as close to her sister as she possibly can. She slams the huge pillow over her head to drown out the noise. She grips with her free hand a portrait of her deceased father. She cries loud and hard until she eventually cries herself to sleep.

One Hour Later

Amber sits in the tub of hot water, scrubbing away when she hears her mother at the bathroom door. She sings the tune to her favorite song while being interrupted by her mother's voice. "Lil Bit," she whispers from behind the door.

"Yes," Amber replies in a sweet and innocent voice.

"I'm going to the store. I'll be right back. After you finish up, it's bedtime. Your sister is already sleep, ok?"

"Yes," Amber replies. In a matter of seconds she hears the kitchen door slam. In less than two minutes the sound of the bathroom doorknob being twisted frightens her to no end. Three light taps on the door sound off.

"Lil Bit?" The sound of her stepfather's voice instills so much fear in her little heart. She sits quietly. "Lil Bit, open the door," he whispers in a soft voice. His voice sounds calm and peaceful but Amber knows better. His voice may sound innocent but his malicious intent is quiet vicious. She sits still as if she doesn't hear him. "Lil Bit," he says a little bit louder. "Open the door," he says as he taps on the door harder. He begins to get frustrated. "Lil Bit!" he shouts with fury in his voice. He now bangs on the door. "Lil Bit, open this fucking door!" he shouts furiously. His words cause her to tremble with fear. "I gotta use the fucking bathroom! Open this motherfuckin' door! The way his words slur from his mouth makes her sure of how drunk he is. She imagines him staggering back and forth as he always does. "Hurry up. I have to use the bathroom, I said. Open the fucking door!" he says before damn near kicking the door off of the hinges. "If I piss on myself, I'm gonna beat yo little ass!" he snarls. The fear of him beating her is quiet frightening but the fear of him molesting her overpowers it.

At the tender age of six years old, her sister's father has taken the liberty of making her a woman as he likes to call it. She involuntarily lost her virginity to him a few months ago. Waking up to the touch of his hands months ago eventually evolved into him actually going all the way. The fear of what he may do to her if she tells keeps her from telling anyone. She also fears that he will kill her mother if she found out and asked him about it. He's promised her many times that he would kill her mother if she told. So instead of being the cause of her mother's death she decides to keep it to herself.

She remembers the very first time as if it were yesterday. Scared and confused she didn't have a clue of what she should do but her common sense told her to hide her blood soiled panties in her book bag and dispose of them in a dumpster near her school.

She just wishes there was someone that could protect her. The feeling of helplessness is too much to bear. She just wishes her own father were here to protect her but he isn't. He was murdered on a street corner two months before she was born.

The only thing she knows about her father is that his braveness and his temper is the cause of his death. She's been told that he was feared by many. Hearing that, makes Amber know that if he were alive he could protect her. She often dreams that her father came back to life and comes to rescue her as if he's her personal superhero. Whenever she's frightened she grabs hold of his portrait, which lies under her pillow. Even with the picture frame shattered into many pieces, she still cherishes it.

One day her stepfather saw the portrait on her bed and slammed it to the floor and stomped on it. Watching that brought pain to her heart but the words he shouted hurt her even more. "Fuck your father!" he shouted. "I'm your father! I feed you, clothe you and love you as if you're my own! He didn't love you! He didn't even want yo ass," he snickered sarcastically. "The punk mufucker didn't even want yo ass and here you are holding onto his fucking picture like he God!" he shouts as the tears poured down her face. His words may have ruined her for life.

"Open this fucking door!" he shouts as he bangs violently on the door. "Open the door you little bitch!" He bangs on the door so hard that he sounds as if his hands are about to bust through it.

The banging continues but the voice changes. The sound of her mother's voice soothes her ears. "Lil Bit?" she whispers. "Lil Bit?" Amber's eyes pop open suddenly as she awakens from the dream. She peeks around with confusion.

She finally realizes that she was having a nightmare. She wasn't trapped in the bathroom. His knocking on the bathroom door was actually her mother knocking on her bedroom door. "Lil Bit, open the door," her mom whispers.

Amber jumps out of the bed and runs to the door. Her eyes are greeted by the gruesome sight of her mother's swollen face. Her left eye is tremendously discolored. Her high yellow skin under her eye is black and purple. She leans over and picks Amber up in her arms holding her tightly as she slams the door shut behind her. She locks it quickly for safety before walking over to the small twin sized bed, where they collapse. They lay nestled close together in each other's arms. She kisses Amber on the forehead. "I love you," she whispers in Amber's ear. Amber looks into her bruised eye and the tears begin to drip from her own eyes down her pretty little face. "Mommy is ok, baby," she says as she tries to comfort her daughter. "I'm ok, and most importantly, we will be ok. One day all this is going to be over and we're going to live happily ever after. I promise you that, baby."

Amber can't take the sight that lies before her eyes. She turns away slowly.

"Lil Bit," she whispers.

"Yes," she replies as she lifts her head up and looks into her mother's eyes.

"Never let a man do this to you. Never," she says sternly. You hear me, baby?"

Amber does not reply. She's confused. How can her mother tell her this when she's allowing a man to do this to her. She's too young to understand. "Baby do you hear me? Never let a man do this to you. This is not love. It's not right. Any man that puts his hands on a woman to hurt her is a punk. This is not love," she says once again. "Love isn't supposed to hurt. A woman should be treated like a queen. Do you hear me?"

"Yes," she murmurs innocently.

"No matter what, you never forget that. No matter what," she repeats as she begins to rock her to sleep.

///// CHAPTER 3 /////

January 12, 1995

Little ten year old Amber walks down the corridor of the luxurious apartment, struggling with the many shopping bags that she holds in both of her hands. In total she holds approximately $1,000.00 worth of clothes that her big sister Ashley has bought her for her tenth birthday, which happens to be today.

"Come on, Lil Bit, hurry!" Ashley yells as she stands at the front door. Amber drags along. She's despising the fact that it's time for her to go home. If she could have it her way she would move in with her sister and never go home again. Being here is so peaceful and serene compared to the living nightmare that she lives at home.

Amber idolizes her big sister as if she's a celebrity. She looks like the spitting image of her big sister. Their high yellow complexions are identical on down to their long sandy colored hair. Ashley dreams of one day growing up and living the luxurious life that her sister lives. Ashley's fortune is all due to her boyfriend who happens to be one of the most successful drug dealers in Newark. He rescued her like a knight in shining armor several years ago. He spoils her rotten and provides a lifestyle that a seventeen year old can only dream of living.

Ashley met him when she was just barely 13 years old. Six years her senior he was already a grown man. At that time he was already 19 years old and was already considered to be ghetto rich. He was able to see beneath her shabby clothes and felt like she was a precious gem that just needed a cleaning up to make her shine like a diamond. In just a few short months of dating her, he moved her out of her mother's house where she left all her problems behind. He took her under his wing and raised her to be the woman she is today. He not only is her boyfriend, he also played the role of her deceased father. Deep inside that was something she longed for. Anything that she knows about life outside the home, he taught her. She lives the life of a ghetto Cinderella story.

Little Amber hops into the passenger's seat of the candy apple red Lexus Coupe as Ashley plops into the driver's seat. As she starts the car up, the sound of Mary J. Blige's "My Life," seeps through the speakers. Amber falls back and sinks into the creamy golden leather interior as disgust sets deep in her little heart.

Ashley peeks at Amber through the corner of her eye. She can actually feel the tension coming from her sister's direction. This is a normal reaction each and every time it's time to drop Amber off back home. It breaks Ashley's heart to see her little sister saddened like this but there's nothing she can do about it at this time. She's promised Amber many times that one day she'll let her move in with her once she gets her life together but the truth of the matter is her selfishness prevents her from doing so. She would love to take custody of Amber permanently and she's sure that with the help of her boyfriend she would be able to provide a much better lifestyle for her. By doing so she realizes that she would have to give up her freedom. Deep inside she knows that she isn't ready to take on the responsibility of raising a child, when she's merely a child herself.

"Lil Bit, stop it," Ashley whines. "Why do we have to go through this every time," she asks while pouting like a baby. Amber totally ignores her, staring straight ahead. "Please, don't do this to me?" she begs. "You know how much I hate to see you sad. Come on, you're making me feel bad," she moans. "You just had a nice birthday weekend. We spent hours of Big Sister, Little Sister time. Just think of all the fun we had this weekend," she says hoping to change her sister's attitude. "In New York yesterday, getting Doobies, manicures and pedicures," she sings. "Then lunch at Red Lobster…caught a movie…then dinner at Olive Garden. Skating this afternoon and spent the rest of the day shopping in Short Hills. Please don't make me feel like a bad big sister. You know how much I love you," she whines. "I promise you, I'll come get you and Star next weekend. You have to go to school tomorrow and on Friday I'll be there right after school. We can do whatever you want to do."

Hearing this alleviates Amber's disappointment. She turns her head and looks into Ashley's direction. "You promise?" she asks with the most desperate look ever.

Ashley turns quickly after stopping at the traffic light. They lock eyes deeply before she speaks. "I promise," she says sternly.

In a matter of two minutes they arrive in front of Amber's house. Just seeing the house disgusts her terribly. Ashley gets out helping her sister. From the passenger side of the car she watches Amber drag along toward the house.

Amber rings the bell and in seconds the door is snatched wide open for her to enter. She looks up only to be greeted by her stepfather. The smell of liquor bleeds out of his pores. The deranged look on his face is not foreign to her due to the fact that she's seen it so many times before. The collar of his t-shirt is stretched out and torn slightly, letting Amber know that she just walked in on another fight.

"Close the door behind you!" he shouts furiously.

"Psst," she sighs under her breath.

Back to the living nightmare.

///// CHAPTER 4 /////

One week later

Little Amber had been waiting impatiently for this weekend to come. She was so anxious that she marked the days off on her Barbie calendar. She's had her and her little sister's bags packed ever since Monday. Amber came alone on account that her stepfather wouldn't let Star come along.

To actually sleep a night in peace without hearing her stepfather beating on her mom is a dream come true which is one of the reasons why she loves to stay at her big sister's house.

Ashley and Amber are finally ending their long and exhausting day. Amber is so tired that she's close to sleep walking up the steps to the house. Ashley hits the remote alarm to lock the car doors. "Home sweet home," she sighs as she inserts her key inside the door of the house.

Suddenly, a shadow appears over Amber's shoulder, followed by a sudden force which snatches her from the ground into the air. She's caught by total surprise. She's wide awake now.

Another man yanks Ashley by her throat and clasps his hand over her mouth. The cold steel handgun rests on her cheek. "Bitch shut up, or I will blow your fucking head off." Ashley looks over at the masked man who holds Amber in the air. She has a gun to her head as well. A third masked man snatches the keys from Ashley's hand. He leads the way as Amber is carried into the house and Ashley is dragged inside.

They all enter the apartment where they find Ashley's boyfriend, sound asleep in the recliner. He's snoring loud and hard until he's struck across his forehead with the nose of the semi-automatic pistol. He wakes up in total shock as he looks right into the barrel. "Move and I'll end your life right now," the masked man threatens.

Amber's mouth is taped shut and her hands are tied together before she's thrown onto the floor. Ashley gets the same treatment but the man holds her by her ponytail, yanking her hair with all his might.

Ashley's boyfriend's hands get tied together behind his back. Next his ankles are tied together. One slab of duct tape seals the deal. Now the bandits are ready to get on with what they've come here to do. "Take me to the money," the man demands as he drags Ashley's boyfriend onto his feet.

"Let's go bitch," the other man barks at Ashley. "Yo, bring the little bitch in here too," he says referring to Amber who sits there in amazement. Once she's dragged into the room she's tossed onto the floor like a doll. She just sits and watches the episode play out.

"We ain't got no time to fuck around with you," the man informs Ashley's boyfriend. "I'm asking you once and that's it. Get me that money!"

Ashley's boyfriend has no problem cooperating. He realizes that he holds the destiny of three lives in his hands and the last thing he wants to do is be the cause of someone dying in here due to lack of cooperation. He murmurs to get the man's attention and with a nod of his head he directs the man to the bed.

"Hit the bed!" the man shouts. The other man slams Ashley onto the floor, face down before running over and flipping the mattress over. On the floor there sits two duffle bags that the bandits can only hope is filled with money. He quickly retrieves the bags and is happy to find out that his hopes are fulfilled.

The man begins brutally beating Ashley's boyfriend with his gun until blood spurts from more places than can be counted. "Anymore in here, nigga? Huh?" he asks as he continues to strike him viciously.

The third man turns the entire room over looking for goods. In a matter of minutes he has located and bagged up anything of any value. He's retrieved enough jewelry to open up a small jewelry store.

The other bandit grabs hold of Ashley and drags her out of the room. As they exit the room she fights as best she can under the circumstances. Her boyfriend is so busy getting beat on that he doesn't even know that she's being dragged out of the room. Amber watches with fear, wondering what's next for her sister. At this point she's so scared that she can't even cry.

He gets her into the bathroom, where he violently pops the zipper of her skin tight jeans. She squirms and wiggles as he pries the jeans down to her ankles. Of all the days for her to be wearing no panties. She wiggles and screams silently as the man bends her over the sink and pins her down. She manages to put up a little resistance until he bangs her head onto the ceramic sink, not once but three times. Blood leaks into the sink instantly. The impact of the blows knock her semi-unconscious

Amber can hear the loud noise of naked bodies clapping against each other and she's sure of what's going on. She tries to block the noise out but it's impossible. Boom! A gunshot sounds off from across the room taking Amber's attention away from the other room where her sister is. She watches as her sister's boyfriend collapses onto his knees in a crawling position. Boom! This shot causes him to fall flat on his face, while he squirms. Boom! This shot stops all his movements. Amber screams so loud that she can actually be heard over the tape that's covering her mouth. The bandit ignores her because it's so muffled. Thirty seconds later, another shot is fired from the bathroom. Amber expects to hear more but not another is fired.

Ashley lays bent over the sink with her head dangling in it as the blood fills the entire sink. The man runs back into the bedroom where his team awaits him. He runs into the bedroom with his gun dangling. Amber watches in fear as he points the weapon at her forehead. It's over, she tells herself. At this point, death would be better because she would hate to live after witnessing all of this. There's no way in the world that she would ever be the same. She closes her eyes awaiting her death.

"Ah ah!" a voice yells from afar. "She's a baby," he says with compassion. "Let's go!"

Amber looks up and sees the other two men standing over her. She has not a clue what all this is about but she assumes that they got what they came here for. Both of the men take off out of the apartment with all the bags, while the third man backpedals away from Amber slowly. All she can see are his eyes through his mask. His look is as cold as steel. He slowly tucks his gun into his waistband before back pedaling out of the apartment.

///// CHAPTER 5 /////

3 Years Later

Amber stands petrified at the hospital bed inside of University Hospital. Just being inside of the hospital gives her the creepiest feeling. The sound of all the machines sends chills up her spine. She keeps her hands tucked tightly inside her pockets, not wanting to touch anything. The thought of all the germs that are lingering around disgusts her terribly.

She stares at her mother with great sympathy. She hates to see her mom in this condition. The tube running up her nose and the IV in her arm are just a fragment of the hospital equipment that she's hooked up to.

She lays there looking like death itself. Cancer has transformed her plus size figure to a tremendously petite frame. Two weeks ago she weighed in at less than 90 pounds. Her complexion is three shades darker than normal and her thick long hair is only a memory now thanks to the chemotherapy. If Amber had not watched her deteriorate over the past two months she wouldn't even recognize her own mom at this point.

Two months ago the doctor broke the news to her that she only had six months to live. The tiny lump in her breast led her to the hospital where she was diagnosed with breast cancer in the late stages. She was already way too late, giving the doctors no time to do anything to help her.

She refused to believe that on the account of her two daughters. She desperately accepted any treatment that they had to offer her, despite the fact that several doctors told her nothing could help her at that point.

Her eyes pop open slightly. She cracks half a smile at the sight of her daughter's beautiful face. Her smile only brings more tears to Amber's eyes. She attempts to lift her arm but doesn't have the energy to do so.

Amber reaches over and grabs hold of her mother's ice cold hand. Her hand feels like the hand of a skeleton. "Ay baby," she whispers faintly from her dry crusty lips. She holds her side as the look of agony covers her face. She keeps her eyes closed tightly for over a half a minute.

Amber hates to see her mother in pain. In fact as she thinks about it, she's rarely seen her in anything but pain. One thing she does know is throughout all of the distress she's never seen her mother shed a single tear, ever. That's ok though because at this point Amber is crying enough for the both of them. Seeing her like this is breaking her heart.

Amber's mom's painful episode eases up momentarily. Her eyes open up slowly. She sees the tears rolling down Amber's face. "Stop crying, Lil Bit," she whispers. "Stop, please?" she begs as she grips Amber's hand with all the strength she has left in her body. "Baby, don't cry. I'm alright. Trust me, I don't feel as bad as I look," she says as she attempts to put a smile on her skeletal framed face. "Lil Bit you have to be strong," she says while gasping for air. "It's almost over. The end is here."

"No," Amber whispers as she shakes her head from side to side. She places her hands over her ears.

Her mom nods her head up and down. "Baby, I'm afraid it's over," she whispers. "I'm tired."

"Mommy, stop...please. You're scaring me. I thought you said you would never give up?"

"And I haven't," she replies. "But baby," she gasps. "How long do you think I can fight like this? I'm all drained out. I fight just to open my eyes."

"Well keep on fighting," Amber cries.

"I will," she gasps deeper. "Baby, listen to me carefully. It's time to step up. You have to become a woman before your time. It's not fair but it's life. I know it's early but you have no choice."

"Why Mommy? Just tell me why this is happening? What did we do to deserve all of this? You're right, it's not fair!"

"Life isn't always fair," she gasps. "But it's the hand that we were dealt. All we can do is play the hand out. Life is a big card game and God is the dealer."

"God," Amber interrupts. "If there was a God do you really think he would be putting us through all of this?"

"Amber never ever say that again. Please, baby, never," she says with sorrow in her eyes. "Sometimes he deals you a winning hand and other times you may get a losing hand. The bottom line is playing your hand to the best of your ability. Anything can happen. You can get dealt a winning hand and one wrong move can declare you the loser. On the flipside of that you can get dealt a losing hand and according to the decisions you make you can become a winner. But regardless of what, whether you are winning or losing, you wear the same face at all times. You keep your poker face on and no one will ever know if you are up or down. When you're down, the devil and your enemy becomes stronger and attacks you harder."

Listening to this makes all the sense in the world to Amber. She could never understand why her mother never shed a tear no matter what she was faced with. Her stepfather was the enemy. Now she understands why she never cried no matter how brutal he beat her.

"Lil Bit, I'm sorry," she gasps. "Your young eyes have seen way too much and it's my fault. I was not a good role model for you. In no way do I want you to follow my footsteps. I have always fallen in love with the wrong man. Men who didn't love me as much as I loved them. I've settled for these men when I didn't have to. Beating me and humiliating me in front of my children, yet and still I stayed. Before I blamed it on fear but in all reality it was stupidity. Never confuse love with desire. It's a thin line. Never love a man more than you love yourself. And never allow anyone to degrade you. Please don't follow my footsteps," she gasps. "Lil Bit, never allow a man to hold you back from being the best woman you can be. They say behind every strong man there stands a strong woman. Baby, that doesn't mean you have to stand in the back. If he's that strong he will know how to step behind you and support you when necessary. Step up and take your destiny in your own hands. I'm not telling you that it's going to be easy. It's going to take a fight but baby you've been fighting all of your life," she gasps again.

"It's going to be tough but follow these rules and it will be a lot easier. As I said before, it's almost over. The doctor has given me less than four months to live. You will have to play mom to Star. I know you will take good care of her. Please be a good role model for her. Craig promises me that he will take care of you as if you were his own."

I bet he will, Amber thinks to herself.

"You will stay with him until you get of age, get a job and you can take care of yourself.

Amber shakes her head from side to side with tears rolling down her face. She refuses to live alone with him and be forced to have sex with him, while no one is there to stop him.

"Lil Bit, I'm sorry. There is no other alternative. I know you hate him for what he has done to me but we have no other choice. I'm sure he would never do anything to hurt you."

You sure, Amber thinks to herself. The truth is burning a hole in her tongue. She's fighting to hold it back. She just wants to finally let it out. She wants to relieve herself. Holding onto the secret for almost 8 years now is driving her insane. The pressure is really starting to get the best of her. "Mommy, I can't go with him," she cries.

"You have no choice."

"Mommy, I can't," she cries harder as the truth shoots from her gut. 'I," she murmurs as she looks into her mother's eyes. She's sure that telling her mother will only make matters worse. To tell her something like this on her death bed would not only kill her faster but it will increase her guilt even more. She thinks to herself before coming up with the conclusion that it's better to keep the secret to prevent hurting her mother anymore. She figures that if she's kept the secret this long she may as well hold onto it.

A shadow appears in the doorway. Both of them face the doorway only to see Craig. Hate quickly fills Amber's heart. She always despised him but his lack of support for her mom when she needs him most makes her hate him even more.

His face is frowned up and distorted. "Come on, Lil Bit! I gotta go. I got things to do!" he shouts not even looking in her mom's direction.

Amber shakes her head with disgust. And this is the man you fell in love with, Amber thinks to herself. "Bye mom," she says before hugging her mother tight and placing a huge kiss on her stiffened lips.

Amber walks away, stepping toward the door, "Amber," her mother gasps. Amber turns around quickly. "Huh?"

"I love you."

///// CHAPTER 6 /////

One Week Later

The gravediggers lower the casket six feet into the dirt. Amber takes one long look before spinning around and walking away. The graveyard is deserted except for the gravediggers and Amber who clutches her little sister's hand tightly for comfort.

Her mom didn't even live forty eight hours after their heart wrenching conversation. As much as Amber tried to prepare for her mom's death, it still tears her apart. Watching her take her very last breath is something Amber will never be able to erase from her memory. Her mom's face appeared to have a smile on it. The smile was actually bigger than any smile Amber ever saw on her mother's face. She assumes she was happy that her pain was finally over. The end of her mother's pain is actually the beginning of her own pain.

She feels more helpless now than she's ever felt. She also feels deserted. It takes all the strength in the world to restrain herself from jumping in the ground with her mother and letting the gravediggers bury her alive. Oh how she wishes she was lying dead next to her mom. At least all her pain would be over with as well.

She can't help but wonder what the future holds for her. Life without her mother isn't worth living. Her mother's love has been keeping her strong. Now she wonders what will give her the inspiration to continue on.

Amber takes baby steps toward her stepfather's car, dreading being alone with him. She's sure that being in the house without the presence of her mother will be far worse. Now whatever his sick mind tells him to do, he will carry it out and there will be no adult there to stop him. The saddest part of it all is that she feels that she will eventually have to give in to him just to keep a roof over her head and food in her stomach.

Amber hops into the passenger seat and sinks low. She hates to even look at him. She avoids doing so by turning around and looking into the backseat where Star sits.

The car smells of alcohol and cigarettes. The pungent odor turns her stomach. As she turns around to face the front, she sees her stepfather through her peripheral. He greedily downs the remaining contents of the E&J.

"Aghh," he gulps before starting the car up and cruising away. Off to the darkness they ride.

Hours Later

Amber dries herself off, while looking in the mirror at herself. Sadness is written all over her face. The feeling of emptiness fills the house without her mother's presence. Even though her mom hasn't been here since she was hospitalized, her presence was still felt.

Amber wiggles into her panties, while reaching inside the medicine cabinet. From the bottom shelf she pulls out a box of maxi pads. She neatly tucks the pad into her panties before stepping into her pajamas. Her menstrual went away almost a week ago and yet she still wears the pad. The pad is the only protection that she has from her stepfather. Three nights he has snuck into her bedroom in the wee hours of the night and curled into her bed beside her. As she pretended to be asleep, he touched her in places that she dreaded to be touched by him or any other man. After feeling the pad, he stopped. She's sure this won't protect her for long when he realizes that it's impossible for her to still be on her period but she plans to ride it out for as long as he allows her to get away with it.

///// CHAPTER 7 /////

One Week Later

It's 3 in the morning and Amber stands in the tub as the steaming hot water pounds on her body. The water smacks her face refreshingly as the tears wash away. She's never felt filthier than she does at this moment. She's totally disgusted with herself right now. She cries like a baby as she scrubs away at herself. "Unghh," she sighs, just thinking of what has just taken place.

Either her stepfather got onto her maxi pad trick or he was just disgusting enough to want it even that way. Tonight is the worse episode that she's had with him. Just as she figured, being there alone with him would be the actual worse. With no restriction it seems as if it took him forever to finish. Normally he rushes, but tonight he took his sweet old time.

Tonight he did something totally different though. Instead of pounding away as he usually does, he was gentle with her. He caressed her and stroked her hair. The worse part of it all is that he even kissed her. That disgusted her totally. The thought of his lips on hers makes her want to tear her lips off of her face.

An hour later both of them were soaking wet in his sweat. The thought of his perspiration on her body gives her the creeps. That was almost as bad as his sexual secretions on and inside of her. Never before has she ever felt this grossed out.

She's been scrubbing away for the past hour and she still doesn't feel clean. "This is it," she whispers. "I can't take it anymore. This is it," she whispers to herself. "I refuse to do that ever again," she says as she drops onto her knees and hurdles over into a human ball. Her body jolts violently as she begins throwing up. The thought of what just happened makes her sick to her stomach.

After throwing up her guts, she just sits there allowing the hot water to bang onto her back. She cries silently. "Never again," she cries. "I'd rather die!" she says with her mouth but the truth of the matter is she doesn't mean it. She can't die right now because if she does she will never get the revenge that she plans to get for him putting her through all of this. She doesn't know how she will repay him but one thing she promises herself is that one day, he will get his just dues. She plans to make him wish that he never did the things that he has done to her. She plans to torture him before his actual murder so he will know exactly what it feels like to be tortured and taken advantage of. "One day," she cries. "One day you bastard. I promise you I will get even," she cries harder. "If I don't do anything else in my life, I promise you I will kill you with my own hands."

///// CHAPTER 8 /////

Amber lies in the living room of the shabby one bedroom apartment. The little raggedy house here on Newark Street is one step away from being abandoned. It's actually colder in here than it is outside. The entire building is rodent infested. As bad as it may sound, Amber feels more comfortable here than she did at her own house with her stepfather.

After the last night he violated her she stuck to her promise. The next morning before she left for school she packed as many clothes that she could into her book bag and off she went with plans of never turning back. It's been a little over a week now that she's been staying with her mother's younger brother. She just appeared at his doorstep and he didn't hesitate to welcome her in. He was very curious as to what led her there. After questioning her so many times she finally made up some lie about how they could never get along and all they do is argue back and forth.

She was so close to telling him the truth but her lack of comfort with him restrained her from doing so. Although this is her mother's only brother he and Amber are not close at all. In fact she barely knows him. While growing up she hardly ever saw her uncle JJ. Before the funeral she hadn't seen him in years. He spends most of his time incarcerated. His crimes range from petty larceny to armed robbery. His biggest felony which was a kidnapping sent him to prison from the time Amber was two years old until she was 11 years old.

Amber is sure that if she could muster up enough nerve to tell what her stepfather has been doing to her he would kill her stepfather. The truth of the matter is she's too ashamed to admit it to him.

Over the past week even though they're living together they still have not gotten any closer to one another due to the fact that he's never home. He stumbles in drunk out of his mind every morning right as she's walking out of the door on her way to school. This morning she opened the door and there he was laying on the doorstep sleep and reeking of cheap alcohol. She was late for school on account of it taking her damn near an hour to get him inside the house.

Today was just one more late day added onto her attendance sheet. Ever since her mom was hospitalized she went from an honor roll student with perfect attendance to a student with barely a C average. On top of that she's added 20 late days and 25 absents. At this point school is the last thing on her mind. She's more concerned with her day to day survival. It takes all the determination in the world just for her to get up and go to school each day and now that she only has 3 outfits, her foolish pride makes it even harder to go. At this rate she's sure to be a 9th grade drop-out.

Amber hated to leave her baby sister behind with the sickly perverted man but she had no choice. She realized that in order to help her sister she has to help herself first. She just hopes and prays that he's not sick enough to molest his own daughter. She doesn't know how she's going to pull it off but one day she plans to go to the house, take her little sister and never look back but right now all she can do is survive the best that she knows how.

This week has been so difficult for her. She can't concentrate on her school work because she can barely keep her eyes open. Her uncle barely has food in the house. Three nights already she's eaten sleep for dinner. If not for school lunch she would have already died from starvation. Bare necessities like soap and toothpaste she now considers to be luxuries.

Three hours ago Amber's stomach growled her to sleep. She lies there peacefully until a huge bumping noise sounds off awaking Amber. Her eyes pop open with fear. She sits up on the edge of the couch. Amber's uncle busts through the door, stumbling harder than she's ever seen him stumble.

"Lil Bit, why? Why? My favorite sister. Why?" he says in a whining voice. "I can't live without her!" he shouts as the tears roll down his face. He stands over her quietly for a few seconds just staring into her eyes. The look on his face makes Amber nervous. Her heart begins to race a mile a minute. "You're so beautiful," he whispers as he looks right through her. Now she's no longer nervous. She's petrified. The look in his eyes makes her feel extremely uncomfortable.

"You look identical to her," he cries. "Just like her. Every time I look at you, you remind me of her," he says as he leans his head back. Amber can't help but see the white powder residue that lies around the rim of his nose. The powder explains the look in his eyes. This look is not foreign to her being that she's walked in on him a few times while he's had his face buried in a small pile of cocaine. "Lil Bit," I'm sorry. I'm sorry," he slurs. "I can't take the sight of you. You're breaking my heart," he cries like a baby. "You gotta leave. Go."

"Huh?" she replies, not believing her ears.

"Go!" he shouts. "Leave. I can't stand to look at you. Go, I said."

"Uncle JJ?"

"My ass...just go!" he says with violence in his eyes. "Get the fuck up! Leave!" Amber sits there confused. "Get up!" he shouts as he snatches her by the hood on her sweater. He drags her out the bed.

"Uncle JJ, please?"

"Get the fuck out! Go!"

"Go where?" she cries.

"I don't know. Just leave. I can't look at you tonight," he says with tears flooding his face and snot leaking from his nose. "Go!" he shouts as he drags her across the floor.

She tries to grab on for her life but his strength overpowers her. By the time she realizes it she's laying in front of the door. He snatches it open wide. "Leave!" he shouts as he pushes her out the door onto the porch. The door slams shut in her face. She lies there scared and confused with no clue of her next move. Suddenly the door opens. Amber looks up with desperation. She hopes that he's come to his senses. Her shoes bang against her head, reassuring her that he hasn't. He slams the door once again.

Hours Later

Amber finds herself walking along Frelinghuysen Avenue in the dark. The light drizzle is now pouring down rain. Her wet clothes weigh a ton and makes her colder. She's been walking so long that her feet are wet as well as aching. She's been crying the duration of the long walk from across town.

At the start of her journey she just walked around not having a clue of her destination. Finally she came up with her only option, which is her mother's younger sister.

She's so close yet she seems so far away. The rain begins to pour heavily, almost blinding Amber. She really wants to run for cover but realizes stopping will only slow her down. She uses her forearm to shield her eyes from the rain. The sound of a horn catches her attention. She looks to her right, where she sees a dark colored two door vehicle cruising alongside of her. At the sight of the vehicle she already starts thinking the actual worse. Her heart skips a beat, thinking of what can happen to her out here all alone. She stares straight ahead, continuing on with her journey. She hopes that ignoring the driver will make him continue on about his business. Instead he honks the horn once again. She continues on for many steps until she reaches the corner.

As she steps off of the curb, her path is obstructed by the nose of the vehicle. She tries to step around it but it inches up preventing her from doing so. This scares her even more. Any minute now she's expecting the driver to hop out and drag her into the car. She now finds herself at the passenger's side door. "Shorty," the driver says arrogantly. She ignores him and attempts to step behind the vehicle but to her surprise he backs up quickly, blocking her path. "Shorty," he calls out again. "What you doing out here in all this rain? Let me get you out of all this mess? I know you freezing."

"No thank you," she says politely. "I'm ok."

"Come on, I will take you where you have to go."

"Thanks but I'm ok," she says with her mouth but deep inside she would love to get out of the rain. For the first time, she looks into his face and is quite surprised to see that he's a young boy himself. He appears to be a few years older than her.

"Come on girl, get outta that rain. I'll take you where you going," he says with a look of pure innocence in his eyes.

"No, I'm alright. I'm only going around the corner," she lies, knowing that she's at least twenty blocks away from her aunt's house.

"I'm only trying to help you," he claims. "Shit crazy around here. You out here soak'n wet, freezing cold on this pitch black hoe stroll."

"Hoe stroll?" she asks, not having a clue of what he means. Using the context clues, she knows any phrase with the word hoe in it can't be any good.

"Yeah, hoe stroll. Only chicks that walk down this block is selling something."

"Well, I'm not selling nothing," she says defensively.

"The next mufucker riding down this block might not look at it like that. I'd hate for the wrong mufucker to ride up on you. You know what I mean?" She knows exactly what he means. And now she's extremely frightened. "Come on, just get in the car. I'll take you where you have to go with no strings attached."

She looks at him closely, examining him thoroughly. He doesn't look like a killer or anything, she thinks to herself. Maybe his intentions are to get her where she has to go safely. But then again, maybe it isn't? A part of her wants to get in the car out of the rain and the other part of her is afraid of what he could do to her. "How do I know that you aren't one of those crazy people that you warned me about?"

"Come on, Shorty, stop it? Look in my eyes," he says while stretching his eyes wide open with a sincere smile on his face. "Look in my eyes," he repeats. "Do I look like I would hurt you?"

This breaks the ice, causing Amber to smile brightly. "I don't know."

"Get in," he says as he pops the door wide open for her. She hesitates briefly. Should I, she asks herself as she peeks around at the oncoming traffic. He doesn't look like he would hurt me she tells herself trying to make herself believe what she's saying. She takes one look at his car to see the make just in case she has to give a description.

"Come on, my seat getting wet," he says.

She drops into the seat and before she realizes it the car is cruising off. She quickly slams the door shut. She looks over to the driver's side and reads the word Acura on the steering wheel. 2 door black Acura Legend she says to herself. Her mind begins to wander. I can't believe I'm in the car with a stranger. Stupid, stupid, stupid, she says to herself.

"Let me give you a little heat," he says in a cheerful voice. "I know you freezing!" he says before blasting the heat and aiming the vent in her direction. The blazing heat knocks the chill right off of her.

The loud sound of Tupac blasts through the speakers. He lowers the volume. "What's your name?"

"Amber," she whispers.

"Nice name. Amber, I'm Mu-Fee. Amber what the hell are you doing out here alone at 12 at night? How old are you anyway?"

"Fourteen."

Fourteen? What, you a runaway?"

"Runaway? No."

"Then what the hell you doing out here? Where are you going?"

"My aunt's house. I don't know the name of the street. I just know how to get there. Go straight."

"Shorty, shit too real for your little ass to be roaming around out here by yourself like that." He stops at the red light and looks her over from her thighs up. The thickness of her thighs hardly looks like the thighs of a teen-ager. They look more like they belong to a grown up. Her drenched hood sweater clings to her body showing off the curves of her c cups. He can't believe how all that is packed into such a tiny package. She appears to be one inch taller than a midget. "Damn, you don't look no fourteen years old. I mean besides your height," he snickers. "How tall are you four foot nothing?" he laughs.

"Four feet 11 for your information," she smiles.

"You pretty," he says as he reaches over and runs his hand through her wet and silky hair. His touch makes her feel even more uncomfortable.

"Keep going straight," she says as she pulls her head away from him.

"Amber you got a boyfriend?"

"No," she laughs goofily like the child that she is.

"What school you go to?"

"Barringer Prep. Keep going straight. How old are you?"

"Seventeen," he replies, shortening his age by almost three years. He presses the buttons on his disc player and the sound of Tupac's voice is replaced by Kace and Foxy Brown's 'Touch Me Tease Me.'

"Make the right at the corner," she instructs. "Right here, right here," she says as he cruises right through the intersection. "Where are you going?"

"Cool out...take it easy. I gotta make one stop first. I have to catch somebody. After that I'll bring you right back here."

"No, you can let me out right here. I'll walk the rest of the way," she says nervously.

"Psst no. I ain't gone let you walk. A couple of minutes is all it's going to take. I just want you to ride with me for the company."

Amber sits back nervously while wondering where he's taking her. Five minutes later he turns into the parking lot of a housing complex. Amber peeks around at her surroundings. Swarms of people occupy the area. From the looks of it, heavy drug activity is taking place. "Where are we?" she asks as she peeks around looking for a sign. It's impossible to do so though being that it's pitch dark out here. All the street lights have been busted out purposely by the drug dealers so it's hard to see out here. This gives them the advantage over the police who come in here. It's easier for them to maneuver being that they know the area well. The police on the other hand are left to fumble around blind. Amber doesn't have a clue of where she is.

He rips the key out of the ignition. "Come on!" he shouts as he opens the door.

"Where?" she asks frantically.

"Calm down. Upstairs. I gotta pick something up then we out. In and out. Don't worry."

"I'll wait right here," she whispers. "Where are we? Why couldn't you just drop me off first? I could have walked! I gotta get to my aunt's house. I should have been there already. I know she's waiting for me," she lies.

"You gone get there," he smiles. "Stop worrying. You in good hands. I ain't gone do shit to you. Come on?"

"No, I'll wait right here."

"Alright," he says nonchalantly. He steps out of the car and slams the door behind him.

Amber peeks around at the scenery. She forces the door open. "Wait!" She hurries to catch up with him and walks close to him with fear.

Finally he leads her to a door. He pulls out his keys and enters the apartment. He opens the door wide open for her and she steps in. The living room is dark except for the light which is coming from the small television. The stale smell of cigarettes and musty clothes fills the air. On every chair there lays a body curled underneath a blanket. On the couch there lays one child on each end. Directly in front of Amber on the floor a pile of blankets move and a head peeks up. She can't believe her eyes. Six people sleeping in the living room. She can only imagine how many people are to a bedroom. And she thought she had it bad.

A frail woman comes creeping toward her from out of the kitchen. As they pass each other, Amber gets a good look at her. She tries hard not to stare but she looks like something from the Dawn of the Dead. They lock eyes. "Hello," Amber says. The woman continues on her way.

"Ma, take yo ass to sleep!" he shouts.

"Mu, can I get five dollars?" she begs.

"Hell no! Get the fuck out my face!"

Amber can't believe the manner in which he's talking to his mother. As the woman passes by Amber the foul smell of the woman's body odor snatches Amber's breath away.

He sticks the key into the padlock that rests on his door. He pushes it open and flicks the light on. To Amber's surprise his room is spotless. It doesn't look like it even belongs in this housing complex, let alone this particular apartment. She peeks around at the many luxuries. Her eyes are attracted to the huge fish tank that takes up the entire back wall. He grabs the remote and turns the huge movie screen on.

"You can sit down," he says as he points to the king sized bed.

"I'm ok. You said in and out."

"Yeah, in and out, just calm down," he says as he walks to his bed where he seats himself. He acts as if he's so in to the television. Suddenly he digs into his pockets, pulls mounds of money. Amber stares at the piles of money in awe. Never has she seen so much money in her life. He takes off his coat and begins sifting through the pile.

Ten minutes pass and he's still counting. Amber begins to get restless. Her feet and legs begin aching from her long walk. She stretches her legs to alleviate the pain. Just so happens he notices her. "Sit down. This might take a minute."

Finally she accepts the offer and sits on the edge of his bed. To her surprise the mattress rolls like a tidal wave almost getting Amber seasick. She assumes this must be a waterbed.

He walks over to his dresser and begins fumbling with the lock on the safe. As the safe is opened, Amber is shocked to see the many stacks of green that fills the inside. Each stack is piled high and held together by rubber bands.

He tosses the money, stack by stack onto the bed, right next to Amber. She tries hard to turn away but she can't help but to stare. She could never believe that a 17 year old could have this much money. She assumes that he must be rich beause she's never seen so much money in her life. After the safe is emptied of the money, he digs his hand in and pulls out a long nosed handgun. Amber's heartbeat speeds up. She sits still as she watches him closely. Click, click, the gun sounds off as he loads it up.

"What you doing?" she asks in a terror filled voice.

"Damn," he laughs. "Take it easy," he smiles as he lays the gun on top of his dresser. He then stacks the money back neatly into the safe. After locking it, he tiptoes behind Amber and sits closely behind her with his legs straddled around her waist. He hugs her tightly from behind while burying his head in the center of her back. "Damn Shorty," he growls sexily as he snuggles with her.

This frightens Amber tremendously. She can't take her eyes off of the gun that he put on the dresser. She wonders what his purpose of taking it out could be. She attempts to squirm out of his grip but he has her pinned against his body. "Get off me," she says sternly as she tries to free herself from his tight clutch.

"Let me get you out of these wet clothes?"

"No, I'm ok."

"Come on?" he insists. "I got a change of clothes for you."

"Come on, please?" she begs. "I have to go."

"Easy Shorty. Why you bugging?" he asks as he plants a series of soft kisses on the nape of her neck. "Cool out," he whispers. The stiffened bulge in the seat of his pants rests on her back, scaring her to death. She realizes that she should have never gotten in the car with him in the first place and this wouldn't be happening. The more she attempts to fight him off the more excited he gets and the harder the bulge gets and the more terrified she becomes.

"Get off me, please? Let's go? Can you drop me off please?" she begs.

He ignores her pleading and begins grinding on her. He grips her breast one in each hand, caressing them gently. She tries to fight him off with all of her energy but she can't get away from him. As he's holding her tightly with one arm, he slides his free hand up her sweater. She pulls away violently, snapping her bra in two. The feeling of his hand on her naked breasts scares the life out of her. With his other hand he begins petting her private part. A sudden burst of energy rips through her body. She squirms and slides off of the edge of the bed. Instead of letting her get away, he jumps on top of her pinning her to the floor. With no room to maneuver, she puts up as much fight as she possibly can. He totally disregards her fighting as he puts his hands on items that he has no business touching.

"Could you please stop?" she begs. "Please?" she says louder. "I'm about to scream," she says before he clasps his hand over her mouth. What a bad decision he's made? She sinks her teeth deep inside his hand until the taste of blood quenches her taste buds.

"Bitch," he growls before slapping her face with all of his might. The painful slap dazes her momentarily. "Fucking bite me. Why you bugging? Stop fighting with me. He leans over and kisser her on the neck. "Come on? Don't you want it? I won't hurt you, I promise." He looks down at her after realizing that she's no longer fighting with him. Her face is flooded with tears. "Stop crying," he says as he removes his hand from her mouth.

"Go ahead" she says. "Take it," she demands. "Just get it over with and drop me off," she cries. Her words catch him by total surprise. He can't believe his ears. "Come on, you want it right? Take it? This is what you wanted right? Ain't this why you picked me up? You don't have to rip my clothes off. I'm giving it to you. It means nothing to me. All my life it has been taken from me," she cries. It's worthless! Take it and drop me off!"

He crawls off of her with sympathy. She rolls over crying her head off while he stands there just watching with a baffled look on his face. He feels terrible right now. He's too embarrassed to let her know how sorry he feels for her. "Get the fuck up," he says. He uses a phony mad voice to cover up his feelings of sorrow. "Come on...get up."

Amber rolls over and crawls onto her feet. The tears pour down her face. "Fucking dick tease," he barks. "You knew what it was. Playing fucking games. Get yo ass in a bad spot. Walking in the dark and jumping in cars with mufuckers. What you think gone happen to yo ass? I was only trying to scare you up," he lies. "So you never do that shit again," he says with a cheesy grin on his face. He grabs her hand to help her up but she snatches away from him. "I just wanted to teach you a lesson. He smiles on the outside but on the inside he feels like a creep.

Fifteen Minutes Later

Amber is so grateful to see her Auntie's house. The driver has spent the entire ride apologizing and trying to make her believe that he was only trying to prove a point to her and teach her a lesson.

"Right here," she snaps.

He stops short directly in front of the house. He lowers the volume on the stereo. "Again, I apologize. For the one hundredth time, I'm sorry," he whispers.

Amber pushes the door open and makes her exit. She steps onto the pavement and walks away from the car, leaving the door wide open. She stomps away in rage. On her way up the steps, she peeks over her shoulders and watches him pull off.

She rings the bell desperately awaiting an answer. Seconds later, she rings it again. This time she rests on it. She really hates to wake her aunt but she has no other alternative.

The sound of the chain lock being slid across the door brings joy to Amber's heart. "Who?" the voice whispers angrily.

The familiar voice sounds like music to Amber's ears. "Amber," she replies.

"Who?"

"Amber."

"Who?"

"Auntie, it's me...Lil Bit."

The door creaks as it cracks open slightly. Her aunt peeks her head from behind the door. Her eyes are bulging from her head. "Lil Bit, what you doing here this time of night?"

"Uncle JJ came in drunk and acting crazy." As Amber is talking her aunt appears to be preoccupied with what's going on inside the house. She peeks back and forth behind her. Amber peeks in to see what her attention is on but she can barely see inside the apartment on account of all the thick smoke that's in the air. To her surprise a butt naked man walks pass the doorway. Her curiosity strikes. She leans in closer to get a feel of what's going on inside. She sees three men and one woman crowded around the broken down table. All of them are naked. One of the men holds a glass pipe close to his mouth.

The pipe explains the entire scene. Amber realizes that she has interrupted their get high escapade. Her aunt peeks back again. Anxiety fills her gut as she thinks of the possibility that they're going to smoke all of the crack without her. "Ay, hold up," she says as she steps slightly away from the door, giving Amber a glimpse of her naked, shriveled up ass. "Here, I come! Not now, Lil Bit. Now isn't a good time, baby. Just come back tomorrow, alright?" she says before slamming the door in Amber's face.

She stands there looking at the closed door. This was her last option, now she's stuck with nowhere to go or no one in the world to turn to for help. Now what, she asks herself as the tears pour from her eyes.

Amber's eyes pop open and she finds herself sitting on the park bench. She realizes that she dozed off momentarily. She wonders what time it is. She realizes many hours could not have passed because the sun still hasn't risen yet. She remembers looking at the clock inside of the Acura as he dropped her off and it read 12:47. Today has been the longest day of her life. She can't imagine what tomorrow will bring and in no way is she looking forward to it.

She closes her eyes and hopes to get at least a few winks of sleep. Sweet dreams.

///// CHAPTER 9 /////

Ten Years Later/ January 30, 2008

The atmosphere in the lounge is strictly for the grown and sexy. It's extremely packed but still calm. Everyone is doing their own thing with their own group. Candle lit tables shine brightly in the dim room. Plush velour couches sit on the Brazilian cherry wood floors.

The beautiful sound of Mary J. Blige's voice rips through the speakers. A woman sitting at a table in the far end of the lounge sings her heart out with the song. "No more tears," she sings. "No more fears!" she says with huge emphasis. "No more drama in my life. No more pain!" she sings looking back and forth to her two tablemates who know exactly why she's so happy to hear this song. The deejay doesn't have a clue but this is her motto song. With all the drama that she's been through in her life, she feels as if Mary J wrote this song for her.

The deejay quickly fades that song away and changes the entire mood when he brings in Kanye West's 'Good Life.' The waitress drops another tray of shot glasses onto the table in front of the three women. The middle woman passes the waitress a small stack of money in return. The woman sitting in the center of the table snatches the glasses and passes them to her tablemates. "Cheers!" she shouts as she holds her glass high in the air.

As they're holding their glasses side by side, another woman speaks. "To what?"

"To the good life," the girl in the center replies arrogantly. "Who said women can't ball?" she asks with a cocky smile on her face. "Fuck the WNBA! We the real Women's National Balling Association! Balling!" she says mimicking rapper Jim Jones.

"I'll drink to that," one of the other girls replies before downing her shot.

"Bitch, you drink to anything," the other girl replies with a smile. The liquor has them all nice and tipsy now.

"I beat the odds," the girl in the center says. "Today, I'm twenty-four years old. Happy fucking birthday to me. I never imagined seeing this age with all the shit I been through. A bitch started with nothing! And guess what? Now I got everything! And didn't have to get on the pole to do it," she smiles. "I did it my way." Kanye West's 'Flashing Lights' interrupts her speech. "Whoa! That's my shit!" she shouts as she pops up out of her seat. In seconds she's standing on the table bopping to the beat. Both of her tablemates follow her lead. The three of them dance seductively, putting on a show for the patrons. The women watch with jealousy as the men watch lustfully. The high yellow complexioned 5 foot woman in the center is by far the feistiest. The two women on the ends of her, dance and grind their bodies against hers, while she two steps to the beat confidently.

Once the song fades away, they seat themselves and transform back into the classy women that they are. Their little dance session has drawn the attention of everyone. They can feel the eyes of damn near everyone peeking at their table. No soon as they're seated, the girl on the end spots two men coming in their direction stepping cockily.

"Oh boy," she snarls. "Unwanted company," she says as she buries her eyes in her lap.

The girl on the opposite end looks the two men up and down. "FCG's (Fake Cool Guys) all the way," she says, while barely moving her lips. They all laugh at the remark. The girl in the center looks them up and down and her radar kicks in. "Hustler start up jewelry kit," she whispers, referring to the cloudy stoned Jesus medallion they both are wearing around their necks. "No karat earrings in their ears. White gold, Canal Street bubble gum machine pinkie rings. Goofy, Invicta watches. Blazer and sweater by Gap. Jeans False Religion not True Religion and shoes by Kenneth Cole or either Steve Madden. Eeelk," she laughs.

"Go that way," the other girl sings causing the other two to laugh hysterically.

"No...be nice," the girl in the center whispers. "Let's have a little fun with them."

"Ladies, ladies," the shorter man says with charm.

"What's good?" his partner follows up.

The girl in the center replies by head nod while the other two engage in a conversation of their own.

"What's your name?" the shorter man asks.

"Lil Bit," she replies, giving him her nickname.

"Hello Lil Bit, I'm Rockafella and this my man New Money."

"Hmphh," the girl on the end laughs in their faces.

"Cute," Amber smiles brightly. "Don't mind her. She's had way too many drinks. She's Deja and that's Sade."

"Hey ladies. How ya'll doing tonight?"

"Ay," Deja replies blandly. Sade, the most conservative of the three doesn't reply. She just lowers her eyes bashfully.

What's the occasion?" he asks.

"Today is my birthday."

"Oh, Happy Birthday! Let me at least buy you a birthday drink. "Excuse me Ma," he says to the waitress. "Give them another round of whatever they're drinking...on me," he says as he grabs the chair and pulls it out from under the table. "Can I?" he asks as he's sitting down.

"You already have," Amber says with a smile.

The other man sits close to Deja.

"So Amber how old are you now?"

"Shame on you," she replies. "Don't you know better than that? There are two things you're never supposed to ask a woman. That's her age and her," she says before he interrupts her.

"And her weight," he says with a smile.

"No, I have no problem telling my weight. One hundred and twenty pounds in all the right places as you can see," she says arrogantly. "No you never ask a woman's age or how many sexual partners she's had, she smiles. "It's senseless. She'll never tell you the truth anyway. She'll tell you you're the third man she's ever slept with even if you're her thirty third."

He chuckles. "I hear that."

This table is like Burger King. A man can really have it his way. Amber is 5 feet 1, 120 pounds, small waist, thick thighs, high yellow complexion, long sandy colored hair, with beautiful hazel eyes. Deja is the total opposite. She stands 5 feet 10. She's as thin as a rail but filled out in all the right places. Her skin is pitch black and her hair is a weave. Sade fits right in the middle. She's 5 feet 6, brown skin, with a short feathered haircut. She has just a few extra pounds as a result of her three children. The majority of the time she's the last choice but if they only knew, she's the best catch by far. She's the most beautiful one inside and out. She's an all around no drama type of chick unlike Amber who has so many men issues and excess baggage. Deja is just an all out problem in itself. She's the definition of the word Bitch.

The other man looks over to Deja. "You're beautiful Ma."

"Thank you but I'm not your mother. Deja is sufficient."

"Sorry Deja. No offense intended."

"Much offense taken."

"You a tough one huh? Where ya'll from?"

"Jersey," Deja replies arrogantly.

"Oh, ok, where at in Jersey?" he asks.

"Newark."

"What part?"

"What difference do it make? If I tell you, you still won't know."

"I know Newark," he says sarcastically. "I fuck around over there from time to time. I got peoples out there. The projects...Prince Street."

How did I know he was going to say Prince Street, Deja says to herself. It never fails. Whenever they're out of town and tell someone they're from Newark the first thing he says is something about Prince Street being that it's the most famous project in Newark. "So you out there a lot?" she asks, winking her eye at Amber on the sneak tip.

"As a matter of fact I was just out there not too long ago."

Deja looks at Amber before speaking. "Baby, I'm sorry to tell you but they blew Prince Street Projects up over ten years ago," she says with a cold look in her eyes.

His charming smile transforms into a tight smirk. The waitress comes back just in time to save him from any further embarrassment.

"So, what's your story?" the man asks Amber. "Married, single?"

"Happily single...by choice."

"Good choice for both of our sake."

"Oh," she smiles. "You think?"

"I'm sure," he says confidently.

"Why are you so sure about that?"

"Everybody deserves to be happy."

"And you think I'm not happy?" Amber asks.

"I mean, you may be happy but it's all a matter of what you consider to be happiness. I think I can make you the happiest girl in the world."

"Uhmm, cocky. I like that in a man."

"Nah, not cocky. I'm just confident."

"Same shit," she smiles.

"Nah, that's real talk. Fucking with a nigga like me, I can change your situation."

"Oh is that so?" This man has no clue of the danger that he's putting himself in. Amber loves a cocky man for the sole purpose of breaking him down. "Look at me," she says while staring into his eyes. "Does my situation look like it needs changing? Who are you...Prince Charming?"

"I've been called that," he smiles.

Another round of shots and thirty minutes of meaningless conversation later the lights come on. The men realize that they've gotten nowhere. They hate to accept the fact that they wasted their time and money here with these women.

The three women get up and put their coats on. They step away from the table giving the men a full view of what they will not be getting tonight. Animal Kingdom are the words that best describe their outfits. It's a shame what has been done to these poor animals just for their pleasure. Amber is dressed in a full length Persian Lamb with alligator sandals on her feet, while Deja sports a three quarter chinchilla with knee-high crocodile boots. Sade, the most conservative one of them all rocks a short mink jacket with ostrich pumps. Animal Rights Activists would have a ball with them.

Both of the men hate to see them leaving and realize that they must say something quick in order to keep them in the game. "How about breakfast?" he asks desperately.

The waitress interrupts their attempt. In her hand she holds the check. She passes it to the man as requested. The three women watch quietly as their eyes set on the bill. The man's eyes stretch wide open as he swallows the lump that forms in his throat. "I think ya'll made a mistake," he says as he passes the check back to the waitress.

She quickly reads it over. "No, that's right. Six shots...Fifteen hundred plus tax."

"That's two hundred and fifty dollars a shot. What the fuck they was drinking?"

"Louie the Thirteenth," she replies.

The man looks at the table and counts 12 empty shot glasses. In total there are 18 of them, which means they bought 12 of their own. That's 3 grand, he thinks to himself. He looks over at his partner who looks like he just saw a ghost. Embarrassment is on both of their faces. They step to the side where they pull out every dollar they have in their pockets. They begin counting slowly. They count over and over hoping that more money will appear. Together they only come up with $620.00. The cheesiest looks appear on their faces, further convincing the women that they can't foot the bill.

To their defense, one of the men speaks. "I ain't paying no fifteen hundred for no six shots! That's crazy!"

"Sir, you ordered it. You ordered two rounds of whatever they were drinking. And this is what they were drinking all night long."

"I ain't know that!"

"You didn't ask," she replies, while giving the bouncer the signal to come over. In a matter of seconds they're surrounded by eight huge gorillas. "Problem?" one of the bouncers asks.

"Yes. He's bickering over a fifteen hundred dollar tab that he has."

"Get Steve," the bouncer instructs another bouncer. In no time flat the bouncer returns walking side by side with the owner.

"What seems to be the problem?" the owner asks.

"He refuses to pay his fifteen hundred dollar tab," the waitress replies.

"Oh, that's not a problem," the owner says as he pulls his cell phone from his pocket and dials the three magic numbers.

Amber and her crew slip out of the crowd sneakily and begin walking towards the exit.

"The police are on their way," the owner says calmly.

"Police!" the man shouts. "You called the police on us and we didn't drink none of that. Them bitches drank it and ya'll letting them leave. Yo, yo! Come back!"

Amber really does want to come back but only to slap his face. There's not one thing she hates in the world more than being called a bitch. Ever since she was a kid she's been called a bitch. She also heard her stepfather always call her mom a bitch and the men who raped and killed her older sister referred to both of them as bitches. Hearing that word makes her snap. She refrains herself from going back over. Instead she just spins around facing the crowd. "When you first came over we were ladies. Now we're bitches huh?" she laughs as they exit the spot.

Three minutes later the police walk in at the peak of a loud argument and the only two who seem to be arguing are the two men who can't pay the bill. As they spot the police they lower their voices. "Officer!" he shouts as he begins to explain their side of the story.

Just as he gets to the part where he speaks of the three bitches, Amber walks in. She squeezes through the crowd and stands face to face with the waitress. "Here Mami," Amber says as she passes the waitress a small stack of crispy one hundred dollar bills. She then snatches the money from both of the men's hands. She hands the six hundred dollars to the waitress. "Tip the bitch," she says sarcastically to the men. "It's the least your sorry asses can do."

They stand there in pure embarrassment as Amber prances sexily out of the club like the Bitch that she is.

///// CHAPTER 10 /////

Amber parks in the parking space directly in front of the sign which reads 'Natural Beauty.' She hops out and steps onto the pavement. She hits the alarm on her key ring and the lights of the snow white Range Rover Sport illuminates the area. She turns to her right where Deja's cherry red convertible Lexus SC430 is parked.

As Amber steps into the crowded beauty parlor the sound of Keisha Cole's voice greets her as it seeps through the speakers. All eyes are on Amber as she struts into the room. She's quite accustomed to the attention. Something about her confident demeanor draws a great amount of attention to her.

"And now we have Miss Lil Bit on the runway," says a male in a high pitched voice. "Miss Lil Bit is blessing the runway in her casual wear. Isn't she stunning?" he asks as he pops his neck like a woodpecker. "Shoes by Prada. Jeans by Seven. Leather jacket by Bally. Handbag, shades and shoes by who else but Gucci," he sings. "Work it girl! Now turn. And tease," he adds as he prances around.

"Shut up Luscious," Amber says with a phony grin on her face. The sight of this 6 foot three, 240 pound man prancing around like this makes her sick. Amber has known him for over two years now. In the beginning she couldn't even be in the same room as him but now he's grown on her. Luscious is the shampoo girl.

Give him an inch and he will take many miles. Once he gets started he can't stop. Now he's in the middle of the floor doing the Vogue and is actually terrific at it. Amber shakes her head from side to side. What a waste she thinks to herself as she looks him over. On many occasions she's mentioned that if not for his sexual preference he would definitely be one hundred percent her type. He has a tall and muscular frame, milk chocolate complexion, ivory colored teeth with dreadlocks that drape down his back. Amber has always been a sucker for a man with dreadlocks. It's too bad that he's more gay than Marvin.

Amber plops into Deja's chair and tries to ignore Luscious as he continues to dance around.

"Luscious!" Deja shouts.

"Yes dear?" he replies as he freezes in the middle of a twirl with his hands held high.

"Lil Bit needs a wash."

"Come to mama, baby!" he shouts.

In one hour Amber's hair is tingling clean and dry. She sits in Deja's chair as Deja teases away. Deja has been Amber's beautician for all of her grown up years. In fact no one has touched Amber's hair besides Deja in over 8 years. Deja has bounced all over the state from beauty parlor to beauty parlor and Amber has followed her faithfully.

Deja's filthy mouth and nasty attitude has gotten her kicked out of every shop that she's worked in. With nowhere else to turn she spent an entire year doing hair in her apartment. That was until Amber came up with the idea of Deja opening up her own shop. Deja was totally with the idea but there was only one problem. She has a spending habit which is way out of control. All the money she's made in a lifetime and she was not able to save one dime of it.

Amber had no problem capitalizing off of Deja's shopping weakness. That was the perfect way for her to slide in and get a piece of the pie. Amber put up the $25,000.00 that it took to put the shop together. It took Deja all of five months to pay Amber $12,500.00. Now they're partners, fifty-fifty. All in all it's not as lucrative as Amber expected it to be but she has to admit that it was a stable investment which brings in a few extra thousand a month for her.

Deja's phone rings again for the third time, frustrating her to no end. She digs into her jacket pocket and snatches the phone. She reads the number on the display and slams the phone onto her work station. "I'll pass...the dick was trash," she sings quietly as she mimics rapper Lil Kim.

Amber sits with a shocked expression on her face. "Girl you are crazy." Although Amber knows how loose Deja is with her mouth she's still shocked at some of the things that come out of her mouth. She shakes her head from side to side with disbelief.

"I ain't crazy. I'm just real," she claims.

"Who was that?" Amber asks.

"The nigga I met at the New Jersey PAC at the White Affair. He is stingy as hell," she growls. "Big truck, big car, big house and a big dick. All that money and he don't wanna let a sister hold nothing," she says sarcastically. "And he can't fuck. What the hell I'm gone do with him?" she asks with disgust. "Just wasted this poor little ol wet coochie," she smiles. "You ever heard of a nigga who just big for nothing? That's what the fuck I get for fucking with these Newark niggas," she smiles. "I should have known better."

Deja is what you call an International Gold Digger. She's a seasoned veteran. Her days of milking the locals are far behind her. Ten years ago she prided herself by juicing all the so called big time drug dealers from Newark. By age eighteen that was no longer exciting or lucrative enough for her which is why she began taking her show on the road. Any event that took place, from All Star games to Super Bowl weekends she was present. She would spend her last dollar just to be there. She considered it a small investment that would pay off due to the quality of ballers that she would have access to. Hundreds of rich hustlers all in one place are the venues that she needs to be in. The quality of dudes that she met there solely depended on her which is why she would be dressed to impress.

Just last year she became bored with that scene which made her take her game to an altogether different level. She decided to no longer involve herself in dating hustlers. Her new venue is the Corporate America scene. She now targets Black Caucus events and political affairs. So far she has been somewhat successful. She's had doctors, lawyers and politicians eating out of her hand and begging for her mercy. Deja lives a lifestyle that most can only dream of. She drives the most exotic cars, wears the finest clothes, lives in the most luxurious homes and not a dime of it affects her own finances. Her entire lifestyle is funded by weak men who will do anything to be a part of her world. Her motto is 'as long as niggas making money she will be alright' and she truly believes that. Her studies have proven to her that the less sex she gives a man the more he will spend on her in an attempt to get more sex from her. Her latest victim who happens to be a CEO of a computer software company, has not had the pleasure of even smelling her panties and still he makes sure that she wants for nothing. Between the beauty parlor and what he does for her she has more material than she knows what to do with but still she can't seem to stay away from what she does best and that is playing the game.

Today she doesn't play the game to obtain material items. She just plays it for the fun of it. The idea of seducing a man into spending his riches on her gives her a rush that can't be explained. The more they spend the more she wants them to spend. To date Deja has sent many men to the poor house and her goal is to send many more.

"Talk to me, girl," Deja says as she tries to change the subject. "Tell me something good. How are things going with your little boy toy?"

"Samad," Amber says sternly.

"Damn," Deja laughs. "He's got a name now? Uhmm, you taking up for him, huh?"

"Girl please," she smiles. "I'm not taking up for him. You know I always hated when you call him that."

"Uhhmm, uhhmm," Deja sighs.

"Anyway," Amber sighs. "I don't think it's going to go much further."

"Huh? Why not? Just last week you were head over heels in love with him and he was the best man you ever met in your life. Now it's not going to go much further?"

"I'm still feeling him," she says in attempt to downplay her feelings for him. "It's just way too much pressure though. He's on some I-spy shit. He questions my every move. I'm in the bathroom, he's at the door waiting on me. I'm not used to that."

"He pussy whipped," Deja interrupts. "That's the power of the pussy, girl," she smiles.

"Whatever," Amber replies. "I hate to feel cramped like that. I don't know how long we can go on like this. I give it a few days and we will be finished," she says with a saddened look on her face.

"Hey, it is what it is," Deja says with no compassion.

"Deja it ain't that simple. I hate to cut him off but I have no choice. I'm not ready to let him into my world and explain everything to him. I mean we are like at the borderline phase. I love him but I don't know if I can trust him. Besides I don't even know if he can handle the truth."

"He probably can't," Deja interrupts. "Weigh your options. Ask yourself really, if you cut him loose what will you be losing. You can get dick from anywhere."

"Deja, this isn't about dick," she replies hastily.

"What is then? It can't be about stability! He ain't got shit. He can't possibly take care of you. He probably can barely take care of himself. Before you think of exposing your whole life to him, you need to think of that. Yeah, I heard you say he has potential but you know that can go both ways...potential to succeed or potential to fail," she says as her attention is drawn to the doorway where a young man stands.

He then starts walking towards Deja's booth. "Ma, how much you charge to do my dreads?" he asks as he runs his hands across the nape of his neck and unravels his long locks. He shakes his head arrogantly as he awaits her answer.

The door is forced open abruptly. "Everybody stay still and shut the fuck up!"

says a gun toting youngster as he runs in and makes his way over to Luscious. Another man runs in behind him. At his entrance, he immediately draws all the blinds and curtains tightly. "Shut that music down!" shouts the gunman as he forces Luscious onto the ground and places the gun onto the back of his skull.

The man standing in front of Deja draws his handgun as well. "Strip bitches, strip!" he shouts. "Money, jewels, everything! Everybody lay down!" he says as he snatches Deja by her weave.

All the women dive onto the floor at his command.

"I want it all. Bitch, you can't hear?" the man shouts as he points his gun in Amber's face.

"Owwwww!" the woman under the dryer screams at the top of her lungs.

"The next bitch that screams loses her head!" the gunman shouts as he bites down on his bottom lip. "You too, bitch," he says as he looks Luscious in the eyes.

"Please don't kill me," Luscious begs as he lays on the floor scared out of his mind.

"Shut yo faggot ass up!" the man says as he slams the gun against Luscious' head. "Give it up, faggot!" he says as he examines Luscious, looking for any jewelry. After snatching a Gucci watch from his wrist, he speaks. "Give me the money," he says as he digs into Luscious' pockets where he retrieves one twenty dollar bill. "Give me the fucking money!"

Amber looks the man square in the eyes without even blinking. She calmly begins to unloosen her watch from her wrist.

"Bitch, I said lay down!"

"Here," she says as she hands her watch over to him.

The icy Rolex gleams like a demon, bringing joy to his eyes, yet and still that isn't enough for him. "I said lay the fuck down!" he says as he rips her diamond fluttered necklace off of her neck. The other man runs rapidly around the room collecting valuables.

"Where the money at faggot?" the man asks Luscious.

"That's all I got," he cries.

"I should spill yo faggot ass just because. You bitch ass nigga," he says before slamming the gun into Luscious' head. "Go ahead and scream and you a dead ass faggot!" he threatens.

Luscious closes his mouth tight and whines to himself in order to save his own life.

"Bitch, I'm gone tell you one more time...lay your stupid ass down!" the man says as he places the gun onto Amber's nose.

Rage fills her eyes. "You already got everything," she whispers in a cool and calm manner. "I'm not laying down on the floor. You got what you wanted, now just leave."

"Bitch, you don't tell me what to do. Who the fuck do you think you are? I'm giving the instructions. Now lay the fuck down!" he says furiously.

"I told you I'm not laying down."

"Come on, let's go," the man says as he runs past them holding all of the goods.

The man pushes Deja with all of his might causing her to fall over the chair, landing on her knees. "Hold up. This bitch think it's a game. Let me bang her stupid ass brains out?"

"Come on, let's go," the man says as he waits at the door. The third man rushes to the door as well.

"I'll see you around," the man says before tapping Lil Bit on the butt. Her face turns fire red instantly. He can see the rage in her eyes. He laughs in her face. He backpedals away from her still aiming his gun at her.

The door slams shut and everyone remains on the floor quietly for seconds, just making sure the coast is clear before getting up. Everyone is scared out of their minds except for Amber who is furious and Deja who is too pissed off to be nervous. "Punk ass niggas!" she shouts as the tears well up in her eyes. "All the drug dealers out there and they gotta run up in a beauty parlor and rob some girls? I swear I seen that short one before! I just can't place his face."

The beautician to the left speaks, "he been here before," she whispers.

"Been in here?" Deja questions.

"Yeah...with Kira. That's her boyfriend. His name is Tragedy."

"Oh," Deja sighs. "Now I get it." Kira used to work here as a beautician until Deja fired her a few days ago when she could no longer deal with her. She constantly kept dilemma in the shop. She bickered back and forth with all the stylists including Deja. Her disrespectful attitude forced Deja to get rid of her. "Oh, so that's how the bitch wanna play?"

"Where is he from?" Amber interrupts.

"From up the hill," the girl replies.

"That bitch gone wish she didn't do this!" Deja claims.

"She sure will," Amber whispers.

///// CHAPTER 11 /////

Two Hours Later

Amber hops into the passenger's seat of the Toyota Avalon. "Hey," she says softly as the driver totally ignores her. He stares straight ahead, deep in a trance. Heavy tension fills the air. "Hello Samad," she says as she looks over to the driver only to be ignored again. He never even looks into her direction.

Suddenly he increases the volume of his stereo as Prince's voice blares through the speakers. "I ain't got no money!" Prince shouts. "I ain't like the other guys you hang around," Prince screams. "This might sound funny but they always seem to let you down."

Hearing Samad listen to Prince shocks Amber drastically. In no way is Prince his type of artist. He's more of a gangster rap fanatic.

"I wanna be your lover!" Prince shouts as Samad increases the volume even more.

Amber's phone rings, interrupting her thoughts. She looks down at the display and her heart skips a beat as she sees who the caller is. She immediately sends the caller to her voicemail. Seconds later the phone rings again from the same caller and she sends him to voicemail again. She then looks over to Samad and wonders why he hasn't pulled off yet. Instead he's now mumbling the words to the song. She finally puts it altogether. She realizes that he must be playing this song for a reason. She listens to the words carefully trying to understand what he's trying to say to her. Just as she is grasping the concept the song fades off. Her phone rings once again and she quickly sends the caller to voicemail.

"Answer your phone," he says as he looks over at her.

"Nah, it's nobody important."

"Shit," he sighs. "You sure?" he asks as he looks her dead in the eyes. His pupils are burning through her soul. "I mean, they calling back and forth, they must want something," he says sarcastically.

"I said it's no one important," she replies in an innocent tone.

Samad stares at her coldly. "Lil Bit, enough is enough. I can't take it anymore. This some bullshit. It's time to lay it on the table. Either you gone fuck with me or you're not. I ain't got no time for the games. I mean, all this secret shit, I ain't with it!"

"Samad, what are you talking about?" she asks, knowing exactly what he's talking about.

"Lil Bit, stop playing stupid or better yet stop playing me like I'm stupid. Everytime I think we're getting somewhere something happens where you show me that we're not. We running in place! I mean for crying out loud I'm in love with a mufucker that I don't even know! I don't know shit about you besides your name and what you drive," he laughs sarcastically. "I been fucking with you for over five months and still I don't even know where the fuck you live. Shit for all I know, you could be a fucking FED," he says as he looks over at her to see how she reacts to his last statement. "I don't even know if I can trust you. I might be getting set the fuck up for all I know! Shit, you know everything about me...where

I live, how I eat and who I eat with."

A FED?" she asks. "You think I'm a FED?" she snickers hastily. "Wow," she sighs.

"I don't know shit. I invited you to my home but I ain't good enough to go to yours?"

"Samad, we already been through this. My last relationship was crazy. Do you know how it feels to be stalked?"

"Nah."

"Oh, I didn't think so. You don't understand."

"Well, help me to. If you don't trust me why do you continue to fuck with me?"

"Cause I love you," she replies without even realizing what she just said.

"You can't love me. How the fuck you gone love somebody that you don't trust? Lil Bit keep it real with me. You got a dude right?"

"A dude?" she questions. "That's what you think?"

"Yeah, I think you live with your dude. You might not want to be with him or you're not sure and you just keep me around as a safety blanket. Maybe you're with him for the dough but you're not happy with him." Amber's phone rings once again, interrupting Samad. "That's probably him right there."

"You got it all figured out huh?"

"You forced me to figure it out on my own. What else am I supposed to think? I don't know where you live. You don't tell me shit. You move like a ghost. Trips back and forth out of town with this nigga while I'm sitting back like an asshole just waiting for you to come back. This ain't me. I ain't never been on no sucker shit like this!"

"I never told you I was going out of town with no nigga."

"That's the thing. You ain't never told me shit! This is it right here though. Either you gone tell me the deal or this little game we playing is over."

Amber sits back quietly. She knew this day was coming but damn. She assumed it would be a few weeks not two hours after her and Deja's conversation. She understands where he's coming from. Although she's in love with him she just isn't ready to open up to him. She can feel his passion about the situation and her heart is telling her to open up to him in fear of losing him.

She would really hate to lose him. This is the first man that she's ever actually loved. Before him she never knew the meaning of love between a man and a woman. Until him she always despised men. She can't even explain how he managed to sneak into her heart. When first meeting him she wasn't even attracted to him. He was the total opposite of her type. She likes muscular, dark skinned, dread heads and he on the other hand is lighter skinned, short and frail with wavy hair. He's more a pretty boy and Amber has always hated the pretty boys until she met him.

He's her first in so many ways. Of course he's not the first man that she's ever had sex with but he is the first man that she's actually made love to. Before him she never enjoyed sex and only did it to please her partner. He's the first man to take her to ecstasy and get orgasm after orgasm out of her.

"Speak now or forever hold your peace," he says.

She considers losing all of this and wonders if it's worth it.

"Well, I guess you answered me without answering me huh? I'm out," he says as he twists the key in the ignition.

"That simple huh?" She realizes that she has to say something to keep him here. "So, that's it? All I been through today for nothing. I thought we were going out to eat. I sat in the beauty parlor for hours, starving just cause I thought we were going out."

"Ay, it is what it is," he says arrogantly. "I hate to say this but when you ready to let me in and deal with me straight up, give me a call," he says as he starts the car up.

"So you putting me out?" she asks.

"No. You're putting yourself out," he says as he straps the seatbelt over his chest.

She opens the door and slowly exits the vehicle hoping that he'll change his mind. Instead he drops the gear into the drive position. She steps onto the pavement and closes the door to her happiness. She stands at the curb and watches him cruise away. The tears drip down her face slowly but her heart fills with sorrow quickly. "What a price to pay," she says to herself as she shakes her head from side to side. "What a price."

///// CHAPTER 12 /////

Later that Evening

Amber steps out of the elevator of the 26th floor condo building. "Hello Miss Baker," the concierge says pleasantly as she passes his desk.

"Hello," she replies as if her last name is actually Baker. She has been using this alias for so long that it comes as second nature for her.

The double doors open automatically. Just as she struts through the doorway the chill from the Hudson River snatches her breath away. She walks gracefully toward the beautiful black CL550 Coupe Mercedes that awaits her. She hops into the car and before she's fully seated she leans over to hug the driver. "Ay, Maurice."

He plants a soft kiss on her cheek. Before pulling off, he leans his head back to shake his dreadlocks from his face. He cruises off to get out of the doorway of the building. He parks in the empty space where they sit and view the sun setting, while they're staring into Manhattan.

"Bust it, we found out everything about him. Apparently him and his little crew known for doing wild shit like that. They been on a robbing spree for the past month. He wasn't hard to find. As a matter of fact we have him right now as me and you speak."

"So why hasn't he been handled yet?" she asks coldly.

"Come to find out he's Sal's people," he says slowly. "Seems that they have some type of rapport with each other which is why he wants to know if there's anything that can be done to squash all of this?"

"Squash it?" she asks in a harsh manner.

"Yeah," he drags. "He said he's sure he can get every piece of jewelry and every dollar back from the kid, Tragedy."

"And then what? Just forget that it ever happened?"

"Well, not forget. Just let it pass I guess."

"Well, as you already know I'm like an elephant. I don't forget shit. And as far as letting it pass, me and you both know it will never pass. If you let him get away with this, what will he do next?"

"So I take that as a no?"

"No, take it as a hell no! You should have heard him in there. Disrespectful bastard! Motherfucker put a loaded gun on my nose. He grabbed my ass," she utters with fury.

"Alright, that's what it is," he says as he starts to dial the numbers on his car phone. "I gave him my word that I would try and I tried," he says as the phone rings. "I'm calling Sal now."

"Big Nigga, what up baby?" the caller asks as his voice rips through the car speakers.

"Bust it," he says before hesitating momentarily. The anticipation wells up in the caller's heart. Maurice moves as slow as a turtle. He takes his sweet time with everything that he does, even talking. "That ain't gone happen."

"Nah?" he asks. "No way?"

"No way."

"Alright," the man whispers before the call dies.

Maurice ends the call as well.

Sal looks over to his passenger. His eyes tell it all. He starts up the vehicle and cruises off.

The passenger snatches his gun from his waistband and quickly releases the safety off of his nine millimeter. He then unrolls his skullcap and his face is quickly covered by a mask. He watches the crowd of men sitting on the porch of the abandoned house. They rapidly approach the group of men. "Right here," the man whispers just as they're a few feet away from the group of men. He forces the door open and rushes out of the van with his gun waving. Boc! Boc! He fires at the crowd just in case anyone decides to draw. He's shocked to see the crowd disperse so quickly. The man sitting on the stoop has no time to get away. His eyes stretch wide open as he sees the gunman coming in his direction. He manages to roll over onto one knee as he tries to retrieve his own gun from his waist. The masked man realizes that he has no time to waste. It's now or never. The last thing he wants right now is a back and forth gun battle. Boc! Boc! He fires as he runs up closer to his target. The first shot rips the man's clavicle forcing him backwards. He tumbles over onto his back. In his right hand his gun is now visible. The masked man fires again to keep him from having time to retaliate. Boc! Boc! Boc! The man rolls around trying to avoid being a target. He's already been hit three times and doesn't want to take the chance of being hit again. His body is exploding with pain. The masked man hovers over him. The young man looks into the masked man's eyes and could actually feel the coldness coming from deep within. Boc! Boc! Boc! He fires as he watches the young man's body bounce off of the cement after every shot. The young man stares at the sky as he watches his young life pass before his very eyes. The masked gunman continues to fire until the man lies there as still as can be. All the life has made an exit out of his body. His gun falls onto the ground, telling the masked man that he's finished. He trots over to the tinted van and the driver peels off.

Twenty Minutes Later

The Mercedes pulls up to the corner of the crowded block which is swarmed with police from corner to corner. Yellow caution tape seals the entire area off.

"Just in time," Maurice says as they watch the coroners dump the body bag into the back of the mini-van.

Amber looks at the body bag and tries to visualize the young man lying inside. For a second, she actually feels sorry for pressing the button. The image of his face is still clear in her mind as well as his voice. She can clearly see the smirk that he wore on his face when he told her that he would see her around. She remembers how many bitches she was called by him. The worst part of it all is how he recklessly pointed his gun in her face. After reliving the experience mentally, any sympathy she had has vanished. "What a Tragedy," she says with no compassion at all.

////// CHAPTER 13 //////

One Month Later

Amber sits in the living room of the tidy apartment as the loud noise of screaming children pierces the airwaves.

"I'm sick to my stomach," Amber shamelessly admits. "It's been a whole month and he hasn't even called. I could have sworn he would have called by now. I guess he really is serious," she whispers.

"Well, why don't you call him?" Sade suggests.

This is why Amber loves Sade. She's so understanding. Deja on the other hand shows no compassion at all. Amber wouldn't dare waste her time crying on Deja's shoulder, only to be told to forget him.

Having Deja and Sade as friends keeps Amber balanced. Hands down, Sade is Amber's very best friend. Sade has been there for Amber during the toughest times of her life. Back when she was homeless Sade never turned her back on her. Although for whatever reason, Sade's mother refused to let Amber move in with them, Sade still snuck her in every chance that she could. She even made sure to wash the few garments that Amber owned. Sade didn't turn her back on Amber which is why she will never turn her back on Sade. In fact Sade is experiencing a tough time in her life and the only person she can count on is Amber. Just as her mother turned her back on Amber in her time of need, she's doing the very same to her own daughter.

Sade has been a wreck for the past few months. Her husband of 4 years and first boyfriend was gunned down a few months ago, leaving her to struggle with three boys. Sade has no job and no skills to land a decent job but still she's alright, thanks to her best friend Amber who takes care of Sade and the kids just as Sade's husband did, if not better. They may have lost a major piece to their puzzle but financially they have not missed a beat.

"Girl, he's just trying to make you sweat," Sade claims. "I bet you he's somewhere just as stressed out as you are."

"You think so?" Amber asks.

Meanwhile Many Miles Away

Samad sits behind the steering wheel of the rented Toyota Avalon. He takes a huge drag of the Sour Diesel smoke before passing the blunt over to his passenger. He watches with lustful eyes as her lips wrap around the blunt. Her eyes are half closed while she puffs away. Either she's doing this purposely to turn him on or he's just a pervert to create something like this in his mind. "Uhmm, uhmm, uhmm," he whispers to himself before taking a swig of the Remy Martin. He leans back in his seat as he views the entire block. People strut along the block consistently in search of crack. This corner is fifty percent of Samad's and the other fifty percent belongs to his best friend D-Nice.

D-Nice walks up to the car and taps on the window. "One minute and we out," Samad says to his passenger as he steps out of the car. He daps hands with D-Nice.

"What's good?" D-Nice asks.

"It's all good, nigga," Samad replies arrogantly.

"How shit looking?" D-Nice asks.

"It's alright. Shit was rocking at like 6 but it slowed down crazily. I scored about three thousand altogether."

They have the block broken up into two shifts. Samad and his crew work from ten in the morning until ten at night. D-Nice and his squad take over from there.

"Shit you probably done got everything, already," he sighs. "What you about to get into now?"

"Shorty," Samad smiles as he looks at his passenger's seat. He pulls a hotel key and two boxes of condoms from one pocket and from the other pocket he pulls three sacks of smoke and a bottle of Remy. "I'm about to hit the Telly, drink like a fish, smoke like a chimney and then fuck like a jack rabbit," he smiles. "I'm gone knock this bitch head off," he says while biting down on his bottom lip.

"I hear that," D-Nice replies with a smile.

"I know so," Sade replies confidently. "I'm willing to bet everything that he's somewhere sitting around with you on his mind, just wishing you would call. Look at you...why wouldn't he be?"

"You're probably right," Amber smiles. "At least, I hope that you're right."

///// CHAPTER 14 /////

Two Weeks Later

Amber is so happy that words can't explain it. After six long, heartsick weeks Samad has finally called her. So many times doing this period she had to restrain herself from reaching out to him. She figured if she wasn't ready to open up to him then it would be better to leave him alone. She realizes doing so would have only made matters worse. Each day became harder to deal with than the last. It's a good thing that he called because she's sure she couldn't have held out much longer. Just last night she almost called him several times. Seeing his phone number pop up was like a dream come true. In no way did she hide behind her foolish pride. She answered the call before the phone could even ring a second time.

He explained to her that his reason for calling is the fact that he was in need of a favor and he went on to say that he hated to bother her but he had no one else that he could depend on. Amber didn't believe him for one second. Of all the friends and associates that he has she's quite sure that there is no way he couldn't find someone else to help him. It wasn't as if it was something top secret. Driving him to get another rental car is something that anyone could have done for him. Amber is quite sure that he just needed a reason to see her and in no way does she have a problem with that.

Samad comes walking towards Amber's truck after making his exit out of Enterprise Rental. He climbs into the truck and plops into the seat. "Psst," he sighs.

What's the matter?" Amber asks.

They don't have shit but a little Ford Focus. I ain't driving no fucking Focus! All the good shit is out and they won't have anything until tomorrow."

"He's calling you," Amber interrupts as she refers to the man who is coming out of the rental spot.

The man walks over to the passenger's side of the truck and Samad rolls the window down. The man peeks around very sneakily before speaking. "I might have something for you," he says as he looks over his shoulder.

"Now?" Samad questions. "I need something ASAP."

"Nah, later."

"Come on, Mike," Samad whines. "I need something now. I'm assed out. I ain't got no way to move around."

"I got your number," the man says. "I got a few pieces that should be coming through in a few hours. I should be able to swing something for you."

"Man, ya'll about to close in thirty minutes. Ya'll don't know how to treat customers in this mufucker. I been fucking with ya'll for over a year now. That's like three thousand a month for sixteen months."

Yo, I got you," the man claims. "I'll call you in a couple of hours," he says as he steps away from the car.

"You can pull off," he tells Amber.

"Damn you giving them three thousand a month?" Amber asks as she pulls off. "Do you realize what you could be driving for 3 gees a month? You could be driving a Bentley GT for that price. You're crazy. You gave them forty eight thousand dollars. That makes no sense. You could have bought two of those little Toyota thingies for that price."

Damn, Samad says to himself. He's never really looked at it like that. "Yeah, I mean you right but it all works out for the best. I drive all day long. I do about two thousand miles a week. I get my money's worth out of it. If it was my car I would have to worry about mileage. If something goes wrong with it, I bring that shit right back. Plus, I can switch up whenever I want to. As soon as the Jake get on to me I change cars. By the time they get onto that one I flip it again on they ass."

"I guess that makes sense."

Five minutes have passed and Amber is cruising down Route 280 through **West Orange**. Samad comforts her by stoking her hair. His touch has her extremely relaxed, making her realize that she misses him more than she really knew. She's so relaxed that she hasn't even noticed his hand which he has sneakily placed on her lap. A few gentle strokes along her thigh lead to him petting her kitten over her dress.

Suddenly, the truck heats up like a sauna. He leans over and grips a handful of her dress, lifting it up and laying it on her lap. He gently rubs the kitten until her moistness seeps through the silk of her panties. He slides his finger along the elastic near her thighs and slides one finger deep within until he reaches his destination. He pokes and strokes until she becomes wet and creamy.

The feeling becomes way too intense for her. "Samad, stop," she says with her mouth but her body begs to differ. Her lips pucker up and grip his finger tightly. "No," she says as the suction from her box draws his finger in. "Stop," she whispers.

"You really want me to stop?" he whispers sexily as he leans closer to her. "You want me to stop? I'll stop," he says as he snatches his finger out of her. "There, I stopped," he says before sticking his finger into his mouth and sucking it bone dry. "Uhhm," he sighs. The sight of that turns Amber on extremely. "Can I kiss it for you?" he asks as he leans his head over and dives face first onto her lap. He gnaws away at her panties until they are soaking wet from his saliva. He teases her by rubbing his tongue over the wet silk. Suddenly his hot breath heats up her entire body. He presses his lips against hers, "Muaahh!"

"Samad, please stop. Don't do this", she whispers as she leans her head back while still attempting to keep her eyes on the road. The feeling of his stiffened tongue being inserted into her drives her wild. She closes her eyes for two seconds, totally forgetting where she is until the swerving of her truck snaps her back in to reality. She tries hard to keep a steady pace but for some reason the needle on the speedometer won't go over 15 miles per hour.

He snacks on her for minutes before feasting away. She looks at the speedometer and realizes that she's now 15 miles above the speed limit but she can't help it. "Stop, oh, stop. Please baby stop," she begs. "I can't take it. I can't take it, oooh," she screams.

Samad knows exactly what this means. He can read her like a book. Her body language tells him what's next. He lifts his head up slightly, awaiting desert. Amber's sexual juices shoot from her fountain. "Aghh," she grunts. She tries to hold back but the feeling is unbearable. Love squirts from her like water squirts from a water pistol. Samad opens his mouth wide as she quenches his thirst.

Amber is what you call a "squirter." She's of the small percentage of women who squirt when they orgasm instead of leaking. She never knew this until she met Samad because she never had an orgasm before she met him. The first time it ever happened it freaked her totally out and made her feel ashamed. She felt like a freak of nature. Samad, on the other hand, finds it be sexy and quite kinky.

Amber slams on the brakes and the truck jolts. She sits still in the middle of the highway as her body quivers. "Aghh," she grunts. "Oooh," she sighs as he lifts his head off of her.

Minutes later she pulls in front of his building and he grabs hold of the door. Amber is praying that he invites her inside. His pussy eating escapade was fulfilling but she's in serious need of his penetration now.

"Thanks," he says as he steps out of the truck.

"Word?" Amber says, feeling totally played. "Like that?" He slams the door and she rolls the window down quickly. "What was that all about?" she asks with a tight smirk on her face.

"What?" he asks nonchalantly. "It wasn't about nothing. I had a taste for some pussy," he says as he spins around giving her his back. He walks away leaving her speechless. Her face becomes cherry red with embarrassment. She pulls off furiously.

///// CHAPTER 15 /////

The Next Day

Samad is infuriated. He's been sitting around his house all day with no means of moving around. So many times he was close to calling Amber and asking her to pick him up and drop him off on the block but he's sure what he did to her yesterday pissed her off. He refuses to let her get one up on him by denying him a favor in retaliation.

In order not to go an entire day without making a dollar and to also keep the block from losing the clientele to another block, he switched shifts with his man, D-Nice just for the day.

Finally, his phone rang twenty minutes ago with his rental car, dude asking where they could meet. Samad stands in the doorway of the Dunkin Donuts, which is at the corner of his block. He's somewhat particular of who he brings to his house which is why they're meeting here.

A black Cherokee cruises into the parking lot. Samad spots his man instantly. The slim man hops out as cool and calm as can be. He's dressed neatly in a suit and tie as he always is. "What's up, Babe?" he asks.

"Damn Mike, I blew a whole day fucking with you."

"I apologize but I'm here now. Better late than never, right?"

"I guess. What you got for me?"

"You looking at it," he says as he points to the Cherokee.

"I never knew ya'll had Cherokees."

"They don't," the man spits out arrogantly. "That's what I wanted to kick it with you about. I'm bout to blow that spot. I got some other shit brewing but I'm just working there until my shit bubble. The bills gotta get paid, ya know?"

"Yeah, I can dig it," Samad replies, not having a clue of where this conversation is going. "So what you trying to do?"

"Well...I'm gone tell you cause I dig your style but please don't mention a word of this to them mufuckers at Enterprise."

"Nah, I would never do no shit like that."

"It's like this...me and my uncle trying to start up our own little rental car spot. We're halfway there. We got the store front and like 4 vehicles. On the real, you know we can't get nowhere with only 4 cars. I just been hollering at a couple of the Enterprise customers that seem cool and try to bring them our way. The last thing I need is for them to rat me out to the big boss. I'm really just using them to get a hold of their customers so we can get on our feet. The goal is to get a whole fleet of cars but you know you gotta crawl before you walk."

"Absolutely," Samad agrees.

"It's a lot easier than it sounds. I'll bring you in if you want. Me and Unck definitely need some investors. Look how simple it is. If you have a couple of dollars you ain't doing nothing with, this is perfect for you."

Oh boy, Samad says to himself. There's the catch. Another get rich quick scheme, he figures. He has heard so many schemes in his lifetime from legal guys who figure every drug dealer is a fool and can be taken for a ride. At this point Samad isn't even interested in hearing anymore. "Unck got A-1 credit but our funds are limited. I'm gone keep it real with you, fuck limited, we don't have any funds," he smiles. "We can get five more cars for about ten thousand dollars total. Off them five cars alone we can rent them each out for a minimum of six hundred dollars a week. That's twelve thousand back the first month. That's two thousand over what you invested already. From there each car will make us over two thousand a month after paying the four hundred dollar car notes. Just five cars is ten thousand profit a month. We already got four, that's another eight thousand a month. That's eighteen thousand a month with just nine cars. All we need to do this thing right is start off with about sixteen cars and we making at least thirty thousand a month. All profit," he adds.

"Wow," Samad says. He has to admit this is the best get rich quick scheme that he's ever heard. It actually sounds like it's foolproof. He's quite impressed with it all. It definitely sounds like a good investment if only he was in a better financial situation. Right now he's having a hard enough time just surviving from day to day. "Damn, sounds real simple."

"It is. All I need is someone to believe in me and fund the project. I ain't got no problem letting a cat eat with me as long as he helps prepare the plate."

"What do you need to get rolling?"

"It's all a matter of what you can handle. I told you ten thousand can get five cars but even if you wanted to buy just one, that will help. Of course it's going to cost more than two thousand. The only reason we can get five for ten is because we buying in bulk. It's up to you though. You know scared money don't make no money," he says in a rather slick manner, turning Samad all the way off. "We will do everything by the book. Legally! You got an attorney? Put you attorney together with mines and let them draw the paperwork up where we both are protected. Just so you know that I'm not trying to beat you."

"Beat me?" Samad asks sarcastically. "I definitely ain't worried about that," he smiles.

"Nah, just so you can see that everything is on the up and up." He explains.

`"Let me think about all that. Like I said, it all sounds good. I just want to tighten up some things on my end before I go dishing money out. Feel me?"

"Of course. Take your time and think about it. The offer doesn't expire. Even if I find another investor you can always come on in."

"That's good to hear. I will definitely keep that in mind. But on this note, what's the ticket on her," he says as he points to the Cherokee.

"Ah," Mike says as he begins calculating figures. "Damn," he sighs. "You're a potential investor so I can't charge you full rate." he smiles. "The best I can do is three hundred a week. I'm at six hundred a month with insurance. That's only six hundred a month profit. Unck gone kill me. Hopefully, he'll understand. At the worse case scenario, I'll eat the loss and let him take the whole six hundred for himself.

"Sounds good," Samad says as he thinks of the extra four hundred a week he will save due to his new rental price. All in all that's equivalent to a half ounce of crack which equals another eight hundred dollar profit. That's another thirty-two hundred a month. "Profit is profit," he whispers to himself.

///// CHAPTER 16 /////

Later that night

Amber sits across from Maurice at the Cafeteria in Manhattan. Candle lit tables, good music, delicious food and stimulating conversation with Maurice and still Amber can't keep her mind off of Samad. The way he played her the other night was the ultimate worst. He made her feel lower than low but still she can't help but to miss him. As much as she misses him, she promises herself that she will never, ever speak to him again. She knows it's going to be hard but she's sure she will eventually get over him. Her mind soars and there she finds herself at the scene of the crime as Samad damn near ate her to death. Just thinking of it makes her moisten her panties instantly.

"Lil Bit? Lil Bit" Maurice says, snapping her back to the present.

"Huh?" she says with a goofy look on her face. She squirms in her seat. The slightest movement has made her panties even wetter than they were.

"What's on your mind?" Maurice asks. "You wasn't even here. You was on cloud nine somewhere."

No, Route 280, she says to herself. "Nah, just got a few things on my mind. Nothing I can't handle though." As she speaks she wonders what Samad is up to this very moment.

Meanwhile

Samad leans back in a deep sleep. It's after 2 in the morning and Samad's body knows it. Samad is used to being sleep at this hour or at least in some girl's bed. As he attempted to watch over the block just as he does in the daytime, he dozed off back and forth. That lasted for an hour until he dozed off and never dozed back on.

Samad being the light sleeper that he is hears a noise which causes his eyes to pop wide open. The first thing that his eyes set on is the shadow that hovers at the window. A hand pops the lock open through the slightly parted window. The door is now being snatched open. Samad leans to his right, away from the person at the window so he can get a view of who it is. He automatically assumes that this could be the police.

"Nigga, give it up!" the raggedy man snarls. This man being police is definitely out of the question. Samad quickly fumbles for his gun that rests under his right thigh. The man realizes what it is that Samad is reaching for. He lifts his gun and fires without aiming. Bloc! The slug rips into Samad's bicep. The impact knocks him over. He leans over in the passenger's seat, trying to shield himself. Bloc! The man fires again. This shot misses his head by only a few inches and slams right into the dashboard.

Samad now has his gun in the palm of his hand. Boc! Boc! Samad fires as the man speeds off into flight. Boc! He fires and to his glory the man is knocked off of his feet. Strangely he gets right up and continues to run like a track star. Boc! Boc! Boc! Suddenly the man stops in his tracks. He staggers back and forth as he grabs hold of his chest. Just as Samad is gaining on him, the man tumbles forward, landing on his belly. Samad stands over the man. His adrenaline is racing so fast that he has totally forgotten about the slug that's lodged into his arm. Boc! Boc! Boc! Boc! Boc! He fires at the motionless target. He continues firing until his gun is completely empty. He then spins around, leaving the dead body. He hops into the Cherokee and burns rubber away from the scene.

Ten Minutes later

Just as Maurice is paying the waitress, Amber's phone begins to ring. She wonders who could be calling her at 2 in the morning. In seconds she finds out that it is Samad. She sends his call straight to her voicemail. "Get the fuck out of here," she whispers to herself. He calls her right back. In a matter of seconds he calls her again and again and again.

"Bitch pick up the phone." Samad says aloud as he rocks back and forth trying to alleviate his pain. The pain that started in his arm has now filled his entire body. "Aghh," he grunts as another painful sensation rips through his body. He dials again but to no avail. She's probably at home sleep with her dude, he thinks to himself.

Samad peeks around nervously. His paranoia takes over and his mind begins to race rapidly. His man D-Nice already called him and gave him the word that police have come through and rounded up people for questioning about the homicide. He wonders if anyone told them anything. He's sure the chances of them not telling are highly unlikely. He's sure all it would take is to grab one of the crack heads up and offer them crack and they would sell him out instantly. He tries hard to remember who was out there at the time but he can't on account that he blacked out. All he can do is assume that all the regulars were there. He can hear it now, all the feigns telling other feigns until everyone knows who committed the murder. He's sure none of them will be able to retain that juicy gossip. For all he knows he can be sitting here in the jeep that every cop in the state is searching for. "Damn," he says to himself. "I'm sitting there minding my business and now this mufucker done got me in a situation. Damn!"

After dialing Amber once again and getting her voicemail, he figures she's not going to answer. He has to get to a hospital quick. He's afraid to go because he fears they may arrest him as soon as he comes in. He looks at the murder weapon that sits on his lap. "Damn!" He considered dumping the gun into the lake in Branch Brook Park but changed his mind after thinking of the chances of them catching up with him and then later finding the gun and linking it all together. "What the fuck?" He begins to text Amber. Pick up the phone, please, he types. I just got shot.

Back in Manhattan

Amber leads the way out of the restaurant and makes her way over to Maurice's huge black on black Dodge Ram 3500 pick up truck. Her phone alerts her that she has a new text. She's sure that it's Samad. She's actually enjoying sending him to voicemail. She can only imagine how furious he is right now. Just as she flips the phone open to read the text a strong force smacks into her behind, almost lifting her into the air. She turns around hastily.

"Tight lil ass," Maurice says sexily as he palm grips both of her cheecks with one hand.

"Stop," she says as she smacks his hand away. She reads the text and her mouth drops wide open. Her heart is pumping vigorously. She nervously begins to type her reply. What happened? Are you alright, she types as she stands at the door, not even realizing that Maurice is standing there holding the door open for her. She climbs in and he slams the door behind her.

Another text comes right in. She reads it. It's a long story. I'll explain it to you later. I'm good but I need to get to a hospital. You have to come and get me. I'm at the Shop Rite in Kearny. Hurry please!

Amber quickly types her reply. I'll be right there, baby!

///// CHAPTER 17 /////

Detectives waited around patiently while doctors removed the bullet from Samad's arm and patched him up. They questioned him and Amber for hours and still they held it down. Samad was quite impressed with the way Amber handled herself under pressure. No matter how they switched it up, her story remained the same. Samad got shot while trying to get away from a carjack situation is what they told the detectives. They told them they were getting into the Range Rover when they got attacked by the assailants.

After the interrogation, Samad was confused as to what he should do next. One thing for sure, he refused to go home. He fears that the police may be waiting for him there, that is if anyone told on him. As much as he hopes that Amber would have invited him to her home and let him stay a few nights until things cooled down, she didn't suggest it not even once. Deep down inside he should have known better. She broke his heart when she asked where he wanted her to drop him off. He went on to tell her how he feared staying home and also he didn't want to stay alone. He hoped that would make her take him to her home but still it didn't. After dropping hint after hint, he finally realized it wasn't going to happen. He's now positive that she lives with a man. After getting over the rejection, he finally told her to drop him off at the motel. When they arrived at the cheap looking motel the look on her face spoke volumes. She told him he could stay there and she would come and pick him up in the morning. She claims that she's never laid in a sleazy motel and she wasn't about to. Needless to say, her expensive taste led them to the Hilton Hotel in Short Hills. He doesn't know the price for a room but judging by the area, he's sure it costs way more than he wants to spend.

Samad has his arms spread wide in a push up position. His back spreads like an eagle. The pain in his arm is excruciating but the pleasure that he's creating for both him and Amber overpowers it. Amber lies underneath him with her legs straddled around his narrow waist. Her arms are wrapped tightly around his neck. He winds his hips while digging hard and deep inside her. The deeper he digs the hornier she becomes. She moans and groans with pure pleasure.

49

He presses his lips close to her ear. "Give it back to me, Mami! Come on, Mami, fuck me," he begs. In seconds she's doing just as he's begged her to do. She winds her hips like a belly dancer. The sensation is mind blowing. Suddenly she grabs him by his lower back and starts to slam herself into him. After a few seconds of that she goes back to winding slow but passionately.

Samad is turned on immensely. Anxiety fills his gut. He's extremely excited and it shows. He bites down on his bottom lip and begins to pound harder and dig deeper.

"Ooh," she grunts as he fills up her insides. Each thrust snatches her breath away. "Easy baby," she begs as he does the total opposite. He snatches her legs from around his waist. He grabs her by the ankles and pins her legs to her chest as he crashes his manhood into her forcefully.

Suddenly Amber's pleasure turns to fear. As she lays there her mind takes her back to her younger years when she was being molested by her stepfather. "Get off me!" she screams out as she wraps her hands around Samad's neck. His oxygen is cut off as she squeezes tighter. "Stop please!" she shouts at the top of her lungs. Samad is now baffled. Amber becomes as strong as an ox. With the strength of ten men, she throws Samad off of her.

Samad lays there on his back with a look of confusion on his face. Amber quickly curls up in a fetal position, turning her back to him. He realizes exactly what has happened. This is the second time that she's done this to him. The very first time she scared him to death. He didn't have a clue what was going on. He assumed she must be bipolar. She shamefully admitted her situation to him so he could better understand her and not think that she was a deranged lunatic. It took all the power in her to admit those details to him. She's never told any man that part of her past. Her story brought tears to his eyes. They laid there and cried together. He can't understand how a grown man could do something like that to a child. To scar a woman like that is terrible. Her story put vengeance in his heart, making him want to hurt the man that hurt her.

Samad curls up close behind her. He strokes her hair gently as he presses his lips against the nape of her neck. "Lil Bit," he whispers. She lays there just sobbing away. "Lil Bit," he whispers again. "Look at me." he says as he grabs her chin and turns her head toward him. "Look at me," he says as she lays there with her eyes closed tightly. Still the tears wring from her eyelids. She's so embarrassed that she can't even look him in the eyes. "Please, Mami, look at me," he begs. Finally, she opens her eyes slowly. They stare in each other's eyes as the tears drip down both of their faces. "Look at my face, "he whispers. "I'm not the one who hurt you. I would never hurt you," he whispers before pressing his lips against hers. "Never," he adds. "You got my word on that. Muaaahhh!"

///// CHAPTER 18 /////

February 7, 2008. Four days have passed and Samad and Amber are still here at the Hilton Hotel. Amber spends her days across the street at Short Hills Mall shopping her heart away while Samad just lays around in bed watching television.

Lil Bit just left a few minutes ago. As she walked out D-Nice walked in.

"So you sure nobody ain't say shit?" Samad asks curiously.

"Nah man. Them niggas know better. They only grabbed up Fu and Shane. You good. It ain't nothing to worry about with them."

"Alright. You know them better than I do. Samad doesn't have much of a rapport with them because they're part of D-Nice's crew. When they switched shifts they switched crews as well. They felt it would be better to keep the designated crew out there at their normal times so they would be familiar with the nightshift operation. Samad would have felt more comfortable if his own crew would have been present. At least he knows who is who. "Yo, I gotta get that Cherokee over to Sal at the autobody shop in the morning to fix that big ass hole in the dashboard. I gotta get out of that ASAP. I'll be damn if they catch me riding around in that. You never know who saw me leaving in that."

"No question," D-Nice agrees.

"Yo, that mufucker caught me slipping. I was sleep like a mufucker. I don't know where the hell he came from."

"I think I know," D-Nice claims.

"Yeah?"

"Yeah. When I pulled up on the scene that night everybody was telling me how the shit went down. You know, praising and cheering and shit. All the while I'm digging the nigga Ashy Mu. His face was sour as hell. He wasn't feeling that shit at all. He was trying to act real regular but his face was looking crazy. Feel me? I think he set the whole shit up. Who else would know you was sitting in a jeep a half a block away? And you never been in that jeep. You just got it that day."

Samad nods his head up and down. "You got a point."

Ashy Mu is an old head stick up kid who just came home from jail about a month ago. He watched Samad and D-Nice grow up. They always admired his style since they were kids but once they started hustling they started to despise him after realizing in this game guys like Ashy Mu are their enemies.

When he first came home he told them that he's turning over a new leaf. He claimed that he was tired of robbing because it's gotten him nowhere. He told them that he wanted to try his hand at hustling. Neither of them trusted him or wanted to deal with him but he begged and begged until D-Nice finally gave in.

"And my lil man told me Ashy Mu took the gun off the dead nigga," says Samad.

"Yeah...that's a no brainer. That had to be his work. I mean it's a good thing he took the pistol cause they would have matched the bullet I had in my arm with that gun and it would have been a wrap." He shakes his head from side to side. "Ashy Mu, I told you he wasn't right!"

D-Nice looks down at his watch. "Damn, let me get out of here. I have to pick ol girl up. Bitches crazy. At first she was pushing her car on me...take it, take it. Now she be bugging, acting like I'm some Herb using her for her car and shit," he says with agitation in his voice.

"Yo, give that bitch the car back and get a rental," Samad suggests.

"Shit! I ain't giving nobody no fucking eight hundred a week for no rental car!"

"Cheap mufucker," Samad laughs. D-Nice has to be the tightest and stingiest dude that Samad has ever met. He'd rather catch the bus than to have a car note and have to gas the car up everyday. "I told you I got the hook up. Three hundred a week, that's it."

"That's still twelve hundred a month," he says as he stands up. "So how long you plan on laying up in here?"

"I don't know. A couple of days till shit cool off. I'm coming out tomorrow though to handle shit with the Cherokee. You got any money on you?" Samad asks knowing what his answer will be.

"Nah, not really," he lies. Never does he leave his house without at least twenty-five hundred on him. Leave it up to him he would love to go back home with the same amount. He'd rather starve than to break a bill. "Like what?"

"About a stack or two?"

"What?" he asks with a high pitched tone. "A thousand or two? Man!" he says while shaking his head from side to side.

"I got you "B"...soon as I get to my house. I don't know how much this room gone cost me and I been eating up that room service shit."

"Man, you laying up in this mufucker and you don't know how much it's gone cost? You bugging "B". Nigga you across the street from Short Hills Mall. That's like being in Beverly Hills. How much you think it's gone be? A grip nigga. You been staying at the Motel! What's the difference now? Let me guess, you trying to impress that bitch, Lil Bit, right?"

"Psst, hell no!"

"Oh she too good to stay at the Motel?" he asks sarcastically. "She gotta lay up in Short Hills, right? Like her pussy don't stink. Why she didn't take you to the crib? Listen man you setting yourself up for failure. You gone fuck around and drop the pot fucking with that bitch. Man, look at that bitch, she got everything and don't work nowhere. She got an '08 Rover, diamonds galore, crazy shoe game. You said the bitch got watches that cost thirty thousand dollars. More than one too, right? You can't buy her one of them mufuckers," he says with huge emphasis. "On the real you gone go broke fucking with her."

"Nigga I ain't spent a dime on that bitch yet."

"Yeah, dig what you just said...yet. She's a professional. She ain't gone ask you for shit in the beginning but when she do it's gone be big. She's gone wait until she know she got you reeled all the way in and you fear telling her no cause you don't want to lose her to the next nigga who can give her what she wants. I just hope you ain't stupid enough to give her everything and go broke behind that bitch. You gotta keep it real with yourself. You can't afford her Bruh," he sings. "Right now it's all good cause she don't need shit. Somebody holding her down but when the well run dry and it's time for you to step up to bat, Bruh," he says as he shakes his head from side to side.

Samad analyzes the entire situation and as much as he hates to admit it, he thinks D-Nice is right. It all makes so much sense after he's explained it. Deep down inside he knows he can't afford her. He figures it may be best to cut her off before she puts him to the test and asks for something that he can't deliver.

"Bruh," D-Nice whispers with his eyes stretched wide open. "You better get out while you still got the chance. Let that bitch go about her bizness!"

///// CHAPTER 19 /////

Days Later

Samad is getting dressed while Amber is in the shower. They're on their way to pick up the Cherokee from the auto body shop. Things are moving as usual on the block from what D-Nice has told him. The Jake hasn't been around in days.

He hasn't been out in days. It's time to get back on the street but first he has to get out of that truck. He will never feel safe riding around in that.

As he's brushing his hair he looks at a receipt that's laying on the nightstand. The figures cause his eyeballs to bulge from his head. "Twenty nine hundred dollars," he whispers. "For five days?" He reads further only to see that the hotel bill has been paid. This confuses him. If Amber is the gold digger that D-Nice thinks that she is, then why did she cover the bill, he asks himself. He thinks about this momentarily. Maybe all this is part of her trap. She does for you so you have to do whatever she asks. If she puts up $3,000.00 for him he can only imagine what she may ask from him in return. "Fuck that," he says to himself.

Amber walks out of the bathroom naked and wet. What a gorgeous sight. Goosebumps cover her entire body. Her pink nipples stand at attention. Her hair is plastered to her face, draped over her shoulders.

She walks over to him and presses her body close against his. She bites down on to his top lip seductively. "Can I get a little more before we leave?" she mumbles with his lip still in her mouth. "Please?" she begs as she grabs a handful of his manhood.

As much as he would like to make love to her he refuses. "Nah, we ain't got time. I gotta switch this truck," he says as he digs into his pocket. "Here," he says as he counts quickly. "Why did you pay for the room?"

"Huh? Psst," she sucks her teeth. "Baby, it's nothing. I didn't ask for the money back."

Oh it's something, he says to himself as he thinks of the trap she may be setting. Maybe today it's nothing but one day it will be, he says to himself as he looks her square in the eyes. "Here," he says as he drops the money into her pocketbook, that's on the nightstand.

Hours Later

A man and a woman stand face to face in the narrow alleyway between two abandoned houses. "Can I get three for twelve?" the woman begs as she stands there rocking back and forth. She watches the bag full of crack closely with greed in her eyes. Her mouth is watering just looking at it.

"Damn Betty, you ain't never got straight money," the man barks as he digs into his zip lock bag. He drops the small plastic bags of crack into the palm of her hand and she quickly passes the money over to him. In seconds she vanishes.

The man quickly counts the money before adding it to the pile that he already has. Three steps away a man scales the wall cautiously. As he gets to the end of the house he steps unexpectedly into the tight alley. The barrel of his gun gets there before he does. The crack dealer looks up. His eyes stretch wide open with fear as they set on the sight that lies before him. Boc! The nine millimeter sounds off deafeningly. The loud noise echoes back and forth between the two empty houses. As the crack dealer collapses the gunman fires again. Boc! The victim's neck snaps backwards sadistically. He lays there on his back motionless. The gunman grabs hold of the money which is laying on the ground. He then frisks the dead man's body until he finds what it is that he's in search of. He snatches the gun from the dead man's waistband and takes off toward the opposite end of the alley.

Once he gets to the other end he spots the get away car which is parked at the curb awaiting him. He quickly climbs into the passenger's seat of the Cherokee and the driver cruises off at a somewhat normal speed. He's trying not to draw any attention to them.

The passenger unties the hood from around his face and snatches it off. His adrenaline is still pumping and his heart is pounding through his chest. He takes a few deep breaths to try and regulate his breathing.

"You finished him?" D-Nice asks anxiously.

"You already know," Samad replies with a blank look in his eyes. "Sneaky bastard. I told you he wasn't to be trusted," he says as he looks at the gun that he took from Ashy Mu. He's positive that this is the weapon that he was shot with the other night. "Here it go," he says as he holds the gun in the air. "Yo, let's go and put this truck up. First thing in the morning I'm calling the nigga Mike. I'm getting the fuck outta this firecracker!"

///// CHAPTER 20 /////

March 21, 2008

Amber and her baby sister Star come walking out of the nail salon slowly. The cheap flip flops smack onto the ground causing them to walk goofily. Amber pops the locks to her truck and they climb inside.

They've spent their entire day making themselves over as they call it. That consists of getting their hair and nails done, their eyebrows waxed and their bodies sugared. Now they both are feeling completely brand new.

Amber loves hanging out with her little sister doing girlie things together but it only makes her realize how much she misses her older sister Ashley. She hates the fact that Star never got to know Ashley. Amber always pictures how life would be if Ashley were alive. She's sure that the three of them together would be one big mess. Ashley may be gone but she's definitely not forgotten. Not one day passes that Amber doesn't speak to her spirit. Each time she looks at Star she sees Ashley. Ashley and Amber favored one another but Star is the mirror image of her; all the way down to the petite waist and the jumbo behind. Amber feels like she was cheated in the ass department. All the women in her family had too much behind. Amber on the other hand feels like she doesn't have enough. Men beg to differ though. She always makes fun of Star telling her that she can fit four asses her size in Star's ass.

Amber enjoys and appreciates Star's company. It's rare that they get a chance to hang out together now that Star is away at school. Star is a sophomore at Morgan University. Star hated to go away but Amber insisted. She said she was willing to do everything in her power to make sure that Star makes something of herself. She promised her mom that on her deathbed and she is not about to go against her word. She refuses to lose her little sister to the street like she did with her older sister.

Amber has had total custody of Star for the past six years. When Star was 13 years old she admitted to Amber that her father had been molesting her for years. It broke Amber's heart to hear that. She felt so guilty because she knew he was sick and still she allowed her to live with him. Amber commends Star for her braveness. If only she had her courage back then she would have told someone. Had she done so he would have been arrested then and her sister would have never been violated but she didn't and now she has to live with that guilt for the rest of her life.

Amber knows the effects that has had on her and still has on her and she assumes that her sister goes through the same thing which is why she spoils her. Deep down inside Amber is trying to erase the pain that she may have but the reality is she knows more than anyone that there's not much that can be done to erase the traces of that experience. To live life after that type of experience, Amber wouldn't wish that on her worse enemy.

Star's father has been incarcerated for six years now. Amber could only imagine how much it hurt Star to get her own father locked up but selfishly she disregarded that entirely. Amber felt like Star was pressing charges on behalf of the both of them being that she didn't have enough heart to stand up for herself. All the trauma he has put them through and he was only sentenced to not even eight years. Amber was hoping for the death penalty or the lethal injection.

"Baby Sis," Amber says. "Run into the bank and deposit this check into your account, through the ATM," Amber says as she hands Star a check.

Star looks down and reads the amount of one thousand dollars. This is Star's monthly allowance. Amber makes sure that she doesn't have to work so she can put her full attention on her schoolwork. Most importantly she doesn't want her sister to need a man for anything. She wants to eliminate any distractions. Amber knows how easy it is to fall victim to guys who take care of you which is why she takes care of Star so well. She buys her any and everything that a dude could buy her and more just so Star is never tempted by what a guy can do for her. That's her plan and up until now it must be effective because outside of her father she has never had sex with another man. It hurts Amber to know that her sister would still be a virgin at almost 20 years old, if it wasn't for her own father.

Star gets out and trots toward the bank. Amber laughs to herself as Star's behind rumbles like an earthquake. Her velour sweatpants don't have enough material to support all of her thickness. Audience clapping is not louder than the noise that she's creating. Thunder clapping is more like it. Those sweatpants are a no-no, Amber says to herself. She can't even imagine Star in those sweatpants without her supervision. She's sure the boys at her school would be flocking to her like bees on honey. "I gotta make sure to hide those sweats before she leaves," Amber says to herself.

Amber calls Samad. She hasn't heard from him since yesterday. She's called him several times but he hasn't answered. She hopes everything is ok with him. She sits there patiently as the phone rings.

Meanwhile

"What's good?" Mike asks as he steps closer to Samad.

"Man, I want out of the Cherokee," Samad says in an agitated tone. He puts his mad face on to pump a little fear into Mike.

"Why? What's wrong?" Mike questions.

"Psst…man, that shit riding fucked up," he lies. He can't tell Mike the truth that he got shot in the truck, caught two murders in it and used it as the getaway car.

"Fucked up? That's a brand new truck. What is it doing?"

"It's sluggish as hell and it be stalling," he continues to lie.

"Yeah? Damn, I gotta check that out. That shouldn't be happening. It ain't even a thousand miles on that truck."

"I know. What else you got?"

"Shit," he replies. "Nothing else but that," he says while pointing to the silver Chevy Impala. "And that's for my personal use so I can get around."

"Alright, let me get that then?"

"Come on man. I kinda like that shit. Today is my first day driving it."

"Come on Mike you know the policy, the customer is always right," he smiles.

Mike shakes his head from side to side. "I can't argue with that," he says as he holds the keys in the air.

Samad snatches the keys and takes off. "Yo, the key is in the ignition!" he shouts. As he gets into the car he reaches for his phone which is ringing. Once he sees that it's Lil Bit's number he just listens to it ring.

He's avoiding her by all means. He analyzed the situation and finally gave in and accepted the truth of the matter that he really can't afford a girl like her. He decided to quit while he's ahead. He figures now is the perfect time to cut off their relationship before either of their feelings begin to go overboard.

His phone alerts him that he has a text message. He quickly reads it. I guess you on that bullshit again, it reads. No hard feelings though. I understand. I'm a big girl. I was just worried about you and wanted to know if you are alright?

He quickly types his reply. I'm good.

Amber reads his reply and her temperature rises to the roof. "All this motherfucker has to say is I'm good?" she says aloud to herself. "You got that," she blurts out as she starts typing away.

Samad reads the message and it looks as if it's jumping out of the phone. FUCK YOU NIGGA! The message leaves him speechless. Little does he know her feelings went overboard months ago.

///// CHAPTER 21 /////

Amber and Deja stand side by side of each other in the crowded bar. The men who surround the bar are paying more attention to them than they're paying to the half a dozen half naked women who are on the stage dancing their hearts away.

This is Amber's first time in a go-go bar. It was Deja's idea for them to come. Deja's long time friend called and told her that him and a couple of his boys were in town and were about to go to Cinderellas. He said he only had a few hours to spare and his boys wanted to come here. He wanted to see her as well so he figured he could kill two birds with one stone by inviting her along. Deja had no problem coming to meet him here. She's sure by just coming here she can get at least $5,000.00 out of him and the good thing about bringing Amber along is that he knows that getting sex from her is out of the question.

Amber had to admit it to Deja that she's actually having fun here. She stands there bopping to Rapper Fifty Cent's 'Candy Shop' as she downs yet another shot of Patron.

"You downing them shots, girl," the man says in a heavy southern accent. The heavyset man is Deja's friend, Tiny. At 6 feet 4 and almost 400 pounds there is nothing tiny about him. He's as big as a house but his bank account is bigger. Tiny is from Texas, so Deja has given him the nickname, Big Texas.

She met him in Cancun about ten years ago and they've been friends ever since. She sees him maybe once or twice a year but his Western Union drops to her are quite frequent. He's up here on business. In all the years that Deja has known him he's never told her what type of business he's into. She's never asked but her senses tell her exactly what type of business it is.

Him and his crew of five other men stand in a huddle as three women stand in front of them dancing away to Fifty Cent's 'Just a Lil Bit.' They're competing for the men's attention. Each of them tries desperately to outdo the other. The men constantly tip away. The singles begin flowing like water and before you know it every dancer on the stage has made her way over to the group of Texans.

"Look at these thirsty bitches," Amber says. "Playing themselves. Look at homegirl. She let this nigga put his dirty fingers in her coochie for a lousy ass dollar? Wow," she sighs, not believing her very eyes.

"Look, look, look," Deja says. "No he didn't just kiss her pussy," Deja says as the man kisses it once again. The girl then turns around on the bar putting her enormous rear in his face. She backs up close to him as he stuffs dollar bills in her g-string. Before you know it he buries his face deep in between her cheeks. He grabs hold of her waist while she waves her tail like a puppy. "Nasty motherfucker," Deja laughs. "And he got the nerve to have on a wedding band," she says as her eyes set onto the huge icy platinum ring. "Now what bitch think her husband is at the go-go bar eating go-go ass?" Deja asks with a look of disgust on her face.

"The sound of Jay-Z and Jermaine Dupri's 'Money Ain't a Thing' comes on. "Ooh, that's my shit," Amber says before singing along with the artists. "I'm about to show these country motherfuckers how we party up top," she says as she digs into her pocket and stacks a small pile of singles onto the bar in front of her. She waves a few bills in the air as bait and suddenly she reels one in. The beautiful Asian girl steps sophisticatedly over to Amber. Her chinky eyes are locked into Amber's eyes the entire time. She stops short directly in front of Amber. Amber hangs the dollar bill high in the air, teasing the girl immensely. The Asian dancer reaches for the dollar bill but Amber lifts her hand higher. She shakes her head from side to side. "Not that easy Ma," Amber says as she waves the girl on to come closer to her. The girl leans over the bar. Her perky rounded breasts sit perfectly on top of the bar. Amber tucks the bill deep into the tight cleavage of her bosoms. Amber tucks another and another. The girl stands up squeezing the life out of her breast in search of another dollar. Using her hand, Amber gestures for the girl to turn around. The Asian girl spins around slowly and bends over slightly, poking her firm little rear in the air. Amber leans over the bar and tucks a bill down the waistband of her thong. She then smacks the girl's butt with a gentle tap. The Asian girl stares at Amber over her shoulder and blows a sweet kiss to her. All the customers sit back and watch Amber's private show. Before you know it all the dancers are swarming around Amber and Deja. Amber has the attention of everyone in the bar.

Ten minutes have passed and Amber is still in control of the spotlight. In front of her and Deja are five huge piles of singles. Amber is enjoying herself so much that she's traded in $1,000.00 for 1,000 singles. One by one she passes a bill to each of the girls. They're damn near fighting for Amber's attention and she loves it. She looks at these girls and can't understand why some of them are doing this. A few of them are drop dead gorgeous with bodies that are to die for. For them to stand here and degrade themselves for a lousy dollar bill is absurd. She figures what they need is for someone to school them to the game. Men are so weak for beauty. Off of their beauty alone they could find a man who would take good care of them; or a woman for that matter.

Rapper Webbie's 'Independent' comes on and Amber absolutely loses her mind. She sings along at the top of her lungs as she bounces around staring into the faces of the men in the bar. "I.N.D.E.P.E.N.D.E.N.T. Do you know what that mean? She got her own house! She got her own car! Two jobs, work hard, you a bad broad!" she sings arrogantly. "When you call her on her cellular she tell you she don't need," she sings as she smiles at Deja. "She got her own house! Drive her own whip! Range Rover all white like her toe tips," she sings as she holds her Range Rover key in the air for everyone to see.

That song quickly fades off and Fat Joe's 'Make It Rain' replaces it. In seconds Amber picks up a mound of singles and in the air she tosses it. The dancers two step seductively, catching money as it showers onto them. Amber tosses the money, mound after mound until the singles are no more.

The tall sexy Latino girl sneakily passes a piece of paper to Amber as she passes by her. Amber looks down at the paper and sees that it's a phone number. She lifts it up to show Deja. "Look," she laughs. "One more," she says as she drops the paper onto the floor where four other numbers lie.

"These bitches crazy," Deja smiles.

Minutes pass and the party is over. Deja leads Amber toward the door when Amber feels a tapping on her shoulder. She spins around slowly and there she stands face to face with her little Asian dancer.

"Ya'll leaving without me?" the girl asks sexily.

Deja stands there with a surprised look on her face.

"Excuse me?" Amber says.

The girl bites down on her bottom lip seductively before speaking. "I said are ya'll leaving without me?" she whispers. "Excuse me, I apologize," she says as she extends her hand to Amber. "I'm Asian Caramel and you?"

"I'm Lil Bit," she replies with a smile.

"Lil Bit, you're gorgeous. I never even consider going out with customers but for some reason, you're different. I mean maybe it was me but earlier tonight when we stared into each other's eyes I felt a connection."

"A connection?" Amber says with a smile. "Mami, you are beautiful, trust me but I'm sorry to tell you that there was no connection. It was all in your mind. You've taken this thing way out of context. On the real I don't go that way. I respect ya'll hustle but I was just having a good time. No more no less."

A look of disappointment covers the Asian girl's face. "I'm sorry."

"Don't be," Amber says. "It's no problem Mami. Nice to meet you anyway though," she says as she turns around and exits the bar. Amber looks at Deja with a smirk on her face. "Bitch crazy," she laughs.

Deja laughs hysterically. "Uhhmm, uhhmm, uhhmm!"

///// CHAPTER 22 /////

April 5, 2008

This has been one hell of a weekend. Here it is Saturday and Amber and Deja have been partying away since Wednesday. Amber has been trying hard to keep her mind off of Samad but it's hardly working. Every clear second she has, Samad fills her mind. She's already let her pride go days ago. She calls him several times a day but he never answers. A few days back she drove through his block to see if she could catch up with him but to no avail. A few times she's driven right past him but being that she doesn't know what he's driving she doesn't know what to be on the lookout for.

Today is an extremely special day for Maurice. They've been here at the Sand Bar in Jersey City for a few hours now. Bottle after bottle has been popped until not one is left in the entire building.

"No more champagne?" Big Nigga asks the waiter. "This some bullshit." Today marks his 40th birthday. Although they're celebrating his birthday, they're partying no different tonight than they do any other day. They party until the champagne is no more. That's their motto. "Aw man," he sighs. "When the champagne gone we gone," he smiles as he looks around at his table of six men, Amber, Deja and three other women.

Amber is familiar with all the men at the table. They're all a part of Maurice's Federation as he calls it. The women on the other hand Amber doesn't know any of them but knowing how sneaky Maurice is she feels it's safe to assume that they could easily be his jump-offs.

The smell of money is in the air. At this table there is a couple of million dollars in jewelry alone. Maurice and the Federation have enough ice on to freeze the entire room. By far this is definitely the coldest area in the room. When they stepped in the building dudes started sneakily hiding their own jewelry shamefully.

The waiter stands at the table waiting for the money. He shivers just standing here. The frost from all the jewelry is causing a major draft. Maurice hands the waiter a stack of brand new one hundred dollar bills. The waiter slowly peels through the stack of 180 bills. In all his years of working at this bar never has he seen anyone drink up $18,000.00.

Maurice then hands him another stack of ten hundred dollar bills. "That's your tip Playboy."

In minutes they're dispersing out of the club. Someone must have turned out the lights becomes the club becomes dark and gloomy once they're gone. The dazzling diamond jewelry they're wearing is now illuminating the dock area.

People swarm the dock along the rail just staring into Manhattan over the Hudson River. It's a beautiful Spring night just barely over 70 degrees. All the people on the dock watch inquisitively as Maurice and the Federation step off of the dock and into his birthday present. Ever since he was a young kid he always loved boats. He promised himself that one day he would buy himself one and today on his 40th birthday he's made his dream come true.

He spent the whole winter boat shopping until he finally found the one to his liking. The 43-foot cruiser yacht is a boat lover's dream come true. It's a 12 passenger with two bedrooms, one bathroom, full kitchen, wall to wall carpet, walnut wooden doors, three televisions, sun bed on the top deck, refrigerator and ice maker on the back deck and a radar and navigation system. Today is his first day actually cruising the Hudson in it. He's totally satisfied with it and believes that it's worth every penny of the $300,000.00 that he spent for it.

As Amber is stepping into the yacht, Maurice runs behind her and sweeps her off of her feet. She wraps her arms around his neck tightly. As her head is dangling in the air her eyes set on a familiar face. She double takes just to make sure that her eyes are not deceiving her. She now triple takes. Please God, say it ain't so, she prays as she adjusts her eyes. There leaning on the rail is Samad.

Standing right next to Samad is D-Nice. A sour look is plastered on Samad's face. He can't believe his eyes. His gut is bubbling right now. He tries to act nonchalant but D-Nice has been around him all his life and can read him like a preschool book.

""Smooth, what up?"

"Nothing," Samad answers in a high pitched tone.

"Shit," D-Nice sighs. "You ain't got that tight ass face on for nothing. Something happened," he says as he looks around nosily.

Samad stands there as hurt as can be. A part of him wants to tell D-Nice but he's too embarrassed. He looks at this group of men who are fully loaded with expensive jewelry, hopping into a yacht and realizes that in no way can he compare to these dudes. D-Nice's point has been further proven; he can't afford her.

He leans on the rail, heartbroken and disgusted as he watches the yacht pull off and coast up the river.

Amber lays on the top sun deck sprawled across the sun bed next to Deja. "Damn," she says to Deja. "Girl, I feel so bad. You should have seen his face. It was so pitiful," she says shaking her head from side to side.

"He'll be alright," Deja says with no sympathy. "Girl, the motherfucker ain't called you in weeks or even answered your calls. Fuck him!"

"No, Deja. You should have seen the look on his face."

Seconds later Amber's phone alerts her that she has a text message. She retrieves it and quickly reads it: Just as I figured. I asked you do you have a dude and you denied. All you had to do is keep it real with me and give me the opportunity to either deal with you like that or not.

She types her reply quickly: I know what you saw but I swear it is not what it looked like.

He reads her message and texts her back: It's all good though. Now the feelings are mutual. You said fuck me. Now it's fuck you. For now, for good and forever.

Amber reads his reply and her heart sinks. "I don't believe this shit," she whispers to herself.

///// CHAPTER 23 /////

Days Later

Amber looks absolutely stunning today dressed in her pinstriped Carolina Herrera business suit. The three inch stilettos not only add height to her but it adds thickness to her already beautiful legs. Her hair pinned up in a bun coupled with the tiny squared frame Cartier glasses gives her a sexy nerd type of look.

She steps stylishly through Newark International Airport. A few steps later, she boards the plane and makes her way to the middle where she locates her seat. She drops into the seat and instantly her eyes drift out of the window. There is nothing more that Amber enjoys in the world than flying. While soaring in the air she feels as free as a bird. She finds flying to be relaxing as well as pleasurable. No matter what it is that she's going through the moment she steps into the airport she starts to feel at ease. As she boards the plane her mind starts to become clear. Once the plane departs her worries seem to disappear.

For the first time she's on the plane doing something other than relaxing. Samad has her mind so tied up that she can't unwind. She decides to attempt to call him one final time before the plane departs. She quickly pulls her cellular out and dials his number. The phone rings twice before it's picked up.

"Hello?" says a woman in the sweetest voice. Hearing this woman's voice shocks Amber to death. She pulls the phone away from her ear and looks at the display. She figures she may have dialed the wrong number. She quickly hangs it up and tries again. "Hello?' the same voice greets.

"Hello," Amber says in a low voice.

"Yes?"

"Yes, can I speak to Samad?"

The woman giggles. "I'm afraid now isn't a good time. Samad is tied up. He'll have to call you later, Dear."

"Excuse me," Amber replies in a sarcastic manner. She then hears the clicking in her ear telling her that the woman has hung up on her.

"Attention all passengers, the plane will be departing in five minutes. Please turn all cell phones and electronic devices off at this time."

Amber is livid. Bastard, she thinks to herself. She wonders if he instructed that woman to answer his phone or she took it upon herself to do so. She hates to feel like the butt of the joke.

Samad stands against the hood of the Chevy Impala which is parked on his block. The Impala is surrounded by four unmarked police cars. Down the block there are two more cars parked on the sidewalk as the police raid the crack house that his crew works out of.

Police are everwhere on the block. They're searching the Impala high and low. One cop is in the trunk. One is in the front seat and one is in the backseat while the last one has the hood popped searching. The young female undercover cop stands a few feet away from Samad. In her hand she grips Samad's cell phones. For the past twenty minutes she's been answering his phone hoping to receive a phone call from potential crack buyers.

Apparently someone down the block made a sale to an undercover cop because when they looked through Samad's money they located a particular bill that they were in search of. Although he wasn't involved in the actual sale he's been back and forth in the midst of the action all morning. Samad has no clue how long they've been watching the block but he does know that he's driven back and forth at least ten times already.

As he stands there alone the thought of making a break for it comes to mind but the tight handcuffs that are ripping through his wrists reminds him that he will not get very far.

The huge white gorilla grabs Samad by the neck and drags him to the police car where he literally slams him into the backseat. "Why ya'll taking me for?" he asks as he tries to play stupid for them. The driver starts the engine up and speeds off totally ignoring Samad. Samad looks ahead where he sees two police cars leading. He then turns around where he sees a string of police cars following.

They ride for a matter of minutes. Samad was expecting to be taken straight to the Sheriff Department's Bureau of Narcotics Division but they're going in a totally different direction. He becomes curious as to where they're taking him until they turn onto the block where he lives. He's now scared shitless. The passenger holds his license up and reads his address off of it.

"You got the keys right?" the driver asks.

"Yes," the female officer replies as she holds the keys high in the air. Samad's phone rings again for the twentieth time. "Damn baby they're blowing you up," she says as she turns around and smiles at him. "You must be a real ladies man?"

I can't believe this shit is happening he says to himself. All this seems like a dream. He's just waiting to wake up. Damn, I'm going to jail. This is Samad's very first run- in with the law ever. He thinks of what he has in his house and becomes sick. He realizes that there is enough evidence in there to send him to prison. Shit, he thinks to himself. He knows it's too late now but he sure wishes he didn't have his address on his license. How stupid, he thinks to himself. I must be the dumbest drug dealer in the world. He prays that D-Nice isn't still in the house. If he is and the both of them get locked up, getting bailed out is out of the question.

The cop parks in front of the building and the driver runs to the building followed by many others. The passenger sits in the passenger's seat quietly. The presence of the police has drawn the attention of all the neighbors. They stand on their porches, their lawn and others are hanging their heads out of their windows. Samad ducks down low in his seat with embarrassment.

In twenty minutes the first officer appears in the doorway. In his hand he holds a plastic shopping bag and in the other he holds two Nike boxes. Samad's heart stops beating. The second cop walks out dragging D-Nice along with him. Samad assumes that he must have still been asleep. He's wearing a tee shirt, boxers and Timberland boots. The officer slams him into the backseat of the car that's parked in front of them.

The driver opens the door and drops into the seat.

"What we got?" the female cop asks anxiously.

The driver dumps the goods onto her lap. A smile pops up on her face as she peeks into the plastic bag where she sees hundreds of little baggies with tiny rocks of crack in them. She then opens one of the boxes where a small yellowish colored brick lies along with a small digital scale. "How much crack is that?" she questions.

"256 grams," the officer replies. Samad can't begin to imagine how much time he will face for this. She opens the second box where stacks of money lie and a 357 revolver. Her eyes stretch open widely.

Damn, $30,000.00 down the drain, Samad thinks to himself. In that box lies all the money that Samad and D-Nice have been able to save together. Both of them have their own personal savings as well. The driver pulls a shoe bag from his hoodie pocket and holds it in the air. Samad recognizes the bag. It's D-Nice's stash where he keeps his personal money. Samad hopes and prays that they didn't find his. "Whatever is in those boxes is what we're reporting," the driver says. "This right here is ours," he smiles. "We found a bag with $11,000.00 in one room and in the other room in this bag we found a little over $20,000.00. That's like 3 grand apiece for all of us. Here," he says as he hands her the bag. "Merry early Christmas," he smiles.

"Thank you," she replies. A gun too?" she says. We got drugs, money and a weapon. That's enough to fry their asses. Dumb motherfuckers, she says. "Don't you know better than to have everything in one place? Ya'll drug dealers need to take drug dealing 101," she teases. "Never have your money and your product in the same place. Dummy!"

How dumb he really feels right now. He thinks of the loss they have just taken. They have lost over fifty grand and another 15 grand in product. They didn't even get a chance to put a dent in the work and here they are getting arrested for it. Samad thinks of the entire situation. Not only are they going to jail and need bail money for the both of them but they also owe D-Nice's cousin $7,500.00 for the 300 grams of crack that he fronted them on consignment.

"Not bad for our first bust of the day," she says.

Not bad for who, Samad asks himself but he does realize that it could be a lot worse. He could still have had the murder weapon and the gun that he took from Ashy Mu in the house. It's a good thing that he took the guns to his uncle two days ago or his life would be over right now.

Samad sits there in disgust as the cars pull off slowly. He can't imagine how he's going to get them out of this situation. What a way to start the day, he says to himself.

/////// CHAPTER 24 //////

Three Days Later in St. Thomas, Jamaica

Amber stands in the dining room of the huge lavish mansion. She stands in the center of the room wearing nothing but her bra and panties. Here she stands half naked in front of four men yet she has no shame at all due to the fact that she's gotten accustomed to it.

The long dread headed Jamaican kneels down in front of Amber as he tapes the kilo onto her thigh. The cocaine is packaged tightly in a rubber casing. After it's tight and secure he tapes another one with an inch of space in between them. After taping three down her thigh he goes on to tape one around her shin. He does the same process on her other leg.

Here it is a half naked gorgeous woman standing in front of four men and they all sit as cool and calm as can be; all except one of them. One man stands guard at the huge mahogany double doors. In his hand he grips an Uzi. Directly across from him stands another man who stands at the window overseeing the land that surrounds the huge estate. The mansion is surrounded by a 20 foot wall. Standing at the only entrance of the wall there are two other dreads who both hold machine guns in their hands as well. In the attic of this mansion there is always a watchman present each day all day. This house is as secure as Fort Knox and it should be.

These men's job is to serve and protect Muhsee. Muhsee sits at the very top of the throne of Jamaica's drug trade. He's earned his position with the help of his army by stomping over and demolishing any and everybody who appeared to be in his way. His huge business is not a secret to anyone, not even the officials who are also afraid to oppose him. With a murder count way above the hundreds they have well enough reason to be afraid.

Amber stands here with a total of nine kilos strapped to her body. The man steps over to a huge closet where he takes one more kilo from the shelves and shelves of kilos. In the closet there are more kilos than can be counted. As Amber is getting strapped she attempts to count the kilos as she always does. To this day she's had no success in getting the exact count. Before she can ever get a third of them accounted for the strapping process is finished. The highest number she's ever counted was a little over 800 and even then she had many more to go. All in all she estimates billions of dollars worth of pure cocaine of the highest quality to be in that closet.

Amber looks around at Muhsee's soldiers. Their demeanor is so frightening. Their eyes are cold and blank. They barely even blink. They only speak when spoken to by Muhsee. There is one more soldier present. He stands a few feet away from Muhsee. He stands about the same height as Amber and weighs nothing. In his hands he holds the biggest gun of them all. He has a baby face but his eyes are arctic. He may look young but his eyes show that he has an old soul. This is her first time ever seeing this particular soldier which tells Amber that he must be a new recruit. Amber peeks at him curiously and wonders how old he is. The number she comes up with is not a day over twelve.

Amber looks around at the many soldiers with their heavy artillery and actually wonders what would happen if the officials did muster up enough heart to come in and try to interrupt the operation. All she can imagine is one huge bloodbath.

The man tapes the last kilo across Amber's flat tummy. "Turn around," he says as he examines her, making sure that she's strapped securely. As she spins around, Muhsee who sits at the head of the dining room table gets a view of Amber's rear which appears so tight and firm. Amber may be small but it's amazing how all her goods are compressed into her compact little body. Muhsee watches lustfully. His eyes pierce through her like a knife. It's as if he's wearing x-ray glasses the way he's removed her bra and panties, just imagining what she looks like completely nude.

Amber faces him and catches him looking at her with lust and perversion. With no shame he continues to stare for a matter of seconds before lifting his eyes and looking directly into hers. She stretches her eyes wide open and tilts her head. "Damn," she says. "So disrespectful," she smiles.

Amber has gotten familiar with Muhsee and learned how to deal with him. His militant demeanor is what instills fear into people as it did when she first met him. In the beginning she was afraid to even breathe around him. She figures the best way to handle him is by treating him regular and ever since she's been doing that she's had him totally confused. He can't understand why she doesn't show him the fear that everyone else shows him. What he doesn't know is she probably fears him more than anyone else in the world but that she will never show him.

Muhsee smiles devilishly. His pink lips part slightly, exposing his bright white teeth. He stands up slowly. His lean but muscular torso is exposed being that he's shirtless. His enormous arms are well-developed and detailed perfectly. His beefy chest tapers off into his undersized waist. His upper body appears to be twice the size of his legs.

Prior to Amber coming here to Jamaica all she knew about it was what she saw on television. After seeing Muhsee she realized that American television does a severe injustice to Jamaican men. They always make them up to look like hideous and unattractive men. Muhsee on the other hand by far is one of the most handsome men she's ever laid eyes on even in the United States. His arrogant demeanor, pitch black skin and his heavy accent are just some of the things that Amber finds sexy about him. Nevertheless, this is business and she would never ever cross the line.

Muhsee steps toward her swaying from side to side with a cocky swagger. "Aren't you tired of this?" he asks with a heavy accent. His accent is so strong that there are times that Amber can barely understand him but over the years she's learned to adjust to it. "When are you going to let me take you away from all of this? You're too beautiful to have to do this. You should be with a man like me who will treat you like the queen that you are. This is not the life for you. Please let me take you away from all of this? You can forget about all of this and you and I can live happily ever after."

"And what, move in here with your ten other wives you got around here?" Amber asks with a smile.

"Psst," he sucks his teeth. "Ten? No way. The women you see are maids and cooks," he claims. "Meaningless women. For you I will throw everyone out of here," he says with a grin on his face. "I will move you far away from here. Buy you a house miles away from here."

"You want to buy me a house? Buy me a house in the States," she says sarcastically.

"That's no problem. I will buy you the biggest house they have there. Money is no object you know. Just marry me and I will give you the world," he says with sincerity in his eyes.

"Muhsee, please," she says as she's putting her clothes on. The two of them go through this each and every time she comes here. Amber doesn't take him serious one bit but she has to admit that his persistence is quite flattering. At times she has wondered what life would be as the wife of a Jamaican drug lord. She imagines it to be way crazier than the life she's already living.

The fact that Amber pays him no mind drives him crazy. His arrogance makes him feel like he's every woman's dream come true. He has money, power and looks and still he can't figure out why Amber pays him no attention. The fact that she doesn't, makes him desire her even more. Muhsee is used to getting everything he's ever wanted at any cost. Little does Amber know he has plans of getting her and he will never give up until he has her by his side.

Now Amber stands here fully clothed in baggy clothing which hides the curves of her body as well as the kilos that are strapped to it. The clothing which is at least two sizes too big for her is perfect. There's not a bulge in sight. She spins around slowly. "How do I look?" she asks looking at Muhsee.

"Beautiful," he says with passion and sincerity in his eyes.

"Boy, shut up," she says playfully. "You think you a real Cassanova, huh? Get me out of here. I have a plane to catch," she says as she examines herself.

Thirty-five minutes Later

For some strange reason Amber's gut is filled with queasiness as she steps through Montego Bay's Sangster International Airport but she manages to maintain her confident swagger. No mater how long she does this she hopes to never get so used to it that she takes it for granted. She constantly reminds herself that if she's ever caught she can kiss her freedom goodbye. With that in mind she's forced to be on point at all times and always move wisely.

Her beauty draws the attention of everyone she passes including the police who swarm the airport. She's gotten accustomed to the tight security and she's learned how to move around them. As soon as she feels the slightest amount of attention on her she immediately puts on her dumb tourist act, pretending to be lost. There have been times that she was under extreme pressure with them watching her like a hawk and instead of avoiding them she did the opposite and went over to them asking for their help.

One thing Amber believes is that police have senses like dogs. They can smell fear and they react off of it. In many cases it's that one look into a cop's eyes that tells him you're up to no good. That sudden look gives him the incentive to check you out. Amber bears witness that the eyes don't lie which is why whenever she works she hides the windows to her soul behind huge dark sunglasses.

The hot and stuffy airport has Amber congested like she's never been. It's extremely hard for her to breathe. Suddenly she becomes light-headed. She stops in her tracks for a second to regain her composure but this only makes it worse. She staggers as her knees buckle slightly. She feels as if she's about to fall. The room begins to spin around before her eyes. She snatches her shades off of her eyes and squints to see her surroundings. She uses her hand to guide her over to the wall, where she leans with desperation as the dizziness settles in her head. Her strange behavior draws the attention of a female passerby.

"Are you okay?" the woman asks as she looks into Amber's delirious looking eyes.

Amber stretches her eyes wide open to adjust them onto the triplets that she sees in front of her. "Yes," she lies as she swallows the lump that's forming in her throat. Her mouth becomes juicy as the taste of salt water gushes from her taste buds. "I'm fine, thank you," she says as she steps away from the woman. What the fuck is going on, Amber asks herself. She's never felt like this in her life. Each step that she takes the dizzier she becomes. The room is now spinning like a roller coaster. Her paranoia kicks in due to these circumstances. She looks around and suddenly police seem to be everywhere. With ten kilos strapped to her body the very last thing that she needs to do is draw attention to herself. "I have to get myself together," she whispers to herself as she attempts to shake the dizziness away. Her mouth fills up with salty saliva until she can hold no more. She swallows but the more she swallows the quicker her mouth refills. Black dots appear before her eyes scaring her to death. A hot flash runs through her body as a fever sets in heating her body up tremendously.

The lights go out and Amber's body collapses. She falls onto her back where she lays there unconscious.

In the States

Deja is having a dilemma of her very own. Five seconds ago she received a call from an anonymous caller.

"Listen, I don't have a clue of who or what you're talking about and I would really appreciate it if you never call my phone again," Deja says as politely as she can

"I will never call your phone again if you never call my man again," the caller replies.

"Listen, I already asked you who your man is and you refuse to tell me who the hell you're talking about so as far as I'm concerned this conversation is over."

"Bitch stay away from my man."

"Bitch?" Deja repeats. "Obviously he's not that much of your man if you're calling me about him. Don't call me. Check your man." Deja has no clue of who this woman could be referring to and really doesn't care the least bit. With the many male friends that she has this woman could be talking about any one of them. In no way is she about to sit here and wreck her brain trying to figure out who she's talking about. Deja has been receiving calls like this all of her grown up life and has learned that the best way to deal with them is to ignore them.

"Don't say I didn't warn you," the woman says. "All the shit that I been through with him. It's been hell maintaining this relationship and just when I think things have gotten better, here you come! I won't sit back and allow you to destroy my life and my marriage. I won't!"

"I'm going to ask you again," Deja says. "Who are you talking about?"

"Damn," the woman replies. "You're fucking so many married men that you can't figure out which one I'm talking about?" she asks mordantly.

"No dear, I have better things to do than to sit here and wreck my brain trying to figure out who you're talking about. I have better things to worry about like which day Neiman and Marcus is having their fifty percent sale," she explains sarcastically.

"What type of skank are you?" the woman asks.

"Apparently a good one," she laughs. "After all you're calling me begging me to stop fucking him. And truthfully dear, for the record, I don't do much fucking. I don't have to. You can have the dick and the heartache. I don't need it. He just gives me the money. Instead of calling my phone pestering me you need to sit back and ask yourself what is it that I can do to be a better wife and keep my husband happy. Cause it's obvious that you're not doing a good job."

"Oh, I'm not lacking anywhere," she interrupts.

"Sweetheart you must be or we wouldn't be having this long drawn out conversation that I'm about to end," Deja says before hanging up in her ear. In seconds the phone rings again. Deja picks it up on the very first ring. "Listen! Please stop calling my phone!"

"I'll stop calling when you stop calling him! And if you don't stop calling I'll track you down and make your life a living nightmare!"

Deja does not do well with threats. "Bitch, is that a threat?"

"No bitch," the woman replies in a sweet voice. "That's a promise."

"Oooh," Deja sighs mockingly. I'm scared," she whines. "You have me shivering in my nine hundred dollar Giuseppes that your man as you call him probably bought me. Such a good man. I don't know what in the world I would do without him. Thanks for choosing such a good man for us. How can I ever repay you?" she asks mockingly. "Let me give you a tip. The less you give of yourself the more he'll want of you. Deprive him and he'll do everything he can to conquer you. Then in no time you'll have him wrapped around your little finger like I do," she explains. "Toodaloo dumb bitch. I'm hanging up, bye," she says before ending the call.

Amber's eyes pop open slowly. Everything is one huge blur. She looks around at the many people who have her surrounded and she can't figure out why. She looks to her right and then her left and what does she see? Two policemen stand over her with solemn looks on their faces. She looks up at the sign which reads Montego Bay's Airport and suddenly she remembers what's going on. She remembers vaguely what happened but she doesn't know why. She looks up and notices two more policemen coming in her direction.

If I don't get up from here I'm going to jail for the rest of my life, she says to herself. She quickly thinks of her loved ones at home who will never see her again if she's incarcerated here in Jamaica. She stands up quickly at the thought of that.

"Slow down, Maam," the paramedic says. "Are you ok?"

"Yes, I'm fine," she replies.

"Do you remember what happened?"

"I wasn't feeling well. The room started spinning and after that I remember nothing. I feel fine now," she says as she looks for her pocketbook which is nowhere to be found until she looks at the policeman who has it gripped in his hand. In the other hand he holds her passport along with a bag of souvenirs.

She reaches for her pocketbook. "Please?"

He slowly hands it over to her. With a heavy accent, he speaks. "Miss Baker your reason for being here in Jamaica is?"

"Vacation," she says in a quite convincible manner. She extends her hand for her passport and her souvenirs. The bag of souvenirs is her front. What type of tourist would she be with no souvenirs?

He nods his head up and down, scaring Amber to death.

"Maam, maybe you need to take a seat," the paramedic suggests. "Would you like to see a doctor?"

"No, I'm fine. I just need to get home. I had an awful vacation. I have been throwing up the entire time," she lies. "I think I'm expecting," she says as she rubs her hand over her belly. "I have to go now. Thanks to all of you," she says as she looks at everyone in their face. "Good day," she says as she walks away. As she's stepping she can feel the eyes of everyone scorching her. She surely hopes that she's not stopped by the police because she's sure that could only result in one thing and that's them taking her to the back room for questioning and make her strip down.

Thirty minutes have passed and Amber is quite grateful to be sitting here on the plane back to the United States. She watches out of the window into the baby blue sky. She sighs with relief as she realizes how close of a call that was. For that she's thankful but she does realize that only half the battle is won. She may have gotten past them now but if by some chance they believe they should have stopped her they can easily alert the officials at Newark Airport to have her stopped.

She replays the entire situation in her mind and wonders what the cause could be. She lied about throwing up and thinking that she could be pregnant, although those are the symptoms. She sits back with a baffled look on her face. I know I'm not pregnant. Can't be, she says to herself.

///// CHAPTER 25 /////

The Next Day

Amber sits in the passenger's seat of Maurice's car. They're parked in front of Amber's building. He hands her a Prada shoe bag. She pulls the drawstrings loose. "How much in here," she asks.

"How much is supposed to be in there?" he asks with a charming smile.

"You know your slick ass," she says as she sifts through the stacks of money. "Always trying to Jew a sister. Always trying to get something for nothing." In total, Amber counts twenty stacks as it should be. "Here," she says as she pulls a few stacks from the bag. "Here's the ten thousand I owe you. Now you can get off of my back."

Amber owes Maurice ten thousand dollars for her Range Rover. She begged and begged him to buy it for her, promising she would pay him back every dime that he spent for it. After all of her pleading, he did better than that. He paid for the truck cash and told her all she had to pay him back was half. She's paid him back a total of $26,000.00, five or six thousand dollars at a time leaving her with a ten thousand dollar balance.

"Now we're even," she says.

"Bout fucking time. Took you long enough. Now I can get off of your back," he repeats. "The original deal was to have me paid off in three months. It's been over a year now," he says as he grabs hold of the money.

"And you really gone take it?" she asks with a shocked look on her face. "Shit, all the shit I do for you I shouldn't have to pay shit back."

"Shit, bizness is bizness," he says meaning every bit of that. "You know that."

Correct he is. Amber has been doing business with Maurice for quite some time now. She's been transporting kilos from Jamaica for him for over nine years now. At the age of sixteen Amber met Maurice. At a time when no one seemed to care about her she met Maurice, a man who appeared to genuinely care about her and her well being.

After a few short weeks he found out that she had no place of her own to stay. He immediately solved that problem for her. He got her an apartment of her very own. Little did she know there was a clause in the contract. She was so happy that she didn't take the time to read the fine print. The catch was her apartment was the stash house where he housed his drugs. She was so happy to have her own spot that she never considered the danger she was putting herself in.

At the time she was only 16 and was already 31. Maurice raised her as if she was his younger sister or more like a daughter; except for the sexual intercourse that they indulged in from time to time. Amber was introduced to all of his girlfriends and even his wife as his little cousin and never has she told any of them any different. She refused to do anything to go against him and take the risk of being back on the street with nowhere to turn. She just played her position in order to keep a roof over her head.

Months later Maurice took Amber to Jamaica for her 17th birthday. She had no idea that their little vacation getaway was work related until the last day when they went to Muhsee's where Maurice talked her into strapping herself with work and bringing it back. She was so frightened that she couldn't imagine going through with it. Maurice walked her through it step by step and made her comfortable enough to go through with it.

For two years or more Amber transported the work for him free of charge. She was just content with her rent being paid and the clothes that he bought her. He may not have paid her but he definitely took great care of her. Finally after hearing how much he paid other transporters, she became wise enough to demand that she be paid for her services. Not completely knowing the value of the job she demanded five hundred dollars for every kilo she brought back for him.

The older she got the wiser she got. Today she's the highest paid transporter that Maurice has. While he pays everyone else one thousand dollars per kilo, Amber is at the top of the food chain, receiving two thousand a kilo. With just one run per month Amber makes close to $400,000.00 a year.

"Let me go. I have things to do," Amber says as she's getting out of the car. "Later," she says before slamming the door.

Maurice rolls the window down. "Lil Bit!"

She turns around slowly. "Huh?"

"That little ass getting fatter and fatter. What you doing taking ass shots?" he says with a smile on his face. He grabs a handful of his manhood. "Let me come up for a little while?"

"Bizness is bizness," she replies with a smile. "You know that," she says as she switches sexily away from the car and into her building.

Maurice shakes his head from side to side as he watches the show that she's putting on for him. "Got damn!"

///// CHAPTER 26 /////

The loud noise of the Black and Decker blenders roar at full volume. In total three blenders are running simultaneously. The table is covered with powder. From the looks of the kitchen table and the sound of the blenders one would think bakers are seriously at work baking until they look closer to see the digital scales. The measuring cups are filled with lactose instead of milk. The powder is ground up cocaine instead of dough.

The man in the center of the table empties the ground up powder from the blender into a tray. He quickly empties another bag of powder into the tray and shuffles it carefully, trying hard to mix it perfectly.

This may be a long and tedious process but it's well worth the wait. For every one kilo of cocaine, one kilo of cut is added to stretch it and make more. The cut that they're using is top notch and better than any other cut available to them. Procaine is the cut that they're using. It's man made cocaine. With not a gram of real cocaine in it, even the most knowledgeable dealer can be fooled by it. The smooth outer texture and the shiny scales of the interior makes it look identical to real cocaine. It even burns like cocaine. The only difference is an addict can smoke an entire kilo of it and he won't get the slightest high from it. Adding procaine does nothing to the quality of the cocaine as other cuts do.

Maurice pays $6,000 a kilo which is a number that dealers can only dream of getting it for. He pays Amber $2,000 for transporting it back to the United States. He pays $500 per kilo of procaine. He pays his bakers as he calls them, little to nothing for their services. All in all he spends less than $9,000 a kilo but he sells them to his family for the price of $18,500. They in turn circulate the kilos to smaller dealers for the price of $20,500.

Maurice's Federation consists of 12 mules (transporters), including Amber, who bring the work back to the country; three men who do his baking as he calls it, and seven other men who distribute the work from here to Atlanta. His twelve women, ten men crew is responsible for generating close to six million dollars a month for Maurice. Each week Maurice sends out four of his mules. Each of them is responsible for bringing back ten kilos. Those 40 kilos are transformed into 80 kilos, which generates $1,480,000 a week.

Maurice pulls into the deluxe suburban apartment complex. He presses the button on the remote and the garage door opens up for him. He pulls inside before pressing the button to close the garage. Before getting out he grabs hold of the bag that lies in his backseat.

He gets out of the car and steps only two steps before getting to the door. He sticks the key into the door and steps right into the kitchen where his bakers are hard at work. They're so busy that they don't even look up to acknowledge him. He drops the bag of ten kilos that Amber gave him onto the table and he leaves the apartment without saying a word.

These kilos are already accounted for. Maurice's lieutenant and long time friend, Sal already has an order for them. In just a few hours these ten kilos will evolve into twenty like magic. In another hour Sal will take them and distribute them to his client from New York. By the morning Sal will turn in $370,000. Not bad for a days work.

Amber sits in the passenger's seat of Sade's R class Mercedes van. She cruises out of the parking lot as Amber sits in the passenger's seat quietly. The van is extremely quiet, not even the music is playing. Sade thinks hard to find something comforting to say to Amber but she can't seem to come up with anything.

Amber sits back with her head glued to the headrest. Her face is as white as snow. She's still in somewhat of a shock due to what she's just been told. Tears dribble down her face. "Pregnant?" she murmurs. "I don't believe this."

Sade looks over to Amber and sees her face full of tears. "Are those tears of joy or sorrow?"

Amber just left her doctor. She went to find out what happened to her the other day and he told her, beyond a shadow a the doubt, she's pregnant. She's already six weeks into her pregnancy.

"Unghh," she sighs as she shakes her head from side to side. "I, I don't know. I mean, I would love to have a child but not under these circumstances. You know I never wanted to be nobody's baby's mother. Call me old fashioned but I always wanted to be married to my child's father, just as you were. You know we both grew up with that fairy tale mind frame."

"Yeah, you said it right, fairy tale. Look at me, I married my children's father and now what? I'm still left alone to raise three knucklehead boys."

"Yeah but at least you stuck to the plan."

"Amber, we plan but God is the best of planners."

"I know but..."

"So are you going to get rid of it?" Sade interrupts.

"Psst, you're asking some tough questions right now, Sade. I can't think right now. My brain isn't even working. I can't bring a child into my madness. Mommy doesn't work a real job but she's going to Jamaica once a month. Mommy will be back," she says in a sweet and innocent voice. "And all it takes is one slip up and Mommy never comes back because she goes away to jail for the rest of her life."

"Lil Bit, you do know that if you have that child the trips will have to stop? You have to do something else."

Sade is always on Amber's back about her occupation. She's never agreed upon it. When she first started transporting Sade thought Amber had lost her mind. As much as she hated it she understood why she did it. She constantly begs and begs Amber to quit. She's more fearful of the consequences than Amber is. Each time Amber's plane departs Sade prepares herself for the dreaded phone call that she will not be coming home. Sade has bubble guts from the time Amber leaves until the time she returns.

"Do something else? Like what? Work at Wendy's? What the hell I'm gone do with a ninth grade education? Fuck a high school diploma. I don't even have a G.E.D."

"There are lots of things that you can do. I'm sure you have some money put away. You can invest in whatever business you want to," she says as she looks into Amber's face which has dropped. Amber's eyes fall into her lap as she sits there without saying a word. "Lil Bit, I know you have some money saved. All the money you make don't tell me you have not saved any of it?"

Amber does not have to say a word because her eyes tell it all. Yes Amber makes lots of money but the truth of the matter is just as fast as she makes the money she spends it even faster.

"What do you think he's going to say about this? Do you think he's really father material? Do you even think he wants to be a father?"

"Honestly I don't have a clue. We never discussed children. Psst, that little penny anny nickel and dime shit he do in no way can provide for me and a child. He can barely provide for himself," she says sounding exactly like Deja. "Anyway I haven't spoken to him in over a week. He hasn't called me or answered any of my calls since he saw me at the Sand Bar. Girl, he's done with me."

"Leave him a message telling him what's going on. If he doesn't call you back after hearing that then you already know. At least you did your part."

"Girl please. Imagine that. Call him and say what? I'm pregnant and you're the father. The last time he saw me I was in another man's arms. He'll never believe me. He already believes that I live with a man. Seeing me with Maurice made that even more believable. I will never play myself like that and leave myself open for him to say how you know it's mine or it ain't mine like I'm some tramp or something." She shakes her head from side to side. "What the fuck have I gotten myself into?"

The ringing of her phone interrupts her self pity party. She slowly lifts it up and sees an unfamiliar number. Her curiosity leads her to answer it on the second ring. "Hello?"

"Amber!" the voice shouts out.

The voice is quite familiar. It's Samad. Her heart skips a beat. "Yes," she replies.

"What's up? Check it, I'm on the three way with my man's little sister. He let me use the phone real quick. I just called to let you know I'm locked up."

"Locked up?" she asks hysterically. The first thing that comes to her mind is the murder he committed. Damn, she thinks to herself. "Where? What happened?"

"Some bullshit. I'm down here in the county. I been here for over a week already. They got me jammed the fuck up. A house raid, a sale to an undercover, a gun, a bunch of bullshit. We'll kick it though. I need you to do me a favor?"

"What? Anything?"

"I need you to go and holler at my rent a car dude. Tell him to go to the block and pick up the Impala. The police left it out there. Tell him, I...I don't know. Tell him something. Tell him I will get with him when I get home. I don't want him to think that I ran off with his car." Samad calls out a phone number. "Please call him as soon as we get off of the phone. Yo, I gotta go. My man has to call his baby mother. Answer your phone. I'll call you later, if not today, tomorrow."

"Wait! Wait!" she shouts. "When are you coming home?"

That's the million dollar question. Samad sits quietly for a few seconds. That answer he can't provide due to the fact of the ransom bail that they've set for him. He has not a dime to go toward the bail even if it was lowered drastically. With D-Nice being here with him, he doesn't even have a way to generate any money either. "I'm just gone ride it out," he whispers. "Yo, the phone about to hang up. I love!" he shouts before Amber gets the dial tone.

The tears pour from her eyes even faster than they already were. She sits there in distress. "What the fuck is today, bad news day?"

///// CHAPTER 27 /////

The Next Day

Maurice sits on the sofa in the living room of the two bedroom apartment. The sound of the money machine rippling through the bills taps loudly, sounding like music to his ears. Sal sits patiently as the last bills are counted. The score is settled. He's turned over the $370,000 he owed Maurice. That deal scored Sal a $40,000 profit for himself.

Maurice packs the money into a small duffle bag and prepares to leave the apartment.

"Yo, I need five more. My Spanish boy from Paterson on his way in about an hour." Maurice points to the closet, gesturing for Sal to go ahead. Sal proceeds to the closet and snatches the door wide open. Inside the closet there lies over 100 kilos.

This apartment is known as the 'Bat Cave.' It's solely for the purpose of housing Maurice's cocaine. One of Maurice's flunkies lives here rent free but his only job is to be here day and night to supply the family with whatever work they're in need of and to count and note any monies that's generated.

Sal retrieves the work, packs them into a shopping bag and together him and Maurice exit the apartment. Once they're outside Sal climbs into his Cadillac pick-up while Maurice climbs into his Dodge pick-up.

"That wasn't long now was it?" Maurice asks as he drops the duffle bag onto the floor of the passenger's seat.

"Long enough," Amber snaps hastily.

"Yo, what's wrong with you?" Maurice asks with fury in his voice. "You been acting like a real bitch all day."

"I ain't no bitch!" Amber says with fury in her voice. "Don't call me no fucking bitch," she says in a sassy manner.

"I didn't call you a bitch. I said you been acting like a bitch," he explains.

"Same shit," she interrupts.

"You bugging!"

Amber sits back for a few minutes and analyzes her behavior today and realizes that her sassy attitude and one word answers could easily have her thrown into the bitch pile. She's just under so much pressure right now, not knowing what to do. She realizes that Maurice has nothing to do with her problem. "Sorry. I just got a lot going on right now. My mind is somewhere else."

"You alright? You need something? You know I'm here for you. Anything," he whispers.

"Nah, I'm good. I'll be alright," she says before silence fills the air.

In a matter of minutes Maurice cruises Newark Airport. He stops short at Continental Airlines Arrival. A frail man comes walking toward the truck. He looks quite peculiar to Amber due to the fact that he's not carrying one piece of luggage. As he gets closer Amber recognizes who he is.

This man is Maurice's younger cousin. He's from Chicago. She knows his face but she doesn't know his name. She's been around him a few times but they have never been formally introduced. Maurice only refers to him as 'The Stalker.' His presence tells Amber that someone is in trouble. He only comes here when there's some dirty work that Maurice needs cleaned up. Every time he shows up in New Jersey a funeral follows shortly after.

The Stalker climbs into the backseat of the truck. "Alright," he says in the same low whisper as he always speaks in. Amber has never heard him talk louder than that nor has she ever heard him say a complete sentence. He leans back in the seat and relaxes himself. His presence alone has created a cold and tense atmosphere.

Everyone in the Federation is familiar with the Stalker and his work but none of them have actually seen him. Maurice keeps his face, name and whereabouts a complete secret to all of them just in case they ever cross over and he has to send the Stalker out for them. Amber is the only one who has seen the Stalker. All the other people who have the non-pleasure of seeing him face to face are no longer here so they could never tell you what he looks like.

Maurice trusts Amber like a sister. In many instances she has proven her loyalty to him and the family. He's even tested her with huge amounts of money that he claimed to have lost and like the honest person she is she turned it over to him. Her honesty and loyalty to him makes him treat her more like a sister than a mule.

As Maurice cruises off Amber is looking in the mirror, applying her lip gloss. She sneakily peeks into the backseat. For a quick second she stares into the Stalker's eyes as he looks out of the window, not paying attention to her. His eyes are dark, blank and bitter. Amber can actually see murder in his eyes. The Stalker looks into the mirror and catches her looking at him. They lock eyes for a second before Amber looks away and slams the visor shut. Goosebumps pop up all over her body from the fear that he just instilled in her by only staring into her eyes.

Damn, she sighs to herself as she remembers the look in his eyes. I wonder who the unlucky person is who is about to have the pleasure of meeting the Stalker face to face?

//// CHAPTER 28 ////

The cozy living room is swarming with loud talking women who all are trying to over talk one another.

"How much for this one right here?" Deja asks as she holds the extra large rubber dildo in her hand. "Yep, this the one I need right here!" she shouts with perversion in her eyes.

"You want that one?' the girl asks as she looks over her price list. One of Deja's customers from the shop gave this Pleasure Party and invited Deja who dragged Amber and Sade along.

The coffee table is covered with every sexual toy ever made from Diving Dolphins to Pocket Rockets to Edible Underwear.

"Thirty dollars for that, Deja."

"No problem," Deja says as she fumbles through her Gucci bag.

"Damn, Deja 12 inches? You a greedy bitch huh?" the girl teases.

"I'm greedy but not this damn greedy," she says with a bright smile. "No way in the world would I jam this thing up in me. It's for show. Let me school ya'll," she says. "This right here is what you call the ego buster, morale breaker," she says as she waves the enormous wand, causing it to dangle. "This is for those arrogant motherfuckers who think they're God's gift to us. This is what you do...when you know he's on his way over place it somewhere you know he's going to see it. You act like you made the mistake of leaving it there. Act like you're embarrassed and all. Go all the way through with it. Girl, you wanna see the big lion turn into a cute little shiatsu?" she smiles. "Beat his ego down! I guarantee you he won't even get hard. Just thinking that you can take all that in will kill his drive. He will wonder how he can ever satisfy you," she claims. "I bullshit you not, a couple of years ago I was hooked up with this nigga who just knew he was the shit. I fixed his ass. One day I'm in the shower, I faked like I forgot my panties and I sent him to my drawer to get me some. Girl, when he came into the bathroom you should have seen his face. Talkin' about in shock!" She laughs hysterically just thinking about the look on his face. "No matter what he tried that night he could not get it up to save his life!" she laughs. "He bitched about that thing for months until I finally got rid of it."

"Girl you a mess," one girl interrupts.

"Keep it up," another girl shouts. "One day you gone get one of those Fun boys on the down low and you gone pull that thing out and he's going to want you to fuck him with it," she says causing all the girls to laugh with her.

"Oh, I'll give him what he wants," she says. "I'm not a selfish lover. Fuck him like he's never been fucked. Ram this thing up his ass until it busts out of his forehead. But as soon as we done. I'm gone let him know that he's every faggot in the book," she laughs.

Meanwhile Miles Away

Maurice sits behind the wheel of his pick-up truck on the dark secluded one way street. He stares straight ahead as he talks to his passenger. "So, I'll hit you in the AM so we can meet from there," he says.

The man hands Maurice a shopping bag which is filled with money. "That's seventy thousand. I'll have the other four in the morning for you," he says nonchalantly.

This man is part of Maurice's Federation and has been for some years now. He owes Maurice $74,000 for four kilos that he got from Maurice over two weeks ago.

"Cool," Maurice replies. "In the AM."

"Absolutely," the man says as he forces the door open and steps one leg out of the truck.

"Oh, hold up!" Maurice shouts. "I almost forgot," he says as he reaches into his middle console where he retrieves a phone. "Here. This the new line."

Maurice and his Federation speak to each other on phones that are solely used for their own communication. Only they have the numbers to each others phone. No outsiders, not even their families are supposed to have these numbers. Although Maurice strictly enforces the no talking business over the phone rule, purely out of negligence there are times that they all slip up. The good thing about it is the pre-paid minute phones are not in any one's name which makes it hard to track the calls back to them. Every few months Maurice collects the old phones and gives everyone a new one.

The man grabs hold of the new phone and hands Maurice the old one in return. "Alright Big Nigga. I'll hit you first thing in the morning," he says before slamming the door shut.

As soon as he's out of the truck Maurice cruises off into the darkness. The man takes a few steps before hitting the remote starter. The locks pop open and the headlights of his champagne colored convertible 650 BMW brighten up the dark block. As he reaches for his door handle, he's yanked by the hood of his sweater. He turns around suddenly where he stands face to face with a totally unfamiliar face. His eyes stretch wide open with extreme fear. Pop! The muffled sound of gunfire sounds off almost quietly. The shot to the man's abdomen causes him to hurdle over at the waist. The gunman yanks him by the hood, snatching him closer to him. He rests the gun against the man's chest and squeezes. Pop, pop. He then shoves the man away from him and as soon as he lets the man out of his grip, he falls to the ground floppily. The gunman then aims at the man's head and fires again. Pop, pop, pop. All three shots thump into the man's head. His aim is so precise that all three bullets land not even a hairs length away from each other. The man's head dangles to the right, hanging over his chest as he lays there motionless. The gunman kicks his head twice in search of any resistance but unsurprisingly there is none which tells him that the man is as dead as dead can be. The gunman peeks around cautiously as he tucks his gun into his overall pocket. He trots away quickly, heading up the block.

Six shots fired and no one has heard a one of them due to the silencer that sits on the tip of the gun muffling the sound. The man turns the corner where Maurice's truck awaits him. He hops into the truck and Maurice peels off. He takes deep breaths in order to regulate his breathing. His adrenaline is racing hard and fast. He immediately examines his clothes and boots looking for any spec of blood but there's not a drop anywhere. He quickly begins unzipping his overalls. Once they're off he dumps them into a garbage bag along with his latex gloves.

The murder victim signed his own death certificate. At one time he was one of Maurice's most valuable players who was accountable for moving close to 40 kilos a week. That was until the larceny and deceit creeped into his heart and he started cutting a side deal with someone Maurice has no knowledge of. What Maurice does know is the man went from shaking 40 kilos a week to only moving 20 kilos a month. Maurice found out about the man's side business from another teammate. He informed Maurice that the man was selling his work in one week and using the money to buy work from someone else. To add insult to injury he even bragged about it to two of the teammates and even tried to bring them in on his caper.

Minutes later Maurice cruises along Routes 1 and 9 south, just minutes away from Newark Airport. He hands the Stalker an envelope stuffed with hundred dollar bills. In total there's $10,000. "Good looking," Maurice whispers.

"No doubt," the man whispers as he looks at his plane ticket. Perfect timing, he thinks to himself. His plane departs in less than two hours.

"What time is the flight?" Maurice asks.

"Eleven thirty five," the man whispers.

Maurice double parks in front of Continental Airline's entrance. "Hit me when you touch."

"No doubt," the man replies as he exits the truck. He struts casually through the double doors and disappears like a ghost.

Maurice presses a few buttons on his steering wheel and like magic his dashboard slides open gradually. He grabs hold of the murder weapon from the floor and dumps it into his secret compartment. He hated to have his man murdered but he feels like his hand was forced. For one he had to prove a point to the rest of the team that deceit will not be tolerated from anyone. He also believes that if you give someone an inch they will take a mile. Today it's a little cross but tomorrow it will be bigger. He believes that a man that will do anything will eventually do everything. He feels that deceit is generated by jealousy and greed which are the same factors that lead a man to snitch if they're ever placed in a position to do so. He may be thinking way ahead of the game into the future but he refuses to take that chance.

He looks at the man's phone and shakes his head from side to side. He lied to the man about giving him a clean line. The phone he gave him was not even activated. He only took the phone from the man so police would not be able to link him to the murder being that he was the last person that called the man before he got murdered. Maurice wonders how the man could ever think that he would get away with crossing him when he knows that Maurice always thinks ten steps ahead of them. Either he thought Maurice was plain stupid or he thought he was just that smart.

"Damn," he whispers. "No loyalty, no honor."

///// CHAPTER 29 /////

Days Later

The heavy downpour of rain gives the cemetery an even creepier look. Massive people surround the grave as the coffin is lowered into the ground. Looks of sorrow cover the faces of the man's loved ones.

Maurice and Amber stand side by side watching closely as the coffin disappears before their very eyes. Amber was quite correct in her prediction. She was sure that after picking up the Stalker from the airport a funeral would be near. She just had no clue that it would be Keith or even a member of the Federation. Amber looks around at the rest of the Federation. They are scattered all over the cemetery. They can easily be spotted by their custom fit suits and dark sunglasses which make them resemble mobsters.

Amber hears a faint voice from afar. Hearing the voice frightens her. It's the voice of the deceased man Keith. He was somewhat of a comedian who always seemed to put a smile on Amber's face. He never called her Lil Bit as everyone else does. He called her Lil Butt and always commented on how perfect her little butt is and she should insure it just as J-Lo did. A smile appears on her face as she thinks of some of the funny times that they've had together.

Maurice stands there as solemn as can be. He thinks of the last time he saw Keith. He can still envision the exact look that he wore on his face as he claimed that they would see each other the next morning. Little did Keith know his life was about to ended with that very next minute. Maurice shakes his head from side to side before taking a huge sigh of distress.

A loud outburst disturbs Maurice's and Amber's sentimental moments. The deceased man's wife falls onto the ground while screaming at the top of her lungs. "No! No!" she shouts. Her performance causes her two young children to start crying as well. Seeing how they're acting sort of touches Maurice. Watching the kids cry is breaking his heart. He can't stand the sight of it. He nudges Amber with his elbow. "You ready?" he whispers before stepping away without giving her time to reply. Together they sneak away from the gravesite and out of the cemetery. The only people who have noticed them leave are the members of the Federation who also vanish from the graveyard one by one.

Maurice holds the door of his black on black 4 door Maserati open for Amber. She gets in slowly, tucking her dress inside of the car. Once she's seated he slams the door shut and proceeds around the car. He gets in and cruises off with no hesitation. He sits quietly as he's driving, just evaluating the entire situation and how it played out. For the first time ever he feels remorse about a decision that he's made. Up until now he's never regretted anything that he's done. His remorse has nothing to do with the man himself but it has everything to do with the man's family. Maurice happens to know Keith's wife and children quite well. Watching them perform as they did put pity and sorrow in his heart. He's never seen the effect of his actions, firsthand. Just to know that his decision has caused misery to a woman and her children. In no way is this the first life that has been taken at his command but it is the first man that he knew on more than a business level.

Amber sits on the edge of the seat and for the life of her she can't seem to get comfortable. Thoughts of Samad overflow her mind. She misses him dearly and wants him so badly that words can't describe. Just to hear his voice would bring her so much joy. Every day, all day she desperately anticipates the ringing of her phone with him on the other end. This baby situation is driving her crazy. She debates back and forth all day about what she should do. She is totally against abortion but on the other hand she does not feel like she's ready to bring a child into this wicked world. The entire thought process is really starting to get the best of her. She shifts her body once again in attempt to get comfortable but this position is worse than the last position. "Psst," she sucks her teeth with frustration. Her mind wanders back to Samad. She wishes he would just call to update her on his situation.

"Lil Bit, what's up?" Maurice whispers. "Tell the truth," he demands. "Say what's on your mind," he says quite defensively. "I can feel it. You think I was wrong don't you?"

"Huh?" Amber questions, not having a clue of what he's talking about.

"You know what I'm talking about. Say it! You think I was wrong for pressing the button don't you? Tell the truth."

Amber was never formally informed that Maurice ordered the hit. She just automatically assumed it being that she saw the Stalker come into town a few days ago. In fact no one was informed of it. Through conversations that Maurice has had with all of them they feel safe in assuming that he did it. Furthermore they know if anyone else would have murdered Keith, Maurice would have sent the army out by now. Being that he hasn't declared war on anyone they're quite sure that the murder was at his command.

"You felt the need to do what you thought needed to be done," she says in a rather cold manner. "What's done is done," she adds. Amber handles death differently than the average person does. She shows no sorrow or compassion. In fact she barely even grieves. The hardest thing for her to do was to stand over her mother and her sister's grave. After the digestion of that, to stand over the grave of anyone else means nothing to her. She watched her brother in law get slaughtered and listened to her sister get raped and murdered so to feel sympathy for anyone else is quite impossible for her. At times she's quite emotionless. "Do you regret it?"

"Real talk...yeah and no. Why the fuck niggas can't just keep it real? Niggas always trying to get over on a mufucker. I'm a good mufucker. I take care of my people. Why they gotta go against the grain and make me come outside my character?"

Amber has never seen or heard Maurice act like this. She sits quietly, just letting him vent. It's apparent that he has a great deal on his mind.

"It ain't even about him. If he would have just kept it real we wouldn't be going through this. "Lil Bit, I don't know if I'm getting soft or what but back in the day I would have went on with my regular day after that. I think the older I get the more I start to think about shit. You know me. It ain't about the bread. It's the principle. I don't even argue over money but I will kill a nigga over principle," he says with murder in his eyes.

Amber sits back quietly, repeating his words to herself. She's heard him use that same phrase over and over since she met him 8 years ago. She is a total believer of his statement. She's watched him let guys slide with owing him six figures at a time and on the other hand he's murdered and had dudes murdered who just made a fucked up statement about him. She can't quite understand his complexity but all in all she vouches that he is fair. She sits back and just listens to him ramble on and on non-stop.

Many Hours Later

Amber lays curled up on the left side of her huge California King Sized mattress. Normally as soon as her head hits the pillow she falls deep asleep but today as soft and comfortable as the pillow top of her mattress is she can't fall asleep for the life of her. She stares out of the window straight into Manhattan. She can not get Samad off of her mind. Just one phone call from him would ease her mind.

Maurice wraps his arms around Amber pulling her body close to him. She tries to put up a little resistance but it's not enough to prevent him from doing so. Their bodies nestle close together. The stiffened bulge that rests on her butt alarms her, telling her that he's expecting sex from her. Oh boy, she thinks to herself. This is what she was afraid of.

After hours of driving with no destination, Maurice finally pulled in front of Amber's building. As she was getting out, he explained to her that he was way too tired to take the long drive to his home in Alpine, New Jersey. He didn't even bother to ask permission to stay with her. He just invited himself there as he always does. She really didn't want him to stay with her but she couldn't muster up the nerve to tell him so. After all he was an emotional wreck and she would hate herself if something happened to him on his way home. She would never forgive herself.

Maurice places his hand in the crotch area of Amber's tight boy shorts and begins petting her kitten. She quickly snatches his hand off of her and knocks it to the side. He still doesn't give up. He places both of his hands over her palm sized breasts and squeezes them gently. She smacks both of his hands away but this only excites him more. The stiffened bulge becomes rock hard. He leans closer and kisses the back of her neck.

Amber nudges him with a gentle elbow to the gut, without even realizing it. The unexpected blow to the gut knocks the wind out of Maurice. She turns around quickly and sees the look of fury on his face. She realizes that she may have just messed up. The fear sets in her heart. She tries to ease his fury with her gentle voice. "Maurice, not tonight, please. I'm not in the mood."

Maurice applies a phony smirk on his face. "I been hearing that from you a lot lately," he says sarcastically. "You're full of excuses. Do you realize me and you ain't did it in about four months?" he asks.

Six months, Amber says to herself. She knows the exact day that they last had sex on. Ever since she started falling for Samad she knew that her and Maurice's sexual relationship was over. Prior to meeting Samad, Amber only slept with Maurice because she had grown accustomed to him over the years. She hardly ever got anything out of it and only did it for his pleasure. Once making love to Samad she knew there was no turning back. Comparing them is like night and day. Size wise Maurice has Samad beat by inches and with all the extra size Maurice still can't reach her heart as Samad does. "No I didn't realize that it's been that long," she lies. "You been counting the days?"

"Lil Bit, keep it real with me. You ain't into me no more? What, you got your eyes on somebody else?"

"No," she replies quickly. "It's just," she stops short.

"It's just what?" he asks anxiously.

"It's just that I want more than you can give me at this time. I'm at a place in my life where I need my own man. Sharing somebody else's man is not enough for me. I'm grown up now. I'm not that vulnerable little girl anymore who you can talk into doing any and everything you want me to do. I refuse to go on sharing you with not only your wife and only god knows how many mistresses you have. I need more," she says very sweet and innocently.

"Oh boy!" he shouts as he covers his ears with his hands. "I can't take no more. What's gotten into you? You actually sound like a." He stops before finishing his statement.

"A what?" Amber asks curiously.

"A girl," he replies. In all the years he's known her he's always commented her on the way she thinks and moves. He said that he's never seen her act on emotions as most women do. He constantly tells her she's like one of the guys.

"A girl," she replies. "Maurice dear, I'm not a girl," she whispers. "I'm a woman."

Her words leave him speechless. Amber has said a mouthful. As much as he would like to debate with her she's left him no room to do so. She spins around, curling up in a fetal position. He stares at her for seconds before curling up close behind her. In minutes they fall in deep sleep.

///// CHAPTER 30 /////

Amber steps into the doctor's office. Glued to her side is her support system, Sade. After hours and hours of debating back and forth Amber has finally come up with what she thinks is the best possible answer. As much as she hates to do this she feels at this point in her life it would be better. She's always been against abortion up until now when it's her situation. She's sure she would make a good mother except for her occupation. She doesn't want to bring a baby into the world under these circumstances and the fact of who the father is doesn't help the situation at all. If she thought he could provide for a child then she would have no problem walking away from her occupation and just be a mother to her baby but she feels the possibility of that is highly unlikely.

Amber still hasn't heard from Samad. She promised herself that the very next time Samad calls she will break the news to him. She feels it is only fair that she does that. There is only two things that can possibly happen. One is he can deny the baby due to the fact that he believes that she has someone else or either he will try and talk her into having the baby for him. She's not looking forward to either of the possibilities. She feels awful that she's about to kill a baby and feels even worse that she has not even given him any say so in the matter.

She promised herself that she would tell him the next time he called but who would have known the next time would be the morning that Maurice spent the night before in her bed. Samad not only called once but he called several times back to back. As much as Amber wanted to answer she couldn't. For one, she's sure that Maurice's eyes and ears would have been glued to her not giving her a chance to talk to Samad. The last thing she needed is for Samad to get wind that Maurice was in her home. She's sure she could never make him believe differently so instead of answering she just let the phone ring over and over again.

"Yes, Doctor Patel," Amber whispers nervously to the receptionist.

"Miss Baker, please have a seat? Dr. Patel will be right with you."

Amber and Sade do as the receptionist instructs them to. They seat themselves directly in the center of the room. As they're sitting there Amber looks around at the other people who are present. Three of them are young girls who appear to be in their teens. Two of them sit side by side with women who appear to be their mothers. The looks on the young girls' faces are looks of fear that they're covering up with rebellion. Amber can't help but to assume what their stories are. She figures that they're probably fast and grown girls who got caught up and their moms are forcing them to get rid of the babies.

A third young girl appears to be about seventeen years old. She seems to be quite different from the other girls. She's talking loudly to a crack head looking woman that's sitting next to her. She pops her gum loud and irritatingly. Her cool and calm demeanor tells Amber that this isn't her first time here and Amber is sure that it won't be her last time either. Amber has met so many like this girl in her lifetime who look at abortion as a method of birth control.

The door opens and two young girls walk in. Both of them are dressed like boys with baseball hats on top of their dreadlocks and their jeans are sagging way below their waist. Amber can only assume that they're gay by their boyish demeanor. They come in looking around as if they are in search of someone.

"Sharon!" the feisty teenager shouts loudly. She pops her chewing gum louder than ever.

The two rough looking girls walk over to her and hug her. "What up Bria?" one of the girls greets. "What you doing here?"

"You already know," she replies loudly accompanied with a boastful smile. "What ya'll doing here?" she asks.

"Some crazy shit," the girl whispers as they sit on the opposite side of Sade. "You seen this skinny long hair chick come out?"

"No," the girl replies.

"She probably didn't come out yet."

"What ya'll doing here?" the girl asks anxiously.

"I told you some crazy shit," she smiles.

"I'm listening," she replies as she waits anxiously for the juicy gossip. Not only is she listening but both Amber and Sade are listening as well. Their curiosity is now killing them.

"Check," the girl whispers as she peeks around. "You know Troy?"

"Troy Troy?" the girl says trying to place the name.

"TR," the girl says in a louder tone.

"Yeah, yeah," the girl replies.

"Anyway, you know he about to get married in a few months and he already done had a baby on his fiancee with some girl from New York. Now he got this other chick from Montclair pregnant. She all crazy in love with him and shit and want to have his baby. Her family is Jehovah Witness and they don't believe in abortion and she's refusing to get rid of it. You know Troy love his fiancée and will do anything for her. He ain't about to lose her for that bitch. Anyway he paid us to bring her here. He paid us $300.00 apiece and said if she don't get the abortion by the doctor then we give her one by beating the baby out of her," she smiles.

"Damn girl, so he making her get rid of it?"

"Yep," she says with a huge smile.

Amber can't believe her ears. The awful story hits a soft spot in her heart. Just to think that someone is being forced to kill her baby and getting threatened to do so. Amber looks at Sade whose eyes are full of sympathy. "That's fucked up," Amber whispers before her attention is drawn to the door where a young beautiful girl appears. She walks out with her head hanging low and her face long and saddened.

The two girls stand up at her entrance. "You ready?"

"Yes," the girl replies politely in a low whisper.

Amber watches as they escort her out of the waiting room.

"See you around the way Bria!"

Amber's heart is filled with grief as she watches the guilt that the young girl wears on her face. What a pity she thinks to herself.

"Miss Baker!" the doctor shouts as he holds the door open. Amber's heart pounds hard and fast. This is the moment that she has not been looking forward to. She gets up slowly.

Sade grabs her hand one last time for comfort. "I'll be right here."

Amber can't force words out of her mouth. She's totally speechless. She just nods her head up and down as the tears start to trickle down her cheeks. She lays her pocketbook on Sade's lap and follows the doctor behind the deadly door.

Meanwhile in Essex County Jail

Samad stands close to the phone waiting impatiently as the phone rings over and over again. Finally Amber's voice mail comes on. "Damn!" he shouts. "Yo, call her one more time. This the last time right here," he promises the other caller on the phone who clicks over and dials Amber's phone once again. The caller has called so many times that he now knows Amber's number by heart. Getting Amber's voicemail is getting somewhat tiring for Samad as well as the caller. They're both starting to get the hint that she doesn't want to be bothered by him. The caller clicks back in and they both listen as the phone rings several times before her answering machine comes on once again. "Damn! Alright. I'll try again later. I'm about to go. I will hit you back later."

Samad hangs the phone up and just stands there for a second. At this point he's highly frustrated with Amber. Whenever she doesn't answer his call his heart drops. His jealousy takes over and causes him to wonder who she's with. He catches himself and stops his mind from wandering. "Fuck that bitch," he whispers to himself trying to psyche himself up. "Money over bitches," he whispers. "Me against the world. Fuck that bitch. I ain't never calling her again."

One Hour Later

Sade cruises out of the parking lot as Amber leans low in the passenger seat. Tears cover her face and confusion floods her mind. She thinks hard, wondering if she's made the right decision today.

"What you think?" Amber asks.

""Girl, you know my position. I'm with you. Whatever decision you make wrong or right I'm gone ride with you to the end."

"Thanks," she whispers. "I don't know what I would do without you. God took the majority of my family away from me but he sent me a guardian angel and that's you," she smiles. "I love you."

"So...who is the godmother going to be me or Deja?" Sade asks with a smile. "And I'm not trying to hear that two godmother shit," she says with jealousy in her voice. "Either me or her. Choose right now," she demands.

Amber spent the entire hour in the bathroom debating. When she came out Sade thought the procedure was over but Amber had to admit that she couldn't go through with it.

Amber looks at Sade through her tearing eyes. "You know you win hands down," she says with a huge smile. "Thanks for being there for me as you always are."

///// CHAPTER 31 /////

In South Orange, N.J.

It's a quiet night here in Voro Lounge and Restaurant which happens to be one of Maurice's favorite spots. In fact this is the only local spot that he will go to. He sits curbside accompanied by a few members of the Federation. They've been sitting here sipping champagne for the past two hours. The music blasts from inside of the bar. The house is packed and the people are jamming but Maurice and his crew have a party of their own going on.

They're at the table popping bottle after bottle while several beautiful women occupy the table right next to them. Maurice has been feeding the women and quenching their thirst for the past hour or so. His magnetic attraction for women has the ladies overwhelmed.

At this point he has the opportunity to take any one or maybe two or three of them with him. Each of them is trying desperately to get his attention and keep it. They all have openly tried to outdo the other to gain his acceptance; all except one of them. The fact that she's the most beautiful one of them all isn't the reason, why in his mind, he's already chosen her. The caramel complexioned, jet black haired, chinky eyed, long legged beauty has been sitting quietly the entire time. His reason for choosing her is the fact that she's barely paid him any attention. More than anything else in the world he loves challenges. The flawless 3 karat stone with the glistening baguettes surrounding it, that's wrapped around her ring finger on her left hand is just another mission that he's sure he can accomplish.

Maurice is and always has been a complete ladies man. One would call him quite debonair. His charm has always been an asset for him. Women have always had a problem resisting him. You can take the most upright, faithful married woman and Maurice has the power to break her. Anyone who knows him knows that if you have a woman that you love you should never bring her around Maurice. His loyalty to his friends would never allow him to cross any of his friends behind a woman but he's not the problem. The women just seem to gravitate to him even if he exerts no effort at all.

The waitress makes her way to their table and blows out the candle, giving them the sign that the night is over. Maurice takes the last drag from his cigar before tossing it onto the street. He stands up, signaling the crew to follow. They quickly follow his lead.

"Ladies, it's been a pleasure," Maurice says as he looks at the table full of women. They all look at him thirstily hoping to be picked. It's almost like they're begging dogs. Their tongues hang out of their mouths and their tails are wagging.

"I'll be over here," Sal whispers as he steps toward the curb.

Maurice continues to look at the table of women. He flashes his arrogant smile and they're all receptive to it. In slow motion he reaches over and grabs his target by the hand. To no surprise at all to him she puts up no resistance. The rest of the women release a sigh of disappointment. He pulls her away from the table and begins to whisper all the right words into her ear. Her blushing tells him that he has her right where he wants her to be.

As Sal paces back and forth along the curb watching the surroundings as he always does, the rest of the crew has made their way into the parking lot to retrieve the vehicles. As the occupants of the lounge disperse, Maurice and the mixed race beauty seem to be the focal point of everyone. Women watch with jealousy towards the girl for actually getting the attention from Maurice while dudes watch Maurice with admiration. Damn near every dude in the spot has cracked on her tonight with no luck and here Maurice has her eating out of his hands. Instead of watching with hate, they're just happy that someone has a shot with her.

In less than three minutes all the onlookers divert their attention from Maurice and the girl to the street where the car show is taking place. The cranberry 650 convertible BMW leads the pack. The black on black convertible S55 Mercedes follows that. A silver convertible Jaguar XK8 creeps up slowly and double parks behind Maurice's black on black Maserati. The rest of the cars in the surrounding area don't even seem to matter much.

To no one's surprise Maurice makes his way over to his vehicle and behind him not even a step away is his prize. He grabs the door handle on the passenger's side and holds it open for her while she seats herself. He then slams the door shut while the driver hops out and runs to the passenger side of the vehicle in front. Sal walks to the driver side of the Jaguar while the driver slides over into the passenger's seat. In minutes the string of vehicles cruise away from the scene as the onlookers stare with awe.

Maurice blasts the tune of 'I Love Your Girl' by singer The Dream. The woman melts into the butter soft upholstery and just enjoys the ride. Maurice remains silent as he cruises into no man's land.

Suddenly the loud noise of screeching tires drowns out the sound of his music. Bright headlights illuminate the block as the vehicle behind him flashes its high beams. Maurice looks over his shoulder to his left where he sees a black Porsche SUV coming at him full speed from behind. Maurice swerves to his right to avoid from being hit by the Porsche. "What the fuck?" he says as he snatches his gun from his waistband.

"Oh my God," the female sighs with terror. "No," she pleads. "Keep going please?"

"What's up?" Maurice asks as he peeks back and forth from the SUV to the female passenger. "Who that?" Maurice questions curiously.

"That's my ex I told you about," she informs. "Please just keep going." In the brief conversation they had a few minutes ago she explained to him that she's in the middle of a divorce.

"Keep going for what?"

"Please?" she pleads.

Maurice peeks up at the driver who is yelling and making strong hand gestures. Maurice stops short at the traffic light as the car before him just makes it through the light. They have not a clue of what is going on. Maurice looks over to the driver who has now hopped out of the vehicle and is running toward the car.

"Yo, pull the fuck over!" he barks viciously. "Pull over!" Maurice holds the gun tightly, ready to fire. He rolls the window down to hear what the man is saying. "You filthy bitch!" he barks viciously. "What the fuck you doing?" he asks as he runs in front of Maurice's car in fear that they may pull off.

The woman locks the door on her side, trapping herself off in the car. "He's crazy. Please keep going."

"Ay my man, please don't run up on my car," Maurice says rather casually.

"Man, shut the fuck up! This ain't got nothing to do with you. This between me and my wife. Bitch, get out!"

"You right, I ain't got nothing to do with it but don't make it my issue. Step away from my car." The man totally ignores Maurice and runs over to the passenger's side and begins tugging on the door handle.

Sal who is now two cars behind sees the mayhem and speeds up to them. He pulls close to the curb and sits there momentarily just watching to see how things are going to play out. This is a quite normal situation for them. Jealous boyfriends have approached them on several other occasions.

Maurice rolls the window down. "Player, step away from my car. I ain't gone ask not one more time. Handle this shit another time. You on my time now. Don't make this about me and you."

By now Sal has called the other members of the Federation to let them know what's going on and they've pulled up to the scene. The man is so busily engaged that he has not noticed that he's surrounded by Maurice's soldiers including Sal who stands away from the crowd at the curbside.

"Mind your business Fam!" the man shouts before reaching into the vehicle and punching the girl square in the face. "I thought we were going to work on our relationship?" he yells out as the punch lands. The impact of the blow sends her head slamming into Maurice's lap. She screams frantically. Maurice looks down and gets furious at the sight. He hates to get involved in this man's issue with his wife but he's forced Maurice's hand by hitting her while she's in his car. Now he feels violated.

Maurice jumps out of the car furiously with his gun gripped in his hand. The man has now managed to open the passenger's door. He flings it open wildly and immediately starts kicking and stomping the woman abusively. "This is how you work on our relationship, leaving clubs with niggas?" he asks as he commences to stomping on her. She screams her lungs out. "Bitch, give me my fucking name back before you start jumping off!" he shouts as he attempts to drag her out of the vehicle. Suddenly he's snatched violently away from the vehicle. Before he knows it he's laying on the ground curled up while he's now getting stomped and kicked by the entire Federation.

Maurice quickly realizes that they have it all under control and starts to make his way back over to the driver's side. The girl watches happily as they beat him almost to death. Suddenly she begins to watch with sympathy.

Maurice hops into the car and cruises away slowly. He looks over to his passenger who has the eye of a heavyweight boxer. It's swollen and half closed. She turns away from him with embarrassment. "You alright?" he asks with sincerity. He feels terrible that this happened in his car. He wonders if this has affected his chances of a happy ending or actually increased them.

The traffic light changes and he speeds off in record breaking time. In seconds he's already two blocks away. He blasts the volume of his stereo and hums along with the song. "Running fingers through her hair, trying to call her over there. I'm like shorty you should go but she like fuck that nigga," he mumbles. "She dropping down to the floor and I'm telling her, shorty you should go but she like fuck that nigga," he mumbles a little louder. "Situation got you mad and I would be too cause boy she's bad, oh so bad," he sings in a low whisper as he looks over to her.

"Watch out! Watch out!" Sal says as he finally gets tired of watching them whomp on their victim. He forces his way to the center of the crowd. Everyone steps to the side giving him an opening. The man lies on the ground half conscious. Sal stands over him, aiming his gun precisely. Boc! Boc! Boc! He fires hitting the man in random spots. He fires once again. Boc! "Let's go," he whispers, leaving the man squirming with pain. They all hop into their cars and flee the scene as the man lies on the ground full of lead.

///// CHAPTER 32 /////

In the Essex County Jail

Here Amber finally sits behind the glass wall after all the hurdles she's had to climb to get here. Although the treatment from the corrections officers was quite humiliating and degrading still it was not a big enough obstacle to get past in order to finally see Samad. At this point she is so desperate that she would have done just about anything to be here.

After finally receiving his call last night he begged her to come and visit him so he could not only see her but also give her the details of his situation.

The door behind the glass opens slowly. Amber's heart beats with anticipation. Her eyes light up with joy as Samad steps toward the glass with his head held high. Seeing him in his jail jumpsuit brings much sadness to her heart yet she manages to keep a phony smile on her face.

Once he gets close to the glass he winks at her sexily causing her to blush like a teenager. Amber looks into his eyes which she feels is the window to a person's soul. She believes that the eyes never lie. Although he wears a smile on his face his eyes show distress.

As he sits, he lowers his head close to the glass and speaks. "Ay Ma," he whispers through the holes in the glass.

"Hey," she replies with joy.

"I'm glad you came."

"Why wouldn't I? You thought I wouldn't?" Samad sits back quietly for a second before replying. The answer to her question he really won't reveal. He really didn't expect her to come. He thought she would leave him hanging and not come to see him. The series of missed calls to her made him think she didn't want to be bothered but even thinking that he just had to try one last time before giving up on her. He shrugs his shoulders. "I don't know. A lot of shit been done and said."

"Samad before we start let me tell you again, what you saw was not what it looked like. I can explain everything and I will once you get out. I been thinking hard these past couple of weeks. I been sick without you. I really miss you. Honestly, I never met anyone like you and I don't want to be without you any longer. If you just give me another chance I will explain everything," she emphasizes. "I miss you," she whispers as a tear trickles down her face. He watches the tear roll down her face until it disappears into the seam of her glossy lips. The sincerity is extremely evident in her eyes. "I miss you too," he replies.

"I've been hurt all my life so I know how it feels to be hurt. Trust me. I would never do anything to hurt you. You believe me don't you?" He looks deep into her eyes without replying. "Huh?" she asks. The fact of him not replying tells her that his answer is no. She shakes her head from side to side.

"Did you holler at the rent a car dude?" he asks totally changing the subject. She replies by head nod. "What did you tell him?"

"Nothing really. He was just happy to get his car back. I told him you had an emergency and had to fly out of town at the last minute. He said contact him as soon as you get back."

"Thanks."

"So, what's the story? Did you get a bail yet?" He looks away from her. "Yeah but I'm waiting for a bail reduction. It don't make sense to post that high ass bail. Mufuckers told me to hold out for a few days and they will lower the bail." Truth of the matter is no matter what the bail is he can't post it. He's just ashamed to admit that to her.

Amber puts him under even more pressure. "So did your lawyer say he can get the bail reduced? You do have a lawyer, right?" He hesitates before replying. He's too ashamed to admit the truth to her. His pride tells him to lie but he can't. "The public defender on it right now but as soon as I get out, I'm going to get a paid attorney," he explains.

"Babe, you can't fight this case with no public defender. Don't you know what people call public defenders? Public pretenders," she informs. "They're not really here to assist you. They work for the state," she says with agitation in her voice.

Samad sits there feeling goofy as can be. "Real talk, shit went crazy for me," he says trying to regain himself after the beat down she just gave him. "Most of my money tied up," he lies. She's put him into a position where he's now forced to lie just so she doesn't know how broke he really is. "Once they lower the bail and I get out I can collect my money that's out on the street and then I can do what I gotta do, feel me? I know I can beat it. I'm not pleading guilty to shit! I didn't make the sale. They found the money on me but shit that ain't nothing. I could have got hold of that bill by giving change to a mufucker. The apartment ain't in my name and they didn't have a search warrant. The public," he says before stopping. He feels silly making this statement but he's already started. "The public defender said he can beat this case all day," he whispers. "All I have to do is get the right lawyer and it's a wrap. It might cost me a grip but fuck it. My freedom means everything to me."

Means everything to me as well, she thinks to herself. She looks into his eyes deeply as she honors the fact that this is the father to her unborn child. Hearing his story makes her reevaluate the situation. Maybe I really need to get rid of this baby, she says to herself but the truth of the matter is she will feel like a murderer if she does so. She came here with the intentions of telling him about the pregnancy but now she's not sure. She doesn't know how this story is going to end. She listened to him clearly. He makes it all sound so simple but Amber knows better. She's sure that he's destined for failure with his life in the hands of a public defender. She knows little about the judicial system but what she does know is that nothing worth having in life is free and a public defender is free.

The door behind Amber opens slowly and the correction officer peeks his head in. "Time is up!" he shouts.

Her heart drops realizing that the visit is now over. "I'll call you later alright?"

She nods her head up and down. "What can I do to help? You need anything?"

"Nah," he says with a fake sense of arrogance. "I'm good," he lies. "I got myself in this situation and I'm gone get myself out of it. I'll call you later, alright?"

She looks at him with sadness in her eyes. I love you."

"I love you too," he says before getting up and walking away. He leaves her sitting there with a million thoughts racing through her mind. Despite the fact that he claims that he's good she knows that he's not and as long as he's not good neither is she. She realizes that something has to be done to get him out of this situation but what, she asks herself.

///// CHAPTER 33 /////

After a few sleeplessness nights Amber has finally come up with a plan to help free the potential man in her life. She stands on the boardwalk a few hundred feet away from her building. She leans over on the rail, staring into the Hudson River. Standing by her side is Maurice.

"I just need to know what the sudden change of movements is about?" Maurice says with a rather stern look on his face. "On more than enough occasions I've asked you to double up on trips when I had no one else that could come through for me and no matter how much I begged you, you always said no. Pissed me off but I respected it," he says as he shrugs his shoulders. "Now you want to make a move when you just went over a couple weeks ago? What happened to your once a month rule?" he asks sarcastically. "What's going on? If you ask me, you sound kind of desperate?"

Beyond desperate, she thinks to herself. She hesitates before replying to him. "I'm in a little jam," she whispers. "It's not really for me. It's Star," she lies. "I just have to handle some backed up tuition issues." She feels bad lying to him but she has no other choice. She knows that using Star is the key to his heart. He loves Star and will do anything for her. In fact he looks at Star like a daughter. He's provided for her financially just as he's provided for Amber.

"Star? What she need? You know I'm always here for her."

"No it's ok. It's nothing I can't handle. The only thing I need for you to do is let me make this run and I will handle it from there." Amber can easily borrow the money that she needs from him but deep down inside she knows it isn't right. To borrow the money from Maurice to bail out Samad would be morally incorrect. That would make her feel downright trifling and if Maurice ever found out she could only imagine how he would react.

Amber contacted a lawyer that Deja recommended to her and put him on Samad's case. He informed her of his fee as well as how much it will cost to bail Samad out.

"Well?" she asks in an innocent voice, while staring at him with sad puppy dog eyes.

He looks at her with a blank look. "Don't give me that sad look," he says. Maurice has no problem with her making another run. He can always use more work. His actual problem is his nosiness. He's extremely private with his business but wants to know every detail of everyone else's life. He hates for anything to go on without him knowing about it.

Amber waits impatiently for his reply, hoping that he doesn't pry anymore and continue to question her. She adds more sadness to her face hoping to reel him in. "Yes...no?"

"Hmpphhh," he sighs. "You know I can't tell you no," he says before turning away.

Amber is a soft spot in his heart. He's like putty in her hands and can and always has been able to manipulate him to do anything that she desires.

When she was a young teenager she had a certain amount of control over him but she didn't realize it. She's just gotten mature and wise enough to acknowledge that she has power over him. Even knowing it, she rarely uses it on him because she's just not that type of woman.

"Yes," she cheers silently. That's only one battle down though. Now for the hardest part. The amount of money that she's in need of can't be obtained by her going to St. Thomas alone. She needs more than twenty grand. She figures she can get someone to go along with her and give them ten thousand while she keeps the other ten thousand. She knows how particular Maurice is and figures it's going to be quite difficult to talk him into it. She's so desperate now that she's willing to do anything to talk him into it.

She has no particular person in mind but whoever she chooses to go along she has to be able to trust them wholeheartedly and also convince Maurice that he can trust them as well. A part of her knows that Maurice is always searching for more trustworthy transporters and normally he wouldn't have a problem with anyone she brought to the table but under these circumstances he may not be receptive.

She thinks long and hard before asking him the next part. Before she does so she has to have all her thoughts together so she will be able to make Maurice believe that she has planned it all out carefully and none of this is an act of desperation. The person has to be trustworthy as well as have the courage to make the move. Damn, she says to herself. Who can I get to go?

Miles away

Deja steps out of her two story townhouse and takes a deep breath intaking the fresh air. She looks around just admiring the beautiful structure of the housing complex. She looks to her right where her car is parked and her eyes stretch wide open. Her windshield is shattered. She runs over toward her car. "What the fuck?" she sighs. A piece of paper tucked under the windshield wiper catches her attention. She grabs hold of it and begins to read.

I begged you to leave him alone but still you didn't listen. Hopefully I now have your attention. This is my second warning and it shouldn't be taken lightly. I'm willing to do anything to save my marriage, ANYTHING. I know everything about you, including your whereabouts. I even sat in your chair at the shop. Please don't force my hand.

Dangerously in Love

Deja looks around nervously as the hairs stand up on the back of her neck. She actually feels like she's being watched. Her heart pounds with fear. At first the phone call was quite funny but now it's become a serious matter. The phone call didn't even make her wonder who the woman was referring to but now that the woman has come to her home this is an altogether different level. This woman claims to know everything about her while Deja has not a clue of who she is nor who her husband is. She has no choice but to find out at this point.

She has dealt with married men in her life but currently no one she even speaks to is married. The few friends that she has all claim to be single but it's apparent that someone is lying. She stands here wearing a few emotions on her face, fear, confusion and fury all at the same time. She has to get to the bottom of this.

///// CHAPTER 34 /////

The sound of someone busting into the hotel room awakens Amber. She stares at the door with alarm as Luscious stumbles into the room. Amber looks at him with pure hatred. She's never been more agitated with anyone than she is with him. She totally regrets the fact that she brought him along but she had no choice. He's pissed her off gravely. He's done nothing but whine and complain since they've been here. He questions her over and over about every detail of the operation. She's sure he's afraid which is why he's asking so many questions but his questions come across as downright nosiness. He wants to know who they're transporting for, who they're getting it from and how long she's been doing this. She hated to bring him in on her secret but again she had no choice. She hopes that her attempt to instill fear in him makes him keep his mouth shut. She told him if a word of this ever leaks out the mob boss she works for will kill the both of them along with their families. The look in his eyes made her believe that he will never utter a word of this to anyone. She hasn't told anyone but Sade that she brought him along. Not even Deja knows. Amber told Luscious to tell her he will be away with family for a few days.

"Miss Lil Bit, what are you doing awake at this hour?" Luscious sings. His eyes are red and glassy. Amber can smell the liquor seeping out of his pores from across the room. "Get your rest honey. You look a mess," he smiles. "You can surely use some beauty rest."

"Fuck you!" she barks.

"Oooh," he sighs. 'You my dear need an attitude adjustment. Unravel your panties. They must be in a bunch."

Amber has taken as much from him as she possibly can. "Listen faggot, don't fuck with me," she says harshly. Never has she disrespected him like this as much as she wanted to.

"Sheesh, lighten up. What's your problem?"

"My problem? You're my problem."

A tapping on the door startles Amber causing her to get quiet. She wonders who in the world it could be.

"Who?" Luscious yells.

"Shh…shut the fuck up," Amber whispers.

"Relax," he says as he peeks through the peephole. "It's for me," he whispers as he looks at her over his shoulders. "One minute," he sings as he runs away from the door. "I have to change into something more comfortable."

"Who the hell is that?" Amber asks.

"Nosey aren't we?" he smiles. "My little friend. We're going out for a nightcap."

"Are you fucking crazy? We're here for business. How in the hell are you going out with a perfect stranger?"

"Easy," he teases. "Don't worry. I'll be alright. Nothing will happen that I don't want to happen," he says with a devilish look in his eyes. "In no way am I an easy date," he says as he's changing his clothes.

"I don't give a fuck about you. Do you realize the seriousness of this matter? Keep your drunk ass here," she says as she thinks of the possibility of who his date could be; maybe a FED or even a robber.

"Coming!" Luscious yells, totally disregarding Amber's instructions. He trots over to the door and snatches it open. A middle aged white man stands there awaiting him. Luscious lifts one leg in the air behind him while staring over his shoulder at Amber. "Don't wait up," he says with a devilish smirk on his face. He quickly slams the door behind him.

"Stupid motherfucker!" Amber is quite furious. She can't believe the stupidity of him. Maybe this was a bad idea bringing him along. Fury is ripping through her gut. She looks at the clock. Although it's late and she hates to awaken Sade, she can't help herself. She grabs hold of the phone and the calling card and begins dialing.

Sade lies in the bed flat on her back. "Finally some me time," she whispers to herself as she takes a sip on her glass of red wine. She's exhausted from a long tiring day with the kids. Never in her life did she imagine it being like this. A single mother raising three kids was never a part of her plan. She hopes and prays that she becomes a proud and successful parent. Her biggest fear is losing her boys to the street. She will do everything in her power to keep them away but judging by the looks of it, it almost seems inevitable; especially her eldest son who seems to be infatuated by the street life. He's always idolized his father and portrays him as a hero. She believes that it is highly likely that he will follow in his father's footsteps. The thought of that makes her tremble.

She takes another sip of her wine to calm her soul. She lays back and without even realizing it she sticks her hand underneath her short terry cloth robe. Her hand greets her bald shaven cat. She slowly pets herself into relaxation mode.

She's so uptight and drinking an occasional glass of wine has been her only source of relaxation. Also, she's never felt lonelier in her life. She's been manless for almost a year now and has not even had the urge to start dating. Her husband was her first and her last. She's extremely lonely but at this point dating is not even an option of hers. In fact she doesn't even know how to date because she's never had to being that she married her first date. She can't even imagine being touched by another man even though she's in need of some sexual therapy. She wishes she had the heart to just find herself a boy toy who she could call on from time to time to cater to her sexual needs with no strings attached but she doesn't, which is why she's forced to cater to her own needs.

For the past couple of months after putting the kids to sleep she's put herself asleep by masturbating. She's done it so much that the touch of her own hand has gotten quite boring and seems to no longer do the job. She feels a great amount of guilt in playing with herself but she'd rather do that than to go out and find a man to play with her. Not only is she not ready to be with another man but she also knows that her kids are not ready to see her with another man.

Her heavy petting has her hot and sticky as it always does but now she's in need of a nice finish. She reaches into her nightstand and retrieves her pocket rabbit that she bought from the pleasure party. She shakes her head with disgust as she looks at it. She always felt that toys were for perverts but at this point she's forced to look at it differently. She takes another sip of her wine to erase her guilt then she hits the power button on her substitute.

Amber finally gets the call to go through. She listens closely as the phone rings over and over. "Come on girl, pick up," she begs. The answering machine comes on. "Damn," Amber sighs as she thinks of the dialing process that she has to go through all over again.

Sade's body is sunken deep into her fluffy mattress. She leans back with her eyes rolled into her head. Chills rip through her body as her vibrator vibrates her soul. Her toes cramp up one by one as the sensation enhances. Her feeling of pleasure rolls from her lips as she moans sexily. She slams the pillow over her face to muffle the noise so the kids will not hear her. She's in paradise right now but the time is coming closer. She's in deep concentration, ready to explode when the phone begins to ring off the hook once again. "No," she whispers with rage. Not only has the phone broken her concentration level she's lost her spot as well. She hasn't had a good orgasm in months but oh how close she was. "Damn," she whispers as she reaches over for the phone. "Hello," she barks hastily.

///// CHAPTER 35 /////

Amber walks closely behind the machine gun toting dread as he leads her into the dining room of Muhsee's mansion. A few feet behind her is Luscious. His heart is beating as loud as a drum. He's scared out of his mind. He thought this would be easy as pie for him to do but after actually getting here he's had second, third and fourth thoughts about it. He's no foreigner to crime. He's cashed a few fraudulent checks in his day and even boosted clothing from the malls but this here is an entirely different ball game from the petty crimes that he's partaken in.

He sits back and watches as this entire situation plays out like a scene in a movie. He can't believe that he's one of the main characters. He's seen how all the movies of this kind end. Right now he's about two seconds from pulling out on Amber. He will just have to reimburse her with the money she spent on his flight. He really doesn't think he can go through with it.

Amber steps into the room and takes a seat while Luscious stands close to her. "Have a seat," she suggests. Luscious is so nervous that he damn near sits on her lap. Amber can feel the heat which comes from the opposite side of the room. She looks over where she sees the young boy gripping the machine gun in his tiny hands. They lock eyes. He stares at Amber coldly as his lips curl with disgust. She's staring at him and not even realizing it. Her long stare makes him feel as if she's challenging him but in all actuality she's looking at him with sympathy. Yesterday Muhsee explained to her the kid's story. He's only twelve years old. All of his life he's been living with AIDS which was passed down to him by his parents at birth. His mom and dad died from the disease when he was seven years old and left him to raise himself ever since. He's just waiting to die as well. Muhsee explained that he's miserable and has nothing to lose which makes him the perfect man for this job. He lives with no boundaries because he knows that he can die any day. He knows that he can murder the Ambassador if he's ordered to and jail means nothing to him because he knows he'll never live long enough to do the time that they sentence him to.

Amber takes notice of his lip which is now quivering with fury. She quickly turns away from him. Muhsee comes into the room right on time. He steps arrogantly toward the dining room table without even acknowledging the fact that they're here. He sits down and watches Amber and Luscious closely. The look in his eyes scares Luscious even more. Amber can feel his body trembling against hers.

"This is like a scene from the movie Belly," Luscious whispers. Amber ignores him as she watches Muhsee watch them. "Girl, I don't think I can go through with this," he whispers. His whispering causes Muhsee to watch harder as he tries to read his lips.

Amber takes notice of the level of discomfort that Luscious is causing Muhsee. "Shhh," she whispers sneakily.

Luscious ignores her and continues to babble on. "Girl, I just want to get out of here. I wish I would have never agreed to do this. I will pay you your money back for the flight and hotel. I can't do this shit," he whispers. "If I make it out of here it will be a blessing. All I need is for the police to bust up in here. We gone be put up under the jail. Americans in a Jamaican jail. Girl, I won't last a minute in there with them Rasta savages. You know how they feel about my kind. They're extremely homophobic. They would probably rape me, torture me and then kill me," he says fearfully. "Look," he says as he points out of the window. "If they wanted to raid this place it would be easy. All they would have to do is come through that little side entrance. Ain't no security over there." Muhsee watches him as he points out of the window but Luscious is so busy running his mouth that he's not even paying attention to Muhsee. "That front yard is big enough to land one of those police helicopters right there," he points. "These little security gaurds won't be able to stop them. They would have snipers surround this place. Probably just shoot us dead to avoid spending the money to feed us in prison. Lord, please get me out of here," he prays.

"Ay!" Muhsee shouts firmly. Seconds pass before he speaks again. Both Luscious and Amber look at him as venom bleeds from his fire red eyes. "Didn't your mother tell you that it's rude to whisper? Do you have something you want to share with the room?" Luscious sits there quietly. His body stiffens with fear. "I'm talking to you botti boy! Stand up!"

"Muhsee," Amber says, trying to save Luscious.

Muhsee points at her with his index finger. "Shhh...I'm not talking to you. Speak when spoken to." He then points at Luscious. "Come here!" Luscious sits without moving. His fear has him glued to the seat. "Now!" Muhsee shouts, causing Luscious to jump out of the seat. Muhsee gestures for him to come over to him. Luscious steps slowly toward him with a terrified look on his face. Finally he stands about five feet away from Muhsee. Muhsee stands up. "Who are you?"

"Lu...Luscious," he stutters.

"Bitch boy, I'm going to ask you again. Who the fuck are you?"

"Lucias Smith," he says as he adds a little bit of manly bass in his voice as he spits out his government name.

Muhsee reaches over and grabs Luscious by his shirt collar. He then rips Luscious' shirt open, popping every button. He closely examines his chest looking for a wire. "You a FED?" he asks with a smirk on his face.

"A FED? No," he whines.

"Strip now!" Muhsee's voice alarms all of his soldiers who come running toward the center of the room. In seconds they have Muhsee and Luscious surrounded. "Strip!" he shouts again. The soldiers now have their weapons aimed at Luscious as he stands there petrified. "Strip before I command them to fire."

"Muhsee please," Amber begs as she stands up. The twelve year old turns his body into her direction and aims his gun at her head. He peeks down the barrel with one eye closed, trying to get an accurate aim. "Sit down!" Muhsee instructs Amber.

She does as she's told. "Muhsee. I would never bring a FED to you," she whispers with fear in her voice.

Muhsee gestures for the young boy to stop aiming at her. "He strips or he dies."

Luscious takes the first choice. He begins unbuckling his slacks quickly. In seconds he's standing there only in his silk bikini briefs.

Muhsee turns away with disgust at the sight of Luscious. He yells out something in his language as he walks away. All of his soldiers follow him out of the room except for the young boy who still has his machine gun aimed at Luscious' head.

Luscious looks back at Amber. A tear trickles down his face as he stands there helplessly. She feels sorry for him but there's nothing that she can do to help him.

She peeks into the other room where Muhsee paces back and forth as he holds his phone to his ear. He's talking on the phone but Amber can't hear a word of what he's saying. His hand gestures and his body language are quite aggressive. She assumes that he must be talking to Maurice on the phone; well at least she hopes that he's talking to Maurice. Maurice is the only one who can save them right now.

Ten minutes pass before Muhsee and his soldiers step back into the room. The heartbeats of both Luscious and Amber can be heard from miles away. They both wait nervously to see what's next on Muhsee's agenda. Muhsee sits back in his chair while his strapper walks over to the closet. He opens the closet and retrieves an armful of kilos.

"Come on," he says to Amber as he walks toward her. "Phew," she sighs as she stands up and begins stripping herself of her clothing.

After he's done taping the kilos to her body the moment he dreads comes. He despises the fact that he even has to touch Luscious' flesh. He barely touches Luscious as he straps the work to him.

The process seems to take longer than ever. Amber and Luscious can't wait for it to be over so they can get out of Muhsee's sight.

Meanwhile in the Essex County Jail

Samad sits alone in his cell. He's finally made it into population. Last night he was released from quarantine and admitted to this tier. In quarantine he was in a cell alone. The seclusion was hard on the mind but easier for survival. Here it's quite chaotic and full of tension. In just a few hours he's learned that Bloods run this entire jail and if you're not Blood, you're helpless. A man can't breathe, eat or shit without permission from the Bloods. Samad has already watched men get their food and sneakers taken from them while they had no ability to do anything. Only one man attempted to put up a fight and that only made matters worse. He was rushed off of the unit with over twenty stab wounds. All the fight he put up and he still left here shoeless. Before he was dragged off of the tier he laid there half dead and bleeding like a pig.

Samad feels safe because a long time friend of his happens to be on this same tier. The fact that his friend is Blood makes it all the better. He's welcomed Samad with open arms. He's given him everything he needs in order to survive until he gets his own commissary. Samad has food, cosmetics and even extra underwear. His friend, Bullet has made him feel as comfortable as he can possibly feel in jail.

Samad wonders how his man D-Nice is making it. After they were discharged from quarantine they both were shipped to different tiers. He just hopes that he doesn't run into any problems. He's more worried about D-Nice than he is worried about himself.

Samad lays back on his bunk, trying to enjoy the music that pours into his ears from the tiny earphones when his friend Bullet walks into the cell. Bullet peeks around sneakily as he tiptoes over to Samad. The look on his face causes Samad to be alarmed. He slowly snatches the earphones from his ears. "Bullet, what up?" he asks with major concern.

Bullet hesitates before replying. "Smooth, you my man," he says while shaking his head from side to side. "I can't just sit back and watch shit happen to you. We like family," he says before going silent again.

"What you talking about?"

Bullet stares into Samad's eyes with sympathy. "The Homies gone move on you," he whispers. "I tried to hold them off for as long as I could but once the call is made ain't shit I could do."

"Move on me? For what? I ain't fucking with nobody. I'm just here doing me. What they gone move on me for?'

"Cause they could, he replies. "You know the Gee I showed you? He made the call. He want them ACG's," he says as he points to Samad's brand new Nike boots.

"He made the call over some fucking boots?" Samad asks as he thinks of how minute that sounds. He quickly realizes what he's dealing with as he recalls how the last man was almost killed over some petty $60 sneakers.

"I had to warn you. I just couldn't let it go down like that."

"So, what the fuck I'm supposed to do, just let them take my boots?" he asks with sarcasm.

Bullet hesitates before replying. "I wanna tell you yeah but at the end of the day I know you a man. I took a chance by even telling you this. If the Homies find out then I got problems. It's like I'm taking your side over theirs."

Samad can't believe his ears. "Bullet, we go back to Kindergarten. You probably barely know these niggas. You supposed to take my side over theirs."

"Smooth it ain't like that," he whispers.

"Fuck you mean it ain't like that?"

"They Blood...you not."

Samad snickers. "So you saying if they try to roll me out you gone sit back and watch? Or you gone roll me out with them?" he asks as he anxiously awaits the answer.

"I ain't got no choice. You know how this shit go. Blood rules over everything. If the Homies roll I gotta roll. Or at least act like I'm rolling on you."

Samad prays that his ears are deceiving him. "Word?"

"It's fucked up but it is what it is. I don't need them type problems with the Homies. I take your side and these niggas fuck around and label me food."

Samad shakes his head from side to side. "I don't believe this shit. So, what I'm supposed to do just sit back and wait for them to move out on me?"

Bullet peeks over his shoulder before sneakily unloosening his jumper. He digs into the waistband of his underwear and pulls out a small jail made shank. The tip has been filed into an extremely sharp point. He passes it over to Samad as he peeks back and forth making sure no one sees him. Here, hurry, hurry." Samad quickly grabs it and places it underneath his thigh. Bullet looks into Samad's eyes sadly. "Don't let nobody know I gave this to you. You my man. My hands tied. Keep your eyes open at all times. Protect yourself cause I can't do it for you," he whispers before he turns away. Samad watches Bullet closely as he exits the cell with his head hanging low with shame.

In Jamaica

Amber leads Luscious through the airport as he follows many steps behind her. He's walking slow and in a trance sort of like a zombie. He's so fearful that his normal feminine prance has transformed to stiff baby steps.

Amber is thankful to be out of Muhsee's grip. She thought for sure that Luscious was about to lose his life in there. Although she was quite agitated with Luscious seeing him scared and helpless like that broke her heart. He cried like a baby in the cab all the way to the airport. He too realized how close he was to losing his life.

"Come on, you have to speed it up," Amber whispers as she reaches back and grabs hold of Luscious' hand. She pulls him close to her, damn near dragging him. His hand is trembling like a leaf from nervousness. She grips it tightly to comfort him.

As she looks ahead she spots several police officers who are scattered around the airport. She immediately prepares herself to pass them. She adds more confidence to her swagger. "Luscious, you have to loosen up," she says reassuringly. Her words go in one of his ears and out of the other. He's in a deep daze that can't be broken.

As they're strutting along a policemen steps out of the restroom unexpectedly. He's walking swiftly toward them. Amber switches along casually but Luscious stops dead in his tracks. His heart pumps with terror. Amber looks at him with surprise. He snatches away from her and with no warning he starts to trot away in the opposite direction. There Amber stands almost face to face with the cop with less than four feet in between them. Oh shit, she thinks to herself, not knowing what to do.

The policeman pays no attention to her but his eyes are glued onto Luscious. Without even thinking she takes off behind him. She quickly catches up to him. She has no idea of how she's going to play this matter off. Without putting any thought into it she snatches the beach towel from around her neck and as she catches up to Luscious she flings the towel popping him across the back of the neck in a playful manner. He turns around with fear. She flings the towel once again. As the towel strikes his chest, she reaches out for him and grabs hold of the collar of his t-shirt. She pulls him close to her. The policeman watches on as he approaches them. Amber acts as if he isn't even there. She grabs Luscious by the back of his head and mashes his face onto hers. They kiss like two lovebirds. Amber makes out with Luscious right in the middle of the floor of the airport.

She stops long enough to catch her breath. "Motherfucker," she snarls. "Are you crazy?" she whispers. Luscious looks over her shoulder where he sees the policeman getting closer. The look in his eyes and the beating of his heart which is jumping out of his chest tells her the cop is near. "Kiss me," she instructs. "Kiss me, kiss me," she demands as she grabs hold of his head once again. She locks lips with him by biting his bottom lip.

Through her peripheral she sees the policeman passing them. Surprisingly, he's not even acknowledging the fact that they're standing there. Amber keeps her lips glued to Luscious' lips until the cop is several feet away. Once he's far in the distance she backs away from him and pulls him along with her as she leads him through the airport.

Minutes Later

Amber exhales a huge sigh of relief as she plops into her seat. She looks over to Luscious who sits in the window seat of the plane. Anger bleeds from her eyes as she thinks of how close of a call they just had. If not for her quick thinking they both would be finished right now.

Safe and sound, she thinks to herself. She looks up to the ceiling of the plane. "Thank you, God."

///// CHAPTER 36 /////

Deja sits at the table sipping on a glass of Pinot Noir. Across from her sits her friend. Ever since the incident with her car window, she's been quite uneasy. She constantly wonders who the woman is actually talking about. In total there are three men who are suspects. She has no clue which one could be married to the stalker wife so she got money from all three of them to fix her window.

She plans to interrogate them one by one and hopefully she will find her culprit. When she does she will set him free to go on with his wife and maintain her peacefulness as well. At this point she feels that she is way too old to be dealing with this type of drama in her life.

Deja stares seductively into her friend's eyes from across the table. "Do you have something you want to tell me?"

"You look awesome tonight," he says with charm.

She smiles but his charm holds no weight tonight. "Besides that," she replies arrogantly.

He stares into her eyes before speaking. "Uh…no," he says slowly.

"You sure?"

"I'm positive," he says as he tries to figure out what it is he should be telling her. "Something like what?"

"Uhm, I don't know. Anything that you feel I would want to know."

"You know everything about me already," he claims.

"Are you sure about that? You know you can tell me anything right? I'm real like that. Your deepest darkest secret you can tell me and I will never judge you. All I ask is that you keep it real with me at all times so I always know what I'm up against. Got me?"

"Uh…I think."

"So, tell me something," she demands.

"Something like what? What do you want to know?"

"I wanna know everything."

"Deja I already told you everything. Where are you going with this? You've known me for almost a year now. What is it that you're looking for? You tell me what it is that you want me to tell you?"

"Ok, you have three kids right?"

"Yeah. You already know this."

"Three different mothers, right?"

"Yeah and?"

"One mother is in Philadelphia, right?"

"Absolutely."

"One mother in New York, right?"

"Yeah."

"And your two year old, her mother is where?"

"Here in Jersey," he snaps. "Deja what are you talking about? You asking questions that you already know the answer to."

"Ya'll broke up how long ago?"

"Last year."

"You sure about that?"

"Why the fuck wouldn't I be sure?"

"I'm just making sure. No dealings with her right? No dating, no sex with her, nothing, right?"

"Right," he answers with frustration.

"So after her there was who?"

"After her I was doing me! What is it that you're trying to figure out? Cut to the chase?"

Deja looks at his ring finger, looking for a sign of a wedding band; an indention from a tight ring or a sun tan line around his finger. She decides to cut to the chase as he said. "Something tells me that you're married."

He laughs in her face. "Married? Let me tell you something. If I was married I would tell you. I would never lie about nothing like that. I would tell you up front and if you couldn't deal with it then oh well," he says arrogantly." His arrogance sort of pisses her off but she accepts it. His cockiness makes her believe that he's telling the truth. "Something tells you I'm married," he says in mockery. "Something is telling you wrong," he laughs. "Married to who?"

Meanwhile Two Cities Away

Maurice cruises along the dark Newark street while Amber rides shotgun. Luscious sits right behind her in the backseat while Sal sits behind Maurice. Tension fills the truck. It's extremely quiet, not even the radio is playing. Maurice's silence is killing Amber. She knows he has so much to say to her. She's been with him for close to an hour and he's barely said two words to her. She hopes he remains silent until they're alone. She would hate to be embarrassed in front of Sal and Luscious.

Maurice instructed Amber to catch a cab to TGIF in West Orange and he would pick them up from there. Once he picked them up he took them straight to the Bat Cave where they freed themselves of the ten kilos apiece that were strapped to their bodies.

Amber is quite sure that Maurice is going to chew her out. The look on his face tells her how furious he is. She hates to hear him chastise her like a child but deep down inside she knows she deserves every word of it. She realizes how bad of a decision it was to bring Luscious along. Her desperation led her to do something that could have easily cost her life.

Maurice cruises up 12th street alongside of the cemetery. Once he gets to the middle of the dark block he pulls over to the curb and stops. Amber looks over to him, wondering why they're stopping here. Her heart pumps vigorously as she thinks of the possibilities. Nah, she thinks to herself. No, he didn't take me for the ride. He wouldn't, she tells herself as she watches him slam the gear into park. He quickly pops his automatic locks open. Amber peeks from side to side wondering what's going on when suddenly she hears the back passenger door being snatched open. She looks behind her with her eyes stretched wide open.

"Oww!" Luscious screams at the top of his lungs as he's being dragged out of the truck. Sal forces him out with all of his might while another man stands outside of the truck pulling and tugging away at Luscious' legs.

"Maurice please," Amber says nervously. He stares straight ahead, ignoring her as if she hasn't said a word to him. "Please, Maurice, don't do this? It was a mistake." Her pleading is not only on behalf of Luscious. She's begging for her life as well.

"Lil Bit, please! Please!" Luscious screams as he's finally dragged out of the truck. Amber is just so sure that she's next until the back door is slammed shut and Maurice peels off quickly. He makes the left turn onto 12th Avenue where he parks in the middle of the block.

Luscious fights like hell as he's being dragged into the entrance of the graveyard. He kicks and screams for his life until he's pounded on top of his skull with the .44 Magnum which dazes him. Everything goes blurry before his eyes and his energy is drained from his body. With no resistance from him at all they drag him into the cemetery.

"Yeah, a mistake! A fucking mistake that could have not only cost you your life but could have blown my entire operation up as well! What are you fucking stupid, bringing that Homo with you? I trusted your judgment and I shouldn't have. You were this close to losing your life over there. I begged and begged for him to spare you. He really thought we were setting him up."

Two gunshots echo in the air, interrupting Amber's scolding. Her body shivers. Oh my God, she thinks to herself. She's sure they've killed Luscious. The saddest part of it all is the fact that she knows that it's all her fault.

"Do you think that talkative ass homo was going to keep our secret? Do you? This would have just been juicy gossip for his faggot ass! For every action there is a reaction? You understand that?" She nods her head up and down slowly. "Do you understand that?" he shouts viciously.

"Yes," she whispers.

"I gave him my word that if he allowed you out of there I would handle the homo. I had no choice it was him or you."

Amber sits there as stiff as a board. Her emotions take over her body. Her heart withers while she cries like a baby. Her face doesn't show a trace of her crying because it's on the inside that she cries. Guilt pours from her heart as she entertains the thought that Luscious lost his life because of her. Damn!

///// CHAPTER 37 /////

Samad sits upright on his bunk with his back pressed firmly against the wall. His eyes are heavy and they're as dry as sand. He rubs them vigorously to ease the burning. It's a strain to even keep them open. He lays back and closes them for a second just to rest them. He dozes off once again but fear awakens him out of his nod. It's 4 a.m. and he hasn't gotten any sleep. Ever since Bullet warned him he's been on point and ready for their attack.

He's been forced to change his sleep pattern on account of the fact that the Bloods in here stay awake all night. They get all their sleep during the day. Sleeping at night puts any man at a terrible disadvantage. No way in the world will Samad be able to sleep in peace knowing those savages are wide awake and each of them have jail made daggers and pokers the size of swords in their possession.

Samad dozes off once again. The sound of someone walking past his cell awakens him. His eyes pop wide awake. He grabs hold of his shank which he has tucked underneath his thigh. He conceals it behind his back as he prepares himself for war. To his glory the man passes the cell without paying the slightest bit of attention to him.

Samad realizes that he can't live like this forever. Sleeping with his boots on, placing all of his possessions underneath his pillow, staying awake all night and day is just way too much to deal with but he has no choice. It's either deal with it or check into PC (Protective Custody.) He refuses to play himself like that. If the dudes on the street get the word that he checked in, he would never live to hear the end of it. He'd rather get killed in here than to swallow his pride and check in.

Samad dozes off once again. His neck hangs over until his chin rests on his chest. In seconds he's snoring loud and hard. Hopefully he can sleep in peace?

Many Hours Later

Amber cruises through the town listening to her Keisha Cole CD. She left the lawyer's office over thirty minutes ago where she turned over a whopping $25,000.00 to him. She feels so good knowing that Samad will be freed. She never imagined herself doing something like this for a man. Never has she cared enough for a man to give him twenty-five cent let alone twenty-five thousand.

She misses him so much that she would have done anything to get him out of there. She can only imagine the questions he will have for her once he gets out. She's sure he will want to know where she got that type of money from to bail him out as well as pay for his attorney's fee. At this point she doesn't know what she's going to tell him. She'll just deal with that when the time comes.

After stopping at White Castle to fulfill her unborn child's craving, Amber finally parks in front of the beauty parlor in an attempt to meet her appointment. She stuffs the last burger into her mouth greedily. She pulls the visor down to make sure her face is clean and out the door she steps to the beauty parlor.

She grabs the door handle and pulls it gently. To her surprise the door does not budge. As she's standing there baffled a buzzer sounds off. Deja signals her to come inside.

Amber pulls the door open and walks in. "What's that all about?"

"Security measures," Deja replies. "Too much bullshit going on." The bullshit that she's referring to is really the stalking woman. The comment she made about being in Deja's chair makes Deja very uncomfortable. Just to know that the woman was that close to her and she had no clue really scares her. She feels a little safer now that everyone has to be buzzed in instead of just walking in off of the street.

The ambiance of the shop is so abnormal today. Normally music is blasting from the speakers while the beauticians are screaming at the top of their lungs but today it's quiet and all their faces are quite saddened.

Amber knows exactly what the long faces are all about. She takes a quick glance at the sink where a huge Poland Spring bottle sits. The word donation is spelled out across the bottle. On the wall behind the sink there is a huge collage which has the words RIP Luscious spelled out with a bunch of pictures of him spread all around. Amber's heart drops at the sight of it. Although she knows exactly what happened she has to play it off. "What happened?" she asks Deja.

Deja shakes her head from side to side. "His mother came here this morning and told us police found his body in the graveyard early this morning. Dead with two bullet holes in the back of his head."

"Yeah?" Amber asks with a phony shocked look on her face. As she's standing here Luscious' screams sound off in her head. "Lil Bit please," he cried. "Please," he begged. Now the sound of the two deadly gunshots ring in her head. The guilt is killing her. Damn, she thinks to herself. "Who would do something like that to him?"

"They don't know as of yet. He told me he was going away with family. He told his mother he was going to Cancun with a friend. She don't know who the friend is or nothing. Apparently he just got back then he got killed. They don't know if the friend he went with killed him or his lover did it. His mother told me that his lover said he spoke to Luscious early that day and he didn't sound right. He said the way he was talking was so not like him. He kept telling him just in case you never see me again just know I love you. It was like he knew he was going to die. He wouldn't tell the lover where he was or who he was with but he told him he would explain later."

Amber feels terrible hearing the story. Maurice had him murdered, thinking he would tell all the business and in all actuality he told no one at all. Amber tries to throw Deja off. "Shit, sounds like the lover might have done it. Luscious probably came back and admitted where he was with another man and the lover probably went berserk. All that other shit might be just him trying to put it on somebody else."

"Nah, his mother said detectives are more pointing to whoever he went away with. They don't know who it is yet but they're on it hard, trying to figure out who the friend is."

What, Amber mumbles under her breath. She can't believe her ears. Oh shit, she thinks to herself. What have I gotten myself into?

///// CHAPTER 38 /////

12:17 A.M. Amber sits behind the steering wheel of her Range Rover. She's quite tired but she refuses to leave. She's been waiting for Samad to be released from the County Jail for the past two hours. She can't wait to see him. It seems like she hasn't seen him in months.

Suddenly a few men step out of the door in spurts. Amber looks closely, hoping to see Samad. All the men come out and start stepping in their own direction. Finally Samad steps out. Amber's heart races with joy as soon as she sees him.

Instead of honking the horn to catch his attention she decides to just sit back secretly, just admiring him. He stands there with his chin high in the air taking deep breaths of the polluted air. He then bends over, lacing his boots up. As soon as he's done, he takes off like a flash of lightening up the hill. His joy of being freed makes him sprint like a track star. He feels they must have made a mistake by even calling his name and he doesn't want to be anywhere near when they realize that they made the mistake. He's sure it had to be a mistake because he doesn't know anyone who could have put that type of money up for him.

Amber starts her truck and cruises up the hill until she finally catches up with him. She rolls the window down. "Excuse me, handsome!" she shouts.

Samad looks over as he's running. His face lights up with joyfulness. He stops short, almost tripping over his feet. He's so delighted to see her that he runs over to her truck. Amber slams the truck into park and hops out quickly. They stand in the middle of the dark street hugging like they have not seen each other in years.

Twenty Minutes Later. "I don't care how much the bail was I was coming for my man," she smiles as she cruises up the block.

Samad's pride is somewhat hurt because it's obvious that she knows that he couldn't afford to post his own bail. Foolish pride, he thinks to himself. He's happier to be out than he is ashamed. He will regain his pride after he pays her every dollar back. His curiosity is running wild, giving him no choice but to ask. "Where did you get fifteen thousand to bail me out?" he asks.

Damn, the dreaded question, she says to herself as she mentally searches for the perfect answer. "Ask me no questions and I tell you no lies," she says with a sexy smile. The look in his eyes tells her that her answer is not sufficient for him. "You're free. We're here together. All your questions will be answered in due time. For now let's just savor the moment," she says as she turns into the garage of her building. She presses the button on her remote and the garage opens up slowly. As she cruises through the garage she starts to have second thoughts. By bringing Samad here she's violating one of Maurice's major rules. He pays the total rent of $4,000 with the clause that she is never under any circumstances to bring a man here. His rule is not just because of his possessiveness and jealousy but it also has to do with the fact that at times he stashes work here.

He never wants to have his work in danger by some man coming in and running off with it. Amber has followed his rule all these years until now. The things that love will make one do, she thinks to herself. She sure hopes nothing bad comes from this.

Chills run up her spine as she thinks of what would happen if Maurice was to find out. She knows exactly what the repercussion would be but at this point she's willing to take the chance. For once Samad has been evicted from his apartment and claims he has nowhere to go. Another reason she's brought him here is to prove to him that she doesn't live with a man. She sure hopes that her plan doesn't backfire like the last one did.

Samad sits in awe as he looks at the exotic cars that are parked in this garage. He's highly impressed yet he tries to act as if he's not. He wonders what it costs to live in a spot like this. That thought only feeds his curiosity even more.

In minutes they make it into her apartment which takes his breath away. Hardwood floors, mahogany stained walls, marble countertops and beautiful contemporary furniture fills the apartment. He looks around in search of any thing that confirms the fact that a man lives here and he finds not a trace. Her pink colored bedroom seals the deal, bringing total satisfaction and contentment to his heart.

An Hour Later. The air sweeps over the balcony causing goose bumps to pop up on Amber and Samad's nude bodies. They conceal themselves with only the huge beach towel that Amber has draped over her back and shoulders. Samad lies back on the lazy boy as Amber straddles her body over his lap. Her legs wrap tightly around his waist. The cold breeze causes Amber's nipples to stiffen. There they stand erect, glowing in the dark like high beams in Samad's eyes. He grabs a handful of her hair and yanks it, causing her to drop her head back. Her eyes set on the moon and the stars as he plants soft kisses from her chin on down to the center of her breast. The feeling of his hot breath on her breasts gives her the chills. He sticks his arms underneath her armpits, and cups her shoulders with his hands. He thrusts himself into her as he forces her onto him. She leans her head back, and moans loud not even caring who hears her. Her voice echoes in the air like the sound of a wolf howling. Her moaning makes him thrust harder in search of more moaning. His duty is to satisfy her. The more she moans the more he feels like he's doing his job. He stands up and Amber wraps her legs around his waist even tighter. As he walks over to the rail, he continues to pound her with short gentle strokes. He hangs Amber's entire torso over the rail. Blood rushes to her head as she stares onto the ground from the 26th floor. Fear of being dropped comes into her mind but the pleasure overrides it. Deep pounding causes Amber to scream at the top of her lungs. The sensation becomes overwhelming for Samad and he can no longer take it. He grabs her tightly as he collapses and lands onto one knee. He pins her body against the rail and thrusts himself deeper into her.

"Aghh," she grunts as she pushes him onto his back violently. She bounces up and down as hard as she can. This goes on for minutes and minutes, getting more and more intense.

Samad leans his head back as Amber sexes him into ecstasy. He's motionless with his mouth wide open. Amber assumes that her lovemaking has taken over him but little does she know that he fell asleep minutes ago.

Being awake for the last 48 hours in the County Jail has finally caught up with him. What terrible timing. Samad snores loud and hard while Amber's juices gush from deep within. "Oooooh," she sighs as she leans over and places her head on his chest. In seconds they both take turns seeing who can snore the loudest. And the winner is?

///// CHAPTER 39 /////

After hours and hours of calling D-Nice's cousin, Samad hated to accept the fact that he may be ducking his call but he had no choice. Samad assumes that he must be avoiding the call, thinking that he's calling to beg for bail money for D-Nice. While they were in the county, D-Nice called him and even called his mother to relay messages to him but still he sits in the County Jail.

Samad hates to feel like he's sweating him but he has to because he has no other way to get back on his feet. D-Nice's cousin is the only person in the town that he has a business relationship with. All his years of hustling, he's only dealt with him and he figures he should have no problem giving him a little work to get started. If for no other reason at all he feels he should give him something just so he can get back into position to pay him the money for the work they got on consignment from him. Samad hopes that he will allow him to pay him back little by little after he works up the money to bail D-Nice out.

His loyalty to D-Nice makes him feel bad that he's free while his main man is still behind bars with those savages. He doesn't wish jail on his worst enemy let alone his best friend in the world. He remembers how much pressure he was under while he was in there and hates to think that his man could be under that type of pressure. That only increases his drive and motivation to get on his job in getting him out of there.

Calling and getting no answer forced Samad to sit out on this block and wait for the man to come through. D-Nice's cousin wholesales cocaine throughout the city but this block is his foundation where he controls all the cocaine that is bought from out here. If he can't be found anywhere else, he can be found here most of the day when he's not making other moves.

After sitting here for half an hour, Samad's eyes light up as he sees the midnight blue 750 BMW pull up and park a few cars ahead. Samad watches angrily as the man hops out of the car. He decides to dial the man's number once again to see if he sends the call to voicemail. Deep down inside he hopes that the man is just not carrying that phone anymore.

Samad dials and watches the man as he steps away from his car. He looks at the display and once he sees the number he just lets the phone ring. "Hmphh, motherfucker," Samad says as he hops out of the driver's seat of Amber's Rover.

Samad had to beg for his life for Amber to loan him the truck. She offered several times to take him anywhere he had to go but he denied. No way in the world was he about to drag her along to watch him beg from this man. That would have made him feel less than the peon that he already feels like.

Amber's only problem with loaning him the truck is Maurice. All she needs is for someone to see Samad driving her truck throughout the town and she's sure all hell will break loose.

"Rah!" Samad shouts as he follows many steps behind. The man turns around and once he sees Samad, he becomes agitated instantly yet he tries to put a smile on his face.

"Oh what up?" he asks in a rather bland tone. "Where you come from?" he

111

asks as he looks around.

Fury wells up in Samad's heart. He forces himself to reach out and shake the man's hand. "I been calling you like crazy."

"Yeah? From what number?"

"The last number that just called you," Samad answers sarcastically.

"Oh, that was you?" he asks with a smile. "I didn't know who the fuck that was. I don't be answering calls I don't know."

"I left you crazy messages and Nice been calling you too." Samad feels that he has squeezed the man into a box with nowhere to run. He wonders what his next excuse will be.

"Man...I don't answer no calls from the building. What up though?"

Samad hesitates before replying. He has to quickly swallow his pride. "I'm fucked up," he whispers. "I been trying to get at you so I can get my hands on some work. I know we still owe you but the only way I can get that back to you is if you let me hold some start up? You know I'm good for it," he adds.

Rahiem stares at the ground the entire time that Samad is talking to him. He really has nothing to say in reply. He looks up and locks eyes with Samad. "What the fuck happened?"

"They raided the crib, got all the work you gave us the night before. An undercover sale, crack, a gun and money. I'm tapped. Every dime I had I spent on bail and a lawyer," he lies. "Twenty-five stacks."

"Man, I told ya'll to stop moving so reckless."

Samad interrupts him. "Man that's neither here nor there right now," he says with anger in his voice. "Shit happened already. Now we just have to do what we have to do. Gotta charge it to the game." He refuses to sit here and listen to him scold him like a child.

Rahiem wonders if Samad is telling the truth or not. His paranoia makes him believe that Samad may have been freed only to set him up and bring him in. The little work that he fronts them and how reckless they manage it, he feels that it's almost impossible for him to be able to come up with twenty-five grand. Rahiem looks into Samad's eyes and studies them. They show sincerity but he still doesn't trust him. His distrust made him avoid the calls just in case they may have had his phone tapped. "What they talking about?" he asks trying hard not to implicate himself in any way, just in case Samad is wearing a wire.

"They talking about twenty fucking years," Samad exaggerates. "I'll deal with that when the time comes. As Samad speaks the screeching of tires interrupts his conversation. He looks in the direction where the noise came from only to see a Cherokee speeding recklessly down the block. He looks at the plate number and is shocked to see that it's the exact same jeep that he rented from his dude, Mike. As the jeep passes he looks at the driver to see if he knows him but his face is not familiar at all. Jealousy fills his heart as he realizes that Mike must be renting cars to others. The jealousy is erased when he thinks of the dirt that was done in that jeep. The fact that he's renting to others could easily work to his advantage just in case the police are looking for that truck, they will never ever be able to prove that he ever had it.

The truck turns the corner out of sight and Samad starts his conversation back up. "Like I was saying...I'll deal with that when the time comes. Right now I gotta get Cuz up outta that building. All I need is like a couple of hundred grams and I can run with that."

Whoa, Rahiem says to himself. He realizes that replying to that statement alone can implicate him. He thinks before speaking, being careful to choose the right words. "Man, I ain't got shit," he lies. "I'm chilling. Shit crazy. Everything on freeze," he whispers as he spins around giving Samad his back. "If something come through, I'll let you know," he says as he walks away leaving Samad standing alone and feeling totally disrespected.

Punk motherfucker gave me his back, Samad says to himself as anger boils inside of his chest. "Hmphh," he snickers with rage as he watches him walk away. His mind tells him to catch up with him and beat him to death but he restrains himself. His plan A is down. He had no plan B, but now he's forced to come up with one. What will it be? Not even he knows.

///// CHAPTER 40 /////

After Samad's meaningless meeting with D-Nice's cousin, Rahiem, he became so discouraged that he came back here to Amber's house. He had a few other people that he wanted to reach out to, hoping he could get a few dollars from them or a little work but he couldn't get to them. The Rover's gas tank was on empty, just barely enough gas to get back to Amber's house. He didn't have a dollar to go toward refueling it.

Samad searched through his mental rolodex thinking hard who he could go to for help but came up with nothing or no one. He has to get back in position soon because he's sure if he doesn't all his workers will have gathered work from somewhere else. The thought of that makes the matter worse.

Samad returned here so lost that he didn't know what to do with himself. He's flat broke with no clue of how he's going to get back in the swing of things. At 4 P.M. he laid in bed and stressed himself to sleep.

It's now 11 P.M. and Amber sits upright in the bed with her head resting on the headboard. She tries hard to drown out the loud noise of Samad's snoring. Her lack of sleep has little to do with his snoring. It has more to do with her unborn child.

She doesn't know how she's going to break the news to Samad or even when would be the perfect time to tell him. It's obvious that now is the absolute wrong time. Although he didn't tell her much about his day she feels that it's safe to assume that it didn't go as he would have liked it to.

When he asked to borrow the truck he claimed to her that he had money on the street that he needed to collect. When her truck returned on E, she automatically figured that he hadn't collected a dime. She had planned to break the news to him today but the look on his face when he returned made her change her mind.

Amber's phone rings, interrupting her brainstorming. She quickly grabs hold of it to prevent Samad from waking up. When she sees Maurice's name and number her heart skips a beat. She lowers the volume and lets the phone continue to ring. What in the world does he want, she utters to herself. The phone begins ringing again. "Shit," she sighs almost silently. What the fuck, she says to herself as she leans her head back. Not even one minute later the phone starts up again. Now she's really curious to know why he's calling back to back. He never does that. Maybe he's having some type of emergency, she thinks. She wonders if he's in some type of trouble and needs her. Her mind is running wild, long after the phone stops ringing.

Maurice speeds across the Pulaski Highway as he holds the phone close to his ear. As soon as he hears Amber's voicemail he decides to send her a text. He figures her phone may be on silent mode but if she gets a text it will alert her.

He quickly reads over his text to make sure everything is spelled correctly. I'm drunk and tired. No way will I be able to make it all the way home tonight. I'm five minutes away from your crib. Get up and let me in. He presses the send button.

Amber has gotten out of the bed. She paces back and forth throughout her living room with bewilderment. She hopes he's not in any type of trouble. She would feel terrible if he is and she can't come to his aid. He's always been there for her and feels she should always be there for him.

Her text alert pops up and she begins reading instantly. Oh shit, she whispers. This can't be happening. She thinks to herself. "Five minutes?" she utters. "What the fuck am I going to do?" she whispers.

The nighttime doorman comes to mind instantly. Him and Maurice are quite cool. Maurice brings him expensive champagne and cigars. He even gives him a hefty Christmas bonus. She thinks of the time her and Maurice had a huge argument and she wouldn't let him in. Maurice bribed the doorman with five hundred dollars to let him up and it worked. He banged and banged on the door for an hour until she finally let him inside. I gotta think fast, she tells herself. He's probably on the block by now.

In seconds she takes off out of the apartment, barefoot with a tank top and ass clenching boy shorts on. She stands anxiously as the elevator takes forever to come to her floor. "Hurry, hurry, please?" she begs in a whisper. Finally she gets in the elevator and down to the ground level she goes. When she gets to the bottom floor, she's surprised to see that the concierge's desk is empty. She looks around and he's nowhere in sight. "Fuck," she sighs. Just her luck he isn't working tonight and no one will be at the desk to stop Maurice. "Shit."

Finally the pleasant tune of whistling can be heard from around the corner of the hall. Amber recognizes his whistling as well as the refreshing smell of his cologne. She runs around the corner to meet him.

"Miss Baker, are you alright he asks as he looks her up and down. His eyes never make it back up to her face. They get stuck on her perky nipples that are cutting through her skin gripping, see through wife beater. Never has he seen her like this.

"Ben," she says with a shortness of breath. She peaks at the door hoping that Maurice doesn't pull up while she's standing here. Then there will be no way that she can tell him that he can't come up. "Do not let anyone up to my apartment. No one. You hear me? Anyone shows up. I'm not home. No one," she emphasis.

"Are you okay?" he asks.

"Yes and no," she replies. "Ben, no one," she repeats.

The look in her eyes tells him that something isn't right. "Are you sure you're alright?"

"Yes but I won't be if you let someone upstairs," she admits. She hated to admit that to him. Ben swears that her and Maurice are a real couple and now he may think she's a slut. That bothers her but right now her image isn't important to her.

"Oh...I got you," he replies with a smirk on his face. Thoughts of blackmail enter his mind quickly. He's sure she would never want Maurice to find out about this. He wonders what she's willing to do to remove it from his memory bank. He looks her up and down seductively.

"Thank you, Ben," she says as she spins around and jogs off.

Ben licks his lips with perversion as he watches her tight little ass bounce up and down vibrantly. "No problem, Miss Baker. No problem at all," he smiles.

As soon as Amber steps out of the elevator her phone rings. He must be here she thinks. How close that was?

Maurice parks his car in front of the building where he always does. It's a fire zone but he pays a small fee to the concierge to park it there. Maurice staggers into the building. "Big Ben!" he shouts as he's passing the desk.

"Money Mo!" he shouts back. Damn, he thinks to himself. How can I stop him? "Mo, you gotta sign in."

"Sign in?" he asks sarcastically. "What's this some new shit ya'll on?"

"Yeah, they enforcing the rules," he says as he steps closer to Maurice with the pad in his hand. "New boss who plays everything by the book. They're taping this whole lobby right now. No more sleeping on the job," he laughs while trying to ease the tension that he sees building up in Maurice's face. Maurice looks at him with his face wrinkled up like a piece of crumbled paper. He signs the book. "As a matter of fact, do me a favor? At least make it look good?" he says knowing that he's pushing Maurice way beyond the limit. "Press her doorbell right here," he instructs.

Maurice is furious now. He presses the bell and waits for her answer but he gets none. He presses again and again but to no avail.

"Maybe she isn't home," Ben says. "Come to think about it I been here since 11 and she hasn't passed me."

"She sleep hard. I'm just gone go up and tap on the door like I always do."

"Damn, Money Mo, I'm afraid I ain't gone be able to let you do that," he says sadly. "New policy."

"Ben, this me baby. You know me," he says as he digs into his pocket. "I pay that girl rent," he smiles.

"I know but it's the rules."

"Rules are made to be broken," Maurice smiles as he holds three hundred dollar bills loosely in his hand.

The money sure does look enticing to Ben but he can't accept it. "Mo, I can't. I told you we're on tape."

"Man, fuck the rules and the tape," he says sternly. Maurice hates to be challenged. "I'm going up," he says as he walks past the desk.

"Mo, please?" he begs. "Let me do my job, bruh?" Maurice stands at the elevator waiting for it to come down. He ignores Ben totally. "Come on Mo, don't do this. You're putting my job in danger. The camera will show you going up without her buzzing you in. Technically I'm supposed to call the police once you pass my desk."

"Do your job then. You'd call the law on me?"

Ben shakes his head from side to side. "No, that's why I'm going to lose my job," he whispers. "Because I won't."

The look in his eyes makes Maurice feel bad. The fact that he said he won't call the law on him makes him respect him as a real stand up dude. Maurice will never get in the way of a man trying to feed his family. He rolls his eyes coldly as he walks away from the elevator. As he exits the building he paces in front as he calls Amber over and over until he finally gets sick and tired of hearing her voicemail.

Amber paces nervously throughout her spacious living room. Her stomach is queasy from nervousness. She tiptoes around quietly in the dark. She hopes that Ben doesn't give in and let Maurice upstairs.

She knows how aggressive and manipulating Maurice can be. She can imagine him forcing his way up here. Any minute now she's expecting him to be banging on her door.

Samad comes walking into the living room. "Ma, what you doing up?" he asks. "Why you in the dark?"

"No reason," she replies in a low whisper.

"Well come to bed," he says as he stands there awaiting her. "I need you next to me."

His words melt her away. "Here I come," she says as she steps toward him. As she passes the sofa, she plants the phone underneath the cushion to muffle the sound of the phone just in case it starts to ring again. She closes the bedroom door shut behind her before hopping into bed. All she can do is pray that Maurice doesn't come up. It's better for both of their sakes.

///// CHAPTER 41 /////

Amber sits at the table of the huge Italian restaurant. It's packed from wall to wall which is the reason for the hour long waiting list. Across form Amber sits Samad. The look on his face is downright pitiful. The look on his face represents the status of his pockets. In his pocket he holds not one dime and he doesn't know where he's getting the next dime from.

If not for Amber he wouldn't even have clothes on his back or even a haircut. All his clothes are padlocked in his apartment and he can't get them out until he pays the rent he owes. It broke his heart when Amber left him a couple of hundred dollars so he could go and get himself a few outfits. The last twenty dollars he had left he spent on his haircut.

The thoughts that have run into his mind should be illegal to just think about them. Never before has he thought like this. His worst thought of all is committing suicide. That thought sneaks into his mind quite often. He can't imagine living like this forever and deep inside he really feels like he will never come out of this situation. He really can't imagine killing himself but at this point he can imagine killing someone else in order for him to come up. If push comes to a shove he already has a victim in mind. In no way is he a robber or a thief but his empty pockets are sure making him think like one.

The suspect he has in mind is D-Nice's cousin. The way he played him erased any respect that Samad had for him. He feels that Rahiem doesn't care about him or even his own cousin so why in the world should he care about him. Samad has already planned the robbery and committed the murder in his head as if it has happened already. He's planned how he can get him, where he will snatch him from and all the details in between. He sure hopes that it doesn't come to that but if his ribs sqeeze together any tighter he will have no choice but to carry out his plans.

Amber puts a great deal of pressure on Samad as well. Seeing the high quality lifestyle that she lives makes him feel worthless because he can't contribute a penny to it. He's used to spoiling his women and splurging on them. Although he's never played on Amber's level he was always at the top of his game. To be at a dinner table with a woman who is paying the tab for his food makes him feel lower than the lowest.

Samad's food has barely been eaten. He's played with the food more than actually consuming it. He hasn't eaten a full meal since he got locked up. His stress overpowers his hunger.

The waitress walks over to their table handing Amber the dessert menu. "Dessert for you?" the waitress asks.

Amber looks over at Samad who shakes his head negatively. "No thank you," Amber replies. As the waitress walks away Amber digs into her pocketbook. "I have dessert for you," she smiles. "You want it?" she asks as she reaches over the table with her hand closed tightly.

"What?"

"You want it?" she smiles. "Here."

"What is it?"

"Just open your hand." Samad gives in. He opens his hand and Amber drops a small black box into the palm of his hand.

"What's this?" he asks as he looks at the box and tries to figure out what it is.

"My remote starter," she says seductively as she bites onto her bottom lip. "Start me up…shut me off at your leisure."

Samad recognizes the look on her face. He's made notice that whenever she gets horny she makes this particular face. "Huh?" he asks as he looks at the little box. The numbers 1,2, and 3 are written in bold letters with a tiny lever on the side.

"Hit it," Amber instructs.

He does as she says. With his thumb he flicks the lever into the three position. Like magic Amber bounces in her seat. The expression on her face looks like she just got struck by a bolt of lightening. She's even surprised at the effect of it.

Samad quickly shuts the power off, not understanding what just happened. He slowly flicks the lever into the two position while watching her face closely. Once again she bounces in her seat. This time she is a little more at ease. The look of pleasure that she displays on her face causes him to keep the power on.

Amber sinks into her seat enjoying and appreciating the moment. Just as her eyes start to roll into the back of her head, Samad shuts the power off. Her eyes pop wide open. "What happened?" she asks.

"What the hell is this?" he asks with a baffled look on his face.

She leans over the table close to him, as she looks him square in the eyes. "You hold the remote to my remote control panties," she whispers sexily.

"What?" he laughs goofily.

Amber is happy to see a smile on his face. She hasn't seen the trace of one in weeks. She knew he would get a kick out of her new toy. She bought it from the Pleasure Party that Deja dragged her to. She invested in the toy purely with Samad in mind. The panties have a built in vibrator right in the center of the crotch area.

Samad hits the lever once again and like magic, he controls Amber like a robot. He goes from slow, teasing to fast and intense at the touch of one button. She sits helplessly as he plays not just with her body but her mind as well. He blasts the speed then just as she's about to orgasm he slows it up and teases away at her. The fact that they're sitting in the middle of a restaurant makes it all the more exciting. No one else in the room has a clue.

Amber sits back with her eyes wide open, trying hard to play it cool and calm. She grips the tablecloth in her hands, damn near snatching it from the table. Her glass of wine tips over, spilling onto the table but she pays no attention to it all. "Oh," she whispers as she sprays her juices from within. In seconds her panties are soaking wet. Samad goes on for minutes and minutes. The sensation is at times unbearable but not a complaint is uttered from Amber's lips. She just sits back while Samad controls the vibrator that is vibrating her mind, body and soul.

///// CHAPTER 42 /////

Deja stands by the cash register in her shop. She sifts through the pile of money while Luscious' mother watches her closely. The pile of money appears to be a lot but it mostly consists of singles.

The middle beautician walks toward them as she digs into her apron. She dumps the contents of her apron pocket onto the pile of money.

"Thank you, baby," Luscious' mother says graciously.

In a matter of minutes a few of the customers donate a few dollars as well. Deja quickly counts the money and is disappointed at the total amount. She looks at Luscious' mom and is quite ashamed to tell her that his closest friends in the world have only come up with $455.00 to go toward his burial.

The door buzzer sounds off causing Deja to look at the door. Saved by the bell, she thinks to herself. "Hit the buzzer!" she shouts as she sees Amber standing at the door.

The buzzer sounds off and Amber prances inside. She speaks to everyone while stepping to the back of the shop. She sees Deja standing there counting money next to the donation jar and automatically assumes this woman is Luscious' mom. Amber's guilt prevents her from being able to look the woman in the eyes. Just to think it's her selfish plan that has gotten a mother's child taken away from her. The thought of that has been bothering her ever since the murder of Luscious.

"Deja, can I speak to you for a minute?" she asks as she walks past the woman with her head hanging low with shame. She quickly steps into Deja's office.

"Excuse me, Miss Smith," Deja says before following Amber into the office. "What's up?" she asks as she closes the door behind her.

"How much ya'll came up with?" Amber asks.

"Girl, not even five hundred lousy ass dollars," she says shamefully. "I feel so bad cause his poor ol' mother struggling with her five grandkids that she got custody of cause the daughter strung out on drugs. She thought she had a few dollars to go toward the burial but the daughter stole her ATM card the night before Luscious got killed. Luscious didn't have no life insurance. She was about to have him cremated cause she knew she wasn't going to be able to come up with the money to bury him. Then me with my big ass mouth gone say hold up we gone come up with the money. I thought we would at least come up with twenty-five hundred. Damn, I'm ashamed to even give his mother this shit. She can barely buy flowers for his funeral with this money. I'm gone have to hit my little stash and take out about a thousand. At least she will have fifteen hundred. It ain't nothing but it's more than what she started with."

"Here," Amber says as she fumbles through her purse. She hands a white envelope over to Deja.

Deja is shocked at the thickness of the envelope and is quite curious to know just how much is actually inside. "How much is this?" she asks anxiously.

"Twelve thousand," Amber whispers.

"Twelve thousand, wow," Deja manages to utter from her lips. She's at a loss of words. She can't believe that Amber would donate this amount of her money on behalf of Luscious when she knows how much Amber actually hated Luscious. She knew that Amber couldn't even stand the sight of him, ever. Little does she know Amber hasn't put up twelve thousand of her money. She only put up two thousand dollars of her own money. The other ten grand is actually the pay that Luscious was supposed to get for bringing the ten kilos back from Jamaica. Amber wouldn't be able to live with herself if she allowed Luscious to be buried like a welfare recipient when she has ten thousand dollars of his in her possession. The two thousand that she's donating is guilt money. "Lil Bit, that's big," Deja says with a shocked look on her face.

"The man needs to be buried," Amber says casually.

"But Lil Bit, you hated his guts."

"I didn't hate him. I hated his lifestyle. You know me I don't do well with gays.

I think it's trifling. It's because of them that AIDS has spread across our country like that. That's disgusting…Eeel," she says as she thinks of it. "But at the end of the day he's still human and I feel sorry that his family can't come up with the money."

Deja thinks of the contribution that Amber is making and she can't even stand him. She realizes that the least she can do as his friend is add a little more money to the pot. She walks over to the huge picture on her wall. She carefully removes the picture and immediately starts turning the lock trying to get the exact number. She gets the safe open and from it she pulls two stacks of money. She shuts the safe and places the picture back on the wall. The both of them step out of the office where Luscious' mom awaits them.

"Miss Smith, here," Deja says as she hands her the envelope. "That's fourteen thousand and five hundred dollars," she whispers.

The old woman can't believe her ears. Never did she imagine them coming up with this amount of money. In all her years of living she's never seen this amount of money at one time. "Oh thank you," she cries. "This is more than enough. Thanks to ya'll my baby will be able to have the best funeral ever." Tears begin dripping down her face at a rapid pace causing Deja to cry as well. Amber turns her head to avoid a guilt tear trickling down her face.

Deja doesn't want to take the risk of something happening to Miss Smith with almost fifteen thousand dollars in her possession. "Uh, Lil Bit, could you please drop Miss Smith off for me? We can't let her walk the street with all that money on her. I would do it but I have ten clients waiting on me." Amber looks at her with disgust. "Please?" she begs.

"Sure," she says with agitation in her voice as she starts to walk toward the door.

Minutes later, Miss Smith straps her seatbelt on as Amber cruises off. Amber can't believe she's actually in the car with the mother of a man who has been murdered because of her.

"Excuse me dear but I didn't get your name," she says in a sweet and innocent voice.

"Am," she utters before thinking of the fact that she may be linked to the murder. "Lat," she's about to say in reference to her alias Latoya Baker but she realizes that is the name that she flew to Jamaica under. "Lil Bit…just call me Lil Bit."

"Ok, Lil Bit. Again I thank ya'll and I know Lucias thanks ya'll. I know he's in heaven looking down at us now." That thought sends chills through Amber's body. She nods her head up and down. "Baby, I won't rest until everyone that was involved in my son's murder has been captured and executed. They slaughtered my baby. I hope they get the death penalty."

Goosebumps cover Amber's body due to the things that the woman is saying. Her curiosity is begging to be fed. "So, no one still knows nothing?"

"Oh no, they know something."

Fear rips through Amber's gut. "Oh yeah?"

"Yeah," she says while nodding her head up and down. "We thought he was in Cancun. Come to find out he was in Jamaica. Whoever he was with he knew and trusted, is what the detectives said. I also found out that my son wasn't just into men. He liked women as well. On his lips and his face were traces of red lipstick…

even on the collar of his shirt."

Amber looks at herself in the rearview mirror. Her red lipstick is plastered neatly on her lips just as it was the day in the airport when she kissed Luscious to throw the police off. Her heart starts to pound like a drum.

"They also found a few strands of hair on his t-shirt as well."

Amber swallows the lump that forms in her throat, sounding off loudly. Oh my God, she thinks to herself.

"Somebody is going to get charged for my son's murder and I won't sleep until they do. I'm not going to let them get away with it and more importantly God isn't going to let them get away with it!"

///// CHAPTER 43 /////

One Month Later Sade sits back in her recliner as Amber vents out to her. Sade doesn't say a word in response. She only listens because it's obvious that Amber has a great deal on her mind and just wants to let it loose.

"Girl, I don't know what to do. How did I get myself into all this mess. My life is a wreck. I'm pregnant," she sighs as she looks down at her stomach. Amber's small frame hides her pregnancy well. To the naked eye the tiny bulge can't be seen but Amber's self conscience makes her believe that she's showing more than she actually is. "And the damn father of the baby don't even know I'm pregnant. I don't know the right time to tell him. It's only going to add to his stress. He's flat broke and can't afford to take care of himself let alone a child. Deja was right. I should have listened to her and I wouldn't be in all this shit. Girl, it's crazy. I can't even sleep at night. I'm up all night stressing. Thoughts of me being dragged in for questioning for Luscious' murder, back and forth debating if I should have this baby or not. I have to figure out what I'm going to do before it's too late to have an abortion. Then Maurice…he calls every night trying to come over. I think he knows something is up because he's never tried to come over every night like he does now. I've ran out of excuses for him. The more I deny the harder he's going to try and get in. I have to get Samad out of there. He has to go somewhere. I mean I love him but he can't live there. Maurice pays the rent for crying out loud. How disrespectful is that?" she asks. "Samad is getting way too comfortable. Last night he asked could he put his clothes in the dresser. This morning he had the nerve to ask do I have an extra key so when he goes to the gym downstairs he can get back in."

"What?" Sade asks with shock. "I know you didn't fall for that one?"

"Hell no!" Amber replies.

"Yeah, he's getting way too comfortable. What did you tell him?"

"I told him that my little sister has the other key." Amber's face becomes more saddened. "But I cleared out a drawer for his clothes," she admits with shame.

"Girl, you just added wood to the fire," says Sade. "Now you're never going to be able to get him out of there. Why would he leave? Everything is laid out for him. Put yourself in his place. A beautiful apartment overseeing the Hudson River, looking right into Manhattan, all the amenities, pool, tennis courts, basketball courts, a gym, and he got you there holding him down. He's living like a king. I'm sure he never lived like that. Where was his apartment?" she asks.

"On Sussex Avenue," she whispers.

"Girl," she says as she shakes her head from side to side. "I'm sorry to tell you this, this late in the game but I didn't want to get in the way of you being happy. The glow in your eyes made me feel good. You deserve to be happy but it's obvious that he's not on your level."

"I know, I know," Amber replies. "Girl, I don't know if I should have this baby." Just as she makes that statement she gets a swishing feeling in her belly. She feels that the baby is giving her a sign that it hears her. She pats her tummy for the baby's comfort. "Sorry Baby," she says in a baby voice. "What the fuck am I going to tell Maurice? He will kill me, Samad and the baby."

Sade sits quietly. In her heart she's sure that what Amber is saying is the truth. At this point she realizes that Amber has gotten herself in way too deep. She wishes she knew what to tell her but unfortunately she doesn't. Amber has gotten herself into this mess and only Amber can get herself out of it.

///// CHAPTER 44 /////

Samad tosses and turns in the bed as he's been doing the entire night and every other night. He doesn't get much sleep. In spurts he may get a wink in here and there but it lasts no more a few minutes. The insomnia is starting to get the best of him. He's tired, agitated and overall disgusted with himself. He walks around all day in a blur. He's only been broke for about 45 days yet it feels like an eternity. He can't understand how a person lives their entire life like that.

Samad lays around in the bed day and night in a state of depression. He always looked at depression as a white person's disease that they just made up for dealing with what blacks call 'life.' He always looked at it as a cop out. Today he realizes that depression is real and it's not just a Caucasian disease. He can't even stand the sight of himself so he barely looks in the mirror. He feels like a total failure. He sleeps the whole day away and lays wide awake the entire night.

A few hours ago D-Nice called as he does every night. In no way does Samad look forward to the calls but he still answers them. It breaks his heart when D-Nice asks him has anything changed yet and he has to tell him no. Samad hates to say it but D-Nice may have to fight his case from the inside and to make matters worse he may have to do it with a public pretender as Amber calls it.

Samad feels extremely guilty because it feels as if it's all his fault that D-Nice is in the situation that he's in. The sale was made on his shift by his workers while D-Nice was home lounging and because of Samad he was dragged into the situation.

Samad's thoughts of suicide pop into his mind now more than ever. He would rather die than to live broke like he is. Each morning he wakes up, he tells himself that he's going to get drunk and blast his brains out. The only problem is he doesn't have the money to get drunk with. It's also a good thing that his gun was confiscated. He doesn't have the means to get another one but if he did he's sure before killing himself he could find something better to do with it like killing D-Nice's cousin and robbing him of everything.

Samad lifts his head up and looks at the clock that sits on the nightstand. He's shocked to see that only fifteen minutes have passed since he dozed off. The feeling of Amber's eyes burning into his back causes him to turn around, facing her. There she lies wide awake just staring at him just as she was doing before he fell asleep the last time and the time before that. "What's wrong?" he asks while staring into her eyes.

"Nothing," she says as she lowers her gaze.

"Bullshit," he replies. "I've dozed off and woke back up ten times tonight and each time I wake up you're looking at me. I know why I can't sleep but what's your reason? You be up at night more than me."

Amber shakes her head from side to side with a troubled look on her face. She has to admit that he's absolutely correct.

"What is it?" he asks. "Talk to me mami," he says as he stares deeply into her glassy eyes. "Something is bothering you and whatever it is, for whatever reason, you can't tell me. Check this out, I'm gone turn around and whatever it is just tell it to the back of my head," he says as he turns around, laying on his side. He stares at the wall, wondering what it could be that's bothering her.

"I don't know where to start," she whispers.

Damn, that much, Samad says to himself. "Just follow your heart," he replies nervously.

Well here goes nothing, Amber tells herself as she prepares to drop the bomb on him. "I'm pregnant," she whispers.

"What?" he asks as he turns around facing her. "By who?" Those words rip through her soul. She has to bite her lip just to prevent from cursing him out. This is exactly why she been dreading telling him. She attempts to speak but her mouth freezes wide open with rage. By who?" he repeats.

"Samad, please turn back around," she begs.

"By who?"

"Please?" He turns around to face the wall again. His temperature boils as he thinks of the fact that he's in love with someone's baby's mother. "By you," she whispers.

"By me?" he asks sarcastically. "How many months?"

"A little more than two months," she whispers.

A little more than two months he says to himself as he starts to calculate in his mind. He quickly realizes that two months ago he was at the Sand Bar watching her being carried onto a yacht by a man. The same feeling that he felt while watching her that night relives itself. "So how do you know it's mine?" he asks arrogantly.

"See this is the exact fucking reason why I didn't want to tell you!" she shouts viciously. "I know it's yours because you're the only man that I'm having sex with. What do you think I am, some whore?" she cries. "Do you think I'm the type of trifling bitch that would put another man's baby on you? I would get rid of it before I do that. It's your baby!"

"What about homeboy? I see you being carried by some unknown nigga two months ago. Now here we lay two months later and you're telling me you're a little over two months pregnant and I'm supposed to just take your word for it right? Why you wait so long to tell me? What…you told him too and he denied it?"

Amber sucks up her tears and cries to herself. She refuses to let him know that his remarks are getting to her. She's hiding her feelings well. The look on her face shows no emotion at all. "I didn't tell you because one, I didn't know if I was going to get rid of it or not and two because I didn't want to hear those words come out of your fucking mouth."

Samad sits quietly for a few seconds before turning around facing her. "Come on ,Ma, how am I supposed to just believe that? I don't even know who the fuck that dude was. For all I know that could have been your boyfriend at the time, could have been your husband. I don't know shit. I'm completely in the dark. For all I know you probably let me stay here cause ya'll broke up. You didn't let me come here before. Why now?"

"You know what?" she says with a smirk on her face. "Niggas always asking for the answers to questions they know they really don't want the answers to, knowing ya'll can't handle the truth. I'm about to give you all the answers you need. If you can't handle it and your feelings get hurt then so fucking what. You can't say that I didn't try to protect your feelings. That man you saw me at the club with," she says with her eyes stretched wide open. "Was he my husband? No! Was he ever my boyfriend? No! He's a very good friend of mine that I've known since I was 16 years old. Have we ever fucked? Yes!" she shouts.

Samad swallows the frog in his throat. Hearing this makes his stomach churn. His jealousy roars from deep within. He really can't handle the truth as she said but still he gluttons for punishment as he listens for more.

"We started fucking back when I was sixteen years old. He was a grown man fifteen years older than me. He was, actually the first man that I had consensual sex with. He not only turned me out but he taught me everything I know. I was never his girl. I was always his side chick. He's married with a bunch of mistresses. Did he take good care of me? Yes! He gave and will give me any and everything I want. Do I care for him? I do more than care for him. I love him but like a brother though. Do me and him have sex now? No! I stopped having sex with him back when me and you first met. I have not slept with him since and that's my right hand to God!" she says as she raises her right hand in the air. "I swear on my mother and my sister's grave and I never do that! Now, did you get what you want? Are you happy? Your feelings hurt? Huh? Good!"

Samad lays there speechless and jealous. He feels like his insides have been ripped out of his body. He lays back, just repeating her words. Her first love and she's admitting that she loves him? Damn, he sighs silently. He envisions Maurice's face in his mind. He plays back the scene as they stepped out of the bar, loaded with gleaming jewelry, stepping arrogantly into the yacht. Samad realizes that the dude has to be wealthy and in no way can he compare to him. Even at the top of his game he's sure he's nowhere near that man's level. He lays there jealous and feeling worthless.

"This entire situation has just been too much," she admits. "I love you but you're killing me. Laying around the house all day and all night depressed and irritated. I can't even say a word to you without you snapping on me. What happened to the old you?"

Samad rudely interrupts her. "What happened to the old me? He went to jail and came home broke!" he admits for the first time with no shame. That's what the fuck happened to him. Of course I'm depressed. I ain't used to this shit and can't get used to it! Waking up with no money in my fucking pockets. Can't even buy myself a fucking can soda!"

"Baby, I understand. I feel your pain but laying here depressed ain't gone change the situation. You have to pull yourself together and try to make something happen."

He feels humiliated. His ego speaks out for him. "Make something happen," he snaps. "What the fuck you think I'm just laying around here happy with the fact that you taking care of me? Do you actually think that? I ain't that type of mufucker. I ain't never let no chick do shit for me!"

"No, I know you ain't that type of dude but..."

"But what?" he asks defensively.

"But I think you gave up." Samad sits back quietly just evaluating what she's just said to him. He will never admit it to Amber but she's correct in her assumption. Actually he's given up many days ago. "I'm in a tight spot," she says. "I don't know if I should have the baby or not. I went to the abortion clinic a month ago but I just couldn't go through with it. There's a little life inside of me. I can't kill it. I couldn't go through with it. Now that I see you sitting around here all depressed I'm really not sure what I should do. If I have this baby, I'm going to need help. I can't do it all by myself. If you don't think you can provide for a baby let me know now so I don't jam myself up. Please?" she begs.

"What you think I'm a piece of shit?" he asks fiercely.

"No, I'm not saying that. I just don't want to make a bad decision. What should I do? Tell me?"

"Do whatever the fuck you want to do." His ego speaks out once again. He hops out of the bed and starts pacing around the bed.

Amber sits upright. She watches him closely as she sees the rage in his eyes. "Samad, baby, calm down."

"I'm calm," he smiles.

"Samad, I will help you in any way that I can. Just tell me what it is that you need to get the ball rolling. I want to see you get back on your feet. Your stress is my stress. Listen, I know you have nowhere to go and that is the reason that I allowed you to come here. I have no problem with you staying here from time to time but this living together thing, I've never done it before. It's all new to me. I have to get used to it."

Oh shit, Samad says to himself. Damn, I've really been a burden on her. This bitch playing me like I'm some scrub. "Say no more," he says arrogantly. "I will have my shit out by the morning."

"Samad, stop, please. I'm not putting you out. I know that you have nowhere to go. I just want you to get right, first. My little sister comes home from college in two weeks for the summer. I've always tried to be a good role model for her and lead her by example. And really I don't have a problem with you living here but like I said I've been on my own since I was 14...well I got my first apartment at 16 and I've always been alone. I have to get used to living with someone. I have no problem getting used to it but now is not the time. When my little sister comes home I can't have a man living here with us. What will she think? That's not the example that I want to set. I hope you understand?" she says as she talks to his back. He paces around the bed acting as if he's ignoring her but in all reality he's listening closely to every soul piercing word that she has said. "Two weeks should be more than enough time to put a couple of thousand together. Just tell me what it is that you need and I will do anything that I can to help you. Anything!"

///// CHAPTER 45 /////

Days Later

Deja stands in the center of her girlfriend's living room, wearing nothing but a tight fitted Juicy Couture t-shirt, a sexy, hot pink, laced thong and 3 inch sandals. She stands there with no shame whatsoever as three sets of eyes are glued onto her as if she's a science project.

A woman kneels down on her knees. Her face is just inches away from Deja's pitch black behind. "See, right here," she says as she drags her index finger across the lower part of Deja's rear. "See the little sagging, right here?" she asks.

"My ass don't sag," Deja replies defensively as the other women giggle at her response.

"Yes it does. Right here," the woman points. "But when I'm done it will no longer," she claims.

Deja is about to get her first butt job. She's no stranger to plastic surgery and implant jobs. In fact she's just about altered every part of her body. Her breasts were tiny A cups that she was so ashamed of. They were dried up like little raisins until she took her first trip to Dominican Republic where her implant job turned them into luscious C cups. Her flat tummy is the result of her last trip to D.R. where she got her tummy tuck to flatten out her slightly protruding belly. Even her smile is not really her own. She owes all the thanks for her pearly white Colgate smile to her dentist who chiseled down her own teeth and placed caps on top of them, giving her a picture perfect smile. Each year she finds something new to do to change her body. All the cosmetic surgery that she has totals out to approximately $40,000.00 but it cost her not a dime. It was all funded by the people who appreciate the changes more than she; her male friends.

Deja could have easily took another trip to D.R. to get this work done but a few good friends of hers referred this woman, saying that she does an equivalent job. Her fee is a little more costly than D.R. but it all works out. In D.R. this entire job would only cost her $250.00 but here it costs $500.00 per cheek. Deja figures it all equals out by the time you include the price of the flight and the hotel stay.

Deja and the two other women are all here for the same job but they're using Deja as the guinea pig. They talked her into going first just in case they don't like the results. Deja has no problem with that because she's seen this woman's work on a few women and feels total confidence in her.

The woman stands inches away from Deja's behind. "Don't move," she says. "Now," she says before snapping away with her camera. "That's the before shot. Then when we're done we'll take the after shot."

"Girl, I better not see pictures of my ass on You tube," she says in a joking manner.

"No I will only post it on Myspace," she jokes.

"Yeah, ok," Deja smiles. "Listen, I don't want no big ol' ghetto stink booty!"

"No, it will be the same size. The shot's are only going to round it off. Because there will be no more sagging it will appear to be much bigger. All the looseness down here, will round off, shifting to the middle and the top," she says while loading her syringe. She holds the needle in the air. "Now, don't move. You have to relax," she says as she gently smacks Deja's solid rear. "Come on loosen it up," the woman says as she smacks it again. This time it jiggles like Jello. "Right there, right there. Don't tense up. You ready?"

"As I will ever be," Deja says as she closes her eyes tightly, trying to prepare herself for the pain.

"Here we go," she says as she pokes Deja and inserts.

"Aghh!" Deja screams at the top of her lungs.

After seconds of excruciating pain, the woman speaks. "Ok, one down and five more to go and this cheek is done."

"Twelve needles?" Deja asks in a high pitched voice.

"Yup, I'm afraid so."

Deja can't even imagine going through this pain eleven more times. "Damn."

Meanwhile Amber sits in her living room watching television when Samad walks into the room. The look on his face is sad as usual.

"Ay Bay," she whispers. "You still haven't told me what you need? Are you avoiding the question?"

Yes, he is. Samad is trying hard to avoid taking money from her. His pride just won't allow him to do so. He's been thinking hard about what else he can do but nothing comes to mind. As much as he hates to take a handout from her he has no other choice. "I can't take a handout from you," he whispers with shame.

"It's not a handout," she argues. "Look at it as a loan. You giving me my money back," she says in a teasing manner. "Just tell me how much?"

Samad hesitates before replying. "I don't know." He's not sure how much he should ask for. He doesn't want to low ball and ask her for such a small amount that he can barely do anything with and then again, he doesn't know how much is too much.

"Tell me," she demands.

"I don't know. I guess like four thousand," he says while looking in her eyes for her reaction. Her baffled look has him confused.

"Four thousand? Is that enough? What can you do with that? Honey, you have a lot on your plate. You figure, you have to bail your friend out, a down payment for an apartment and still after that you have to have money to keep it all going. Do you really think you can do all of that with a measly four grand," she asks making him feel ashamed that he asked for such a small amount.

He instantly feels the need to defend himself. "I'm saying...I'm a hustler. I can take it up from nothing," he says with arrogance. "Yeah, that's chump change but I will be able to get it poppin' from there."

"I think I can do a little better than that for you," she smiles. "Give me about a week and let me see what I can put together. Don't worry. I got you, Bay," she says as she winks her eye at him seductively.

Eleven ass tightening shots later and Deja still stands in the center of the room with a swollen and extremely painful ass. The woman snaps away with her camera once again. "There," she says. Deja holds the mirror behind herself, staring at her new booty. "How does it look?" the woman asks.

"Swollen," Deja replies although she can see a little difference.

"Once the swelling goes down you will see the difference. It will be a little irritated for a few days but once the pain is over, it will be perfect."

"All the pain I just went through, it better be," Deja replies.

"Ay that's the price we pay for perfection," she says with a smile. "Congratulations on your new booty. Use it wisely," she smiles. "Take good care of it and it will take care of you."

///// CHAPTER 46 /////

One Week Later. Amber pulls up to Newark Penn Station, cruising slowly. She peeks around in search of her little sister.

Finally she spots her. She pulls up to the curbside where she sees Star accompanied by her good friend Tara. There they stand side by side looking like two video girls. They're dressed in tight jeans, fitted t-shirts, high heeled sandals and oversized designer sunglasses. They're definitely candy to any man's eyes. They're rocking designer everything on down to their luggage.

Amber pops the hatch of her truck open and sits while they drop their luggage into the back of the truck.

Tara hops into the truck first. She seats herself in the backseat. "Ay Lil Bit," she greets politely.

"What's up, Tee?" Amber replies as the passenger's door is snatched open. Amber's eyes are drawn to her sister's wide hips and thick thighs which have apparently stretched out miraculously since the last time she was home.

Star parks her wide load into the passenger's seat. Her eyes light up with joy at the sight of Amber's face. "Ay Sister!" she greets as she reaches over and gives Amber a huge hug.

Amber returns the hug rather coldly. "You couldn't find no bigger jeans than that?" she asks sarcastically.

"Oh boy, Sister," she sighs. "Not even a hello first?"

"What's that a size zero?"

"Sister, stop," Star says in a teasing manner, hoping she will ease up off of her. "This is a seven/eight, as I always wear."

"Well, I think it's time to start shopping for a nine/ten," she barks as she thinks of all the attention she may be getting from the boys at her school. "I think you are one cheeseburger away from a nine/ten. You better slow your ass down." Amber is trying to use reverse psychology on her. She's trying to make her believe that she looks fat in her clothes and hopefully she won't be so quick to reveal her body. In all reality, Amber knows the truth though. She has eyes and can see clearly. Star's juicy thighs and enormous behind extends from her tiny waist. With all her thickness, surprisingly she does not have an inch of fat anywhere on her body, not even her naturally flat tummy. Amber hopes her tactics work.

Star is done with her classes for the semester a few days earlier than expected. Amber was hoping for the total opposite. She hoped that Star would be a few days later instead. That would have given her time to get Samad out of the house before Star came home for summer recess. Unfortunately things have not gone as Amber expected which means she has a lot of explaining to do to Star about Samad. For the past ten years Maurice has been in Amber and Star's life. He's played the father role to Star for so long that she actually respects him like a father. Ever since she was eleven years old she has referred to Maurice as her sister's boyfriend.

Amber never explained to Star that Maurice is a married man. She's just allowed her to believe that they're a couple. Now to see Samad living here with her she wonders how Star will look at the situation. She also wonders show Star will look at her. She has no clue what she's going to tell her but she has to come up with something and quick.

Meanwhile Many Miles Away. Deja lies in her bed feeling so weak that she can barely move and when she does muster up enough strength to move, her body aches fiercely. She's been throwing up for days now. Her body is stiff and sore. She feels as if she's going to die. In fact she would rather die than to go through this type of pain. She had an allergic reaction to the shots. The woman explained to her that this may happen but she didn't say it would be this intense.

In the beginning she thought the pain would go away but it hasn't. Instead it's gotten much worse. She can't take another second of the pain. She's been debating for the last hour if she should go to the emergency room or not. The only thing that's stopping her is the fact that she will have explaining to do. What she did was against the law because the woman who did the work is not FDA certified. How embarrassed she would be to have to admit that she had a bootleg booty job done.

Deja pulls herself together and works up enough energy to drag herself out of the bed. She limps slowly across the room, trying hard not to apply too much weight onto her aching legs. The pain in her legs is excruciating but the pain in her butt is unbearable. The swelling has yet to go down, instead it has swollen even more.

She leans over to look in the mirror dreading to do so because she hates to see what her beautiful face has transformed into. Pity fills her heart as her eyes fix on what's in the mirror. She can barely see through her puffy, half closed, eyes. The bags that are underneath them are puffy and swollen as well. Her lips are double their normal size. She wonders if this is God's way of punishing her for altering her body and not being grateful for the body that he's given her.

"Please God," she prays. "Forgive me for not being grateful. Please don't let me die in here," she begs. "Please don't curse me forever. Please remove the pain from my body and turn my face back to the way it was. I promise I will be more grateful. If you just help me though this I promise I will never do anything to alter the body you have given me, nor will I ever complain again. God, I know we have been here before and you've heard me make promises to you before but this time, I promise to keep my word. I have learned my lesson. Please God, please?" she begs as the tears slide down her hideous face.

▰▰▰▰▰ CHAPTER 47 ▰▰▰▰▰

Amber has been in the company of Muhsee for hours. The entire time she has been listening to him talk. She's never heard him talk this much in all the years that she's known him. She now knows everything about him after him discussing the details of his childhood and even how he transformed from a poor kid here in Jamaica to the filthy rich drug lord that he is today.

The constant running of his mouth is all a result of the Jamaican Rum that he's been downing the past two hours or so. She's actually gotten a better understanding of him and now realizes that underneath his monstrous exterior he's actually a sensitive man. He only capitalizes off of fear to transform that into money and power.

After an hour long tour of his enormous and lush mansion, they finally end up in the tiniest room of the entire place. Muhsee opens the door and the loud creaking sound spooks her. He holds the door open for Amber to enter but instead she just peeks around attentively throughout the dimly lit room. The deep basement has the same extremely high ceilings as every other room does but has none of the luxuries that the rest of the mansion has.

"Enter," Muhsee demands quite impatiently. The tone of his voice makes her do just what he says. As soon as she steps inside her breath is snatched away by the foulest smell she has ever smelled in her life. The smell is a cross between feces, throw up and blood. She holds her breath in order not to smell it. The door slams shut loudly behind Muhsee. "This is the dungeon," he says as his voice echoes throughout the hollow room. The creepiness of the room pumps fear into Amber. She stands there wondering what he's going to tell her about this room.

Muhsee grabs hold of Amber's hand and leads her toward the center of the room. He stops short at two classroom desks. As Amber studies the desks she notices that they're not ordinary. On the legs of the desks, shackles are attached. Shackles are also attached to the table tops of the desks as well. Across the table tops are homemade looking harnesses with an opening in the center. "These are the only luxuries in this room as you can see."

Amber exhales quickly and sucks up another breath of air. She holds her lips closed tightly, trying to avoid the odor from seeping into her mouth. She looks around closely and notices that shackles are hung along all the walls. She quickly assumes what they could be used for. Muhsee walks further, leaving her in the center of the room. Finally he stands inches away from the cement wall. He turns around facing her. "This room I call the 'Many faces of Death.' Aghh," he grunts after taking another sip of the liquor. The liquor heats up his throat on contact. The burning sensation then blazes his esophagus on down to his belly. The look on his face becomes demonic. "In this room victims have been beaten to death," he says as he points at a dried-up bloodstain that marks the wall. He slowly points to another and another. "They've been tortured to death and even fried to death," he says as he points to a small incinerator. An evil smile appears on his face, frightening Amber even more. He steps toward her slowly. The closer he gets the more scared she becomes.

He stands face to face with her. He extends his hand toward her and she flinches with terror. Surprisingly, he strokes her hair from the top of her head down to the last lock which drapes down her back. Their eyes intertwine momentarily before he speaks again. "I've never been in the presence of a woman more beautiful than you."

Fear has Amber speechless. She wonders what deranged thoughts are floating through his mind right now. "Thank you," she whispers. "Muhsee, can we leave now? I have to be up bright and early. My flight departs at 7.am," she explains. The fear has overpowered the foul smell or either she's just gotten used to it. "This room gives me the creeps," she admits.

"Why?" he asks. "Are you afraid of death? Death is promised to all of us. With all of the madness going on in the world birth should be feared not death. Death should be celebrated because the day to day struggle is over. The same way a woman feels when she gives birth to a baby…the satisfaction and pride she feels, I feel the same way when I take an individual out of the world," he says with a smile. "When a child is born the mother has no idea that her child may grow up to spread corruption or to be a thief, a rapist, or what have you. Had the mother knew that then maybe she would have done the right thing from the start and abort the bastard."

Damn, Amber thinks to herself. Is this sick bastard actually making sense? How about her unborn child grows up to spread corruption in the world, she thinks.

"Me, I get enjoyment doing what they should have done. Removing those individuals from this earth is like providing a service to the world free of charge," he smiles.

He's scaring her terribly. She's never seen him look like this. It's like this room has him acting crazy. "Muhsee, please? Let's leave from here, please?"

He ignores her and continues to speak. "You see this chair right here?" he asks as he grabs her hand. He stands directly in between the two desks that sit side by side. "This seat right here was close to being the seat that belonged to your friend, the botti boy. If not for the begging of your boss, this would have been his final destination. He would have been forced to sit in this seat where we would have shackled his ankles. Here we would have shackled his hands. And here," he says as he lifts one end of the harness. "He would have rested his head," he says as he slams the block of wood onto the desk. "His neck would have been secured," he smiles demonically. He reaches underneath the desk. He lifts his hand in the air and in his grip he holds an old fashioned sword holder. He snatches the sword from the holder. "And who do you think this seat would have belonged to?" he asks with a smile. "Who?" he asks with fury.

"I, I don't know," she stutters. "Muhsee," she whispers.

"Take a wild guess," he smiles. He waits seconds before speaking again. "Still no answer? Let me help you? Who else but you?" he smiles.

She's heard and seen enough. She flees away from him with fear. She damn near snatches the door off the hinges, leaving him all alone to sulk in his craziness.

///// CHAPTER 48 /////

Amber exits the elevator and steps sluggishly toward her apartment door. For some strange reason today's flight seemed to be the longest flight ever. Amber isn't sure if the turbulence of the plane was more than usual or if her pregnancy just makes it seem like that but she suffered from nausea the entire flight. She hates to admit it but something tells her that her days of transporting will be coming to an end sooner than she thought. She has no clue what she will do when that time does come.

"Home sweet home," she whispers to herself as she inserts the key into the lock. She pushes the door gently and steps inside. She exhales a huge sigh of relief as the peacefulness of her home greets her.

She drops her purse onto the sofa and makes her way to the bathroom to unstrap the kilos from her exhausted body. The work has her body weighed down terribly. She can't wait to relieve herself. As she's stepping toward the bathroom a peculiar noise stirs her attention. The sound of heavy gasping and deep moaning stops Amber dead in her tracks. Her heart stops beating momentarily as she stands still just listening closely. What the…No, it can't be, she says to herself. The sound of the sexual moans makes the hairs on her neck stand at full attention. Her curiosity leads her into the direction of Star's room where the noise seems to be coming from.

The closer Amber gets to the room the louder the moaning gets. I know this isn't happening, she says to herself as she envisions Samad and Star engaging in sexual intercourse. I invite him into my home and this is how he repays me by fucking my baby sister, she utters. Star wouldn't do this to me. The thought of it makes her more than enraged. The closer she gets to the door the slower she walks. She's actually afraid to set her eyes on the sight but her curiosity continues to lead her to the room. I'm gone kill his ass, she utters to herself as she stands at the door trying to prepare herself for what lies within the room. She takes a deep breath before snatching the door open forcefully.

As her eyes set onto the Queen sized bed her bottom lip drops to the floor, leaving her mouth wide open. Paralysis takes over her body. She stands there in awe with her body as stiff as a board. What lies in front of her is a sight for her sore eyes.

Star lays flat on her back swaying her head from side to side. She roars like a porn star. In between her moaning and groaning she desperately fights for air. Her legs are spread apart with her toes damn near touching the ceiling as the imprint of a head is buried between Star's legs. The bright white linen sheet covers the head of the person who is causing all the damage.

Rage fills Amber's heart. She looks to her right and grabs hold of the first thing in her reach. She grips the miniature aluminum baseball bat and runs toward the bed at full speed. Her loud stepping causes alert. Star looks up with a surprised look on her face. She locks eyes with Amber as Amber is only steps away. Fury is in her eyes.

Both fear and embarrassment covers her face but the fear is extremely dominant. "Owwww!" she screams. She scatters to the opposite side of the bed where Amber is. The bulge in the sheet pops up just as Amber stands over the bed. Amber draws the bat, lifting it high in the air. Just as she's about to smash the bat onto the head of the culprit, the culprit peels the sheet back. They lock eye to eye. Amber drops the bat in mid air as she stands there in even more surprise.

She stands here emotionally crushed. She can't believe what she's just witnessed. She wants to say something but she's speechless. She slowly backpedals away from the bed and out of the room. Never before has she felt so many emotions all at one time. She feels rage, embarrassment, confusion and most of all disappointment.

After Amber is completely out of the room, Star feels a certain amount of safety. She looks at her best friend Tara. They gaze into each other's eyes. Embarrassment is plastered onto both of their faces. They both lower their heads with disgrace.

An Hour Later. Amber lies across her bed, trapped inside her room. She's heartbroken. No way in the world was she prepared to see what she just saw. She can't believe that her little sister is gay. She's extremely furious and hurt at the same time. The hate she has for homosexuals is beyond imaginable.

She sure hopes that was just a first experience that she happened to have walked in on and not something that Star is actually into. A part of Amber wishes it was Samad in the room with Star instead of Tara. Either way it would have broken her heart but at least if it were Samad, she could just chalk it up as a loss. She would never let a man come in between her and her sister. This situation is just a little more difficult to chalk up. She just can't accept the fact of the matter.

She wishes she could erase from her memory what she saw. A part of her wants to talk to Star but she's too ashamed to do so. She can't even face Star right now. She's shameful as if she's the one who was caught in the bed with another woman. Until she gets over the embarrassment and is able to look Star in the eyes she plans to hide here in her room.

Amber's bedroom door opens up and in comes Samad. He's dressed in his gym attire. "Ay lady," he greets joyfully. "I missed you."

"Ay," she replies rather blandly.

"Ay? That's it?" he asks. "Wow," he utters with a smile.

"Samad, not right now," she says with aggravation in her voice. She's really not even in the mood to be around him. She just wants to be alone so she can think. Her sister rolling around like that in the bed replays in her head over and over again. Amber wonders if she's responsible for Star turning out to be gay. She's always done everything in her power to prevent Star from dating. She wonders if she pushed her into the arms of women. Back to back thoughts overflow her mind.

Samad stands there just staring into Amber's gloomy eyes. She rolls her eyes with disgust as she looks away. "What's wrong with you?" he asks.

Amber gets up from the bed and makes her way to the walk-in closet. She wonders if Samad knows. Star and Tara stayed here with him the nights that she was away. She wonders if he heard anything strange in the room. She wonders if he joined them.

Her reason for letting Tara stay was to keep Samad and Star from being here alone. Just to think she may have made it all the better for them. Amber shakes her head from side to side trying to shake that thought away. She's always trusted her sister but she knows the power of a man and how manipulating and conniving they can be. After seeing her sister in action like that she really doesn't know what to believe. Never in a million years would she have suspected them to be gay. "Nothing," she whispers as she steps into the closet, where she disappears.

Samad walks to the opposite side of the room. He steps inside of the bathroom and in a matter of seconds fog from the hot shower water seeps into the bedroom. He stands at the doorway relieving himself of the sweaty gym clothes. He tosses them into a small pile on the floor.

"Here," Amber whispers into his ear as she stands directly behind him.

He turns around abruptly. His eyes are drawn to her hands that she holds at her waistline. In them she holds a sky blue, rectangular shaped balloon. "Here," she repeats as she lifts it closer to him.

Samad reaches out and grabs hold of the balloon. He has no clue what it is. The weight of the balloon is light but it seems to be filled with something. "What's this?" he questions as he juggles the balloon in his hand. The contents seem to have a sandy feel to it.

"You don't know what that is?" she asks, while staring directly into his eyes. She looks over onto her dresser and snatches a small finger nail file. She sticks the point of the file into the rubber and slides it gently across a small section of the balloon. Once an incision is made she jabs the file into the rubber and cuts right through the shrink wrap covering. When she pulls the file out, snow white powder covers the entire tip.

Oh shit, Samad says to himself while trying to keep a nonchalant look on his face. He feels totally ashamed of the fact that he didn't know what was inside the balloon. He's never seen it packaged in this manner.

"Now do you know what it is?"

"Of course," he says arrogantly. Wow, he thinks to himself.

"I told you I had you, right?" she asks with a cocky smile on her face. "So how much do you normally pay for one of those?"

"Huh?" he utters as if he didn't hear her.

"A kilo," she whispers. "How much do you normally pay for one?"

Samad hesitates before replying. The fact of the matter is she's giving him way too much credit. She's asking him how much he pays for a kilo when the truth of the matter is he's never paid for a kilo. The most cocaine he's ever had is 300 to 400 grams and he's never had to pay for the work up front on account of D-Nice's cousin, Rahiem, who has been giving them product on consignment since they first started hustling a few years ago. In the beginning he only fronted them half a ounce at a time, then ounces. Eventually they worked their way up to an eighth of a kilo and a quarter of a kilo. Only twice they had half a kilo and both times they messed the money up, coming up short when it was time to repay Rahiem. It seems the more product they have to manage the harder it is for them to manage it. When they have smaller amounts of work they make the expected profit each time but whenever they go over their limit they tend to think they have more room to make mistakes and that is exactly what they do; make silly mistakes that they would not normally make.

Samad starts calculating in his head. He knows there are 1,000 grams in one kilo. He quickly multiplies 1,000 by the twenty-four dollars that he pays for a gram. "Twenty-four thousand dollars," he replies.

"Twenty-four thousand?' she repeats with shock. "Are you serious?"

"Yeah, twenty-four dollars a gram," he replies.

"Wow," she whispers. She can't believe that he's actually paying that price but she understands how it goes. She realizes how fortunate Maurice is to have the connection that he has. Dealers would do anything to have a connect like Muhsee who has unlimited kilos for that cheap of a price. To get kilos for the price of $6,000 is unbelievable for most, when the average dealer can't get a better price than twenty or twenty-one thousand dollars a kilo. Maurice owes his fortune to his family lineage. His great grandmother was Jamaican and as a kid he spent every summer in Jamaica with her. He dreaded going there but as he got older one good thing came out of it. He stumbled across Muhsee who at that time was nowhere near the stature that he is today. He was only an aspiring kingpin. When Maurice went to Jamaica to bury his great grandmother he ran into Muhsee and it's been on ever since.

Maurice has taught Amber that the smaller the kilo is broken down and the more people who touch it the more expensive it gets. A kilo that starts out at $17,000 can end up going for $24,000 easily, depending on how many hands that it passes through. The original buyer may buy it at $17,000.00 and score two points off of it by selling it to the next dealer for $19,000. That dealer will score a point and a half profit when he sells the kilo for the price of $20,500. That dealer normally starts to break the kilo down, selling it a hundred grams at a time, by the ounce or even as low as by the gram at $24 per gram. At the end of the flip when it's all sold, he scores a three and a half point ($3,500) profit. By this time the kilo has no wholesale value left in it. All the equity has been drained out of it, leaving the street dealer with no room to do anything but take it to the ground. He has to chop it up and put it into small vials and sell them for five and ten dollars.

The street dealer is the last man on the totem pole and may seem to have the pettiest position but actually he has the largest profit margin. By breaking the product down he gives himself the opportunity to almost double his money. A half an ounce that he pays $336.00 for, he will flip it and turn that into close to $800.00. One hundred grams that he pays $2,400, he will flip that and turn that into close to five thousand dollars and so on and so on.

Hearing Samad admit that he pays $24,000 tells her just how low on the totem pole he is. "Listen Bay, a word for the wise," she whispers sternly. "From here on out when you purchase product be sure to buy by the kilo and not by the gram. When buying a kilo you shouldn't be charged the same number as a guy who is buying by the gram," she explains. "Let me tell you something else...everyone is always so quick to say it's 1,000 grams in a kilo and how wrong they are. A kilo is actually 1008 grams, so if that's the case are they giving you those eight grams for free? No, if you're paying by the gram, but yes if you're paying per kilo. Get it?" she asks. "If you ask the price and he says $24 a gram, you simply tell him I'm not looking for the price by the gram, I'm buying the kilo," she says with a cocky look on her face.

Samad sits back quietly as if she read his mind as he calculated 1,000 by $24 per gram. A part of him feels humiliated because he's being schooled by a girl but the other part of him is just grateful to be receiving the valuable information.

"Listen Bay, no more twenty- four thousand. You hear me? That number is absurd...trust me. Always remember that everything is negotiable and don't let anyone tell you different. A dealer's goal is to move the work. His greed won't allow him to let one dollar pass him. You capitalize off of his greed and parlay the deal to your advantage," she says before winking her eye at him. "Is this enough to get you on your feet?" she asks. "Or you need more?"

Her arrogance makes him smile. "Nah, this more than enough," he smiles. Get back on my feet, he says to himself. I never been on my feet like this to start with, he thinks to himself.

"Alright...and you ain't paying no twenty- four grand for it either. How long do you think it will take to finish this off? How long do you need?"

Samad starts figuring. Three hundred grams normally lasts him and D-Nice about four days. At that same rate it will take him close to two weeks to move a kilo. Suddenly his ego speaks out. "About a week," he says arrogantly. Damn, he says to himself, realizing that he may have just put his foot in his mouth.

"One week it is," she says. "That's what I will tell him," she lies as she tries to make him believe that the work belongs to someone else and not her.

Tell him, Samad whispers under his breath. His jealousy now speaks out. His emotions are taking turns talking. "Who is him?"

"Bay, please. You need to get in position right? And your girl has resources that you can use. It's that simple. Don't take it for anymore than that. Ask me no questions and I will tell you no lies. Just know one thing...I have not done anything to disrespect what me and you have. I will never do anything to disrespect what we have. Know that!" Amber gets quiet as she wonders what number would be fair to charge Samad for the work. She wants to give him a number where he has the flexibility to do all the things that he needs to do. She only paid $6,000 for the kilo and would really love to give it to him at that number but she's sure that would lead to a bunch of other questions. "Twenty thousand, five hundred," she blurts out as she thinks of the number that the members of the Federation distribute the work at. "Is that number good enough for you?" she asks with hope that she may have taken his mind off of where she got the work from.

"Bet," he says with a huge smile. He thinks of what he can do at that number. Never having a kilo to himself leaves him clueless to just how much he can make off of it but he's sure it's way more than he needs.

Amber feels quite guilty and deceitful overcharging the man she loves. Her guilt vanishes shortly after she realizes that love doesn't pay the bills. Bringing the kilo back for Maurice would have normally scored her a profit of two grand. This particular kilo will score her $14,500 in seven days. It's all business, she thinks to herself as she silently sings the words of Tina Turner's hit song 'What's Love Got to Do with It.'

Samad is grateful to have the tool he needs to get in position but his jealousy won't let him leave well enough alone. He automatically assumes that Amber must have got the work from the man he saw her with at the Sand Bar. "Ma, I appreciate this but begging for work from another nigga to give it to me, that just ain't my twist," he says while shaking his head no.

"Hold up, hold up," she interrupts. "I didn't beg for this," she snaps. "I don't beg for shit! I work for mines," she barks hastily.

"Nah, not like that. Please, just tell me where you got it from?"

"I already told you, ask me no questions and I will tell you no lies."

"But," he in interrupts.

Before he's able to say another word Amber places her finger against his lips. "Shhh," she says as she presses her finger gently against his lips. "No...but," she whispers. "Everything after but is bullshit. Now get money!" she says arrogantly.

////// CHAPTER 49 //////

Deja sits in the passenger's seat of the beautiful pea green body, baseball glove colored gut convertible Bentley GTC. In the driver's seat is one of Philadelphia 76'ers most valuable players. The two of them just shared their first date which happened to be quite entertaining. Now they're cruising the lovely city of Manhattan just enjoying the view.

Deja met this man just a few days ago when she was at a hair show in Philadelphia. Once they chatted on the phone Deja found out that he would be coming up to New York in a few days for business. Once he got here, even before handling his business, Deja was the first call that he made.

As they cruise along the congested block, the sound of singer D'Angelo's 'Lady' bleeds through the speakers. The bright lights of 42nd Street are hypnotizing. Deja plays the passenger's seat like the superstar that she is. Her silk Chanel scarf is tied loosely around her head. She uses the scarf to protect her weave and keep it in tact. The roof is peeled back which causes the wind to bombard into the vehicle. It's after 12 midnight so the dark sunglasses that cover her eyes are quite useless. They're purely for fashion purposes. She likes to refer to them as her 'hater blockers.'

Today is Deja's first date since her life threatening disaster. She's so happy to be completely back to normal. Her face and body bounced back together days ago. As grateful as she is for that, she has already come up with a few more cosmetic surgery ideas. She's so happy with her new booty but now she feels that the only thing she's missing is size. She feels if she had just a little more plumpness her booty would be picture perfect. Despite the promise she made to God, she has already set up her trip to the Dominican Republic for next month. A part of her feels guilty that she's breaking her promise to God but deep down inside she takes for granted the fact that he will forgive her.

They cruise through the Big Apple for minutes with no destination; well at least that is what Deja thinks until the driver pulls up front of a building on 5th Avenue and 52nd Street. He parks directly behind a row of exotic cars. The smell of money is in the air. She takes a sneak peak around the surrounding area where she sees so many Maybauchs that her head begins to spin. They are so common that they look like taxi cabs. The drivers of the cars hop out as the valet parking attendants stand at the door ready to replace them.

Deja has no clue where they are. She looks up and what she reads disturbs her tremendously. "The Peninsula," she utters to herself. "I know you didn't bring me to no fucking hotel?" she shouts with venom. "Who the fuck do you think you are? Better yet who the fuck do you think I am?"

"Hold up, hold up," he says casually. "Be easy. No disrespect intended. This is where I'm staying. I was just hoping we could hang out a little longer. I'm not expecting anything."

"Shit! You better not be expecting anything! We don't even know each other! Listen, I'm sorry if I gave you the wrong impression but you got the wrong one."

"Listen, you didn't give me any impression. I'm just enjoying your company and I'm just not ready for the night to end. That's it…real rap."

Deja looks into his eyes and for some reason she can feel his sincerity but still she has to make sure that they're clear on this matter. "Be honest. What did you think? Did you think I was going to be so overwhelmed with the night and so pleased to be with you that the night would end with me and you rolling around in your hotel room? Be honest?"

"Never came to my mind," he claims with a straight face.

"I bet," she smiles. "Well let me make sure we're clear on this. I'm not one of your little groupies. I never even heard of you until the night after we met. I went online just to see if you were who you said you were. Really I couldn't care less. I don't even follow basketball so in no way can I be one of your fans. Be clear that you bouncing a ball up and down a field means nothing to me."

He laughs in her face, interrupting her. "Court not field," he smiles.

"What the fuck ever. That's how much I know and trust me I care even less. Any thoughts of you blowing my mind and getting into my panties you might as well erase them now."

"Honestly those thoughts never crossed my mind. Like I said, I'm just digging your company. We're both grown right? We should be able to chill in a hotel room without sexing each other, right?"

"Hmphh, I can. I don't know about you."

"To be honest with you, I have not looked at you sexually not once tonight."

"Hmphh, that's a first," she smiles.

"Nah real rap. I mean you're gorgeous and all but I don't know why my mind hasn't gone there yet. Anyway we can just hang out with no strings attached. I will not try anything. That's my word on everything," he says just as the parking attendant opens the door for her to exit the vehicle. "I promise," he says as he makes a cross over his chest as if he's crossing his heart.

The innocence in his eyes causes Deja to smile. She sure hopes that he's a man of his word. In any attempt she's sure she can handle herself against him. She's sure the last thing he needs in his early career is a rape charge. She thinks about it momentarily before she speaks. "I'm telling you if you try to even touch me, I will never speak to you again in life," she threatens.

"Yo," he interrupts. "I promise."

Deja steps onto the asphalt. The driver walks around to her and grabs hold of her hand. "This isn't considered touching you is it?" he teases.

"You know what the hell I mean," she barks. "You ain't stupid," she says with a smile.

He leads her into the hotel as the valet cruises away with his car. At the entrance of the hotel Deja's attention is stolen by the huge marble stairway that sits in the center of the lobby. They walk up the steps and it seems as if it takes them forever to reach the last step. The top of the staircase flourishes into an open lounge area.

Deja looks around and notices how diverse the crowd is. There are men in here walking around with jeans on and flip flops on their feet while others are dressed in formal tuxedos. The women are quite diverse as well. Her attention is automatically drawn to the women who are dressed in sexy evening gowns. She's been to enough of these types of places to know that these women are just upscale prostitutes that are here hoping to land on the lap of some rich millionaire who is horny enough to pay them a hefty fee for a nice evening. "Can't knock the hustle," Deja mumbles under her breath.

The man leads Deja to the bar where he orders drinks for them. Deja and him sip on wine and chitter chatter as they people watch.

Meanwhile across the Water

Amber sits on the huge rock, staring at the brightly lit landmark buildings in Manhattan. Sitting close by her side is Star. Amber has ducked and dodged Star for days and although she realizes the act was quite cowardly she continued to do so because she was in no way prepared to face her yet.

Finally Star took control of the situation. Not even five minutes ago she marched into Amber's room and asked if she could talk to her and now here they are.

"Sister, I really don't know where to start," Star whispers shamefully.

Amber looks away with shame. Her head is full of questions that are ready to explode from her mouth but she wants to give Star ample enough time to say whatever is on her mind before she unloads on her. Suddenly she can't resist the urge any longer. "How long has this been going on?" she asks as she looks at her little sister with pure disgust on her face.

Star allows seconds to pass before answering. "For over three years," she admits with embarrassment.

Amber's heart drops. She hates to believe it but she now realizes that Star is officially gay. She was hoping that situation was only an experiment. The look of disgust on her face increases drastically at the thought of that. Damn, she says to herself. "Three years? So all this time ya'll were acting like the best of friends?'

"We weren't acting. We are the best of friends. Outside of you, Tee is the only person in the world who knows and understands me."

"But how?" Amber asks. "Why?"

"How?" she repeats before exhaling. "We started out as best friends and I guess in spending so much time together feelings that we couldn't control started forming. I swear to you I never looked at her like that or even any other woman but I really can't remember when we started acting on our emotions. It's like it just sort of happened. The first time I was confused but really it didn't seem so bad. It was weird but I had no guilt. It felt like it was supposed to be. It felt natural," she says with a baffled look on her face. "Before I knew it the situation became more and more normal feeling. In fact the only time I realize that it's not normal is when I come back home and we have to pretend to you like we're just friends," she admits. "Sister, that is the hardest thing in the world for me to do. At times I can't wait to get back to school so I can feel free again. Sometimes it's hard to suppress my feelings for her in front of you."

Amber's stomach is turning and her blood is boiling. She'd rather crawl up under a rock and die than to hear this come out of her sister's mouth. "So everyone in school knows about ya'll?" she asks in a high pitched voice.

"Sister, it's been almost four years."

"Let me ask you, when did you realize that you were that?" she asks not even feeling comfortable enough to say the word gay.

"Sister, the word is gay."

"Yeah that," Amber replies. "Do you even like boys?"

"Of course I see men who I think are attractive. I have eyes. I can see when a man has style and swagger but do I find a romantic attraction for them?" She shakes her head from side to side. "No. I've never seen a man that I've wanted for myself. I never even wanted to give it a try."

"Well maybe you should!" Amber can't believe she just said that. All these years she's been trying to keep Star away from men and now she's damn near ready to push her into the bed of the first man that she sees. Hopefully she would enjoy the experience and she would revert to what Amber considers to be a normal state. "You never know, you might like it."

"Seriously Sister, I highly doubt it. The actual thought of being with a man disgusts me. Everything about it. The smell of his sweat, the touch of his rough hands, his beard, his hairy body, eelk," she says with a look of hatred on her face. "I view all men as nasty, sex crazed, perverted individuals."

Wow, Amber says to herself. She understands it all perfectly clear now. This situation has derived from the fact of Star's father sexually abusing her. Damn, she thinks to herself. She realizes that her hatred for men has everything to do with what her father did to her. She also realizes that this could have easily been her own story. The situation has had many effects on her as well. She thanks God that her issues are mainly trust and affection issues. She just wishes it were the same for Star. Amber fights hard to keep the tears from welling up in her eyes.

"Sister, I have no use for men whatsoever. I could never share anything with them. I despise them and I could never ever trust one. Please, just understand me?"

Amber shakes her head from side to side. She hates to admit it but she really does understand her. How could she ever trust a man when the man she loved and admired put her through hell? "But what about Tara? Has she ever been with a guy? What if you later find out that this is just a phase that she's going through and she realizes that she wants to live a regular life?"

"Sister, this is a regular life. Maybe not for you but for many this is the only life they know or even want to know," she explains. "No, Tee is bisexual. She's dealt with a few guys but she claims that she never completely feels fulfilled when in a relationship with a man. She's told me that she tried to suppress her attraction for women because she felt like a freak. She said once we met she no longer felt the urge to suppress her feelings and she refused to blow the opportunity to be happy with who she really is and finally get that feeling of fulfillment that she's always been chasing."

Damn, Amber says to herself as she listens to what sounds like bullshit to her. Even the gay girls got game, she says to herself. She starts to think of her sister's feelings and hopes that Tara isn't just playing with her. She would hate for her little sister to get her heart broken. Even worse she would hate for her to be played with. What if Tara is just leading Star on only to bring her in on a ménage a trois with one of her boyfriends? She quickly shakes the thought from her mind. "Well, what if she decides that today she wants a man in her life and just leaves you?"

"Well, in the game of love we all take that chance. Of course I will be heartbroken but what can I do? Life goes on. It's a risk that we all take. The chance of her doing that is as equal as the chance of your friend, Samad waking up and leaving you for another woman. It's different for you because you're not gay but at the end of the day it's the same situation. Love is love," she claims. "Sister, I'm sorry that I may have disappointed you. I know you only want the best for me but you have to realize that this is what makes me happy," she cries. "It doesn't make me less of a person. I'm still your little sister and I promise I will still make you proud. My sexual preference will not get in the way of that. You've worked so hard to get me here in this position and I will not let your hard work be in vain. I promise you that. All I ask is that you accept me for who I am and also accept Tara for who she is to me. I'm ashamed that you walked in on that but a part of me feels relieved. I no longer have to live that lie that I've been living for the past three years. I feel free...free to be me. I just hope that you can love me the same," she says as she stares into Amber's eyes. "After all, your approval means more to me than anything in the world."

Amber looks at her closely. Star's words have touched her heart tremendously. As much as she opposes this lifestyle she has no choice but to accept it on her sister's behalf. She hates to do it but she just chalks it up as cause and effect. How can she be mad at her sister when she's the victim? The culprit is Star's father for altering her feelings and emotions. "I have no choice but to love you the same," she whispers. "You know I'm totally against that lifestyle but as you said, it's your preference. If you're happy I'm happy. I just want the best for you," she says as she wraps her arms around Star and hugs the life out of her.

Star exhales a deep breath as she hugs Amber even tighter. "I love you, Sister."

"I love you too."

Meanwhile in Manhattan

Deja and her date have made it up to the hotel room which has her blown away. In all the places that she's traveled she has yet to see a hotel room more prolific than this one. She finds the room to be well worth the $1,500 a night that it costs.

She's impressed with the entire layout from the 18th Century Victorian furniture on down to the silk drapes and 800 count Egyptian cotton sheets. She's more amazed with the tiny details such as the 18kt gold plated china.

The bathroom must have impressed her the most because by the time they stepped into it, the both of them were completely naked. Either the limestone floors and the wall to wall mirrors turned her on or it must have been the many glasses of wine that they sipped on.

One thing that Deja found out is that his word means nothing because as soon as they got into the room he could barely keep his hands off of her despite the promise that he made to her. It's obvious that her word meant nothing as well because at the current time she lays back in the huge soaking tub. The Christian television show which is playing on the television that's built in the wall is making it extremely hard to get into her sexual zone. She tries hard to tune it out. She lays her head back onto the edge of the tub. She cracks her eyes open and looks up at the many mirrors that cover the ceiling. She gets a clear view and is quite surprised to see how sexy she looks laying here with her legs sprawled wide open. One foot touches the wall while the other foot dangles over the tub.

The deep sea diver takes yet another dive into the lukewarm water. As soon as his head submerges, he uses the tip of his nose as his navigation system. In no time at all he locates his destination. He uses his tongue to pry open her treasure chest. He digs deep with hope of retrieving the treasure. Deja grabs the back of his head, guiding him to the right spot. The feeling is so awesome that she totally forgets the fact that she has his head submerged under water until he smacks the water with the palm of his hand to get her attention. The splash snaps her out of her zone. She lets go of his head allowing him to come up for air. A few seconds longer and he may have drowned. He lifts his head up above water. He takes a series of short breaths to regain himself.

In a matter of seconds he submerges into the water once again and immediately starts to please her. The sensation gets so good to Deja that she does something that she hardly ever does. She totally lets herself go. She slouches lower in the tub and spreads her legs even wider as she slow grinds his face.

The way she sways her hips from side to side makes him lose his bull's eye. He grabs hold of her tiny waistline to keep her body restrained as he licks, nibbles and eats her alive. "Wwwwbbbbb," he growls while shaking his head from side to side causing a feeling that she has never felt. The withering of his tongue is driving her crazy. She can't hold back any longer. She grabs his head and pumps his face erratically. The sensation that she gets brings tears to her eyes. She cries with pleasure. As the tears drip down her face, juices also seep from her lips, turning the entire tub into saltwater. The taste of her sweet juices makes him even more exited. He would love to just stay here and drink from her fountain of love but he must come up for air. He pries her hands from around his neck and lifts his head up. "Whew!" he sighs. He takes a few deep breaths before preparing to dive back in. Deja grabs his head, holding it tightly. "No, no more. I can't take no more," she pleads. "Fuck me?"

"Just like I figured," he whispers to himself. This sounds like music to his ears. All that she said to him about sexing him was all a front just as he figured. It totals out to be nothing but nonsense. He hops out of the tub before she can change her mind. He quickly takes off into the next room. While he's gone Deja keeps herself occupied by teasing away at herself.

In seconds his third leg enters the room before him at full attention. Just the look of it causes Deja's body to heat up even more. Oh how hot she is for him. She fiddles with herself just that much more. She watches anxiously as he straps up. "Hurry up baby, please?" she begs. Deja stands up, while still caressing herself. She hops out of the tub and grabs hold of his hand. She leads him over to the sink where she bends over. "Take it," she demands as she looks in the mirror at her new found booty which looks perfect from this angle. It's her booty and it has her turned on so she can only imagine what it's doing to him.

The anxiety is killing him. He grabs her by the waist and thrusts himself into her. Deja holds her breath at his entrance for what seems to be an eternity. He digs deep until he can finally go no further.

"Aghh," she exhales.

He arches his back and curls his body close to hers. "Damn, you feel good," he whispers into her ear as he takes another stroke. She grips him like a glove making the sensation that much more amazing. "Girl," he whispers. "Damn."

His slow stroking is only teasing her. "Baby, give it to me," she whispers. "Please?" she begs. "Come on baby, bang it, bang it, please?"

He slow strokes her once again, trying to get accustomed to her. "I got you baby," he whispers. Just hold up for one minute," he says before stopping his stroking. He stands still to try and alleviate the sensation.

Deja longs for his pounding and his sexual abuse. She has a desire for pain that he just isn't fulfilling. "You're teasing me baby," she whines. "Give it to me. Fuck me please," she pleads. Fuck me!" she snarls. The sound of her words coupled with the swaying of her hips and the contracting of her walls causes his anxiety to roar. He grabs hold of her waist tighter and digs as deep as he can dig. He strokes her once. "That's it right there baby," she cheers. "That's right, give it to me!" He strokes her twice. "Uh huh, yes! Come on baby!"

"Aghh," he roars as he explodes like a bomb.

The stillness of his body alarms Deja. I know this motherfucker didn't, she thinks to herself. She turns her head in slow motion. She watches with rage as his eyes roll into the back of his head as if he's having a seizure. At this point she wishes he was having a seizure and just die right here. Yes, this motherfucker did she says in reply to her own question. Finally he opens his eyes. The look in her eyes humiliates him. He lowers his head with shame. "I know you're not serious? Tell me you're playing?"

"Nah, just hold up for a second. I can bounce right back.

Deja walks away from the sink with rage in her eyes. She steps into the bedroom. "Don't even bother!"

///// CHAPTER 50 /////

The Next Morning

Silence fills the air as Deja and last night's date cruise through the city of Newark. Not even the radio is playing. He's so consumed in his thoughts that he doesn't even realize that he hasn't turned the radio on the entire ride. He feels so low right now that he can't even look her in the eyes.

After his premature situation he tried hard to redeem himself but Deja wouldn't give him the opportunity. He begged over and over but still she denied. If she didn't know her body well enough to satisfy herself she may have given in. Unfortunately for him she does.

What she did do was torture him. She pleased herself obtaining orgasm after orgasm until she finally collapsed and fell asleep. It was pure torture for him as she allowed him to look but not touch.

He hates himself right now and wishes he could play the night back but he can't and has to live with this forever. He promises himself the next time will be better and hopefully she will one day forget about that disaster. He now truly understands the meaning of the saying 'you never get a second chance to make a first impression.'

He steers his car into the parking space in front of her beauty parlor. Damn, what can I say, he asks himself. He wonders what he can say to redeem himself at this point. She starts to collect her belongings. "You disappointed in me huh?" he asks, assuming that he already knows the answer she's about to give him.

Deja cracks the door open before he even gets the chance to put the car in park. "Of course I am," she says as she steps out of the car. She slams the door shut and looks him directly in the eyes before speaking. "It doesn't matter anyway though because I told you if you tried anything I would never speak to you ever again. Unlike you, I stand by my word." He sits there with the cheesiest look ever on his face. Her statement just cut through his heart like a dagger. "So long," she says as she switches away sexily, giving him a good view of what he will never get again in life.

Meanwhile

It's bright and early in the morning and Samad has already been up for hours. This is the first time that he's been up early in weeks. His state of depression has had him pinned to the bed but today he got a burst of energy. Thanks to Amber he's up and ready to not only face the world but conquer it as well. Amber and Star left out an hour ago to go shopping and he's sure that could take all day. That gives him more than enough time to do what he has to do.

Samad has been up banging pots in the kitchen since the moment Amber and Star left. The noise that comes from this kitchen can be compared to the noise of a busy restaurant. The smell of his cooking is nostalgic to him but maybe stomach turning to others. The smell of burning cocaine blazes the entire apartment.

He takes a huge sniff of the air. "Aghh," he exhales. There's no fragrance sweeter to him than the smell of cocaine when it's cooking. Crack addicts think of getting high when they smell that aroma but he thinks of money when he smells it. Thick fog is in the air, making it quite difficult for him to breathe. Just inhaling the vapors is enough to get anyone high.

The timer on the microwave starts chiming and Samad immediately starts running over to it. He snatches the door open and his eyes light up with joy. "Viola!" he shouts as he stares at the smooth, bright white sheet of crack that lies before his eyes. He's shocked to see the crack come back this color. He's used to seeing crack in a dingy yellow shade but it's obvious to him that the purity of his cocaine has everything to do with this shade. He touches it in a few places to see if it's as hard as he wants it to be. He then lays it on the countertop to dry out completely.

Samad is multi-tasking. He's so anxious to get rolling that he's using every method of cooking cocaine that he knows just to speed up the process. He quickly runs over to the stove, where he looks into the huge pot of simmering cocaine. He grabs a small bag of baking soda and dumps it onto the pot and allows it to marinate before he begins stirring it as if it's stew. In a matter of minutes he rushes to the refrigerator where he snatches a tray of ice from the freezer. He quickly snatches the pot from the flame and starts dropping the ice into the pot cube by cube to let it cool off. After he's dumped the entire tray into the pot, he sits the pot on the stove and leaves it unattended for a few moments.

He grabs the remainder of the cocaine that he has and drops it onto his digital scale. It reads 258 grams. The powder is so light and fluffy that it hardly needs grinding. He quickly begins dumping baking soda on the scale until the numbers finally reach 62.5.

The way he adds, subtracts, divides, multiplies and even measures he should have been a scientist or a mathematician but instead he's a street level chemist. He has it all broken down to a science. For every quarter of a kilo (250 grams) he adds 62.5 grams of baking soda.

Samad is stunned at the purity of this product. Each time before he starts his actual cooking process he takes one gram and cooks it up. Normally when it's all done he comes up with one or two lines short of a gram. Even with the baking soda and water added it still loses once the cut has burned away. With this product he put a gram on the scale and after it was cooked it weighed in at 1.2 and in another case 1.3. He couldn't believe his eyes and thought he was making a mistake until he tried four different times.

So far Samad has transformed 750 grams of cocaine into 1,027 grams of crack. He's already whipped up Amber's money many grams ago along with a hefty profit so everything from here on out is all extra. Using the same method he plans to stretch the 258 grams to the maximum. He's going to add his normal 62.5 grams of baking soda. That coupled with the extra two lines per gram that come back will give him a minimum of 340 grams.

He can't wait to hit the streets. Thanks to Amber his spirit has been lifted. His hopes and dreams seem to be limitless at this point. He's never had this much product in his life but something tells him this is only the beginning. His new motto is 'you think big, you get big.'

When he finishes this flip he will be right where he needs to be. He's sure he has more than enough product to pay Amber back, bail D-Nice out, get himself an apartment and keep the ball rolling. He picks up his pen and starts calculating. He jots down the number 1,367 which is the total number of grams that he expects to have after he finishes. He normally makes $70.00 off of every gram. At that rate he expects to make $95,690. He stares at the whopping number and his eyes damn near pop out of his head. Damn, he thinks to himself. He will more than quadruple his money. After the original $20,500, he will be left with over 75 grand before paying his crew. He pays them one dollar for every nickel of crack that they sell. That equals out to another $20,000 split up amongst his workers. After it's all said and done he still walks away with close to 55 grand profit. "Damn," he sighs once again.

His ring tone sounds off and he bops to the beat of 'Duffle Bag Boy' for a few seconds before answering the call. He snatches the phone from the countertop. It's D-Nice. For the first time in a long time he's actually happy to hear from him. He hasn't heard from him in days and can't wait to break the good news to him but first he decides to have a little fun with him.

"Hello?" he answers in a saddened voice.

"Yo," D-Nice replies in a sadder tone. "What's good? Nothing new yet?" he asks with desperation.

"Nah, shit," Samad lies. "On the real I was thinking you might just have to plead guilty and take a plea."

D-Nice can't believe his ears. He hopes that he's heard him wrong. "What?"

"Yeah, take the plea. I'm gone keep it real with you, I can't come up with the bail money to save my life. Shit fucked up," he whines. "I mean if you get anything less than 15 years you made out good."

"I made out good? Nigga what type shit you off?"

"Nigga I'm off some real fuck the world shit!" Samad yells. "Nigga fuck you and everybody else."

"Fuck me? Nigga fuck me? Nah nigga fuck you!"

"Yeah fuck you more nigga! Pack your shit nigga!" Samad says with a change of voice. "I'm coming for you nigga!"

"What?" D-Nice asks with a confused tone.

"You hear me nigga? I'm coming for you! Pack your shit! In a couple of days you outta there! You hear me nigga?"

"Yeah?" he questions.

"Yeah, like that nigga. Let me get off this phone so I can do me. A couple of days, that's it! Tell moms I'll be in touch with her in a few days."

"That's what it is!" D-Nice shouts.

"I'm out!" Samad says arrogantly before slamming the phone onto the countertop.

///// CHAPTER 51 /////

2 A.M. The light drizzle is increasing to a heavy downpour. Eight men stand in a small huddle in the middle of the pitch dark graveyard. The only noise out here is the sound of the raindrops splashing into the many puddles and ditches. A great deal of tension fills the air as Maurice stands quietly with a solemn look on his face. Each man except for Sal wonders who and what the topic of this meeting is all about. While they stand glued in their spots, Sal leans casually on a tree a few inches away from them.

Maurice called an emergency meeting an hour ago and this is always the designated place. Each member knows there has to be a problem when they meet here. He paces back and forth without saying a word. His pacing creates more tension and inquisitiveness in the men.

Finally he stops at the center of the huddle. He bends over while running his hands across the nape of his neck unloosening his cluster of locks. He stands up slowly, slinging his dreads wildly. He then takes a seat on the 3-foot tombstone. "Word is in the air that a certain individual has either already gone against the Federation or has plans to do so." All of the men's heart skips a beat at that statement. They listen attentively to hear more. "The mentioned individual has been speaking against me. Supposedly he has plans on making a move. Ya'll know me. I like to nip shit in the bud. I don't get involved in he say she say bitch gossip but I feel the need to address this matter," he says before pausing briefly. He has the full attention of all the members of the Federation. They all wonder who he's talking about and hope that they're not the individual that he's referring to. "Smurf," he says. Everyone directs their attention to the smallest member of the group. They all exhale silently, just happy to know that this meeting isn't about them.

Smurf stares at Maurice attentively. His heart has skipped several beats. On his face he wears a look of astonishment. He wonders what Maurice could be referring to.

"Your man Dirt...what's his motive?"

Smurf hesitates, not knowing what to reply with. Dirt is a good friend of his for many years. He's just come home from doing a 4-year bid in prison a couple of months ago. Smurf and Dirt have been friends much longer than Smurf has been a part of the Federation. "What you mean?" Smurf asks defensively.

"I mean, what's his motive," Maurice replies sarcastically.

"His motive? His motive is the same as the rest of us. Hoping to get rich, stay alive and out of the pen."

"Oh yeah?" Maurice questions.

"Yeah, he's a good earner. Responsible for moving ten joints a week for me. And he a good dude."

"You sure about that?" Maurice asks putting a ton of pressure on Smurf.

"Positive," Smurf replies. "I give him the work. He shakes it. He's always on time and the money is always correct."

"Good work ethics have nothing to do with him being a good dude. He could just be a good businessman. Anyway his work regimen is not what I'm referring to. You think he may have a hidden agenda?"

"What kind of hidden agenda?"

"Do you think he could be using you to get closer to me?"

"Get closer to you? Nah, I don't think so. He just happy to be eating. He ain't a greedy dude but I mean at the end of the day who wouldn't want to get closer to you, expecting you to change their financial situation?"

"I don't mean closer to me for that. I mean closer to me to get me out of the way," he explains.

"Get you outta the way? Like do something to you?"

"Exactly," Maurice replies firmly.

"Pssst," he sucks his teeth. "Hell no!" he says with confidence.

"You sure about that?"

"Positive, Bruh," he says with even more confidence.

"That's not how I'm getting it."

"Come on, Mo? I know this nigga. He ain't on no shit like that. That's one nigga I can vouch for."

"Hmphh," Maurice snickers. "You vouch for him?"

"One hundred and ten percent," he says boldly. "I put my life on that," he adds.

"Oh yeah?" Maurice asks. "You'd put your life on the line for another man? That's real but it's also a huge statement," he says with a demonic smile. "I commend you for your loyalty but sometimes we're loyal to mufuckers who don't have our best interest at heart and have no loyalty for us."

"My loyalty to anyone has nothing to do with what they hold for me. I'm just that type of dude whether they give two shits about me or not. I have a certain code and honor that I live by. Fuck the next mufucker. At the end of the day it's who I am. But nah, that's one man that I would put my life on the line for," he says while shaking his head up and down.

Maurice places his hands high in the air while shrugging his shoulders. "I got the word from a reputable source who I hold very dear in my heart. It was stated that the entire time your man was down Rahway he never had a good word to say about me."

"Mo, he doesn't even know you," Smurf interrupts.

"My point exactly. Which makes the irrational side of me think that he just naturally has hate for me or either someone who does know me is feeding him bullshit," he says as he looks coldly into Smurf's eyes. "He babbled on and on about what he's going to do once he touch. He has the plan on getting inside and getting all the info he needs to make a move and the score of a lifetime. He claims it will be easy because he has a good friend of his who moves around with me. Are you listening?"

"Yeah, I'm listening," Smurf says as he looks away. "Come on Mo, you of all people know that niggas gone talk. They probably trying to get shit started up between ya'll. You know how niggas is. He doing alright for himself now and niggas probably hating on him."

"First and foremost my man ain't the type of dude to get shit started. He's one of the most honorable cats in this town. Furthermore, let's keep it real, we all know what your man's M.O. is. "Keep it real, he may be your man but he's one of the slimiest cats in the town. After all his name is Dirt," he says with a smile. "Supposedly you will give him all the info he needs to make his come up. Any knowledge of that?"

Smurf stands there in awe. "Wow," he utters with a cheesy looking grin on his face. "You're really asking me this?"

"Any knowledge of that?" Maurice repeats.

"Hmmpphh," Smurf snickers. "I can't believe that my loyalty to you and the rest of the squad is at question. After all we've done together I would think my honor would be solidified. I live and die for the Federation. As far as my man, he wouldn't even put me in a situation like that. He knows what I'm about and he would know better than to come at me like that even if he had that in mind, which I highly doubt."

"So you're saying that it's not true?"

"Absolutely not," he replies with confidence.

"Ok," Maurice whispers. "Remember you vouched for him," Maurice says as he stands up slowly. He throws his head back swinging his dreads once again. He shakes his head from side to side before speaking. "I find out anything other than what you're telling me, it's your problem," he threatens as he steps away from the circle. He looks back over his shoulder as he's walking. "You said you'd put your life on the line for him, right? I'm going to hold you to that statement," he says before turning away and walking out of the graveyard. Everyone follows closely behind Maurice except Smurf.

At this point Smurf gets the feeling that it's the Federation against him. It hurts him to think like that but watching the look on their faces as well as judging by their body language they made it quite clear for him. In no way is Smurf a coward but he would hate to go against them.

Smurf follows the crowd many steps behind. He loves his man Dirt dearly and hopes that he hasn't put him in a cross like this. He has to get to the root of this problem. Hopefully for the both of their sake it's all just gossip.

///// CHAPTER 52 /////

It's 8:A.M and Samad has already began his day. He feels like a brand new man. He's fully rejuvenated and ready to conquer the world. He has big plans of taking his game to another level. In his couple of months of being at what he calls the bottom of his career he's learned so much. He's promised himself that he will never be broke again for as long as he lives.

Being around Amber has helped him to see things so much clearer. She's taught him more than she can imagine. She's highly motivational for him. She inspires him to reach the top of his game. Of course he wants to soar to the top to provide a better lifestyle for himself but he isn't the only person that he has in mind. He realizes that Amber is high maintenance and probably can't be impressed by much being that she has everything but he at least would like to be able to accommodate the equivalent lifestyle of what she's used to living. The fact that she's used to the finer things in life makes him strive harder. He's grateful to have her in his corner. He had no one else to turn to for help and she came through for him. The assistance that she's given him makes him feel like he owes her dearly. He considers her to be a lifesaver.

Although she has everything that a girl could want he still wants to give her more. It may take a great deal of work but he now has all the drive and motivation that he needs to make it happen. At this point he feels that he's at the bottom and there's nowhere else to go but up. He truly believes that the sky is the limit.

Samad sits on the abandoned porch across the street from where his crew is posted up. His mind drifts off and suddenly he imagines living the life he's always dreamed of. He can see it all so clear, him pulling up to the block in his Mercedes with Amber sitting in the passenger's seat while the baby is strapped in the car seat in the back. He hops out of the car fully loaded with expensive jewelry and a pocket full of money. At his presence everyone runs over to him, flocking to him like a ghetto superstar. He dazes off into space, just visualizing that picture. Suddenly he snaps back into reality and looks at what lies before him, nothing but a couple of young dealers standing huddled up waiting for a sale to come their way.

From where he's seated he can view all the activity that is taking place which happens to be very little at this particular time. The weeks that he's been gone has dried the block out. Their customers have been forced to find other places to purchase product from.

It may be dry out here but still Samad has not the slightest bit of fear. He has nothing but faith due to the quality of work that he holds. He passed out a few samples of the product to his most valued customers and all of them were amazed. He's sure with the help of them the block will not only be up and running in no time but it will also generate a wider range of clientele as well.

Samad has started each of his 5 workers off with a five hundred dollar pack. After giving them the work he held a brief meeting where he gave them the pep talk of a lifetime. Teamwork was emphasized throughout the entire meeting. The look in their eyes proved to him that he must have moved them. A few promises of them all blowing up together as a team led them to agree to working for free of charge. They all agreed to bring him every dollar back, not taking their pay. He explained to them that D-Nice has to be bailed out and he needed the help of all of them to make it happen. In return he promised them that they all would be compensated and he would be sure to make it very much worth their while. Little do they know that Samad plans to work them like slaves for free until he sells every gram of crack that he has. He figures after obtaining the $95,000 he will be in the position that he needs to be in order to take his game to an all time high.

As he's sitting here a Dodge Charger cruises up the block and parks in the space directly in front of the porch that he's sitting on. He watches closely as the passenger window rolls down slowly. "My man, Samad," the driver says cheerfully.

It's his man, Mike, the rent-a-car dude. "Mike what's the deal, baby?" he says as he jumps off the porch and runs toward the car. He hops into the passenger's seat and instantly gives Mike a firm handshake.

"You back huh?" Mike asks.

"No doubt. I had to get away for a minute and regroup," he lies. "This your new joint?"

"One of them," he replies arrogantly. "I been making major moves. Shit got crazy since I last seen you. I got with a couple of investors. I copped like five more cars. Shit is finally coming together. I told you it would! Right now I got ten cars cruising through the city and by next month I plan to have ten more," he says with excitement. He stares into Samad's eyes. "The offer I made to you still stands. Listen, it ain't never too late to get in."

Samad quickly calculates in his mind the profit that Mike is making. He remembers Mike telling him he rents the cars out for $600.00 a week. Ten cars will make him $6,000 a week, $24,000 a month. Good legitimate money, Samad thinks to himself. "Damn, that's alright," he blurts out.

"That's more than alright," he smiles. "Better get in while the getting is good."

"I'm definitely gone fuck with you on that," he says as he thinks of the extra money he can make with Mike as his partner. He figures this would be the perfect way to clean up all the dirty money that he plans on making. If all goes as he expects it to he plans on giving Mike a few thousand to buy in. "Just give me a few weeks and let me put a few dollars together and we gone make this shit happen."

"Alright, I'm here."

"So, this is what you got for me?"

"Yep, this is it. Everything else is out. I really got this for me so I can have something to get around in. I just copped it two days ago," he says as he points to the dashboard. "Look, not even 200 miles on it. It still got the plastic on the seats," he says as he points to the upholstery.

"So, what you gone charge me for it?"

"Come on baby, I already told you your price. You gone take it right now? All you gotta do is drop me off to my raggedy little Chevy. I can get around in that. Everything is for sale! It's all business!"

Samad smiles at him. He tries to come up with an excuse quickly. He's penniless right now. The only thing that he holds is a pocket full of hope but he's in dire need of a vehicle. Not having this car right now will slow him up tremendously. "Alright, just squat up for a second. I ain't bring no money out with me. Just sit out here with me until I get it. It shouldn't take no more than forty to forty-five minutes."

"Sit out here and wait?" Mike says with sarcasm in his voice. "I ain't no babysitter," he says as he looks Samad in the eyes. "Man, drop me the fuck off. Do what you have to do. I ain't about to sit here and watch you make the money. I trust you. What you gone do run off for three hundred punk ass dollars? "I'm parked on Lyons Avenue in Irvington. Take me there. Just hit me when you get it."

Damn, Samad thinks to himself. He didn't expect Mike to let him get away with that. The fact that he did just won him over. Now that he has all the pieces in place he doesn't see any reason why his puzzle can't be put together.

///// CHAPTER 53 /////

Amber sits in the beauty parlor underneath the hot dryer. Her face is buried into a book as she reads the novel 'Caught 'Em Slippin' by her favorite author. She sits on the edge of her seat with her undivided attention on the book. The door opens and her senses tell her to look up. She sniffs the air as two men enter the beauty parlor. Her nose relays the message to her that cops are close. Her senses have never failed her. She lowers her head into the book, pretending like they're not even there but really she has both eyes on them.

They walk right past her without even looking her way. Amber watches closely to see where they're going. She wonders why they're even here. They stop as soon as they get to the back where Deja stands at the counter. Amber tries to watch their lips but she can't from this distance. They both flip their badges and in seconds Deja is leading them to her office.

Amber's curiosity is driving her crazy. She wonders what exactly could be going on. A few ideas come to her mind and all of them are attached to her. She gets nervous when she thinks of the robbery that took place here months ago. Maybe the girl told the police that Deja is behind the murder of the man who committed the robbery. After all the girlfriend did work for Deja and they absolutely hated each other. Amber gets even more nervous when she thinks of the fact of how Deja may crack under pressure. That will result in Deja telling the police that Amber had the boy murdered.

A more recent situation comes to Amber's mind as well. She hopes and prays that they're not here for that reason. "Please God?" she begs. Her gut tells her to leave now while she still has the chance but her curiosity tells her to stay. She closes the book and eases to the edge of her seat. Just as she's about to get up she sits back down. She's in a state of confusion, not knowing if she should stay and get locked up or leave and go on the run. Damn if she does, damn if she doesn't.

"Miss Johnson how are you?" the detective asks rather politely. I'm Detective Rodriguez and this is my partner Detective Hanks the man says with a heavy Latin accent.

"Hello," the black detective says before looking Deja up and down slowly.

She doesn't even acknowledge the other detective's presence. The way he looks at her makes her feel uncomfortable. It's as if he can see right through her. She tries hard not to lock eyes with him. She concentrates on the eyes of the other detective.

"Miss Johnson do you know why we're here?" he asks while staring directly into here eyes.

"No," she answers innocently. "I don't have a clue."

"Uh, Lucias Smith...your former employee. He was murdered recently," he says slowly. "We're assigned to his homicide and we're out here searching for clues."

"I don't know anything," she replies defensively.

"Maybe you know something without even knowing that you do? Any arguments that you've known him to have?"

"No," she replies.

"How about friends? Are you familiar with any of his friends, male or female? We are aware that he lived an alternative lifestyle. Do you know of anyone that maybe could not accept his lifestyle? Maybe this is an act of gay bashing? Are you familiar with anyone that absolutely hates gays?"

Deja stands there quietly. Amber comes to her mind quickly. "No," she lies. "Everyone that we know in common loved Luscious. He was lovable and would help anyone. He never gave anyone a reason to hate him."

"How about the argument you and him had a couple of months ago? What was that about?"

Deja is shocked. "The argument we had? How do ya'll know about that?"

"Like I said we're out here investigating. We're finding out all types of information. Some is bullshit and some is worth looking into. It's an investigation. Let's just say that him and his mother were very close and he told her about the argument."

Bitch ass nigga Deja says to herself. She can't believe that a grown ass man runs home and tells his mother everything. Hmpphh, she sighs under her breath. Why should I be shocked? After all he is a faggot she says to herself. Damn, I tried to help his mother and here she is trying to get me charged for his murder. "We had an argument about him eating some food that I left in the refrigerator without my permission. I would never have him murdered for that. Matter of fact I would never have anyone murdered," she says trying to clear up her last statement.

"No one is suspecting you for having him murdered. Why would you think that?"

"Nah, just the way ya'll coming off," she says in a sassy manner.

"Maam, excuse me if you think we're coming off any particular way. We're just doing our job. Not too long ago, a robbery occured here in your place of business. The assailants jumped on him and beat on him brutally. That was after your disagreement. Someone believes you could have set that up," he says attempting to get a reaction from her.

"Over some fucking Red Lobster takeout? Ya'll gotta be kidding? He told his mother that too? Listen I have to go. I have clients waiting on me. As I told you in the beginning, I know nothing. I had no issue with him. He was not only my employee, I loved him like a brother, or a sister whatever you want to call him.

And if ya'll are finished with me, I have to go?" she says as she makes her way to the door.

They follow right behind her. "Listen maam," the black detective says. "We're not suspecting you as my partner said but we have strong reason to believe that it was a woman involved in his murder. We're on this case until we crack it. With all the gay rights and Governor McGreevey coming out of the closet making it acceptable, they're never going to sweep that under the rug. These people have a world of their own. You may as well get used to us cause we gone be here. Here take my card and call me if you hear anything, ok?

"I sure will," she lies just to get him out of her face.

"My after business number is on that card as well. Don't hesitate to call anytime you like," he says with a flirtatious look in his eyes. "Anytime."

He has no idea how much she despises cops. Please, she says to herself. I wish I would fuck with a cop she says to herself. "I will not hesitate to call if I hear anything," she says as she rushes them through the beauty parlor. She snatches the door open and holds it for them to exit.

"Good day," the detective says.

She slams the door without replying. She turns around quickly and instantly locks eyes with Amber. The look on her face scares Amber to death. Her face looks like she just saw a ghost. Her cocky demeanor is now broken.

Amber lifts her head from underneath the dryer and sits on the edge of her seat. "What was that all about?"

"Luscious," she says slowly. "That was Robbery and Homicide. These motherfuckers come in here accusing me of his murder. Like I had him killed. His ugly ass mother gone tell them that me and him had an argument right before he got killed. I told them we had a fucking argument over some fucking old ass Red Lobster. He even told his mother that the robbery that went down was set up by me because of the argument. I don't believe his faggot ass or his ugly ass mother. I should have let her broke ass burn his body and spread his faggot ass ashes all over the gay parade," she says with fury in her voice.

Weeks ago Amber would have found that to be absolutely hilarious but now after finding out that Star is gay she doesn't find it funny at all. Damn, Amber thinks to herself as she thinks of the fact that the detectives even know about the robbery. That scares her to death. She wonders if they have put it together that the same person that had the boy Tragedy killed is the same person that is involved with the murder of Luscious. Her blood pressure races to the roof. "So they think you're behind it?"

"They said they're just investigating the murder and searching for any information. They said I'm not a suspect but they have a lot of reason to believe that a woman is behind his murder."

Oh my God, Amber says to herself. This stress is just way too much for her. It's so unbearable that she wishes she could just remove herself from the world. She's suffocated with problems to the point that she feels like she can't even breathe.

She's in need of a getaway. She's taking Star away for her 21st birthday in a few days. It's the perfect time to go, right while all the madness is taking place. She can't wait to disappear. She has a good mind to never come back here to this chaos that she has going on. It's starting to be way too much for her. Samad, Maurice, the pregnancy that she hasn't told Maurice about, her sister being gay, the murder of Tragedy, the murder of Luscious, and the kilo that she got from Muhsee. Everyday she wonders if Muhsee will tell Maurice. If he does she knows what will happen to her. She can't understand how she gets herself into situation after situation. Damn, I need to get away.

///// CHAPTER 54 /////

Maurice sits in the living room of the "Bat Cave." The loud noise from the money counting machine stops short. The 'Accountant' as Maurice calls him jots numbers down onto the pad and quickly comes up with the total of $277,500. This amount comes from one man who at the beginning of the week took 15 kilos.

Maurice runs his operation on a weekly accord. Every Saturday night everyone is to turn in whatever they have made for the week even if they're not done. If by chance they have not moved the work they are still responsible for giving him the balance of whatever they have taken.

The Accountant hands the slip of paper over to Maurice who looks at the numbers to make sure that everything appears to be correct. He then looks over at the man who sits across from him. Maurice wonders why his workload is lower than normal. He's usually good for at least 25 kilos a week. "You only took 15 this week?"

"Yeah, I got to a late start this week," he explains. "I been on cruise control. I'll turn it up this week though."

"You don't have to!" the man standing in the doorway shouts out. "Keep on cruising. Leave more for me," he smiles.

The money machine starts up all over again sounding like music to Maurice's ears. Maurice has already received $1,387,000 and all the money for the week hasn't been turned in as of yet. In total there is close to two million dollars in cold cash in this apartment.

The men go on joking and babbling as they always do. The moment they all get together alone they transform from stone cold organized crime family members to immature little boys. Maurice goes to the closet as they are busy joking around. He retrieves two duffel bags that lie in the corner. He carries them and dumps them onto the coffee table. He quickly starts stacking the squares on top of each other, ten kilos high. When he's done he has six and a half piles.

Sal, what you say you need out of here?" Maurice asks. Sal always gets first pick at the work.

He stares at the pile before replying. "That's all that's left?" he asks as he counts out 65 kilos.

"That's it," Maurice replies.

Sal realizes that after these are gone they will be dry for at least three days. Whatever he doesn't get right now he will not get. The rest of the squad realizes this as well. They each hope and pray that he doesn't take his normal fifty and leave only 15 for them to divide. If he does so they will have a terrible week. "Just give me five to hold me until we get back up." They all sigh with appreciation.

They watch with greed. They are all scared that the work will not make it around to them. None of them wants to leave here empty handed. It would kill them to go three days without work.

"Listen ya'll, as ya'll can see it's only these left. I want to make sure all ya'll get work. We will only be down to about Wednesday." Maurice will be sending five mules out first thing tomorrow morning. They will lay around until Tuesday.

One by one on different flights they will come back. Each one of them will be bringing back ten kilos. By no later than Friday those fifty kilos will be stretched out into 100 kilos.

Friday night he will send another crew of five out. That crew will be coming back throughout the course of the day on Monday. Maurice has his set regimen. Every three to four days he sends a crew out. They alternate like clockwork. The operation runs smoothly. To this day none of his mules have ever been popped and he has never gone one single day without work. In fact this is the first time that he has even gotten low in fifteen years.

Normally he has more than enough work on hand. For some reason it's getting harder and harder for him to keep work. Although that's a good problem he still wants to find out what the drastic spurt is about. In the last two weeks he has gone from selling 100-150 kilos a week to moving almost 200 kilos a week. He loves the increase in his finances but his paranoia constantly alerts him, telling him that maybe somebody from the crew has connected with a FED and not know it. The increase in purchases could easily be them trying to build a bigger case against the Federation.

Maurice slides the first stack of ten kilos across the table to the man who is sitting in front of him. "Here, ya'll," he says as he separates the second stack. The men stand in line as if he's giving away free lunch. In seconds the coffee table is bare. The men drop the kilos into their shopping bags to conceal them. Suddenly Maurice realizes that someone is missing. "Anybody heard from Smurf?" It's not like Smurf to miss a meeting. The only thing that comes to Maurice's mind is their last meeting in the graveyard.

They all look at each other with puzzled looks on their faces while shaking their heads from side to side.

"Hmphh," Maurice snickers as he looks over at Sal. Their eyes speak a language of their very own. This isn't a good sign. Smurf's absence makes Maurice take away the benefit of the doubt that he has given him. Deep down inside he doesn't believe that Smurf would cross him but now that he hasn't showed up he really doesn't know what to think. Maurice knows how wicked the streets can be and before he allows anyone to take him away from his wife, his children and his many girlfriends he has no problem removing anyone that he has the slightest bit of doubt about. "Yo! Somebody get that nigga on the phone." The sound of his voice causes four phones to appear. Each of them tries to dial the number faster than the other. Once the winner puts the phone to his ear the rest of them stop dialing. The man listens patiently as the phone rings while the rest of them watch with anxiety.

"Voicemail," the man replies as he dials the number again. Seconds later," he speaks again. "He's not answering."

Maurice snatches his phone from the coffee table. He holds it in the air just staring at it. He's hesitant about dialing because he fears that Smurf may not answer. If he does that the benefit of the doubt will no longer be. He's sure his gut feeling will tell him to not only finish off Dirt but to finish Smurf off as well. Maurice never goes against his gut feeling.

He dials the numbers slowly. Once he's finished he listens while the phone rings over and over until his voice mail comes on. Fury bleeds from his eyes. "Hmphh," he snickers, trying to ease his rage.

"Let me call him?" one man suggests. "Maybe he's caught up and can't get to the phone," he says trying to once again give Smurf the benefit of the doubt. He quickly snatches his phone from the case and starts to dial.

"Nah!" Maurice shouts sternly. "No need. Don't call him. He'll surface," he says with an evil grin on his face. "One way or another."

Meanwhile Two Cities Away. The driver of the Denali is escorted out of the truck by the police officer. "Officer, what is the problem?" the man asks.

"Sir, please just step out of the vehicle?" the officer asks politely.

"I gave you all of my paperwork. What's the problem?"

"Sir, are you aware that your registration is expired?"

"I wasn't. Can't be, man," he says with a look of fear on his face.

The officer drags him to the front of the vehicle and slams him against the hood of the truck. He immediately starts to search him thoroughly. Another officer snatches the passenger's door open and pulls the passenger out of the seat. "Yo, easy man," Smurf says aggressively. The officer pushes him to the back of the vehicle and slams him against the truck. "Yo!" Smurf says as he turns around and looks the cop dead in the eyes. He shoves Smurf harder and quickly begins searching him.

Smurf looks up ahead at the crowded block of Central Avenue. Many police cars, at least 20 police, orange colored cones, and brightly lit flares are lined up the street. Smurf looks up at his man Dirt. How the fuck he missed all of this he can't understand. They lock eyes. "You dumb motherfucker," he says under his breath. Dirt reads his lips clearly. Smurf can't believe that Dirt rode right into a police inspection roadblock. The fact that his paperwork isn't legit makes it even worse. Smurf shakes his head from side to side as he looks at a third officer going into the truck. His hear beat speeds up. Damn, he mumbles to himself as he realizes that they're on their way to jail.

"Cuff them!" the officer shouts. The officers restrain them securely as they start to put the cuffs on them.

"Yo, easy man, I ain't running no fucking where," Smurf says arrogantly as he puts his hands behind his back. The cop steps out of the vehicle happily. In his hands he holds a minimum of three to five years. The chrome nickel plated nine millimeter glistens like jewelry in the darkness. While the officers were snatching Dirt from the car Smurf tossed the gun under the seat. He's a man and will always take the weight for any of his actions but he refuses to admit right here that it's his gun. Admitting it now will make it hard for him to plead not guilty later.

Five other cops run to the scene and they wrestle Smurf and Dirt onto the ground. In seconds both of them are being dragged from the ground and shoved into the back of the police cars.

The door slams in Smurf's face. He watches closely as the police search Dirt's truck. He looks over to Dirt with rage in his eyes. "You dumb motherfucker."

////// CHAPTER 55 //////

Three Days Later

Samad lays back in the car with his head against the headrest. He can barely keep his heavy eyes open. He dozes off every few seconds. In the past 72 hours he hasn't slept a full hour. He takes a 20 minute power nap in between shifts.

He's so tired that nothing can keep him awake. He's drank so many red bulls that the look of the can turns his stomach. Not only is his system immune to it but also the sugar rush that he obtains from them has now crashed making him even more tired.

He hasn't been home since the morning he left on his mission to get rich. He calls Amber every couple of hours just to reassure her that he's alright. His hair hasn't been combed, his teeth haven't been brushed and his clothes, not even his soiled underwear have been changed. He's so focused that not even the foul smell of his body odor is an incentive for him to go home. Sleep will come later he tells himself every time he finds himself yearning for sleep.

He refuses to go home until he's gotten close to his goal. In all actuality he's nowhere near his goal. He thought for sure he would have at least put a dent in the work he has. The first day his crew struggled with the little work that he gave them. His night crew had an even harder time creating a flow. Between both shifts he was lucky to make $1,600. The next day he did a little better, scoring just over $2,000. Today the block seems to be moving in slow motion as well. He expected today to be the best day of all but the block generated nowhere near what expected. The day shift is less than an hour away from ending and he has only pulled in a little over $1,200. That sort of tells him what to expect from the night shift which he predicts to be little to nothing.

Three days in and he's only made approximately $4,900. He understands that it's better than a blank and just three days ago he was dead broke. He's grateful but a part of him is still disappointed. He expected so much more. He was hoping to at least be fifteen to twenty thousand dollars in by now and would be if the block hadn't been dry for as long as it has been.

If he was moving on his own accord it wouldn't be so bad but unfortunately he isn't. The burden that he has on his back is breaking him. He told Amber that he would have the money he owes her in seven days but now he doubts that will happen. At this rate it will take a miracle to accomplish that. The last thing he wants to do is to have to tell her that he needs more time to get the money to her. That would cause him even more embarrassment than actually taking the handout from her in the first place. The last thing he wants to look like in her eyes is a complete failure.

Samad's phone rings in the middle of his sulking. He looks down at the number and instantly his stress level increases. Damn, he thinks to himself as he stares at D-Nice's mother's number. He debates whether he should answer it or not. He thought for sure that he would have made the money to bail him out by now and he hates to tell him he still doesn't have it.

"Yo?" he answers sadly.

"Yeah," D-Nice replies. "What up?" The sound of his voice is quite different than normal and Samad notices the difference instantly.

"Shit. Just out here trying to make it happen."

"Yeah," he asks with sarcasm in his voice. "Hmphh."

The sarcasm in his voice is starting to aggravate Samad but he's trying to refrain himself from saying anything about it. "What's that all about?"

"All what about?" D-Nice asks as if he doesn't know.

"The little laugh thing."

"It ain't about shit."

"Yo, what's up with you?" Samad asks.

"Shit, I'm in jail. That's what's up with me. I ain't on the street, you forgot? I been in here for more than a minute. It's the same old shit for me day in and day out. The highlight of my day is calling you so you can beat me down with some bullshit about coming to bail me out," he says.

Samad is shocked at what's heard. He's so shocked that he doesn't know how to reply. "You bugging Son."

"I'm bugging? I'm bugging?" he laughs. "Nah, you bugging Son! If this shit would have been the other way around, see how fast I would have made shit happen to get you out. No way in the world I would let you sit in the box for this long. No way in the fucking world!"

"What the fuck is you talking about? You think I'm out here bullshitting while you in the building?"

"It ain't what I think. It's what the fuck I see. You out there and I'm in here. You bailed out a minute ago."

"Yeah mufucker I'm trying to get it right! It just ain't happening fast enough."

"It happened fast enough for you to bail out. Why it ain't happen that fast for me?"

"Nigga you already know I was fucked up just like you. Where the fuck was I supposed to get the money from?"

"The same place you got the money from to bail yourself out," he replies sarcastically. "Real talk, before I would have bailed out and left you stinking, I would have stayed here with you. That's just me. It's the principle. This was your beef. Not mine!"

"What? How much fucking sense that would make to stay in with you and both of us fucked up and can't help ourselves do nothing? You talking fucking stupid!"

"The same sense it would make for one of us to get out and shit on the other one while he in jail."

"Shit on you? That's how you see it? You think I'm shitting on you?"

An automated service interrupts their conversation. "The jail will end your call in one minute."

Samad continues on. "Nigga I would never shit on you! You bugging! Them steel bars eating away at your fucking brain!"

"No, nigga, you eating away at my brain," he replies sarcastically. "It is what it is though. Real recognize real and you're not looking familiar," he sings. "I bet you wouldn't leave your bitch in the building would you? Hell no!" he shouts. "That's priority right there. Gold digging ass bitch got you so fucked up that you forgot who love you nigga. That's why I'm still in here. You can't get the money up cause you busy laying up in the Short Hills Hilton and shit...eating Filet Mignon and Lobster. That's some bullshit. That bitch don't love you. She just trying to find a meal ticket. You sucker for love ass ni...," he manages to say before the phone shuts off.

D-Nice has never talked to Samad like this. Samad figures that D-Nice must have been holding onto this for some time now because it seems that once he got started he couldn't stop. He can't believe that D-Nice would ever believe that he would shit on him. He understands that jail is stressful and the pressure is probably taking control of his mind but still that doesn't take away the pain his words have caused. Samad's mother has always told him 'what comes out of a person's mouth is nowhere near what they hold in their hearts. The words he just said were brutal so Samad would hate to find out what he really holds in his heart.

In seconds Samad's anger replaces his sadness. For him to attack Amber and not even know her, pisses Samad off dearly. He has no clue that without Amber, the gold digging bitch, he would still be in jail and D-Nice would not have a chance of getting bailed out. Just for saying that, Samad has a good mind to let him sit.

He shakes his head from side to side as the single tear drips from his eye. Those words ripped through his soul causing extreme pain. He bangs his head onto the headrest and exhales. "Phew!"

///// CHAPTER 56 /////

Amber stands in the full sized mirror stark naked. She spins around, freezing momentarily in between positions. She stands still at the side angle longer than the other positions. She looks closely at the small bulge that has grown in the pit of her belly. The sight of it brings tears to her eyes.

Her tears should be tears of joy but they're not. They're tears of fear and confusion. She's already three months into her pregnancy and she still hasn't told Maurice yet because she doesn't know how to. She can't come up with the perfect way to break the news to him. Although he is a married man she still feels guilty as if she's cheated on him. The fact that he's always been there for her makes her feel like she owes him loyalty and devotion for the rest of her life.

The reality is one day she will have to tell him whether she wants to or not.

She owes him that out of respect at least. What the outcome will be when she tells him she really doesn't want to find out.

Before Amber knows it tears are flooding her face uncontrollably. Amber has cried more in these past couple of months than she's cried in her entire life. She's normally stone cold and shows no emotion but this pregnancy has turned her into an emotional wreck. As big of a cry baby as she's become she still manages to hold back from letting anyone see her cry though. She learned that from her mom years ago and never forgot it.

She's been through a great deal in her life but by far this is on the list of the top stickiest situations that she's ever been in. The more she looks at her stomach the more depressed she becomes. Every time she gets out of the shower she finds herself weeping away. She continuously promises herself that she will stop looking in the mirror but the mirror keeps calling her name. She figures to avoid the crying and depression she may need to take every mirror down from the walls.

Abortion comes to her mind on a regular but killing her baby she can't even imagine going through with it. Her only reason for considering abortion is because of Maurice. She feels foolish to be thinking of how he feels about her baby when he has babies with his wife.

She quickly puts her satin pajama top on to suppress her depression. She sits down on the edge of her bed. Her attention is drawn to an envelope that lies on her nightstand. The envelope is filled with airline tickets.

Star's birthday is only a couple of days away and Amber wants to make it her most memorable one yet. Amber looks at the vacation guide and the sparkling water and palm trees dry up her tears instantly. This vacation is supposedly for Star's birthday but Amber is looking forward to it more for herself for her own sanity. She's hoping that stepping out of the mayhem will help her to put everything into proper perspective. What she doesn't realize is the vacation is only temporary wherein the situations at hand are forever. They will affect her entire life.

Meanwhile a Few Cities Away

Two men sit in the Ford Taurus station wagon. Silence fills the air. No one has said a word in minutes. Both men are extremely agitated. They have been parked here for hours now. Maurice ordered them to do so. He assigned them to sit here and stake out Smurf's house.

Maurice has been calling Smurf for days now. He now feels disrespected. Listening to the phone ring was frustrating him but now that the phone is no longer ringing and going straight to the voicemail he's pissed to no end. At this point he's so mad that he's ordered a C.O.S (capture on sight) on Smurf. If any member of the Federation spots him they have been ordered to snatch him and bring him to Maurice. The only reason the C.O.S. is not a T.O.S (Terminate on Sight) is the fact that Smurf is in Maurice's pocket $370,000 deep. He hated to make that order but he's angry and feels disrespected that a plot was developing right under his nose and he had no clue. Thanks to his good friend he is now aware. Now it's time to handle the situation.

///// CHAPTER 57 /////

Samad is busy at work in what he calls the laboratory. He's rented the kitchen of one of the neighborhood's feigns. He sits at the small raggedy table inside of the empty apartment. On the table in front of him there lies a shopping bag full of tiny crack filled vials. On the opposite side of the table there lies a table full of small empty clear medicine jars.

Despite the aggravation of sitting on the slow block one good thing has derived from being out there with nothing going on. He had all the time in the world to think. While sitting there desperately awaiting sales to come through he had more than enough time to come up with a new idea. He now has a plan that he believes is fool proof. His objective is to shut down every block in the area. He plans to do so by giving the customers more crack for their dollar.

He drops three vials of crack onto the plate in front of him. He then slides the pebbles of crack into one of the medicine jars. He screws the top onto the jar, holding it in the air, up to the light. Crack fills the jar up to the very top. The jar is designed to create the illusion that it's more crack inside than it actually is. He spins it around slowly just appreciating the view. "Yeah," he mumbles under his breath. He looks over to the crack addict who stands in the doorway, watching with greediness. "Here," he says as he holds the jar in the air. The addict runs over at top speed. "What you think about that?" he asks. "What would you pay for that?" The saliva that drips from the addict's mouth speaks volumes. He's sure every feign in the neighborhood will react the same way once they lay eyes on this.

Glory fills the man's eyes as he's enticed by the beauty of his passion. He can barely speak on the account that he's ready to blast away into the twilight zone. "That's a twenty all day," the man replies with joy in his eyes.

"Oh yeah? You think?" Samad asks with sarcasm in his voice. "Maybe on somebody else block but not mines. These our new dimes."

"A dime?"

Samad believes this is the master plan of a lifetime. Increasing the quantity may cut down his profit margin but he's sure it will also increase his cash flow. By giving away three nickels for the price of a dime he will decrease his gross by over $27,000. He's calculated it precisely and although his margin will decrease drastically, he's ok with it because of the clientele that he plans to generate. His expected $95,690 will now be reduced to a little over $68,000 by using this method but he's more than sure it will be well worth it. He will not only rip through the work faster but he will also make it harder for the smaller dealers to compete with him. If they don't have the amount of work that he has on hand, there is no way possible that they can stand up to him in battle. It will be senseless and quite difficult. He's sure that he will be giving away more than the average dealer has to begin with.

"You done lost your mind!" the man shouts. "You about to shut the whole town down with these!"

Samad smiles with joy. "My plan exactly," he whispers confidently. The look in the man's eyes gives Samad a new spurt of life. "Game over!"

Meanwhile. Amber lays sprawled out on her couch. She just woke up not even two hours ago and here she is going to sleep again. Her energy level is at an all time low due to her pregnancy. The baby seems to steal all the life out of her. Normally she's so energetic and alive but now it seems as if all she wants to do is sleep. She can barely muster up enough energy to stay awake an entire day.

She dozes off into la la land when her cell phone rings. She grabs hold of the phone and answers it with her eyes half closed. "Hello?" she utters groggily.

"Lil Bit!"

Maurice's voice rejuvenates her giving her a sudden burst of energy. "Yeah?"

"I'm downstairs!" he shouts at the top of his lungs.

Oh boy, she thinks to herself. Her heart skips a beat. Damn, she says to herself as she quickly fumbles for another excuse not to let him upstairs but she can't come up with a single one. She's run out of excuses long ago. "Huh?"

"I'm downstairs," he repeats. "Where is Star?"

Thank God, she says to herself. I'm safe, she thinks. "She's in her room."

"Tell her to come down!" he shouts with joy. "I got something for her.!"

The excitement in his voice makes her wonder what this is all about. "Ok," she replies.

In less than three minutes Star steps through the huge double doors of the apartment building while Amber stands many steps behind her. She watches nosily to see what it is that he has for her.

Star steps out and looks to her right where she finds Maurice sitting on a bench all alone. He stands up energetically. "Happy Birthday, God baby!" he shouts before extending his arm in the air.

Star looks in the direction that he's pointing in and the lights of a beautiful brand spanking new, candy apple red convertible BMW 335I illuminate the area. Her mouth stretches wide open with awe. She's speechless. The temporary tag in the back window mesmerizes her. She has to rub her eyes just to make sure that she's not dreaming.

Amber watches with awe as well. Just to think that Maurice has spent over fifty grand on a birthday present for Star makes her mind wander. She's not jealous but she can't help but to think of all the heartache and headaches that Maurice has caused her over the years and Star gets the best treatment from him free of charge. She quickly chalks it up and accepts the fact that it was all for a good cause. She hopes and prays that no matter how the story ends with her and Maurice after she tells him about her pregnancy that it doesn't affect the relationship that him and Star have. She knows how much they both mean to each other and it would break her heart to ruin the bond that they share. She's sure that the bond her and Maurice have will be destroyed but she prays that theirs will remain the same.

"Here!" he shouts as he passes her the keys. "Take it for a spin."

Star stands there in a baffled state. "I don't even know how to drive," she snickers goofily.

"Learn. Here," he smiles. "It's paid for and insured," he says arrogantly. "Crash this one and I'll cop you another one just like it. Fuck it!"

///// CHAPTER 58 /////

Smurf is just six hours out of the County Jail for possession of a loaded weapon for an unlawful purpose and here sitting on his lap lays a bigger and a higher caliber one. The black .40 caliber is fully loaded and ready for action. He lays back in the driver's seat of the black on black Nissan Quest van. The dark tinted windows make it hard for him to see outside but it's impossible for anyone to see inside.

A bunch of men exit a building and disperse into their own separate directions. Smurf pops up in his seat and watches attentively. He quickly spots his prey. A couple of men come walking in his direction. He sits still long enough for them to pass his vehicle. He then allows the other men to go on their merry way as well but he doesn't allow his victim to get out of his sight.

In a matter of minutes there is no sign of life on the dark block except for his target. He twists the key back in the ignition and up the block he cruises. His adrenaline is pumping vigorously. His palms are sweating and his mind is racing. He hits the button for the window to roll down. He takes a long drag of his cigarette just to ease his nervousness. He then flicks the burning cigarette butt out of the window.

He races up the block at full speed. He approaches the corner just as his target is crossing the street. He slams on the brakes causing the man to turn around with alarm. He extends his arm out of the window. With less than two feet between the gun and the man's face, Smurf fires. Bloc! The sound of gunfire rips through the air. The victim grabs hold of his face after the heated slug burns through the flesh of his cheek. He stumbles backwards. Smurf fires again and again. Bloc! Bloc! The man staggers before finally falling flat on his back. Smurf forces the door open and jolts out quickly. In seconds he stands over his prey. He peeks around at his surroundings hoping that the coast is clear.

The helpless man looks up at Smurf with fear in his eyes. A look of confusion appears on his face as he realizes who the shooter is. "Smurf?" he utters as blood drips from the corner of his mouth.

The sight of this touches Smurf's heart. He almost can't go through with it but he realizes he's already started so he has no choice but to finish the job. He aims at the man's head and closes his eyes before he starts dumping the shells consecutively. Bloc! Bloc! Bloc! Bloc! Bloc! Bloc! Bloc! Bloc! The noise of the empty chamber snapping back awakens Smurf out of his zone. His eyes pop open and set onto the lifeless man. He shakes his head from side to side before peeking around nervously. He slams the empty gun into his waistband. Two giant steps and he's back in the van. He peels off recklessly before pulling the door shut.

The smell of gunfire mixed with burned rubber from his tires fills the air. As soon as he bends the corner he resumes a normal speed. He exhales a huge sigh of relief. Pity fills his heart instantly as the look on Dirt's face freezes in his mind.

As much as he hated to do it he felt that he had no choice. Smurf already had the murder planned before he was released from jail. He planned to meet Dirt here at the County Jail as he's being released and that he did. He just hopes that the murder won't be linked to him.

After a brief conversation with Dirt in the County Jail he realized that everything Maurice said was true. At first Dirt denied it all but after a while he admitted to saying some of the statements. He downplayed it by blaming it all on just jailhouse chitter chatter but Smurf could not look at it as being so minute. Those statements could have easily caused Smurf to lose his life. He knows the only way he could prove his innocence to the matter is by murdering Dirt. Dirt is his long time friend and he hated to murder him but he understands that was the only way to prove his loyalty to Maurice and the Federation. What a price to pay.

///// CHAPTER 59 /////

The women's section of Neiman and Marcus here in Short Hills Mall looks more like a runway filled with beautiful women prancing around half naked in bikinis. The salesman sits back discreetly enjoying the show as Amber, Deja, Sade and Star try on various swimsuits. He can't keep his eyes off of the beautiful women in skimpy bathing suits even if his job depended on it. There is enough booty and boobs exposed that the room should be rated Triple X. The sight of them is so beautiful that no man can restrain himself from gawking at them. In fact that is the exact reason why the few men who were here were enviously dragged out by the women they accompanied.

"Sister, how is this?" Star asks as she stands in front of Amber.

"Scandalous," Amber barks viciously as she views the way Star's vivacious body swallows her bikini bottom, making her appear to be naked. Her breasts ooze all over the place as if she's topless. "Back to the dressing room."

"Psst," Star sucks her teeth with frustration. She's tried on so many bathing suits and not one of them reaches Amber's standards.

"Girl, ain't nothing wrong with that suit or none of the other ones she's tried on. She can't help it if she has a beautiful body," Deja interrupts. "Come on Lil Bit, ain't nothing wrong with her showing a little skin. After all it's her 21st birthday. Lighten up. You ain't gone be there all the time, girl. Eventually she gone have to get some," she smiles.

Amber laughs to herself. Little do you know she already getting some, just not what you expect her to be getting. "Well, while I'm here there won't be none of that," she says firmly.

"Shit, you was getting some at 21, wasn't you?"

Amber looks in Deja's eyes with a cold stare. The look tells her that she may have crossed the line. Amber plays no games whatsoever when it comes to Star. "Deja, I'm not even going to entertain this conversation with you. She's not wearing that skimpy shit, end of discussion," she says firmly.

Deja quickly gets the hint that Amber is not in the best of moods right now. She quickly begins spinning around in the full sized mirror shamelessly. The attention of the men in the room causes her to perform even more. She stands still looking over her shoulder at her rear end. The black and gold two piece Dior bathing suit looks as if it was made just for her. She looks as if she's been torn right from a swimsuit magazine. "They are not ready for this," she says as she taps her backside gently causing her behind to jiggle vigorously. The only thing that separates her from being ass naked is the thin chain, g-string that parts her cheeks. She sways her hips from side to side like a belly dancer while she watches and enjoys the view. "I'm so in love with myself," she says conceitedly.

Sade stands in the far corner of the room. She twirls around bashfully in her one piece bathing suit. She peeks around nervously to see who is watching her. In her best dream she wouldn't wear a two piece bathing suit. In her younger years she had the perfect body to do so but she never had the heart to expose her body like that in public. Now thanks to her three children that body is merely a memory. She's tried on at least twenty bathing suits and this one is the one that hides her most troubled area; her tummy. Her shapely hips, luscious thighs and voluptuous behind are no problem at all but her modesty forces her to keep the cotton-wrap tied tightly around her waist.

As much as Amber would love to sport a two piece and really does have the body for it, she refuses to do so. Although she still isn't showing she has a huge complex. In her mind that tiny pouch in the pit of her belly is a round bowling ball. She stands in front of the mirror with satisfaction finally as her eyes lay on the Emilio Pucci one piece bikini, stars and stripes bathing suit. The sight of the price tag would cause the normal woman to see stars upon laying eyes on it but in no way is Amber the normal woman. The $735.00 price tag is meaningless to her.

After two hours of dressing up and dressing down it's finally over. Close to forty bathing suits have been purchased and over seven thousand dollars have been spent. Finally shopping for the vacation is over. Just a couple more days to go and they will all be laying on a sandy beach, tanning while watching the ocean water wave.

Meanwhile

In Tops Restaurant in Harrison, New Jersey another deal is being discussed. Maurice and Sal sit side by side in the booth while two Latin speaking men sit in front of them. The two men are long time friends of Maurice's from New York.

Maurice met them over a decade and a half ago when he was just a small time hustler going over to them to buy a kilo or two at a time. After linking up with Muhsee he no longer had the need to visit them but still he kept in contact with them from time to time. One thing that he's realized is if he had never linked up with Muhsee there's no way in the world he would ever be the man that he is today. Dealing with these men would have only stunted his growth. For some strange reason they never allowed him any room for improvement. They would only give him what his money could buy, never allowing him an extra gram on consignment. With that strict harness around his neck his movements were limited. Dealing with them taught him how not to do business. He promised himself way back then, if he ever got on top he would give everyone the opportunity to eat. Now that he's on top that is exactly what he does.

Yesterday evening he received a call from them requesting a meeting with him. He's quite sure that the meeting has everything to do with the major cocaine bust that he heard about on the news the day before yesterday. That bust is the second biggest bust of the decade. Two weeks prior to that a boatload was caught by the Coastguards. Seeing that report eased Maurice's mind concerning the major increase of kilos that he's been moving. Something tells him that it's not over and he has no problem with it. The more kilos caught the more his business picks up.

"So, what's the urgency?" Maurice asks as if he's ignorant to the fact.

The Spanish man peeks around cautiously to make sure no one is eavesdropping. "Please tell me you know something good?" he asks with desperation in his eyes.

"Something good like what?" he asks, playing the game.

The man peeks around once again before speaking. "Material," he whispers. "The streets are dry. No one has nothing. Nobody," he adds. "It's a drought. We search everywhere and can't find nothing. Last week we get lucky and come across the last of it."

"Damn," Maurice says with no concern.

"Yeah, Miami...nothing. Texas...nothing. Everything is dry. The price go up sky high," he says as he stretches his eyes wide open. "We pay way too much for the work last time. The connection raise the price three points. Before we pay seventeen for a kilo. Now he charge us twenty. He say maybe he will have more this week but the price will go up four more points. Twenty-four thousand," he adds.

Of all the man has just said the only thing that sticks in his mind is the seventeen the man claims that he normally pays. He thinks back at how they raped him, charging him $22,000 a kilo, claiming that they only score a thousand profit because they pay 21,000. He smiles at the thought of it. How greedy they are he thinks to himself. Greedy people starve, he says to himself.

Dollar signs flood his mind. At $24,000 a kilo he will be able to score $41,000 profit after stretching one kilo into two. That is a profit to dream of. He's in a position to keep the price the same for them but he refuses to do so because of how they treated him when he was just a young man trying to come up. They never gave him a break. They wouldn't even let him go for a lousy dollar. He's sure they could have given him a better number but their greed stopped them from doing so. Now that the tables have turned he will drag them as far as he can just to repay them for their selfishness.

"I just may be able to help ya'll," he bluffs.

Both of the men's eyes open up widely. They look as if he has just saved their lives. "Thank you," the man whispers.

"The price though, I'm not sure of. At the best I can probably give them to you for about 21, 5," he says as he looks at them closely to see how they react at that number. He can actually beat that price but why would he. As long as he beats the price that they're paying he's sure they will be grateful.

"No problem," the man says with anxiousness. "How fast can you get them?"

Maurice thinks of the thirty kilos that have come in already. As they sit here those kilos are evolving into sixty. Another 20 will be coming in late tomorrow night. "How fast you need them?"

"We need them like yesterday," the man whispers. "The entire Washington Heights area is as dry as a desert. Not a gram of cocaine anywhere. Me, my amigo right here and my cousin, together we control all of Washington Heights. We supply everyone there. Together we can come up with the money for 100. How fast can you get them for us?"

Maurice quickly calculates the figures. Off of the 100 kilos he will gross $2,150,000. At the price of $6,000 per kilo and the mule's fee of $1,000, his overhead on fifty kilos is $350,000. That's a profit of $1.8 million off of this one deal. There's only one problem though. The 100 kilos that he has are already accounted for. His team is waiting desperately for them.

He weighs his options carefully. He can either distribute the 100 kilos to his team on consignment for $18,500.00 a kilo and wait for the money at the end of the week or he can tell his team to hold off for a few days and sell the work for $21,500.00 per kilo, straight money. Uhmm, he grunts as he debates. $1,850,000.00 at the end of the week or $2,150,000.00 up front, C.O.D. It doesn't take a scientist to figure out which one he will choose. "How does tomorrow night sound?"

"Sounds like a deal," the man says as he reaches over the table for a handshake. He nods his head up and down with a huge smile on his face. "Sounds like a deal."

///// CHAPTER 60 /////

The Next Morning. Maurice and the entire Federation sit in the living room of the Bat Cave. Everyone is present in the apartment except for Smurf. Smurf has some nerve being late to a meeting that he's called.

Everyone lays around restlessly when Maurice's phone sounds off. "Yeah?" he answers casually. "Open the door," he says as he shuts the phone off.

Smurf walks in with his head hanging low. The guilt of murdering his good friend is ripping him apart. He hasn't been able to get a wink of sleep yet. He can't even live with himself. He can't believe that he actually murdered someone so close to him as a token of his loyalty to a bunch of men who really mean nothing to him. The root of their relationship is purely based on money. If they didn't have business ties they probably would have never come in contact with each other. Dirt on the other hand was completely different. They were friends long before the money. When they both had nothing they still had each other.

The worst part of it all is the phone call that Smurf received from Dirt's girlfriend an hour after the murder. She claims that he was the first person she called the minute she found out. It broke his heart to sit there and try and console her and Dirt's sons who he is the godfather of. If they only knew the hands he patted their backs with are the same hands he murdered their father with. The guilt tore him apart but still he had to keep a genuine look on his face. He hasn't been able to erase the look on Dirt's face from his mind. It's as if it's frozen in his head. He's sure that will haunt him for the rest of his life.

As soon as Smurf enters the apartment everyone's attention is drawn to Maurice to see how he's going to react. Maurice sits back with no expression on his face whatsoever. He waits to see what Smurf has to say. Silence fills the air. The room is extremely tense. Everyone is quite eager to hear what Smurf has to say.

Smurf makes his way over to the coffee table. He lays the plastic shopping bag onto the table directly in front of Maurice. "That's 370," he says as he gives Maurice the money he owes him for the 20 kilos he was given before their last encounter. He then digs his hand into his pocket, retrieving a folded newspaper clipping. He unfolds it and slams it on the table in front of Maurice as well.

Maurice quickly picks it up and reads the article about a murder of a Newark man who was just released from the County jail minutes before he was murdered. "Jonathan Ross?" Maurice asks not having a clue of who the man is.

"Dirt," Smurf blurts out, bringing the room to a total shock. "My kid's mother informed me that some suspicious cars have been lurking around my neighborhood for a few days. All the cars she named I recognized. All of them belonging to our Federation. Of course I was too ashamed to admit to her that an organization that I belong to, people who I call my family are staking out my house in search for me," he says with anger in his eyes. "At the end of the day all ya'll know me. I'm a man," he says firmly. "I don't run or hide from no one."

Maurice interrupts him. For some reason he feels challenged by Smurf's statements. "We called you over and over but got no answer," he says arrogantly.

"You got no answer because I was locked up. I got pinched in a roadblock with a gun in the car. Me and Dirt spent a day and a half in the County. While in the County I found out that everything you said was true. He felt that the things he said were harmless and he really meant nothing by it, but me, I saw it for what it was. We all have known niggas who have died for less. Before that I had no knowledge of any of it. Needless to say I handled the situation the way I felt it should be handled," he says as he stares Maurice in the eyes. "It breaks my heart that my loyalty was ever at question. I would hate to be a part of a squad who could turn on me over hearsay," he says as he looks around slowly, staring into the eyes of each of the men. "My level of comfort with ya'll will never be the same. Because of that I am resigning from the Federation," he says as he looks Maurice directly in the eyes.

Maurice stands up with a cocky demeanor. He nods his head back slinging his dreads wildly. He stands there quietly just looking Smurf in the eyes. A part of him feels bad that he sent them out to stake out Smurf's house. He jumped to conclusions and feels that is he wrong for doing so but he will never admit it.

Everyone stares at Maurice awaiting his reaction. They're quite shocked at Smurf's aggressiveness. He hesitates just to build even more anticipation. The blank look on Maurice's face makes it hard for them to read him right now.

Maurice stares right through Smurf. The fact that Smurf is staring back into his eyes and not backing down is infuriating him. Finally he opens his mouth to speak. "I didn't beg you to come here and join the Federation and I'm damn sure not going to beg you to stay," he says before spinning around giving Smurf his back. He steps away with his normal arrogance. He flings his head back once again, untangling his dreads. "I'm out!" he says before he exits the apartment and leaves a quiet and extremely tense room.

They are all confused including Smurf. One thing they all know about Maurice is he hates to be challenged. They also know he is one the sneakiest, revengeful dudes that has ever walked the face of the earth. Leaving the room like this is like a cliff hanger. No one knows exactly how this story will end; except for Maurice that is.

///// CHAPTER 61 /////

The Next Night. It's 1 A.M. and Samad should be out watching over the second shift but he isn't. Instead he sits on an old full sized bed inside of a tiny room in a small apartment a few blocks away from his block.

He sits at the foot of the bed with a pile mostly made up of dollar bills in front him. He sifts through the money carefully placing each bill face up. He quickly counts the stack in his hand once then twice before passing it over to the female who sits on the opposite side of the bed. She snatches it from him and shuffles the stack until the bills are neatly fashioned. Once that's done she ties a rubber band around the stack firmly and drops it onto the pile of five stacks that are already lined up behind her.

Samad's eyes are brightly lit as he's fumbling through the bills. Judging by the hefty amount of money that lies before him, he gets the feeling that today is going to be much more lucrative than yesterday. He can't wait to finish counting it all up to get his total. The fact that he doesn't know gives him a rush that he's never felt.

Transferring his nickel bottles into dime jugs was the best move that he could have ever made. As a result of his wise business decision he scored a grand total of $12,000 yesterday between both shifts. That's not bad for the first day and he's sure it's only going to get better with time.

He watched yesterday, as well as today, as customers poured in from everywhere. The block stayed packed all day without a slow spurt in between. A flow like that is expected at the first of the month but at the end of the month it is unheard of.

Yesterday was beautiful but today was even better. The first shift has barely ended and he's already topped what he made yesterday by this hour. Last night at this time he had only made $9,000 and right now he already has $8,000 stacked in front of him. Looking at the huge mess of bills makes him sure that there's more than a thousand dollars left to count.

The girl stands up from the bed and walks away sexily. Normally the tight wife beater and skimpy thong would bring out the beast in Samad but today it's not fazing him the least bit. He's not sure if the love he has for Amber is suppressing it or the fact that his mind is on money. He takes a quick glance at her body as she stands at the mirror before he turns away and buries his face deep into the pile of dead presidents.

Samad and this girl have been somewhat of an item for many years. They have never had any real commitment to each other. Their situation has always been a mere sexual one. She's just the neighborhood girl that knows how to play her position. At any hour Samad can call her and she will come running. She will sit with him and keep him company while he's busy at work. She will hold his drugs for him at her mother's house. She'll also sit in his passenger's seat and carry the gun and drugs for him while he's driving from point A to point B. She's the perfect around the way girl. She does it all and expects nothing in return. What Samad likes most about her is the fact that she's extremely low maintenance. She's content with a pint of pork fried rice, a couple shots of Remy Martin and a blunt filled with

Arizona.

Samad wraps the rubber band around the stack of bills and tosses it onto the pile. He looks at the eleven stacks with pure satisfaction. Today has been record breaking. He's scored $11,000 and the night is still early. He wonders what the rest of the night has in store for him and he can't wait to find out.

Unlike the rest of the slower days and nights he's not the least bit tired. Watching the money flow generously keeps him wide awake. He's been watching closely as every dollar is made.

He grabs hold of the loose bills that lie on the bed and tucks them into his pocket. He grabs hold of his pistol as well. As he's making his way to the bedroom door he stuffs the gun into his waistband. As he walks past her he palm grips her left cheek. "I'm out, Ma. Put that up for me," he says while pointing to the stacks of money. "I'll get with you next day. It's time to make the donuts," he sings with delight.

///// CHAPTER 62 /////

Amber is busy doing her last minute packing. She's so happy to finally be leaving. It feels as if this day was never going to get here. She paces throughout the apartment back and forth with the thought in her mind that she's forgetting something. She stands at the door staring at her Louis Vuitton luggage. Bags and suitcases of every size and shape are here. She's only staying for one week but judging by the many pieces of luggage one would think that she's staying for a month or two. "Airline tickets!" she blurts out as it comes to her memory. As she's on her way to the bedroom to retrieve the tickets she starts dialing numbers on her cellular phone. As the phone rings, she hits the speaker button.

"Lil Bit, what up?"

"Maurice now you sure everything is everything, right?"

"Lil Bit, I got ya'll," he replies with agitation in his voice. "I told you he left two days ago. I just spoke with him. He should be touching a few hours after ya'll."

"Ok, if you say so. Now you know this is the biggest part of the surprise?"

"Lil Bit," Maurice interrupts. "He gone be there," he says firmly. "I'm hanging up. I'm in the middle of something. Call me when you get there. Bye," he says before hanging the phone up.

Maurice parks his pick-up truck in front of the huge abandoned warehouse building. As soon as he pulls up the group of Mexicans that occupy the front of the building all get up and make their way toward him. "Como Estas?" he says as he gets out and takes a huge stretch. The hour long drive in the morning rush hour traffic has taken a toll on his mind and body.

As he's walking to the back of his truck he examines his surroundings. He snaps the hatch of his truck and starts unloading the supplies. The supplies range from tools, aluminum, metal, to lumber. The Mexicans fill their arms up until they can carry no more.

Just as successful as Maurice is in the drug game he's had the same amount of success with the Real Estate game. A few years ago he started dibbling and dabbling in the house game. He began by buying abandoned homes for dirt cheap. The next step was to hire cheap laborers. He would go to the lowest slums of the ghetto and search high and low through the many addicts to find the most skilled plumbers, electricians and carpenters. By hiring junkies he saved himself hundreds of thousands of dollars, putting him way ahead of the game.

Although Maurice made millions of dollars with that hustle, he's gotten tired of it. The game is now so heavily saturated by drug dealers who are trying to legitimize their dirty money that it's no longer worth the effort. Maurice is always steps ahead of the game. Last year he decided to step his game up to the next level. He's sold all of his residential properties and now he's only investing in commercial properties. He has a few properties in Newark and he's branched out to Pennsylvania as well. His goal is to own commercial properties all across the country.

This property here is Maurice's biggest investment. With all of his prior investments joined together they can't compare to this one. Maurice deals with this one extremely carefully. He knows one thing and that is if he plays his hand right this one property alone can make him a millionaire overnight legitimately. Maurice's dream is to be a taxable millionaire recognized and accepted by Uncle Sam. This property will help his dream come true.

This old industrial building has been vacant for over 30 years. The building is 8 floors high, 300,000 square feet and it stretches out to approximately 12 acres of land. It's just enough space for what he plans to do with it. He plans to build condominiums, office space and also some retail stores. The location is the ideal spot. Maurice feels that his idea is just what this area of 110th street here in Harlem needs. It's right in the heart of the city directly parallel to the FDR which makes the building accessible from anywhere.

Maurice paid a total of 18.5 million dollars for this property. He spent 5.2 million dollars of his own money and borrowed the rest. He plans to borrow another 50 million to start his development.

Maurice knows how to play his position. He knows when to lead and he also knows when to follow. His game is cocaine and he knows that he's good at what he does. The Real Estate game he doesn't have the same confidence in. He knows one slip up can bury him which is why he's surrounded himself by trained professionals. His architect, developers, financial advisor and attorneys are all the best that money can buy. With a powerful team coaching him every step of the way he's sure he will not go wrong.

If all goes well and he's quite sure it will, he's expecting 25 million dollars up front plus a continued income of 8 million dollars a year for his pocket. This will make him a legal millionaire.

Maurice leads the pack of Mexicans toward the building. Following closely behind is Sal who also lugs supplies in his hands.

Meanwhile in Jersey City. Amber's house phone starts to ring. "Hello," she screams into the cordless phone.

"Miss Baker, you have a guest," the concierge says in a rather polite voice. "The gentleman's name is Samad."

"Ok, let him in," Amber says as she continues rambling throughout the apartment. "Star! You ready?"

"Two minutes!" she yells back from her room.

The doorbell rings and Amber back tracks through the living room. She pulls the door open and is shocked at what is before her eyes. Samad looks nothing like himself. His eyes are baggy. His used to be wavy hair is now thick and wooly. Dark stubble of hair covers his face. His clothes are baggy and wrinkled. His entire appearance is beat down.

"Ay Smook," he says as he walks past her. The smell that seeps from his mouth is enough to knock Amber off of her feet. Since she's been pregnant her sense of smell has grown keener. His breath smells so bad that if she had no sense of smell she could still get a whiff of it. The foul odor of his body and his stale clothes kind of just lingers in the air. The odor resembles that of a homeless person.

"Damn Babe, you look a mess and smell one too," she says as she cups her hand over her nose. She slams the door shut and just stands there with a sour look on her face.

"I'm grinding," he says arrogantly. "Here," he says as he hands the plastic bag to her that he holds in his hand. "One week as promised," he says with certainty. He says it so confident as if he was never worried about it. Being able to keep his word to her brings so much joy to his heart. The way things were looking he thought for sure he wasn't going to be able to pull it off. The last thing he wanted to do was ask her for an extension after what she had already done for him. He would have hated to belittle himself any further. Being able to repay her rebuilds his self esteem. He no longer feels like the piece of shit that he felt like. He sighs with relief silently.

He owes it all to the wise business decision that he made. If not for that none of this would have been possible. Last night's second shift was record breaking. He's never seen it like that before. The first hour or so the cash flow inched along but at about 3 a.m. things picked up significantly. Between the hours of 3 am and 6 am Samad raked in over $3,500. At 6:30 the early morning rush bombarded the block bringing in another $1,200.00.

Samad left the block at approximately 7:15 with another $5,200 to add to the $11,000 that he made from the first shift. Never in all his years of hustling has he made this type of money in one day. It's hard for him to believe that a block could generate this type of money. If he hadn't seen it with his own eyes he would never believe it.

It's hard for him to believe that just last week he was dead broke and had no clue how he was going to dig himself out of the ditch he was in. Now here he is a couple of thousand dollars richer. He owes all the thanks to Lil Bit. If not for her he would still be contemplating his suicide. Now that half of his battle is won a huge burden has been lifted from his shoulders. She's paid and he still has over $40,000 worth of product left. That's all the money he needs to do everything he has to do.

Samad gazes in Amber's eyes. "Thanks for believing in me," he says with sincerity. He opens his arms wide for a hug. She despises even the thought of hugging him and taking the chance of his funk spilling over onto her clothes. He snatches her and grabs her with a tight bear hug. The odor suffocates her. Her stomach does flip-flops. She can't hold her breath any longer. "Thanks Baby," he whispers. Each syllable is life threatening as the polluted air exits his mouth.

She pushes him back forcefully. She exhales a huge breath of air. "You're welcome, Babe. No problem at all. We're a team. Without you there's no me," she says with sincerity in her eyes. Her words are close to bringing tears to Samad's eyes. "Now get to the bathroom! You stink!" she shouts with a smirk on her face. "Go straight to the shower. Don't stop! Don't sit nowhere and leave that funk there, especially not my damn bed," she smiles.

Samad smiles and walks away from her. He takes a glance at his watch and realizes that he has no time to waste. The first shift will be starting in a little over an hour and he has to be there to open the block up. As he enters the bathroom she goes into the kitchen where she begins counting the money that he's given her. In minutes she's done counting through the twenty and a half stacks. She separates six of the stacks and places them onto the counter. Those belong to Muhsee. She now stares at her profit. The fourteen and a half stacks she holds in her hand is well appreciated.

She makes her way to the living room. She opens her pocketbook and dumps the stacks of money inside. The purse is stuffed now, thanks to her investment. Seven days later and she's scored close to fifteen grand. Samad thinks she's done him a favor and correct he is. What he doesn't know is she's done herself an even bigger one. "Teamwork," she whispers with a devilish grin on her face. "Yeah right," she laughs.

This money has come back at the perfect time. She was just minutes away from soaring off into the sky. Although she has plenty of spending money for the trip she can never have too much. Now that Samad has paid her, she won't have to be away on a budget. "The more money you earn, the more you burn," she whispers.

Maurice paces back and forth while the Mexicans are busy at work. Suddenly his phone rings. He looks at the display and lifts his head up to look over at Sal. "They're here," he whispers as he walks over to the window. "Hello?" he shouts as he observes the white Toyota Camry pulling in front of the building.

"We're here."

"I see," Maurice replies. "Pull to the back and park back there. I'm coming down now." Just as the Camry is pulling off a Ford Taurus station wagon pulls a few feet behind. Maurice watches as the two cars pull into the entrance on the side of the building. Just as he's about to go out back and meet them he notices a Ford WindStar pulling up as well. "They deep as hell," he says as he gives Sal a head nod. Sal quickly takes his gun from his waistband and slams one bullet into the chamber.

Minutes later Maurice stands at the back door, while holding it open. He looks out into the open field where he sees the two Spanish men that he met with the other day. He peeks around at the other men who occupy the field. Maurice expected maybe another one or two men to come along with them for security but the extra three men causes extreme suspicion.

The men get within feet of Maurice at the door. "Dominicano, what's with all the guests?" Maurice asks as he watches the men coming toward him. A few feet behind him, directly by the staircase stands Sal with his gun in his hand, fully loaded with his finger on the trigger. One suspicious move and he's prepared to open fire. "Tell them to stop now."

"Huh?" the man asks as if he can't understand Maurice.

"Dominicano, tell them to stay where they are," Maurice says as he opens the door wide enough for them to see Sal standing in the background.

The men stop dead in their tracks. As he's standing there he says a few words in Spanish and everyone freezes where they are. "What's the problem?"

"Too much company," Maurice replies. "Who are they?"

"You met my amigo here," he says as he points to the man standing next to him. He then points to the next man who stands a few feet away. "That's my cousin, I told you about. The girl and the old man are my drivers. And over there is security," he says with shame. "It's not my idea. I trust you but my cousin doesn't know you. I told him you're good but he no trust nothing."

"And he shouldn't," Maurice replies. "Ok, you, your amigo and your cousin come in first. Your security can come in but the girl and the old man have to wait out here until we need them."

The man shouts a few words in his own language and the girl and the man walk away from the building. The rest of the men make their way into the building one by one. Maurice leads the pack while Sal swaggers way behind with his gun in hand. In seconds they pass by all the Mexicans who are so busy at work that they don't even notice the company that has just come in. Maurice leads them all the way to the back of the place. They enter a spacious room. It's empty all except for an old office desk. Maurice pulls out his phone and starts to dial. "Alright," he says casually. Seconds later, the door opens and a man walks in lugging two duffel bags. He hands them over to Maurice who hands them over to his Spanish friend. He quickly opens the bag and pulls a kilo from inside. "The money, Papi." The Spanish man gives his cousin a head nod and he hands his duffel bag over to Maurice. Maurice quickly passes the bag to the man who stands at the door. "He's going to count it. Which one of ya'll want to go with him? Only one," Maurice adds.

The man who Maurice is most familiar with speaks up. "I'll go. They can stay and check out the work," he says as he follows the man out of the room. The other two men unload the kilos from the bag and examine them one by one while Maurice and Sal just watch them quietly. Minutes later the sound of the money machine rippling through the bills sounds off faintly in the background while the loud noise of drills and hammering echoes throughout the building.

Quite sometime later the 'Accountant' comes walking into the room. Two steps behind him is Maurice's Spanish speaking business associate. The Accountant walks over to Maurice. He leans over sneakily and whispers, "Two million, one hundred and fifty thousand, even."

Maurice nods his head up and down. "You and Hank go through the side door. Load the money into the box and head straight back to Jersey non-stop," he whispers. "I'm going to hold them here for another five minutes. I don't want ya'll leaving with them."

The whispering is making the men nervous. "Maurice is there a problem?"

The Accountant rushes out of the room like lightening. "Not at all, everything is good. Call your drivers and tell them to meet us at the back door."

The man makes the call as he's zipping the bags up. He throws one over his shoulder and his cousin grabs the other one. They follow Maurice and Sal down the back stairs. The security follows close behind with their guns drawn just in case anything strange comes about. Once they get to the door Maurice opens it for the drivers to enter. The man and the girl grab hold of the bags and exit the building.

In less than two minutes the Taurus wagon is cruising through the open field. The van follows several feet behind.

"Dominicano, I'm aware that a lot of bread is on the table but hopefully next time there will be no need for security and guns drawn. Not only does that put a strain on our relationship, I also find it to be very disrespectful. Back in the day I came all the way to 192nd street with no weapon and never did I feel threatened or intimidated. I trusted you and felt that you wouldn't allow anything to happen to me. Give me the same respect. I'm still the same guy," he says followed by a charming smile.

"Sorry, Maurice. I do apologize but again as I said it's not me. It's my cousin." Once the field is clear the two men make their way out of the building. "Maurice, thanks a million. I will be giving you a call in a few days."

"Please do." Maurice watches as the men cruise the open field and disappear. He exhales. All is well that ends well, he thinks to himself. He looks over to Sal who stands by his side. "Life is beautiful. A two million dollar deal sealed while a half a billion dollar deal is in process," he says arrogantly. "Life is good!"

///// CHAPTER 63 /////

Samad's eyes pop open slowly. He looks around with cloudy vision as he tries to figure out where he is. His deep sleep has erased his memory momentarily. He looks around and suddenly realizes where he actually is. He looks over at the alarm clock which reads 11:30. He sits up quickly. "Oh shit!" he shouts as he realizes that he's an hour and a half late for the first shift. After showering he sat down to lotion himself and ended up collapsing onto the bed. The last time he looked at the clock it read 9:53. He planned to take a quick power nap just to rest up before opening the block.

He jumps out of the bed and rushes over to the dresser to get fresh clothes. He's pissed that the block has been dry for over an hour. This means many customers have spent their money on other blocks. The thought of that makes him quite jealous. He gets even angrier when he thinks of the time that he's put in the past few days to build the block up and here it is customers have been forced to go elsewhere.

He grabs his underwear out of the drawer. As he steps into them his eyes are drawn to the balcony where the lights of the Manhattan skyline are shining brightly. He becomes confused as he looks into the darkness of the sky. He looks at the clock once again. "Eleven forty one," he whispers as he scratches his head with perplexity. The bright stars in the sky reassure him that it is not morning time. He realizes that he has slept the entire day away.

He grabs his phone and is shocked to see that he has over thirty missed calls and most of them are from his crew. Two of the calls are from Amber and the last three are from some of the dudes who work the nightshift. Suddenly he entertains the thought that he may have slept more than one day away. Right now he's quite groggy and feels like he may have slept too much but he really does feel well rested and rejuvenated.

He starts dialing Amber's number. The phone rings and rings for seconds before she finally picks up. "Hello!" she shouts at the top of her lungs over the noisy background.

"Lil Bit!" Samad shouts but she can't hear him over the loud music that is playing on her end.

"Hello!" she shouts again.

"Yo! Where are you?" he asks.

"Huh? I can't hear you!"

"Where you at?" he shouts even louder.

"In Miami. What do you mean where am I?"

"Yo! What's all that fucking noise?"

Amber hesitates before replying to him. "I'm in the club!"

"Yo! What's today?" he asks.

"Huh? What's today? Thursday! What are you talking about?"

Samad realizes that he didn't sleep more than a day away. He's only slept the first shift away. "Nothing," he says, feeling quite stupid for even asking her that. "What time ya'll got there?"

"Like 2!"

Samad is starting to get a headache from all of the noise and the screaming and shouting. "Yo! Just call me when you leave the club."

"Ok!"

Samad ends the call and gets dressed quickly. In no time at all he's stepping out of the door. As the door slams behind him he realizes that Amber didn't leave him the key which means that he will have nowhere to stay until she returns from her vacation. A part of him is stunned at the thought of it but truthfully he doesn't have the plan of sleeping anywhere until he finishes the work he has and handles all of his business that needs to be handled. Having nowhere to stay will just be more motivation for him.

He's already missed the entire first shift and an hour of the second one. He has to hurry because he refuses to blow an entire day without making a dime. He has goals to accomplish and one day can set him back enormously.

He hops into his rental car and off to Newark he goes, speeding recklessly.

Amber slips her phone into the pocket of her linen pants. She looks over to her left where she sees Star and her friend Tara dancing away to the music. From the sound of the loud music one would think that it's a huge party which is packed wall to wall, instead, only the three of them are in the room.

The sight of them together is sickening to Amber but she tries hard to suppress her true feelings on the strength of the love that she has for her baby sister. To anyone else their dancing together may look innocent but just because Amber knows the situation she believes that someone may get the feeling that it's not innocent at all.

Amber hated to invite Tara along for the vacation and she was extremely close to not doing so but she realized that would be mean of her. After all it's Star's birthday and not spending it with her best friend wouldn't be right. Amber put her own opinion of the matter to the side and paid for Tara's trip just as she did everyone else's. This entire vacation has been funded by Amber. It cost her a few thousand dollars but to make her sister happy it's well worth every dollar.

The music is so loud that Amber can't even hear herself think. She steps to the far end of the room. The music has been blasting for hours and she needs a break. She slides the screen door open and steps onto the deck. As she steps out the pungent smell of marijuana snatches her breath away. She looks to the right only to find Deja and Sade standing side by side along the railing. They're passing the blunt back and forth to each other.

Amber follows the trail of the sweet fragrance. As soon as she gets there Deja extends her arm with the blunt dangling loosely from her hand. "Hit this motherfucker," she smiles.

Amber stares at the blunt with desire in her eyes. The blunt is screaming her name and as enticing as it is she refuses. "Nah, I'm good," she says with her mouth but her mind, body and soul beg to differ. She refuses on the strength of her unborn child.

"Here!" Deja shouts as she pushes it closer to Amber's mouth.

The smoke seeps through her nostrils luring her in even more. "Damn, talk about peer pressure," Amber smiles. "I'm good," she laughs.

Deja looks at her with a stunned look on her face. She's never known Amber to pass on some good smoke. "First time for everything," she says before taking a huge drag of the Haze. She doesn't know why Amber refuses but she really doesn't care. She looks at it as just more smoke for her. She has no clue that Amber is making this sacrifice for her unborn child because she knows nothing about Amber's unborn child.

Amber hasn't told Deja that she's pregnant. She's ashamed to tell Deja that she's pregnant by Samad. She's not quite ready to hear Deja run off at the mouth to her. She's sure Deja will look at her like a fool for getting pregnant by him.

Deja continuously downplays Samad and Amber knows the exact reason why. Deja feels that Samad isn't worthy of Amber. The fact that he makes her happy has nothing to do with it in Deja's eyes. Deja judges a man by his worth and not by his heart. Because he's not a successful businessman or big time drug dealer she has no respect for him. She feels Samad is worthless and Amber is wasting her time even dealing with a loser, as she calls him. Not a day passes that Deja doesn't express that to her. Knowing that, Amber refuses to tell Deja until she is prepared for any slick comment that Deja may come at her with.

Amber is sure that she will say something that will infuriate her and right now she has way too much on her plate to add to it. An argument with her good friend will only make matters worse. She plans to continue to keep it a secret until she's prepared to fight that battle with Deja. Right now she's weak and doesn't have the strength to stand up to her. There's so much going on in her life and she's quite overwhelmed.

Amber stands close just inhaling the aroma of goodness. The Haze is so strong that the contact of the second hand smoke is enough to get her high. It's nowhere near the same as actually smoking it but it will do for now. Amber stares into the water that they're sailing on. Just watching the waves is so peaceful. She momentarily loses sight of all of her problems and just gets caught up in the waves.

The moment the plane took off Amber's mind became at ease. It feels great to leave her problems back in Newark. She does realize that it's only temporary though. In one week she will have to go home and face every one of the problems that she has. Hopefully this trip will help her come to some type of solution for all of her madness.

Amber snaps out of her daze. She looks around at the many beautiful yachts that sail around them. Some are much smaller and some are much larger. She's seen some yachts that make this one look like trash. She's amazed at the entire experience. She thought soaring in the air was the ultimate experience but now she feels different. Sailing the Intercostal Waterway here in Miami makes flying seem as bland as riding a bicycle. This is something that she will never forget. Just another dream that Maurice has made come true for her.

Days ago Maurice hired a captain to sail the yacht here to Miami as part of Star's birthday present. After their flight landed here, Amber got the call from the Captain two hours later stating that he had arrived. They've been sailing throughout Florida for hours and all of them are enjoying every second of it.

Amber told Samad she would be in Miami but she never told him they would be using Maurice's yacht. She knew that would only ignite a great deal of friction in their relationship. He already has trust issues with her concerning Maurice. That would only make matters worse than they already are. She knows that Samad won't be able to handle that, which is why she didn't tell him every detail of this vacation. She feels terrible that she is keeping things from him but she figures what he doesn't know can't hurt him. Well at least she hopes so.

///// CHAPTER 64 /////

The Next Morning

Amber stares over the beautiful city of Miami from the balcony of this thirty story condominium. From the penthouse the view is spectacular. A huge body of water surrounds the building as if it is on its own island. Amber inhales a deep breath of freshness. The air is dry and humid today but the gust of wind that blows briskly off the water is quite refreshing.

Amber couldn't have picked a more comfortable place to stay. No hotel of any magnitude would be equivalent. Again, Amber owes all the gratitude to Maurice. This waterfront condo belongs to him. Maurice is so in love with Miami that at one particular time he spent every weekend here. It was like a second home to him so he decided to make it his second home. He purchased a spot here so he would have a place to stay. The money he was spending on hotels every week was costly and he figured he would do better by purchasing a spot. Now he's gotten so busy with business that the apartment is going to waste because he barely has the time to come here.

Just being here in this luxurious condo makes Amber consider actually relocating to Miami. She can really picture herself living here and probably for half the money she spends in New Jersey. She loves her building but this building is on an altogether different level. It makes her building look like a low income building.

The location of this building is great. Although it's not in South Beach it's not too far away either. The building sits in the Aventura section of Miami which is just twenty minutes north of South Beach. It's only twenty minutes away in distance but it seems like a completely different land. It's not as congested with tourists. The buildings are more upscale and even the air is different. Amber loves that a great deal. It's close enough to be a part of the action when she chooses to, but far enough not to get caught up in the action.

The view is magnificent. The apartment quadruples the size of hers and Maurice pays less money for mortgage than she pays for rent. It has three bedrooms, unlike the two bedrooms that she has. It also has 2 and a half bathrooms. The bedroom floors are bamboo. The bathroom floors all have glass tiling. The kitchen floor is limestone. The countertops are marble and granite. Of all the luxuries that fill this condo, what Amber loves the most is the skylight ceiling made of glass which soars over the entire apartment. Waking up and looking into the bright sky gives her the feeling of no limits and no boundaries, making her believe that life has no roof and the sky is the limit.

Amber exhales into relaxation. Suddenly she realizes that she has not heard from Samad yet. She's gotten used to his early morning call. She immediately starts dialing his number on her cell phone. She listens to the phone ring back to back until his answering machine finally comes on. She dials again with no hesitation. In half a minute the voice mail comes on again. Nervousness starts to fill her gut as she considers the possibility that something could have happened to him. She thinks back quickly recalling the last time she heard from him which was at 4 A.M. She quickly dials him again.

In Newark

The Dodge Charger's engine purrs like a kitten as it sits parked idling. The sound of Rappers, The Clipse' hit song 'Grinding' blasts at full volume. Samad sits in the driver seat. Scattered all over his lap is a pile of loose bills. In both hands he grips a bunch of bills as well. His head is pinned against the headrest. He's snoring loud and hard. The lack of sleep is really starting to get the best of him. While tallying up his earnings from the night shift he fell asleep in the middle of the process.

The block rocked nonstop from the time he distributed the work to his squad until the very last second of the shift. It's as if the absence of his product for the first shift affected the block for the better. He thought they would lose customers but instead the customers flocked from everywhere as if they feared they would run out of product and there would be no more. Every second a new herd of customers formed. The dealers distributed the work with no organization. Never before had any of them seen a flow like that. They didn't have a clue of how they should handle the packs and packs of people. Each dealer ripped through $500 pack after $500 pack until Samad eventually lost track. The last he remembers is giving each of the 4 dudes at least 4 packs a piece.

The constant vibration of his phone in his lap awakes him. His eyes pop open gradually, fixed onto his lap at the enormous amount of bills. He looks around and realizes that he must have fallen asleep. Fear fills his heart as he thinks of the danger that he's put himself in by falling asleep with a lap full of money and a waistband full of lead from his semi automatic nine millimeter. He could have awakened to a gun toting stick up kid at the window or even worse, the police. He could have easily lost his life or his freedom.

The phone stops buzzing but it starts up again right away. He reaches for the phone and places it against his ear. "Hello," he grunts groggily as he lowers the volume of his stereo.

"Yeah!" Amber shouts in a feisty manner. "What the fuck you doing?"

"I was knocked the fuck out in the car," he explains. "I'm slipping."

"Are you crazy, boy?" she asks as she considers the danger he put himself in. "You need to go to sleep."

"Sleep is the cousin to death. I'll sleep later. Right now I have to get this money."

"Samad that money ain't going nowhere. You're speedballing. You have to be careful. Slow down."

"I got you, I got you," he says trying to brush her off. "What's up with you though?"

"Worried about you. That's what's up with me," she says in a sassy manner. "You know when I don't hear from you I start thinking the worse."

Amber's compassion makes Samad feel good. Never has he dealt with a woman who he felt actually cared about him. Her attentiveness to him and his well being is one of the characteristics that he loves the most about her.

He smiles with appreciation. "Don't think the worse. I'm good even when I'm not good," he says with arrogance as he starts ripping through the bills in his hand. "What ya'll getting into?"

"On our way to the beach."

"Oh, ok. Just hit me later," he says as he attempts to rush her off of the phone. He's anxious to finish counting his earnings and find out what he scored for the night.

"Alright, I see you ain't beat for me," she teases.

"Psst," he sucks his teeth. "Knock it off. I got my mind on money, money on my mind," he sings.

Lately Amber has been seeing a trait in Samad that she doesn't like and that's greed. She understands his hunger and wants him to fulfill his wants and desires but for some reason she feels like he's the type to let money control him. "Bay, money is good and all but it's not everything."

"Yeah, tell that to a broke mufucker," he says sarcastically. "My ribs touching and I gotta eat."

"Remember these two sayings ok? Greedy people starve. Man makes the money, money don't make the man."

Yeah, whatever, Samad says to himself. "I got you," he says as he looks to the sky with no interest in what she's saying.

"I'll call you later," she says.

"Yeah, do that."

"Alright, love you."

"Why wouldn't you?" he replies in a playful manner.

"Boy bye," she says before ending the call.

Samad immediately blasts the volume of the song that plays on his stereo. The music is so loud that it feels like he's inside of a huge speaker. He's had this same song on repeat for the past 12 hours. The song motivates him so much. "Grinding!" he shouts as he starts counting away.

Two Hours Later

Herds of people spread out along the beach. The sun is blazing and the water is waving viciously. People seem to be enjoying themselves, playing soccer, frisbee, football, and volleyball. Others just lounge around lazily.

From the moment Amber and the crew stepped foot onto the sand they turned heads. Their arrogance and charm attracted the attention of everyone. They stepped elegantly across the beach sporting their exclusive swim suits. They did just what they expected to do; stop the show.

They all lay out in the sand as the hot sun bakes away at their skin. Deja pops up slowly. The group of men a few feet away automatically locks eyes in her direction. They have been anticipating this moment for an entire hour.

She stands up with her back facing them. In a raunchy manner she slides her index finger along the elastic of her bikini to remove the wedgie that she has. That sight is picture perfect to the men. They watch her perversely. Now for the finale, she thinks to herself. She turns toward them to give them what they have been impatiently waiting for. She wears an innocent look on her face but there's nothing innocent about what she's doing. Her naked breasts stare at them as she stands there shamelessly. "I'm done," she says to her group. "Bitch black enough already. If I get any darker ya'll won't be able to see me," she smiles. At the sound of her voice the women all pop up from the sand. The scene is almost pornographic as the five women stand in the middle of the beach topless, exposing their half nude bodies. None of them except Deja had plans of removing her top. Everyone hates a dare and Deja knows that so she used it to her advantage. After removing their tops they all appreciated the feeling of freedom. The spectators appreciated it as well. They showed very little shame because after all they don't know anyone here and the chance that they will see any of them ever again is rare.

The women spin around giving the men full view of their skimpy bikini covered behinds. The men reveal their immaturity level by clapping their hands. The women walk away, paying no attention to them at all. The loud noise of the applauding of the women's behinds drowns out the clapping of the men's hands. All the men watch with lust as the women exit the beach. What happens in Miami stays in Miami.

///// CHAPTER 65 /////

The Next Day

Maurice sits in the living room of the Bat Cave with his crew sitting around him. All of his men sit with long saddened faces as they stare onto the table where two small piles of kilos are stacked. "Listen ya'll, it's only twenty of 'em. Just divide these up. We got another twenty coming in tomorrow."

Disappointment covers all of their faces. In no way are twenty kilos enough for them to divide when each of them has at least one client that buys twenty. They've never had to go through this before and they don't know how to deal with it. Maurice has spoiled them over the years. They've never been without work. When no one else in the world has cocaine they know they can depend on him to have a full supply.

Selling the kilos to the Papis from New York has made Maurice a couple of dollars richer but it's caused his men to lose money. With the drastic increase of kilo sales Maurice is encountering a real problem. He's in dire need of more transporters. Five people going out a week is no longer sufficient. He finds himself sending the same people out over and over and realizes how much danger is in that. He realizes he has to add more people to the team so he can allow weeks in between the time each mule goes over.

"Yo, you sure we gone have them by tomorrow?" the man asks from across the table. Desperation fills his eyes.

"Indeed," Maurice says confidently as he thinks of the twenty that came in last night. His team of chemists as he calls them is at the table now doing their magic. "By the morning I will have that twenty."

"Please make that happen," the man begs. "I got a fifteen sale tomorrow. My cousin coming up from Baltimore. He said ain't no coke nowhere. It's dry from Philly on down to V.A."

Maurice nods his head up and down. Just as he figured. He knew the effects of the cocaine drought would soon be kicking in. "I know. Ain't no work out there nowhere. They just caught two boatloads last week," he informs his crew.

"Well, whatever you do just have them fifteen for me please? Those twenty right there, ya'll can count me out. Ya'll go ahead and split them up. I'll get mines tomorrow."

"Listen to me when I tell ya'll shit bad out there. I hope it gets a lot worse. Everywhere is dry from New York to Miami. A drought every now and then is good for the game though. It cleans up the streets forcing the petty niggas out of the way. The petty mufuckers who are barely hanging on, fall on their face during the drought. The broke mufuckers go broker while the rich mufuckers get richer. The team with the most work wins and we happen to be that team," he brags. "We got work so we control the game. If we move strategically we get richer. The downside to that is mufuckers gone go broke and they're going to be forced to come up with ways to eat. Anybody with some sense knows better than to step in the path of the Federation but when a mufucker starving his logic goes out of

183

window. Niggas gone be on the prowl so keep your eyes open. It's gone be easier for the wolves to see you moving cause ain't nobody else moving. Ain't no other distractions. With that being said, watch your movements. Let's play ball!" he says powerfully. "We got the work we got the power to dictate. I'm raising the price a point and a half to twenty thousand even on a bird. Ya'll go up two and a half to three points according to your clients. No more twenty and a half. The bottom number I want ya'll shaking these for is twenty three. Everybody understand?" They all nod their heads up and down. "Now, let's get richer!"

Meanwhile In Miami

The convertible Rolls Royce Phantom Drophead Coupe glides down Collins Avenue. It doesn't feel like a car. It feels more like a boat. It's a coupe but it's damn near the size of two ordinary cars joined together. By far this is the most gorgeous vehicle on the road in this vicinity. It has a creamy white filling covered by a deep royal blue body. The main attraction of this vehicle is the stainless steel hood. In total this is $423,000 worth of car but it's only costing Amber $1,500 a day to rent it.

Amber sits behind the wheel of the vehicle as if she actually belongs here. No one in the world can tell her that she doesn't qualify to drive this vehicle because she won't accept that. Deja rides shotgun while the other three women are squeezed comfortably in the back seat.

The sun beams on their heads as they fly down the block like a bat flies out of hell. Necks snap as the vehicle speeds by them. The car is moving so fast that people on the side can't even determine what type of car it is. It zips by like a huge streak of blue lightening. The sound of the stereo is so crisp that it sounds as if Lil Wayne and T-Pain are actually riding in the car with them singing and rapping live.

All the women sing along with T-Pain as they rip through the street. "If you got money. Yeah!" T Pain shouts. "And you know it. Yeah! Then take it out your pocket and show it and throw it like this a-way and that a-way! Ah hah! This a-way and that a-way," he sings. "Getting mugged by everyone you see then hang over the wall of the V.I.P. like this a-way, that a-way!" he sings.

Amber pays close attention to her rearview mirror. She's picked up some fans. The canary yellow Lamborghini has been following them for two blocks. It's tailing her extremely close almost touching her back bumper. It's so close that she can actually feel the engine of the Lamborghini growling and rattling the ground under her. The faster she drives the more she feels the ground trembling. Finally they're stopped by a red light. She slams on the brakes abruptly. The Lamborghini misses her bumper by inches. It cuts around them precisely and pulls side by side with them. The women look straight ahead singing along as if they don't even notice the car on the side of them.

The driver of the Lamborghini is doing everything in his power to get their attention as his passenger sits on the edge of his seat. The women stop singing along and try to play the classy role for their spectators. Lil Wayne shouts at the top of his lungs. "One for the money! Two for the show! Now clap your hands if you got a bankroll." Deja turns to her right facing the driver of the Lamborghini. She looks him square in the eyes as she starts to clap away. The traffic light changes and Amber speeds off, turning left, leaving the Lamborghini sitting there at the intersection. They all sing along again. "Like some clap on lights in this bitch," he whines. "I'm gone be clapping all night in this bitch!" he shouts as they all clap in rhythm.

Amber makes the right turn onto Ocean Drive. She speeds up the block recklessly until she gets to her destination. She pulls in front of the little Italian Restaurant. The sidewalk is loaded with people eating at small tables.

The loud music coupled with the extravagant car full of beautiful women has everyone staring at them. Lil Wayne continues on. "Bitch ain't shit but a hoe and a trick!" he shouts. "But you know it ain't tricking if you got it!"

The Valet service stands at the doors of both sides waiting to escort the women out of the vehicle. They sit there allowing Lil Wayne time enough to spit his last verse. They take their time with no regard for the men who stand at the doors awaiting their exit. "Bitch, I'm the bomb, like tick...tick!"

///// CHAPTER 66 /////

The Next Morning

The yacht sails slowly to the deck of the Bal Harbour. After it has come to a complete stop the girls exit and in minutes they're standing at the entrance of the mall. The entire scene is playing like a scene from Sex in the City and they're the stars of the show. Lifestyles of the Rich and Famous is how it can best be described as they sail the sparkling water and anchor to the dock of a huge mall to go shopping. It's hard for them all to believe that they're actually living a dream right now.

They look at the many yachts that sit side by side. They secretly watch the women who have traveled here by the same way. They enter the mall casually as if this is their normal routine. They appear to be from all walks of life. There is no telling who is amongst the crowd of women. Some could be actresses, wives of sports figures or even self-made women. They could just as well be ghetto chicks just playing the role just as Amber and the crew are.

There they stand like kids in a candy store not knowing which store to go into first. Seeing all the different boutique shops here underneath one roof has them all captivated. Not knowing which one to start with they follow their hearts into Luca Luca. After an hour of pleasurable shopping their feet finally lead them out of Luca Luca and into Giuseppe Zanotti where they try on so many shoes that their feet get sore. Two stores down and they have many more to go. Altogether there are five women with quality taste, pocketbooks filled with cash and hard plastic with unlimited credit. This shopping spree can go on for days.

Meanwhile back in Jersey

Samad cruises up the block in the white Ford Five Hundred. He's driving slowly as he's busy multitasking. He's driving, talking on his cell phone and stuffing his face with French fries all at the same time. He hated to leave the block but the growling of his stomach forced him to his favorite fast food restaurant.

He steers the car around the corner, turning onto his block. His face is buried deep into the bag of goodies. He looks up momentarily only to lock eyes with a car full of police who are cruising the block in the opposite direction as him. His face muscles stiffen at the sight of them. His eyes stay glued on them for seconds before he turns away. Fear makes him turn back for one last look.

His heart beat speeds up. He watches his rearview with hope that they will continue on their way. Those hopes are crushed when he sees their unmarked car busting a wild u-turn in the middle of the intersection. His first thought is to step on the gas pedal and take them for the ride of their life but the three year sentence for eluding the police quickly erases that thought.

They're coming behind him at full speed. The closer they get to him the more nervous he becomes. He's worried and really has no reason to be. He's clean. He has no drugs in his possession or a gun. He has a valid driver's license and all, so he really shouldn't worry about them but his fear of police still makes him uncomfortable.

He slowly passes his block at a moderate speed, hoping they will just run his plates and let him go about his business once everything comes back legit. Suddenly the flashing lights in the grill of their car tells him that is not going to happen. "Got damn," he blurts out. "Yo, let me hit you right back," he tells the caller on the other end of the phone. He drops the phone into his lap sneakily. Once again, stepping on the accelerator at full speed enters his mind but instead he steers the car to the right and parks in the empty spot. He slams the car into the park position and quickly raises both of his hands out of the sun roof to avoid another Amadou Diallo case.

In a matter of seconds four humongous red necks are out of the car and walking toward his car. Terror fills his heart as he sets eyes on a familiar face. One of the cops who raided his home is amongst the group.

That cop is the first to step to the driver's side of Samad's car. He snatches the door open aggressively. He then snatches Samad out of his seat even more aggressively. His feet never touch the ground. The cop slams Samad onto the hood of the car violently.

"Samad Brown," the cop says. "What you doing in this neck of the woods? You coming to make your drop off or your pick up? You don't get enough huh?"

"No reason. I'm just driving through," he claims.

"Yeah I bet."

Samad watches nervously as two of the cops get inside of his car and begin searching high and low. He looks over to the fourth cop who stands a few feet away from him. He becomes frightened when he sees what lies in the grip of the cop's hands. The small plastic bag filled with glassine vials of crack is all he needs to send him off for another visit to the County Jail. At this point that is the last thing that he needs. "Please God, don't let them plant these drugs on me," he prays under his breath as he keeps his eyes glued on the cop's hands.

"You got anything on you Samad?" the officer asks as he frisks him from head to toe.

"No Sir," he replies politely hoping that his politeness will prevent them from planting the drugs on him. The last thing he wants to do is piss them off and give them a reason to do so.

Once the cop is done patting him down for a gun he turns Samad around. They stand face to chest. The cop pats Samad's right pocket where a huge bulge of money rests. "What's this, drug money?" he asks as he digs his hand into Samad's pocket. He snatches the hefty roll of bills and starts fumbling through them. "How much is this?"

Samad hesitates before replying. Damn, he thinks to himself. He realizes that there's no logical explanation that he can give for the $4,300 that he's staring at. This is what he has obtained in the few hours that he's been out on the block today. He wishes he would have dropped the money off but everything was moving so fast that he didn't have the chance to do so.

"How much is this?" the cop repeats.

"Twelve hundred," Samad replies, hoping the cop takes his word for it and not count it. It's sad to say that the cop does the total opposite of what Samad hoped for. He looks at the bag of crack that's in the other cop's hand and realizes this money is the key to their puzzle. He already has a good idea of how this story is going to end and he's sure it's not going to be a happy ending.

The cop turns away from him and walks toward the backseat of the car where the other cops are still searching away. Minutes later the four of them stand huddled together whispering to each other. His life flashes before his eyes when they all come walking toward him. He has a good mind to make a run for it but they get to him before he can get his feet in motion.

The cop who is holding the money stands directly in front of Samad as the other cops surround him. His heart is racing like a marathon. "Here," he says as he hands the money over to Samad who stands there in total shock. "Count your money," the cop demands. Samad does just that and is shocked to see that he's $3,100 short. He looks up and stares the cop in the eyes. He can't force the words from his lips. He's too afraid to say a word. "How much you got there?" the cop asks.

"Twelve hundred," he replies sadly.

"That's what you said you had right?" he asks with a straight face. "Mr. Brown, have a good day," he says as he turns around and walks away. The other cops follow his lead by a few steps. "Don't let me see you out here for the rest of the day!" he shouts as he's getting into the car. They pull off, leaving Samad standing there in rage. He can't believe that he's been robbed by them.

As he considers the fact of how things could have went he soon becomes grateful. He quickly looks at it like a blessing that they didn't plant the drugs on him and lock him up. He charges the loss of the $3,100 to the game and looks at it like bail money without an actual charge. It all evens out, working out for the better.

///// CHAPTER 67 /////

The Next Day

Maurice stands in the kitchen of the small two bedroom apartment. Standing directly in front of him is his first cousin. "Here," Maurice says as he hands the stack of airline tickets over to the man. "Three round trip tickets in there. It's simple Cuz. Play it real smooth and we will have no problems. Ya'll going to look like ya'll on a family vacation. You, your wife and the baby. Who would suspect anything?"

Maurice's cousin is the newest addition to the team of transporters. He's a good, hard working man who tries to do the right thing all the time. Normally he would never even consider doing anything like this but the recession has him by the balls. He just lost his job two months ago. Now he's stuck trying to provide for his wife and newborn baby with no income whatsoever.

Maurice couldn't have propositioned him at a better time. The offer was so good that he persuaded his wife to aid them as well. $20,000 cash money right now will solve all of their money issues. Although she's extremely afraid she allowed her husband to talk her into strapping her body with kilos as well.

It all works out perfectly. He looks at it like a work/vacation. With money being tight there would be no way he could possibly afford a vacation. Now he will get the opportunity to take his family to a foreign country, enjoy themselves on a beautiful island and make a half a year's income while doing it.

"Tomorrow morning I need ya'll at the airport at eight on the dot. Go there and enjoy yourself. Look at it as a getaway and not work. With all the shit you got going on I know you need a break."

Nervousness fills his heart for the millionth time as he thinks of the jeopardy that he's putting his family in. If his back wasn't against the wall he would never consider doing something like this. The fact that his wife is willing to help in order to get them out of their financial ditch really touched his heart. Over the years she's proven her loyalty and devotion to him but this takes the cake.

"But what if?"

"Man later for buts and what ifs. Don't even allow yourself to think like that. Don't look for nothing and there won't be nothing. This is simple, baby," he says trying to reassure him. "It's gone be the easiest twenty grand you ever made in your life." The truth of the matter is he's never seen twenty grand at one time let alone made it.

Maurice winks his eye arrogantly. "Trust me when I tell you."

Meanwhile

Amber and the crew sit around the huge swimming pool in the back of the Delano Hotel in South Beach. They're sipping Mai Tais from the Tiki Bar and nibbling on appetizers. Their bikinis are dry, not a hair on their head is out of place and their lip gloss is popping. Unfortunately they're not the only gorgeous, attention attracting women here. The topless models who are floating throughout the enormous pool are capturing everyone's interest, stealing the show.

They didn't come here to actually swim in the pool. Their sole purpose for coming here is for the atmosphere. Sitting shoulder to shoulder with legitimate millionaires gives them the rush of a lifetime. Being around money inspires them to make money.

They refuse to ruin their elegant stature by getting in the pool, drenching their bikinis, smearing their make-up and soaking their hair. Instead they plan to sit back and soak their pedicured feet in the pool while looking classy and beautiful doing it.

Deja's phone rings. She grabs it and places it to her ear. "Yello?" she says in the phoniest voice ever. "Deja speaking," she says putting up a front for the people at the neighboring table. The caller on the other end says a few words. "Excuse me?" she utters politely. "Who is this?" she asks as a look of hatred covers her face. The woman's last statement enrages Deja. She loses it. "Bitch!" she shouts at the top of her lungs, totally disregarding the people who are sitting around them. Her shouting has captured all of their attention. Amber looks at her with embarrassment as the rest of the crew look on with confusion. "Get a fucking life!" she shouts before hanging the phone up on the woman.

The call was from her stalker, threatening her life if she doesn't stay away from her husband. She was calling Deja every so often but the calls stopped for a short period. She's now been back at it for a few weeks. She still can't figure out who the woman could be referring to, not even if her life depended on it. Judging by the threats the woman makes Deja's life may depend on it. She's questioned every one of her male friends and none of them admit to being married. At this point she realizes that someone is not keeping it real. The question is; which one is it?

Deja exhales with frustration. "Dumb ass bitch! I'm tired of her fucking threats. Fuck her and her fucking husband!" she says cursing like a sailor. She looks around and notices that all the attention is on her. She realizes that the classy image that they were trying to portray has been tarnished. "Oh well," she utters to herself.

You can take the woman out of the ghetto but you can't take the ghetto out of the woman.

///// CHAPTER 68 /////

The Next Morning

Samad feels like he can finally breathe again. Despite the three thousand dollar loss he took yesterday he's still way ahead of the game. Thanks to Amber he's two goals short of everything he had to do.

Each day is getting better and better for him. Yesterday he scored a grand total of approximately $18,000. Of course three grand of that went to the police but he's accepted that fact. Taking 17.5% of his earnings for the day is better than getting locked up and spending two days in the County Jail. That would have made him lose close to forty grand. He would have had to post a five thousand dollar bail and he would have had to spend another five grand for an attorney to beat the case. He estimated that as a damn near fifty thousand dollar loss when it would have been all over with. With all that in mind he appreciates the petty change that they took from him.

He feels so good today. More and more each day he's starting to not only understand what life is all about but appreciating it as well. He's grateful for his quick turn around in life but he's sure it will get much better. Yesterday's earnings took him over the top. Now he can finally relieve himself of the biggest burden of all.

As he cruises along up Lyons Avenue on his way to his destination he dials Amber's phone number. He's a few hours late for his early morning call to her. The fact that she hasn't called him to check up on him makes him wonder why.

He holds the phone up to his ear and listens patiently as the phone rings over and over again. He doesn't take the voicemail for an answer. He quickly dials again and again getting no answer from her. By the sixth call his jealousy kicks in. His suspicions take over and strangely he envisions her laying up with another man. Not answering the phone is unlike her. He assumes that is the only reason that she wouldn't answer.

He doesn't have a face to put on the man. All he can envision is Amber laying curled up next to a man's body. Suddenly a face fills the blank. The face belongs to the man he saw her with at the Sand Bar. All types of crazy thoughts fill his head. He thinks that maybe she didn't go away with just the girls. He gets enraged at the thought of that. He starts to dial the numbers, pressing hard with fury.

Meanwhile In Miami

Four women cruising down Collins Avenue on motor scooters, wearing nothing but bikinis is a beautiful sight for perverted eyes. G-strings and wedgie encrusted cotton expose their naked behinds which are propped up high on top of the seats of the bikes. The sun beams on their helmet-less heads. The sun is hot but it's nothing compared to the explosive heat in between their thighs. The heat from the engine burns through their naked skin. The faster they ride the bigger the rush they get. The more they accelerate the more the engine roars, giving them a vibration between their legs that is almost orgasmic for two of them but actually causes an orgasm for the other two.

Deja and Sade ride side by side while Star and Tara ride a few feet behind.

Back in New Jersey

Samad is now furious. He's called Amber so many times that his battery has died. He no longer pictures her and the man laying side by side. He now pictures Amber straddled on top of the man in her favorite sexual position. He knows more than anyone else how much she enjoys riding on top. She's told him on many occasions how dominant and in control she feels on top compared to the feeling of submissiveness she gets while laying on her back. The days of her being sexually molested by her stepfather have affected her to the point that she absolutely hates to be on the bottom.

His stomach bubbles while his blood boils with anger. He can't wait for his battery to charge up so he can call her again. He refuses to let her enjoy herself. He has plans of calling her over and over hoping to spoil any pleasure that she may be having.

Finally he pulls to his destination. He parks directly in front of the small house here on Coit Street in Irvington. He snatches the Prada shoe bag from the passenger's seat and hops out of the car quickly. Before he gets to the house the front door opens and a small woman appears in the doorway. "Ay Ma!" he shouts with joy. Samad has known this woman all of his life. She's like his second mother. His first mother is his grandmother who just died a little over a year ago. Deep down inside he's always envied D-Nice and his mother's relationship. His real mother was never in his life. She gave his grandmother custody of him when he was under two years old. Instead of raising her own child she chose to run the streets, getting high.

"Hey Baby," the woman says as she opens her arms wide awaiting his hug. "Come in," she demands. He steps into the hallway and closes the door behind himself. "Did you eat?" she asks. "I have breakfast on the stove. Pancakes, turkey bacon, eggs and home fries."

The thought of the food makes his stomach growl. He's grown up eating her meals and would never admit it but loves her cooking more than his grandmother's. His mind wanders back to Amber being with another man. The bubble guts that he gets from that thought coupled with the hunger growl causes an eruption. He's seconds away from soiling his underwear. "Nah, I just ate," he lies as the smell of the food smacks him in the face. As he gets into the kitchen the pleasant smell increases even more.

"You just missed his call."

"Oh yeah?" Samad asks with phony concern. He's still quite annoyed about what was said to him during their last conversation. "Here," he says as he hands her the shoe bag. "That's ten thousand."

Her eyes light up with joy. "Thank you, Baby. I miss him so much," she says with genuineness in her eyes. "You know ya'll worry me so much. Ya'll got to get it together. This ain't no life for ya'll. Ya'll are good kids...I mean young men. I pray for ya'll everyday," she sighs. "Lord knows if ya'll don't straighten up ya'll gone give me a heart attack."

Samad looks her in the eyes but in no way is he paying her the least bit of attention. His mind is consumed with thoughts of Amber. At this point there's no room for anything else in his mind. The entire time that he's been standing here all he can think of is getting back to the car so he can start calling her all over again. D-Nice's mom continues to talk to Samad while he stands there with a spaced out look in his yes. Right in the middle of her chastisement he interrupts her without even realizing it. "I gotta run now, Ma. Tell him to call me the minute he gets home. Ok?" he says as he gives her his back.

"Will do, honey."

Samad flashes out of the house like lightening. He trots quickly to his car. Before he's fully seated he grabs hold of the phone and starts to dial. He listens with fury as it rings.

In Miami

The bathroom is hot and hazy. The shower is running at full pressure. The loud noise of grunting sounds off over and over again. A completely nude Amber is on the floor on both knees, holding onto the toilet for dear life.

She lifts her head to take a quick breather. She tries to regroup but dizziness overpowers her. "Oh my God," she cries before the salt water seeps through her taste buds. Suddenly her mouth fills up and she can no longer hold it. She throws up her guts for minutes until every drop of fluid in her body has been released.

This has been going on for hours. She woke up this morning to a terrible case of morning sickness. Since she's been pregnant she has been sick a few times but nothing to this magnitude. She's never been this sick in her life. Not even her worst hangover can compare to this. This sickness alone is enough to make her never want to get pregnant again in her life. She can not imagine going through this for her entire pregnancy.

She felt so bad this morning that there was no way in the world that she could have left with the girls. The only person who knows what she's going through is Sade.

She told the others that the food from the Delano yesterday didn't agree with her stomach.

Minutes later she finally gets herself up from the floor and gets into the shower. When she's done she feels refreshed but her tummy is still quite bubbly. Just as she's walking into the living room, the ringing of her phone catches her attention. She grabs hold of it, hoping to catch it before it stops.

Samad's heart is somewhat relieved when he hears the call being picked up. Silence fills the line. Amber fumbles with the phone before placing it to her ear. "Yo!" he shouts like a madman.

""Yeah?" Amber says in an extremely weak voice. She's thrown up all the energy that she had.

He feels relieved to hear her voice but the anger is still there. "Where you at, yo?"

Amber hates when he addresses her by 'yo'. Normally she would read him but right now she doesn't have a bit of fight in her. "I been calling you all morning. Where the fuck you been?"

The sound of his voice is infuriating her but again arguing is not an option this morning. Ooh, she sighs to herself. Who the fuck does he think he's talking to she asks herself. "Throwing up all morning," she replies.

"What?" Samad barks.

"This baby is kicking my ass today. I'm sick as hell."

This feels so good to hear come out of her mouth. Being sick isn't good but it's better than laying up with another man. His heart softens up until its like putty. "Damn baby, I'm sorry to hear that."

Amber's curiosity strikes. She wonders what made Samad speak to her in that fashion. "Where did you think I was at?"

He chuckles aloud. He's too ashamed to tell her. "I ain't even gone tell you what I was thinking."

///// CHAPTER 69 /////

Samad sits behind the steering wheel of the Ford, just staring into the pitch darkness. He has the stereo low so he can concentrate. The customers scatter all over the block like roaches do when the lights are turned on. The constant running back and forth is hypnotizing.

He takes a long drag of the blunt and pauses momentarily before taking an even longer one. This drag caves his face in. He damn near coughs up a lung afterwards. Seconds later he takes a shorter drag. The car is now funky and hazy. Everything is a blur due to the thick clouds of smoke that fill the car. Samad takes one more drag before passing the blunt to his passenger.

D-Nice reaches for the blunt in slow motion as his eyes stare before him in a daze. The weed has him in the Matrix. Being that his system has been clean for many weeks, it's easy for him to get high. He was blasted after the second pull but every pull after that was just pure greed.

D-Nice was released from the County Jail late last night. Being free is like a dream come true. This morning when him and Samad linked up it was like a face off. Both of them stood there stubbornly as they both tried to outstare the other. Neither one of them wanted to be the first to say something to the other, in fear that the other would think that he cared. Eventually Samad gave in by asking did he really believe he would leave him in jail. D-Nice said that he was just stressed out and he knew for sure that Samad was coming for him. That's only what his mouth said because the truth of the matter is he had already lost faith in Samad coming to get him weeks ago.

Their loyalty to each other is not at question. D-Nice knows Samad will do anything for him. What makes him uneasy is Lil Bit. The power she has over him is quite disturbing to D-Nice. He watched his best friend go from a male chauvinist, gigolo to a sucker for love all in a matter of months. Something tells him that she's no good for him and she will be the key to Samad's demise. He's tried to warn Samad several times already but he refuses to listen. A part of him just wants to leave Samad alone and let him learn the hard way so he can say 'I told you so.' The downside to that is they're so close that if Samad destructs D-Nice will destruct right along with him. It's like two houses that are joined together. If one burns the flames will catch onto the other.

D-Nice passes the blunt back to Samad after two pulls. "Here," he says slowly with his voice dragging, sounding like a broken record. He starts to cough ferociously.

"Nigga, hit that shit," Samad demands. "I'm good," he says denying the blunt.

Instead of hitting it again D-Nice just lets it burn away in his fingertips. He sits there with amazement. He's never seen a flow like this. Customers are running back and forth, some hide in alleyways smoking their crack, while others are bold enough to smoke in the open while walking down the street. Watching this is blowing his mind more than the weed. It's hard for him to believe that just a short time ago this same block was damn near a ghost town. The money that he's witnessed the block generate in the past two hours would have taken them two shifts to score. He can't believe that the block has excelled to this level in such a short time. "Damn, this some New Jack City shit," he whispers.

"Yeah nigga and I'm Nino Brown," Samad says with an arrogant smirk on his face. "You can be whoever the fuck you wanna be. Welcome to the Carter!" he smiles. "Nigga look at this shit!" he shouts. "I told you, you was gone be shocked. This shit on fire! Between both shifts we scoring damn near twenty stacks!"

D-Nice sits there in awe. "Word?"

"Yeah!"

"Got damn!" D-Nice barks. He starts to calculate. Twenty grand a day he says as he thinks of the crack that it takes to supply the block. He wonders how the hell Samad could be getting that much crack from when they both were just dead broke. His curiosity strikes making him wonder how Samad has been able to supply a block of this magnitude. He really wants to ask but he hopes that Samad will tell him without him having to ask. Samad would love to tell him but at this point he can't. Amber made him promise not to leak a word of it to anyone. Deep down inside he hates to keep a secret from his best friend but after all a promise is a promise.

"Yeah like that, nigga!" Samad brags.

D-Nice sits back quietly, just wondering how he's going to fit into this big picture.

"Shit about to be on another level. Here," Samad says as he passes D-Nice a roll of money. "That's three stacks right there. Hold onto that. It will get greater later," he promises. "Give me a day or two and I got something real nice for you." He looks D-Nice straight into the eyes. "We been on the sideline long enough watching niggas bubble around us. Fuck second string. We been riding the bench long enough with our asses full of splinters. You know we always dreamed of having our own connect? And what we said we would do if we ever got one?" he asks. "We been screaming for years, 'coach put us in!' Begging for a chance to prove to the world that we can really ball. Now it's our turn! The coach has finally put us in the game," he says arrogantly.

D-Nice sits back and he's getting more hyper by the second. He has one question though. He asks himself for he refuses to ask Samad at this time. Who the fuck is the coach?

////// CHAPTER 70 //////

"The Mansion" here in South Beach is one of Miami's hottest clubs. Tonight the place is jam packed as usual, packed from wall to wall and everywhere in between. The crowd is well diversified with every nationality and sexual gender from male to female to homosexual to bisexual and even tri-sexuals who will try anything.

The small table at the corner of the VIP section is loaded with champagne bottles. Out of the eight bottles there, not one of them is even half empty. Amber and the crew have been popping bottle after bottle purely out of competition against the men who sit one table away from them. All this is done for the sake of women's equality. They buy a bottle every time the men buy a bottle. Amber refuses to let men beat her at anything.

The women sit around the table in laid back baller mode. Dark shades in which they call 'hater blockers' hides the eyes of all of them. Deja looks at the table next to them. It's occupied by four men who appear to be in their mid thirties. She has a keen sense of smell when it comes to money. She can sniff out a fake baller a mile away but the smell that seeps through her nostrils from their direction is the sweet smell of success.

She admires everything about them. They all seem to be confident but laid back. They sit back quietly just enjoying the company of each other. They're pretty much letting their bottles do the talking for them. They've been here longer than the girls and it shows on their tables. The girls only have eight bottles of champagne compared to the men's 13 bottles.

Deja's built in price scanner starts up automatically as she watches the men secretly. From behind her shades she examines them from head to toe. They're accessorized with iced out Presidential Rolexes and Breitlings, yellow stoned earrings and diamond fluttered pinkie rings. The jewelry is sparkling clean and flawless with quality and not gaudiness. Deja despises gaudiness and looks at it as tasteless and way too much. With these men it just seems to flow naturally as if they're not trying at all.

The man at the center of the table raises his hand to get the waitress's attention. "Bring five more out," he says flashing his five fingers in the air. He whispers loud enough only for the waitress to hear but Amber manages to read his lips.

She raises her hand as well. She's buying bottle after bottle for the sole purpose of competition. Due to her pregnancy she hasn't taken one sip. Five more bottles will cause the men to lead this game into a blowout. The men are winning but she plans to catch them in the long run. "Uh, excuse me," she whispers. "Bring seven over here."

In less than five minutes the bottles are being lined up on both tables. Corks begin flying into the air as the explosions pop off like the fourth of July from both tables. Mean looks come from the women who hover around the velvet rope that separates the VIP section from the dance floor. If looks could kill Amber and her crew would have been slaughtered minutes ago. Those women stand there desperately hoping that one of the men will invite them into their section. Until then they will continue to mean mug the table full of women who are there doing their own thing.

"Damn!" Deja says as she locks eyes with the woman who is giving them the hardest stare. Coincidentally the deejay fades in the perfect song. "Hustle hard!" rapper Maino shouts. "Stack paper! You see me! Hi haters," he sings. "Hi haters!" he shouts as Deja stands up. The rest of the crew stands up along with her. Together they start waving at the crowd singing along with the song. "Hi haters! Hi haters!"

Once the song goes off the women get back into their seats and sit there as if they haven't just put on a performance. Their audience watches with hatred in their eyes. Deja's attention goes back to the table of men. Surprisingly she locks eyes with the man sitting on the far end of the table. She quickly turns away from him as if she's not paying him any attention. She looks in the total opposite direction, staring directly into Amber's face. "This nigga all in my face," she whispers while barely moving her lips.

Amber looks in that direction. "Here he comes," she whispers to Deja out of the corner of her mouth. "He's on his way over here."

Deja preps herself. She immediately puts on her 'I don't want to be bothered face' knowing damn well that she really does want to be bothered. She's been watching him since the time they got here. She will never let a man get the idea that she's desperate. Her motto is the harder a woman plays to get, the harder a man will try to get her.

As he's getting closer to the table she watches him out of the corner of her eye but she keeps her head facing the dance floor. He diddy bops to the table. Deja looks down at her cell phone just as he gets there.

"Hey lady. How are you?" he says as soon as he gets there.

Deja looks up with a look of agitation on her face. Surprisingly she finds him standing directly in front of Star. The look of agitation is replaced by a look of pure embarrassment. She's so ashamed that she can't even look Amber in the face.

Amber laughs hard to herself as she makes it worse by staring at Deja. That's what the fuck she gets, Amber says to herself. Deja has always been good for that. For some reason she makes herself believe that whenever a man is looking at their group he has to be looking at her. Amber is so happy that today that isn't the case. She hopes that Deja has learned a valuable lesson from this.

Amber looks at her little sister. She figures she must really feel like like a grown woman right now. The fact that he picked her over the rest of the women at the table speaks volumes. She watches quietly as the man attempts to win Star over with charm. That is something that she never does. Normally by now she would have stepped in and fought the man off of her baby sister, trying to protect her from gaming men. Today she's not doing so. She looks the handsome man up and down and deep down inside she prays that he has the magic touch to persuade Star to come back to the other side which is a heterosexuality.

"That's my sister," Star says as she points to Amber. "This is my best friend," she says pointing to Tara who watches with extreme jealousy. "And these are my good friends," she says with a smile. Although she hates men she plays it off really amicable. Her bright smile may actually make him believe that he has a shot with her.

"Tell your friends to get with my friends," he says pointing to his table. "And together we can all be friends," he smiles. "Ya'll mind if we come over and join ya'll?"

Star looks at Amber for her approval. Amber shrugs her shoulders nonchalantly while Deja looks away as if they are not even there. Star shrugs her shoulders. "I don't care," she whispers.

"Yo, my man," he says as he taps the waiter who is walking by. "Join those tables together. We about the get shit popping right here," he points. In a matter of seconds the tables are joined together and the men are mingling with the women as if they've known them for their entire lives. A total of 33 bottles now spread across the tables. "Yo! It's my girl's birthday!" he says to the waiter. "Bring three more bottles out."

"Uh, excuse me?" Amber interrupts. She refuses to let them outdo her. "Make that eight. I'm paying for five," she says.

When the eight bottles arrive a total of 41 bottles of champagne circulate throughout the VIP section. A few of the bottles even trickle out onto the dance floor. Everyone is mingling except for Deja. She sits back with massive attitude. Only Amber knows what the attitude is all about.

Suddenly Deja's attention is forced to the left of her where she sees a slim framed man creeping into the area. She watches him subtly as he steps toward the table and starts shaking the hands of the men who stand here. He then stands to the side just looking around sneakily.

Deja looks him up and down. He doesn't even appear to fit with the rest of these men. It seems as if they don't have anything in common. They're loaded with diamonds and he's not. They're extremely social and he appears to be anti-social. Deja locks in on him and her scanner kicks in. He's wearing fitted Rock and Republic jeans that she calculates at $300.00. She looks to the ground and is shocked to see his neatly pedicured toes exposed. "Damn, flip flops," she whispers to herself. The Gucci thong flip flops she's sure he paid at least $400.00 for. She's not a fan of men in flip flops but she's willing to give him a pass. "After all this is Miami," she rationalizes with herself. His bright white v-neck t-shirt clings to his lean but muscular torso. The hat that he wears on his head is a negative. He becomes suspect to her. He loses a point due to the Ferrari hat. "Not a good look," she whispers under her breath. She assumes that he may be perpetrating the fraud as a Ferrari driver.

Since they've been down here they've seen so many broke dudes driving big cars that they've blew every dime they have just to rent them. She understands that in Miami anything goes. After all they're down here moving around in a half a million dollar automobile their damn selves.

To rent the car is one thing but to buy the hat to go along with it is way over the top. To her, that's just too much fronting. She looks at his hand in which he twirls his key ring. Her eyes stretch wide open. A few keys that are on the ring catch her attention. Not only is a Ferrari key on the ring but a Mercedes key and a Porsche key are on there as well. She quickly removes all doubt from her mind.

He reaches over her for a bottle of champagne and her eyes pop out of her head. She realizes that he is definitely the real deal. The watch that he sports on his left wrist is the watch of all watches. She admires a man with a nice watch. She believes that a man's watch determines his character. Wearing this watch she assumes that he must be full of character. To the average Joe this watch may appear to be an ordinary watch but Deja isn't the average Joe. She considers herself to be a watch connoisseur. Collecting watches has been a hobby of hers ever since she was a little girl. She actually knows more about watches than she knows about styling hair. She studies the watch carefully. The leather band, rose gold bezel watch has not a diamond in sight. It's a limited edition Roger Dubois Excalibur. 'Just for Kings' is the title of it. She realizes in order for him to be able to afford a $260,000 watch he must be a king.

She's studied him long enough. She feels it's time to go in for the kill. She refuses to wait another second and allow someone to steal this one from her like the last one was stolen from her. Now she looks at it as a blessing that Star did get the other man. If she hadn't she would have messed up her chances of getting next to the King. She slides the bottle closer to his reach.

"Thank you," he whispers politely.

She smiles seductively. "Nice watch," she compliments.

"Thank you," he replies casually, not thinking much of the compliment.

"What number is that twenty eight?" she asks. Deja knows that this watch is of an extremely limited edition wherein they only made 28 of them in the world.

"Nah," he replies with a stunned look on his face. He's shocked at her question. Her shouting out the magic number 28 tells him that she knows exactly what she's talking about. "Not at all," he smiles. "Number 3," he says arrogantly as he points to the hand painted number 3 that's on the face of the watch.

Damn, he got the third one made in the world, she says in her mind. Impressive, she thinks.

It's always noted that watches are conversation pieces. That statement is the bridge she needed to get where she wants. Before she knows it, he's pulled his chair next to hers and they engage in watch talk for hours. For the first time in his life he's found someone who has even more passion for watches than he does. He's just shocked that it's a woman.

Many hours pass and the club is now closing. The waitress comes over and drops the two checks onto the tables. They're so heavy that they damn near cave the table in. Amber managed to break a tie with the men. It's a draw at 25 bottles apiece. She's almost afraid to look at the bill. She can't believe that she allowed her ego to get her into this mess.

She peeks through one eye and the only thing that stands out on the bill is $13,670. Got damn, she says to herself. She can feel everyone's eyes on her as they try to see how she's going to react. She remains cool and calm as she tucks her hand into her purse. "Never let them see you sweat," she whispers to herself. She pulls her hand out and smacks the Platinum American Express card onto the table. The men stand in a huddle putting their ends together. Amber sits there gloating as if she has won. She's paying for the tab all alone while they're chipping in paying together.

The waitress grabs hold of Amber's card and steps away from the table. "Hold up," says the man who has been in Star's ear all night. The waitress turns around. "Give her the card back. We got it," he says as he stands there with several rolls of money in his hands.

The waitress does as she's instructed to. Amber is hesitant to pick the card up. She doesn't want them to pay her way and besides if they do they will win. "That's ok," she whispers politely.

"Nah, we got it," he replies. "We ain't doing plastic tonight," he says arrogantly.

You got it, she says to herself. Later for the foolish pride shit, she says in her mind. "Thank you," she whispers with a smile. A part of her feels like she has lost the game though.

"Eeelk!" Deja shouts. Her loud outburst causes everything and everybody to stop. They look at her to see what the outburst is about. Silence fills the air. She stares at the man who was with Star. The look on her face is of pure disgust. Everyone realizes that she's looking at him and they look at him as well to find out what the disgusting look is all about.

He stands there with a huge bulk of money in his hand. The look on his face is clueless as he looks himself up and down trying to see what is wrong with him. "What?" he whispers with a baffled look on his face.

Everyone looks at Deja awaiting her reply. She points at the man with an obnoxious look on her face. "He got ones in his cake!" she says referring to the dollar bills that he has mixed in his money. The women begin rolling with laughter. She's crushed him. He stands there with a goofy look on his face. Deja feels like she's gotten even with him for the embarrassment he put her through earlier tonight. "Checkmate motherfucker," she utters under her breath.

An Hour Later

The party may be over but now it's time for the after party. The string of high line cars are parked in the parking lot of the Bal Harbour Yacht Club. After paying over $27,000 for the champagne, they left a three thousand dollar tip for the waiters and waitresses. The men walked out as if they felt they may have really impressed the women. Little do they know that Amber is quite used to that. Maurice and the Federation do that in every spot they attend.

Deja refused to let her new friend get out of her sight. It was her idea to link up with them afterwards. Amber and the crew followed her lead. When they got to the parking lot the valet attendants pulled up in a Lamborghini, a Bentley GTC convertible, a Maybauch and last but not least the Ferrari that Deja's friend is driving. When the Rolls Royce Drop head Coupe appeared the show stopped.

In no way did they believe that the women actually owned the Rolls Royce but they were still highly impressed. The looks on their faces makes her feel that she is now ahead of the game. They may have won in the bar but she's determined to catch up and beat them in the long run.

Amber prances arrogantly across the bow of the yacht. A few steps behind her is her crew. Many steps behind them are the men. She decided to show them how to really play. Sailing the yacht through Miami should take her way over the top.

In these men's mind they believe that the women may have rented the yacht here in Miami for a night. Even having that in mind they are still impressed with the whole movement. As they're stepping onto the yacht the men's attention is drawn to the New Jersey registration tag. It causes them to reevaluate. Maybe it is theirs, they all think. Amber can see the curiosity in their eyes. That gives her great appreciation. Just as she figured; she would beat them in the long run. She laughs to herself. "Game over!"

///// CHAPTER 71 /////

11:00 A.M.

Samad sits on the edge of the bed counting through stacks and stacks of money. "Hey what about this one?" Shakira screams from the head of the bed. Samad turns around toward her. Without looking upward he continues to sift through the bills. "One bedroom in Irvington, thirteen hundred a month," she reads. "One and a half months security."

Samad is in dire need of his own apartment but with the block banging like it is he doesn't have the time to search for one. He hired Shakirah for the job. She's been on the case day in and day out for the past week. She's the only one he can trust outside of Amber. He's shared some of his deepest darkest secrets with her and never has he heard a word of what he told her come back to him.

"Nah," he interrupts. "No Irvington, no Newark and no East Orange." Amber must have rubbed off on him because never before has he ever cared so much about where he chose to live. She continuously tells him how security is first and foremost and there's no price too steep to pay for it. With his newfound success he now understands exactly what she's talking about. With the high volume of crack that he's selling he's sure some bad days are to come. The last run in that he had with the law taught him a valuable lesson. His next spot he plans to move so far out of the way that no one will be able to find him.

"How about West Orange?"

"That's cool, I guess."

"The rent is a lot more though."

Before his new found success he was limited to the places that he could live due to the fact that he couldn't afford to live outside of Newark. Now he feels assured that he can live just about anywhere he wants to. "Doesn't matter."

"Here goes a good one, sounds like anyway. One bed," she says before he interrupts her again.

"Nah, two bedrooms," he says with his main man D-Nice in mind. He doesn't make a move without him in mind.

After he finds his apartment, all of his goals have been accomplished. He thought that was the last of his problems but now he's encountered another one. In front of him there lies over twenty grand. He has only enough work to last him for the rest of the day if he's lucky. The problem is he doesn't have a clue of where or who he can get more product from. Having money is senseless if you don't have the means to make more. Without a connect his show will stop.

As he thinks of his problem his mind races. He's put way too much energy into the block to let it go dry due to lack of product. He sits back in deep concentration as he tries to figure out who he can go to in order to get what he needs. The only person he can think of is D-Nice's cousin Rahiem but after the way he treated him the last time they saw each other he told himself he would never deal with him again in life. Whether he wants to accept the fact or not, he really has no other alternative.

Meanwhile In Miami

The girls are all laid out sleeping in the living room of Maurice's condo. Normally at this hour they would be lounging out on the beach but today they're way behind schedule. The night didn't end until after four in the morning and even then the men didn't want it to end. It was evident that they all were expecting the night to end with them laid up in the sheets but that didn't happen. What they didn't realize is the whole idea of the boat ride was to allow Amber to rub her glory in their faces. The two hour boat ride was all the time she needed to make a lasting impression on them. The women were so tired when they got in that they collapsed right in the living room.

Amber's light sleeping is interrupted by the noise of the door opening up. She looks up only to find Deja attempting to sneak in. She's quite surprised to see them all lying here. She was hoping to sneak in without them knowing what time she got in.

The after party led to a nightcap for her. When the night was ending for everyone else and they all went in their separate directions, Deja left in the passenger's seat of the Ferrari with her new friend.

"I told you not to wait up," Deja says with a cheesy smile on her face.

Amber looks at her through one sleepy eye. Even through that one eye she can see that Deja looks a mess. Her hair is all out of whack and big bags lie underneath her eyes as if she hasn't slept a wink. As she passes Amber on the love seat Amber looks her up and down. The thong that peeks over top of her tight fitted, hip hugger jeans screams for attention. Something tells Amber that Deja has not been a good girl. The tag being on the outside of her thong is a dead give away. "Your thong is on backwards," Amber says in a teasing manner.

Deja reaches behind her and tucks the thong down her jeans. "Oh is it?" she asks casually, not once looking in Amber's direction.

"Tell me you didn't give him none on the first night?"

"No, I gave it to him this morning," she replies with a half a smile.

"Girl, you a trip. I thought you really liked him? Aren't you worried about what he may think of you for giving it up so fast?"

"Not at all. I'm grown," she says firmly. "Let me tell you something. If you give it to him on the first night or make him wait for a year the results are still going to be the same. Bitches believe the longer you make him wait the more he's going to respect you and want to settle down with you. Bullshit! Just cause you make him wait don't make you wife material in his eyes. If that's the case why do motherfuckers marry sluts?" she asks with a cocky look on her face. "That's the biggest misconception ever. If a nigga's main objective is the pussy, the minute he gets it he's going to leave anyway. Whether it's one day or a year later it don't matter cause his mind is already made up from the time he meets you. If that's his goal, to just fuck you nothing is going to change his mind. Unless you got the bomb pussy," she smiles. "That can alter his whole chain of thought. Trust me when I tell you that."

"So you're not worried about him never speaking to you again? After all he got the coochie already."

"See, you don't give him everything all at once. You give him just enough to make him want more. It's like giving him a sample," she explains. "Just enough to reel him in. Fortunately, my sample is more filling than most chicks full course," she says with a seductive smile. "The way I put it down, I doubt very seriously that he will never not speak to me again."

Amber looks at Deja with her mouth stretched wide open. She's shocked at the words that are coming out of her mouth. Being that she's been around her for years she shouldn't be. Just when she thinks Deja has outdone herself she finds a way to further outdo herself. "I hope you're right."

Deja's phone rings. She looks at the display and a smile pops up on her face instantly. "Excuse me," she says politely. "Hey babe," she says as she winks at Amber arrogantly. "You're going to live a long time. I was just talking about you," she says smiling from ear to ear. "Of course. Nothing but good things." She places her hand over the phone to prevent him from hearing what she's about to say to Amber. "With me, what happens in Miami doesn't stay in Miami. Believe you me," she whispers with a devilish smile.

Many Hours Later

"Damn Cousin, I needed you and you didn't come through for me," D-Nice says with sadness in his eyes as he stands before his cousin Rahiem. "I can't believe you let me sit. I would have got the bread back to you."

Rahiem stands in front of D-Nice but his attention isn't on him at all. He's busy watching his surroundings. For some reason he feels like he's being set up. He peeks around looking for any sign of police who may be around watching them.

His first alert was Samad making the high bail. That made him suspicious. Now that D-Nice is out as well he's way beyond suspicious. He wonders how the two broke individuals managed to come up with so much money in such a short time. That's hard to understand when they are the same guys who could never come up with money to buy their own work in all of the years he's been dealing with them. The entire situation seems shady to him and he refuses to get caught up in the trap that they're setting. He can't believe that his cousin would try and set him up though.

Rahiem looks across the street where Samad is sitting in the Ford 500. The hard stare that Samad gives him forces him to turn away. Samad can't stand the sight of him at this point. It takes everything for him to restrain himself from getting out of the car and beating him to a pulp. He thought for sure that Rahiem would at least come through for them if they needed him, especially after all the years that they've been doing business together.

Samad promised himself that he would never say a word to him for as long as they both live but the fact that he's in need of work made him break his promise. Still he couldn't force himself to talk to Rahiem which is why he put D-Nice up to it.

"Right now, that's neither here nor there," D-Nice utters. "That ain't even what I'm here for. We need to get hold of some twirk (work). We need a joint ASAP."

"A joint?" he asks as if he doesn't have a clue of what he's talking about.

The look in Rahiem's eyes is the same as the look in D-Nice's eyes when Samad told him how much work they were in search of. D-Nice couldn't believe his ears. That only increased his curiosity more. He still can't believe that Samad hasn't told him how he's escalated to this level. This is like a dream come true for D-Nice.

He never thought the day would ever come that he would be buying a kilo. He has to admit that it feels as good as he always thought it would feel.

"A key," he barks arrogantly. "What you gone charge us?"

The word key rips through Rahiem's eardrums. This seals the deal for him. At first he thought they may be working with the police but now he's sure they are. In his mind there's no way in the world they could have come up like this. They're claiming to have money for a kilo when they have never even bought a quarter of a kilo on their own. He looks D-Nice square in the eyes. "I ain't got shit."

"Nah? Damn! When you gone have something?"

"I ain't doing nothing," he says loud and clear, hoping that every word is heard just in case D-Nice is wired and the FEDS are listening in. "I'm done."

"Well turn me onto somebody?" he begs.

The desperation in his eyes further convinces Rahiem that something isn't right. Now that they can't trap him they're just ready to bring in anyone. The thought of that pisses him off seriously. Bitch ass niggas, he utters under his breath. "I don't know nobody to turn you onto. I don't know nothing. My ear ain't to the street like that."

D-Nice looks around at the block. What he's saying is hard to believe when the block is jumping with activity. He can't quite understand what this is all about. Suddenly he starts to consider the fact that maybe his cousin is trying to hold him back from doing his thing. He becomes frustrated at the very thought of that. He snickers with agitation. "Alright, cool," he says nodding his head up and down. "If something come through holler at me," he says as he starts to backpedal away. "Later!"

D-Nice gets into the passenger seat of Samad's car. Before he can even get seated, Samad attacks him eagerly. "What's the word?"

D-Nice sighs with frustration. "He said he ain't got shit. He said he fell back. He done."

"He done? Since the fuck when? When he saw us pulling up?" he asks sarcastically. "Look at the block! Do it look like he done? What's up with that nigga? Yo, if he wasn't your cousin I would do something to him!" He watches Rahiem standing in the center of a small huddle. The sight of him infuriates him tremendously. The truth of the matter is, at this point not even the fact that the two are cousins is enough to stop him from doing something to him. His mind is already made up. What Samad doesn't know is that Rahiem has some plans of his own and the fact that D-Nice is his cousin is not enough to stop him from doing what he plans to do either. The reason for that is what he plans to do, consists of doing it to D-Nice as well.

///// CHAPTER 72 /////

Several Hours Later. Samad's spirits have been lifted. After making just two phone calls he landed himself a potential connection. He finds the price to be absurd but his hands are tied. He realizes that the only option he has outside of buying it at that price is to actually go without. He remembered what Amber told him about paying cheaper for the whole thing as opposed to buying it by the gram. He tried to exert the authority he thought he had but it didn't work. What he didn't realize is when dealing with middle men there is no flexibility. They have no room for haggling. Before they allow you to talk them out of their cut they will let the deal walk away from them. They would rather both parties lose than to let you win.

Samad hops into the passenger seat of the older model Jeep Cherokee. At his entrance he hands a bag over to the driver. The driver then passes the bag to a man who sits quietly in the backseat. The man immediately starts counting through the many stacks of money.

As Samad is listening to the bills flicking he gets even more pissed off. He feels like he's being played for a sucker. $27,500 is a big difference from the $20,500 he just paid Lil Bit for a kilo. If he had any other option he would never pay this amount but unfortunately he doesn't. "Yo, Dee, tell your man he gone have to do something about that price. That shit crazy," he says looking at the driver but referring to the man in the backseat. Even though he's in the car with him he's not saying a word to him because he doesn't know him. He only knows the driver. When they spoke earlier he said he knew someone that had work. His man Dee is nobody and he has nothing. He just runs around brokering deals.

The man in the backseat finally finishes counting. He hands the plastic bag up to Samad. "The price is the price baby. Shit dry everywhere. Ain't nobody got shit. You can check everywhere. I'm one of the only mufuckers in the town with work. And ain't nobody gone be able to beat my price."

Samad listens as he slits an opening in the tape that houses the brick of cocaine. He examines it closely. It's pure white and shiny but the texture is as hard as cement compared to the soft and fluffy powder he just had. "You sure this shit correct, right?" Samad asks.

"Psst, Dee, tell your man about me. I don't play them type games. All my work is guaranteed."

Samad listens to all the big time talking that is coming from the backseat and wonders if it's really like that. He's talking like a millionaire but the hooptie that he pulled up in is not the car that a man of his stature should be driving. His appearance doesn't seem to match up to his arrogance. Samad figures that either he's on the super down low or he's just flat out fronting. "I'll hit you in a couple of days."

"Yo, if anything, just hit Dee. He'll get in touch with me," the man says making it perfectly clear that he can't deal with him directly. He has to go through Dee.

Samad hops out of the Cherokee and walks a few steps up to his car. He gets into his car and cruises away slowly.

The man digs into the bag and grabs hold of a one thousand dollar stack. He passes it over to Dee in the driver's seat who looks at the money with appreciation.

He just scored a grand for making a phone call. Brokering the deal is the easiest job of them all. Not once did he have to put one finger on the drugs. The saying is true; it's all about who you know.

The man hops out of the backseat of the Cherokee and walks across the street to his raggedy Buick. He pulls off and cruises up Springfield Avenue for two traffic lights before he pulls over into the Auto Zone parking lot. He parks directly next to a black Range Rover. Before getting out he digs into the bag once again, snatching another thousand dollar stack. He quickly stashes the stack into his pants pocket as he's getting out.

He snatches the passenger's door open slightly. "Good looking Big Bruh," he says as he hands the driver the bag which now holds $25,500 in it. "I'll hit you up," he says before slamming the door shut.

The Range Rover zips out of the parking lot making a right turn onto Springfield Avenue. At the corner of Irvine Turner Boulevard the driver makes another right turn. While riding he removes a stack of bills and places them in his glove compartment. After traveling for a few blocks the driver steers to his right and turns onto Avon Avenue. He parks directly behind the midnight blue 750 BMW. The driver hops out of the Rover and trots over to the passenger's window of the 750, where he sneakily drops the bag onto the seat. "Rah, good looking. That's $24...5. I'll get with you later. My man from Camden supposed to be coming through later. You gone be around?"

"Yeah definitely," Rahiem replies as he slams the gear into the drive position. "I'm about to go and get right, right now. I'll be ready when he gets here."

"Alright bet. Be safe," the man says as he makes his way back to the Rover.

"No question," Rahiem says as he pulls out of the parking space. It doesn't take a scientist to figure out that this Rahiem is the same Rahiem who is the cousin to D-Nice. Just as they figured he's still in operation. If Rahiem only knew where that kilo traveled from. That bird has flown throughout the entire city, getting more expensive each time it landed. Lucky for him that they're not working with the police because if they were he would be dead busted.

Rahiem cruises up Clinton Avenue on his way to his destination. That was the last kilo that he had. Now it's time for him to re-up. He grabs his cell phone from the middle console and starts to dial. He listens in silence as the phone rings. "Yo, Rock I'll be at the spot in five minutes. Cool," he says before ending the call.

In three minutes flat, Rahiem pulls into the parking lot of Pathmark on Lyons Avenue. As he cruises the lot the high beams of a GMC truck flashes twice to get Rahiem's attention. Rahiem cruises over and parks side by side with the truck. Before getting out he snatches a stack and half from the bag leaving $23,500 inside. He then presses a few buttons on his steering wheel and his dashboard pops out slowly. From it he grabs a plastic bag which holds $69,000. He dumps it all in one bag and slides out of his car and into the truck.

He drops the bag of money onto the man's lap. In return the driver gives Rahiem a bag filled with four kilos. Rahiem hops out without hesitation and the driver speeds off. As the driver cruises the parking lot, he picks up his phone. "Big Nigga, where you at? I'm coming through."

Yes, there's only one Big Nigga and that's Maurice. This man in the driver's seat is one of the six members of the Federation. What a small world.

/ / / / / CHAPTER 73 / / / / /

Maurice stands in the living room of his cousin's apartment. He unzips the duffle bag and starts to drop the kilos inside. The kilos have been disappearing at a rapid pace. Just as fast as the bats land, they're flying out of the cave. Today alone he has three transporters coming through. The thirty they're bringing in and the twenty that he has in the bag will make up the 100 that his Spanish boys from New York have put their order in for.

"Yo, Cuz thanks for the opportunity. The vacation was beautiful and now thanks to you I will be able to get out of the hole."

Maurice hands a bunch of bills over to his cousin. "Twenty stacks as promised."

"Thanks Cuz," the man says gratefully. "Anytime you need me I'm here."

"Don't say that," Maurice says with a grin as he makes his way to the door. "I will call your bluff. Later!" he says as he exits the apartment.

The man leans against the wall, just flicking through the crisp one hundred dollar bills. He holds them up to his nose while shuffling the money. The sweet smell of the dirty money gives him the rush of a lifetime. This is the easiest twenty grand he ever thought of making. He just may have found himself a new occupation. To go to work for less than $2,500 a month sounds ridiculous to him right now. Just one trip for Maurice and now he's turned out. He places the money up to his lips and kisses it. "Sonny was right," he whispers quoting a line from the movie 'A Bronx Tale.' "The working man is a sucker!"

Meanwhile

Amber, Sade and Tara hop out of the cab in front of Miami International Airport. As they're walking into the automatic opening double doors, Amber spins around looking behind her. "Where the hell this damn girl at?" she asks referring to Deja. "She claimed that she was right behind us with her lying ass. She can keep playing around if she wants to. She gone miss the damn flight," she says as she starts to dial Deja's phone number.

Deja lays back in the creamy golden gut of the cranberry CL55 Mercedes Benz Coupe. Her friend was forced to put the Ferrari up and pull out the Mercedes. There was no way in the world that all the items that he bought for her during yesterday's $10,000 shopping spree could fit in the Ferrari. It's just barely enough room for the items in the trunk of this car.

Deja looks around just admiring the view when her phone rings. When she looks down and sees Amber's name on the display she just ignores the call. She assumes that Amber is calling to ask where she is just as she has been doing all morning. She zooms in on her beautiful surroundings. Last night it was so late when they got in that she couldn't get a clear view of everything that's going on here. Last night she thought the condo here on Williams Island was beautiful but now that she's seeing it in the daytime she sees it as magnificent.

In total her friend has 3600 square feet of pure luxury. The panoramic view from the 30th floor apartment is breathtaking. He claims to have paid 1.2 million dollars for the apartment and Deja finds it to be worth every dollar of that if not more.

As they're making their exit from the underground garage Deja has to put her sunglasses on to block the bright sun rays that are peeking in through the skylight ceiling. As they exit the garage she looks to her left at the beautiful waterfall. It's gorgeous now but at night it turns completely blue. All in all this place is almost unbelievable.

She looks around and is amazed at the many yachts that are lined up around the island like cars. As they cruise a little further her attention is captured by a huge swimming pool which has gigantic frog sculptures sitting inside, spitting water from their mouths. "This is beautiful," she whispers.

"Thank you," he replies modestly just as they approach the front gate.

Palm trees swarm the area making it resemble a jungle. Two men stand on opposite sides of the gate. Both of them are wearing safari hats and all white linen. They stand there stiff like statues until the car passes them. They then salute as if he's the General. Damn, this is really something impressive she says to herself. A bitch can really get used to calling this home, she says in her mind. If I play my hand right it will be home, she says grinning to herself devilishly.

"Bitch ain't answering the phone," Amber says with attitude. "Alright. When this plane leaves, I'm leaving on it. She just gone be a left bitch." What Amber doesn't know is at this very moment Deja really has no problem with getting left. She's sure with the help of her new friend she could make a new life for herself right here in sunny Miami.

They're all sad to know that the vacation is over. Now it's back to the rat race. Sorrow filled Amber's heart from the moment she set eyes on the airport. Her mind has been at ease all week. She barely thought about the troubles that she has back at home.

One good thing though, she found a solution to her biggest problem. She plans to break the news to Maurice the minute she gets back. She can't go another day living this lie. After all he's a married man and he should understand that she's ready to go on with her life. She feels like a slave to him and that's not fair that she has to live her life like that. She wants and needs more out of life than just being his playmate when he wants to play.

The last few months their relationship has been beautiful. It's been all business. They have not bickered or argued about anything. With just a business relationship they have nothing to argue about. She hasn't slept with him in quite some time so her emotional ties to him have been watered down. Normally she's the one to start all the arguments. After they would have sex she would find some reason to start an argument with him. The fact that she felt used after sex with him would make her pissed to no end. She has way too much pride to let him know her true feelings so she would just start an argument about anything else.

Hopefully Maurice will understand when she breaks the news to him. She realizes that she's taking a big risk and putting a lot on the line by doing this. She realizes that she will have to tell him one day because she can't hide her pregnancy forever.

By revealing this she is not only endangering herself but Samad will be in even more danger. She's sure Maurice is going to have a lot of questions for her. He will want to know how long she's been dating him, how did they meet and the most dreaded question of all, who he is. Regardless, Amber will not disclose that. That may result in the love of her life being murdered.

While Amber is checking her bags in, her cell phone starts vibrating. She looks down at the display and seeing Maurice's name causes her stomach to bubble. The moment of truth is only a few hours away. She picks up the phone on the fourth ring. "Yes?"

"What's up Baby?" he sings with joy. "I need you bad! What's up with tomorrow afternoon? I know you tired and all from flying and vacationing but I need you. I'll take care of you for sure."

Maurice thinks she will have a problem with flying right back out but truthfully this is the best news she could hear right now after blowing through so much money this week. A trip right now would be perfect. It will give her a chance to replenish her bank account that she ripped through.

She doesn't want to seem desperate and blow any incentive that he may be willing to offer her. "Damn Moe. I'm beat," she whines.

"I know, I know. I got you Ma. I'm gone make it worth your while. And on top of that I got something else real special for you," he whispers. The sound of his voice tells her that he's referring to sex. "You know it's been a long time don't you? I want you so bad right now that I can taste you through the phone."

Oh my God, she thinks to herself. The fact that he's hoping for sex with her makes her not even want to go home. His horniness will make her job of breaking the news to him just that much more difficult. She looks back at the many cabs that are along the ramp and it takes everything to keep her in the line. At this point she wants to just stay here a few more days but she realizes she can't run forever. It's time to go home and face the music.

///// CHAPTER 74 /////

Later that Night

Maurice sits in the driver's seat of his pick-up truck which is parked on the dark secluded block. Not a bit of movement is taking place. In his passenger's seat sits Smurf.

Smurf sits back quietly, just staring straight ahead as Maurice speaks.

"Ay man, you know how this shit goes. In order to survive out here you have to be on any and everything. You gotta stay ten steps ahead of the game. You get a lead, you gotta move on it. Slip up and you outta here, just that simple. You can lose your life. I'm trying to be here. I gotta wife and I got kids. Before I let anybody take me away from them I will tie any loose end. It ain't personal and I hope you don't take it like that. I'm here doing something that I never do and that's apologize. I'm here man to man, hoping you accept my apology. I already had my mind made up before hearing you out and that was wrong. Even after you explained your side of the story I still believed what I wanted to believe. I didn't even give you a fair shot. I just accused you. We got too many years in. I'm supposed to take your word over anybody who ain't a part of us. I didn't and because I didn't, I'm apologizing," he says as he looks at Smurf who is looking straight ahead.

In all actuality hearing Maurice apologize means a great deal to Smurf because he's never heard him do that before. For sure the apology won't bring back his good friend Dirt though. Smurf will have to live with the guilt for the rest of his life but he has to chalk it up as a huge price to pay to prove his loyalty to his squad.

"You accept?" Maurice asks.

Smurf looks him dead in the eyes. He shrugs his shoulders. "You already," he replies arrogantly. "This Federation of ours, I breathe this, I shit this. I am this. I live for this shit, I'll die for this shit and as you already know I'll murder anything that attempts to come in between me and my niggas."

"Say no more. I'm glad to hear that," Maurice says as they shake hands. "Now, let's get back to business. I got 15 bats at the cave waiting for you. The ticket is twenty one a pop."

"Twenty one?" Smurf asks, not believing his ears.

"Yeah, twenty one. Shit just went up again yesterday. Shit crazy out here. Ain't no coke nowhere."

Maurice doesn't have to tell him that. He knows first hand. For the past couple of days he's been trying to get his hands on some work and has had no luck at all. That's probably the best thing that could have happened though. Had he got hold of work he may have signed his own death certificate. Maurice doesn't believe in leaving stragglers around. Once a dude has been noted as a part of the Federation he's that for life. They make an oath that states until death do us part. Needless to say there are no former members traveling the land.

Maurice is well aware of the fact that members have been exposed to so much. They've heard a lot and witnessed even more. The information they have is valuable and can cost many their freedom. To leave a straggler around and allow him to link up with others and take the risk of secrets being revealed, he would rather finish them off first. Smurf is well aware of that. Understanding the possibilities of him possibly losing his life was enough of an incentive to make him reinstate his membership to the Federation.

Meanwhile A Few Miles Away

Samad pushes the door open and walks into D-Nice's room. "What's up nigga?" he says to D-Nice who sits on his twin-sized bed playing X-Box. Being in this room makes D-Nice feel like a child again. Once he moved out he thought he would never return. Now here he is cramped up in this tiny room, sleeping on this tiny bed. This entire situation has been one huge reality check for him.

One thing he realized while he was in the County was the nickel and dime petty hustling that they were doing was really meaningless. Now he understands that they really were in the way, obstructing real hustlers. The little money they drained from the game could have easily helped a real hustler get that much closer to his dreams. For them it was just enough money so that they wouldn't have to work a real job. It was in that County Jail that he made up his mind that either he was going to go hard this time around or just get out of the way.

Samad drops a plastic bag onto D-Nice's lap. "What's this?" he asks as he presses pause on his game controller. He looks in the bag only to find a nice chunk of crack.

"That's the key to your future," he says with a smile. "That's a half a brick."

D-Nice stares at the bag of hope. All of a sudden his future looks that much brighter. Now he can go ahead and make his come up. He feels bad that he even thought like that. "How much I owe you on it? What I gotta bring back?"

"You don't owe me shit. It's yours. I want for my brother what I want for myself."

Samad cooked up the entire kilo and was quite disappointed with the results. He expected to whip up close to an extra 500 grams as he did with the kilo that he got from Lil Bit. This kilo only allowed him to whip up an extra 200 grams.

True indeed both kilos are from the Muhsee network but the one Amber gave him was still in its purest form. Once Maurice gets them and stretches one into two the work loses a great deal of the purity, making it just barely above average cocaine. The reason they control the streets is because they have access to so many kilos. Also no one can beat the number that they move them for. All in all it's a win-win situation for the Federation.

"You got a half a joint and I got a half joint," he lies. He's not including the extra 200 grams that he kept for himself. Another secret that he's keeping to himself is the fact that he has purposely given D-Nice his work while it's still slightly wet. If it were completely dried out it would be 30 to 40 grams short of 500 grams. D-Nice doesn't know any better either because they have never bought cocaine or transformed it to crack on their very own. They always bought it as crack already. Until recently neither of them even considered the advantages of cooking it themselves. Now that Samad knows, will he keep the recipe to himself or will he share it with his business partner? "You know I been thinking? We're grown ass men with our own goals and aspirations. All these years we been penny pinching. You complaining every time I spend a dollar more than your cheap ass spent," he says with a sarcastic smile. "Now we ain't gotta penny pinch no more. You do you and I do me. At the end of the flip we meet at the crossroads. Then we do it all over again. I ain't in your pocket and you ain't in my pocket. When we flip we match money. How does that sound?"

D-Nice listens with joy. All of a sudden his future looks much more promising. Now he can finally make his own come up. For some reason he felt as if Samad was going to string him along with a bunch of bullshit promises but never actually bringing him all the way in. He now feels bad for even thinking like that.

Also while in the County D-Nice drew the conclusion that Samad has always held him down to a certain degree. It seems like they could never get ahead of the game and just continued to run in place. D-Nice could go through an entire flip without spending a dime wherein Samad spends money foolishly. The end result was them barely having any money to split after paying D-Nice's cousin the money they owed him. Now with his own work he can soar as high as he wants with no one and no thing holding him back.

He nods his head up and down. "Sounds like a plan."

Samad puts his fist in the air. "The last one to the top is a rotten egg," he says like a child.

"Hmphh," D-Nice snickers as they bang fists. "I'll smell you when you get there."

///// CHAPTER 75 /////

The Next Day

Amber cruises out of the Post Office parking lot on Springfield Avenue. Signs of agitation are all over her pretty face which is crumbled up like a sheet of paper. It's not even afternoon yet and she's had a bad day already. She's heard nothing but back to back nonsense since she woke up this morning. The shocking news she just received in the mail was the icing on the cake.

On top of everything else she got into a huge argument with Samad early this morning when she told him that she wouldn't be home for a few more days. She lied to him because she knew she would be leaving back out for Maurice today. She just wanted to avoid his question and answer session. When he accused her of cheating she lost it and cursed him out like she's never done before. Needles to say that wasn't the end of her dilemma. She then called Deja and explained to her that she was going out for business and needed Deja to lay low for a few days because she told Samad that they were still on vacation. Deja blacked out on her for even caring what 'the broke motherfucker' in her words thinks or even feels. In return Amber let her have it as well.

Amber has gotten to the point where she can no longer control her emotions. The pregnancy is definitely getting the best of her. Another reason for her tension comes from knowing that she has to break the news to Maurice. A part of her can't wait to get it over with but the other part dreads to do so. She does hope that after telling him, a great deal of her burden is decreased.

She pulls into the parking lot of Popeye's Chicken. As soon as she spots Maurice's pick-up truck her heart starts to pop out of her chest. "Please God, give me the strength to go through with this," she prays. "And please don't let me get killed while doing it, please?" she begs.

Maurice walks confidently to the passenger's seat of Amber's truck. In his hands he holds the computer print out for her airline e-ticket. He snatches the door open and climbs in. "What's up, lady? I miss you, crazy!" he says as he leans over and tries to plant a kiss on her lips. She leans her head back out of his way to avoid the kiss but he just keeps on coming until he backs her into the corner. He grabs her head and forces his mouth onto hers. "Muuuuaaahhh. Muaaah."

She sways her head from side to side trying to shake him off of her. The more she fights the harder he kisses her. All the fighting is turning him on. He climbs onto the chair on his knees and continues to kiss her until the bulge in his jean shorts becomes harder than steel. The stiffened bulge that rests on Amber's forearm causes her to get even more disgusted with him. She pushes him away with all of her might but he still continues to hold her down. Finally he backs off of her. "Get the fuck off me!" she shouts. Her face is cherry red with frustration. The smile on his face doesn't make it any better.

"Damn baby, calm down," he says. "I'm just happy to see you. You not happy to see me?" he asks as he sneakily reaches over and drops his hand onto her lap. Before she knows it her spandex covered kitten is being groped by him. He pets the cat twice before. "Smack!"

Without even realizing it Amber's anger has taken over and slapped him. He shakes it off with a look of shock on his face. After the state of shock wears off his reflexes kick in and causes him to jump over onto her seat. He's straddled over her lap with both hands wrapped around her neck. "What the fuck wrong with you?" he asks as he chokes her. The back and forth rocking of the truck causes a few people to sit and watch them without them even realizing it. "Don't you ever put your fucking hands on me," he says as he chokes her over and over while she gags away. "Are you crazy?" he asks while totally ignoring her gags.

She's furious. Her anger brings out the tiger in her. She digs her claws into both sides of his face until the skin breaks. Even then she attempts to sink them even further into the white meat. The pain that comes from the wounds causes him to choke her even harder. "Stop scratching me," he demands. She gags but her stubbornness makes her continue to claw him.

Finally the burning sensation in his face he can no longer take. He lets her neck go and grabs hold of his face. When he looks down and sees both palms full of blood, he hauls off and smacks the daylights out of her.

She reaches over to smack him back but he catches her tiny wrist in mid air. He squeezes it with no mercy expecting her to cave in but instead she lifts her leg high in the air. Using all of her might she drives her three inch stiletto heel into the beefy part of his muscular chest. The pain infuriates him. He chokes her wrist even harder before palm gripping her head and mashing it onto the headrest.

She sits there awaiting his finish. He draws his huge fist high in the air while marking her nose as his target. She closes her eyes and prepares herself to absorb the pain. Seconds fly by and she feels nothing. She pops one eye open only to see him backing away from her. He lets go of her wrist, slightly and slings her arm toward her.

Maurice pats the blood from his face while Amber gets herself together. She pulls her visor down to look at herself in the mirror. She sways any hair in place that may have gotten out of whack. She slams the visor shut. "Get out," she demands without even looking in his direction. He totally ignores her. "Get the fuck out!"

"Shut up! I ain't going nowhere," he says looking at her coldly. "What the fuck ya'll looking at!" he barks to the spectators.

"Fuck it, I'll go then," she says before forcing the door open. She hops out of the truck and slams the door. She peeks in the window. Now explain all those scratches to your wife. Ah hah," she teases, infuriating him to no end.

"Fuck you!" he shouts.

"You wish you could fuck me again!" she says as she switches away angrily.

He grabs the door handle and is seconds away from chasing her down and beating her to a pulp when his anger dissolves. He now starts to feel bad for putting his hands on her. Although she smacked him first he wishes he could have restrained himself. After all the smack was painless. "Lil Bit! Get over here!" She steps onto Grove Street as if he hasn't said a word to her.

He pushes the door open and gets out. As he's walking away something comes to mind and forces him to double back toward the truck. From the floor he grabs hold of her pocketbook and from the seat he grabs her airline ticket confirmation paper. He walks away from the truck, leaving the door wide open and the engine running.

///// CHAPTER 76 /////

Amber decided to give it a second shot. She cruises up Bloomfield Avenue in her Rover. It's a wonder she still has her truck after Maurice left it running in the car theft capital of the world. The minute she saw his truck pass her yesterday on Grove Street she took off in flight to get back to her truck. Never did she imagine he would leave it in the parking lot still running. Knowing how ignorant and stubborn he can be at times, she shouldn't have been shocked in the least bit.

She makes a right turn into the shopping center and creeps throughout the parking lot in search of Maurice's truck. After obtaining more than enough sleep she finally regained temporary control of her emotions. Before falling asleep, she promised herself that she would never speak to him again. When she woke up and realized that he's her source of living she immediately realized that she would have to break that promise.

Maurice is well aware of how stubborn she can be which is why he took her pocketbook. He hoped that her wanting it back would be reason enough for her to stay in touch with him. He also knew that her pride wouldn't allow her to call him for it so he called her instead. During the phone call he expressed to her that he had a lot to say to her and it should be said face to face. At this point her reason for coming had nothing to do with the pocketbook or the talk he wants to have with her. Her sole reason for coming is because she's in real need of the money that she will make for making his run to Jamaica.

She parks a few feet away from the Staples entrance, directly across from Maurice's pick-up truck. As soon as she slams the gear shift into park Maurice comes stepping toward her with her pocketbook in his hand. He climbs into the truck and closes the door behind him.

At his entrance, she turns away stubbornly, looking out of her window. He gets agitated instantly as soon as he hears the voice of singer, Jennifer Hudson's voice singing. Lil Bit bops her head mumbling the words along with her. "I don't like...living under your spotlight."

Maurice drops her purse onto her lap. "Yo, you got something you want to talk to me about?" he asks while looking in her direction. She doesn't reply with words just a shaking of her head from side to side. Damn, she says to herself. Now would be the perfect time for me to break the news to him. If only I had the nerve to do it. "You sure?" She nods her head up and down. "You positive?"

He's starting to make her nervous. What is he talking about she asks herself. Does he know something? "What are you talking about?" she asks nervously.

He peeks to the right of him before sighing. "Hmphh. Bust it. I did something I shouldn't have done but fuck it. It's done already. I looked through your pocketbook," he admits shamefully.

"You what?" she barks. Her heart pumps vigorously as she thinks of what he could have seen in the pocketbook. She desperately tries to remember everything that she has in there. "How the fuck could you invade my privacy like that?"

"I was bugging. The way you been acting lately made me feel like you're up to something. I was hoping to find out what it is that you're up to. I been thinking. This shit ain't me. Begging for pussy, looking through your pocketbook

213

and fighting you and shit. I'm playing myself. Seems like to me, you got your mind made up already. It's obvious that somebody got your mind all twisted and I ain't got time to untwist it for you. I ain't gone try to talk you out of nothing that you want to do. You a grown ass woman. Do you. I was out of place yesterday and I apologize. From here on out we can keep this all strictly business. I won't cross the line ever again. Whenever it get to the point that me and you physically fighting, somebody gotta step up and end it. I'm gone be the one to do so. You still my little peoples," he says as he looks at her waiting for a reaction.

Little peoples, she repeats to herself. It burns her up inside but she restrains herself from saying something because she knows that's exactly what he wants.

"I just can't fuck with you like that though. Here," he says as he passes her the print out of her flight information. "From here on out this is what it is, no more no less," he bluffs while hoping she tries to talk him out of his decision. He passes her six, one hundred dollar bills. "Your flight leaves out at eight tonight."

She wonders what he could have seen in her pocketbook that has him reacting like this. Whatever it is has served the purpose. She feels good to know that everything she wanted to say, he has. The only thing not mentioned is her being pregnant. She wonders if he knows. Damn, did I leave something in my pocketbook from the doctor, she asks herself. Maybe my iron pills, she says. Her curiosity is driving her crazy. She almost wants to go through the pocketbook right here in front of him.

He pushes the door wide open and steps one foot onto the asphalt. "Oh, so they let ol boy out huh?"

"Huh?" she asks as she wonders who ol boy is.

"The piece of shit ass nigga, Craig," he says, referring to Star's father.

A light bulb pops up in her head as she thinks of the letter she received from the State. Yesterday she received a letter in her post office box that ripped her apart. The letter was a part of the reason she was so pissed off yesterday. The letter stated that under 'Megan's Law' her and Star had to be notified that he was being released from prison.

Reading that letter brought her into tears. All the trauma he's forced them to live with for the rest of their lives and after only a few short years he's released from prison, free to go on with his life. Her faith in the justice system at this point is none.

"I can't believe you invaded my privacy like that. You had no business in my pocketbook in the first place."

"Why didn't you tell me?"

"You didn't give me a chance to before you got in touching shit you had no business touching," she says referring to him groping her.

"Oh yeah?" he utters with sarcasm. "That's how you feel about it, huh? It's all good," he smiles. "I won't be touching shit else that I shouldn't be touching. Not on you, anyway," he says as he slams the door and walks away from the truck. "You can bet your bottom dollar on that!"

"Thank you," she whispers.

////// CHAPTER 77 //////

Two Days Later. The black on black Chevy Envoy cruises through the darkness of the quiet suburban housing complex. It's 3:30 in the morning and there's no movement whatsoever. Samad peeks around attentively in search of any car that he might be familiar with. As of right now he sees not a single one.

This apartment complex seems to be the perfect little lay low hideout. After Shakirah located this spot for him he was more than willing to take it but his final judgment depended all on this tour. He decided that the perfect hour to check out the area would be late at night. He believes by this hour, the majority of people are home sleeping, which gives him the opportunity to find out who his neighbors will be. That strategy was taught to him by who else but Lil Bit?

"What you think?" Samad asks from the passenger's seat. He looks over at D-Nice awaiting his reply.

"I don't recognize none of these cars," he says while looking around. "It looks like a go."

"That's what it is then."

Meanwhile Miles Away. Maurice sits in the living room of the Bat Cave. He lounges out on the loveseat, barely able to keep his eyes open. He's been dozing on and off for hours. After a deep nod, he peeks into the kitchen that he calls the laboratory.

In the lab a group of men crowd around working like slaves. So many kilos are stacked on the kitchen floor that no one can move throughout the room. It's almost 4 in the morning and their job is barely half way done. They've already converted all the kilos and now they're repackaging them.

Once that process is completed, 200 birds will be ready to fly out of the cave and that they will. The cocaine drought has been great for Maurice's business. Each day his crew is picking up more and more clientele. He has never worked this hard in all his years of hustling. Trying to keep his clients supplied has been a full time job.

By noon all these kilos will be distributed and he will be back at square one, trying to find more transporters to send on his journey. All 200 of these have been pre-ordered days ago. The ten that Lil Bit is bringing back is accounted for as well. Lately his work seems to never end.

Maurice picks up his phone and starts dialing. As he listens to the phone ring, he leans back with his eyes closed. The caller picks up. "Yo?" he whispers groggily.

"What's the word?" Maurice asks.

"Everything is everything," the caller replies.

"Cool. She should be coming through any minute now. Don't move until I call you. Hit me," he says before ending the call. As soon as that call is ended he starts dialing again.

"Yeah?" the man utters from the passenger's seat of the black on black Buick Enclave. Through the dark tinted windows the passenger as well as the driver keep their eyes fixed on the huge factory building.

"What up?" Maurice asks. "Ya'll on point?"

"No question," the man whispers.

"Ok. Hit me as soon as."

///// CHAPTER 78 /////

The Next Morning

D-Nice's mom stands in the kitchen area of the empty two bedroom apartment. She leans over the countertop as she signs her name on the dotted line of the lease. "Here we go," she says as she passes it over to the Caucasian woman that stands before her.

In return the woman hands her two sets of keys. "Ok, Miss Bey. Enjoy your new apartment."

Minutes later Miss Bey walks out of the apartment and gets into the Chevy Envoy. "All done," she says as she passes the keys to the backseat where Samad sits.

Samad looks at the keys in his hand with great appreciation. All of his goals have been met at this point. He exhales a big sigh of relief. He suddenly feels light as if the burden on his shoulders has been lifted.

As D-Nice exits the parking lot of their new home, both him and Samad entertain their very own thoughts. Coincidentally they both have the same thing on their mind and that is meeting their next goal of conquering the world.

Meanwhile in Jamaica

Lil Bit sits on one end of the long marble table while Muhsee sits at the other end. On the table before them there sits a huge spread which consists of fruits, vegetables and many Jamaican dishes that Muhsee calls breakfast.

She has sampled everything on the table and finds only one thing to actually taste good. That happens to be the fresh squeezed orange juice that she's getting full off of. Just as she gulps the last swallow of juice that's in her glass a middle aged woman runs over to the table and fills her glass once again for the tenth time.

Muhsee coughs hard after taking a pull of his weed. Before eating or drinking, the first thing he did was light up his smoke. After the coughing session, he finally speaks. "Thank you for blessing me with your beauty this morning," he says with great charm.

She blushes away. "Thank you, Muhsee."

"No...thank you," he says while staring into her hazel eyes.

His eyes penetrate her soul, making her feel extremely uncomfortable. "What?" she asks with a goofy looking smile on her face.

He shrugs his shoulders. "Nothing. I'm just admiring your beauty. What would it take to bring you into my world? I have everything as you can see," he says as he opens his arms wide. "To the naked eye one may think that I'm happy. Most would be if they had just a fraction of what I have. I have money, power and respect and still I'm miserable because I have no one to share it with. What's the use of having it all if you have no one to enjoy it with you? Having you here with me to share and enjoy it all would make me the happiest man in the world. I would then be complete," he says before taking another drag of his smoke. "Just name it. Anything! Name your price."

"Muhsee, I'm not for sale. Money can't buy you love."

"I'm sure enough of it can," he replies arrogantly. "We can take it all one step at a time. He pulls the smoke once again. After letting it marinate in his mouth he blows it out through his nostrils. He coughs again. "First step is moving in with me. You can fall madly in love with me later."

She smiles. "Muhsee," she whines.

"What?" he asks with a smile. "You move in and we don't even have to sleep in the same bed. We don't even have be in the same part of the house. You can have the back quarters all to yourself, just you and your servants. They will wait on you hand and foot. You won't have to scratch you own ass if you don't want to," he says with a grin. "You don't even have to see me if you don't want to," he says with desperation in his eyes.

"Muhsee, what kind of relationship would that be?"

"Our relationship."

Muhsee's persistence turns Amber on. The harder she fights to push him away the harder he fights to get close to her. His desire for her overrides his loyalty to Maurice. She tells him over and over that her and Maurice are a happy couple but that seems not to matter to him.

He realizes he should never mix business with pleasure and at no cost should he allow a woman to get in between him and a client. Maurice is one of his most valuable clients and he would hate to lose him but Lil Bit is so irresistible to him that he can't help himself.

"How can you be happy with your situation?" he asks. "You claim to love him right?"

"Yes," she says in reply.

"Well, did you ever think that maybe he doesn't love you the same? How could he? If he loves you would he allow you to risk your life and your freedom, sending you back and forth here? Strapping your body with enough kilos to send you to prison for the rest of your beautiful life?"

He just stabbed her in the heart. She can't deny that he's speaking the absolute truth. She does believe that Maurice has love for her but she doesn't believe that he was ever in love with her. She's sure if he really loved her the way she loved him at one time, he would never send her over here. This is more of a reason to chalk their relationship up as business and not even care how he feels about her moving on with her life.

As Muhsee is puffing away, he thinks of the possibility of Lil Bit going back to the States and telling Maurice what he said to her. He's sure that could have a negative effect on their business dealings. He bears witness that women have started wars. This is definitely one war that he's willing to fight if he was guaranteed to get the woman in the end. At this point there is no guarantee of that so as of now he would hate to lose Maurice as a client. It would be meaningless to lose Maurice as a client and blow his chances of getting her.

"I trust that what's said and done in my home remains in my home. Between me and you right?" he asks with a look of coldness in his eyes. She finds the look to be extremely threatening. "Everything is not for everybody," he adds.

She covers her fear with a bright smile. "I trust that you will remember that as well."

///// CHAPTER 79 /////

The Next Night

Lil Bit stands in front of her building as Maurice pulls up. She walks to the passenger's seat of his truck. In her hand she's carrying a small suitcase which is packed with the ten kilos of cocaine that he sent her for. Another successful trip and hopefully many more are to come.

She climbs into the truck. "Hey," she says rather casually. As soon as she's seated he presses the secret code buttons to his stash box and his floor opens up. He dumps the suitcase into the box and hits a few more buttons. In seconds the floor is back to normal. He immediately pulls off. "Where you going?" she asks curiously. "I didn't lock my door."

"It's cool. We'll be right back," he says before blasting his stereo at high volume. The Big Payback by James Brown blares through the speakers. Hearing this song makes her wonder what his purpose is in playing it. They cruise without saying a word to each other. They're just listening to the song play over and over.

In approximately twenty minutes, Maurice makes the right turn onto the small, dark, one way block of South Fifth Street. Amber watches attentively. Halfway down the block he pulls over and parks behind a vehicle that she's completely familiar with. The Buick Enclave is one of the Federation's vehicles. Both worry and confusion sets in her heart quickly because she knows when this vehicle comes out something isn't right. But what, she asks herself.

"Come on," he says as he's getting out of the truck. He peeks around cautiously making her really panicky. She's quite hesitant to get out with him but still she does. She follows him a few steps behind. She peeks around nervously as they walk toward a big abandoned looking house. Maurice leads her to an extremely dark and narrow alley.

She stops at the entrance. "What's back there?" she asks nervously. All kinds of crazy thoughts start to fill her mind. She wonders why he's taking her back there. After their last episode she doesn't trust him. The way that he's been acting is kind of crazy to her. She still wonders what exactly he saw in her pocketbook. She looked throughout the pocketbook over and over and didn't find anything leading to Samad or her pregnancy unless of course Maurice took whatever he found. Maybe that is why she couldn't find it?

Suddenly an even crazier thought comes into her mind. Maybe Muhsee told him about the work that she's taken from him? She didn't even have to ask for it this last time. He talked her into taking it. Maybe it was all a trap just to see if she would fall for the bait and cross Maurice? Or maybe Muhsee just told on her before she could tell on him. She sensed it in Muhsee's voice yesterday that he was a little bit nervous of her telling Maurice about his proposition to her. That thought makes her even more afraid to go in the back with him. "What's back there?" she asks again with even more nervousness.

"Come on," he demands. "I got something for you," he says before walking into the darkness. "Come on!" he shouts from the back of the alley.

She slow steps with worry as Maurice taps on the side door of the raggedy house. Just as she gets closer to him, the door opens. Maurice holds the door wide open while she steps inside into the pitch darkness. The foul smell of the funky old house is stomach turning. Her heart races a mile a minute as she hears the creaking of the door behind her. It's all playing out like a scene from a horror movie.

An image stands before her. She can't see the man's face but she does recognize his voice. It's Black, a member of the Federation. "This way," Black says as he leads them down a small staircase. She can't see in front of her so she grabs the back of his t-shirt and holds on for dear life.

"Maurice what is this all about?" she whispers with fear. "Why are we here?"

"Just walk," he demands. His aggression is scaring her.

At the bottom of the staircase a faint light shines dimly in the background. Black stops at the entrance of the doorway waiting for Maurice to catch up. "That way," he points into the direction of what appears to be the bathroom. He leads them right into that direction. They climb over radiators and garbage just to get there. Lil Bit peeks into the room where three other members of the Federation stand in the candlelit bathroom. They stand around the tub in a huddle. She tries to peek over their shoulders to see what they're looking at but she can't see over them.

Maurice pushes her gently toward the tub as she puts up a little bit of resistance in fear of what may happen to her. "Watch out," he says to his crew. They slide to the side, giving Lil Bit full view of what is in the tub. What lies before her eyes instills massive fear into her heart. She turns away from the sight quickly. "What's wrong?" he asks. "We put him on ice to preserve him for you until you got back," he says demonically. She trembles with fear.

In the tub, lying on a bed of tiny ice cubes lays a man. He's barely conscious. He's ass naked and hog tied. His face is so swollen that at first he doesn't look familiar to her. She fixes her eyes on the man, studying his face and in seconds she knows exactly who he is. Seeing him laying here sends a chill up her spine.

This man is Star's father. His body is badly bruised and swollen as well. Bloodstains cover his face and his body. New blood drips from his swollen eye as if the wound just happened. On his chest are spots where the skin has been burned off of him down to the pink meat. From the looks of him, he's been beat severely.

"Give him more ice," Maurice demands. From the floor each man grabs a bag of ice in their latex glove, covered hands. They dump the ice onto him, emptying their bags. As the cold ice touches his naked flesh, he trembles frantically. He looks up with fear in his eyes. He's so weak that he doesn't have the energy to utter a word. They've come close to beating the life out of him for an entire day now.

After jotting down the man's address from the letter Lil Bit received, Maurice ordered his men to stake out the man's house and follow him. They tailed him from home to work and back home again on one day. The next day they kidnapped him a few blocks away from his factory job. He's been here getting tortured ever since.

The man peeks through his half closed eyes. He sees Lil Bit and now it all makes sense to him. Up until now he had not a clue of what any of this abuse was about. He just thought he was living out a long nightmare. Through the look in his eyes he begs for his life. "Lil Bit," he manages to utter from his chalky, blistered lips. She looks at him and all the torture that he's put her through comes to mind. She actually reenacts in her head the things that he's done to her. Her mother's screams and pleas can be heard clearly in her mind. Suddenly she pictures him molesting her little sister. She shakes her head from side to side to shake the vision away but it won't go anywhere. All of a sudden she becomes highly enraged. The look in her eyes is of the devil himself.

"It's the big payback!" Maurice shouts as he lifts his foot high in the air and drops his size 12 onto the top of the man's head. "You like touching little girls, huh?" he asks as he kicks him again. "Huh?" he asks before stomping the man brutally. "What you got to say for yourself now?" Maurice kneels down and gets close to the man's face. Amber watches with great appreciation. She always said she would get even with him but she never really believed that the opportunity would present itself. "Now, you're at her mercy," Maurice smiles satanically. "What the fuck you have to say for yourself now? You filthy, perverted piece of shit! You wanna beg for mercy don't you? You want to apologize don't you?" he says with a smile. "I know you do but guess what? We're not accepting," he says as he looks up at Lil Bit. She's never seen him this angry. His face looks like that of a demon. Foam is building up in both corners of his mouth. "Black give her your gun." Black does as he's instructed to. "Take it!" Maurice demands as Lil Bit stands there frightened to death. "Take the gun!"

She grabs it with fear. She looks at the huge revolver that is dangling loosely in her hand. It trembles like a leaf.

"Lil Bit, grab the gun tight," he instructs her. "Grab it! Now aim it right at his bitch ass head," he says as he steps behind her. He nestles his body close to hers, reaching over her shoulders. He clasps his hands over hers around the gun. He looks down the barrel, aiming at the bull's-eye which is the center of the man's forehead. He begins to whisper in her ear. "All the pain he put you and little God daughter through," he whispers. "Violating ya'll and taking advantage of ya'll. Now it's your turn to get even. You always said you pray that you can get even. Well, your prayers have been answered," he whispers. "He's at your mercy. Don't you want to get even? Look at him," he whispers. "Look in his eyes. He's as scared as you were when he entered your bedroom at night. What about your mother?" he asks. "He beat the poor woman to a pulp before your eyes. Get even for her. You know she's watching. Do it for her," he says as he backs away, leaving her standing there with the gun tight in her grip and aimed precisely. She's a wreck right now but she refuses to let Star's father and any of the other men see her cry. Instead she lets the tears drip down her heart. As he looks up into her eyes, he begs for sympathy but she feels none for him.

"On the count of three, I want you to squeeze the trigger and blow his fucking head off! One!" Maurice shouts. Amber stands there trembling. Her heart is racing and her palms are sweaty. "Two!" She's now scared out of her mind. She closes her eyes and tightens her grip. "Three!" She stands there with her eyes still closed trying to make herself squeeze but she can't.

Boc, boc, boc, boc! The gunshots sound off, leaving a ringing in everyone's ears. The smell of gunfire fills the air. She opens one eye at a time only to find the man lying lifelessly in the tub, with his head dangling onto his chest. His face is a bloody mess. The tub of ice is filled with blood now as well, making the tub look like one huge blood slushie. She looks to the right where she sees Maurice standing over the man with his gun still aimed. Boc! He fires once again.

"Let's go," Sal whispers as he grabs hold of any loose ends that could lead to them. He then trots toward the door and the other four men follow him. Maurice pries the gun from Lil Bit's grip as she stands there in shock. He grabs her by the arm and drags her out of the room, leaving her dead stepfather, lying in the tub leaking like the filthy pig that he is.

It's the big payback!

////// CHAPTER 80 //////

Samad cruises at a moderate speed up Route 280 West. He's just left Lil Bit's house. She called him this morning an hour and a half ago stating that she's returning his call. The only problem with that is he's been calling her ever since 10:00 last night.

After last night's episode Lil Bit was in a state of shock and just got hold of herself this morning. She hasn't been able to sleep a wink. The murder of her sister's father replayed over and over in her head all night long. She was so consumed with those thoughts that calling Samad didn't even come to mind. She just sat in her room in a trance. She totally isolated herself. She didn't answer the phone nor answer Star who knocked on her door several times. Although Craig was what he was, he's still Star's father. She couldn't even face her sister let alone tell her what had happened. This is one secret that she will keep from her sister for the rest of their lives.

The moment Samad walked into the apartment he started ranting and raving. They haven't seen each other in ten days and he should have been happy to see her but instead he walked in the door full of rage. She told him she would be back last night at ten and he expected her to be. After calling over and over and getting no reply, he automatically assumed she was with another man. Lil Bit gives him no reason to believe that she's messing around on him but his lack of trust comes from his own self-esteem issues. Deep down inside he doesn't believe that he's worthy of her. He's sure she could have a man of more stature than him. As long as he believes that, he will be haunted by those thoughts.

She had no logical explanation to give him for returning his calls this morning. There's no way in the world she would ever tell him what she witnessed last night. That was for her eyes only. She gave him a weak story about how she fell asleep the moment she got in. He didn't buy that for one second. He was hoping to hear a better lie than that. Feeling disrespected that she would even play on his intelligence, he didn't hesitate to let her have it. He accused her of all his suspicions.

Little does he know she heard not a word of what he was saying to her. His yelling went in one ear and out of the other. The more causal she appeared to act the more frustrated he became. He had no clue that she was not in a stable frame of mind. Right while he was in the act of shouting his head off like a baby, she found the perfect way to pacify him. She handed him the souvenir that she brought back for him and in minutes his shouting and screaming was all over with.

Samad spots a State Trooper sitting in the cut, up ahead about a mile away. He looks at his speedometer which reads 73 miles an hour, he immediately steps on the brakes, trying to decelerate. Just as he approaches the trooper he looks at the speedometer once again. He still happens to be going just a little bit faster than he should. He looks straight ahead as he passes the trooper. The last thing he wants is for them to lock eyes. That usually results in getting pulled over. Just as he gets a half a mile away, he looks in his rearview mirror and happens to see the trooper peeling out of the cut. His lights are flashing and he's speeding.

"Oh shit!" Samad shouts out. "Damn," he sighs. He's scared shitless. He looks over to the passenger's seat where the plastic shopping bag sits. Inside the bag is the souvenir that Lil Bit brought back just for him. As soon as he grabs the bag a huge whiff of pure cocaine blows into the air. The vapors fill the entire car. He tucks the bag under his seat. He then straps his seatbelt as he watches the trooper through his rearview mirror. He's catching up with Samad rapidly. His heart is jumping out of his chest.

To get caught with this kilo will be a living nightmare. He's sure that there is no coming back after that. He's going to have a sky high, ransom bail that he can't make and once he's convicted he's sure he'll get sentenced to life. "Damn," he whines, just thinking of all of this. Anxiety takes over his body, causing him to black out. Suddenly, he stares straight ahead in a deep zone. The zone is so deep that he doesn't notice the trooper fly right past him. It's not until the trooper gets two miles away and pulls another car over that he finally snaps out of the zone. Samad zips right past the trooper. "Phew," he sighs.

Meanwhile In Jersey City

Lil Bit sits on the edge of the couch, staring over the coffee table into Sade's eyes. At this point Lil Bit really needs to vent and the only person in the world that she trusts enough to vent to is Sade. "So, he takes me into the basement of an abandoned house," she says as the scene replays over in her mind. "When I get down there, he was laying in a tub of ice, naked. He looked a mess. You could tell he had been beaten severely."

"Who is he?" Sade asks, not having a clue of who she's talking about.

Lil Bit ignores her and just continues on with her story. The look in her eyes is quite delirious. "Then they gave me the gun and told me to squeeze the trigger," she says as she shakes her head from side to side. "I gripped the gun and closed my eyes. As bad as I wanted to I couldn't kill him."

"Him who?" Sade asks with frustration.

"Then I hear boom, boom, boom, boom. I open my eyes and there he is laying in a pool of icy blood."

"Who is he?"

"Oh...Star's father."

"What?" she barks with shock. "He's out of jail? When did he get out? How did ya'll find him?"

"I didn't find him," she says defensively. "He was released a couple of days ago."

"So, how did ya'll find out that he was home?"

"When I checked my p.o. box, I had a letter from the state about Megan's Law and all. Whenever a sexual offender is being released, people have to be notified. And the rest is a long story," she sighs. "Me and Maurice got into a big fight the other day. I ended up hopping out of my truck leaving him there. He takes my pocketbook and looks through it. He finds the letter and when I got back they got him in the basement. All the middle details I know nothing about," she claims. "I had nothing to do with it, Sade. I swear!"

Sade watches with sympathy. "Damn girl. I have to be honest with you. This doesn't look good at all. You get a letter telling you that he's been released and the next day he's murdered. What if they try to charge you with it? After all you do have all the probable cause in the world to murder him."

With all of the problems that she has going on in her life at this point does she really have room for one more? "I know," she says as the tears build up in her eyes. "I know."

///// CHAPTER 81 /////

Four Days Later. Samad sits back in his rental, puffing the last of his smoke and sipping on Remy. He's dead tired and can't wait to get to Lil Bit's house. The only thing that has been on his mind the last few hours has been crawling up in the bed next to her. It's been quite some time now and they are both way overdue.

His shift is a few minutes short of ending. Today has been another productive day for him. Now that D-Nice is home it has not been as lucrative because now they're back to splitting up the shifts. Before, everything that came in was his alone. In that little time he had gotten quite used to that. Although the proceeds are being divided, Samad still has nothing to complain about. He still averages from eight to ten grand a day on his shift.

D-Nice pulls up in his rented Envoy. He double parks right next to Samad. The window rolls down slowly. "What's good, nigga?" he greets.

"Same shit," Samad replies casually. Samad peeks around cautiously. Just like employees punching the clock, members of D-Nice's shift are pulling up and parking. They're ready to put in their hours. They line their cars along the block. Just as they're parking, the members of Samad's crew are walking toward their cars.

Samad has gotten rentals from his man Mike for the entire block. He promised them that he would take care of them for helping him out during his crisis and this is just the beginning. He paid for the first week for everybody's vehicle but it's their duty to pay the tab on them, though. They don't realize that paying $6,000 for each of them to get a car is nothing compared to the money that they made him. They're all just happy to be driving.

Mike said that $6,000 was just the push he needed to really get things popping. He said he will now be able to get another 3 cars. All in all he has close to twenty cars speeding through the streets of Newark. Samad plans to invest with Mike the moment he can see above water. Mike's plan appears to be foolproof.

"Yo, how you looking?" D-Nice asks.

"As far as what?"

"As far as work? I'm working on my last bit tonight," says D-Nice. "You got a lot left?"

"Yeah," he replies. Of course he does. The kilo that they split up has been finished. He's now working on the kilo that Lil Bit gave him. A part of him feels guilty that he's holding out on his good friend but the other part feels like he owes him nothing. He bailed him out and he's set him up with a half a kilo. What more can he ask for?

The kilo Lil Bit gave him is just what he needed to take him over the top. He couldn't believe that she was still able to give him the kilo at $20,500 which is seven thousand dollars cheaper than what he paid at the last deal. That can only be blamed on ignorance. She has no clue that a drought is going on and the entire town has raised the price of their work. Samad has no plans on telling her either.

The half a kilo and the extra 200 grams that he whipped up scored him approximately $35,000. The kilo Lil Bit gave him this time was even better than the first one that she gave him or either he is getting better at whipping. This time he managed to squeeze a little bit short of 500 grams extra. When it's all said and done he will be in the best position of his life. All in all he's in a good place but he can see that it can get a lot better.

Just a couple of months ago he couldn't even feed himself. Now he has close to fifty grand saved up. Before now he's never seen fifty grand at one time. On top of the fifty grand he has over sixty thousand dollars worth of crack. If all goes well he should be touching his first hundred thousand real soon. He's sure once he achieves that goal nothing will be able to stop him.

"Damn, I'm gone need some work," D-Nice sighs. "After tonight, I'm stuck like Chuck!"

All of a sudden Samad gets a bright idea which consists of him capitalizing off of D-Nice's desperation. The look in D-Nice's eyes and the sound of his voice tells Samad that he will do anything to get hold of some work. Samad wonders if he should ask D-Nice to help him sell his work so they can speed up the process. He realizes that would be outright deceitful but it will help him to achieve his hundred thousand dollar mark that much faster.

"Come on 'B'! We gotta do something," D-Nice says desperately. "I need work! Call the coach!" he shouts with sarcasm.

Meanwhile in Jersey City

Lil Bit lies in her bed tossing and turning with much aggravation. Her phone starts to ring for the hundredth time. After the third ring the phone beeps, letting her know that her battery is now dead. "Thank you," she sighs. "Finally," she says as she rolls over onto her stomach and slams the pillow over her head.

Maurice has been calling her for the past two hours. She answered the first time and he apologized about his behavior the other night. He explained to her that when he said that he wanted to keep it business that was just talk. He asked if she could ever forgive him. Although she has already forgiven him she didn't tell him that. She plans to ride this wave for as long as she possibly can. She just hopes that he eventually gets tired of her rejecting him and finally let her be.

He told her that he was on his way to her house and she told him not to. He begged and pleaded with her but still she denied. Her plan was to break the news to him but it's better that she didn't have to. By him starting the argument he did the work for her. He may have started the beef but she sure as hell plans to finish it.

Maurice paces back and forth in front of Lil Bit's building. He's been here for the past hour and a half and doesn't plan on leaving until she lets him in. The phone is glued to his ear as he awaits the phone to start ringing. Instead it goes straight to voicemail. "Lil Bit, please just hear me out. I made a mistake and now more than ever I realize what you mean to me. I need to talk to you. You may as well come downstairs cause I'm not leaving until you do!" he says with determination. "I ain't going nowhere."

One Hour later

Maurice has finally gotten tired of calling and getting no reply. He zips up the block with anger. He's so angry that he almost runs through the red light. He slams on the brakes abruptly. His huge highbeams illuminate the dark block. The entire street is bare all except for the small car that sits across the street on the opposite side, at the traffic ligfht as well.

Samad sits at the traffic light, barely able to keep his eyes open. In just a few seconds he has dozed off three times already. The bright lights coming from the huge pick-up truck hypnotizes him, causing him to keep his eyes open and glued onto the grill of the truck.

Suddenly the light changes and the two vehicles pass each other. Samad attempts to look into the truck but the windows are too dark. Little does he know the driver is staring into his car as well. They both watch their rearview mirrors until they are out of each other's sight.

///// CHAPTER 82 /////

Two Days Later

Lil Bit steps into the beauty parlor and all eyes are on her as usual. All the customers here know her and respect her. They all have high admiration for her. They secretly watch her and try to copy her style. They look to her as if she's a Vogue magazine. She sets the trends and they follow.

Normally she prances in here like a supermodel but today she doesn't feel sexy at all. She's dressed in fitted Juicy Couture sweatpants and two dollar flip flops. The black Juicy t-shirt, she wears strategically to conceal her pregnancy. The enormous Dior sunglasses she wears to make her nose, which has spread across her face, appear smaller.

She walks toward Deja's empty chair. Deja stares her up and down, making her feel way uncomfortable. Lil Bit slowly snatches her shades from her face and looks away shamefully. She feels like Bozo the clown because her conscious tells her she has the biggest reddest nose.

"Damn girl, something about you is different today," Deja says while examining her. Her statement has put Lil Bit on full blast. Now everyone that heard her is staring as well. Lil Bit looks around in every direction but Deja's. "I can't put my finger on it but something is different though. You glowing girl," she smiles. "Somebody getting it in," she teases.

"Girl, please," Lil Bit blushes.

"Nah, your white ass glowing like a lightening bug."

Lil Bit seats herself in the chair while Deja has her eyes glued onto her. "Girl, do my hair please!" she smiles.

Deja spins her around to face the mirror. She has Lil Bit's hair in a bunch, pinned into a pony tail. She stares at her closely. Suddenly a grin pops onto Deja's face. She leans over close enough to whisper in Lil Bit's ear. "I know you not pregnant?" she asks as she curiously waits for a reply. Lil Bit smiles bashfully without replying. "Well, are you?"

Meanwhile

Samad walks out of the corner store. The record breaking heat of 99 degrees beats on him. He stands there just watching the activity of the block as he sucks on a 25 cent freeze pop to cool him off. Today is going great just as all of his recent days have gone. Something tells him that better days are to come now that he's talked D-Nice into helping him move the work that he has left. In order to get his hands on some work, he had no problem signing on his crew members to shake Samad's work on his shift. He knows one hand washes the other and right now he needs his hands washed. Between two shifts, Samad figures it shouldn't take him longer than 4 days to finish the work. In less than a weeks time he plans to be the 'Hundred Thousand Dollar Man.'

As he walks up the block to get back to his car, the loud noise of tires screeching snatches his attention. He turns around in that direction. "Freeze!" shouts the suit and tie wearing detective. His gun is aimed right at Samad's head.

The detective walks from the passenger's side slowly. Suddenly tires screech from every direction. In seconds Samad is surrounded by three more unmarked police cars and two unmarked police vans. Detectives hop out of all those vehicles as well. All of them have their guns drawn and aimed.

Samad looks around with fear in his eyes. "Move and you'll make the news!" the detective threatens. "Front page," he adds. "One move and today you will rest in peace! Hands on your head!" Samad looks at all the .40 caliber guns and does exactly as he's instructed. "Now drop to your knees!" Samad collapses onto the ground with extreme fear and the moment he lands on the ground three detectives swarm him. One of them tackles him onto the ground and starts frisking him immediately.

He lays there wondering what this is all about. The detective snatches him by the arms and cuffs him. "Yo, what's up? What I do? Ya'll must have the wrong guy. I didn't do nothing," he says with fear. The detective lifts him by the cuffs, choking his wrists terribly.

As Samad stands there in pain, another detective walks over holding a stack of papers in his hand. The detective stares at Samad, examining his face and then he looks down at the paper. "This you, right?" he asks as he shoves the paper close to Samad's face. "You Samad Brown, right?" Samad looks at the mugshot of him and paralysis takes over his body. "This you right?" He doesn't even bother to answer the detective. He stares at his photo with his mouth shut as the detective reads him his rights.

He looks around and realizes that this can't be drug related because all of his crew members are huddled up down the block looking at him. "Under arrest? For what?"

Deja spins the chair around as she teases away at Lil Bit's hair. Lil Bit faces the glass window and what she sees before her eyes sets fear and despair in her heart. The pearl white Harley Davidson motorcycle parks directly in front of the shop. Even though the glare from the sparkling chrome trimming has her blinded she still knows exactly who the rider of the bike is. "Phew," she sighs as she sees Maurice walking toward the door.

Deja spots him as well. She presses the buzzer immediately to let him inside. He walks in wearing a tight wife beater, exposing his bulky, muscular frame. His half a helmet would expose his face if it were not for the huge, dark, aviator shades that cover his eyes and the black bandana that covers his nose and drapes down over his neck. As soon as he snatches the helmet from his head, he slings his head back arrogantly, shaking his dreads loose. All the women watch him lustfully.

He looks in Lil Bit's direction as he pulls the bandana from over his mouth. A stern look appears on his face as he snatches his shades from his eyes. The look in his eyes is quite intimidating. "Can I speak to you for a minute?" He turns around and walks out, leaving a room full of women with soak 'n wet panties. Lil Bit's panties are wet as well but not from lust. She's so afraid that a little urine has trickled. She dreads to go out there but realizes that she has no choice. She doesn't know what to expect from him because his last calls to her were quite threatening. She hasn't answered his calls and now she wishes she would have.

She walks out of the door cautiously. She looks Maurice square in the eyes with a look of submissiveness. "Maurice, don't embarrass me out here," she says. Her voice is full of demand but her eyes are full of fear.

"Embarrass you?" he says with signs of agitation on his face. "I'm embarrassing now?"

"Maurice, that isn't what I'm saying."

"Well, what are you saying then?" She looks away without answering him. Although she's looking away she keeps her eyes on him just in case he tries to make a move on her. Never before has she ever been afraid of him but now her guilt has her terrified of him. "No answer huh?"

"Maurice, please don't cause a scene?" she begs.

"Why not? If you would have answered the fucking phone I wouldn't be here. This what I gotta do now to speak to you? I gotta trap you the fuck off? Is this what it done came down to? I'm not even worthy of you answering my calls now? I stood out there for hours," he lies in search of her sympathy.

"I told you not to come," she whispers.

"Lil Bit, what is it? Tell me the truth. It's another nigga right? Keep it one hundred with me."

You must think I'm a fool, she thinks to herself. You think I'm gone tell you that so you can kill me out here. Oh how she wishes she could tell him but she knows now is not the time. Embarrassing her would be an understatement. "Maurice it was your own words to keep it business," she reminds him.

"I told you I said that out of rage. That's not what I want."

"See, that's the problem. It's always what you want when you want it," she whines. "What about what I want? Fuck that! What about what I need?"

"What the fuck do you need?" he barks hastily.

"My own man," she blurts out. "I already told you I need more than what you can give me. I can't go on like this. What am I supposed to do just let you come in and fuck me whenever you feel like it? Whenever you can get away from your wife, just let you come in and spend the night. Then wait around until you can get away again? Tell me what am I supposed to do? Just get old and die as your mistress of many mistresses?"

"Lil Bit, you already know my situation," he says in defense of her attack.

"Yeah, yeah, I know," she says rudely. Heard it all before, she sings to herself. "You're married to her but you don't love her. The only reason you're still with her is because of your daughters. Ya'll don't even sleep in the same bed. No need to tell me again. You have already expressed that to me a million times already."

Maurice stands there with a pitiful look on his face. He really feels like he's losing her and it's killing him inside. He's so used to having his way with women that he doesn't know how to handle it when it's not going his way. "Lil Bit, listen without interrupting me please? I been sitting back these couple of days and I realize that I love you more than I've ever loved her."

"But you married her, not me. That was your decision. You chose her over me…simple as that."

"Lil Bit, at that time you were a child, not even seventeen years old," he whines.

"Oh, I was old enough for you to fuck me but not consider me for marriage, right?"

He shakes his head from side to side with hopelessness. "If I knew you would grow up to be half the woman you are today, I would have married you."

"But you didn't. You made your decision and we all have to live with it. Now let me make mines."

"And what is your decision?"

"I want to go on with my life. I want to be somebody's number one."

"You can be my number one," he whispers.

"Maurice, listen to yourself. You're making no sense. How can I be your number one?"

"I'll do anything to make this right. Anything. I told you I don't love her."

"You have your family and I don't want you to leave them for me. Maurice, outside of my sister, I love you more than anybody in this world. It's like you're a brother but you're not my brother because we shared intimate moments. I no longer want to be your playmate." She looks him deep in the eyes as she shakes her head from side to side. "I wish you were my mother's child so I could always be a part of your life and know everything that's going on with you. I want to be supportive of you and I want you to be able to share your deepest darkest secrets with me. I just don't want to share intimacy with you. Honestly, I think I outgrew that...I don't even want to call it a relationship. I think I outgrew our situation." She can see the pain that she's causing him and it's scaring her but she's on a roll and can't stop now. She's almost afraid to say what she's about to say. "I just wanna do me," she whispers.

That phrase tears his heart into shreds. He never thought he would see the day that she would be telling him this. "Do you? And what the fuck does that consist of?"

"Whatever I want to do," she whispers. "Without you governing my movements."

"Somebody got your head all fucked up. Somebody got your mind. All I'm gone tell you is whoever this nigga is he's good. Ask yourself though, is he worth it? Is he worth losing what we have?"

"Maurice, we have nothing."

"Phew," he sighs. "Listen," he says as he digs into his pocket. "Here, take this," he says as he hands her a piece of paper. She reads it over and realizes that it's an airline confirmation print out. Her alias, Latoya Baker is on the top of the paper. "I got two round trip tickets. One for you and one for me. To Hawaii. I know I promised that trip to you almost ten years ago but here it is. Let's just go away and figure out what our next step is."

She stares at the print out. He is absolutely correct. He promised her that vacation back when they first met, ten years ago when she told him that as a child she dreamed of going there. Needless to say, he never kept that promise to her. "Ten years ago that would have been a dream come true to go to my dream place with my dream man. Today it's not that important," she says with sorrow in her eyes. "I can't accept this ticket," she says as she extends her hand toward him.

Tears build up in his eyes. His only back up plan has fallen through and he doesn't know what else to do or say. He backs away from the paper. He stretches his glassy eyes open wide to prevent the tears from falling. "Hold them," he whispers. He backs away quickly trying not to drop a tear in front of her. Tears may be in his eyes but rage is on his face. The tears come from the fact that he realizes that he may have lost her forever. The rage comes from the same fact. He doesn't lose well. He doesn't know how to deal with rejection because he's never been rejected.

He stares at her through his glassy eyes with fury bleeding through them. "Lil Bit, I refuse to let it end like this. Trust and believe me when I tell you, before I lose you to a nigga I'll fuck the game up for everybody," he says before putting his sunglasses on. Just as he does, a single tear drips down his face. He straddles himself over his bike, while strapping his helmet on. Lil Bit watches with confusion. For some reason she takes that as more than a threat and maybe she should.

In minutes he pulls off and speeds up the block recklessly, leaving Lil Bit standing there in a terrible state of confusion. After getting herself together she walks into the beauty parlor. She's in a complete daze. Everyone can feel the tension by the look on her face.

Coincidentally, the song 'Take a Bow' by singer Rihanna rips through the speakers. Rihanna sings beautifully, "You look so dumb right now, standing outside my house, trying to apologize. You're so ugly when you cry. Please! Just cut it out." Her voice stops and the chorus fill in. Deja sings along with them. "But you put on quite a show. Really had me going but now it's time to go. Curtains finally closing. That was quite a show. Very entertaining but it's over now. Go on and take a bow."

///// CHAPTER 83 /////

In the Essex County Jail

Samad sits in the small room dressed in his County Greens. Sitting in front of him is a Caucasian detective. Another Caucasian detective paces back and forth behind Samad, creating an even more tense atmosphere.

Just two minutes ago he finally found out what he's been arrested for. Samad tries hard not to stare at the photos that lie on the table face up. By looking at them he feels he may appear to be guilty to the detectives. He looks over them as nonchalantly as he can. One photo is of a man that he doesn't know at all but his face is quite familiar. The other photo is of Ashy Mu who Samad now knows as Gerard Sanders.

"So, you're telling us that you've never seen these two men in your life?" the detective asks with sarcasm.

"Never," he replies. He attempted to answer it with confidence but the weakness of his voice tells them that he's not telling the truth.

"So, you didn't murder these two men?"

"Murder them?" he asks in a high pitch voice. "Hell no!"

"Well, Mr. Brown we have witnesses who say that you did."

Witnesses, damn, Samad says to himself. But who? The detective comes from behind Samad and sits on the edge of the table right in front of Samad. They sit so close that Samad can smell the onions from the detective's lunch seeping out of his nostrils as he breathes. He sits there quietly. The silence creates even more tension in the room than them actually speaking. "You didn't commit the murders?"

"No," he replies as confidently as he can.

"Okay then take the polygraph test," he suggests as he hands Samad a sheet of paper.

Samad becomes more terrified now. By denying the test he will look guilty but by taking the test they will be sure that he's guilty. They have him between a rock and a hard place. He's damn if he do and damn if he don't.

"Sign the consent form," the detectives urges as he forces the pen on Samad.

Samad sits there not knowing what he should do right now. He realizes anything he says can incriminate him later. He's seen enough cop shows to know that. "I'm not doing anything or saying anything without the presence of my attorney."

Meanwhile. Amber has been in a serious state of depression after receiving Samad's call last night informing her that he's been arrested. He didn't give her any details because he only knew very little. He expressed to her that he would call her the moment he finds out what the deal is.

More and more each day she realizes that maybe she should have listened to Deja about dealing with Samad. She always wanted to be madly in love but never did she think it came at such a high price. She did the analysis and ever since she met him her life has been falling apart. He's starting to be more of a liability than an asset. All her problems are centered around him. She's really starting to believe that having a baby with him may be the dumbest thing that she's ever done. One of the main reasons for believing that is the fact that she's sure to be killed once Maurice finds out. She can't believe that she's put herself in this situation.

Lil Bit sits on the extremely uncomfortable chair, listening attentively as her doctor speaks. She has just completed her pre-natal check up. "The baby seems to be perfectly fine but you are the problem," he says with concern. "There's no way your baby can be healthy if you're not. Your iron is down and your pressure is up at an all time high. I thought you were going to work on your stress issues. It seems as if it has gotten worse. You have to find a way to suppress your stress and keep it to a minimum. Your baby's life depends on it." Easier said than done, she thinks to herself as he's speaking. "What is it that has you like this?" he asks. "I'm sure it can't be that bad."

You think so, she says to herself. Three men have been murdered and all of them link back to me, she says in her mind. One murder was at my command. One murder I'm not the blame for. The other I'm all the blame in the world for. There are two more that I'm going to be accountable for when they finally take place. One of them is the father of this baby and the other is my own life. She shakes her head with misery. If this doctor was a mind reader she would be put under the prison.

"What is it?" he pries.

"Trust me, you don't want to know. If I told you I would have to kill you," she says in a playful manner. I mean that literally, she says to herself as she looks in his eyes.

///// CHAPTER 84 /////

In West Orange. Lil Bit sits in her Rover which is parked in the quiet housing complex of Seven Oaks. She received the call from Samad last night, stating that he's been charged and indicted for a double homicide. There was no need for him to go into anymore details because she knew exactly what murders they're accusing him of.

She called his lawyer first thing this morning so he could get on it ASAP. Right now she's waiting for D-Nice to come out and bring the money needed to get this process rolling and free her dude.

D-Nice walks out casually with a backpack on his back. A look of aggravation is on his face. The sight of Lil Bit makes him furious. "Money grubbing bitch," he mumbles to himself as he steps toward the truck. He hates the fact that Samad even told her where they live. This apartment was supposed to be on the low and he was under the impression that not even Lil Bit was supposed to know. He wishes she didn't because he doesn't trust her as far as he can throw her.

He gets in and sits down in the passenger's seat without even greeting her. His coldness makes her feel uptight as well. She can sense that he doesn't like her but she has no idea why. This is actually their second time ever being around each other. Instead of trying to figure out why he's acting like this toward her, she just gives him her I don't give a fuck attitude as well. "You got that," she says in a manner that is sure to get under his skin.

"Hmphh," he sighs almost silently. "Pull off." She pulls off with no hesitation. Just as they get almost a block away he speaks again. "You can let me out at the corner. I will walk back," he says as he lays the back pack on the middle console. "Here."

"What's in there?" she asks.

"Forty stacks," he replies with a little bit of an attitude.

"Forty? He told me that you had sixty five for me."

"Oh that's what he told you?" he asks sarcastically. He doesn't trust her nor believe a word that she's saying. He feels that she's trying to take the rest of the money and do who knows what with it. That isn't going to happen as long as he's in control. He snickers to himself. You may have my man fucked up but I ain't him, he says to himself. "Oh, he ain't tell me that. You gone have to take that up with him when he get home. That's forty. If he need more, tell him to let me know," he says putting major emphasis on the word me.

She gets the feeling that he doesn't believe what she's telling him. She laughs to herself.

"I'm good right here," he says. He forces the door open while the truck is still rolling. She slams on the brakes unexpectedly causing his body to jolt forward. He hops out and slams the door shut without saying goodbye.

She watches him angrily as he steps away. Suddenly a smile appears on her face. "You little broke ass bastard. I should have left your sorry ass stuck in jail. Sorry ass nigga," she laughs.

He turns around and sees her watching. As he turns his head back to face his direction, a smile appears on his face as well. "Fucking gold digging ass bitch," he mumbles to himself.

Now is that anyway to think about the coach?

Meanwhile

Samad lays back on his bed. He just got moved into Quarantine where he is supposed to be for a week. He has no plans on being here by the time the day is over. Being confined to this tiny cell for 24 hours is not part of his plan. He's pissed off. The last time he was here he promised himself that he would never be here again. He's highly frustrated yet he tries to restrain himself. In just the little time that he's been confined he feels as if he's losing his mind.

The last time he was here he thought being in jail with no bail money was the worst situation a man could be in. Now he realizes that being in here with money is worse. When he was here with no money he thought he had no way of making bail so he just accepted the fact and made himself comfortable here. Now that he has money he refuses to get comfortable. This is a real battle for him. The anticipation of knowing that you're going to make bail but not knowing when is enough to drive a man crazy. He's literally counting the seconds away until his name is called.

Many thoughts run through his mind at a rapid pace. More than anything else the money and drugs that he has left behind is his main concern. The sixty five grand he ordered Lil Bit to take from D-Nice was done out of fear of D-Nice possibly spending the money. He knows that D-Nice isn't a thief but he figures he may try and make a flip with the money.

The money is starting to take over his mind. His greed for the dollar is starting to get the best of him and he doesn't even realize it. He shakes his head from side to side with grief as he thinks of the drugs that he has left. He has just enough to last for about three days. He can't imagine what move D-Nice is going to make after that. All he can pictures is D-Nice messing the money up and him having to start from scratch again. The thought of that scares him to death.

He realizes that he's gotten himself into a sticky situation. A double homicide with witnesses is more than enough to get him sent away for the rest of his life. In the few hours that he's been here he's found a solution to his problem. Without witnesses they will have no case against him. Getting rid of the witnesses will be the easy part of the battle. The harder part will be finding out who they are and locating them. He's more than willing to accept the challenge because his freedom depends on it. Things are just starting to look up for him. He can't imagine going to jail right now. He hasn't had a chance to even live yet and he refuses to let anyone end it for him.

///// CHAPTER 85 /////

Five Days Later

Lil Bit cruises around Newark Airport. In the passenger's seat there sits Deja. She's on her way to one of her favorite places in the world, Dominican Republic. She's not going there as a tourist nor to vacation. Her purpose is solely to enhance her beauty. The beauty enhancement will not cost her a single dime. It's all funded by her new friend in Miami.

"I have to admit, you proved me to be politically incorrect," Lil Bit utters. "I thought for sure he was going to hit it and quit it."

"You actually thought that?" Deja asks arrogantly. "I didn't entertain that thought not one time," she boasts. "To date, no one has ever just hit this and quit it. I've never had that problem. If anything I can't get rid of them after they hit it," she smiles. "See, the difference with me and a lot of women is, I don't get caught up with what a nigga has. Most women get caught up in the money and will give up their soul to him cause he has money, not me. I'll treat a rich nigga the exact same way that I treat a broke nigga," she smiles. "That's how you break them down to size. Rich niggas hide behind their money. Me, I strip them of all that and there they stand in front of me butt naked, just me and him. I get to the core of who he really is. The man he is without the money which is usually an unconfident, low self-esteem having little boy. Once I dig to the core of who he really is, he can't talk to me the way he does other women and he can't treat me how he does other women. Cause deep down inside he feels like I can see right through him and all of his bullshit."

Lil Bit smiles. "Girl, you should be a Gold Digger Professor," she giggles. "You got it all figured out. Bitches would pay you to get all that valuable information you got." At times Lil Bit wishes she had the heart to be like Deja but she doesn't. Even at her lowest point in life when she was a teenager with nothing, she couldn't allow herself to do that. She had many men that would step to her offering her the world but the fact that she had no feelings for them made her deny their offerings. The majority of women would have used them to put themselves in a better position but she couldn't do it. "Girl, I always tell you that I envy the way you move so carefree and heartless. I wish I had that in me but I don't."

"Nah, it's not a matter of being heartless. Lil Bit, I'm a little bit older than you. Next month I will be thirty-five years old. I been around. I been through a lot and I seen a lot. It's a dog eat dog world. Everybody thinks I'm just a gold digger but it's more to me than that. If you come in the door talking about how much money you got, I'm gone put you to the test. At the end of the day if it don't work, who cares? Nothing from nothing leaves nothing. Our relationship was based on money. I like money and he claims to have money," she says sarcastically. "Outside of that we had nothing in common. If bitches could get that concept in their heads they would be alright instead of sitting around broken hearted when these niggas move onto the next bitch. They gotta realize these niggas only playing games. Me, I play right along with them but I set the rules. Lil Bit, my daddy was a hustler before he got murdered. So were all my uncles and my brothers. They always had plenty of money. My daddy brought me home from the hospital when I was four days old in a Mercedes. When I was five years old I got my first dozen roses. It was Valentines Day and he had them delivered to my school. I was chauffeured to my eighth grade graduation in a Rolls Royce. In high school I wore Gucci and every other hot designer. My weekly allowance was five hundred dollars. He was murdered right before my twelfth grade prom so I can only imagine what he would have done for that. My mommy would always tell him to stop spoiling me because he was gone make me worthless. She said he was going to spoil me so bad that no man was ever going to be able to deal with me. She thought he would mess me up for life when in all actuality he prepared me for my life. There's nothing a nigga can do for me or show me that my daddy never done for me or showed me. I can't be teased or manipulated with money because I've always been around money. You gotta do something else to get through to this heart," she says as she taps the center of her chest.

Lil Bit steers to the right as she gets close to the ramp. Deja snatches her suitcase from the backseat, before hopping out. "Later, Girl. I'll see you in a couple of days!" she says as she slams the door shut. She takes two steps before she turns around. She gestures for her to roll the window down. Just as Lil Bit is doing so, Deja begins speaking. "Take your last look at this cute little rear of mine because when I get back you won't even recognize it," she smiles. "It will be a full-sized wagon," she says as she switches away, wagging her tail from side to side like a frisky puppy.

"Crazy Bitch," Lil Bit says to herself. The ringing of her phone interrupts her moment of laughter. She pulls off while answering the phone. "Hello?" The automated service tells her that she has a call from the County Jail. She accepts the call. "Hello?"

"What up, Ma," he says energetically. "What's the deal?" No one could have ever told him that he would still be in here five days later. This time the money isn't the issue. The problem he has seemed to be minute but is actually a bigger deal than coming up with the money. "Yo! My man D-Nice mother said she will sign for me. All you gotta do is go past the house and it's done."

"Ok, good. My girl Deja, she already signed. We just gotta come up with three more signatures."

"Yo, anybody you can think of, let them know I'm willing to put the bread up," he mumbles. "You know what I'm talking bout?"

"Don't worry, I got you. I'm on it. I got some people that I'm going to holler at. I got you covered. Trust me."

"You already know! But yo, dig this, I'm bout to go eat. I'm gone try and call you back later. Be a good girl, you heard?"

"I heard," she laughs.

"Love you!" he shouts before hanging up the phone, not giving her a chance to reply. He spins around and standing before him is one of Newark's terrors.

The scrawny little man appears to be frail and harmless but he will teach a person to never judge a book by its cover. He stands about five feet nine inches tall and only weighs about 135 pounds when he's soak 'n wet. His heart is as big as a lion's and it's made of pure steel. In every aspect of the phrase he's what you call a wolf in sheep's clothing. His huge alien shaped head appears bigger than it is because it's propped onto his skinny frame. His bald head, no facial hair and no eye brows coupled with his cinnamon complexion makes him look sickly like a cancer patient. The only sickness he has is from his diseased heart which makes him as cold as ice.

"Samad what the deal, Big Bruh?" he greets with open arms. His eyes shift sneakily.

"Man, you already know!" Samad feels good to once again come in contact with a familiar face. "Off The Chain, what up!"

"How long you been in here?" he asks.

"I just got out of quarantine. How long you been down here? I ain't seen you in forever."

"Phew," he sighs. "About ten months. It's a long story, Big Bruh. What's up with you though? I hear you doing big things out there."

"Knock it off," Samad replies with modesty.

"Nah, real talk. Your name ringing in here. I heard you got that block on fire."

"How you hear that?" he asks.

"Man, this shit just like the street. As a matter of fact shit travel down here faster than it do on the street. It's like that. Trust me it's not a secret, Big Bruh. What's the deal with you though?"

"Shit…trying to bail out. They got me in here on some bullshit," he claims. "They trying to put two bodies on me," he whispers as he peeks around with caution.

"One of them bodies, the boy Ashy Mu, right?" he whispers. Samad is shocked out of his mind. The hairs on his neck stand up at attention. "I told you the word travel. Samad watches him nervously. "Big Bruh, this ain't no place for you. Jail is for losers like me," he smiles exposing his yellow, raggedy teeth. "Man, I can't seem to get it right to save my life," he says sadly.

The look in his eyes touches Samad's heart. He's known this man since the 1st grade, way before he earned the name 'Off The Chain.' He met him back when he was just plain old Jason Flemming. Later he grew up to be a wild and reckless dude who would rob and extort drug dealers throughout the town. No one wanted a problem with him because they knew that there was no limit to the craziness that he would partake in if he didn't get his way. He's known to double cross friends and family but with Samad it's completely different. He has the utmost respect for Samad and has never done anything to tarnish that. For what reason Samad has no clue but he's grateful.

"I ain't gotta tell you," he whispers. "You know me and where I come from. I remember I was in third grade and couldn't spell cat. Mufuckers clowned the shit outta me. Not you though. What you do for a nigga?" he asks as he looks Samad square in the eyes. "You tutored me at your house until I learned how to read," he whispers with no shame. His eyes begin to get glassy. "I never forgot that shit," he adds.

Wow! Samad says to himself. He even forgot about that being that it was so long ago. Up until now he could never figure out why Off The Chain has never showed him anything but love.

"I don't know if I ever took the time to thank you so I'm going to do it now. Thanks man," he says with gratefulness.

This is starting to be a sentimental moment and Samad can't take it. "No problem 'B'," he says casually as he tries to harden up the moment. "That loser shit, I ain't trying to hear it. Tell me what you want to do and let me see if I can make it happen. Maybe I can bring that winning streak out of you," he smiles.

"Man, I ain't gotta be the MVP. I'm cool with just being on the winning team for once in my life.

"What you got in mind though?"

"Big Bruh, real talk, I'm tired. This jail shit is for the birds. You know I started jailing in the youth house when I was ten years old. I already gave them crackers fifteen years of my life altogether. I ain't got another day in me. I'm just waiting for my court date. Hopefully I'll beat this shit cause it's something light. Even if I don't beat it, it's all good cause the charge only carry like three years. I don't want to do a day but three years I can do that shit standing on my head," he brags. "But after that I'm done. Man, look in my eyes. I'm beat up. They done got the best out of me. I been getting four and five year bids for dumb shit! I ain't never made a dime off of nothing I ever went to jail for."

"I can change that for you," Samad claims.

"Honestly speaking Big Bruh, it's too late in the game for that. To get to 27 years old and just start hustling, that's crazy. I ain't got no room for no mistakes. The judge already told me, if I ever stand before him again, it's a wrap! Straight career criminal. I can't J-walk let alone get caught up with some drugs."

"I mean, what you gone do then?"

"I just wanna play my position," he says as he looks away sneakily. "For instance, you in here for murder. You outta position. That shouldn't be. You ain't got no business in here. You supposed to be out there running the operation. Now the operation probably suffering cause you in here. Let me play that position? That's what I do. A nigga step out of pocket, I'll pluck him. Just keep me stashed somewhere, feed me, pay my rent, and keep a couple of dollars in my pocket and I'm good," he claims. "We don't party together, eat together or nothing but I'll be just one phone call away," he whispers. "That's all I can do these days. I can't be running around and getting into trouble cause I can't stand it, feel me?"

It all makes perfect sense to Samad and he can definitely see the use in having him on the team. "I definitely feel you. What's your bail?"

"Big Bruh, I'm ashamed to tell you," he says with embarrassment. "I'm here on some super light shit. Ready for this?" he asks. "My bail $250.00," he whispers. "Tell me that ain't some loser shit? I ain't got no love out there. I done burned all my bridges. I done fucked everybody who I could but real talk I only crossed mufuckers cause I knew they was only using me. They ain't never gave a fuck about Jason Flemming. They only feared Off The Chain. So, why should I give a fuck about them? On my grandmother, I would never cross you! I always had respect for you before the money. All I ask is you give me the chance to prove my loyalty."

"Say no more."

"I'm telling you, just give me a shot and I will show you what I'm really made of," he says as he tries to further convince Samad.

"Yo!" Samad says with a look of agitation. "It's a wrap, a done deal!"

///// CHAPTER 86 /////

Two Days Later

After going a few days without work, D-Nice finally located some earlier today. At the price of Thirty dollars a gram, he purchased a half a kilo (500 grams) of pure garbage. He's been getting complaint after complaint ever since the first sale his crew made. He can't even imagine how he's going to move over twenty-five thousand dollars worth of nothing.

All he can do is hope that he doesn't lose his money due to this mistake. He's been giving customers their money back in good faith to keep their trust. All in all he just prays he can at least make his fifteen thousand dollars back.

As D-Nice sits on the porch soaking in grief, his phone rings. "Hello?" he answers with sadness.

"What's up, nigga?" Samad shouts. "Why you sound like you dead, nigga? I'll be back! They ain't gone have your boy down here forever! You sound like it's the end of the world," he teases.

"Nigga, whatever," he says with a little more cheer.

"What's good though?" Samad asks.

"Shit," he sighs. "Literally 'B'. I hollered at my man today. Straight Kabook (garbage) nigga, you heard?"

"Yeah, I heard."

"Yeah, straight ass," D-Nice says.

"You ain't go hard did you?"

"Hard enough, halfway," he mumbles. "Just trying to get my money back.

Yes, Samad cheers to himself. Hearing this has made his day. Each day he fears more and more that D-Nice may be getting ahead of him. Deep down inside he loves to hear things like this to reassure him that he's still ahead of the game. For some reason this doesn't seem like friendly competition. The whole meet you at the top comment may be more than just a friendly gesture.

"Damn, that's fucked up," he says with phony concern. "Ay yo, the broad gone come through for the cheese, you heard?" he says referring to the sixty semi grand that D-Nice has for him. He was able to move all the work that Samad had left. The selfish part of Samad makes him believe that D-Nice will use his money and come up off of it. Before that happens he's going to stop any chances of it. "I'm gone call her and tell her to get with you alright?"

You stupid motherfucker, D-Nice says to himself. He can't believe that she's gotten hold of his mind wherein he trusts her with his life savings. "Yo, you sure about that? You trust her like that?"

"Definitely. I'm bout to hit her and ya'll get it together, alright?"

"Whatever."

"Peace," Samad shouts before ending the call. He quickly starts to dial Lil Bit. He waits patiently as the phone rings.

Meanwhile

Star's BMW is parked right in front of the high rise building. Both, the passenger's door and the back passenger's door is popped wide open. The trunk is open as well. The car is stuffed to the maximum with Star and Tara's clothing.

Star slams the backdoor shut just as Lil Bit makes her way to the trunk. She's so busy pulling the heavy suitcase that she doesn't realize that her phone is vibrating in her pocket. She leans the suitcase on the car so Star can dump it in the trunk.

Suddenly the sound of loud music catches all of their attention. They all turn their heads into that direction, only to see Maurice's CL550 pulling into the entrance. The sound of Rapper Jay-Z's 'Song Cry' seeps out of the car and travels through the airwaves. There's no doubt in Lil Bit's mind that he's purposely playing this song for her. He hops out of the car and walks right past Lil Bit as if she isn't standing there. "Ay Lady," he says as he touches Tara's hand. "God daughter, what up? You ready to get back to school?" he asks followed by a charming smile. He reaches into his front pocket and pulls a hefty stack of hundred dollar bills. He counts through the stack five times before he passes it over to Star. She hugs him tightly. "That's five thousand," he whispers into her ear. "That should hold you for a minute. Hit me though, alright?" he says as he backs away from her.

"Thank you," she says with a huge smile.

"That's nothing. You my baby. You know you can get anything I got. Regardless of what I'm always gone be here for you," he says as he walks right past Lil Bit once again as if she's invisible. He hops into the car and presses repeat on the stereo. Jay-Z's voice sounds crisp and clear. "A face of stone was shocked on the other end of the phone," he says. "Word back home is that you had a special friend. So what was oh so special then? You have given away without getting at me. That's your fault, how many times have you forgiven me? How was I to know that you was plain sick of me? I know the way a nigga living was whack but you don't get a nigga back like that! I'm a man with pride, you don't do shit like that! You don't just pick up and leave and leave me sick like that. You don't throw away what we had, just like that," he says with sorrow. "I was just fucking them girls, I was gone get right back. They say you can't turn a bad girl good but once a good girl has gone bad she's gone forever. I'll mourn forever," he says sadly. "Shit, I gotta live with the fact that I did you wrong forever." After that verse, he mashes the gas pedal. The tires screech as he burns rubber. He busts a u-turn at the end of the parking area. As he passes them on his way out, he finally looks at Lil Bit for the first time. They lock eyes just as the chorus is singing. "I can't see 'em coming down my eyes so I gotta let the song cry." A few seconds of music plays before the rapper speaks again. "That's fucked up, girl," he says as he rolls his eyes away from her with rage.

Seeing him like this really touches her heart. Never did she imagine them going through this. At this point she really wonders if Samad is actually worth all of this drama. She may have gained a lover but she lost a friend.

Tara hops into the driver's seat while Star gives Lil Bit the hug of a lifetime. At this point she's in real need of it. "I love you, Sister. Cheer up," she whispers. "Whatever he's going through he'll get over it," she says as she backs away.

Lil Bit smiles to cover up the hurt that she really feels. Sister, you don't know the half, she thinks to herself. This is only the beginning. Worse days are sure to come.

///// CHAPTER 87 /////

Two Days Later. Lil Bit cruises along Raymond Boulevard in Newark. A heavy burden has been lifted from her shoulders a few minutes ago. She's been on her grind day and night and it finally has paid off.

Her phone rings and she answers it on the third ring. "Ay, Baby," she says with cheer.

"What's up, Mami? Tell me something good," he says with desperation.

"It's all done. I just got the last signature over to the lawyer. Now all he has to do is take it before the judge and hopefully from there you will be free."

"Damn Baby, I don't know what I would do without you. You my ride or die!" he shouts joyfully. "Don't ever think I take you for granted. One day I'm gone be in a position to pay you back for everything. I'm gone give you the world," he says with confidence.

"We'll see," she replies as if she doesn't believe him.

Minutes later, she steps into the Post Office. She opens up her box and grabs hold of the stack of mail that's stuffed inside. She slams the box shut and turns around facing the table behind her. She lays the mail onto the table and one by one she opens and reads each piece.

After reading through the majority of junk mail, she grabs hold of a certified mail slip and walks to the front counter. She gives the woman the slip. In less than two minutes the woman returns with a certified envelope in her hand. What could that be, Lil Bit thinks to herself. She's full of curiosity as she signs her name on the line to confirm that she's received the letter. "Thank you. Have a good day," she says before walking away from the counter.

She makes it halfway to the door before she's forced to rip open the envelope. She can't take it anymore. She's not expecting anything and can't imagine what could be inside. She digs her hand into the envelope and pulls out a single sheet of paper. The raised seal which reads Prosecutor's Office snatches her breath away.

Her heart begins to beat like a drum as she's reading through the letter. The letter informs her that she has 72 hours to report to their office before they come looking for her. She wonders what they could be looking for her for. Suddenly, Luscious' face pops into her mind. His begging and pleading sounds off in her mind. Now, the scene plays right in her mind, the day the coroners took the young boy's body from the crowded block. Now, her sister's father's face pops into her mind. The gunshots ring off clearly in her head. She wonders which murder they are after her for. Or is it all of them?

She begins to hyperventilate. She stands there in a trance momentarily. Suddenly everything around her gets blurry. The pounding in her heart is nothing compared to the pounding in her belly. Her stress level has the baby doing aerobics in her stomach. There's more kicking and flipping going on in her belly than a karate flick. She bends over, grabbing hold of her tiny pouch of a stomach. The pain eases up long enough for her to consider making her way to the door.

She stands up slowly and takes a few steps before her knees get weak. The entire room starts to spin just as the pain in her stomach starts right back up. This time the pain is unbearable. She takes the last step toward the door and suddenly her legs are no longer there. She faints and collapses onto the floor where she lays unconscious.

///// CHAPTER 88 /////

Several Hours Later

"That was an extremely close call," says Lil Bit's doctor. "The baby is good, thank God. You were this close to a miscarriage," he says as he holds his fingers together with a tiny space in between them. "Now you should take that as a lesson. I warned you more than enough times about the stress and the hardship that you're putting on this baby."

Sade stands side by side with Lil Bit as she does any other battle that Lil Bit has had in her life. She shakes her head side to side with grief. She feels so bad to see her best friend going through so much. She's been watching her fight battle after battle since they were children. Through the toughest situations Lil Bit has fought her hardest and by being here after all of it she reigns champion in Sade's eyes. It really hurts Sade that Lil Bit still has to fight. Through all the madness that she's been through she's never seen Lil Bit this weak. She can actually look in her eyes and see something that she's never seen in them and that's defeat.

Sade will never admit this to anyone but deep down inside she almost wishes Lil Bit would have lost the baby. It may have hurt her for a little while but at least that way she could cut the risk of losing her best friend to homicide by Maurice. Sade believes that God does everything for a reason. When she was first called here to University Hospital she first thought was that Maurice had done something to her. After getting here and seeing Lil Bit laying here looking safe and sound she immediately figured that God took the baby away to save Lil Bit's life. Now that he hasn't taken the baby away Sade wonders what the reason is behind that.

"I'm going to have to assign you to bed rest," he says with sternness in his eyes. "I mean that. It's for the life of your baby," he warns. "Just lay down and relax. Don't lift a finger if you don't have to." He stops talking long enough to fill out a prescription for her. "Here take this. Take these pills once a day. Ok? Any problems, call me immediately. Ok ladies, have a goodnight," he says pleasantly as he steps toward the door. He holds the door open slightly. "And no sex," he whispers.

"No sex?" she asks.

"No, until further notice," he says as he shakes his head from side to side before walking out of the door.

The moment the door closes behind him, Lil Bit gets up and pulls the hospital gown over her head. "Damn, no sex," she sighs with a smile on her face.

Sade looks down at the little pouch of a belly that Lil Bit has developed. Sadness fills her heart as she realizes that the pregnancy is starting to be noticeable. She fears the day when she can no longer conceal it from Maurice.

Lil Bit catches Sade staring at her. She doesn't want to make Lil Bit uncomfortable the least bit. "What happened?"

"Girl, the last thing I remember is standing in the middle of the Post Office reading my mail and the next thing I know I'm in the back of the ambulance. My life is over," she says as the tears drop down her face.

Even more sorrow fills Sade's heart. For the third or fourth time in their lives, she's seeing Lil Bit cry. She's sure it must be something well worth the tears. "What now," Sade asks as she prepares herself for the latest. Lil Bit digs deep into her purse. She passes the letter over to Sade who reads over it quickly. She lifts the paper up high enough to shield her face. The tears drop rapidly as she considers the fact that maybe her life is over. She gives the tears time enough to dry up on their own before she lowers the letter from her face. "So, what are you going to do?"

"Flee the country," she says with a cheesy smile on her face. The tears are still flowing from her eyes. "Just kidding. I really have no choice. I'm turning myself in," she says as the tears now pour from her eyes. "My life is a wreck right now but something tells me it's going to get a lot worse," she says as she stares at the Prosecutor's seal on the top of the paper.

///// CHAPTER 89 /////

Later That Night. Here in Montclair, New Jersey, Diva Lounge is packed well beyond capacity. The V.I.P. section only consists of two groups; the Federation and a group of a lower echelon. The entire Federation is shining as usual as opposed to the other group where only one man is laced with diamond encrusted jewelry. It clearly shows that particular man doesn't fit in with the rest of the men in his group. He has a different glow about him. Although their clothes may be clean and fashionable, their looks and their demeanor depicts that they're the grime of the city.

Maurice and the Federation sit at their table sipping away. By now they're all good and tipsy. Smurf stands up with his cell phone glued to his ear. In seconds he fades out of the V.I.P. section.

The man in the center of the other table is sparkling like a bright disco ball. He fumbles with a cane that leans on the table beside him. Discreetly, he watches Maurice and the rest of the squad. "Yeah, that's them," the man whispers to the man that is sitting next to him. He smiles, "One thing about me, Trauma...I don't forget a face. See the one with the dreads? That's the one she was in the car with."

"Yeah? That's the boss," Trauma says. "His name is Maurice. They call him Big Nigga," he adds. "He got that grip. For sure. Which one of them actually shot you though?"

"On the real, I don't know. The sucker ass nigga shot me from behind. Coward wasn't even man enough to look me in the eyes. Real rap though, I want that big nigga. He had a lot of mouth that night. I told him the beef me and my lady was going through had nothing to do with him but he was on some Captain

Save A – Hoe shit. Any real nigga wouldn't have got into a situation between a man and his wife."

"So now we gone show him why he should have stayed out of it," Trauma whispers with an evil grin on his face.

One hour has passed and there's only fifteen minutes left before the bar lets out. The members of the other group all get up from their seats as Maurice and his squad continue doing what they do. After the man at the center of the table finally gets up, he leans onto his cane and limps away. He follows the rest of his group a few steps behind. In a matter of minutes, the Federation has the entire V.I.P. section all to themselves, while the other parties disperse out of the club.

Maurice sits down fumbling through his money. Tonight the tab is a mere joke to him. They didn't have enough champagne in the building to supply them. "Here," he says as he hands the waitress, 46, one hundred dollar bills. His crew stands around him as he finally comes to his feet. They quickly form a tight huddle around him as they always do. They walk through the club, guarding him as if he's the President of the United States.

The Porsche SUV sits parked as the engine races so quietly that it doesn't even sound like it's on. Trauma sits in the passenger's seat, focusing all of his attention on the door of the lounge. They're parked in the perfect spot. They're a half a block away but still they're close enough to see everything.

"What about that cop at the door?" the man asks from the driver's seat.

"What about him?" Trauma asks with sarcasm. "You seen that young punk?" he smiles. "He's straight out of the academy. He ain't ready for no action. All he gone do is duck for cover. Trust me."

Rock leads the pack as they step close to the door. He peaks from left to right to make sure everything is cool before he steps his other foot out of the door. The Federation follows his lead. As soon as they're out of the building, they walk to their left in the direction that they're parked. Smurf pops up at the corner and blends right in with them.

As they're walking, a man watches them carefully from across the street. He sits on the curb in between two parked cars. As they're crossing the street, he darts out of his hole at top speed. Suddenly the sound of footsteps makes all of them turn their heads in the gunman's direction.

Bloc! Bloc! Bloc! Bloc! He fires, aiming randomly at the crowd. All of them disperse in different directions. Maurice and Black take off in the same path. Smurf grabs hold of his .40 caliber and starts to let loose. Boc! Boc! The gunman manages to fire once at Maurice and Black. As he swings his arm around to fire at Smurf, a ball of hot steel crashes into his chest cavity and slams him backwards many steps. The rest of the men are now able to get on the curb to safety where they duck low, just watching the scene play out. Smurf dashes at him with pure aggression, firing with each step he takes. Boc! Boc! Boc! Boc! He continues until the man is laying flat on his back. Boc! Boc! He fires, aiming at the man's head.

Smurf leads his pack though a small one way street where their cars are parked. A Toyota Avalon comes speeding down Bloomfield Avenue at top speed.

As he gets close he bends the corner in pursuit of the Federation. Pop! Pop! Pop! Pop! The passenger fires hitting nothing but parked cars. Boc! Boc! Boc! Smurf fires as the car passes him.

The cop at the door grabs hold of his gun with one hand and his walkie talkie with the other. He radios in for back-up as he makes his way over to the scene of the crime. He steps carefully to the middle of the street where the man lays motionless with not a drop of life left in his body. The sound of police sirens rip through the airwaves from every direction.

Maurice and the crew hop into their cars and back up out of the one way block so they don't have to come out onto Bloomfield Avenue. The sirens are getting louder and louder as they take the back road to safety.

In a matter of seconds six police cars surround the cop who is checking the man's neck for a pulse. The Porsche SUV cruises by the scene just as the cop is standing up and facing all the other officers. He shakes his head from side to side negatively. Trauma looks at his soldier lying on the ground and a great sadness fills his heart. He doesn't say a word. He just nods his head up and down with fury in his eyes.

///// CHAPTER 90 /////

The Next Morning. Lil Bit sits in the passenger's seat of Sade's R Class Mercedes as Sade cruises up Morris Avenue in Union. Lil Bit is a nervous wreck. She's in need of a cigarette and she doesn't even smoke. She's tried her hardest to calm her nerves for the baby's sake but nothing seems to work.

She calls Maurice once again for the one hundredth time and still he isn't picking up. She's left messages telling him how urgent it is for him to call her back and still he hasn't. "I don't believe him," she whines. "This is the wrong time for his stubbornness. I could be dead right now and he doesn't even give a fuck. That's why I can't fuck with him," she raves. "Right here," she says as she points to her left. Sade pulls into the parking lot.

Once they're parked they step into the building. Both of their eyes scan the building directory. "There it goes," says Sade. "Attorney at Law," she reads aloud. They hop onto the elevator and off they go.

24 hours have already passed and Lil Bit has 48 more hours to go. She refuses to step into the Prosecutor's office without legal representation. She's sure if she goes there without an attorney present they will eat her alive which is the reason why she's been trying to contact Maurice. She needs him to direct her to the best attorney that money can buy. Her life depends on it and she can't believe that he would ignore her right now. After all his life is on the line as well, being that he's the one who has ordered and committed the murders in the first place.

She spent all of last night on the internet searching for lawyers before she recalled Maurice telling her about a lawyer being in Union who he referred to as the best in the business. Supposedly all the major hitters use this attorney and the majority of them walk away scot free. All she can do is hope that she is of the majority.

Lil Bit and Sade stand at the door reading the sign before they actually ring the bell. The buzzer sounds off and they both walk in nervously. "Yes, may I help you ladies?" the beautiful dark complexioned receptionist asks.

"Uh, yes, Tony Austin, please?" Lil Bit says in her most pleasant voice.

"Uh, one second, please?" the receptionist replies as she looks them up and down with no shame. The look she gives them makes the both of them feel uncomfortable. She presses the button on the intercom.

"Yeah?" the male voice answers casually.

"Yes, Mr. Austin, two beautiful young ladies await your presence," she says with sarcasm.

Lil Bit senses her sarcasm and shoots her a dirty look. They stare at each other until the sound of the door opening snatches Lil Bit's attention away. She then rolls her eyes with disgust.

A smooth and debonair, slim framed man comes strutting into the waiting area. Both of them are quite impressed with his dress code. His pink linen, short sleeved shirt tapers closely to his model physique. So does his slim fitted denim jeans. His Gucci flip-flops reveal his true sense of fashion. "Hello ladies. Tony Austin," he greets as he gently shakes their hands. "Uh, may I help ya'll?"

"Uh, yes, I'm in need of some legal advice," Lil Bit whispers.

He shrugs his shoulders. "Let's step into my office," he says as he leads the way. They follow him closely as the receptionist watches them like the hawk that she is. He holds the door open for them to step inside the plush office. "Have a seat," he suggests. He gives them time to seat themselves before he sits behind his desk in the oversized leather recliner. "Ya'll mind?" he asks as he grabs hold of an extremely long cigar. Without giving them time to reply he immediately bites the tip and sparks it up. In seconds, he's screened by a thick fog. He coughs. "Excuse me. So what brings you two here?" he asks as he looks Lil Bit in the eyes. "Hold up, before we get started let me first say with all due respect, I am no longer practicing law. I need to make you aware of that before we go any further. The only reason my doors are still open is because I have a few more cases to finish up before I can actually close the doors for good."

"No, please, just hear me out," Lil Bit begs without shame. "I'm sure one more case isn't going to hurt."

He shakes his head from side to side negatively. "It's just not part of the plan right now. Besides it took a great deal to get to the point that I'm just about ready to walk away from it."

"Don't walk away just yet, please? After this you can walk away as fast as you want to," she smiles.

"Nah, easier said than done. I love what I do and if I take another case that will lead to two then three and before you know it I'm full blown all over again," he says with determination.

Lil Bit senses that his mind is made up and something has to be said. It's obvious that the batting of her long eyelashes isn't working. "My boyfriend sent me," she lies.

"Who is your boyfriend?"

"Maurice," she whispers. "Maurice Strickland.

"Maurice Strickland...Strickland," he repeats. A smile pops up on his face.

"Slow Moe?" he asks. "Oh my man. How's he doing?"

Jackpot, she thinks to herself. "He's doing well."

"Good man but I'm afraid that not even he can pull me out of my pre-retirement."

"Could you please just consider it?" she asks as she holds the letter from the Prosecutor's office.

Without even reading it, he speaks. "I'm afraid not," he says before taking a huge pull of his cigar. He turns his head to the side as the long train of smoke seeps out of his mouth. "As much as I love my profession, I'm walking away from it. The politics involved in this game have gotten to be way too much. Bottom line, mufuckers ain't playing fair," he smiles. "You definitely don't want me to represent you in any case, not even a traffic situation. Not in the State of New Jersey anyway. I'm taboo. Just walking in the courtroom with me will get you the maximum of any sentence. I can't do that to you, knowing what the consequences will be."

"No, please," Lil Bit replies. She has always had a problem taking no for an answer.

"You don't understand. My last case was an upset. I busted my ass for years trying to get not just my client but a good friend as well, free of all charges and just when we had the case popped, he embarrassed me in front of a Federal Judge, two Federal Prosecutors and two Federal Agents. Not only was my ego crushed, my career was bombed. My winning streak now tarnished and I'm the laughing stock of the decade."

"Listen, I can't take no for an answer. Please just read the letter before telling me no."

"You're determined, huh?"

"Very," she replies.

He reads over the letter quickly. "This doesn't say anything. Report to them for what?"

She hesitates before replying. She knows she would be a fool to tell him what she thinks it's about. If she reveals the fact that she knows anything she may look guilty in his eyes. Her best bet is to play dumb. "I don't know which is why I'm here. I received this letter in the mail."

He gazes into her hazel eyes. His eyes pierce through her soul. "You have no clue of what this could be about?" he questions.

"Not at all."

"No possible clue?" he further questions.

"Not a clue," she lies.

His expertise of these types of matters tells him that she knows more than she's telling him. That coupled with the fact that he knows Maurice quite well. He's helped members of Maurice's crew shake gun charges, drug charges and even homicide charges. One thing he knows for sure is any girlfriend of Maurice's is in no way as innocent or ignorant as she may be acting. He's sure she knows something but what she knows he has no clue. "No clue at all?" he asks with sarcasm.

She stands firm in her spot. No matter how many times he asks her, her answer will remain the same.

"Uh, Mr. Austin," the receptionist's voice comes through the intercom. "Can I speak to you for a minute?" she says with a demanding tone.

"Excuse me," he says as he gets up and walks to the door.

Once he steps out, Sade speaks. "Lil Bit you have to tell him the truth," she whispers.

"The truth about what?" she replies. "If I tell him anything I will look guilty."

"You're trying to get him to represent you. If he's your lawyer you're going to have to tell him something."

Lil Bit looks at her with pity. She's been sheltered her entire life and has no idea how the real world works. With that in mind she forgives her for making such a goofy statement. "Not that," she whispers. "If he finds out what they're suspecting me of then he can defend it. Until then I don't know what the letter is about. I don't trust no fucking lawyer. How can you trust anyone who lies for a living?"

The door opens and they both turn in that direction. His frowned face transforms into a pleasant smile quickly. "Ladies, there's nothing I can do to help you. I wish I could but I'm done. Sorry."

Lil Bit sighs. "I don't believe this shit," she whispers. "I got 48 hours to report to them. I can't go in there without legal representation," she whines like a baby.

"Take it easy. It may be nothing at all. You could be here willing to spend money for no reason." The look in her eyes reassures him that she knows a lot more than she's admitting to knowing.

"Well, could you at least refer me to someone else?" she asks with hope.

"I'm afraid not. Real talk, I don't fuck with people like that."

"Mr. Austin," the receptionist says over the intercom. Extreme agitation is in her voice.

"Ladies sorry I can't help you," he says. "I wish you all the luck. Hopefully this is nothing," he says as he holds the door open for them. They get the hint that he's now putting them out of his office.

They both get up and make their way out. "Thanks for nothing," Lil Bit says as she passes him.

When they get to the receptionist's desk, tension awaits them. She watches them with jealousy as they pass her. "Hmphh," she purposely sighs loud enough for them to hear her.

///// CHAPTER 91 /////

Trauma stands in the center of the little basement apartment, as fifteen members of his Unit lounge around him. They listen and note every word that he says as if it is law. Once he says something it's etched in stone. Any command that he gives, no one can stop them until they carry out his mission.

Signs of mourning cover all of their faces. "No need to cry over the lil homie. He died doing what he did. Ya'll know him just like I know him. He loved being in the middle of the action. I'm sure the homie gone rest in peace cause he went out the way he always said he wanted to, with his gun in his hand," Trauma says with aggression in his voice. "As for the situation at hand, niggas definitely gotta pay for that loss though. We gone hit these streets today and every other day until we get every nigga that was involved or even affiliated with them. The Federation," he smirks. "Well, we gone be the ones to shut the Federation down. Move smart cause these niggas ain't the typical niggas," he admits. "The nigga Maurice, aka Big Nigga ain't your average rich nigga hiding behind stacks of money. He play too. As a matter of fact, they all play which will make all of this even more fun. It's even. A game of warfare. We ain't got no room for no mistakes though. Take ya'll time out there. Don't rush. Make every move count. Let's move strategically. Be patient and these niggas gone walk right into our hands. You know how it goes. These niggas rich. How did they get rich? By grinding and putting in work. They love the dough! They gone be so busy chasing that paper that they gone fall right into our hands. It's that simple."

Meanwhile

Maurice paces back and forth throughout the living room of the Bat Cave as his crew just watches him closely. The fury in his eyes set the tone in the tense room. "In all the years that I've been running around this town never before have I been played out like this." More than anything else his pride and his ego is hurt. "I never thought I'd see the day that a mufucker will cross the line. Either these niggas don't know who we are or they just don't give a fuck," he smiles. "I got the 411 on everything. You know the streets talk. Them little filthy ass niggas at the table next to us in the VIP, was Trauma and his Unit. Remember the nigga on the crutches?" he asks. "That was the nigga from Voro's that time."

Maurice feels good to have it all figured out. Last night they left the scene believing it was a potential robbery situation. Through rumor and gossip he learned the real story.

"So, that nigga part of the Trauma Unit?" Black asks.

"I don't know if he with them or just surrounds himself with them for protection. It really don't matter cause even if he ain't with them, he gone die with them," he says with a cold look in his eyes. "By this afternoon I will know the whereabouts of each and everyone of them. Money talks and that bullshit walk," he sings. "I put a ten thousand dollar reward out for anyone that gives me information that leads to the murders of Trauma and his Unit. Nigga, it's a recession and a drought on top of that, so you tell me how fast niggas gone start spilling their guts. They gone tell everything they know!" he says with a sinister smile.

"I heard the niggga Trauma good for putting his nose in business that ain't got nothing to do with him. He gone wish he didn't get into this beef though. Right now I heard they moving around up there in the Vailsburg section. They like gypsies. They don't stay no one place too long. They migrate from area to area wherever they can muscle their way into. I heard he has a huge following though because wherever they go he picks up more and more members. Just pay close attention to your surroundings," he warns. "As far as moving around goes. All that is on freeze until we get control of this situation. Until I say so, I don't want anyone selling not even a gram. Shut the operation down! We can't afford to be out here making moves. All you need is to answer a half a bird call and them niggas sitting right there waiting for you at the meeting spot. At this point we don't know who is with them, feel me? Them lil dirty niggas don't get no money. They ain't got shit going on which means they got all day to sit around and plot on us. We gone knock these pussies off one by one. They're probably expecting us to be out here riding up and down the street shooting out of the window at them. They don't know we on some totally different shit. They ain't never beefed with niggas like us. I guarantee you that. The first one gone be down by tonight. Trust me. I got it all figured out."

///// CHAPTER 92 /////

New York, New York

Maurice sits at the table inside of Smith and Lewinsky's Steakhouse. Across from him sits the mixed race beauty that all the chaos evolved from. "Damn, you look awesome tonight," he says with charm.

"Thank you," she says as she blushes from ear to ear.

His phone vibrates in his lap. He peeks at the display and once he sees that it's Lil Bit, he presses ignore once again.

This woman is torn. Before her husband was shot she had her mind made up that she wanted no more to do with him. After he was shot, he ran the guilt trip of a lifetime on her which happened to work. He made her feel responsible for him getting shot and that alone worked. She allowed him back into her life. She may have accepted him back but not once did she even consider forcing Maurice out of her life. She's there for Maurice's taking anytime he wants to take her. Her husband doesn't have the slightest clue, which makes it even more fun for the both of them.

It's amazing what ten inches of solid pipe, the strength of a mule's back kick and the know how of what to do with it all, can do to a woman. When used properly the bearer of those characteristics can have her moving at his every beck and call as Maurice has her doing. She's so captivated by him that she would betray her own family if he asked her to. Never would he do that though. Even in a time like this, when her husband attempted to have his life taken he still wouldn't ask her to cross him. He's sure she would though but there's no need to even ask her a single question about him because everything he needs to know he already asked weeks ago after their situation. She's told him every detail without even realizing it. He knows every detail of his operation as well as all of his locales.

She looks down at her pink faced, diamond bezel Presidential Rolex and a bit of nervousness creeps into her gut. Damn, she thinks to herself as she realizes that she will never make it home the time she told her husband she would. She becomes jittery as she thinks of the trouble she's going to be in when she does get home late. His lack of trust for her makes him keep her under tight watch. Even under his tightest watch she still manages to see Maurice whenever he wants to see her. Some may say that he has more control over her than her husband does. Maurice knows that but rarely does he exert his authority.

She picks up her phone and starts dialing. "Shhh, please," she whispers as she presses her finger against her lips. Maurice nods his head up and down. "Bay, you're not home yet right?" She already knows the answer to her question. She knows his routine like the back of her hand. He gets in the house every night by 11:30, which means he should be on his way. "Because, there's no way I'm going to be finished here on time. I don't want to leave the baby with your mother overnight. So, can you stop by there on your way and pick her up? I should be about an hour behind you. I promise," she says to reassure him. His suspicions are now raised and she can hear it in his voice. She overlooks his lack of distrust. "Thanks, Babe. I love you," she says with a sense of sincerity in her voice. Hearing this makes him believe her story wholeheartedly. For some reason he's foolish enough to believe that she wouldn't say she loves him when she's in the presence of another man. Maybe any other man would be offended but not Maurice. He couldn't care less.

Maurice presses the keys on his phone. He texts Sal informing him that the man is on his way. At the current moment, Maurice has the man's home, his mother's home and his stash house guarded by members of the Federation. Tonight he will be murdered. It's inevitable. Having her right here with him makes the perfect alibi. He's sure if anything was to happen to her husband, he would definitely be on the top of the list of suspects. Being that they're here together, she could never suspect him.

Twenty minutes later, they're cruising through Manhattan on their way back to Jersey. They're both fatigued and quite full from the steak dinner. The only thing that could top this night off is him and her rolling around in between the sheets. She's looking extremely sexy and all night he pictured them indulging in erotic sex but he knows that time isn't on either of their sides. She's on the clock so he just settles for the mouth that she's been giving him since they pulled out of the parking lot. It's so intense that he can barely keep his eyes open. She's sucking him into tranquility.

The man hops out of the Porsche and slowly walks toward the one family house on the quiet suburban block. He uses his cane as an aid to help him walk. The bullet that is lodged deep into his hip makes each step painful.

Just as he steps onto the bottom step, a bright orange flash lights up the area, followed by Boom! The hot wind greets his face before the slug actually caves it in. He stumbles backwards before tripping and falling onto his stomach. The gunman pops up from behind the tall bushes that surround the front of the house. The victim rolls over onto his stomach as he attempts to get up. His vision has been stolen from him. He's as blind as a bat. All he sees is pitch darkness. He hears Boom! Boom! Boom! His head smacks onto the concrete. The gunman fires one more shot to the head, just for the sake of doing so. He then kicks the man's lifeless body before trotting through the alley toward the getaway car that awaits him on the next block.

Just as Maurice's Maserati speeds out of the Holland Tunnel, the 'brain surgery' is at an all time high. He grabs the back of her head and makes love to her mouth. In the middle of the action, his phone starts to rattle the console. He grabs hold of it and looks at the number 1 that's on his screen. That's the code number that they planned to use to tell him that the job is done. He feels a sense of glory in knowing that he's now dead as planned. He drops the phone onto the floor and continues to rabbit pump her mouth with short but filling strokes.

In a matter of minutes the 'mouth off' is interrupted by a series of phone calls to her phone. As much as she would like to answer it, she was always taught not to talk when your mouth is full. Besides, she can tell that she just about has him ready to submit to her. She's been working too hard for this moment to stop now. Her jaws are locking up and she refuses to stop and have to start up all over again. Come on, she thinks to herself as she stretches her jaws. She starts cheating by stroking him crazily with one hand as she wrings his neck with her lips. Viola, she says to herself as he grabs the back of her head and erupts. He roars like the king of the jungle as he peeks through one eye at the traffic in front of him.

"Pop," is the sound that her mouth makes as she lifts up off of him. She puckers up her lips. "Muaahh," she utters as she gives it one last kiss. "Uhmm," she sighs as she bites down on her bottom lip. "You straight now?" she asks with a seductive smile that exposes her pearly whites.

"You already know," he grunts.

She quickly reaches for her phone and immediately starts dialing the number of the last caller. "Hello?" she says as soon as she hears her sister- in-law's voice. "Shonda?" she attempts to shout over the loud noise in the background. She hears the sound of her own daughter's voice in the background as the little girl is crying and shouting. She's both startled and confused. She can also hear her mother- in-law crying as well. "Hello?" Finally her sister- in-law gets the words together to speak. "What?" she asks as her mouth drops wide open. Maurice knows exactly what she's just been told. He continues driving as normal as he possibly can. "No!" she cries.

. He looks over at her. "Yes…bitch," he mumbles to himself as he cruises moderately.

///// CHAPTER 93 /////

Two Days Later

Lil Bit stands in front of the full sized mirror getting dressed. She's a nervous wreck. Judgment day is here. In just a couple of hours she will be sitting in the Prosecutor's Office and she is not looking forward to it.

She wonders what exact questions they will be asking her. She's rehearsed over and over her answers to the questions that she thinks they may ask her. She's not sure what murder they may have called her in for which makes it even worse. She preps herself to answer various questions of each murder. God forbid if they're calling her in for all of the murders. She's sure all the preparation in the world isn't going to help her against the trained professionals though.

The ringing of the phone interrupts her thoughts and saves her from a potential nervous breakdown. She walks quickly over to the dresser and snatches the phone. For once in a long time she's actually happy to see Maurice's name on the display. Although she's glad, she refuses to allow him to know it. "What?" she barks.

"Dig, the dude you went to meet in Union the other day?" She listens closely. "It's a go. Meet him at his office in one hour on the dot."

She wonders how Maurice knows about the meeting. Hearing this removes the huge burden from her shoulders. Her coldness to him is now broken. "You sure?"

"Hit me when ya'll done. Let me know how things go," he says before hanging up the phone and leaving her holding onto a dead line.

One Hour Later

Lil Bit sinks into the soft leather interior. The creamy white filling of the snow white convertible Bentley GTC makes her feel like she's a banana stuffed into the creamy filling of a powdered donut. The attorney closes the door behind her and makes his way over to the driver's side. He hops in, starts the car up and instantly Young Jeezy's raspy voice rips out of the speakers. "Let's get it!" Tony raps along with him. "The flow is back, your boy is too. Let's take 'em back to 93 and make one brick two!" he says with hand motions to go along with it.

Lil Bit is shocked to know that he even listens to hip hop. In fact she's shocked at his swagger altogether. Something tells her that he knows something about turning one brick into two. She's sure whoever his wife is, has to be the happiest woman in the world. He has the complete package; the swagger of a hustler but the stability that they can't provide. "Uhmm," she sighs as she admires him for a second. "Beautiful car."

"Oh, thanks," he replies modestly for a change. "It was a gift from a client."

Twenty five minutes pass and the moment of truth has arrived. Her heart is banging out of her chest as they're walking through the corridor. Her nervousness turns into pure terror the moment she spots detectives walking the floor. It seems as if her and the lawyer are the only people in this building who don't have a holster on their hip. This gives her the feeling that everyone is against her and the sad part is she may be right.

"You nervous?" he whispers to her.

"Yeah," she admits with shame.

"Don't be," he says arrogantly. "That's what I'm here for. To eliminate any fear that you may have. I will tell you when we should be nervous. I got you. Just follow my lead," he says with charisma.

His passion for this would never allow him to refuse a client, especially a client like her. He's always been a sucker for long hair, a fat booty and a bright smile. He could never deny a woman with all the above ingredients. As she sat before him in his office he already had his mind made up to accompany her here. Even his wife, the receptionist is aware of his fetish for that type of woman which is why she reacted the way she did. She banned him from taking on this case but still he couldn't avoid it. This is just another secret that he will have to keep from her.

His loyalty to Maurice made him hold off until he got the word from him that it was ok to represent her. He's made hundreds of thousands of dollars through Maurice over the years and in no way could he reject anything that he needs from him. After speaking with Maurice and getting the green light on the situation, he didn't hesitate to accept the job.

Tony enters the room with great confidence. Lil Bit tries to feed off of his energy and puts up a false sense of confidence. "Good day, gentlemen," he shouts at his entrance. The two middle-aged Caucasian men reply by way of head nod. The both of them are familiar with Tony and despise him just as every other person who is on the opposite side of the law does. The dirty looks they give him only boosts his confidence. It feels good to know that he still has the power to get under their skin even when he's not trying to.

"I'm here on behalf of my client here," he says as he points to Lil Bit who is now trembling like a leaf. "Reporting as you said she should," he says with a smile. "Can I ask what all this is in reference to?"

"No need to ask," the white haired man replies with sarcasm. "We will get to that in time." He rolls his eyes with disgust. "Miss Jones. Have a seat, please," he says with great demand.

She seats herself slowly. Her heart is racing rapidly. Here we go, she says to herself. She places both of her hands underneath the table to keep them from seeing the trembling. The moment of truth is here. All of her rehearsing was in vain because right now she can't even remember her own name. She peeks over to Tony who is leaning against the wall nonchalantly. Seeing him so calm eases her nerves just a little.

"So, Miss Jones, how are you?"

"Ok," she whispers.

"Do you have any idea of why you are here with us?"

"No," she replies with false sincerity.

"Ok, well let me start from the top. Your sister, who you are the guardian to, pressed charges on her father for sexual molestation." Lil Bit sighs silently. Now at least she knows what murder she's here for. Not that it makes a difference. She just knows what she has in front of her. "Under Megan's Law the victim is to be notified when the person is released from prison. By chance did you receive a letter about his release?"

Trick question, she thinks to herself. It ain't gone be that easy she tells herself. She shakes her head from side to side.

"Are you sure about that?"

"Positive."

"Well, Miss Jones, your sister's father was found dead in an abandoned house in Newark. He was badly beaten and tortured before having his brains blown out."

"Wow! Are you serious?" she asks with her eyes popped wide open as if she's really surprised.

"You knew nothing about that?" he asks with mockery.

"How would I know anything about it?" she asks with a grin. "I haven't seen or heard from him since we were in court over six years ago."

"Just for the record, where were you on April 15th?"he asks.

Uh oh, she thinks to herself as her knees knock with fear. "On April 15th," she asks as if she's actually has to figure it out. She doesn't want to just spit the date out and make it seem as if she rehearsed it, knowing he was going to ask about that particular time. "On April 8th, I went to South Beach. I returned on...the 15th."

"What time?"

"Uh, I don't know. My flight came in that evening."

"Oh, funny," he chuckles. "He was murdered that evening."

"Enough," Tony interrupts. "Are you suspecting my client of his murder?"

"No, just interrogating. We don't think she committed the murder. But we do believe she knows who did commit it."

"What makes you so sure of that, if I may ask?" Tony questions.

"A threat was made in the courtroom after he was sentenced. Quote unquote, six years is nothing. I should have served justice on my own and I will. I promise you that," he says in a high pitched voice. "Does that sound familiar to you, Miss Jones?"

Tony looks at her awaiting her reply. "No," she replies.

"Think hard, Miss Jones. You don't remember saying that to Miss Jeffries, your sister's aunt?"

She remembers it oh so clearly. She told her that in the middle of a heated argument they had over the phone when the woman called Lil Bit and accused them of lying on her brother. Lil Bit looks at Tony and the look in her eyes is begging for him to rescue her. "So you're insinuating that she had him killed?" Tony asks with a smile. "What year was that, 2002? Six years ago, right? Miss Jones how old are you?"

"I just turned twenty-four a few months ago," she replies.

"Oh wow, at eighteen years old she made a statement and six and some years later, you're trying to blame her for this scum bag's murder? You have to be kidding," he smiles. "She never received the letter from the state. She has no contact nor does her sister have contact with anyone from her family," he says with hope that he's speaking the truth. "Which means there's no possible way that she would ever know that he was released. Furthermore, the man's a sexual offender. Maybe he did the same thing to someone else and they done it to him. Maybe a prison beef caused him to be murdered. Oh and if none of those are the case let me just remind you of the fact that the murder and torture took place in Newark. How many murders we have noted this year already, sixty something? Maybe someone just murdered him just for the fuck of it," he says with spit shooting out of his mouth.

"Yeah, maybe the gang that your client is affiliated with committed the murder," the man says. "You care to tell us about your gang affiliation?" he says with a huge grin.

"Gang?" she asks with a smile. She looks at him as if he's just said the most foolish thing in the world. "I'm not gang affiliated."

"Are you sure? That's not what Miss Jeffries said. She informed us about, in her own words, a black mafia that your boyfriend is the head of and apparently you're, in her words again, a mafia princess."

"A mafia princess?" she smiles. "First of all I don't care what Miss Jeffries said. She's a crack addict."

Tony interrupts once again. "You know what...enough said. This is absurd. Let me ask, are you charging my client with the murder?"

"No, just simple interrogation."

"Well, ok at this point, I feel she's answered enough questions. She never received the letter. She was on vacation hundreds of miles away when the murder took place. She made a threat when she was a child," he barks. "Any statement, you need her to give I'm sure she will be more than willing to do so. Do you need a statement?" he asks. The man sits quietly as Tony takes control over the room. "Ok, well we're gone. I think we've wasted enough time here. If you give us the okay, we will be leaving right now?"

"Leave," he smiles, exposing his yellow coffee stained teeth.

"Ok, gentlemen, have a good day," he says as he reaches over and grabs Lil Bit's hand. He leads her toward the door.

"Uh, Mr. Austin, remember, every goodbye ain't gone," he says with an evil grin. "We're on it. One slip up and we will find her," he threatens. "And everyone knows you can't afford to put yourself in another situation." Both of the men laugh in his face. "You may just be in need of some legal representation yourself. If need be, don't hesitate to call me. I know a few good criminal attorneys," he says with major sarcasm.

"Ha ha," Tony chuckles. "You're a real comedian huh? I thought you just looked funny," he smiles after his attack. "If it's going down, let's get it over with. I never turn down a challenge. You know me, I'm like the Eveready battery. I just keep going and going," he smiles. "No one or nothing is ever gonna change that. Hopefully you find that slip up that you're looking for. I'll meet you front and center. Me and whoever ya'll put me up against. No dirty tricks, just straight up law. Head up, ya'll don't stand a chance against me. This will be the perfect opportunity to redeem myself," he smiles. "Good day, ladies!"

///// CHAPTER 94 /////

Two Days Later. Deja hops out of the passenger's seat of Lil Bit's truck. She just flew back in from D.R. Her trip was a success. She's completely satisfied with her recent addition and the best part of it is she had no brutal side effects, unlike the boot leg job she had done months ago. The crazy part is she hasn't had her new booty for three days yet and she has already found some more surgery that she plans to do.

"Thanks, Girl," Deja says as she grabs her suitcase from the backseat.

"Mark me down as the first customer in the morning," Lil Bit says. "I will be there when you open the door."

"Ok," Deja says as she forces the door open.

Lil Bit watches closely, just waiting to see the results on Deja. Deja hops out one leg at a time. Her terry cloth coochie shorts grip her like a glove. Lil Bit watches with great admiration. What lies before her eyes is more than picture perfect. She can't believe what she's seeing. The perfectly rounded bottom explodes from her tiny waist and is plastered onto her stick legs. She didn't overdo it wherein it looks big and raunchy. She did just enough to make a man's mouth drop open just as Lil Bit's mouth has.

Deja turns around to give Lil Bit a peek of the profile. She looks as if she has a football in her back pocket. She slams the door right before spinning around and walking away. She steps away, purposely switching extra hard. Each ass clenching step has Lil Bit hypnotized. Never before has she ever considered cosmetic surgery but seeing Deja like this has given her a change of heart. Deja stops suddenly and spins around. Her fingers are pointed at Lil Bit like two guns. "Made you look," she smiles.

Meanwhile. The pitch black Customized Ford Conversion Van is so dark that it can barely be seen. If not for the blue headlights the van could camouflage into the darkness. All the windows on the van are tinted including the windshield. Even the tires have black rims.

The smoking beauty growls as it cruises up South Orange Avenue. The driver makes the left turn onto Salem. Maurice sits in the passenger's seat, watching ahead while Sal peeks through the smoky windshield. Maurice fades into a zone as his favorite song comes out of the speakers. He sings along with Rapper, Young Jeezy. "Mafia! Mafia! Bitch I'm in the Mafia!" he shouts at the top of his lungs. Trauma was correct when he said Maurice isn't a rich nigga who hides behind his money. He could easily hire people to handle this situation for him but truthfully he'd rather handle it himself. He also figures by showing his team that he's willing to go out on the front line with them they will respect and love him more. "Mafia! Mafia! Bitch I'm in the Mafia!" he shouts. Hearing him shouting these words gets all the other passengers excited. In the backseats of the van the members of the Federation sit with military assault weapons on their laps.

The artillery in this van is enough to fight off an army. In total they have over 1,000 rounds of ammunition on hand. The M60 can fire 500 rounds in 60 seconds, with the option to either spit them out at a rapid rate or fire five rounds at a time. The SKS holds a 30 round clip. The MP5 has a 25 round clip. The AR15 also has a 25 round clip and is almost the same as the MP5 except that it's designed for close range shooting and the AR15 can hit it's mark up to 600 feet. Last but not least the M1 which only holds 7 rounds but is the most deadly weapon by far. It is used by snipers and can penetrate a hummer a mile away.

They all stare up ahead at the small huddle of men that are gathered in front of an abandoned house near the end of the block.

"I wonder if these dudes was there that night," Sal says from the driver's seat.

"It don't matter," Maurice blurts out. "This one of their spots. Even if they wasn't, the niggas who was will get the message."

Sal slams on the brakes. "Yo, it's only like six mufuckers out here. No need for all of them to hop out and waste fire," he says as he looks into Maurice's eyes.

"Fuck that!" Maurice says with rage. "Everybody getting out. Let's show these mufuckers what we working with and make them realize that they fucked up this time. When we pull off from here I don't want nobody breathing. I want six dead mufuckers. That will get our point across."

"That's what it is then," Sal confirms. "Ya'll hear that? Ready?" At the sound of his voice they all pull their ski masks snug over their faces and grip their weapons. "Let's go!" Sal shouts as he steps on the gas pedal. The back door is pushed open slightly so they can hop out quickly. The adrenaline of every man in this vehicle is now pumping hard. The closer they get the more anxious they become.

The men standing in front of the house watch cautiously as the dark van approaches them. The fact that they can't see inside makes them more attentive to the van. They look down at the license plate but even that has a tinted cover on top of it. Their eyes are glued to the van as it passes right by them.

Sal slams on the brakes unexpectedly and the machine gun toting men spill out onto the curb. Before they're all the way out of the van gun shots are echoing, causing all six of the men to flee in their own direction. The AR15 rips uncontrollably. A man who was sitting on the banister has been knocked off by the power of the weapon. He falls flat onto his back into the dark alley. The SKS sounds off but hits no one. The bullets ricochet, causing windows to shatter and wood beams to be split in half. In seconds the entire porch is caved in. The MP5 and the MP60 are being fired simultaneously, singing the same tune. The shooters are spraying with no particular target in mind. They just rock back and forth, up and down and side to side until the men before them are no longer standing. The man holding the M1 watches closely as one young man appears to be getting away. He aims low. Just as the man gets a few feet away, the gun starts popping off. The impact of the weapon rocks the shooter after each shot but he manages to keep it under control. Before he knows it seven shots are unloaded. Before the fourth shot sounds off, the man is tackled to the ground by the bullet that crashed into the back of his head.

"Come on, come on!" Maurice commands. Without hesitation, they all climb into the van one by one. The last man slams the door behind himself. Sal steps on the gas pedal and speeds away from the scene leaving behind a bunch of casualties.

The men all sit quietly as their heart beats slow down to a normal pace. The brutal scene replays in their heads. "Damn," Sal says with fury. "That nigga Trauma wasn't even out there."

"Don't matter," Maurice says calmly. His time coming soon. Trust me," he says with a smile. "We got time. We're just getting started!"

///// CHAPTER 95 /////

The Next Afternoon

The 4-foot high Round River Bend Stone wall shields the huge one family, five bedroom estate. A beautifully manicured lawn and uniformed shrubbery surrounds the house as well. Luxurious cars are lined up the driveway. The CL550 starts the line up. Next in line is the Maserati Quadraport. Then the Dodge pick-up truck. The last vehicle sits parked mysteriously. It's concealed by a vinyl covering. Underneath the cover is a Fayalite Green colored exterior, Tobacco Brown colored gut, 2 door Mercedes Benz convertible SLR Mclaren. The only thing that can be seen is the Florida license plates. Never has this vehicle been driven in New Jersey. It was bought for the sole purpose of ripping through the streets of beautiful Miami.

The multi-million dollar beautiful estate here in Alpine, New Jersey may look lavish to most but is actually the least expensive house in the entire area. With all of its beauty most of the residents that live in this town will frown upon it as a disgrace to this gorgeous town.

This town prides itself on exclusiveness and privacy and because of that not a house here has an address attached to it. Instead of addresses the homes have names that the owners have given. Not a single mailbox is attached to the homes either. The only source of incoming mail is through the local post office where the owners rent mailboxes. All this is to protect the privacy of the people who reside here which makes the perfect hideaway for any man who prefers to keep his business all to himself.

Maurice lays back in the lazy boy lounge chair in total peace away from the drama filled life that he's created for himself back in Newark. He resides here without the least worry of any of his negative dealings affecting him. Not even in his worse nightmare does he dream of anyone being able to find him here. His home is safe and sound from the underworld.

This is a huge advantage for him. He can go to Newark and do whatever he chooses and at the end of the night he can come home and play family guy with no worries, wherein his enemies are vulnerable because they live in the same place that they do all their dirt in.

Maurice lays back, watching his three beautiful daughters splash around in the huge in-ground swimming pool while the smell of burned charcoal and Black Angus beef seeps through his nostrils. The serenity he feels while being here in the lap of luxury in total comfort with his family makes all the chaos that he deals with on a daily basis more than worth it. He sometimes wishes he was a normal family man but the downside to that is the fact that he knows the normal family guy would never be able to provide the life that he's created for his family. He wouldn't trade it for the world.

Maurice dials Lil Bit's number as he wonders if she's going to answer. He hasn't called her or answered her calls since telling her to meet with the lawyer. He's been updated on the entire situation at the prosecutor's office by the lawyer. In no way does he even worry about Lil Bit and the situation that she's in. He has total confidence in her. In fact he has more faith in her than any man that is a part of his organization. He believes that there's no amount of pressure that can be applied to her that will make her crack. He also has complete confidence in the lawyer. He's sure that even in the worst case, Tony will manage to maneuver her out of any situation.

"Hello?" she answers hastily.

"What up?" he asks.

"What up? Now you want to know what's up?" she asks with attitude. "You know what, don't ever call me again and I won't ever call you again!"

"Who are you showing off for?" he asks. "Your little friend must be right next to you huh? You making him feel like a big man by talking to me like that in front of him. Guess what though? He will never be the man that I am and he can never make you happy as I have. He's probably laughing away but tell him I said laugh now cause he gone cry later. That is if he gets the chance to," he adds. "I promise you, I'm gone get the last laugh."

"There you go with that shit," she replies. "Why? Ain't you happy? Why can't I be happy?" she asks. She knows how bad that gets under his skin.

"Oh, now you're protecting that mufucker? You can't protect him. You gone be too busy trying to protect yourself." Lil Bit sits back quietly. That remark sends chills up her spine. She knows better than to take that threat lightly. She's sure he will make her life miserable if and when he finds out the truth. That is if she has any life left. "Why are you so quiet now?" he teases. "Talk slick now," he says as he peeks through the opening in the wall and sees the stainless steel colored GL 500 Mercedes SUV parking behind his car. "I'm gone get the last laugh. Remember I told you that," he threatens as he rushes off of the phone.

A short stout woman hops out of the vehicle and makes her way up the long walkway. This woman in no way can compare to the looks of the women he plays around with but still she's the mother of his kids and his wife. He looks her in the face and can actually see the misery and the heartache that he's caused her over the years. Her eyes tell the complete story. At the young age of 30, she looks to be about 50.

When he met her she was quite petite and beautiful but stress and three babies have evolved her into what she is today. Her face looks somewhat beat down and wrinkled. That is the result of all of her crying and constant frowning. She lives in the lap of luxury but still she isn't happy. She appears to have it all but in all reality she has nothing.

She often tells him how she would trade it all, in a heartbeat just to live a stress free life with the man of her dreams who happens to be him. She's well aware that he's not monogamous but still she loves him dearly. He keeps her away from it all but still she knows that it exists. He banned her from going to Newark or even associating with her friends from Newark and tells her his reason is to keep her out of harms way. She knows for sure a part of that is true but the biggest reason he doesn't want her there is to keep her from finding out about his many women. She's found numbers and even pictures of his women. She's gotten so accustomed to it that she doesn't even bring it to his attention anymore.

She finally makes it over to him. She stands there quietly for seconds before even speaking. The look in her weary eyes is blank. She shakes her head from side to side with great suffering. She tries to refrain from saying something to him but she can't keep it in. "On the phone with one of your bitches, huh? Had to rush off of the phone before I got here," she teases with a foolish grin on her face. "You can keep talking. I don't care," she lies. "I already know they exist. You may as well talk to her right in front of me. You been disrespecting me for over ten years. There's no need to stop now. I'm immune to all your bullshit."

"Here we go again," he sings. "I ain't even gone argue with you," he says. The truth of the matter is he can't argue with her because she's absolutely correct. He looks into her eyes and feels terrible that he's beat her down emotionally like this for so long. The sad part is he can't help it. His obsession for having multiple women supersedes his guilt. Deep inside he knows he could never commit himself to just one woman.

"You're sickening," she says with disgust. Her eyes are filled with hate. "Why don't you just leave me? I don't deserve this. What did I do so bad that I'm getting all this hurt?" she asks. "Just leave me alone so I can be happy."

"Psst," he sighs with frustration. Another bitch with this leave me alone so I can be happy shit, he says to himself. Hearing this coming from her mouth pisses him off but doesn't bother him no where near as much as hearing it come from Lil Bit's mouth. The truth of the matter is, he loves his mistress more than he loves his own wife.

She stands there awaiting some type of response from him. She looks into his eyes which are blank and carefree. She then looks into his mouth as he begins to speak.

"Whatever," he says with very little concern. "I ain't going nowhere. You so miserable then why don't you leave me so I can be happy?"

///// CHAPTER 96 /////

7 A.M. the next morning

Lil Bit just enters Newark on Route 280. She speeds recklessly, trying to make her appointment with Deja. All of a sudden she gets a text alert on her phone. She peeks down at it to see who it's from. Maurice's number is on the display screen. She is so pissed with him that she really doesn't want to open it but her curiosity leads her to do so. She opens it and it reads: The weatherman announced a heat advisory in Newark. Hot and sticky out there. Stay cool! She reads the text and doesn't know how she should take it. Is this a threat about him possibly doing something to her? Is this a warning about maybe the police?

Yesterday part of the reason for his call was to inform her to stay out of Newark. The last thing he needs is to have her traveling the land and Trauma and his Unit attack her. As pissed off as he is with her, he will not be able to live with himself if something happens to her because of him.

Lil Bit cruises through the streets with nervousness. She wonders if his warning is because of Feds or could it be something else? His general statement has her confused out of her mind. She's peeking around at every car that comes close to her. Her nerves are already beat down. This is the last thing she needs right now. She will do exactly what he told her to. After her beauty parlor visit she's going back to Jersey City out of the heat as instructed.

Meanwhile

Maurice and the Federation sit around in the Bat Cave. Only a few days have passed and his crew is already feeling the effect of the war. Even though they're winning, they're losing financially. The drought has gotten worse. Not a sprinkle of cocaine can be found anywhere. They're sitting on kilos and kilos of work and can't make a dime. They can't wait for the war to blow over or until they capture Trauma, whichever comes first. They're eager to be able to get money again.

Maurice on the other hand is only being affected by the war partially. He may not be getting a dime from his Federation but just yesterday he scored $2,600,000. He shook one hundred kilos at the price of $26,000 per kilo. The price may sound ridiculous but to many that number is way beyond fair. At this point the average kilo is being sold at $30,000.

At that rate he scored a profit of approximately $2, 200,000 off of that deal. With a profit margin like that he hasn't missed a beat. As long as he's scoring like that with his Dominicans alone, he can afford to continue the war without losing a dime.

The Dominicans in turn will break each kilo down. They will grind it down into the simplest powder form and add a half a kilo of cut onto each kilo. They will use procaine or lactose, whichever best suits the grain of the material. When it's all said and done they will repackage the cut up kilos and have them ready for resale.

The 100 original kilos they bought will be turned into 150 kilos. They will sell the work gram for gram to small time buyers for $33.00 per gram. For their kilo customers they will charge $30,000 a kilo. At the bare minimum, if they only sell kilos and not break them down, they will have $4,500,000. At the end of their flip they will be a few hundred thousand dollars short of doubling their money.

Just as Maurice said, the drought affects the smaller dealers but it makes the already rich more rich. At this point of the drought all the cocaine on the streets is pure garbage. A certain amount of the purity is already decreased once Maurice stretches one into two. Once the purchaser steps on it, there's very minimal purity left. Even at the lowest level of purity, customers still buy the work with no hesitation because material is so scarce throughout the land that they're just happy to have some material. At this time, even garbage cocaine is feasible to sell.

"As you all see, we are in total control," Maurice gloats. "By now, I'm sure they realize that we're not bullshitting. I bet you they are ready to throw in the towel," he smiles. "We already got their source of money out of the picture. Without him they're harmless. You can't go to war without financial backing. We got all the backing in the world! We can do this forever," he says as he looks at their faces. The looks in their eyes beg to differ. "I talk to ol girl everyday and she has not a clue of who is behind the murder," he says with a smile. "Hitting that block up, was a big statement but it ain't over. We got a lot more to say. We're going to hit up every spot in this town that they're known to be. Yesterday we missed a whole day without striking. That's not a good look. The art of war is to strike continuously so the enemy never gets time to think and come up with a plan of their own. As long as we keep them on the defense they will never get the opportunity to be on the offense. We have to suffocate them! How the hell they gone breathe with no air?"

Meanwhile

Trauma leans back in the raggedy recliner in the living room of the shabby basement apartment. A few of the members of his crew stands before him as he talks on and on. They watch and listen closely as he's speaking. They're quite anxious to hear what the plan is. Fear has found a place in their hearts but none of them will admit it. In just a few days a number of them have been murdered and a few more have been severely injured. Each of them have the secret fear that they could easily be the next murder victim.

Up until this beef they have never been retaliated against. They're used to doing what they choose to do to whoever they choose to do it to, with no repercussions. The whole situation has them off balance because they never had to go this far before.

"Yeah," Trauma says while nodding his head up and down. "We lost a few but that's the game. Sometimes you have to give up a few pawns to move across the board and get the king. It's warfare." He stands up actively. "I love this shit!" he shouts with animation in his eyes. "These niggas think they can't be touched. They move around on the outskirts, slipping in town and out of town, thinking they're safe because they don't live in the hood. But you know what their downfalls are?" he asks as he looks in the eyes of them one by one. "I don't give a fuck if you a rich nigga or a poor nigga, working class nigga or a street nigga, all niggas got one thing in common," he says before pausing for a few seconds. "Every nigga loves a hood bitch. You can move a thousand miles away from the hood but at the end of the day the hood nigga in you gone have to come back home. The hood nigga in you always gone crave some hood rat pussy. I don't give a fuck how far up in the moon you go or how deep into Hollywood you go, it ain't the same. Ain't nothing like a good, dirty, filthy hood rat that will do any and everything you want her to do with no limitations. Hollywood bitches ain't the same," he smiles. "They got too many rules and regulations. They don't want to fuck in the ass. They don't want to swallow. Eventually a hood nigga gotta come home and get blown away by his hood rat bitch. Ain't nothing like a nasty, raunchy, dirt on the bottom of her feet, fishy smelling coochie hood rat. Everybody got at least one rat laying in the cracks and crevices somewhere," he says with an evil grin.

///// CHAPTER 97 /////

One Day Later

Lil Bit rolls around in between the black satin sheets. All of her life she's never had a huge sexual appetite due to the affects of her childhood. Something about this pregnancy has her horny the majority of the day. With Samad being locked up most of the time and not able to relieve her of her sexual frustration it just makes it worse. She's forced to keep that energy pinned up inside of her and makes her a sexual beast when she does get it. Her doctor may have banned her from having sex but he said nothing about oral sex. With their bodies nestled together in the 69 position Lil Bit and Samad please each other like they've never done before. The loud noise of sucking and slurping echoes throughout the room.

Samad is finally home from his small vacation. He's fresh out of the County and hasn't been home for an hour yet and already they're indulging in some heavy sexual business. Lil Bit was so horny that she tackled him at arrival, not giving him a chance to say a word. Samad on the other hand didn't even have sex on his mind. His mind was purely on business just as it has been over the past months.

This is just a fraction of the business that he has to handle. In the couple of weeks that he's been gone he's left his woman sexually deprived and he's also left his block dry. He has enough sense to know that depriving either one of them can result in him losing them to another. He can lose the clientele to another block and he can lose his woman to a man who is willing to give her what she needs. Once he's done servicing his woman, he can tend to his business. He's missed so much money over the weeks and plans to grind extra hard until he gets every dime that he has missed.

Once again he sat in that County Jail and thought like he's never thought before. It seems as if he can only gather his thoughts when he's in jail. When he's on the street he just moves without thinking. He has definitely learned the dangers in doing that. He has no plans of ever going back to the County again. From here on out he knows he has to tighten up so he never falls into the belly of the beast ever again.

As for the first case that he caught, his lawyer promises him that he has nothing to worry about. He feels he has the case beat, hands down. The fact that Samad has no priors on his record is an even better look for him. The lawyer explained that, the worse case scenario, he will get sentenced to a couple of months at Delaney Hall in the drug rehabilitation program.

The double homicide is a bigger issue though. The lawyer informed him that they have witnesses who have identified him and explained the entire situation down to the very smallest details. The stories coincide perfectly. From the looks of things Samad can see that they're trying to send him away for the rest of his life. Things have just started going good for him. He believes that he's just started living and he refuses to allow them to stop his life. He looks at it as if they're trying to stop his shine before it even starts. There's only one way that he can think of that will help him to remain a free man. Two things stand in between his life and his demise and he's determined to remove both of them out of his path.

///// CHAPTER 98 /////

The white Toyota Avalon creeps along Bergen Street with no destination. Both the passenger and the driver peek around nosily in search of any trace of their enemy. The only thing they know about their enemies at this point is what type of cars they drive. They've been combing the streets with a fine tooth comb for hours and they're determined to keep searching until they find what it is that they're looking for.

"They definitely playing the peek a boo game," Trauma says from the passenger's seat. "Popping in and out like suckers. Niggas, come out in the wide open and let's get it on," he says as he realizes how stupid he sounds. Still he goes on. "Let's beef like men!" He wishes it was that easy. To get them to be out in the open would make his job so easy. Not being able to find them is frustrating him tremendously. The more frustrated he becomes the more apt he is to do something foolish. The little common sense that he started with has now vanished. He will do any and everything he can to get even with them.

Meanwhile

Samad is just minutes away from his meeting with his last resort. He's made call after call to everyone he can think of who may have an inkling of where he can get some coke from. Desperation made him get D-Nice to call his cousin once again but to no avail.

The effects of the drought are severe. No one has even a spec of cocaine anywhere in the city. He just hopes he can get hold of anything right now. He would be happy with having garbage right now. Anything beats a blank.

Samad pulls up to the AppleBee's on Springfield Avenue. At his entrance, his man Dee and his partner get out of the Cherokee. Samad's hopes are semi shut down when he sees the looks on their faces. "Psst," he sighs as he looks over to D-Nice. "These niggas ain't got nothing," he barks. "I can tell by the looks on their faces."

Samad parks and gets out. He shakes both of their hands as he stops right in between them. The last time he met with this man he claimed to be the biggest thing in the city. He bragged on and on about him being the only one with work during the drought. Samad prays that he's still singing the same tune. "What's good?" Samad asks with high hopes.

"Not a damn thing," the man replies with sadness on his face. "Ain't no work nowhere," the man says from his white chalky lips. "From the looks of his dry mouth and weary eyes he appears to be starving. Samad assumes that the drought is getting the best of him. "I ain't had shit in about a week but I'm supposed to get my hands on a few tomorrow," he lies. He tells Samad this just to keep him on standby just in case something happens to come through. "I could have had something yesterday but the price was too high. It didn't make sense for me to get it at that price," he lies in order for Samad to keep faith in him.

Samad calls his bluff without even knowing it. "What price was that?"

This question catches the man off guard. He thinks quickly. "They wanted me to pay thirty-four dollars a gram. The best I could have sold it for is thirty-five, thirty-six," he says thinking the numbers will deter Samad.

"Get it. I'll give you thirty six for it," Samad says desperately. The price is sky high but he realizes that having it now is more beneficial than not having it. Even if he barely makes a profit, at least the block will be up and running.

"That's over," the man mumbles. "I called back an hour later and it was already gone," he lies.

"Damn," Samad utters with rage. "So, what time tomorrow do you think?"

He shrugs his shoulders. "Dee got your number right? The minute they come in I'll tell him to hit you," he says as he extends his hand to Samad. Samad returns the handshake and their meeting is over.

A Few Blocks Away

The Toyota Avalon cruises up Avon Avenue into the sunset. More frustration fills Trauma's heart as he looks at the bright orange sun and realizes that another night is coming to an end. Another day has gone by without him touching his enemy. All their cruising up and down the street has been in vain. They got nothing out of it but an empty gas tank. The driver slows down at South 11th Street and makes a left turn onto the block.

A half a block away, a Nissan Quest van starts to pick up speed. It barely slows down as it approaches 11th Street. The white Avalon is slowly approaching the traffic light at Springfield Avenue, which has just turned red. "Now!" Maurice shouts from the passenger's seat. Sal steps on the gas pedal and keeps his eyes glued to the back brake lights of the Avalon.

They just happen to be cruising through the town, not expecting to see Trauma or his squad anywhere when all of a sudden Sal spotted the Avalon. He recognized the car from the night at Diva's when they came speeding through the block shooting out of the window. They now have been following them for a few blocks, just waiting for the perfect time to pull up on them. Trauma and his driver are so busy on the hunt that they don't even realize that they're being hunted as well.

Sal catches up with the Toyota quickly. Maurice hits the button and the window rolls down automatically. "Pull up close as you can," he instructs. "As they approach the car, he looks inside where he sees Trauma laying low in the seat in relax mode. Perfect, Maurice says to himself. By the time Trauma realizes what is going on it will be way too late. Maurice lifts up, hanging his torso out of the window. His long arm stretches out like the arm of the 'rubber band man.' In his hand he grips an eleven shot .45 automatic. "Stop, stop, stop!" he shouts. The van is almost bumper to bumper with the Avalon and they don't even sense their presence. Maurice fires with vengeance. Bloc! Bloc! The back window on the driver's side shatters instantly. Sal inches up as Maurice fires again. Bloc! Bloc! The driver peeks to his right to see where the shots are coming from. Quickly he then looks to his left. He sees the huge handgun aimed at his head and darts out onto Springfield Avenue with no regard of the oncoming traffic. Sal takes off right with him. The loud noise of tires screeching sounds off loudly before the loud sound of gunfire drowns it out. Sal has the van pinned side by side with the Toyota. Trauma draws his gun and aims. Before he can fire Maurice fires two more shots. Bloc! Bloc! In seconds the driver of the Avalon's head bangs into the steering wheel and the car swerves to the right. The car bounces onto the sidewalk out of control. The loud sound of the car crashing into the stop sign can be heard from blocks away.

"Go, go!" Maurice shouts. Sal mashes the gas pedal and speeds away from the scene. "Got his ass!" he barks. "Another one down!" he shouts with glory. "The driver outta here," he says with certainty as he replays in his mind, how the driver's head banged onto the steering wheel lifelessly.

////// CHAPTER 99 //////

Lil Bit cruises along the Newark International Airport yet another time, on her way to drop Deja off. "Yeah, I'm going down here to give him a return on his investment," she says referring to her friend in Miami. "It's time for him to cash out on his profit. It's the least I can do," she says with a seductive smile. "I'm gone go down here and put the mufucker on him," she says with confidence. "I'm gone show him how this little amount of money he spent on that job is the best investment that he could have ever made.

"Huh," Lil Bit sighs. "I think he done already put the mufucker on you. I done seen you go through many friends and I think you really like this one."

"He alright," she replies.

"Alright?" she teases. "I think you open."

"Open?" Deja repeats. "I don't get open. I do the opening! He been open. Girl, the nigga was talking about me relocating to Miami the next morning. He done already proposed to me three times already. How open is that?' she asks with a huge smile.

"Girl, I know you ain't falling for that shit, Deja. You're way too smart for that. The nigga is loaded. That little money he's spent is nothing to him. Don't confuse that with love. You could easily be his trophy for now and once he gets tired of you he will toss you to the side like a bad habit."

"Lil Bit, let me educate you once again," she says arrogantly. "I don't get tossed to the side. Indeed, no matter how beautiful a woman is a man can get bored with her. Every man yearns for different pleasures and adventures. You know how you supply that for him and keep his attention? You have to create the illusion that you offer variety and adventure."

"How do you do that?" Lil Bit asks with inquisitiveness.

"Look baby, a man is easily deceived by appearances. They have a weakness for the visual, so you have to first create a strong physical appearance. The first step is done because your beauty has him trapped already. He won't get bored with you and he won't be able to toss you to the side if you keep him distracted and never, I repeat, never, let him see who you really are. That will make him chase you forever.

Lil Bit sits quietly just absorbing the lesson that she's being taught.

"It's all about conquer. In order to do that you must have two qualities. You must have the ability to make him chase you so hard that he loses focus of himself. You also have to give him a challenge. Challenge is seductive to a man. An extremely sexy appearance always does it. Make him desire you. You have to be careful not to come across as a hoe or a groupie. If you do then he will chase you only to get the coochie and then when he does he will kick you to the curb. Instead, you have to remain mysterious and distant. You'll make his fantasy come to life. Those qualities will make him chase you hard. The more you make him chase the more he will want you. In his foolish mind he will believe that he's chasing you because he wants to and never will he realize that you're manipulating him. Challenge adds spice to a relationship. It's appealing to men. Why do you think the good homebody housewife gets shitted on for the go-go dancer?"

Lil Bit sits back with her mouth wide open. She's awestruck.

"And last but not least, you must make him fear losing you. Never let him get too close. That makes him keep the respect for you. You can't let him get close enough to notice that you have shortcomings. Never give him an inkling that you're human. Even shitting or farting in front of him will make him realize that you are normal. You don't want that. You always have to be bigger than life in his eyes. Now for the fear part. Do you know the best way to make him fear you?" she asks. "Sudden mood swings. You have to go from the perfect woman to the worst bitch in the world right before his very eyes. That's how you keep him fearful of you and off balance."

Lil Bit steers her truck toward the curb in front of Continental Airlines. She slams the gear into the park position as she looks at Deja with pure amazement. She's amazed at what Deja is saying to her. To the average man Deja appears to be just another gold digging hoochie but Lil Bit knows her underneath the surface and respects her highly. Despite what anyone else may think, she believes that Deja definitely has her shit all together. Just as Deja is getting out, Lil Bit finally finds the words to speak. "Where do you get all this shit from?"

"Where?" she repeats. "The Art of Seduction by author Robert Greene," she whispers with a smile. "Reading is fundamental. Bitches need to stop reading all those urban novels. I see them in the shop everyday wasting hours and hours underneath that dryer reading, Block Party and shit like that. Not me," she utters. "They need to read something that's going to stimulate their minds and enhance their game," she barks hastily as she hops out of the truck. She stands on the curb as she reads over the ticket to see which gate her flight is departing from.

Lil Bit can't help but notice the words First Class on her ticket. Why shouldn't she fly First Class when she's a First Class Bitch, Lil Bit says to herself. Deja slams the door shut. Bye, girl. I love you!" she shouts before switching away.

"Love you too! Lil Bit shouts through the open passenger's side window. "Ay! Where's your luggage?" she asks thinking that maybe she was rushing and forgot it at home.

Deja spins around briskly. "At home," she replies. "He told me not to bring any luggage," she says nonchalantly. Lil Bit shakes her head from side to side as she looks at Deja with a bit of admiration. "Remember reading is fundamental!" she shouts as she switches her way into the airport.

Meanwhile

Trauma comes stepping out of the bathroom with just his boxer shorts on. The young woman lays sprawled out ass naked on the air mattress that lies flat on the hard wood floor in front of him. She looks him up and down seductively. As her eyes set onto the crotch area of his shorts, a tingling sensation tickles her kitten. She gets wet and horny just thinking of the hours and hours of sweaty, funky, back breaking sex they indulged in last night.

He lays back down next to her as she watches him with a twinkle in her eye. As he lays there he too replays the scenes of their raunchy sexcapade. This woman has the make up of the perfect woman. She's gorgeous with a body that puts 'Buffie the Body' to shame.

The best part of it all is the fact that no, isn't a part of her vocabulary. She does it all. To the naked eye she appears to be a woman who has her shit all together. Her clothes are top notch. She has over fifteen fur coats, thirty designer pocketbooks, a closet full of shoes and diamonds for days. Everything about her seems to be flawless until you step into her nasty, raggedy one bedroom apartment in which the only furniture she has is the air mattress that lies on the floor in her bedroom. You then find out that she's just Tamika from down the block. She's a ghetto celebrity to those who don't know her but to those who do she's just another hood rat.

Trauma has been dealing with her on and off for years with no real commitment. Both of them come and go as they please. Even when she's committed to someone else that doesn't stop their situation. No one can come in between them. He will do anything for her and vice versa.

The woman crawls closer to him and cuddles up under his wing. She plants her face onto his chest. The feeling of her soft, naked flesh gives him an instant hard on. As much as he would love to bang her back out again, he has a more serious situation to tackle. "Tamika, I need a favor," he whispers.

"What's that, baby?" she asks thinking that he may be in need of a few dollars.

"I got a situation that needs to be situated. Your little friend Rock," he whispers. "I got a problem with him," he says as he looks down into her eyes.

"Huh?" she asks hoping that she's hearing him wrong.

A part of him feels leery about coming to her like this because he's not sure of how she really feels about Rock. For all he knows she could be madly in love with him and his plans could be reversed. After all, Rock spends thousands of dollars here while Trauma rarely spends a dime. Tamika has been dealing with Rock for the past two years wherein Trauma has been around for three years before that. He knows that he's taking a huge risk but if she accepts the proposition it's well worth the risk for him.

"We going through it," he says. "His squad is gunning for me. That shit that just happened to Little Butter?" he asks while nodding his head up and down. "That was their work. So was that shit that happened to Baby last week. I'm out here with my back against the wall. I don't know shit about these niggas. I'm ass naked."

Tamika lays there quietly just taking it all in. "So, what favor you need from me," she asks with a naïve look on her face.

"I need you to do one of two things," he says as he looks deeply into her eyes. "Either you can lead me to him or you can bring him to me." Tamika can't believe her ears. She can't believe what he's actually asking her to do. She's shocked that he would even come at her like this. "My life depends on it," he says as he tries to convince her. "These niggas gunning for me hard."

Rock comes into her mind. She's not in love with him but she does have love for him. Her real passion for him comes from what he does for her. His contribution to her ghetto fabulous lifestyle is about fifty percent. She has a few more dudes on her roster who make up the other fifty percent. She analyzes the situation and wonders how her life will be affected if Trauma was to murder him. "I don't know, Trauma," she sighs. "I'm not that type of girl," she whines.

"Psst, these niggas gunning for me and you just gone let it go like that? Word up? All the time we got in together? All the shit we done did for each other? All the shit we done been through and you gone let these niggas take me off the map? You letting him come in between us? You choosing him over me?"

"No, Trauma stop. Don't do that. I just don't know."

"You in love with that nigga like that? That nigga don't love you. You his jump off. That nigga got a wife somewhere up in the hills. He don't give a fuck about you!" His words are eating her alive. "Never mind," he says. "Forget that I even asked you for the favor. If these motherfuckers slaughter me, I hope you're happy then."

Tamika now considers the fact of how her life would be without Trauma. The guilt trip is definitely working on her. Sure she may like Rock but Trauma on the other hand, she loves. She can't imagine living without him. If something was to happen to him she would be ruined. "What you need me to do?"

///// CHAPTER 100 /////

The charcoal gray Ford Five Hundred cruises up the block. The driver, known as Fuquan is a part of D-Nice's squad. He's been chauffering D-Nice and Samad around for hours with no apparent destination. D-Nice sits back in the passenger's seat with a million thoughts running through his mind while Samad sits in the backseat with only one thought in his mind.

"Man, it's over," Samad sighs. "Tomorrow is another day. Take me to my car. Hopefully tomorrow will be a better day." Another day has passed without him having work. He fears the fact that he may end up spending his savings during the drought and have to start all over again. He feels like he's so close but yet so far. "Something gotta give!"

"Word up," D-Nice agrees.

Minutes later the driver bends the corner onto the pitch black block. Halfway down the street, he pulls behind Samad's rental and parks. "Next day," he mumbles as he extends his hand to give D-Nice a pound. They dat each other and just as their hands slide apart. Boom! Boom! The driver's torso folds over at the seams of his waistline. His chin rests on his right knee.

The look on D-Nice's face is of pure terror as he stares at the driver all bent out of shape. Samad lifts up from the backseat and aims his gun once again at the head of the man. D-Nice squints his eyes, not really wanting to see this. Boom! Boom! Boom! D-Nice cringes with each shot.

"Bitch ass nigga!" Samad shouts with rage. "Come on, let's go," he says as he peeks around making sure the coast is clear. He forces the door open, gets out and walks casually to his car as if nothing has happened. D-Nice follows in a state of shock. Never before has he witnessed anything like this.

They hop into Samad's car and cruise away from the scene, leaving the dead man in the car with the engine still running. "Rat bastard," Samad says. The dead man happened to be on the block working the night Samad murdered the stick up kid. He also happened to be one of the dudes who the detectives took in for questioning. Needless to say he was one of the witnesses they had on file. "Nigga ain't nobody gone get in the way of me getting this money! It's my turn, you heard?" Samad says as he looks over into D-Nice's eyes.

The look in Samad's eyes D-Nice has never seen before. He looks like a madman. It's as if he doesn't even know who Samad has become. He can't understand this side of him nor can he figure out where all this frustration has come from. Just a few months ago before they caught the case, the both of them were just two young men trying to get a couple of dollars for their pockets. Now this? What the fuck is going on, D-Nice asks himself.

What he doesn't understand is Samad has been turned out. Actually having kilos was only a mere dream for him. Now that he's had that dream come to life before his eyes, that alone gives him a sense of power that he's never had before. Once you give a dog a steak, he will never want dog food again.

"You heard?" Samad asks again with even more rage in his bloodshot eyes.

D-Nice nods his head up and down with fear and confusion. "I heard."

Thirty Minutes Later

Lil Bit sits in her living room all alone, just sulking in sorrow. A total of thirty-two birthday balloons have soared to the ceiling. Dozens of roses are lined along the coffee table. The lights are dim and music plays at top volume. 'Ask of You,' by singer Raphael Saadiq plays at high volume. This cassette that is playing, Lil Bit just found in a shoe box full of her deceased older sister, Ashley's belongings. Lil Bit treasures this box because it's the closest thing she has to having her sister.

Ashley was in love with this song. She would play it over and over. Lil Bit can actually hear her sister's voice singing along. She can still remember the facial expressions that she would make as well. A quick glimpse of her sister's face causes her to crack a slight smile.

Today would have marked her 32nd birthday. Each year on this day, Lil Bit celebrates Ashley's birthday as if she's here with her. She does the exact same thing on her mother's birthday as well. She actually buys them gifts and she sings Happy Birthday too. The various gifts that she has bought over the years, she stores in the closet and she plans to never part with them. Some may call it strange or a bit extreme which is why on this day she alienates herself from the world.

She lounges on the couch with a photo album on her lap, just fumbling through looking at the many memories of her childhood. Although her childhood was rough, she had her mother and her older sister with her and now that seems to matter more than anything in the world.

She looks at a photo of Star when she was a baby and it causes a smile to pop up on her face. It saddens Lil Bit that Star has no memories of their sister Ashley or their mom. At times she wonders where Star would be without her in the picture. She would be here with no one to guide her. That thought makes her grateful to be here.

The house phone rings, interrupting her sentimental moment. She grabs the phone. "Yes?"

"Uh Miss Baker, good evening. I have a Samad down here," the concierge says.

"Let him in," she says before ending the call. She quickly gets up and leans over the coffee table. She blows the candles out on the birthday cake. She then runs over and turns the lights on and the stereo off. She prepares the apartment for Samad to come in. The last thing she wants is for him to think that she's lost her mind.

He taps the bell and she lets him in. When he steps in, he kisses her on the forehead. He looks around at the many balloons and becomes confused. "It ain't your birthday," he says as he tries to recall today's date. Sitting in the County Jail all those weeks has him slightly off balance.

"No," she whispers. "It's Ashley's birthday," she says as she points to the huge portrait that leans against an easel a few feet away.

"Who?"

"My older sister," she says.

Samad stares at the beautiful girl. He's amazed at how much alike her and Lil Bit look. The lips, nose and forehead are identical. She even has freckles just like Lil Bit. He stares at her in astonishment for seconds until her hazel eyes appear to come to life. An eerie feeling overtakes him. He quickly turns away. "What's up, Ma?" he asks as he starts toward the bathroom.

Minutes later, he stands in the glass enclosed shower. He scrubs away at his body thoroughly as if he's trying to wash his sins away. Every few minutes the murder plays in his head but he mananges to shake it away. He blows it off as something that had to happen.

This murder is completely different from the first murder he caught which was done out of pure reflex. He had no time to think about it at all. It just happened and before he knew it, it was over. Ashy Mu's murder, on the other hand, was done out of part rage and the other part fear because he didn't trust whether Ashy Mu would retaliate for the murder of his friend. This murder here was done as an act to remain a free man. He has not the slightest bit of remorse because he feels like his life depended on it.

At this point he can now be considered a bonified murderer that can murder and go on with his life as if nothing has happened. It takes a certain coldness to be able to do that. Some can't live with themselves after murdering while others pay no attention to it at all. Samad has reached that level of immuneness.

One more life has to be sacrificed in order for him to live his life as a free man. He plans to make that sacrifice as soon as the opportunity presents itself.

Many minutes later, Samad lays flat on his back as Lil Bit lays curled up beside him. He rubs his rough hands gently over her pregnant belly as he thinks. This drought is driving him crazy and he feels as if he can't go another day without work. He just wishes there was someone somewhere that he could run into that has what he needs.

Samad hates to ask Lil Bit this question over and over again but he can't help himself. "So, you don't know nobody that got it right now?" he asks with a look of desperation in his eyes.

"Uhhm uhhm," she replies. It touches her heart to see him looking like this. She hasn't seen him sad like this since the month he laid around here dead broke. The look in his eyes is the same. She couldn't take it then and she can't take it now. She may not be able to help him today but she will be able to help him soon. It's just about time for her monthly run. The timing could be no more perfect for Samad right now. "I can't help you now," she says sadly. "But give me a few days. Breathe easy," she says casually. "I got you."

///// CHAPTER 101 /////

The cranberry colored 650 BMW cruises up the quiet suburban block of Montclair. At the end of the long block the driver makes the right turn into the driveway of the two story house. At the end of the narrow driveway he stops the vehicle and hops out. Exhausted from a tiring and stressful day, he walks sluggishly toward the back door of his house.

As he gets within a few feet of the door, the bright light of the motion detector on the house next door lights up. The dark yard is now illuminated. Rock stops dead in his tracks with surprise. His eyes fix onto the house where he sees the image of two men standing alongside the other house. He reaches for his gun that rests in his waistband as he backpedals away.

The conversation Trauma had with his good friend Tamika convinced her to do exactly what he hoped she would do, lead her to him. As much as she hated to get herself involved in the matter, she did so because she felt that she owed him this.

Trauma wanted her to make his job that much easier by calling him while they were in the car together or better yet let him in Rock's house without him knowing it. She couldn't imagine putting herself that deep in. Fear of being dragged into this potential murder and having it all fall back onto her made her refuse. Trauma wasn't totally happy with that but he settled for it. His plan is to make a come up by robbing Rock of all his money and jewels before murdering him.

Trauma stands there with an open face. He notices Rock reaching for his weapon but he has him already beat to the draw. Before Rock can even get his off of his hip, Trauma aims the .44 cannon in Rock's direction and squeezes the trigger. Boom! Boom! Just hearing the explosion makes Rock spin around and take off into flight. Boom! He hears from behind him, causing him to run that much faster. Finally he gets his gun out. He turns his body halfway around, while still running. Without even aiming he fires in attempt to keep them away from him. Boc! Boc! Boc! Right after his shots are fired, the sound of another gun fills the air as well. Bloc! Bloc! Bloc!

As Rock is approaching his car his mind tells him to get in the car and pull away but the gunfire sounding off behind him makes him realize the danger in that. He proceeds on his foot chase as he passes the car. The gunshots rip through the air randomly as Rock tries desperately to get out of the way of them.

Rock spins around again, ripping a shot of desperation. Boc! Both Trauma and his accomplice flinch and stop in their tracks. He turns back around and runs for his life. Trauma and his accomplice stand side by side. Determination is on both of their faces. The last thing they want is for him to get away and blow their attack. Boom! Trauma fires once again with fury. His accomplice takes the lead, leaving Trauma in the dust. He sprints behind Rock like an Olympian track star but instead of catching up, Rock runs that much faster. The man begins firing ruthlessly. Bloc! Bloc! Bloc! Bloc!

In between Rock's high step a sudden crash to his right buttock causes his leg to buckle. As painful as it is he manages to continue on. He looks at the end of the driveway as his finish line and he tries his damnest to make it there but the pain in his behind is effecting his step more and more. He slows down drastically as the gunman behind him catches up with him even more. He can hear the steps coming closer behind him. He flings his arm behind him while running, once again. Boc! Boc! Boc!

Only a foot and a half away from the finish line and the man fires two more shots. Bloc! Bloc! Just as the second shot rings a hot ball of fire pounds into Rock's back, causing him to fall forward. Without realizing it, he tumbles over the finish line. With desperation, he grabs hold of the fence and pulls himself onto one knee. He peeks back and sees his enemy coming closer to him. Fear of losing his life picks him up onto his feet. He darts to his right out of their sight.

Seconds later, the man makes it to the end of the alley where he slows down. He's quite hesitant to pop out of the alley, not knowing if Rock will be standing there waiting for him. He leans low, almost crawling until he gets to the edge of the house. He aims his gun first then he looks to the right. To his surprise, not a trace of Rock is left. He stands there baffled when Trauma finally catches up with him. There they stand side by side with defeat in their eyes. "Damn!" Trauma shouts. "You let that mufucker get away?" Trauma is furious. He can't believe they were that close to getting even. He realizes he was wounded but he isn't satisfied with that. He wanted him dead. He considers the fact of tracking him down because he's sure that he couldn't have gotten far.

Right he is. Rock lays fearfully underneath the compact car just a a few feet away. He's scared for his life. He watches the two men standing there with hopes that they will give up instead of coming at him but he's sure that isn't going to happen. They've come too far to lose. He looks at his gun in his hand and a bright idea pops into his head. He lifts the gun off of the ground as high as he can. Boc! Boc! Boc! He fires. Loud bells ring in his ear almost deafening him.

Trauma and his accomplice look around not knowing which direction the shots are coming from. They realize that he has the upper hand because there is no way they can fight the unseen. They duck low and back pedal away with their guns drawn. Both of them turn around and trot away. Boc! Rock fires once again just to keep them going.

///// CHAPTER 102 /////

One Week Later

Lil Bit lays curled up in her bed with a variety of emotions. Many days have passed and she still hasn't heard a word from Maurice. Not only has he not called her to set up her monthly run, he also hasn't called her to give her this month's rent. Every fifth of the month faithfully since they've been dealing, he's met with her on that day to give her the money. She's gotten so accustomed to it that she never worries about it or even attempts to pay it on her own.

Although she has the money to pay it herself, she still feels that she shouldn't have to. She's sure that he's doing it out of spite. She believes that he is doing this to get even with her. One thing she knows about him is he uses his money to control people. Maybe he thinks she can't pay the rent and she will have to call him. She can only imagine how he would use that in his favor which is why she would never call him and give him that satisfaction.

She gets up and storms over to her dresser and grabs hold of her checkbook. She fills the $3,800 check out with anger. She signs her alias on the bottom line and all of a sudden she gets a feeling of independence. This check is just her first step toward her independence and it feels great. She realizes that without his financial support she has no commitment to him. Outside of their business relationship, she will owe him nothing. The more she does for herself, the less control he will have over her life. She understands it all so clearly right now. She just hopes that he understands it.

Meanwhile

Maurice and Sal cruise along Clinton Avenue in search of anyone that is even affiliated with Traum and his Unit. The fact that a member of the Federation has been touched puts a bad taste in Maurice's mouth. He feels violated and disrespected. He hoped they would get through this war without any of them being harmed. The fact that Rock has been injured scorns Maurice's ego. Now more than ever he realizes that they're not as untouchable as he always thought they were.

Rock has no clue of how Trauma found out where he resides. Tamika isn't even one of his suspects. In fact she was the first person he called after speaking to Maurice. The fact that none of them knows how Trauma knew where to find them has all of the Federation walking on eggshells. They wonder what else he knows.

The shot to the buttock was harmless but Rock had to undergo surgery for the wound to his back. After Trauma and his accomplice fled the block, Rock entered his home where he hid the weapon and bleached his hands of any left over gun powder. He made a call to the police and hung up just to have it on record that he called. In no time at all the police were at his door. His call didn't do it but the calls from his neighbors did. He stuck to his story about a carjacking all the way through. The gun that his neighbors reported him having, he denied totally.

When Maurice received the phone call from Rock, no one rushed to the hospital. There was no need for them to be there when he had Tamika there waiting on him hand and foot just as any other good woman would do. Instead they hit the streets with vengeance. They've been on the street day and night but to no avail. The entire town is like a ghost town. The emptiness of the streets has very little to do with their war. It's due to the lack of cocaine which leaves dealers with no reason to be on the street. "Yo, man," Maurice whispers from the passenger's seat. "Somebody gotta pay for that. I ain't going in tonight until somebody does."

Sal looks at him from the driver's seat. "I can dig it."

///// CHAPTER 103 /////

Samad received a call from Mike the rent-a-car dude minutes ago. He claims that it is imperative that they meet. The sound of his voice was demanding, which pissed Samad off dearly.

Samad sits parked in the white Nissan Murano as the silver Toyota Hybrid Highlander comes speeding up the block recklessly. Mike slams on the brakes at the sight of the Murano. He parks across the street and jumps out with rage. Samad hops out of his vehicle with equally as much rage. Mike storms across the street as Samad awaits him. The look in Mike's eyes makes Samad add that much anger to his face.

Finally they stand face to face. Samad speaks first. "Yo, 'B', I don't know what the fuck you take me for but you better check your tone when you talk to me," he says with seriousness in his voice.

Mike ignores him totally. "Yo, why the fuck you didn't tell me that boy was murdered in my fucking car?"

Samad hesitates before replying. He stands there with a false look of confusion on his face. "What boy?"

"Whatever the fuck his name is. The one who had my gray Ford."

"Gray Ford, gray Ford? Who Fu? Murdered? Where? I ain't seen him in days."

"Yeah, I know you didn't cause he's dead. I got a call from Robbery Homicide a couple of hours ago stating that I have to come down there and claim my car and they want me for questioning," he says with fear in his eyes. "Apparently, they found his body in my car last week. What the fuck am I supposed to tell them mufuckers?"

Now Samad gets nervous. He sure hopes this doesn't lead back to him. "Shit," he mumbles. "Tell them you don't know shit."

"I gotta tell them mufuckers something!" he shouts. "Damn!" He stomps like a kid who is having a temper tantrum. He starts pacing back and forth in front of Samad. "Just a few days before that another motherfucker got murdered in my Avalon over there on 11th Street," he whispers as he grabs hold of his head. "Fuck! I ain't even go to claim that one yet. This shit crazy. It's all starting to be one big headache. Every week I'm picking up one or two of my cars from the pound. Niggas getting in shoot outs with my cars. They getting locked up with drugs and guns in my cars. Mufuckers ain't got no license or nothing," he whines. "My uncle on my ass. He said I'm putting his license on the line."

"Ay man, no need to cry now," Samad says casually. "You knew them mufuckers ain't have no license when you rented the cars to them. You gotta watch who you renting cars to. All money ain't green. You ever heard the saying, greedy people starve?" he asks, repeating the words that Lil Bit once said to him. "I know you're trying to expand your business but."

"Fuck!"

Meanwhile. Extreme silence and deep concentration fills the room here in the basement apartment. A total of four chess games are going on all at once. Trauma paces back and forth, catching a short glimpse of all of them. Him and his crew sit in this basement day after day. He forces them to play game after game with hope of them sharpening up their minds. He compares war to chess and figures once they master the game of chess they will become better warriors. He tests their skills every couple of days by playing head up with them from time to time just to see if they're advancing as players.

Trauma grabs his phone and starts dialing Tamika. "Yo," he whispers, not trying to break their concentration. "What's good? Anything new on old boy?"

"He might be getting discharged from the hospital tomorrow. He's up and walking but his fever won't go down. That is why they have not released him yet."

"Alright keep me posted. Later," he says before ending the call. He paces back and forth with his mind running wild. It's time for another attack. Who and where he hasn't quite decided as of yet.

"Yeah!" the young man shouts from across the room, breaking the silence. "Checkmate, bitch!"

/ / / / / CHAPTER 104 / / / / /

Samad has finally accepted the fact that no product is out there. He's lost all hope of finding something. He's called every person he knows that has a plug; more than once at that. They all have his number stored and he hopes they will give him a ring if something comes through.

Today he didn't even bother going outside. He finds it to be senseless, just riding around up and down the street for nothing whatsoever. With gas at $5.00 a gallon, he can burn $50.00 a day easily. Speaking of burning, his smoke habit exceeds way above $100.00 a day. He blows through at least 5, $20.00 jars of 'Sour' everyday. On a good day he may breeze through ten jars easy. His Ciroc and Gatorade habit comes out to another hundred dollars. His excessive weed smoking and his vodka drinking gives him 'the munchies' as he calls it. He eats at least $60.00 worth of food a day. All in all it costs him close to $500.00 a day just to go outside.

Never before was it like this. He's never been this reckless with money. What he spends in a week now used to be his profit for the whole week. Now that he's gotten a taste of the good life he's gotten extra loose with his spending habits. The drought has had one advantage. It has helped him to put things back in their proper persepective. He hadn't even realized how far gone he had gotten in such a short time. He proved the myth to be really true, 'Fast money, you get it fast and you spend it fast.'

Samad stands on the balcony, just staring over the Hudson River. The many yachts that are sailing along bring joy to his heart. He just wishes that one day he will be able to play like that. His attention is diverted across the water at the beautiful buildings in New York City. Living in New York is also a dream of is. He nods his head up and down with great appreciation. Something about this view inspires him to take his game to the next level.

He pulls the 'Sour' filled blunt from his pocket and sparks it up. He takes a drag of the smoke as he looks at the spectacular view. He exhales slowly. The smoke seeps from his mouth. He coughs violently. "Swww, sww, sww," he attempts to keep the smoke in his lungs. He watches as the smoke ascends high into the air. "Sky is the limit."

Meanwhile a Few Miles Away

Maurice has gotten frustrated with this entire situation. He searches high and low but not a sign of Trauma is evident. He leaves not a trace. He could have easily had this war ended long ago but he wanted to handle it alone just him and his crew. It started with them and he wanted it to end with them. At this point he's just outright tired of the cat and mouse chase altogether and just wants it to be over with. His aggravation leaves him no other choice but to call in a trained professional.

He sits parked in front of U.S. Airways departure ramp as the slim framed, sneaky looking man walks toward the car that Maurice is sitting in. The man is so average looking that he doesn't spark the attention of anyone. The only thing noticeable to the average onlooker is the fact that he's traveling with not a single piece of luggage. He snatches the passenger's side door of the van open and climbs inside. "What's good?" Maurice asks.

"You already know," the Stalker says with an ice cold look in his eyes. "Murder she wrote."

///// CHAPTER 105 /////

More days have passed and still no word from Maurice. Here it is the middle of the month and she's pissed off that he hasn't called her. For all he knows she could have gotten kicked out of her apartment. The thought that he doesn't give a fuck makes her not give a fuck about him, even more.

Stubbornness makes her hesitant to call him but it's time to go to work. She should have been there and back almost two weeks ago. She hates to call him but at the end of the day it's all business she tells herself.

Lil Bit listens patiently as the phone rings. "Yeah?" Maurice answers with an agitated tone. He's quite sure that she's calling about the rent money. He can't wait to hear her come out and beg for it so he can really let her have it. He's been waiting for this day to come. She's been playing him for weeks, getting slicker and slicker with her mouth, he feels. Now it's his turn.

"Uhm, I'm calling for my schedule," she says making sure she picks the right words. She knows to tie all ends when talking on the phone. The FEDS could easily be listening on their line. "What day am I to go in?" she asks as politely as she can.

"Going in where?" he asks as if he's clueless.

"To work."

"Oh that?" he replies sarcastically. "Oh, no one told you? Uhmm, I'm sorry to tell you this but the recession is killing us. I had to let a few employees go. The sad part is you're one of the ones who we had to let go. We're no longer in need of your services," he says with a smile. Finally he feels as if he's gotten even. What can she do without money, he says to himself. Now let's see if her new friend can take care of her. $4,000 a month for rent alone will send the average nigga to the poor house, he smiles. "If things pick back up, I'll let you know. Look at the bright side. We're expecting a tremendous 2009," he says sarcastically. He sits back awaiting her reply. He's expecting her to beg and plead with him. He plans to play hard ball with her until she's willing to play by his rules.

She's burning up with rage. She has to bite down on her lip to prevent from cursing him out. It takes all the strength she has to be able to remain cool and calm. Finally she opens her mouth and she's not sure what is going to come out. "Okay," she says surprisingly. She ends the call in peace. "You black bastard!" she shouts furiously. "Ooooh!"

Maurice holds the phone in his hand just looking at it. He's shocked at the way it all played out. He expected her to lose her composure and she didn't. The fact that she didn't makes him even more livid. He feels like she got another one up on him.

He sits back and suddenly he feels played. He considers the fact that maybe she has that much faith in her new friend that she believes he can take care of her. Even thinking this enrages him even more.

He feels like she's laughing in his face. The nerve of her to ask me to pay the rent when she ain't fucked me in I don't know how long. This bitch must think I'm a super duper sucker, he tells himself. She may be laughing now but he plans to get the last laugh at any cost. "I got something for your little ass," he thinks aloud. "Let's see how hard you gone laugh then."

Meanwhile

The Stalker sits behind the steering wheel of the black Buick Lacrosse that Maurice rented him just to do what he needs to do. Maurice has his own business to handle and doesn't have the time to babysit the Stalker.

The Stalker holds a computer printout from the Department of Correction's website. The print out is a photo of a 32-year old man by the name of Horace Jackson. This man is known to the city as Trauma. The Stalker stares at the photo until the man's face sticks in his mind like a magnet. He lays the photo on the passenger's seat.

He then pulls a duffle bag from underneath his seat. He digs his hand inside and pulls out a .40 caliber handgun. An infra-red beam is attached to it. He grabs hold of a magazine filled with hollow tips. He slams the magazine into the butt of the gun. He goes through this once more before tucking the guns on both sides of his waistline. He digs further in the bag where he finds a silencer. That will be perfect just in case he's in a public place. He can do what's needed and keep it moving.

He plants the bag under his seat before starting up the car. He slams the gear shift into the drive position and he cruises up the block enroute to his manhunt. Trauma's exact whereabouts, he has no clue. The only details he has are the few that Maurice has given him. Along with the photo he has a map of New Jersey and two fully loaded handguns. His goal is to get his man and that, he's determined to do. Afterall, no Trauma, no check.

///// CHAPTER 106 /////

2 A.M. Samad walks slowly around the back of Lil Bit's high rise. He's busy puffing away and thinking. Suddenly his thoughts are interrupted by music. The sound of rapper Jay-Z's 'Song Cry' gets clearer and clearer with each of Samad's steps. Finally Samad encounters the vehicle that the music is coming from. He takes a quick peek at the tinted pick-up truck and thinks nothing of it. He just continues on his way, cooking his brain.

Behind the tinted glass there sits Maurice. He's been sitting out here for hours. He parked right here knowing that this is the perfect spot. He has a clear view of who is coming in and out of the building. He hopes to one day catch Lil Bit and her friend dead in the act. He's sure she has a friend although she denies it. For some strange reason he just wants to see it with his own eyes.

Maurice looks at the man walking and smoking and not a thought crosses his mind. The saggy jean, oversized t-shirt wearing kid doesn't spark any suspicion. In his wildest dreams he would never imagine Lil Bit even considering a dude like him. More than anything else he figures he taught her better than that. He knows he groomed her to want nothing but the best. He believes that he has raised the bar. He assumes that the dude that she's with must be of at least equal stature to him, because his ego won't allow him to believe that a man of higher stature than him even exists.

Maurice thinks he has it all figured out. He thinks whoever the dude is he must be from out of town because he doesn't believe Lil Bit would be foolish enough to get involved with a dude from this town and take the risk of him finding out. He knows that she is well aware that he knows anyone who is worth knowing.

Maurice takes one last look at the young boy who appears to be one step above a peasant. "Nah," he mumbles to himself. How wrong he is.

Ten Hours Later

Samad cruises through the parking lot on Halsey Street, downtown Newark. He hops out of the driver's seat and proceeds toward the parking lot attendant. D-Nice gets out of the passenger's seat and from the backseat a man gets out as well. The three men step out of the lot and make their way toward Branford Place.

Halfway down the block they step into New Era. "Born, what up?" Samad shouts with joy.

"What up, Bro!" the man says from over the tall counter.

"Born, this my man, Off the Chain," Samad says in introduction. "Take care of him. Give him anything he want."

"Anything?" Off the Chain asks with greed in his eyes.

"Yeah, anything. Do you."

Meanwhile

Days have passed since Deja left Miami. Still she sports her Florida tan which makes her as black as tar. The tan makes her look like an African statue. Even with the tan her glow still shines dazzlingly. Her glow is from the happiness that she feels. The few days that she spent with her friend were nowhere near enough. In just those few hours that they spent together he managed to make her the happiest girl in the world. It's possible to believe that Deja has been bitten by the 'Lovebug."

"See," Deja shouts at the top of her lungs while all the women in the shop listen to her with their undivided attention. "The problem with ya'll young girls is ya'll got it all fucked up. Ya'll busy out here chasing the big ballers. Fucking with bosses been played out. Them niggas done came up in the ranks already. They got their wives already who been by their side from day one. She was with him when he was hand to handing, when he put his team together and finally when he blew up. He ain't gone leave that bitch for nothing in this world. He may get a little pussy on the side but that's it. What ya'll need to do is go for the little ugly dude with the potential cause he's next on the come-up. If you play your cards right, you can come up with him. Even if you don't come up with him you can still have your way with him," she says with her eyes stretched wide open. "They're easier to work with or should I say work?" she says with sarcasm. "He's young and prideful which means he has everything in the world to prove to you. The streets are filled with niggas who doing it and your little ugly duckling knows that you could easily be fucking with one of the niggas who got it. Deep down inside he knows he has nothing compared to the real ballers. That will make him try to compete with them just to keep you. He will do anything to prove to you that they have nothing over him. You ask him for something and even if he can't afford it he will try his hardest to get it for you. Even if it breaks his bank doing so," she adds. "He would rather go broke than to admit to you that he doesn't have it."

Deja's attention is broken by a huge flatbed that has pulled up in front of her shop and parked across the parking lot. After a quick glance, she continues on with her gold digging lesson. "Now a boss on the other hand. He has nothing to prove cause he knows that he got it and because he has it he thinks you should be happy just to have the opportunity to be with him. In his mind he thinks that he makes you look good just by being by his side. He knows that he boosts your popularity so in return he will give you nothing. He doesn't care if you think he has it or not because the rest of the city knows that he has it. He will sex you over and over without giving up a dime. Believe that!" she says before she's interrupted by the ringing of the shop's doorbell. She looks at the door and sees a short Caucasian man standing at the door. She hits the buzzer to let him him in. He walks in holding a sheet of paper.

Deja laughs to herself as she looks at the short orange colored man. "Looking like a lil carrot," she whispers secretly causing all the women to bust out laughing. "Yes, may I help you?" she asks politely.

"Yes, I have a delivery for a Deja," he says trying hard to pronounce her name correctly.

She stands there in a baffled state. "I'm Deja."

He walks over to her. "Sign here please," he says as he hands the sheet of paper over to her.

"What is it?" she asks as she signs the paper. "Who is it from?" she asks anxiously. She hands the paper back to him and in return he hands her two sets of car keys. She looks at the keys with confusion as he walks toward the door. She watches him as he climbs into the driver's seat of the flatbed and starts backing up into the second parking space.

He hops out of the truck and begins unloading a small vehicle carefully into the parking space. Quickly Deja puts it altogether. She knows just who the gift is from. The flatbed driver with the orange Florida tan and the Florida license plates on the back of the flatbed are both a dead give away.

All the women watch with admiration and amazement. She's a star in all of their eyes, even Lil Bit who sits quietly at the far end of the room. In a matter of minutes everyone's eyes are fixed on the beautiful brand new fire engine red, S5 Audi Coupe with the pure white interior. A big red bow dangles from the rearview mirror.

Deja is blown away yet she remains as cool as a cucumber. She knows exactly who sent the $60,000 gift to her. While in Miami she happened to make a comment about an Audi that she saw on the street and now just a few days later here she has one. Just when she thinks he can't make her any happier, he manages to outdo himself and change her mind.

She looks over to her number one fan, Lil Bit. They lock eyes. Lil Bit is speechless from it all. Deja shrugs her shoulders slowly. "Ay what can I say?" she whispers followed by an arrogant wink.

///// CHAPTER 107 /////

Days Later

Lil Bit can't get over the way Maurice acted the last time she spoke to him. The more she thinks about it the angrier she becomes. She understands the whole idea of him no longer paying her rent due to the fact that they're no longer sleeping together and he senses that she has another man in her life, but she can't get with the fact that he's doing something that he always taught her not to do. He always warned her about doing business with her heart. He says that's the difference between men and women. With that being said she feels it's only fair to say that right now he's being a bitch ass nigga.

She wonders if he's just trying to prove a point or if he's really cut her off. That part scares her tremendously. The trips to Jamaica are her only source of income. The little money she makes as Deja's partner at the shop in no way can provide the lifestyle that she's grown accustomed to living. All she can envision is her life going downhill from here.

She's pregnant with no income to provide for her child. Samad's inconsistency lets her know that she can't depend on him to take care of her and a child. In all reality he needs her more than she needs him and they both know it. Her future is starting to look cloudy and that scares her more than anything else in the world. She refuses to sit back and watch her life go sour. There's no way in the world that she's going to allow a man to send her back to the poor house where she's lived most of her life.

A part of her believes that Maurice will give in soon but the other part thinks he may not. She knows more than anyone else in the world how stubborn he is and how far he will go to prove his point. She just doesn't know how long she should wait to find out if he's going to have a change of heart. The whole situation is a sticky one. It's like she's sitting around waiting for her destruction and that she just can't do.

She's thought about it over and over and finally she thinks she's come up with the right answer. The answer could easily cause her to lose her life but at this point she feels like she really has nothing to lose. She already considers herself a dead woman walking.

She walks onto the balcony where Samad sits just watching the water through the darkness. She stands there looking at him as she debates if she's doing the right thing or not. "Hmphh," she sighs. Here it goes, she says to herself. "Bay, how much money can you put your hands on right now if you had to?"

This question takes Samad by total surprise. "Huh?" he replies defensively.

"How much money you got right now?"

The revised question he finds to be more offensive than the original one. "Why you ask that?"

"Listen Bay, I ain't trying to get in your personal business. I just came up with an idea. You need work and I know where to get work from. How much can you come up with?"

Now he understands more clearly. His ego still won't allow him to open up his bank account to her but he realizes now isn't the time to hide behind his foolish pride. He thinks carefully before speaking. "I got fifty that I can touch right now but a few cats got a couple of dollars they owe me," he lies. "I'm just waiting around on them."

Lil Bit begins calculating like an accountant. "Would you be willing to trust me with that fifty?" she asks with uncertainty.

Good question, he thinks to himself. That he's not sure of. Giving her all of his money is a big gamble that he isn't sure if he should take. Giving her all of his bank and having something go wrong will lead him back to where he started from; dead broke. Having this money with no outlet to get any work will eventually lead him to the exact same place; dead broke. "Damn, he says to himself. "You sure?"

"Bay, I only talk about what I know. If I wasn't sure I wouldn't have came to you with it. Yes or no, are you willing to trust me with the fifty?"

"But where you gone get it from?"

"Listen, ask me no questions and I will tell you no lies. Yes or no? It's that simple."

He sits back quietly just analyzing everything from start to finish. Finally he speaks. "Without you I wouldn't have the fifty in the first place. I have no choice."

"Good. Get the fifty to me with no questions," she says with great emphasis. "Give me a couple of days to do my magic and I guarantee you it will be the biggest and the best investment you ever made."

That's music to his ears. He's sold on it. "Say no more."

▰▰▰▰▰ CHAPTER 108 ▰▰▰▰▰

Two Days Later. Samad has covered his end of the bargain with Off the Chain. He bailed him out as promised. He's clothed him and put a few dollars in his pocket. Now it's time for Off the Chain to cover his end of the deal. His first assignment has been issued.

It's the middle of the night and the only sign of life on the streets are the crack heads who are desperately in search of crack. Samad cruises the dark secluded block while D-Nice plays the passenger's seat. In the backseat there sits Off the Chain. On his lap sits a 16 shot Ruger which is fully loaded with the safety off and ready for action.

"Wait till she gets a little further out of the light," Samad says as he watches the frail crack addict closely. She walks down the block with her eyes glued to the ground as if she's hoping for crack to be lying there waiting for her.

This woman is the only barrier that stands in the way of Samad's future. After a little research he found out who the name Deborah Miles is attached to. She is the second witness to his homicide. He doesn't recall her being out there that night. So much was going on that he didn't see her but apparently she saw him. He knows how dirty cops play and assumes that they used crack or money for crack as an incentive to get her to sign the statement. Too bad that a five minute high is about to cost her, her entire life.

"Here we go," Samad says as he steps on the gas pedal. "You ready?" he asks as he looks at Off the Chain through the rearview mirror.

Off the Chain lifts the Ruger from his lap, gripping it tightly. "I was born ready." D-Nice's heart pounds like a drum. All this is starting to be too much for him. Murdering a crack head woman seems crazy to him but strangely he kind of understands it. He just wishes he wasn't a part of it. He wouldn't be a part of it if Samad didn't force him to come.

Samad slams on the brakes, cutting the woman off. She stops dead in her tracks. There she stands cluelessly. Her eyes stretch open with fear as Off the Chain crawls out of the backseat. He stands in front of her with his face concealed by his hood which is tied tightly. He lifts his gun in the air and fires. She's so petrified that she can't move a bit. "Boc! The bullet rams into her chest, sending her backwards a few feet. Off the Chain steps closer to her as he fires again. Boc! This time he aims for the head but miraculously it sinks into her shoulder causing her to twirl around like a ballerina. He fires again. Boc! This shot smacks into her back, forcing her to fall face first onto the asphalt. She tries to crawl away but the pain has her body weighed down. Off the Chain stands directly over her as he squeezes the trigger once again. Click...Click! He looks at the gun with surprise before aiming at her once again. Click...click...click!

"Oh shit!" Samad shouts. "The fucking gun jammed," he whines as he lowers himself into the seat. He sits there in fear of being seen by her. Click...click...click, he hears before him and Off the Chain lock eyes. Click...click! "Come on!"

Off the Chain runs to the backseat and hops in. Samad pulls off before he can even close the door. "Got damn!" he shouts with anger and fear. The fear comes from the fact that he may just have made the situation worse.

Meanwhile. The go-go bar is packed wall to wall. Gorgeous half naked women decorate the room beautifully but tension is still evident. With all the gorgeous dolls here inside of the Doll House but there's no one to play with them. They're doing their job and still no one seems to be interested. Mischief still covers most of their faces. They seem to be more focused on starting trouble than playing with the dolls.

The Stalker sits quietly in the far corner of the room, just sipping orange juice. From the angle he sits he can see everyone that comes in and goes out of the bar. His purpose here isn't to play with the dolls either. He's here for the sole purpose of tracking down his prey. One of the details that Maurice gave him is that Trauma loves go-go bars. Supposedly he frequents these types of bars on a regular. The Stalker hopes to catch him during one of his random visits so he can carry out his mission.

The Stalker is so busy watching his surroundings that he hasn't even noticed the thick chocolate bunny that has creeped up behind him. He looks her over from head to toe, one good time. Her thick frame is well proportioned. Her tiny bikini top and skimpy G-string bottom makes her look naked. "Ay Daddy," the woman says as she climbs onto his lap. He tries to push her away gently but she resists. All eyes seem to now be on him and the woman. "Wanna lap dance?" He looks around and sees everyone staring. The last thing he wants to do is to make everyone suspicious of him. He agrees to the lap dance. He sits back paying no attention to her at all as she grinds her soft naked ass on his lap. She runs her hands over the nape of her neck while she grinds away sexily. The entire time she's working, he is as well. He watches the door with no interruption. Finally she gets tired of wasting her time and she gets up. He hands her a twenty dollar bill for her services.

The lights come on, signaling that the night is over. As soon as the lights dim the Stalker walks out sneakily. The night may be over for most, but his night is just beginning.

///// CHAPTER 109 /////

Days Later

Lil Bit is back safe and sound. The moment she got here she made the call to her lover. She can't wait to see the look on his face when he sets his eyes on what she's brought back for him. With all the danger that she's put herself in she just hopes that he's appreciative.

The entire time that she was in Jamaica she thought back and forth if she was doing the right thing. There's no doubt in her mind that she definitely did the wrong thing. A few times she almost pulled back but her fear of not being able to provide for herself made her continue on.

Surprisingly Muhsee didn't ask her a question. The bullshit story she had prepared for him was not even necessary. She realizes exactly why he's participating in the act. For one, he's a businessman. His business is selling kilos. Two; he will do anything to get close to her. He actually thinks that he has a chance with her. He's always believed that but now more than ever he thinks he's gotten to her. Why does he think that? She made him believe that. This particular time she wasn't so reluctant to his flirting. She didn't exactly flirt with him but not once did she shut down any of his outrageous gestures. Instead she just listened to him with a bright smile on her face. That smile turned him into silly putty in her hands. Deep in her heart she feels terrible about playing with his mind but in the words of Deja 'sometimes you have to use what you got to get what you want.'

Lil Bit holds the door open for Samad to enter. "Ay Mami," he says with cheer. His joy has very little to do with seeing her and everything in the world to do with the work that she has for him. She closes the door behind him. "What's up? Talk to me," he says with anxiousness in his eyes.

"Damn, Bay no kiss, no hug, no how are you," she says with a smirk on her face. She makes her way toward the bedroom and he follows her with anticipation. She steps inside the room while he stands in the doorway. She points to the bed without saying a word.

His eyes pop wide open. He pinches himself to see if this is a dream. What the fuck, he says to himself as his eyes set on the stack of kilos that are there. She told him it would be the biggest investment he ever made but still he didn't imagine this. He runs over to the bed and lifts one of the kilos into the air. He kisses it gently. "Muaah."

"Damn, you kiss that and you didn't even kiss me? Wow!"

"I will kiss anything you want me to kiss on you," he says seductively as he walks over to her. He hugs her tightly and kisses her like he's never kissed her before. His passion makes all this worthwhile. After a minute or so he snatches away from her and goes back over to the bed. He quickly counts the stack of kilos. "You got ten?" he asks with astonishment. "Who all these for?"

"Who else?" she asks with sarcasm.

"Mines?" he asks.

"No...ours." She corrects him letting him know clearly that they're now partners.

"How the fuck you pull that off?"

"Ah," she says as she puts her fingers across her own lips. "Remember, ask no questions and I will tell you no lies."

"Okay, okay. What's the verdict on them?"

"Twenty-thousand, five hundred," she says.

"Yeah?" he asks. He was expecting to hear a much higher number than that. At this time that number is as extinct as the Dinosaur but he will never admit that to her. Lil Bit has no idea that the average going rate is ten thousand dollars more right now. "So, what do I have to bring back?" he asks as he calculates ten kilos multiplied by $20,500. He then deducts the fifty grand that he gave her up front. "A hundred and fifty-five thousand right?"

"Correct," she replies.

Samad's eyes are filled with gratitude. His dreams have come true thanks to her. She's put him in a position that he could have never gotten into on his own. What he doesn't know is she just put herself into an even better position. Lil Bit took his fifty grand and added ten grand of her own money to it. She wired the money to Muhsee by Western Union into the twelve designated accounts. The sixty grand paid for all ten kilos, leaving no balance at all. That she will never tell Samad though. She will keep that in total secret from him. $14,500 profit on ten kilos will score her $145,000 at the end of this deal.

Samad runs to the closet and comes right back out in no time at all. He stands before her as he changes his sneakers.

"What you doing?" she asks with attitude.

"Bout to hit the street. I got work to do," he sings. "Ain't no coke nowhere in the town and now I got it. Ain't no time to waste."

She shakes her head from side to side. "Not tonight, you're not," she says as she pulls rank that she's never pulled on him before. "The streets ain't going nowhere. It's after 11. Ain't nothing out there but trouble at this hour. You got all day tomorrow to do whatever you have to do. You're not leaving here. You might as well take your clothes off and take it down."

Samad stares into her eyes. The graveness in them lets him know that she already has her mind made up. Instead of disputing with her, he does as instructed. As he's peeling his clothes off he stares at the kilos with joy.

Dreams do come true.

///// CHAPTER 110 /////

It's 7 A.M. and Samad is up bright and early. He couldn't sleep a wink. He tossed and turned like a young kid does on the night before the first day of school. He can't wait to hit the streets. He just hopes the streets are still dry and no one has work. If so, he has some major plans.

As soon as he gets into his car he starts dialing numbers on his phone. He listens impatiently as D-Nice's phone rings until the voicemail comes on. He refuses to take that for an answer. He quickly dials again and again until D-Nice's groggy voice comes through the phone. "Hello?" he says with attitude. He hates to be awakened out of his sleep.

"Yo Son!" Samad shouts through the phone almost bursting D-Nice's eardrum. "What the fuck you still doing in the bed? It's a beautiful day in the hood. The sun is blazing and the birds are chirping." He pauses to give D-Nice time to register his words into his sleepy head. "I said, the birds are chirping, you heard?"

D-Nice catches on to what Samad is telling him and suddenly he's no longer half dead. His spirit has been awakened. "I heard," he sings. "Where you at?"

"On my way to you."

Twenty Minutes Later. Samad steps into the kitchen of their apartment. D-Nice watches with excitement as Samad lays the shopping bag onto the kitchen table. He slides the two kilos from within and D-Nice's eyes light up with joy. "Yeah nigga! We back and guess what? We the only niggas in town with that twirl! And there's a lot more where that came from."

Samad would have loved to show the stack of kilos off to D-Nice just so he could feel that feeling that he felt when Lil Bit showed them to him. He tried to bring all of them out but Lil Bit denied. She figured with his luck he would end up getting locked up with all ten of them. Then all the risk she took would be in vain. Right now she can't afford that. She needs him more than ever right now. He's her only source of income and she has to protect him from any bullshit that he can get into.

She knows that he has never played on this level. He's brand new to the big league. She's been around it for quite some time now. She plans to raise him and teach him almost everything that she knows about the game. Then hopefully they will blow up together. Then she won't need Maurice for anything.

She's still having second thoughts about what she's done but she realizes it's too late to second guess it now. It's already done so she may as well make the best of it.

"What's the ticket?" D-Nice asks.

"Nigga, you already know you get it for the same price they gave it to me for. Twenty five," he utters.

"Yeah?" D-Nice replies as he thinks of how low the price is compared to all the other numbers that he's heard floating around. He's so happy with that number that he doesn't even consider the fact that it could be lower. He would be hurt if he knew that even at this number his best friend will score $4,500 off of him.

Samad doesn't feel the slightest bit of guilt for overcharging his best friend. Maybe last year or even a few months ago he would have but today he looks at it as business.

"Damn, I only got seventeen," D-Nice sighs.

"Don't worry about it! It's nothing. Just give me the first eight thousand that you make and I'll give it to them. I got the coach in my pocket," he brags. "We ain't got nothing but time on our side. Nigga hit the shelf and get the bake and the blender. I'm gone show you how to make this cake, you heard?"

"I definitely heard!"

///// CHAPTER 111 /////

The Next Day. The block is fluttered with so many people that it resembles the block of 42nd Street in Manhattan. Instead of bright lights and tourists, the block is filled with crack heads and raggedy houses. The only bright lights on the block are the lights from their Bic lighters as they spark up their pipes in the alleys.

The addicts swarm the block with gratitude in their eyes. The town has been so dry that some of them have been forced to venture off into other drugs as a substitute while others have traveled many miles away just to get a half ass high. Now to find a block that is filled with the best crack is like a dream come true for them.

Samad watches over the block with pure satisfaction on his face. Not only is this the only block with crack, he's the only dealer with material. That gives him a feeling of power that he never imagined him having.

Anyone else in his position of power would have down sized their bottles. At this point he could give them little to nothing for their money and still they would have no other choice but to buy it. Instead, he's giving them the same amount which was too much before the drought and now it's way too much.

By paying such a low price he still has the flexibility to give away the same amount. The only thing he did was add way more baking soda to stretch the work. Normally he would have never gambled like that. Instead of whipping up an extra half a kilo, he whipped up 750 extra grams. Off of the $20,500 he spent for the kilo, he will make $85,000 off of it after paying his workers.

He's expecting to make at least a half a million when it's all over with. He has it all figured out. He's going to only allow D-Nice to take three of the kilos while he selfishly keeps the other seven. He's getting greedier and greedier by the day. The more he makes the more he wants to make. It's like a disease.

It's surprising that he taught D-Nice how to stretch his work. It was the least he could do after lying about the price they're paying for the material. Doing that eased his guilt to the point that he hasn't thought twice about it.

Now thanks to the coach, they're both going to be in a position that they never dreamed of being in.

Meanwhile

The small block looks quiet and abandoned except for the small crowd of men who are gathered around in the middle of the block. They stand there passing the blunts back and forth to each other, getting high out of their minds when a black Pontiac Grand Prix cruises the block and stops short in front of the group of men. They all step toward the vehicle, just talking back and forth.

The Stalker sits back in his car a few cars away from them. This block is supposed to be another block that members of the Unit frequent regularly. The Stalker squints his eyes as he places the tip of his ball point pen onto his little pad. He carefully scribbles the plate number down underneath the eight other numbers that he has listed already.

He's starting to realize that this job may be a little more tedious than he expected it to be but it's nothing to him. He loves to be challenged just to sharpen up his game for future jobs. He's sure this is going to take time but time is all he has.

///// CHAPTER 112 /////

Two Days Later. The cranberry 650 creeps up the small dead end block. At the end of the one way street, Tamika slows down before making the left turn. From the passenger's seat, Rock reaches over onto the driver's side visor and presses the button on the small key pad. In seconds the middle garage opens up automatically. As it's openening, Tamika slowly pulls the car inside.

Tamika hops out of the car and runs over to the passenger's side. She snatches the door open and grabs hold of his arm to help him out. He rises out of his seat slowly. With the slightest movement the pain increases. It's so unbearable that he's scared to move. He takes a huge breath before lifting his leg and stepping out of the car. Once both feet are planted, he exhales. He takes babysteps, leaning on Tamika as she escorts him into the house.

This is Rock's hideout apartment. This is the one apartment that he absolutely takes no one to. Not even Tamika has been here before. He's taken a few people to his other spot, male and female which is why he can't put a finger on who could have set him up. Although he doesn't know exactly who it was, he has a list of possibilities of who it could have been. This spot here, he feels safe and sound because he's sure no one knows about it. With Tamika he feels his secret is safe.

Hours Later

Samad walks into Lil Bit's apartment. On his back he wears a medium sized Louis Vuitton backpack. The backpack looks so out of place on his back. The sight of it almost turns Lil Bit's stomach. "What's with the pocketbook?" she asks. She knows exactly what it's about. She is well aware of the fact that he's following after the rappers 'Duffle Bag Boys' lead. She hates to even believe that her dude is even corny enough to jump on this bandwagon.

"This ain't no pocketbook," he says defensively. "This is a man bag."

"It's a fucking pocketbook! And I don't want to ever see you with it again for as long as we're fucking together," she says without cracking a smile.

"I paid twelve hundred for this," he says in his defense. With him knowing how fashionable she is, he thought she would appreciate his bag.

"I don't give a fuck if you paid twelve thousand for it. It's corny!" she says humiliating him even more.

He pulls the bag from his back and hands it over to her. "That's forty-one thousand," he says, hoping to change the subject. He's paying for the two kilos he took the other morning. He's just turning the money in but he actually had it for her at the end of his shift on the first day.

Never before has he scored close to twenty-five grand during his shift but now thanks to the drought he has broken a record. The second shift was record breaking as well, bringing in over fifteen grand. In less than three days the block has generated over one hundred grand so far and D-Nice's shift has just begun an hour ago so there's no telling how much more will be generated for the night.

At this rate they both expect to be millionaires in no time. As long as the drought is in effect their expectations can be met with no problem at all.

"Dig, break me off another one," he demands.

"You done already?" she questions.

"Yeah," he lies. He's not exactly done. He has a little over fifteen thousand dollars worth of crack left. He doesn't expect that to carry him throughout the day. He has to get the ball rolling so he doesn't miss a dime.

Lil Bit is quite impressed. "Damn, Bay," she says with a smile.

"I told you Ma, ain't no stopping me from here," he says with confidence. "All I needed was somebody to believe in me. Now the world is ours!"

///// CHAPTER 113 /////

Days Later. Maurice hops into the passenger's seat of the vehicle. "What's going on, baby?" he shouts at his entrance. Tension is in the air of the car. The stereo isn't even playing. The Stalker sits in pure silence. He doesn't even say a word in reply to Maurice's greeting. He just nods his head up and down once. "Alright, I got something for you," Maurice says with joy as he holds the sheet of paper. He hands it over to the Stalker and he reads it slowly. "That's the barber shop he goes to and the breakfast spot that he goes to everyday."

The Stalker sits there in silence, barely breathing. After a few seconds he speaks. "Where his mother live?" The Stalker knows one thing for sure and that is if all else fails you can always find a dude at his mother's house. It's inevitable.

"Hmmphh," Maurice sighs. "If it was that easy I wouldn't have had to call you here. His moms ain't around. I got the word from my man that last year Trauma got into some shit with some old head Muslims and they went straight to his folk's house. They wasn't bullshitting. They straight slaughtered his pops. The rest of the family packed up and blew the joint. Word is they down South some fucking where. Fuck them though. He ain't down South. He right fucking here and he's gone have to come out sooner or later and when he do."

"You already know," the Stalker interrupts. "Lights out."

Meanwhile

Samad has just been called to the block by D-Nice. As he's pulling up he spots D-Nice's cousin Rahiem's car parked in front of the spot. He looks further only to see the two of them standing side by side. Seeing Rahiem's face enrages Samad. He hates him so much that he can't even stand the sight of him.

Samad hops out of the car and walks toward them. He skips right over Rahiem and shakes D-Nice's hand. "What up?" he asks not even acknowledging Rahiem's presence.

Samad's arrogance and aggression makes D-Nice feel uncomfortable. "Let me kick it with you over here," D-Nice says as he pulls Samad toward him.

Once they get a few feet away, Samad speaks. "What that mufucker want?"

"Work."

"Work?" Samad repeats. "Get the fuck outta here," he barks. "Nigga wouldn't even serve us now he need work. Look at how the tables fucking turned! Tell that nigga to eat my dick!" he barks atrociously.

"He want four keys."

Samad starts calculating automatically before his ego kicks in. "How he know we got it?"

"He don't. Smooth, we the only niggas in town with coke. You know the word gone travel. He came here hoping we could turn him onto somebody."

"Turn him onto my nuts," he barks hastily. Suddenly he realizes that he can profit off of the situation.

"That's four joints," D-Nice says with excitement in his eyes. "We can score some p.c. off the nigga."

Samad is considering selling the work to him but his greed steps into the picture. He realizes if he sells the work to Rahiem they will no longer be the only block with work. There's no telling how far he will stretch out. Samad's fear is Rahiem spreading the work throughout the city and decreasing their flow. He looks at it on the flipside of things. As long as they score tremendously it will be well worth their while. "What is he willing to spend?"

"I don't know. We didn't talk about that. Are you willing to talk to him?" The greedy look in Samad's eyes answers the question. "Come on."

"Listen our price is thirty-two a joint. The seven thousand we gone split, alright?"

"Bet," D-Nice replies. "That's high as fuck but what we got to lose? Come on, let's talk to him."

They step over to Rahiem. "What up?" he asks Samad, trying to break the ice.

"You need four? I can get them for you. The price is thirty-two a joint," he says as he looks at his face to see his reaction.

"Damn thirty-two? That's high as hell!" he says with a sound of agitation in his voice. "Is that the best you can do?"

"Nah, I can do better but that's the best that I'm gonna do."

That frustrates Rahiem to no end but his hands are forced. He has no choice but to accept his bullshit from him if he wants to get a hold of the product. "Deal"

"Alright, we'll hit you in an hour," Samad says as he steps away from the man leaving him and D-Nice standing there.

One hour later and they're meeting just as Samad said they would. Rahiem passes the duffle bag from the backseat. "A hundred and twenty-eight cash," he says. The thought of him buying work from them infuriates him. He never thought he would see this day. These are the last two mufuckers in the world that he wants to buy work from and if there was anywhere else that he could get it from, he would. He's tried to figure out where two petty dudes like them could have ever landed a connect but he can't figure it out to save his life.

D-Nice hands Rahiem the work and he vanishes almost instantly. Samad pulls off feeling good. He just made the biggest deal of his career and it feels great. He's never been so much in control in his life. Selling the kilos for thirty-two thousand scores them a grand total of forty six thousand dollars profit to split if they were actually splitting it.

By lying to D-Nice that the price is twenty five thousand a kilo, Samad scores an additional forty-five hundred off of him per kilo. D-Nice will walk away from this deal with fourteen thousand in his pocket while Samad will walk away with thirty three thousand. Although they won't be the only one's with work any longer, their huge profit margin made it all worth while. Afterall, if it makes dollars it makes sense.

"Damn, that's a hell a move," D-Nice says with excitement. He's just happy to have brokered such a lucrative deal. "I didn't think you was gone fuck with him."

"Why wouldn't I?" Samad asks sarcastically. "Let me tell you something about me. I do business with my mind not my heart. I'm not an emotional dude. You can't do business with emotions. I ain't gotta like a motherfucker to do business with him. At the end of the day we getting money. We ain't even gotta talk. It's simple. I got what he want and he got what I want."

D-Nice sits quietly, just sipping on the drink that Samad is dropping. How true he is, it's just too bad that these aren't his words or his real feelings. He made the move purely out of greed. The great words that he just spoke are not even his. It's just another quote that he's stolen from who else but the Coach.

///// CHAPTER 114 /////

The Next Morning

Samad stands before the groggy eyed Lil Bit. He hands the shoe box over to her and she opens it half asleep. Peeking through one eye she sees the stacks and stacks of money. In total the box is filled with sixty-four thousand. He took the $114,000 from the $128,000 that Rahiem gave him. The other money he stashed away.

He's now ahead of the game. In just four days he's paid Lil Bit for all the work. Now he owes nothing and the last three kilos belong to him. Less than a week ago he was holding onto his last fifty grand for dear life. Now today he has stashed away an additional $100,000 on top of that fifty. He still hasn't even started on his second kilo that he took from her. Once that's done he will be adding another ninety thousand to his stash.

He's calculated his stash at close to $210,000 before even touching the last three kilos. Just to think he was so close to not giving Lil Bit his money. That would have been the biggest mistake of his life. He's so happy that he took the gamble. Just like the lottery, you have to be in it to win it.

Meanwhile

Maurice and Sal cruise through the city still in search of Trauma and his Unit. Although he has the Stalker on the case, he still can't rest.

Sal makes a sudden turn onto a street for no apparent reason. What they both see before their eyes is mind blowing. Addicts are running back and forth crazily. This block seems to be in a world of its very own. It's jam packed unlike the rest of the city which is deserted.

"What the fuck?" Maurice says. "This shit look like 1983 in Harlem," he says referring to the birth of the crack era. "I ain't never drove through this block in my fucking life." He looks at the addicts trying to determine what's being sold out here. They're extremely jittery and hyper which tells him that they're not on dope which would make them sluggish instead. He automatically assumes this must be a crack set. He's now baffled because in order to produce crack you must have cocaine and at this time being that they run the city, no one should have any cocaine. He quickly considers the fact that maybe one of his men has went against his ruling and served someone from this block. He doubts that seriously. He's confused because if they haven't that means someone has gotten their hands on work and it hasn't come from them. The thought that someone is capitalizing off of their lay over, drives him crazy. He refuses to sit back and let anyone get rich while they're not getting a dime. "Somebody got some work," Maurice mumbles.

"No bullshit," Sal replies.

"Who in charge of this lil spot? You know?" Maurice asks.

"Not at all."

"Find out."

Across the street, D-Nice sits on an abandoned porch as he waits for Samad's call. Samad not only went to drop off the money to Lil Bit, he also went to get another kilo for D-Nice. As he's sitting, he notices the Ford Edge SUV slow rolling past him. Sal and Maurice stare at him as they pass by. He squints his eyes to get a clear view of their faces but realizes that he's never seen them before. Their long stares make him feel uncomfortable. "Who the fuck is that?" he mumbles aloud.

Hours Later

Heavy traffic congestion causes the cars to be bumper to bumper for miles here on Fifth Avenue in Manhattan. This area is one of Lil Bit's favorite places in the world. The herds of people that swarm the streets gives her the rush of a lifetime. She loves coming here to shop in the boutique stores. Of course she can get the same items from Short Hills Mall but there's something about shopping on Fifth Avenue.

She's extremely happy that the ten kilo deal went through without one problem. She scored $145,000 off of the original $10,000 of her money that she invested. Of course she's been around money all of her grown up life but to have orchestrated a deal of this magnitude on her own gives her great satisfaction.

She creeps through the street with a pleasant smile on her face. A nice late summer breeze blows through the sunroof of her truck. The bright sun bounces off of her Gucci sunglasses. The fact that the traffic isn't moving a bit is not bothering her at all. Nothing can upset her right now. She's in her zone.

In the backseat there lies Samad's 'man bag' as he calls it. It's filled with $15,000. She plans to spend every dime of it on herself and Sade who sits low in the passenger's seat. This is one of the things they have in common. They both are in love with New York City. She sits there just staring ahead enjoying the scenery as well.

Lil Bit hits the repeat button and bops her head to the beat of singer Neyo's 'Miss Independent.' She sings along with him. "She's got her own thing! That's why I love her, Miss Independent." She hums along before singing again. "She walk like a boss, talk like a boss, move like a boss." Lil Bit feels as if Neyo wrote this song just for her. "She work like a boss, play like a boss. She's made for a boss and anything else she telling him to get lost," she says as she nods her head up and down while looking at Sade. "Everything she got best believe she bought it!"

Meanwhile
"Dig," Maurice says from the passenger's seat of the Stalker's car. "Niggas in the town getting money while we going through this bullshit. I can't have that. Something gone have to give. I need this nigga finished so I can put my squad back to work. I hate to put pressure on you but I need you to speed this thing up."

The Stalker looks at Maurice with a look of coldness in his eyes. He sits quietly for seconds without saying a word. "I'm on my job. If you have a problem with how I work, you can drop me off at the airport. Go about it the way you know how," he says in a low whisper. "Let me know right now. You want me to continue or you want me off the clock?"

Maurice looks at the Stalker with hatred in his eyes. He has a problem accepting the way that he just spoke to him. He sits quietly before replying. "Do what you do."

Many Hours Later
Lil Bit dropped Sade off thirty minutes ago. Now she's a few minutes away from her home. Her and Sade spent the entire day shopping. Together they managed to blow every dime of the $15,000 that Lil Bit set out to spend and some more. They ended the night with dinner at the Bone Fish Grill in Secaucus.

Just as Lil Bit is pulling into the parking garage she catches a glimpse of a familiar car out of the corner of her eye. What she thinks she may have just saw causes her heart to race. She zooms in on the pick-up truck through her passenger's side mirror. "I know this motherfucker ain't," she whispers to herself. She looks down at the front license plate. "Yes the fuck he is," she says as she looks through the rearview mirror to make sure that he's not coming behind her. She tries to keep her eyes glued onto the truck. The backseat is so full with shopping bags that it's hard for her to see through the mirror. She's trying to see if he's in the truck but she can't tell because the tinted windows are so dark. She peeks around nervously as she pulls her swipe card from the visor. She feels as if he's about to pop out of the garage on her any second now. Her heart races rapidly. She feels like she's the star of a horror movie.

She quickly swipes the card. She looks back to make sure his truck has not moved. Her tires screech as she zips into the garage. She constantly looks back to make sure that he hasn't come behind her. She can't believe that he's actually stalking her like this. She can only imagine what would have happened had her and Samad been together. Tonight would be the night that the three of their lives would have been ended.

A part of her wanted to jump out and embarrass him by letting him know that she saw him but then again he may have forced his way upstairs after that. She feels like she did the best thing by acting as if she didn't see him. This frightens her to death. She wonders how long he's been sitting out here and how long he's been doing this. She realizes the danger in this. "Fuck this," she whines like a baby. "I ain't fucking living like this!"

///// CHAPTER 115 /////

Two Days Later

In just the few days that the block has been back up and running, it's managed to be the talk of the city. The word has spread like a virus. Just a few months ago this block wasn't even on the map. Now no one can believe what it has become. Everyone has to come through here just to see it with their very own eyes. Once they get a glimpse of the action, they bear witness that what they heard is true. Thanks to the non descript, Samad, this block is now a tourist attraction.

Off the Chain sits across the street from the action, trying to keep himself out of any trouble that can come about. He watches his surroundings attentively as he fiddles with a Black and Mild. His attention is drawn to a silver Chevy Impala that is creeping through the block suspiciously. The windows are so dark that the interior can't be seen. Off the Chain sits there in a state of confusion. He doesn't know if these are cops or bandits. He puts himself in position to grab hold of his gun if they're bandits as well as to take off into flight if by chance they're police.

The car slows down even more as it gets within feet of Off the Chain. He keeps his eyes glued to the car. Through the dark window he finally finds a small area of light in which he happens to see the passenger passing a blunt to the driver. He quickly stands up and reaches for his gun. He grips it in his hand in the back of his waistband. He stands there with his hand behind his back as the car stops in front of him. He snatches it from his waistband as the window is rolling down. He sneakily slides his arm from behind his back bearing his weapon.

"Don't even do it to yourself," the man says from the passenger's seat. "I already beat you to the draw," he says as he holds the chrome cannon in the air. Off the Chain watches with confusion. He hears the voice but he's paying more attention to the gun. "Off the Chain, what's good my nigga?" the passenger shouts with excitement.

"Trauma, what up baby?" he asks as he runs over to the car. He tucks his gun in the front of his waistband but he never lets it go. He has no trust at all for Trauma.

"How long you been home?"

"Bout a week," Off the Chain replies. "What's up with you though?"

"Psst, the same shit. I'm just breezing through, doing what I do. What you doing around here?"

"I'm waiting on my man to come through," Off the Chain replies.

Trauma looks around at the action. Crack addicts swarm every inch of the block. "Got damn, this shit on fire. Who behind all of this?"

Off the Chain knows Trauma well. The both of them have a certain level of respect for each other. They are of equal danger. The only thing that differentiates them is the fact that Off the Chain rolls alone while Trauma does not.

"Who run this?" Trauma repeats his question, thinking that he must have not heard him the first time. Off the Chain heard him clearly but is agitated by his nosiness. He's sure his reason for wanting to know can result in a messy situation.

"My peoples, you heard," he says hoping that Trauma will get the hint that this block is off limits.

Trauma nods his head up and down. "I heard. Like your peoples peoples?"

"Yeah, my strong peoples. My family," he revises. "Any bullshit come through, I'm here to straighten it out. Everybody got a position to play, feel me?"

"Absolutely. I ain't trying to bring no bullshit through here," he says while looking Off the Chain directly in the eyes. The look in Trauma's eyes tells Off the Chain that he's willing to go against the grain if he has to. "Do me a favor? Get with your strong peoples and see if they can make a little room for us. We ain't trying to take nothing over. All we need is just a little corner in the cut somewhere, you dig what I'm talking bout? Tell him that will definitely eliminate any bullshit that may come through," he says with a sinister look on his face.

"The bullshit I ain't worrying about," Off the Chain says with a smile. "As long as a mufucker don't start none it won't be none," he says letting Trauma know that he's willing to go all the way as well.

"I'm with you a hundred percent on that. I'm gone come back through lets say, tomorrow. Just let me know something," Trauma says before looking over to the driver. "Go," he whispers.

The car cruises away leaving Off the Chain standing on the curb. Something tells him that he has his work cut out for him.

///// CHAPTER 116 /////

One Week Later

Just a few days over two weeks and Samad has taken every kilo from Lil Bit. When he got to the last two kilos he selfishly wanted to keep them for himself but he didn't. He kept one and gave the last one to D-Nice.

He has safely stashed away close to $300,000. Thank God for the crack game he says to himself over and over each day. This is the only game that he knows of where you can be flat broke and then out of nowhere you can be a little more than a quarter of a millionaire.

He's already been in Lil Bit's ear about making another move. She's so in love with the quick profit that she didn't refuse. She just doesn't want to go over just yet. She promised him that she would make another trip the moment she feels it's safe for her to do so.

Samad has no idea how long that will be so instead of rushing through the last kilo and having no work for God knows how long, he came up with a bright idea. He decided to break down his bottle size. Instead of selling dime jugs, he has downsized to regular dime bottles. Now instead of making $85,000 off the 1,700 grams he will now make close to $100,000. Hopefully that will give him a little less of a dry period while he waits for Lil Bit to bounce back. Of course the feigns will frown upon the decrease but Samad realizes that they still have no other choice but to buy it.

Samad stands a half a block away from the action. As he's standing there one of his most loyal customers comes walking toward him. "Smooth, what's happening?"

"You," Samad replies. He can look into the man's eyes and see that he's looking for a handout as he always is. Samad looks away as if he isn't standing right next to him.

"Ay you heard about Lil Debbie?"

"Who?" Samad asks.

"Deborah Miles."

Hearing her called by this name makes him well aware of who the man is talking about. "Nah, what about her?"

"Aw man, somebody tried to take her out a couple of weeks ago."

"For what?" Samad asks, just trying to see how much the man actually knows.

"Something about a murder she witnessed. The dumb mufuckers came back and shot her and didn't kill the bitch. How fucking stupid are they? World's dumbest criminals," he laughs.

He's burning up inside but in actuality he knows that the man is speaking the truth. Everyday he thinks of how stupid it was. "Where she at now?" He got the word that she's in the hospital in critical condition. He heard she was fighting for her life. He prays that she loses the fight for his sake.

"Quiet as it's kept, she's in the witness protection program. They moved her away from here so nothing else happens to her before the trial."

Oh shit, Samad says to himself. He can't believe what he's hearing. He's sure he's going to jail forever now. He's murdered two already. The tampering of a witness, he's sure they will give him triple life for that. He feels as if his life is over at this point. This is the worst news he could ever hear. "How you know?" he asks hoping that this is just gossip.

"I know her brother, Chuck. He told me last night when we were together at his family's house."

"Oh yeah? Where's that at?" he asks with desperation.

"Right there on Orange Street," he says without a clue of why Samad has asked. Samad stands there putting a plan together in his head. He's come too far for him not to go all the way with it.

After a few minutes of silence the man speaks again. "Smooth, I hate to bother you but can you let me get two until later? Please man?" he begs.

Samad was well aware that the information would cost him. The only reason the man unleashed the gossip was to set up for his begging. It may have just been small talk for him but it's priceless information to Samad. "Go tell Q to give you two. Matter of fact tell him to give you four...on me."

"Thanks," he says as he runs off down the block.

"No. Thank you," Samad mumbles aloud.

Meanwhile. Lil Bit sits in Deja's chair as Deja teases her hair. "Girl your hair is growing so much," Deja says. "What are you doing to it?"

Lil Bit knows the exact reason for her hair growth. Keeping this secret from Deja is killing her. She wants to tell her but she doesn't want to hear the nonsense that she's sure will come with it. She just wants to unleash the secret and relieve the stress that's coming with keeping it trapped within. She sits quietly as she debates if she should tell her or not. "I ain't doing nothing to it. The baby doing it for me."

"Baby?" Deja asks with a bright smile on her face. "You pregnant?"

"Shhh, that ain't for everybody, " Lil Bit utters.

"I knew it," Deja whispers. "How many months?" Deja is blushing from ear to ear. "I'm so happy for you. How does Maurice feel? What the fuck is his wife going to say?" she asks with a devious smile. "They still together right?"

"I'm almost six months," she whispers.

"Six months? Wow. You're carrying so small," she says with a surprised look on her face. She looks down at the small pouch that is quite evident now that she's been told. "How did I miss that?" she smiles. Lil Bit looks down at her stomach nervously. Deja's last statement has just made her feel self-conscience. "Your hair is growing so much. That means you're having a boy. A little Maurice," she smiles. "What the fuck is his wife going to say?" she asks again.

Now, here goes the hard part. Lil Bit shakes her head from side to side. "It's not Maurice's baby," she whispers with shame.

"What?" she says as her smile turns to a frown. "Who baby is it?" she asks as she looks into Lil Bit's eyes. They say it all. "Uhmmm," she grunts.

"Deja, I don't want to hear your bullshit. That's why I took so long to tell you," she admits.

"I ain't got nothing to say. You're grown," she says as she continues to tease away at Lil Bit's hair. "What did Maurice say about that?"

Lil Bit hesitates before replying. "He doesn't know."

Deja looks at Lil Bit with disturbance. She shakes her head from side to side, just holding back the rage that she would like to spit from her mouth. She doesn't have to utter a word because Lil Bit can read what she wants to say through her eyes.

"I know, I know," Lil Bit says with shame.

"Have you lost your mind?" Deja asks.

Lil Bit says not a word aloud. This is the same question she's been asking herself over and over again and she has finally come up with the answer. She shrugs her shoulders sadly in reply as she nods her head up and down.

////// CHAPTER 117 //////

Sal cruises up Madison Avenue while Maurice lays back in the passenger's seat. As Sal approaches 12th Street, he turns his left blinker on. He stops short at the traffic light. A silver blur appears on the right of them as the compact car zips alongside of them, squeezing into the tiny area between their car and the sidewalk. Maurice looks over and, Boom! He hears the noise before his eyes can set on the man who has his entire upper body hanging out of the sunroof. The glass shatters in Maurice's face. He ducks low, almost laying in Sal's lap.

The element of surprise has captured them, giving them no time to retaliate. "Oh shit," Sal sighs as he attempts to make the left turn but the oncoming traffic won't allow him to. Boom! Boom! Boom! The gunman fires again as the silver Impala rides alongside of them until Sal bends the corner. The back window caves in after the last shot.

The silver Impala zooms up Madison Avenue. Trauma falls into the passenger's seat still gripping his cannon.

"Yo, you got his ass," the driver says as he replays the way Maurice fell down into the seat.

Satisfaction sets on Trauma's face.

Sal bends the corner recklessly causing the rear of the car to fishtail. Maurice's body shifts from side to side like a ragdoll. He's still laying low for safety. As he's laying there he notices blood on his forearm. He looks down with amazement. "Oh shit. I'm hit," he says as he examines his arm for a hole.

"Word?" Sal asks as he peeks over at Maurice. Maurice sits up while staring at his arm. To his surprise he doesn't see a sign of a bullet hole anywhere. He pats his upper body with his hand to see where the blood could have come from. Suddenly he touches the area where his shoulder and chest meet. His fingers sink into the mushy cotton of his soaking wet shirt. The heat from the wet blood plasters to his chest as he pats it. He pulls his hand away to look at it and there he sees a palmful of blood. Seeing his blood sends him into a state of shock. He immediately starts to panic and as sooon as he does the pain kicks in. "Aghh," he grunts. He takes a deep breath before grunting again. "Aghh." The bullet wound pulsates with pain. "Uhmm," he grunts. "Get me to the hospital. Aghh. "Hurry up, man."

Meanwhile

Lil Bit hasn't been able to get a bit of sleep since she saw Maurice stalking her house that night. He has her scared to come in and out of her own home. She's so worried about what he's going to do that she hasn't allowed Samad to come over since. The past couple of nights she has played sleep when he calls, just letting the phone ring over and over.

She refuses to live in fear like that. He has her living like a prisoner in her own home. She's thought long and hard about what she should do and she thinks she's come up with the perfect answer.

Lil Bit stands at the window staring at the gorgeous view of New York City. She looks across the Hudson River, trying to locate her building. "What you think?" she whispers as she looks over to Sade who stands close to her side.

"I think it's beautiful," she says "But."

Lil Bit knows exactly what Sade is about to say. "I know, I know," she interrupts. She's sure Sade is about to say something about the rent here being expensive. She agrees but at this time she's so in love with the apartment that she doesn't want to hear a negative word about it.

Lil Bit figures this apartment here on 44th and Lexington will be the perfect getaway from Maurice. Midtown is so congested that he will never be able to find her here. Most importantly she has no plans of him ever finding out that she's even moved.

"So, how soon are you looking to move?" the realtor asks.

"Yesterday!"

////// CHAPTER 118 //////

The Next Morning. Maurice lays up in University Hospital. He's in extreme pain but his fury exceeds it. He can't believe he's been touched. Everytime he replays the scene and sees Trauma standing inches away from him he gets angrier. How disrespected he feels.

He's so pissed that he doesn't realize how lucky he is to be alive. Just a few more inches and this whole thing would have played out differently. Right now his wife would be at the funeral parlor making his funeral arrangements.

He lays across the bed fully dressed, waiting for the doctor to come in and give him his discharge papers. Last night they refused to release him stating that they wanted him under their supervision for the night. Luckily, the bullet didn't do anything but scar the tissue. The pain is more overwhelming than the actual damage of the wound. The tiny hole in his chest is more aggravating than anything else. The pain that comes from the huge exit hole in his back is brutal.

Maurice hasn't even called his wife to tell her what happened to him. The last thing he needs is to hear her mouth. Telling her this, will only add to the dilemma that they're already having.

He hasn't heard from Lil Bit in quite some time. He's been fighting his urge to call her because of his stubbornness. This is the longest they have ever gone without speaking to each other and it's killing him. All he wants is to be in her presence just once again. By her being away from him for so long, he's more than sure that her feelings for him have faded away.

He thinks right now would be the perfect time to call her. He's in need of her sympathy. Maybe this call could be the way back into her heart. He has no doubt in his mind that if he can get the opportunity to be in her presence just once, he can make her remember why she fell in love with him in the first place.

He quickly dials her number and listens to the phone ring.

Meanwhile. Lil Bit hands the copy of the lease over to the realtor. She then passes him the $13,600 check. As she looks at the check, butterflies fill her stomach. The rent on this apartment almost doubles the rent on her other apartment. She realizes $6,800 a month is quite expensive. She always thought $3,800 was too much and she never paid her own rent. Now being responsible for this on her own is a huge step. It's been worrying her to death. She's second guessing as she does with every other decision she makes. It's way too late though. The lease is already signed.

The rattling of her pocketbook tells her that she has an incoming call. She digs deep and pulls it out. As soon as she spots Maurice's name she presses ignore. Suddenly all her worries of the costly rent vanish. She understands that there's no price too steep when it comes to your safety and security. At this point she will pay more than this to get away from him.

She now has a safe haven. Now the hard part is maintaining it. How is she going to do that? "Hmphh," she sighs. "I definitely gotta get this money now," she says to herself. "Jamaica, here I come."

///// CHAPTER 119 /////

Hours Later. Maurice has nothing on his mind but revenge. He sits in the parked car a quarter of a mile away from the exit ramp of 280 Eastbound, headed toward New York City. He sits there in silence with rage erupting from his gut.

Through the rearview mirror, he sees the black Charger pull up and park behind him. The Stalker gets out and walks sluggishly toward the passenger's seat of Maurice's car. He snatches the door open and plops into the seat without saying a word.

Maurice is so angry right now that he can't hide it. "Listen mufucker, I hired you to do a job and it still hasn't got done. Because of you I got shot last night. Since you're not doing your job I still have to be out here on the prowl. Either you get down to business or you gone get your ass back on the first plane to Chicago," he says before he exhales.

The Stalker sits there as calm as can be as if Maurice didn't just talk to him as if he was a child. He stares straight ahead with a blank look on his face. Slowly he turns his head to face Maurice. "First and foremost that's the first and the last mufucker I'm gone be. You blaming me cause you got caught slipping? Nigga you been on those streets longer than me. You know how this shit go. I ain't taking the blame for that. If you don't like the way I move then fire me," he says with rage. "You and your Federation can take it from here. Here," he says as he hands Maurice the sheet of paper with all the license plates numbers listed, as well as a bunch of other memos. "This car right here is the car your boy moving around in," he says as he points to the last license plate on the page. "All the other cars on here are rentals. This one is his personal vehicle. Personal as in baby seat in the back, personal. Baby Mama drive it to work everyday. This is baby mama's work address. This is baby's school address. I did all the homework already. Here goes the blueprint. Even a bunch of idiots can take it from here. With that being said, I know your Federation can handle it from here. Now take me to the fucking airport, if you don't mind," he says as he stares straight ahead.

Maurice is shocked to hear all of this. He really thought the Stalker was running around here just wasting time because he's never took this long to find and murder in any of their situations. He hates it but once again, he has to swallow his pride. It seems as if he's been doing a lot of that lately. "I hired you for the job because I got faith in you. Man to man, I apologize for the way I just talked to you but this shit is getting frustrating. You've come way too far. I would never snatch you away from a job. Finish it off."

"Good enough. Now do me a favor and stay out of my way so I can do what I do."

Meanwhile. Lil Bit sits in the Newark International Airport waiting to board her flight to Jamaica. She dials Sade as she's sitting here. After two rings, Sade picks up. "Yeah?"

"They done yet?"

At this exact second Sade is in New York at Lil Bit's apartment. She's just sat here while the furniture people set up Lil Bit's new bed.

Now that she's out of harm's way, hopefully she can now rest in peace.

"They just finished. I'm headed back to Jersey now."

"Good," Lil Bit replies. "Thank you so much. I don't know what I would do without you. I will hit you when I return," she says with arrogance as if she just knows she's going to make it home. Sade on the other end doesn't have that same cockiness and doesn't take one trip for granted. She's fearful each and everytime Lil Bit leaves. Her guts start bubbling right this very second. "Later, Girl!"

///// CHAPTER 120 /////

Two Days Later

The Stalker pulls into the parking lot that surrounds the huge office building. He circles the entire lot once as he peeks at his surroundings. After finding the coast to be clear, he pulls to the far end of the lot. His eyes are fixed onto the white Honda Accord that's parked in between a truck and a SUV.

He zips over and parks to the right of the truck. He takes one long glance around as he reaches for an object that he has laying on the passenger's seat. He walks behind the truck, using it as a shield until he gets to the Honda Accord. He stands at the Honda's passenger's side door, looking straight over, watching everything, as he slides the long, flat metal object alongside the window down into the door panel.

He uses deep concentration as he fiddles the object around until he locates his target. Bingo, he says to himself. He slowly lifts the Slim Jim until he hears the lock pop open. He snatches the door open and quickly slides inside, sitting in the passenger's seat. He snatches the glove compartment open and what he's in search of he finds instantly.

He grabs hold of the insurance card holder and reads over it slowly. "Monique Johnson," he reads aloud. "84 Springdale Avenue, East Orange, New Jersey," he says slowly, trying to register it into his head and lock it in. "Got it," he says as he places it back into the glove compartment. He slams it closed and crawls out of the car sneakily. He slams the door as well as he steps away from the car casually, with his Slim Jim held close to his leg. "Monique Johnson, 84 Springdale Avenue, East Orange, New Jersey."

Meanwhile

Samad cruises through the city with no destination as he's been doing for the past two hours. He's just smoking blunt after blunt. Right now he's cooking. He's deep in a trance, stuck in the seat. It's a wonder he can drive in the state that he's in.

The block is dry and for once he can actually say that he doesn't mind. The break is really good for him. He's enjoying the downtime that he has on his hands. While Lil Bit is away he plans to take advantage of having no work. He will use the next day or so to just sit back and put together some future goals for himself.

As he makes the right turn onto Orange Street, a familiar face catches his attention. For a second he believes that he's seeing things. That is until he fixes his eyes on the woman who hops up the block using crutches. "Oh shit. That's her," he says aloud. He can't understand how it could be when she's supposed to be away in the witness protection program. What he doesn't know is she was away. They sent her so far away that she didn't have the convenience of buying crack on the local street corners and she couldn't live with that. She snuck back into town days ago.

Samad's heart races as he thinks of what he should do. He wishes he had his gun on him so he could finish off the job. He quickly considers going to get his gun. Nah, he says to himself. Maybe that wouldn't be smart. It's rush hour and someone is bound to see him and be able to ID him. Furthermore, a part of him is scared to bother her at all at this point.

He watches the woman hop into Cooper's Deli and Liquors. As soon as she's inside, he parks. He gets out and storms into the store behind her. He looks through the glass on the door and sees that the store is packed with customers. There she stands at the end of the line.

As the door closes behind him, she turns around to see who is coming in. When she sets eyes on him her face goes pale. He steps right behind her. He's so close to her that he's breathing on her neck. She stands there scared to death but trying to act as normal as she can. She's trapped and has nowhere to go. She's so terrified that urine has trickled into her crusty panties, creating mud.

"Ay," he whispers.

She turns around as if she's just seeing him this very second. "Huh?" she asks with her eyes stretched wide open.

"You recognize me?" he asks with murder in his eyes.

She shakes her head from side to side. "Uhmm, uhmm. I never saw you a day in my life."

"You sure?" he asks in a rather calm manner.

"Positive. I mind my business. I don't see nothing. I don't hear nothing. I don't know nothing."

"That's best for you," he says as he walks out of the store, leaving the poor woman petrified.

///// CHAPTER 121 /////

Two Days Later

Samad is well rested and ready to go to work. In the backseat of his car there lies three kilos. Two are for him and one is for D-Nice. He's now on his way to the lab to perform his magic. Now that he's fully loaded with work he plans to go back to the original dime jugs and continue to spoil his clientele as he started doing from the very beginning.

Twenty minutes ago Lil Bit got in his car and passed him the three kilos. She claimed to be going home to shower. What she didn't tell him is which home she was referring to.

Meanwhile

Lil Bit and Sade step into the spacious apartment. "My new home," she sings. "Girl, I love this place. We got a lot of work to do," she says as she looks around at the many boxes that are sitting throughout the livingroom.

"So, did you decide what you're going to do about Samad?" Sade asks.

"I don't know, girl. I really don't want nobody to know about this place. If I could afford both of them I would keep that one too. That's just too much though.

That's ten thousand a month," she utters. "It's not that I don't trust him. I just don't trust his mouth and his recklessness. A lot of shit he don't understand. I can see it now, him bringing somebody over to my house or bragging about living in the City. He really doesn't understand. He's just so far behind. It's like skipping an immature first grader all the way to college courses. You can't expect him to comprehend. Can you believe he had the nerve to come to me with his ears pierced today?" she says with disappointment in her voice. "That ain't the worse part either. When he popped that jewelry box open and I saw them big, goofy, cloudy stoned earrings I wanted to throw up in his face," she says causing Sade to fall into laughter. "Girl, I had no idea how country he really is. I guess he was broke and couldn't buy the shit he really wanted. Now that he got a couple of dollars, all his countriness is coming out. I think I liked him better when he was broke."

Back in Jersey

The Stalker cruises up Springdale Avenue in East Orange. He watches the addresses closely as he passes by them. Once he gets into the seventies he slows down. He quickly locates the house that he's in search of. "84," he says aloud. He cruises to the corner and busts a u-turn in the middle of the narrow street.

He finds an empty parking space and pulls in it sloppily. He scouts the surrounding area. He's in search of certain things like, neighborhood watch signs, beware of dog signs and finds none. He also looks for motion detectors on the houses on each side of Trauma's girlfriend's address. He doesn't see a sign of them either. He nods his head up and down. "Perfect."

///// CHAPTER 122 /////

Samad speeds through the streets like a Nascar driver. He got an alarming call from the block a few minutes ago. He doesn't know what the problem is and that makes it worse. The more he wonders what it is the faster and more reckless he drives.

Finally he pulls up and parks in front of the spot. He hops out quickly, leaving the car running. The moment he steps out all his workers form a huddle around him. "What up?" he asks as he looks onto their faces. Worry is evident. None of them say a word but one man nods his head in the direction of the middle of the block. Samad looks into that direction and is shocked to see a group of about fifteen men crowded around. They're spread out on the sidewalk, looking extremely comfortable as if they belong out here. "Who the fuck is that?" They all shrug their shoulders as if they don't know. He looks at the group of men once again and realizes that he knows not a one of them.

One man speaks. "They just pulled up about an hour ago and been sitting over there watching over here."

As Samad is watching them they notice him and in return they start to stare. Samad subtly slips his gun from his waistband into his front pants pocket. "I'm about to go check it out," he says before stepping away from his men. He storms across the street with rage. As he's coming toward them they form together standing in a small huddle. He steps onto the sidewalk. "What up?" Instead of answering him they stand there in silence just watching him. Judging by the looks on their faces, they have little to no concern for his presence. There's nothing more in the world he hates than to be ignored. "Ya'll alright?"

"We good. You alright?" the man in the center of the huddle replies.

"Ya'll waiting for somebody?" Samad asks.

"Why you say that?"

"Cause ya'll just over here camping out like it's alright."

"It ain't alright?" the man asks sarcastically.

"Nah, not at all. I got shit going on over there and ya'll presence is making mufuckers uncomfortable."

"Oh, you got shit going on over there?"

"Yeah. Can't you see it?"

"Yeah, I definitely can see it. So, this your situation?"

Samad nods his head up and down with arrogance. "Yeah."

"Oh my lil man Off the Chain told me about you. He ain't tell you about me? I'm Trauma and this is my Unit," he says as he points to his men. "What's your name?"

"If he told you all about me you should already know my name."

"Breathe easy, baby. I talked to him the other day about running something past you. He didn't?"

"Nah," Samad says while shaking his head no. "Why don't you run it past me?" Just as Samad says that Off the Chain pulls up in his rental.

"Speaking of the devil. There he go right there. I'll let him talk to you about it first."

"Nah, you talk to me."

"Nah, I'll let him tell you. It's obvious you don't know who you dealing with. If you were familiar with me, you would never walk up on me brandishing a weapon unless you're prepared to use it right then," Trauma says as he looks at the handle of Samad's gun hanging out of his pants pocket. "I'm gone let him talk to you. My resume speaks for itself but he probably can tell you who I am and what I'm about better than I can. I'm gone use him as my reference."

"Yo man I," Samad says with rage just as Off the Chain walks up and interrupts him.

"Yo, Off the Chain, what's hood with your man? He walking up on mufuckers with his thing in his hand and talking too much. He don't know no better. Tell him he supposed to shoot first and ask questions later. That's what we do. Anyway, I thought you was gone talk to your peoples for me?"

"Wasn't nothing to talk about," Off the Chain replies.

Trauma smiles a devilish grin. "So, I take it that we got the green light then? Ya'll got room for us? Great," he says with a goofy smile on his face.

"Nah, this situation already situated. We got this to the neck and we keeping it like that. Ain't no room out here for nobody else."

"You sure?" Trauma asks as he looks at Samad who stands there in the dark. He doesn't have a clue of what all this is about.

"Positive," Off the Chain replies.

"Enough said. That's all you had to say in the beginning. Come on ya'll," Trauma says. They pack into the four cars that are parked one behind another. As Trauma is getting into the passenger's seat of the last car, he speaks. "Off the Chain, this a big party to only have one bouncer working it."

Off the Chain stands there quietly for a second before replying. "Trauma, you know me. Ain't nothing change. I'm still a one man army."

Trauma shrugs his shoulders casually. "So, you saying everything is a go?"

Off the Chain points his finger at the traffic light up ahead. "Look, green light. Go for it."

Trauma shrugs his shoulders with arrogance. "That's what it is then."

///// CHAPTER 123 /////

Maurice is doing just as the Stalker has asked him to do and that is stay out of his way. It bothers him to do so because he wants revenge so badly right now but he's fighting back his urge to go out there and get the revenge that he wants. Today is the first time in a long time that he's spent the entire day with his family.

He knows more than anyone that his homelife needs fixing which is exactly what he plans to do. Afterall, his wife has been by his side since day one. He knows she truly deserves more than he's giving her at this time but he plans to straighten it all out. He hopes to one day be able to be the family man that she wants him to be. Not today though because he has so much more running to do.

Maurice sits across from his wife as they're eating dinner at the fine Italian Restaurant in Saddle River. Their daughters sit around them engaging in childish chitter chatter. Him and his wife might as well not even be together because they haven't said a word to each other since they've been here.

He sits back at the head of the table as he rudely texts away on his phone. He's so indulged with his many text conversations that he doesn't notice his wife staring at him. The look in her eyes could kill. She shakes her head from side to side just to refrain from lashing out at him. The majority of the times she can't stand the sight of him.

Her reason for staying with him is purely for her daughter's sake. She would hate to leave him and have to raise her daughters without their father. Even though he's barely home his presence is still felt. She's a product of a broken home and wouldn't dare put them through that if she can help it. If it wasn't for them she would have left him years ago when she first started hearing news of babies that may be his.

Over the years Maurice has managed to strip her of her self-esteem and any drop of confidence that she had. He always tells her that no man in his right mind is going to deal with her and three children. She questions that as well, which is more reason for her to stay.

For all the drama that he's put her in she hates him dearly for it but deep inside she still loves him more than life. The only thing that she wishes is that she and their daughters could have him all to themselves without interruption from the many side pieces that he has.

Maurice looks up in between texts. They happen to lock eyes. He sees the hatred in her eyes and it hurts him but he doesn't show it. His arrogance and huge ego won't let the pain shine through. He immediately lowers his eyes and continues his text messaging.

Meanwhile

Samad sits in the driver's seat of his rental while his man Dee sits in the passenger's seat. In the backseat there sits the man that Samad calls 'Mouth Almighty.' Just a short time ago he acted as if he was the head of a cocaine cartel and now he sits here in search of work.

"Ay man, I got customers lined up from everywhere. They're just waiting on me. My peoples on vacation. That's the only reason I ain't got nothing," he lies.

Samad doesn't know it but this man has no solid connect of his own. He's never had a connect of his own. Every dime he's ever made came from brokering deals as a middle man. His only real source of obtaining work is through D-Nice's cousin Rahiem. Rahiem has work but being that it's scarce he's handpicking who he's giving it to. At such a high price he can't afford to take any losses.

The man continues to speak. "If my peoples was in town, this drought wouldn't mean nothing to me."

"I can dig it," Samad interrupts. He's quite fed up with the man's babbling. "Uhm, time is money. Talk to me baby. Ya'll need work and I got work. What's the deal?"

"I'm saying, no matter how many you got I can shake them. All you gotta do is let me know what number we at. Right now I wanna see if I can get like one just to hit my smaller customers. Once they know I got it again, they will spread the word to my big customers."

"Ok, alright. For ya'll, I'll do it for thirty."

"Thirty? Got damn! That ain't gone leave me no room to do me."

"Yes it will. The same amount of room you left me at twenty-seven to do me," he says with sarcasm.

The man realizes the game that he's playing and he can't find a word to utter in his defense.

"So, go get your duffle bag and get with me. I ain't really trying to wholesale like that but I'll do it for ya'll on the strength that ya'll was there for me when I needed ya'll. I'm taking all my shit to the ground bottle for bottle."

The man sits back in silence. "I'm saying shit all fucked up. The drought killed me," he lies once again. Never did he have any real money. "If you could just let us hold one to start, we can get right. Your money good with us," he claims. "Right Dee?"

Samad sighs. "Oh, you ain't got no money," he says rubbing it in. He looks into the man's eyes. Just as I figured, he says to himself. The man has been fronting all the while and now he's been exposed.

This is what the drought does. It separates the real from the fake and apparently he's of the fake. During the drought only the real can survive. The real ones are the ones who actually have money to buy. All the consignment dudes go out of business.

"Man, that's tough," Samad says. "How can I give away work on consignment when it's a million cash mufuckers coming at me looking to buy? It doesn't make sense."

The passenger finally speaks. "Come on Smooth?" he pleads. "I'm hurting baby. When you came to me I did what I could do. Just help us out."

Samad looks in his eyes and can see the hunger. He knows that hunger very well. Just a few months ago he had that same look in his eyes. If it wasn't for Lil Bit he would still have that look. That is if he didn't kill himself already. Being broke taught him one thing and that is everybody needs somebody at one point and time. Just because he knows that feeling he would never wish being broke on his worst enemy. "Say no more. Give me an hour and I'll meet ya'll back here. I can't give ya'll no whole one though. I got a half for ya'll."

"Bet!" the man in the backseat shouts with joy. "Thanks man!"

"No need to thank me. Thank Dee."

"Yo, what's your number?" the man asks as he holds his phone in his hand, ready to lock the number in.

"Ah hah. Holler at Dee and he'll holler at me," Samad replies, using the same line the man used on him before. How the tables have turned.

Back in Alpine, New Jersey

Maurice's wife lays in the king sized bed. To the left of her lies her youngest daughter. To the right of her lies her middle daughter. At the foot of the bed lies the oldest one. They lay this exact same way everynight. Maurice peeks in the room and his wife happens to catch him looking in. She rolls her eyes with disgust. He just continues on his way.

He walks down the hall to the guest bedroom. When he steps in, the middle-aged Swedish live-in housekeeper is just finishing making up the bed. "Thank you," he says.

"Good night, Sir," she says as she closes the door behind herself.

He locks the door behind her. He wastes no time before he starts dialing numbers on his phone. He crawls into the bed and curls up under the sheets to muffle his voice. "Hey baby," he whispers. "I miss you. You been on my mind all day," he says with a cheesy smile. "I'm out of town but I will be back tomorrow."

The games never stop.

///// CHAPTER 124 /////

Trauma sits in the basement apartment with his men crowded around him. They stand there at full attention as he speaks. "Dig, the nigga Rock he laying low but I got old girl on the case. As soon as she gets word on where he's laying up, we going in. As far as the big nigga goes, he was hit but unfortunately he ain't down. Right now he probably laying low too but he a man. I'm sure he gone come back up for retaliation real soon. Until then we have to get on with our affairs. We ain't ate in a while and I'm starving. I got a plan though. That block rocking, hard body! Sure we can go out there, slaughter all of them and take it over but that may take too long. I'm hungry right now. I figured out a way that we can eat ASAP. We gone go through there, snatch the nerd nigga and hold him for ransom. I seen it in his eyes, he ain't built! We gone hold him until he make the call. I'm sure with that block banging like that he can get somebody to bring us a hundred stacks as a trade for his life. That's the plan!"

One of the men speaks. "What about Off the Chain?"

"Don't worry about him. He just playing his position. He gets paid to protect and that's what he's doing. It's his livelihood. I ain't mad at him. Anyway, I fuck with the nigga. Once we snatch his man and get that hundred we gone bring him in with us. Watch what I tell you."

6:30 A.M. the Next Morning. Hunger has Trauma up bright and early. The only way to fill that hunger is by carrying out his plan of kidnapping Samad. He jams a .40 caliber down the waistband of both sides of his hips.

All of his men are in place, just waiting on his call. They will meet up and head straight to Samad's block, where they plan to sit until he shows up. He's figured it all out. Only two things can come out of this. Either Samad will make the call to get the hundred cash to them or he will die if he doesn't. There's no middle road in this situation.

He walks out of the house, down the steps and on his way to his car. He hits the remote and the locks pop open. He snatches the door open and seats himself. The engine roars as he starts the car up. He slams the gear shift into reverse before putting his hand on the headrest of the passenger's seat. He turns around to see behind him. His eyes stretch open with terror as he looks into the barrel of the nine millimeter. He peeks at the unfamiliar face behind it.

The Stalker squeezes the trigger. "Boc! The bullet exits the gun and slams into Trauma's forehead. Blood gushes out of his face and splashes back into the Stalker's face. One second later, his brain matter splatters onto the windshield before the glass shatters everywhere. A loud thump sounds off as Trauma's body bangs into the door. He lays there open eyed and twisted.

The Stalker gets the rush of a lifetime by seeing him like this. He's at an all time high right now. The smell of the fresh blood is getting him more excited. He raises up from the backseat and does something that he hardly ever does and that's fire a second shot. Boc! This shot is senseless but he's caught up in the moment. Trauma is already as dead as can be.

Normally he hates to waste bullets. He looks at each bullet as another $10,000.

By wasting them he feels he's blowing good opportunity.

He peeks around before forcing the back door open. He steps out of the vehicle before his memory serves him correctly. He quickly snatches the Slim Jim from the backseat. He sticks his gun into his waistband before getting all the way out of the car. He slams the door behind him and walks away without remorse. His face is blank, showing no emotion at all. Business is business.

One Hour Later. Maurice pulls up to the airport. He's never been this happy in his life. "Job well done," he says as he hands the stack of one hundred dollar bills over to the Stalker. "This is a lil extra for all the overtime you put in," he says as he hands him another stack. "That's ten more."

The Stalker grabs the stack with gratitude. He quickly stuffs them into his pockets. He then pushes the door open and gets out. He closes the door quietly and eases away mysteriously until he vanishes from the scene.

Maurice pulls off slowly. "Back to business," he sings. He feels like a heavy burden has been lifted from his shoulders. He can't wait to get his crew back to work. He even plans to put Lil Bit back to work. His only real purpose for doing that is to have contact with her. He hopes that will bring them back together.

Her face pops up in his head, making him realize how much he really misses her. Not a second passes and he has his phone in hand and dialing. He listens as it rings over and over.

Hours Later. Lil Bit sits in Deja's chair when she feels her phone vibrating in her lap. She looks down and sees Maurice's name. "Psst," she sighs as Deja spins around to face the mirror. Thin micro braids cover her entire head. "You like it?" Deja asks.

"Ah," she whispers.

"Ah, my ass," Deja barks. "You got me up at 4:30 this morning to start this shit and you talking bout ah? I don't know why you wanted to put braids on top of all that pretty hair you got. It was looking so full and healthy."

"I told you it's starting to be too much," she says as she slam dunks a White Castle cheeseburger down her throat. She follows that with a huge gulp of her Yoo Hoo drink. Without a second in between she digs into her bag of goodies that she travels with. She rips into the gigantic bag of Doritos that sits on her lap. "This baby has me so tired that I don't even want to bother with this hair of mine. All I want to do is sleep and eat," she says as she slams another white castle into her mouth to fulfill her craving.

What she's saying is true. She just isn't telling all of it. Maintaining her hair is starting to be a tedious job for her. The other part of the equation is Maurice. Speaking of the devil. She looks down as he calls once again. This time she presses ignore. She figures by not having to come to the beauty parlor she will cut her risks of running into him. The apartment in Jersey City and the beauty parlor are the only places that he can track her down. Her apartment in Jersey City she's getting rid of so that will no longer be an issue. After today she will have very little reason to even come to Jersey. She figures she should have no more problems.

Her phone starts to vibrate again. "Psst," she sighs. "Hell no," she whispers as she presses ignore once again. "Get a fucking life."

///// CHAPTER 125 /////

Maurice sits in the Bat Cave, lounging in the plush recliner. On the coffee table there sits 120 kilos, ready to tear the city up. All his men except for Rock are here. Anxiety fills their guts. They wish he would hurry up and save them the long speech so they can disperse into the land and get all the money that they have been missing.

"Bust it," Maurice says. "The town been dry for a minute now, so I know mufuckers willing to pay anything to get work. My Spanish boys over the water getting forty thousand for the whole thing and Forty-four by the gram. Niggas paying that with no problem. One thing for certain they control the entire Washington Heights area, so anybody going over there to get it we know can't be paying less than forty. We gone raise the price and make up for some of that money we lost fucking with that dumb ass nigga, may he rest in peace," he says sarcastically. "Give me back twenty-nine," he says. "And I want ya'll at thirty-seven, thirty-eight. The Dominicans over the water at forty so I just need ya'll to beat them out so a nigga has no reason to go over there." They can't believe their ears. They've never scored nine thousand dollars profit off a kilo. This makes them more eager to hit the streets. "Alright ya'll, let's get this money. Sal, what you need out of here?"

All the men listen with fear. They wonder exactly how many he's going to take from the 120. There has been times that he's taken 100 and left them with only 50 to split up amongst the entire squad. They hope today isn't one of those times.

"Give me like 25."

"Alright, that's like 14 apiece for ya'll. No, damn, 13. I forgot all about Rock," he says as he dials Rock's number. The phone rings twice before it's answered.

Rock picks up the call. "What up, Big Bruh?" he says as he's driving down the Garden State Parkway headed to Newark.

"Where you at?" Maurice asks.

"I'll be right at you, Big Bruh. I'm dropping wifey off," he says as he looks over into the passenger's seat. Tamika holds his hand over the middle console. When she hears that statement she grips it that much tighter. She's earned her keep. The way she's been taking care of him and nursing him back to life has taken her from the jump-off basket to the wifey position.

She sits back quietly just repeating his words to herself. It sounded like music to her ears. Now that Trauma is dead her and Rock can live together in peace.

"Ten minutes, big bruh!"

Maurice ends the call. All of his men have loaded their duffle bags and disappeared, even Sal. They can't wait to start grinding again. Maurice stares at the table at the last ten that he's holding for Rock.

By raising the price he will make a record breaking profit. At $29,000 per kilo he will score almost $3.5 million dollars. It only cost him less than a half a million to do it. This drought has been a nightmare for most but a blessing for him.

Back to business, he says to himself as he starts to scroll through his phone.

It's time to start sending his mules out. He's sure with the town being dry, his squad is going to breeze through their work in no time. The last thing he wants to tell them is they have to wait. They've been waiting long enough.

He dials his number one transporter, Lil Bit. He knows she's good and hungry right now and he believes that she will bend over backwards for $20,000 right now. At this point he's willing to give her a bigger incentive to get her back on the team. He's willing to double her pay, giving her $40,000. He will do anything just to speak to her. He listens as the phone rings.

In Jersey City

Lil Bit cracks the door open. As she's standing at the door, her phone starts vibrating. She peeks down sneakily and sees Maurice's number on the display. She becomes alarmed thinking that maybe Maurice saw Samad enter the building. Damn, she thinks to herself. Suddenly her attention is diverted from Maurice when she sets eyes on the frosty necklace that Samad has draped around his neck. The huge Superman 'S' dangles over his stomach.

She slams the door shut behind him, as he blows right past her. He slams the shopping bag onto the table. "That's money for four," he says. "Eighty-two stacks," he adds as he watches her approach him. He has to double take at her before he realizes what she has become. He can't believe that the gorgeous little petite woman that he fell in love with has transformed into a totally different package. It happened so gradually that he didn't pay attention to it until now.

He examines her from head to toe as she stands there wearing nothing but a sports bra and his boxers. Her long silky hair has been substituted with braids; something that he hates dearly. Her cute pointed nose has been replaced with the nose of an old boxer, which is flat and spreads across her face. Her handfuls of breast are now the size of cantaloupes. Her flat belly which was able to be concealed for all these months has managed to expand to the size of a bowling ball. It seems to have happened overnight. Her hips have spread widely and her thighs have stretched out as well. Last but definitely not least, her used to be cute little feet have swollen up looking like pig's feet. Got damn, he utters to himself. This doesn't change the love that he has for her but it does make him wonder if she will ever be able to snap back into the gorgeous woman he fell in love with.

Lil Bit fights back the urge for as long as she possible can. This new necklace is the straw that broke the camel's back. Each time she sees him, he's bought something new. She can't sit back and allow him to spend his money so foolishly. He may not know better but she does. "Bay, how much did you pay for that chain?"

"You like it?" he asks. He's been waiting to hear her opinion on it.

You don't really want to know the answer to that, she says to herself. A fucking superman medallion, she says to herself. This motherfucker getting countrier and countrier by the day. She could easily let him have it but she decides to spare him. "How much did you pay for it?"

"Altogether, Forty-seven stacks. Forty for the medallion and seven for the chain," he says with a smile. "Crazy right?"

"Yeah, you crazy alright! Have you lost your mind? What are you thinking about? This is starting to be too much. I haven't seen you with the same outfit on twice. You don't take your underwear and socks to the laundry. You just throw them away. You also throw your sneakers away if you get a spec of dirt on them. Look at you," she says as she points to his tattooed covered arms. "Every other day you getting a new tat. You looking like fucking Lil Wayne. Big earrings in your ear. Last week it was the sixteen thousand dollar watch. Now it's a chain for forty-seven thousand. What's next? Bay, you can't blow through your money like that."

He turns his head away from her with disgust. Hearing her talk to him like this is quite irksome. Instead of listening and taking heed, he looks at it like she's chastising him like a child. "Hmphh," he sighs.

"Bay, you might not want to hear me but keep this in mind. A great man told me this and I never forgot it. Listen, you can't think like the grasshopper. He only lives for the season. When the season is over, he's over, finished. You have to think like the ant. He stashes a little over there and over there and over there," she whispers, repeating the words of Maurice.

The drink she just dropped has broken through his wall of defense. He slowly takes it in and the more he repeats it to himself the more sense it makes it to him. This makes sense just as everything else she has taught him does. A smile appears on his face as he nods his head up and down. This is why she's the coach.

///// CHAPTER 126 /////

D-Nice's cousin Rahiem walks up on the black GMC truck. In the driver's seat sits Rock from the Federation. This is his work vehicle. Not fully healed and he's back at it. Rock extends his hand out of the window. "What's good, baby?" Rock asks. "I just came through to let you know I'm back in business. I know that's good to hear, right?"

"Yeah, no doubt," Rahiem replies. He's definitely happy to hear that. Now he can go back to copping his work from Rock and leave Samad and D-Nice alone.

"Yeah, the only thing is the numbers sky high though. It's beyond my control though. The best I can do is 38."

"Got damn! 38? Man, I'm doing way better than that. I just copped one yesterday at 32," he brags.

"32?" How, Rock asks himself. He wonders who can be in a position to let it go for that cheap at a time like this. He knows that he's breaking the code but he figures it's worth the try. "Who got it that cheap?"

Rahiem smiles. "Come on, Rock. You know I can't do that."

"I can dig it," he says. "I'm sure we will find out though. I'm quite sure of that."

Meanwhile

Samad sits in the driver's seat, while D-Nice plays the passenger's seat. Dee hands Samad a plastic bag from the backseat. "That's fifteen stacks," he says.

Samad accepts the money gratefully. In just two days he's scored a quick five grand off of Dee without exerting any energy. This makes him realize that wholesaling is actually the way to go. The profit is smaller but the risks are smaller as well. He plans to only sell kilos and half a kilos in the future but right now he's breaking everything down until he gets his money up to where he feels comfortable.

Samad digs underneath the seat and grabs hold of the brown paper bag. He hands it back to Dee. "That's another half."

"Good looking, bruh. Oh here," he says as if he's forgot. He hands Samad a stack of money. "That's thirty-five hundred, everything we made off of the half."

"Nah," Samad denies. "Hold your profit."

"Nah, it's alright. My man Flip said give it to you as a token of our gratitude. We know it ain't much but we don't want to keep coming to you empty handed with nothing to contribute. Thirty-five hundred today, maybe in a couple of flips we should be able to cop our own joint.

The truth of the matter is they have never had anyone give them the chance that Samad gave them. Normally they are only allowed to take the work from point A to point B while the owner waits around the corner for the money. Samad gave them the freedom to do what they needed to do and for that they are grateful. Also they don't want to mess that up for anything in the world.

Hearing those words come out Dee's mouth makes him gain so much respect for them. It also reminds him of himself a few months ago. Before this conversation, he clowned 'mouth almighty' for being broke. Now he realizes that they're not broke. They're just upside down for the moment. As long as they have drive they could never be flat broke. One thing that he has learned is everyone needs somebody. You can't do it all alone. Because he understands their story he plans to bring them up just as Lil Bit brought him up. Somebody gave him a shot so he believes it's only fair to give somebody else a shot.

Samad takes the money and the man hops out of the backseat. The moment he's out, Samad pulls off with speed. He picks up his phone and dials. "Yo!" he shouts into the phone. "I'll be right there," he says before hanging up. One deal down and one more to go. After four minutes of riding, Samad parks in front of Branch Brook Park. A young Puerto Rican dude gets into the backseat of the car. Samad immediately hands him the $3,500 Dee gave to him. "Here. What you got?"

"Bubble gum," the Puerto Rican dude says as he hands Samad the bag of smoke. The moment it hits the air, the pungeant smell fills the entire car.

"Yeah," Samad sings. "You smell that?" he asks as he looks over at D-Nice. "Alright, I'll hit you in a couple of days," Samad says looking in the rearview mirror. The man hops out of the backseat instantly.

Samad has gotten spoiled. He no longer goes to the local weed spots to buy smoke by the bag or by the jar. He has his delivered to him by the pound by his own dealer. He no longer smokes the regular smoke. He now smokes the best of the best, straight from the country of Amsterdam.

He pulls a blunt from his pocket and passes it along with the pound of smoke over to D-Nice. "Nigga, roll that up," he demands.

An hour and three blunts later the both of them are high out of their minds. Samad drives throughout the city as slow as a turtle. He's not even paying attention to the heavy horn blowing behind him. He's holding traffic up for at least a half a block. The stereo is blasting at full volume as they both hum along with Rapper, Young Jeezy. "I'm rolling in my rental. We post up in the club and we smoking like it's legal. And this is our hood we ain't worried bout them people. We post up on the curb and we serve them like it's legal. We do it like it's legal, like it's legal, like it's legal," they repeat as their heads wobble back and forth, up and down like bobble head dolls. "We do it like it's legal, like it's legal, like it's legal.

After a few minutes of head bopping and shouting, Samad finally lowers the volume. He's moving in slow motion. He looks over at D-Nice. "Nigga you stuck," he says in a slur. "Look at you. You can't even move." He laughs hysterically for a second for no apparent reason. The smoke is taking control of him. "Yo, we having our turn," he says now with a seriousness in his eyes. "Shit feel good too. Just dead broke a few months ago and now look. I got a few hundred of my own," he admits. "Now all the shit we dreamed of doing we gone be able to live it out. Cars, yachts, the whole shit. Sky is the limit!"

"I can dig it," D-Nice replies. "But that ain't really my big picture. I just want to get moms a house that's it."

"That's it? Nigga you could go to work and buy moms a house. You gone risk your freedom, your life just to buy moms a house? Nigga, go to work for ten years and you'll be able to do that. Save yourself a prison bid, a hospital bed, or worse a grave plot. I'm doing what I do to live the life that I wouldn't be able to live doing a regular nine to five. Real talk!"

"Smooth, you know me. I always been a real simple nigga. Once I get a half a man (million) or even close, I'm out. In the legal world, I can turn a half a man into a nightmare. Won't be nothing that I can't do."

"So, you sitting here, telling me that you doing all this dirt to go back into the real world and start from the bottom with a business venture? That's the dumbest shit I ever heard. My whole purpose in doing this is so I ain't never gotta do nothing else in my life. I just wanna lay back when I get old. Risking your life to invest in something that you could lose everything that you worked for? That's hustling backwards. Man, real talk, thanks to the coach, I'm in the game. I'm only a hundred and some change short from a half a man, a midget, whatever the fuck you wanna call it. I got damn near a half a million. I'm gone tell you the truth. If all you looking for is a couple of hundred, I'll give you every dime I got and buy you out. Let you get on with your way while I take the entire block. If that's all you want. I ain't stopping now. I ain't stopping at a man (million) or even two men (million). I'm riding this shit until the wheels fall off!"

///// CHAPTER 127 /////

One Week Later
It's time for Lil Bit to make another trip to Jamaica. They don't have a grain of cocaine left which means she has no time to waste. Things are going great for the both of them. Just two trips and she has scored close to a quarter of a million dollars. A few more trips and she will be an official member of the millionaire's club if all goes well. There's only one problem though.

She stands in the bedroom in front of her mirror, naked as a Jay Bird. What she sees in the mirror brings tears to her eyes. Her little pouch has evolved to a full grown pregnant belly out of nowhere. It seems to have happened all of a sudden. Seeing this makes her realize that her trips to Jamaica have come to an end. She's sure if Muhsee sees her like this he will know that his chances of getting her are shot. Him knowing that will make him cut off her lifeline or maybe even worse; tell Maurice.

She has to come up with a plan and quick because there's no time to waste.

Meanwhile

Maurice and the Federation meet in the Bat Cave. Surprisingly today Maurice didn't call the meeting. It was called by Rock. "Yeah, I went to one of my customers to let him know that we're back in business. I offered him the work at thirty-eight and he literally laughed in my face. He said that he's getting it at thirty-two."

"Thirty-two? Where?" Maurice asks.

"That I don't know," Rock replies.

Maurice sits back wondering who not only has work during this drought but how can they afford to let it go at such a low number. Suddenly, he remembers the little block that they rode through that was fluttered with customers. He automatically assumes that whoever is in charge of that block must be dealing with the same supplier. This makes him curious to know who the supplier is. He considers that supplier to be more than a competitor because he's actually beating their price. This can be a problem for the Federation which will create a problem for whoever the supplier is. "We gotta get to the bottom of this."

Miles Away

Samad is in his attorney's office, Downtown Newark. "Listen, this is the situation," the attorney says. "The judge and the prosecutors are fired up and ready to go. I can sense the confidence in all of their voices. Something tells me that they feel that they have you beat. Normally a murder case goes on for years before they get the courage to go in. They drag along until they build up enough evidence and their confidence. With this situation, they're ready in record breaking time. I don't know why they're so confident but whatever the reason is they believe in it. Whatever you want to do, I'm with you. We can see what kind of plea bargain they're willing to offer, or we can take it to trial and prove your innocence? What do you want to do?"

Prove my innocence, Samad says to himself. Wow, he thinks. He thinks it over carefully. Hearing about their confidence makes him worry. He wonders why they're so ready to go. He thinks of how well things are going for him and he would hate to interrupt it by going to jail forever. He can easily hold out to see what plea they will come at him with but even a day in jail is too much for him at this point. He's just started living the good life and can't imagine it coming to an end right now.

He pulls a hefty stack from his pocket and slams it on the desk. "Here," he says. "Get it post-poned." Fuck that, he says to himself. I got too much living to do.

///// CHAPTER 128 /////

Sade parks her vehicle in her driveway and hops out. She walks toward her house, carrying Samad's 'man bag' over her shoulder. In the bag there is two-hundred thousand dollars of Lil Bit's savings.

Lil Bit ordered her to hold onto it for her. She feels that it's completely safe with Sade. God forbid anything was to ever happen to her she knows that she can depend on Sade to come through for her. She not only has the money, she also knows the hands to put the money in to get her out of any situation.

Meanwhile

Lil Bit and her aunt board the flight of Air Jamaica. They take their seats and her aunt continues to babble on as she's been doing since they got together. She's as high as a satellite right now. The grams of cocaine that she's consumed have been funded by who else but Lil Bit.

Lil Bit hates her aunt with a passion. Her hatred for her is deep rooted from the time that she turned her back on her when her mom died and she had nowhere else to go. Because she didn't take her in, Lil Bit was forced to live on the street, homeless. For that she will never forgive her.

The only reason that she reached out to her is because she was desperately in need and had nowhere else to turn. There's no way that she can strip down naked in front of Muhsee with that belly. She knows that will be a definite deal breaker. Instead, she will let them strap her aunt and accompany her as she brings the work back to the states. Lil Bit doesn't know how he will take that but hopefully all will go well.

Back In Newark

Samad sits in the passenger's seat of the brand new Chrysler 300M. Mike the Rent a car dude has brought this car here to trade with Samad for the vehicle that he's been driving for the past week.

"Money Mike," Samad says as he looks toward the driver's seat. "I need a huge favor."

"What kind of favor?" Mike asks with caution.

"I got my eyes on some wheels. I got the bread to pay for it but I don't have a name to put it in. I was wondering if you could put the car under your company name? Ya'll doing legit business. They won't check out where the money came from. No need to worry about nothing, no car note, nothing. I'm gone cash the joint all the way out and pay the insurance up for the year."

Mike takes in what Samad is asking him to do. He quickly realizes the danger in doing it and that doesn't sit well with him. "Samad, I don't know about that," he sighs. "Unck ain't gone go for that. If it was me by myself I would do it but unfortunately the company is under both of our names. I can't make a move like that without running it past him first. Let me talk to him and see what he thinks about it."

"Nah, I understand. Talk to Unck. Ya'll think about it first but here," he says as he hands Mike a bulky stack of hundred dollar bills. "That's twenty stacks. Ya'll can get eight more cars with that. At least," he adds. "Eight cars at eight hundred a pop is sixty-four hundred more a week. That's another twenty-five grand a month," he says, pouring it on thick. "That should make it worth ya'll while," he says with a charming smile. "Don't even worry about getting a dime of that back to me. And that ain't got nothing to do with the money I plan to invest in ya'll company. That offer still stand right?" he asks in attempt to make the deal seem that much sweeter.

Mike stares at the money with astonishment. "Y, yeah," he stutters. "I told you that offer has no expiration date on it. Whenever you want in, you in."

"Ok, cool. I'm planning to drop like a hundred stacks on you and just let you do you. Just give me a second. Mike, what you could do with a extra hundred?" he asks with a cheesy smile.

"Man, I can knock Enterprise out of business with a hundred."

"Yeah, I'm sure you could," Samad smiles. "Now run that pass Unck and let me know what he say. I'm sure he can think a lot clearer with all that in mind."

///// CHAPTER 129 /////

Samad and D-Nice have been parked here on Orange Street for hours. Samad is sure that the woman should be coming through soon. He doesn't feel comfortable with the last encounter that he had with the woman. Something tells him that the reason the judge and the prosecutors are so confident is because they have her as a key witness.

He now feels that scaring her may not have been the best way to handle the situation. Fear may only make her tell on him faster, just to get him off of the streets and out of her life. He now believes that he's found the best way to handle the situation.

"There she go," he says as he points to the raggedy looking woman. "Go ahead now," he says with force.

D-Nice sighs silently. He hates to get involved in this but Samad insists. He forces the door open and gets out slowly.

He walks up the block and meets the limping woman at the corner. She recognizes his face and fear fills her gut instantly. She immediately thinks that he's coming to finsh the job. She wants to scream but for some reason her voicebox doesn't seem to be working. She looks around with hopes that someone is watching. She also hopes that he's not crazy enough to do anything to her while they are watching.

"Deb, what up?"

"Nothing," she replies in a fearful, crackling voice. "Please," she begs. "I don't want no trouble with ya'll. Please just leave me alone and let me be. They forced me to sign the statement or they was gonna lock me up for all of my old warrants. I ain't got no money to bail myself out," she sighs. "Anyway, I wasn't planning to go to court anyway. I swear on my dead son!"

"Deb, I ain't really got nothing to do with this," he says to clear his name. "The niggas who do, told me to tell you they don't want no trouble either but they are willing to do anything to keep you from going to court. As you can see," he says as he points to the crutches that she's leaning on. "If you promise not to go to court, they will not only leave you alone, they will also make it worth your while. Here," he says as he hands her the puffy envelope. A hefty stack of greenbacks peek through the opening at her. Her eyes light up with joy as she locks eyes with Ben Franklin and a bunch of his twin brothers. "That's three grand. That's nothing. That's just for you to pay your hospital bill. The rest you will get after you don't show up for court. Trust me they gone hit you off lovely. You gone be happy. By not showing up in court they will be happy. This way everybody will be happy, see?" he asks with a grin on his face.

She's beyond happy. She sifts through the pile and the only thing on her mind is how happy she will be while smoking the crack that she's on her way to purchase. She's already calculated the number of dime jugs she will be able to buy with $3,000.00. If they're lucky she will die from an overdose. "I'm not coming to court. I promise you that!"

///// CHAPTER 130 /////

The Next Day

Lil Bit stepped out of the hotel room hours ago. She left her aunt here all alone with a half an ounce of pure cocaine. She's smoked pebble after pebble until her entire body is numb. She's gotten as high as she's going to get, hours ago. She's now smoking just for the sake of doing so because she has the cocaine in her possession.

She loads the tiny pebble into her stem, sparks the tip and places it to her lips. She blasts away to the moon like an astronaut.

Meanwhile. Lil Bit sits across from Muhsee in the huge Jamaican Restaurant in Kingston. This is the very first time that she's ever left Muhsee's house with him. He always begs her to go out with him. Tonight she accepted the invitation. She only accepted it as a token of her appreciation for all that he's done for her. She looks at it as a small investment that she hopes will keep him in the position that she needs him to be in.

Muhsee has no clue why she's going out with him. In his mind he believes that he's getting closer to reaching his goal of obtaining her. Although she's only playing the game with him she has to admit that the evening is quite impressive. He's given her the red carpet treatment ever since the night began. They were chauffeured here in his Maybauch. When they entered the restaurant, Muhsee had the entire place shut down. He paid for every customer's food before he had them thrown out of the place. Now they have the entire restaurant to themselves as every waiter and waitress caters to them.

"You look awesome this evening," he says with delight as he stares at her over the table. Lil Bit smooths out her loose fitted black linen dress over her protruding belly. She made sure to pack the biggest clothes that she owned, just to hide her pregnancy from him. She feels good knowing that he's not taken a second look at her stomach. "Thank you for blessing me with your company this lovely evening," he says with a smile. "Are you enjoying yourself?"

She looks at him with a seductive look in her eyes. The look melts him away. "Why wouldn't I be?"

Back in the States. Samad and Mike stand face to face on the dark secluded block. Mike called him to meet here, claiming that he had news for him. He never stated whether it was good news or bad news. Samad can't wait to find out which one it is.

"Yo, I talked to Unck," he says before pausing.

"Alright...and what did he say?"

"He with it," Mike says with a smile. "He's all in."

Yes, Samad cheers to himself. "Cool," he says rather casually.

"It's on you. What you trying to buy?"

"Well, I been online trying to locate the perfect joint. I found one in California but it's not the color I want. If worse come to worse, I'll take it though. Just give me a couple of days and I'll get back to you."

"Alright, it's on you. We in!"

///// CHAPTER 131 /////

Samad stands before Bullet. The last time he has seen him was the first time that he was in the County. Samad stares him up and down with hatred. He's still pissed off at him for admitting to him that he had no choice but to take the Blood's side over his. He respects his honesty but still he doesn't like it.

Samad wonders what has brought the man here to his block. "What's good?" he asks as he passes the 'White Rhino' filled blunt over to D-Nice. "What brings you around here?"

"Just bame to holler at you," he says mispronouncing the word came wrong purposely. Because he's Blood he doesn't use the letter C because it represents Crip. "I got some valuable information," Bullet replies. "I ain't gone beat around the bush. I'm gone bum straight at you with it. These ain't my words, alright? I just bame home yesterday, feel me? The word done got back to the Homies that you eating! That's all fine and well but the Gee ain't smelling that. You ain't Homie and you don't got no Homies with you. You ain't spreading no love with the Homies, smell me?"

"Nah," he says with arrogance and confusion. "What that mean?"

"I'm saying like, anywhere you go, whoever eating hard got a Homie somewhere in the picture. Some way or another they paying homage. Whether you let the lil Homies pump some work for you out here or put a big Homie on the payroll to put that twirk in. However," he grunts.

"Oh, ain't no Homies pumping nothing out for me and I ain't paying no Homie for protection either! You know I ain't with none of that gangbanging bullshit. I hate that goofy ass shit!" he says, using massive hand movement. Off the Chain who is sitting in the car a few feet away reads Samad's body language and senses that there's a problem. He gets out of the car immediately. "And if I find out that any of my lil niggas Blood or Crip they getting the fuck off the block!"

Bullet is shocked to see Off the Chain coming over. He immediately changes his tone. "Easy Smooth. You my man. This ain't me talking. These their words. I'm just telling you what's on their mind."

"I don't give a fuck who words they are! Blood rules. All ya'll together, remember?"

"Nah Smooth it ain't like that," he says as he keeps his eyes on Off the Chain. They don't know each other but everybody knows who Off the Chain is. "If that's the base I wouldn't be here warning you. Remember in the building, it wasn't much I was able to do but I did what I did, smell me? I just bame here to tell you what they talking bout doing. They talking bout straight bumming through and doing what they wanna do. Niggas like, he ain't built like that. They hearing different situations you got into in the past and they saying shit like, he wasn't like that in 13th Avenue School."

"13th Avenue?" Samad asks with an agitated look on his face. "Nigga none of us was like that! We was fucking kids. Nigga I left there when I was twelve years old! Nah, I wasn't like that. Nigga, I had holes in my sneakers and hand me down clothes. I ain't have shit to defend. I got shit now though! I got a few hundred stacks and a block that's doing fifty stacks a day. I'm like that now," he says nodding his head up and down. "I got a lot at stake and I'll murder to keep it," he says with a stone cold look in his eyes. "Anyway, who could have said that? None of them mufuckers went to 13th Avenue with me. You the only one who knew me back then. Them niggas don't know me from a can of paint!"

Off the Chain reads the body language and feels that the time has come. He draws his gun sneakily. As he lifts it Samad looks at him and shakes his head from side to side, telling him no. "Nigga this how we gone do it," Samad says. "You go back and tell them red niggas, ain't nothing! And they can take it how they want to take it! When ya'll press the button, I hope ya'll ready to go cause I'm gone go and I ain't gone stop until I get to Trenton State Prison, where I'm gone live forever for multiple homicides on ya'll mufuckers! Straight like that!"

///// CHAPTER 132 /////

Two Weeks Later

The shining automobile zips throughout the streets floating like a boat with the speed of a train. Both windows are rolled down and the sunroof is peeled back like a banana. The late Summer breeze gushes throughout the car, blowing the new car smell past the noses of the onlookers as the car passes. They stand in awe as they try to figure out what type of car it is but it's out of their sight before they can determine it.

The sound of Young Jeezy's 'Put On for My City' rips through the speakers and bleeds onto the streets. The car bends the corner so fast that the screeching of the tires can be heard from miles away. All the activity on the block ceases as the car is approaching. Suddenly the windows are rolling up and the sunroof closes. The darkness of the windows has changed the look of the vehicle giving it more of a mystique appearance.

The car stops short in the middle of the block. The glare of the huge chrome rims damn near blinds the onlookers. Everyone is eager to see who the driver of the never before seen car is. The triple black Audi R8 is not just a rare commodity here. It's rare all over the world. This happens to be one of the few that are even in the country.

The Pennsylvania license plates throw everyone off, making them believe that the driver must be an out of towner. The driver blasts the volume of his stereo even more, as he steps on the gas pedal, revving the car up crazily. The engine roars like a race car, blowing steam from the four pipes that are in the back. The six speed, V8 420 horsepowered vehicle is actually the fastest Audi ever made. "I put on for my city! On on for my city! I put on! I put on!" The driver's door opens while everyone watches with anticipation. The driver stalls to create more of a build up. Suddenly he steps out.

Once the onlookers see Samad their faces drop with amazement. Cheering and applauding sound off like they're at a concert. He walks around to the sidewalk slowly, just admiring his new investment. He can't even believe his eyes. There's no doubt in his mind that this car is worth every dime of the $115,000 cash that he paid for it. He wanted it so badly that he paid an additional $20,000 just to put his name ahead of the three month waiting list.

This car is the biggest thing that has ever happened to him in his life. What a great feeling he's experiencing right now. It feels better than he actually imagined. It's just too bad that he can't share this moment with the love of his life, Lil Bit. If she finds out that he blew close to one hundred and fifty thousand on this car he knows she will be too through with him. Because he knows that, he plans to never tell her about it.

He blew close to half of his savings on this car but he's not worried the least bit. He still has a hefty amount and the work is still rolling in. He plans to buckle down after this and discipline himself. That's his plan but what he doesn't know is; once you start rolling it's hard to stop.

"Yo Smooth, you fucking snapped!"

Samad stands there gloating like a champion. One thing he's sure of is his crew will now be highly motivated. Seeing this car now brings everything he's told them to reality. He's shown them proof that it can be done with hard work and determination. He knows this will only inspire them and in return they will work harder than they have ever worked before. "I didn't do this for me," he says with arrogance. "I did this for ya'll."

///// CHAPTER 133 /////

Days Later

Samad leans back in the driver's seat of the rental car, blowing away on the White Rhino. His phone starts to ring. He passes the half a blunt over to Off the Chain while he picks his phone up. "Yo?" he answers with the dry cotton mouth.

"Bay," Lil Bit says in her sweetest voice. He's sure with that voice she needs him to do something. "Can you do me and your baby a favor?"

Phew, he sighs silently. "What?"

"The baby wants Taco Bell," she says.

Damn, he says to himself. Her cravings are starting to get on his nerves more and more each day. He knows that it's his duty to be there for her but that doesn't stop the frustration that he gets when hearing her whining voice. "Ma, I'm in the middle of something right now," he lies.

"Please?" she begs.

"Psst, ma, I'm making moves," he says as he reaches for the blunt that dangles from Off the Chain's fingertips.

"Pretty, pretty please with cherries on top?" she begs. "Speaking of cherries, can you bring me some cherry vanilla ice cream with that too?"

Samad takes another long drag. He realizes that she's not going to give in. "I'll be there in a little while!" he shouts before ending the call. "Got damn!"

Meanwhile

"Yo Dee, are you really serious about me sleeping on the couch?" Big Texas says as she hands him a comforter and a pillow.

"Yes," Deja replies.

"Shit, I could have got a room at the hotel if that's the case. Some hospitality you showing a nigga."

"I told you, you would have to sleep on the couch."

"I thought you was bullshitting." Big Texas flew up here today for business purposes as he does every so often. Normally Deja lets him sleep in the bed with her but this time she refuses. It's quite evident that Deja has been shot by Cupid's arrow. Her Miami boyfriend is approximately 1,500 miles away and would never find out about her and Big Texas but she still can't do it. "This some bullshit," he says as his phone starts to ring. Deja walks away toward the bathroom. The tone of his voice causes her to slow down and ear hustle. "Come on man! Ya'll bullshitting. Why the fuck ya'll tell me to come the fuck up here then if you wasn't sure? Man fuck that! I don't need you to pay for my flight. You know what I need!"

Minutes later, Deja walks out of the bathroom, draped in her robe. The sweet smell of Love Spell reaches Big Texas' nose before she even steps foot into the livingroom. His manhood stands up instantly as she passes him. "Good night," she whispers.

Just as she steps into her room and starts to close her door, he calls out to her. "Dee!" She turns around quickly. "I need to rap to you for a second."

"Tex, good night," she says, thinking that he's about to ask to sleep in her bed again. "Whatever you want to ask, the answer is no. Good night."

"Nah, hold up. I'll sleep out here. I have no problem with that. I need to ask you something else."

She walks over to him. "What's up?"

He hesitates before replying. "Phew," he sighs. "You know you my people right? And I ain't got nothing but love and respect for you right?"

"Yeah."

"You know I don't ever involve you in my business but right now I'm stuck in between a rock and a hard place. I flew all the way up here to meet with some cats out of Bergen County, I think it is. Now I'm here and they saying they can't do nothing for me. I wasted a fucking trip but bigger than that, I got people waiting on me. Shit dry everywhere. Them niggas was my last resort. Please tell me you know something good? I know a woman of your stature know all the big niggas. Hook me up with one of them. I ain't gotta meet him. Everything can go through you."

Deja shakes her head from side to side. "Tex, I ain't no drug dealer."

"I know, I know, Dee. I'm sorry to come at you like this but I'm desperate. I can't go back home with nothing. Do you know anybody? I will make it worth your while. I got ten grand for you if you can connect the dots for me."

Wow, she thinks to herself. He's definitely talking her language now. Ten grand sounds good to her right about now. But who can she call, she thinks to herself. She quickly thinks of every dude she knows in this town. "I mean what exactly are you looking for?"

"I need birds, kilos. You know anybody with that coke?"

She quickly thinks of every dude that she knows who could possibly have what he needs. "Like how many you trying to get?"

"Well, let me tell you like this, I got my man driving up with money for twenty in the car. Whatever the ticket is, it don't matter. I'll just add more if I have to."

"How much does twenty cost?"

"Nah Dee, it don't work like that. Holler at them niggas and see what they letting them go for. Then we take it from there and negotiate and shit." He digs into his pocket. "Get on it quick. The ten waiting for you," he says as he shuffles the stack of money in her face.

Hours Later

Samad steps into the Jersey City apartment. Lil Bit slams the door behind him. Samad floats on thin air as high as a kite. He's on cloud nine right now. The hours of weed smoking has him 'cooking down' as he calls it. In slow motion, he hands Lil Bit the bag of Taco Bell and the ice cream that she requested.

She snatches them from him rather rudely. On her way through the livingroom, she drops both bags in the wastebasket. She's infuriated with him. His high is blown away. "Yo, I know you ain't just throw that shit away after I drove all the way on 22 to get it and drove all the way over here to bring it to you?"

"Yeah, I threw it away," she says with attitude. "I called you three fucking hours ago!"

"I told you I was doing shit!" he shouts back. "You think every fucking thing supposed to stop when you call. Shit don't work like that!"

"Oh, it don't work like that? When you was in that County jail both times and needed me on point, it was like that. When you needed work, it was like that but now it ain't like that. I can go thousands and thousands of miles away to bring you what you need but I ask you for fucking Taco Bell and you got your ugly ass face frowned up making a big deal about it? Boy, bye! "You know what? Fuck you! I won't ask you for shit ever again!" she shouts as her eyes begin to water. Her emotions are getting the best of her. "Nigga, you need to check yourself. You are getting way too big for your fucking britches. Always remember, in order to know where you're going, you have to remember where you came from. It's obvious that you forgot where you came from so I know you don't have a clue of where you going. I'm gone tell you where you going, nowhere. And fast too. You are running in fucking place! You came from nothing and you gone end up with nothing!" she says lashing out at him. "I hope you saving your money because I'll be damn if I'm gone keep risking my life for your ungrateful ass."

She's letting all of her frustrations out and it feels great. She's been holding onto this for some weeks now. She doesn't know if her hatred for him is because of the pregnancy or she just flat out hates him.

Samad's ego comes to his aid in defense. "I ain't forget where I came from and I know where the fuck I'm going. Yeah, I started with nothing but I got something now!"

"You call that something?" she says sarcastically. "I guess it all depends on what you call something," she adds.

He feels like she just hit him below the belt. His pride is hurt and he has no choice but to strike back. He's been holding onto this for quite some time now but he realizes that the timing is perfect now. "Whatever you say, fat ass," he says casually as he walks out of the room.

She stands there in awe, not believing what she's just heard. This absolutely breaks her heart. She opens her mouth to speak but nothing comes out. She tries again and again until finally, "You wack ass , man bag carrying, no karat earrings, dumb ass superman chain wearing, wanna be! Get the fuck out!"

He swallows the lump in his throat. His face tightens up with anger. "I'm getting!" he shouts as he walks toward the door. A part of him feels like he got the best of her because he knows every woman is self-conscious about her weight. To be a preganant woman on top of that, makes it all worst. The other part of him feels like she scored big on him with that last statement. He wonders if she really feels like he's wack or she said it out of anger.

He snatches the door open and steps out. Before he can get out of the doorway, she slams it banging him in the back. She backs up against the door and slides down to the floor, where she cries like a newborn baby.

///// CHAPTER 134 /////

D-Nice packs the last of his clothes and belongings into the trunk of the rental car. He slams the trunk shut and walks to the driver's side. Living with Samad has become unbearable. His arrogance has grown to an all time high. Day and night he brags and brags and brags. That's the easiest part to deal with for D-Nice. The hardest part is actually sleeping in the house with a closet full of guns, several hundred thousand dollars and a few kilos at a time. Even though Samad knows better than to move like this, he still does.

They both learned their lesson the hard way when the police raided their home last time but Samad is so cocky right now that he doesn't pay attention to the most important things. The money has gone to his head, making him believe that he's above the law and as long as he has money he can buy himself out of any situation.

D-Nice can't understand how he's become like this. The person he grew up with no longer exists. He realized the other day when they were talking that they no longer share the same vision. D-Nice enjoys the simple things in life while Samad is shooting for the moon. That makes D-Nice understand why Samad is willing to live and die for this game and he is not. It was after that conversation that D-Nice decided that it was time to go their separate ways.

All of this is way too much for D-Nice. Every couple of nights, Samad brings different people to their home. Off The Chain, who D-Nice doesn't trust at all, also spends the night at times. D-Nice has been sitting back watching murder after murder, the shooting of the woman and all Samad's other reckless situations. He's positive that Samad is just one big mistake waiting to happen and when it does he doesn't want to be anywhere near it.

That is the reason that he's now moving in with his girlfriend. He hasn't even told Samad. Each day little by little he takes more of his clothes out of the house while Samad isn't there. Today he's taken all of his clothes but he left his television and his furniture just to keep Samad from knowing that he's moved.

D-Nice pulls out of the complex development slowly. As he pulls away, he sighs with relief. Deep down inside he feels as if he's removed himself slightly from all the mess that he can see coming. His next step is to break away from Samad altogether.

Meanwhile. Maurice stands before Black with rage as he listens with full attentiveness. "I ran into mufucker screaming that thirty-two shit," Black says.

"Listen, I'm sure that shit ain't gone be around for long. Somebody probably got hold to it before the shit went sky high. Anyway, I'm sure at that price the shit can't be no good. I know niggas in Florida who paying thirty-seven, thirty-eight. Big niggas," he adds. "It's probably compressed. That's the only way I can see them being able to sell it that low."

Black shakes his head from side to side. "It ain't compressed. On the real, I heard the shit is better than ours."

"Impossible!"

In Hoboken, New Jersey. Deja searched high and low, asking every dude she knows and shes still come up with nothing. The ten-thousand dollar bonus is enough to keep her on the hunt though. She's now depending on her last resort.

She sits across from Lil Bit inside of Ruth Chris' Steakhouse. They're here on Deja's treat. She hopes she can pay for this meal out of the ten-thousand dollars she scores if all goes well and Lil Bit can lead her to some work.

"Listen, Big Texas came up yesterday," she whispers. "He's been trying to get hold of some kilos but he hasn't had any luck. He doesn't want to go home empty handed. He offered me ten-thousand just to hook him up with somebody," she whispers. "Maurice sells cocaine right?" she asks. "You think he can supply Big Texas?"

Lil Bit peeks up at Deja without saying a word. Deja is clueless to the entire matter. She has no idea what Maurice actually does because Lil Bit has never shared it with her. Also she has never even shared with Deja what she does for Maurice. She's never trusted her enough to tell her anything about it.

Deja takes her silence as an invitation to continue speaking. "We can split five thousand apiece," she says as her eyes light up. Lil Bit sits back quite uninterested in the entire conversation until, "he wants 20 kilos," Deja whispers.

Lil Bit swallows the lump in her throat. She automatically begins calculating. 20 kilos at $14,500 profit, she adds up to be $290,000. Deja has her full attention now.

"Do you have any idea what one of those costs?" Deja asks. He said he's willing to pay anything for it. Girl, he's desperate."

"Yeah?" Lil Bit asks.

"Yeah, desperate as hell. Do you know where we can get twenty from? Do you think Maurice will do it?"

Lil Bit sits back quietly as her mind races. "I might," she says as she shakes her head from side to side. "I just might."

///// CHAPTER 135 /////

Later That Night. Samad walks into the bedroom of Lil Bit's apartment. He looks at the dresser where four stacks of bills lie. He's quite surprised that it's still there on the sixth of the month, when he's left it there days ago. The money he left for her to pay the rent with.

Lil Bit planned to get rid of this apartment but out of nowhere Samad gave her the money for the rent. She then had no reason to get rid of it. It all works out for the better though because she had no idea how she was going to get out of taking Samad to her new home. At first she wasn't sure if she wanted him to know about it. Now she's sure that she doesn't want him to know about it. It would have been impossible to maintain a relationship without taking him there. Now that he's paying the rent on this apartment, she can keep it, for the time being.

Her fear of Maurice's stalking still exists but she moves around carefully to avoid him. She knows she can't avoid him forever which is why she plans to move out of this apartment within the next month or two. She plans to tell Samad that the lease is up. She doesn't know what she will do from there. Maybe she will tell him that she's moving in with Sade temporarily.

Until that time comes she plans to do as she's been doing for the past few weeks. She's been juggling apartments. She only stays here on the nights that they spend together. All the other nights, she stays in The Big Apple all alone.

Lil Bit walks into the bedroom and brushes right past him without even looking in his direction. "You didn't pay the rent?" Samad questions.

"I paid it," she replies still not looking at him.

"Why didn't you use the money?"

"I didn't need it. Fat ass got her own money," she says as she walks out of the room. Throughout their little beef, Lil Bit has had time to sit back and think. She's noticed a great deal about him. She now realizes how selfish he really is. All the expensive things that he buys for himself and he hasn't bought her one gift. He even complains when she asks him to bring food in. As far as he knows she's getting the work for him and not making a dollar off of it. It's a good thing that she is charging him or she would be starving if it was up to him. At first she felt guilty for making a profit off of him but now she longer feels like that.

In a matter of seconds the stereo blasts at full volume. Singer Beyonce's 'Irreplaceable' seeps out of the speakers. "To the left, to the left," Lil Bit sings along.

He gets pissed off immediately. She plays this song every time they get into an argument. She plays it over and over until he turns into a madman. Hearing this song cuts him like a knife normally but today he has something for her. He has a secret weapon that he's been holding onto just waiting for the next time she pulled that off.

He walks into the living room, fully aware that she will leave as soon as he comes in. At his entrance into the room, she does just that. "Everything you own in a box to the left," she sings as she passes him.

He presses eject on the CD player. He grips the Beyonce' CD in his hand and flies it like a frisbee into the bedroom. The CD bangs into the wall and shatters into tiny pieces. Lil Bit storms into the living room with fury, just as a new song starts to play. Singer Babyface's voice comes through the speakers. "If you don't love me, somebody else will," he sings as Rapper Lil Wayne's voice fades in.

"Somebody else will!"

"Don't you...get too...comfortable," Babyface sings.

""Yeah!" Samad shouts along with Lil Wayne. "To the left, to the left," they say as they mimick Beyonce'. "If you wanna leave, be my guest. You can step. Feeling irreplaceable, listening to Beyonce, well I'll put you out on your B-Day."

Babyface interrupts once again. "All I ask is you don't take this love for granted. My love for you is real. If you don't love me somebody else will."

Samad and Lil Wayne start up and again. "Babygirl, don't you ever get too comfortable," they sing. "Let me catch my breath. Talking bout leaving and you ain't left yet. And if you leave, leave correct. And I'm gone send a jet to pick up the next. And if you leave you leaving the best. So you will have to settle for less. And I am no Elliot Ness. I don't handcuff, I don't arrest. Baby, you blessed, now just don't jump your nest. Babyface sings once again before Lil Wayne and Samad interrupt. "Irreplaceable huh? Don't get too comfortable," Samad repeats looking in Lil Bit's direction.

Rage bleeds from her eyes. At the end of the song she storms into the bedroom and slams the door. He watches with satisfaction as the door slams in his face. He accepts that as a victory. He smiles from ear to ear. In the next room Lil Bit plops onto the bed and cries her eyes out.

///// CHAPTER 136 /////

Lil Bit cruises around the Newark International Airport. Deja sits in the front seat while Lil Bit's aunt sits quietly in the backseat. Deja is as nervous as she's ever been in her entire life. She sits there trembling in her seat. The only reason that she's even considering this is because of the thirty thousand dollar incentive that Lil Bit offered her.

Lil Bit is going to pay her two thousand dollars for each of the ten kilos that she brings back and a thousand dollars for each one that her aunt brings back. Her aunt only gets $500.00 a kilo. Sure Lil Bit knows that the job is worth more than that but she feels like her aunt owes her for all the heartache she endured from her rejecting to help her when she needed it most.

Everything is in perfect order. Muhsee is expecting them. He accepted her lame excuse on why she couldn't make it. Lil Bit is sure the reason for that had everything to do with her going out to dinner with him the last time.

The money has been wired to him throughout the course of the day and this morning. Their hotel is paid for. Now all they have to do is make it back here safe and sound and everybody will have scored.

"Listen, it's simple," Lil Bit says. "Call him when you get to the hotel and he'll do the rest. It's a piece of cake," she says trying to calm Deja's nerves. "Listen, he's a charmer. "Be careful with him," she smiles. "Every woman in his home has had sex with him. Don't let him have his way."

"Girl, please. Now what about coming back?"

"What about it? Come back the same way you come back from any other vacation. You know how to do that right? Lay on the beach somewhere, get a tan and everything will be the same."

"It won't be the same. I never come back from vacation with a Cuban cigar, let alone with twenty kilos strapped to my body. I have to stand naked in front of him?" she asks as that comes to mind.

"Yes, but girl don't act like that. This won't be the first time you been ass naked in front of a strange man," she teases. "Just kidding. Let me make it easier for you. Think of the $40,000 you're going to make when all this is over with. Does that help?" she asks as she stops short in front of the Air Jamaica ramp.

"Ok," Deja says as she forces the door open. She gets out slowly while Lil Bit's aunt hops out anxiously. "Girl, I hope it's as simple as you say it is," she says before slamming the door shut.

"Girl, how long I just told you I been doing this shit? Almost ten years and I never had a problem. It's that simple. I promise you," she says with her fingers crossed.

Later that Night

Lil Bit's phone rings. The unknown number makes her unsure if she should answer it. She figures it's Deja calling to let her know that she's reached Jamaica but it could easily be Maurice blocking his number. She takes the gamble and answers it anyway. "Hello?"

"Yeah, we here."

"Good. You called him?"

"Not yet. I called you first."

"Ok, call him and he'll take everything from there. Where ya'll at, the hotel?"

"Yep."

"Where's my auntie?"

"In the bathroom."

"That figures. She'll be there the entire vacation. Don't mind her. That's what she do. Don't let her go too far where she starts acting stupid though. And don't ever leave them two alone together."

Deja sighs with nervousness. "I don't know how you talked me into this."

"Girl, it's gone be alright. Just follow the plan. Trust me."

"Alright, I'll call in the morning."

"Ok, later," Lil Bit says before ending the call. While the phone is in her hand she gets the urge to call Samad. She hasn't heard from him all day. She hasn't called him and he hasn't called her either. In the beginning of their relationship they couldn't go an hour without speaking to each other but now they can go an entire day. Lately they don't get along more than they do get along. Lil Bit hopes that it's the pregnancy that is making things like that. She prays that their relationship will snap back into place after the baby arrives.

Her stubbornness almost prevents her from calling him but a part of her really wants to hear his voice. She's still pissed off at him over their last episode and she feels that he won that battle. She's sure she will get even though. She's going to call and start an argument with him to piss him off then hang up on him. She knows he will get even more pissed when she ignores his calls for the rest of the night. That will only make him come to her apartment in Jersey City and he will lose his mind when he finds her not to be there. She's in Manhattan.

She dials his number and surprisingly it goes straight to his voicemail. She gets pissed when it tells her she can't leave a message because the mailbox is full. She dials again and again and again but still the phone isn't even ringing. She gets angrier and angrier with each call.

Suddenly her rage vanishes and she becomes worried. This isn't like him to have his phone turned off. He's become so greedy for money that he could never go without having his phone off. He's too worried that he'll miss a dime sale. Lil Bit slowly walks over to the huge living room window. She stares over the balcony at Times Square. The bright lights hypnotize her momentarily. She then looks over to New Jersey, while thinking, just where in Jersey he could be right now.

She starts to think of the absolute worse case scenario, first. Not about him being locked up. That's the second worse case scenario. The first thought she had was maybe Maurice has finally caught up with him and right now he's laying dead in an abandoned building somewhere. Nah, she thinks to herself. Maurice would have called her to let her know what he did. After all he said he would get the last laugh.

"I hope this nigga ain't did nothing stupid and got his stupid ass locked up again," she speaks out.

In the Short Hills Hilton

The smell of perspiration, Victoria's Secret lotion and marijuana fills the air. The sound of two sweaty, nude bodies clapping together sounds off loudly. The thick bodied female is bent over the bed with her head mashed in between the hardwood headboard and the soft mattress. Samad rams himself into her doggystyle. He's driving hard and fast like a madman.

The doctor assigned Lil Bit to bedrest with no sex but he said nothing about poor old Samad. Getting no sex at home isn't totally the reason for his cheating. There are more reasons than one for that. The sad part is even if he could have sex with her, most likely this would still be happening.

Samad feels sad to admit that he no longer finds her to be sexually attractive. He has three reasons why. One reason is because now that she's so far into the pregnancy, he would be too afraid to have sex with her and interfere with the pregnancy. The second reason is, he sort of holds her on a pedestal. She's the mother of his child. With that in mind, he can't even imagine doing the raunchy sexual things to her that he's done to her in the past. The third reason is during the past month or so of her pregnancy her body has stretched out so drastically that he no longer desires sex with her.

The fourth reason he doesn't even realize himself and that is, the money has gone to his head, making him believe that he's God's gift to every woman. His new found success has every girl in the neighborhood checking for him. He's become so arrogant that he actually believes that they're after him and not his money. The pressure is too much for him and he can't fight them away. Truthfully speaking he isn't trying to fight them away.

He grabs the girl by her waist and rams her as hard as he can as she attempts to get away from his wrath. He traps her by mashing her face deeper into the mattress, pushing her down. She moans with agony which excites him even more.

He grabs her by her weave, lifting her up from the mattress. He snatches a handful of weave with each thrust of his hips. The pain is exciting her as well. She starts to throw it back at him. "Yeah, like that Mami."

In the Big Apple

Lil Bit stands at the window, staring into the gray sky. "Please God, don't let him be in any danger," she prays. "Please don't let him be locked up," she begs.

If only she knew. She would be happier if he was locked up right now.

///// CHAPTER 137 /////

Days Later. Deja has made it back safe and sound to her surprise. Everything wasn't as smooth and simple as Lil Bit explained it to be but it was no way as complicated as she expected. She's so grateful to be seated in the comfort of her own home and not somebody's prison in Jamaica. Even though she was only gone for a few days that was even too long for her.

Sitting across the coffee table from her is Big Texas. He examines the work brick by brick without saying a word. He looks up slowly after checking the very last one. He stares into her eyes as she awaits his response. Finally he speaks. "This that shit!" he says.

"What, it ain't no good?" she asks.

"Good? This the best! It was crunch time and you came through for a nigga!" he says as he hands her the duffle bag that lies in front of him.

"Shh," she whispers. "I got neighbors," she says as she peeks at her windows nervously.

"That's four hundred and thirty thousand," he says as he slides the bag closer to her. "You ain't even got to count that. Me and my peoples counted it at least fifty times."

Lil Bit set the price of $20,500 per kilo which comes out to $410,000. The extra $20,000 in the duffle bag belongs to Deja. She added another $1,000 to the price of each kilo he bought. She felt with all she had to go through to get the work here she deserved more than that. After seeing how desperate he really was she had no choice but to capitalize off of it. When she told him the price he didn't even blink. Even with her adding her number on top of it, it's still a couple of thousand dollars cheaper than he was originally going to pay with his own connect.

"Here," he says as he slams a few stacks onto the table. "That's the ten I promised you and an extra five, for my appreciation."

Deja has never seen this much money in her entire life. In less than four days she has scored a grand total of $65,000. "Thank you," she says gratefully.

Meanwhile. It's broad daylight but Samad isn't going to let that get in the way of him doing what he feels needs to be done. After sitting back and analyzing the situation with Bullet, he feels that Bullet was trying to use his Blood affiliation to get in where he thought he fit in. Samad understands that Bullet thought he saw the perfect opportunity where he could get in and make a couple of dollars for himself. Samad would have respected it more if he had come to him straight up and asked to be brought in. Instead Samad feels like he tried to extort him, which is the reason that he feels so disrespected.

"Let's go!" Samad says as he steps on the gas pedal and cruises up the block. They've been sitting out here for hours waiting for Bullet to come out of his house.

It took no homework at all to locate him because this is the same house that he's been living in since his family moved to the neighborhood back in 1989.

Bullet makes it three houses away from his by the time they reach him. Samad is careful not to stop suddenly because he doesn't want to alarm Bullet.

He's sure there's a great possibility that Bullet may be armed with a weapon of his own and he doesn't want to take the chance of him blasting away at them first.

He steps gently on the brake pedal and Off the Chain hops out armed and masked up. He aims his gun high as he trots behind Bullet. Samad and D-Nice sit back watching it all play out like a movie. By the third footstep Bullet turns around but it's already too late. Pop! Pop! Bullet ducks low as he backpedals with fear and surprise. He attempts to reach under his shirt but Off the Chain rushes him. Pop! He fires again, striking him in the abdomen. Bullet drops to his knees as Off the Chain stands over top of him. He aims the gun at the very top of his head. Pop! Pop! Bullet slowly melts onto the sidewalk and Off the Chain empties the rest of the clip into his head. Pop! Pop! Pop! With each shot he squeezes with more and more aggression. Pop! Pop! He's charged up and bursting with energy. Murder gives him the rush of a lifetime. Pop! Pop! By now, he's hopping off of the ground with each shot. Pop! Pop! Pop! Pop!

///// CHAPTER 138 /////

One Month Later. Samad cruises throughout the city in his pride and joy. He hardly brings it out so when he does it's greatly appreciated. Right now him and D-Nice are cruising up South Orange Avenue on their way to Short Hills Mall.

They're busy blazing as usual. Samad is so high that he doesn't even realize that he's not even going 20 miles an hour. He has the power of 420 horses at his command and right now he's using none of it. Suddenly a blood red blur passes by him like a flash of lightening. This wakes Samad up slightly.

The vehicle stops at the corner as it's caught by the traffic light. The out of state license plate catches his attention. Less than a minute later, Samad pulls alongside of the vehicle in which he spots a beautiful female driver. Just as he sets his eyes on her the light changes and she speeds off. He takes off right behind her. He quickly passes her, leaving her in his dust. Gradually he breaks his gears down, giving her a chance to catch up with him. As she does, he adjusts his speed so they ride side by side. He peeks over and they lock eyes. He winks at her seductively.

They're both caught by the traffic light in South Orange Village. She stops short before inching up ahead of him. As he pulls up next to her he rolls his window down. The smokey haze seeps out of his car and pollutes the air. He looks over to her as he whispers to D-Nice. "I don't really eat chocolate," he says referring to the woman's creamy dark chocolate complexion. "It makes me break out but every now and then I crave a piece," he whispers as D-Nice laughs at the comment. Samad taps his horn causing her to look over at him. He gestures for her to roll the window down and she does but the look on her face clearly says that she doesn't want to be bothered. Still he goes for it. "Wanna race? I'll give you a headstart. If I win, I get to have your heart," he says with a smile.

"I don't have a heart," she says with all seriousness on her face. "I'm a stone cold bitch," she says as she turns away with attitude. She looks up ahead of her before stepping on the gas pedal and speeding away once again. He takes off right behind her.

He catches up with her at the next light and decides to try again. "We both from out of town, Ma. What you trying to get into?" he says quoting a verse from his favorite Jay-Z song. It's obvious that she knows the song as well because she cracks a smile. That's all he needs. "Pull over," he says as he points up ahead. The light changes and she pulls off slowly this time. Just a little past the corner, she pulls over. He passes her and parks directly in front of her to give her full view of his 'Black Beauty.'

She pays notice to his Pennsylvania license plates. He hops out confidently. He pimp steps toward her car. She can't help but notice the frosty 'S' on his chest which is swaying from side to side. The diamonds glisten vibrantly in the sun. The rainbow reflection is quite blinding.

He stops at her window. "His and hers," he says as he points to her Audi. "That's a good look for us, right? See, we already have two things in common. I'm from out of town, lost," he lies. "And so are you. And we got the same taste in cars. I can't wait to find out what else we have in common."

"Why are you so sure that you're even going to find out?" she asks with a smile.

"Cause I know me," he says with his normal amount of arrogance.

"Well, don't be so sure. And anyway I'm not lost. I know where I'm going."

"Where is that?" he asks nosily.

"To the mall."

"What mall? Short Hills?"

She nods her head up and down. "Yes."

"That's the same place I was headed. See, another thing we got in common. We both know quality. I'm a quality nigga and I can see that you're a quality chick," he says as he looks at her diamond watch and her expensive looking accessories. "What's up with a little quality time?"

She interrupts him rudely. "Look, you're holding me up. I got less than one hour before it closes. Talk fast nigga."

"Nah, that, I'm not going to do. It won't work cause I ain't no fast talker. I don't do nothing fast. I like to take my time," he says with a seductive look in his eyes. "Dig, what I'm gone do though. I'm gone give you my number and you hit me when you got more time on your hands. Ok?"

"I'll see," she says as she grabs hold of her phone. "What's the number?" He calls the numbers out to her and she stores it safely. "What's your name?"

"Smooth."

"Nah, I ain't storing that in my phone. What's the name your mama gave you?"

He smiles. "Anything for you. Samad," he utters. She looks up with surprise and quickly she looks down at her phone. "I didn't get your name."

"Cause I didn't give it to you," she smiles.

"Ha, ha, ha," he grunts. "For real though?"

"Ebony."

"Alright Ebony, I'll be waiting for your call," he says as he backs away from her car. She zips around him and speeds up the hill at rapid speed.

Samad gets back into his car. "What happened?" D-Nice asks curiously. "You got her?"

"Did I get her? What's my name? Why wouldn't I get her? That's what I do...

bag bitches! Nigga, I'm like a rock star. I stay hell a high, fuck hell a bitches, and get hell a money. From now on don't call me Samad or Smooth no more. Call me the black Bruce Springsteen!"

Meanwhile

Maurice and his Federation sit around in the Bat Cave. Maurice hoped the situation wth the cheaper priced cocaine would pass but it hasn't. Hearing how potenent the work is makes him curious to find out how true that is. He knows there's no cocaine available to man that could battle with his when it comes to purity. That is when his product is in it's purest form. He's really considering the fact of not cutting the kilos just to make a statement on the street. That will affect his pockets dearly though. He's so spoiled that he's gotten used to the outrageous profit that he's been making and he can't see it any other way. The truth of the matter is he may have to.

His curiousity leads him to want to know just how good the work is that everyone is talking about. He looks at his men with sterness. "I got a plan to find out how raw it is."

In the Big Apple

Lil Bit's phone rings off the hook back to back while she is busy counting through stacks and stacks of money. Finally she's finished. She stacks the money into her Gucci overnight bag and hands it to Sade. "Here, that's four hundred," she says. Sade looks at Lil Bit with concern on her face. Lil Bit is sure that she has something to say. "What?"

She shakes her head from side to side with sadness in her eyes. "Lil Bit when is enough? I'm holding onto close to three hundred thousand already and now you're giving me another four hundred thousand. You got more than enough already. You're pressing your luck now. All good things come to an end."

Samad comes to Lil Bit's mind after hearing that statement. Tell me about it, she utters to herself. "Come on girl, don't start. You scare me when you start talking like that."

"Good cause that's what I'm trying to do. This can't go on forever. You need to stop while the getting is good."

Lil Bit's phone rings. "Yes, saved by the bell!" she shouts as she looks at the display. It's Deja. "Ay bitch," she says with cheer.

"Takes one to know one," she sings in reply. "Ay, your Samad, does he drive an Audi?"

"Audi?" Lil Bit repeats. "What kind of Audi?"

"The new one. The hundred thousand dollar one."

"Shit, not that I know of. Why?"

"Nothing, never mind then. Different Samad then," she says as she blows the conversation off.

"You sure?" she asks with concern.

"Yeah, that's a different one. Anyway this one is from P.A. It ain't him. I was just making sure. Better safe than sorry."

▮▮▮▮▮ CHAPTER 139 ▮▮▮▮▮

Two Weeks Later. Rock from the Federation stands directly in front of D-Nice's cousin Rahiem. "Yo, I went through hell trying to shake them joints that I had. I lost money on them because nobody wanted to pay that price. I ended up selling them for what I paid for them. I need you right now, lil bruh," he says with desperation in his eyes. "I was wondering if you could get me a couple from your peoples? Just like one or two so I can make some of my money back."

"Yeah, no doubt." In his mind he has already figured out how much he is going to tack onto the price. Nothing in life is free, he thinks to himself. "That's not a problem at all."

Meanwhile. It's early evening and the rowdy crowd has yet to start pouring in. The small private room here in the 40/40 Lounge in New York City has only a handful of people in it. All of them being women.

Congratulations balloons and gift wrapped presents are piled up in a corner of the room. The women stuff their faces as they have been doing since they got here. The pregnant Lil Bit waddles like a duck around the room as she thanks and entertains. Even while pregnant she's still the most fashionable woman in the room. Her pregnant glow and her rounded belly make her look that much more beautiful.

Deja and Sade planned this baby shower together. In attempt to keep this an exclusive event, they didn't just invite any and everyone that they know. If that was the case they would have had to have it in the Meadowlands Arena. They handpicked which women they were going to invite. They were careful to invite women who they think would keep their mouths shut. Both Sade and Deja now know the importance of keeping Lil Bit's pregnancy on the low. Afterall, her life depends on it.

"Ok ya'll!" Deja shouts over the music. She stands in the center of the room. "Now we're going to present the gifts to mommy," she says as she sets a chair in the center of the room. She then makes her way over to the corner and grabs hold of the gifts. As she's doing so, Lil Bit waddles to the center of the room.

In a matter of seconds Lil Bit is ripping through the many gifts and thanking each person responsible for their gift. The creaking of the heavy door behind her sounds off. She becomes alarmed. In her mind all she can think of is Maurice showing up at this shower. All hell would break loose. She slowy turns around. Her and every woman watch as the three men step into the room.

The guests stare at the three unfamiliar faces, wondering who they are. Samad, D-Nice and Off the Chain step into the room, bashfully. They can feel all the attention on them. Samad looks at Lil Bit and she starts blushing like a goofy teen-ager. Samad then looks past her and his eyes damn near pop out of his head when he sees another familiar face.

Him and Deja lock eyes momentarily before he realizes who she is and looks away. Oh shit, he thinks to himself. That's Ebony. D-Nice recognizes her as well. He nudges Samad with his elbow. A strange look appears on both of their faces as they stand there goofily. Deja looks at them with a devilish smirk on her face. Samad wishes he could just disappear right now.

He becomes even more nervous as Deja steps closer to Lil Bit. They meet at the center of the room and stand on opposite sides of Lil Bit. Samad turns away from Deja and plants a soft kiss on Lil Bit's forehead. She blushes even more at the touch of his lips. His heart is racing right now.

"Samad, this is Deja," Lil Bit whispers as she looks up at his superman medallion. Suddenly she becomes quite embarrassed. "Deja, this is Samad."

Deja, he repeats to himself. Oh shit, I played myself. Lying bitch said her name was Ebony. "He nods his head nervously. "Ay."

"Hey, Samad. It's a pleasure to finally meet you," she says with sarcasm. "I heard so much about you that it's like we've already met. Your face looks so familiar. I seen you somewhere before," she says as she scares the life out of him.

He stands there with a cheesy grin on his face. He prays that she doesn't blow up his spot. He anticipated her call for the past two weeks and was actually disappointed that she never called. At this very moment he realizes that it's a great thing that she didn't call him.

He's heard so much about Deja that he feels that he knows her personally. Lil Bit has told her everything about her except for the small detail that she drives an Audi with Florida license plates. That threw him off totally. Lil Bit has also told him how outright bold Deja can be at times. That makes him fearful that she just may put him on blast. If what he does know about her is correct, he's sure she will.

Deja stands there quietly. She applies more pressure to him as he squirms with fear. He can't even look her in the eyes. "You little piece of shit," she mumbles so he can read her lips. She looks him up and down. I told her she should have left his broke ass on the street corner that she met him on, she says to herself. Wack ass buster, she says to herself with rage. She could easily rip him right now but she isn't going to. She in no way is saving him. The only reason that she's not going to cause a scene is because of her best friend Lil Bit. Now would be the perfect time to say I told you so but she would never do anything to embarrass her friend like that. Besides she feels just being with that low life should be embarrassing enough.

A few minutes pass and Samad finds the perfect time to escape. He sneakily walks to the door where D-Nice and Off the Chain are standing while stuffing their faces. He peeks around to make sure that no one is watching. "Come on," he whispers. "Let's get the fuck outta here." Damn, he thinks to himself. He knows there's no way in the world she's going to keep that secret away from Lil Bit. I done fucked up now. Damn, he thinks to himself

As they're walking to the parking lot Samad's phone vibrates. He looks down at the display and spots an unfamiliar number. The 305 area code throws him off. He answers. "Hello?"

"Ay, Smooth," says the female voice.

"Hello?" Samad says again. He doesn't recognize the voice.

"Yeah, it's me Ebony," she says. Samad doesn't say a word. He knows that anything that he says can be held against him. He wonders if she has Lil Bit listening on the line. He's debating if he should hang up on her or not. "Samad," she sings. "You there?"

"Hello?" he whispers not knowing what else to say.

"Why did you leave so fast? They're just about to cut the cake. Samad," she sings again. "Why are you so quiet? The other day you had so much to say to me.

You were a real poet. I love the way you put words together. Come on Don Juan, tell me something sweet. Please?" she begs. "Pretty please?" Samad is at a loss of words. Instead of apologizing and further incriminating himself, he decides to plead the Fifth Amendment by not saying anything at all. "Samad?"

"Yeah," he whispers.

"You know you fucked up right?"

///// CHAPTER 140 /////

Samad speeds down Route 280. He sings along with Young Jeezy at the top of his lungs. "You niggas want word play but I'm bout bird play. Third of the month, we call that bird day. Just look at them fly. Just look at them fly!"

He just left his house where he picked the work up from. He has a two bird sale waiting for him. Lil Bit no longer stores the work in the Jersey City apartment. She turns them all over to Samad, giving him full control of everything.

He's been doing this long enough now that she feels a certain amount of confidence in knowing that can handle the operation. She also knows that if something goes wrong he has enough money to at least cover what she came out of her pocket with. At least she hopes that. The way he's been blowing his money lately, it's hard for her to tell if he has a dime left.

She also lets him take the work with him to eliminate the back and forth trafficking. All it would take is one time for them to meet up at the apartment while Maurice is sitting there stalking the place and it's all over for the both of them.

Minutes later, Samad is cruising into the mini mall on West Market Street. He slowly drives through the parking lot. The headlights of the Ford Taurus flash brightly. Samad zips over and parks right next to it.

Rahiem hops out of the Taurus and snatches the passenger's door of Samad's car open. "What up?" he asks as he sits down. Samad doesn't utter a word in reply. Before Rahiem can even get seated, Samad drops the plastic bag onto his lap. In return he hands Samad the plastic bag that he holds in his hand. Without saying another word, Rahiem slides out of the car and gets into his. He cruises off without hesitation. As soon as he exits the parking lot, Samad pulls off as well.

Meanwhile

Maurice sits parked in his Maserati on Court Street. In his passenger's seat sits Rhonda, who is one of his many side pieces. He's given her the nickname 'Young Tender.' She's a ghetto supermodel. She's drop dead gorgeous and should be on somebody's runway but instead she's trapped in the hood exploiting her beauty to manipulate young drug dealers to obtain her wants and desires. If only she had an ounce of class to go with her looks she could soar to the top. Too bad she doesn't.

She's been on his team for about two years now and still she is at the bottom of the list. Her big mouth, sassy attitude and disobedience are all the factors that keep her growth stunned. She drives him crazy as he tries to not only keep up with her but to control her as well.

He tells himself over and over that he's going to cut her loose but he keeps finding himself with her. 'The Snapper' as he calls it has him hooked. She may be hard headed and feisty but at only 20 years of age, her youth and tenderness makes him overlook it. Sex with her allows him to relive his youth all over again. Each time he's with her he feels like he's knocked 20 years off of his age. Holding onto her as her tight wetness envelopes him, makes him feel like he's being cheated by dealing with his other girls.

He finds her to be a cool person to hang around and he enjoys her company but at times her mouth can be overbearing. If she would learn to keep quiet and just play her position she can't imagine how fast she would shoot to the top of 'The Chart,' as he calls it.

"So, how come you weren't at the baby shower?" she asks.

"Baby shower? What baby shower?"

"Oh, you don't know," she says as she smacks on the mouthful of cherry Now and Laters candy. "Never mind," she says as she looks away. She knows exactly what she's doing. Right now she's reeling him in.

He bites on the bait just as she knew he would. "What the fuck are you talking about?"

"Nothing, forget I even said something. I thought you knew about it. If you were not invited then it must wasn't meant for you to know."

It's obvious that she shouldn't know either and she wouldn't if she didn't work at the shop. She's been working there since the shop first opened. She's been secretly creeping with Maurice for close to two years now. Even though Sade and Deja handpicked the people they gave invites to, it's quite evident that a bad seed has managed to slide into the mix.

For so long now Rhonda has watched quietly as Maurice catered to Lil Bit. Whatever she didn't see with her own eyes, she heard as Lil Bit bragged on and on in the shop about the places they go and the things they do. She just sits back and accepts the fact that Lil Bit was there before her and is and will always be his number one side piece. It's a tough pill to swallow but still she manages. The only thing that keeps her going is hope. She hopes that one day she will get that number one spot. At times she feels cheap and worthless, knowing that he takes good care of Lil Bit, while he gives her nothing outside of an old semi-hard cock that's no good to her after a few minutes before he collapses like the old man that he is.

She's laughing hysterically inside as she thinks of how he's always held Lil Bit on a pedestal and now she's played him for a sucker.

"Yo, what the fuck are you talking about?" he asks angrily.

She can sense his anger but she doesn't fear it the least bit. She's so unlike the rest of his women who are scared to death to get on his bad side. She gets a kick out of getting him all aroused and bothered.

She realizes the valuable information she holds can very well take her to the top of his chart. After revealing this secret she's sure she will go platinum. Now that the top spot is empty, she's sure if she plays her hand right she can very well fill that spot.

"Yo, stop fucking playing with me," he grunts.

"Ok, calm down," she says as if she's really worried about him. "Maurice you ain't heard it from me," she says. "My job is on the line and I know you ain't gone take care of me," she says as she looks into his eyes to see his reaction. "Your Lil Bit had a baby shower the other night at the 40/40. It was real exclusive, only invited guests. I just happen to be on the list because I'm exclusive."

Maurice sits there in a trance. He hasn't heard a word after Lil Bit's baby shower. It was then that his air was cut off and his spirit was snatched out of his body. She babbles on and on as Maurice stares straight ahead in a deep zone. "She got big as hell out of nowhere. She still look cute though, I ain't gone hate," she says as she smacks on the candy in her mouth. "She already like eight months. She don't come to the shop that much no more ever since she got her braids." She goes on and on digging deeper and deeper. When it's all said and done, she hopes to fill that number one side piece spot.

Meanwhile

Rahiem snatches the passenger's door of Rock's truck. He doesn't get in. He just uses the door as a shield to cover his body. He drops the plastic bag onto the seat and Rock hands him the bag of money. "That's 33,5," Rock says. "I'm saying though. You could have let me get it for 32 like you get it for."

"Come on, Rock. This business, baby. You know how it goes. If I touch it, I gotta score off it. I had to transport this shit all across town to get it to you."

"I can dig it. Thanks though, lil bruh."

"No problem," Rahiem says as he slams the door shut and walks away.

Rock grips the kilo in his hand and can't help but to notice how soft and fluffy it feels. It's completely different from the rock hard work that he gets from Maurice. Now it's time for the real test. It's time to take it to the lab and see what it is.

///// CHAPTER 141 /////

The Next Day

Maurice is walking around in the same trance that he went into the moment he heard about Lil Bit. Hearing that stunning news shattered his heart. He's never felt so betrayed in his life. For some reason he thought Lil Bit would be his forever. Although they've been going through their dilemma there was no doubt in his mind that they would eventually get over it.

He's mourning over her like she's dead. In fact it would probably be easier to deal with if she were dead. At least that way she would be gone and not with another man. Many sick thoughts have crossed his mind like killing her and the other man but really he doesn't have the energy to do it.

His sorrow has drained him thoroughly. Sadness overpowers his rage. He can't understand how she could do this to him. To be with another man is one thing but to actually have his baby is altogether different. That means she really loves him. That's the part that kills him inside.

His ego makes him question what this man has that he does not. He considers the fact that maybe the man has more money than him or maybe he's a better lover than him. Whatever it is, the bottom line is he's won the prize. That will make it harder for him to live with. Not knowing where he lost out makes him do something that he's never done and that's doubt himself. Never has his self-esteem and confidence been beat down like this.

He's told himself that he's going to leave her alone but he can't; not until he gets clarity on this matter. He plans to get that one way or another. One thing for sure is he isn't going to be able to accept this loss. He refuses to allow them to be happy while he lives his life miserably without her.

Right now he's sitting back in total silence in his truck. He's parked a few cars away from her garage. For some sick reason he wants to see them with his very own eyes. He tells himself over and over that violence isn't the answer but in no way does he believe it. He tells himself that he only wants to talk to her face to face to get clarity but the loaded gun on his lap tells him differently.

He's been sitting out here for hours, hoping to catch her coming in. In his mind he pictures her riding side by side with her child's father and that enrages him even more. He's even pictured himself running up on the truck and murdering the both of them. As hard as he tries to shake away that vision it keeps coming back.

He picks up his phone and before he realizes it, he's already dialed her number.

In the Big Apple

A half sleep Lil Bit answers her phone. "Hello?" she says groggily.

To Maurice's surprise she has answered. His heart pounds in his chest as soon as he hears her voice. He tries to calm himself down so that he doesn't say something that makes her hang up on him. She hasn't answered his calls in quite some time and he would hate to go another day feeling like this. "Yeah, what's up?" he says as he tries hard to suppress his anger.

"Hello?" she says again as she realizes that she's actually answered his call. She was half sleep and didn't pay attention to the number on the display. If she did she would have never answered. Now she's fully awake.

"Yeah, what's up?" he asks again. "Why you been avoiding my calls? I been trying to get in touch with you. I need you. I got your ticket to the game," he says, talking in code. "Front row seats," he adds which really means First Class seats. "You going or what?"

Lil Bit sits quietly as she decides how to answer him. Damn, she thinks to herself. Why did I answer this call without looking, she asks herself. "Maurice... no," she whispers.

"Huh?"

"Ah hah," she replies softly.

"No?" he says with agitation in his voice. He's just lost his composure. "Yo, what's the deal? Is there something you're not telling me?"

"Maurice, I told you everything months ago."

"Nah," he laughs demonically. "You didn't tell me everything. Talk to me?"

"There's nothing to talk to you about."

"Oh, there's a lot to talk about. You just ain't talking! Come downstairs so we can talk face to face."

Her heart skips a beat. "Come down stairs?"

"Yeah, I'm in front of the house. Come in the lobby. You don't have to let me in. We can kick it right there."

"Maurice, why are you at my house?" she asks innocently.

"Oh, what? That's a problem now?"

"Please?" she begs.

"Please my ass!" he shouts. "Please bring your ass downstairs so we can talk!" he demands.

"We're talking right now."

"No…face to face. Come down or I'm coming up. It's your choice."

She's not there but she can't let him know that. She's sure that will only make matters worse. So, instead she plays along as if she's there. "Maurice, what is it that you want from me?"

"I want clarity, damn it! I want to know how you just gone let a ten year relationship go down the drain just like that."

"I already told you."

"Bitch, you ain't tell me nothing!"

Now she's furious. "Maurice, I'm hanging up now before I say something that I'm sure you will make me pay for later."

"Bitch, you already done something that I'm gone make you pay for. Not later, right now, bitch! That's why the fuck you ain't coming down. That's why the fuck you been ducking me."

She's never been called this many bitches in her life. She gets alarmed as she wonders what he's talking about. Does he know about her pregnancy or the trips to Jamaica? Or maybe he knows about both, she thinks to herself. "What are you talking about?"

"Bitch, you know what the fuck I'm talking about. Now you're playing me like I'm fucking stupid! I got you," he says in a threatening manner. "You know what? You ain't gotta come down now but you gotta come out sooner or later. And guess what? I'm gone be right here when you do. I ain't going nowhere!"

She's now terrified. "Maurice you're going to make me do something that I've never done before. If you continue to stalk my house and threaten me, I'm going to have no choice but to call the police."

"The police? Oh, now you fucking with the police? Bitch, call the police! I'll make bail and when I do, I'll fix yo ass!"

"Maurice, I'm hanging up."

"You can hang up but before you do, listen to this. You listening?" he asks slowly. "I'm gone get the clarity I need one way or another. You crossed me bitch and I need to know why. You gone repent to me, whether it be on your two feet, standing face to face or either me standing over top of you, while you laying in a pool of ya'll blood."

Enough heard. She ends the call with fear.

"Hello? Hello?"

///// CHAPTER 142 /////

Lil Bit pulls hesitantly up to the parking garage, while Samad lays back in a deep sleep. She swipes her card and the gate opens up slowly. Once the gate gets halfway up, she zooms underneath it. Suddenly bright headlights illuminate her truck. She turns around only to find Maurice's pick up truck coming behind her. The gate is closing slowly. "Please close," she whispers. "Please close," she cries as Maurice approaches the gate. Just her luck, the gate gets stuck midway and Maurice speeds through recklessly, damn near ripping the top of his truck off.

She mashes the gas pedal as hard as she can but the sluggish Rover seems to be moving in slow motion. The harder she tries to get away from him the slower the truck seems to be going. Loud screeching sounds off as both vehicles' tires grip the slippery floor of the garage.

Lil Bit zooms up the narrow path, ripping many mirrors off of cars that are parked on the sides of her. She peeks through her rearview mirror and sees that Maurice is almost bumper to bumper with her. Suddenly he rams the back of her truck causing her to lose control. On both sides of her are cement columns. She turns the wheel with what she thinks is enough to squeeze between the columns but apparently it was not. She slams into the column with massive force. She tries to back off of it and keep it moving but for some reason her truck has shut off. "Come on!" she shouts to Samad. Who looks at her with dazed eyes. He has not a clue what this is about. "Let's go, hurry!" she shouts with fear.

The both of them bust out of their doors simultaneously and take off into flight. Suddenly, Lil Bit hears gunshots behind her. Boc! Boc! Boc! Boc! This makes her run even faster but her heavy load makes it quite difficult. Samad's screaming echoes throughout the garage.

She peeks over her shoulder to see what is happening. There she sees Maurice standing over top of Samad. He fires twice more. Boc! Boc! A tremendous pain rips through her belly. She grabs it with both hands, cupping the bottom of it. Another blow strikes but this one is double the pain as the first one but still she manages to continue running. Fear carries her body.

She peeks over her shoulder once again and sees Maurice who is now close enough to reach out and grab her. "Now bitch!" he shouts. "Where you gone go now?" he asks. He's close enough to grab her but instead he uses a sweeping motion of his foot to knock her clean off of her feet.

She falls face first, landing on her stomach. She fearfully rolls over, looking square into his bloodshot red eyes. "Now talk slick bitch!" he says as he aims his gun at her stomach.

"No,no," she cries. "No, please!"

"Lil Bit...Lil Bit," she hears before her eyes pop wide open. She raises up in the bed and sits there staring straight ahead. She looks around, not knowing where she is. The room is somewhat unfamiliar to her. "Lil Bit," Samad says once again. "You alright?" he asks. Lil Bit's screaming and tossing and turning awoke him.

Her heart is pounding vigorously. Her clothes are soaking wet with sweat. She tries to calm herself down before speaking. "I had a terrible nightmare."

The last conversation she had with Maurice is affecting her terribly. All she can hear are the threats that he made to her. She's so afraid that she hasn't been to the Jersey City apartment since that night. She's been staying in New York. Tonight she's here at Samad's house only because he begged her to stay with him.

Maurice hasn't called her since then and that only makes her more fearful. She knows that he's coming for her. She just doesn't know when.

"Hold me," she says as she backs her body up to his and falls into his arms. He hugs her tightly with comfort before planting a reassuring kiss on the nape of her neck.

She lays there thinking of the nightmare as Samad lays there thinking of his own dilemma. He can barely sleep himself. All day and night he wonders when he's going to get that call from Lil Bit about Deja. Each time she calls him he dreads to answer it, thinking that she's calling about that matter.

That situation has him on his best behavior. He has not complained about anything that she's asked him to do. Nor has he said one slick comment to her no matter how much she attacks him. The pressure has him doing things that he's never done. Tonight he even massaged her swollen feet until she fell asleep. It almost made him sick to his stomach doing it but still he got through it.

Meanwhile

Maurice, Sal, and Rock are the only members of the Federation who are present in the Bat Cave right now. The fourth man in the apartment is Maurice's chef. He's here to examine the kilo that Rock bought from Rahiem. He will cook it and test it out to see just how it matches up to theirs.

Rock hands the plastic bag over to Maurice who digs into the bag anxiously. He looks at the material with amazement. He's quite shocked at the way the kilo is wrapped. It's wrapped identical to the ones that he gets from Muhsee. He stands there in silence as he cuts through the rubber balloon casing. He then rips through the cellophane. To his surprise he looks in the center of the fluffy powder and can see traces of what appears to be the Jamaican Coat of Arms, which is Jamaica's National symbol.

Never before has he seen this stamp on a kilo until he started dealing with Muhsee. He automatically assumes that this had to come from Muhsee's cartel. "No wonder why everyone is amazed at the purity," he whispers to himself. But who could be plugged onto Muhsee, he asks himself. "Where the fuck did you get this from?"

///// CHAPTER 143 /////

The Next Day

Maurice is laying on his back on the edge of the guest bed when his wife parts the door open and peeks inside. His loud snoring lets her know that he's deep asleep. He hasn't been home this early in years. His reason for doing so is he has to be up bright and early for his flight.

Tomorrow he's going directly to the root of the problem which is Muhsee. For the life of him he can't understand how Muhsee has plugged into someone else here in the States. When he gets there he will get to the bottom of it and also he plans to give Muhsee an ultimatum. Either he deals with him exclusively as they've been doing or he loses their business relationship.

Maurice is so furious about this that his sadness about Lil Bit has eased away for the time being. That situation with her isn't over though. He just has to handle this with Muhsee before he can get back to it. That problem will exist until he solves it.

Maurice's wife tiptoes back into her room, where she is all alone. The girls are sound asleep in their own beds where they hardly ever sleep. She walks into the huge walk-in closet. A total of eight suitcases are stacked on the floor in the corner. In four of the suitcases are clothes of hers and the girls. Every item that means anything to any of them is packed away in the suitcases. The rest of their belongings will be left behind.

Maurice has not a clue that the moment he leaves for his trip to Jamaica, his family will be leaving as well. His wife has taken the last of the abuse that she's willing to take from him. She's totally fed up. She's been planning this move for years now but she's just got the heart to go through with it. She knows that their daughters will be affected by her decision but she can no longer live her life like this.

There's no doubt in her mind that Maurice is going away to Jamaica on business. She's completely aware of his connection with Jamaica. That's not the problem. The problem derived when she went through his pockets this morning while he was asleep and she found two First Class E-tickets. One had his name on it and the other was a female name. She's pretty much familiar with the women that he deals with regularly by her prying but this woman's name she's not familiar with.

In any case at this point it no longer matters because she's done with it. She will not even try and figure out who the woman is. Enough is enough. Her and the girls are out. She hasn't even told them yet. She doesn't know how she's going to break the news to them but plans to do so to the best of her ability.

They're going far from here leaving everything behind. They're only taking the bare necessities, her Bank of America Card and PNC Bank Card. With those two cards there is enough money there to not only start a new life somewhere else but to actually enjoy it as well.

She's been stashing her money for years in preparation for this move. For the past couple of years she's saved every penny that he's given to her. He hardly ever takes her anywhere so she's just trapped inside this house. She realized long ago that it was senseless to continue spending money on expensive clothing only for her daughters to see. Besides she never gets dressed up because her mood doesn't call for that. Putting new clothes on only makes the exterior look beautiful, while the interior is worn out and her spirit is beat down.

Maurice knows nothing about her bank accounts. What she has saved in her accounts is not even one percent of what lies in the other four suitcases. Her bank accounts can only hold them for a minute but there is more than enough in the suitcases for them to be able to live for the rest of their lives. A part of her feels guilty for stealing his money but the other part of her feels like she deserves every penny of it for all the heartache that he's caused her over the years.

She's sure he won't miss the money at all. He has so much money lying around that he even loses track of where he's put it. She could have robbed him for mony millions without him even knowing it.

Maurice is a multi-millionaire many many times over. He has more money than he knows what to do with. He could have stopped a long time ago but greed and addiction to the lifestyle keeps him in the game. At this point, he's hustling just for the sake of doing so. He already has more money than him and his family could spend in a lifetime. So many times she's asked him to stop living the reckless lifestyle that he's living and just be a father to his daughters and a husband to his wife. It's a shame that he couldn't make that sacrifice for his family. Now she's forced to make a sacrifice of her own. Should she stay for her daughters' sake and be miserable for the rest of her life or leave in search of happiness? As selfish as it may sound she chooses to leave. He's going away to solve one problem but little does he know that when he comes back he will have an even bigger one to deal with.-

///// CHAPTER 144 /////

The Next Morning in the Big Apple

It's not even 10 A.M. yet and Lil Bit is already out and about. Her craving for Butter Pecan Ice Cream dragged her out of the bed this morning. She sat inside Baskins and Robbins as she destroyed two double dipped cones. The third one she took to go.

Right now she's around the corner from her apartment building. She's in a world of her own, secluded from the world as she licks the ice cream cone like a little kid. Being here in New York, she feels safe. This is the only time that she doesn't worry about Maurice. She plans to stay away from him and out of the danger that he can put her in.

The past day or so she's been nowhere near Jersey. Every errand she had to run she handled from right here in the City. She even opened up a P.O. Box here in her real name as well as her apartment here is. Latoya Baker may reside in Jersey but Amber Jones is an official New York resident.

Meanwhile. Maurice sits in the First Class section of the Air Jamaica flight. He's as anxious as he can be. His gut is boiling. He can't wait to talk to Muhsee face to face and get to the bottom of this matter.

He looks to the right of him where a beautiful young woman sits. She's looking pleasingly fashionable. Her long and silky Doobie drapes well past her shoulders. Her eyes hide behind huge Dior sunglasses, giving her more of a mystique appearance. Her clothes fit her petite frame closely without revealing anything.

The woman sits in her seat, just staring out of the window. She appears to have so much class until she blows a bubble gum bubble the size of her head. In seconds the bubble bursts and sticky gum splatters onto her face, hair, and her sunglasses. "Huh," she chuckles goofily.

Maurice turns away with embarrassment for her. Rhonda would be the perfect woman to sport on a man's arm if she would just keep her mouth shut and do what she does best and that is look beautiful.

This is Rhonda's first time actually going somewhere with Maurice. Until now they've never been seen in public together. Normally it's drive through Wendy's and straight to the hotel from there. This is real progress that she's making. Rhonda can see herself climbing up the chart. She's sure the valuable information she gave him is the reason for her sudden growth spurt. It is all working out just as she thought it would.

In Alpine, New Jersey. Maurice's wife buckles the seatbelt over her smallest child and quickly slams the door. She hops into the passenger's seat of the rented Chrysler van and slams the door shut.

"Ready?" the woman asks from the driver's seat. This woman is her sister. It's hard to determine who hates who more, her or Maurice. They hate each other equally. She continuously intervenes in their business which is why Maurice does everything in his power to keep them separated. He's done a good job up until now. In all the years that they've lived here this is her first time here. Unfortunately for him this will be her last time too.

"Been ready for years now," his wife replies.

The woman pulls off slowly as Maurice's wife says her farewells to her beautiful home. This house started out as her dream home but has turned into a living nightmare. Maurice had it built from the ground up to her liking. She hates to leave it but if he has to live in it with her she would rather leave it. She's sure there is a better life out there for her somewhere.

She can't believe that she's actually going through with this. She looks up the driveway at all of the cars that are lined up. Her Mercedes stands out the most. She's in love with that vehicle as well and hates to leave it but she realizes that she can't take the risk of being tracked down by him through the LoJack system that's on it. That's not a problem though because she has more than enough money to buy herself another one, once she reaches her destination. "Bye," she whispers as the tears drip down her face.

////// CHAPTER 145 //////

Hours Later. Maurice is here in Muhsee's mansion finally. He's come alone. He left his girl Rhonda back in the hotel at the pool. He didn't bring her along because he doesn't trust her. The truth is he may never trust her. He can see it now, her telling the entire town about his operation. To avoid that he's told her that they're on a three day get away. What she doesn't know is she could easily be coming back strapped with ten kilos on her body, all depending on the vibe that he gets today. It would be like killing two birds with one stone as he always says. He's blown so much money on these tickets that ten kilos right now would make it all worth the while.

One thing he knows for sure is Rhonda is nothing like Lil Bit. He trusted Lil Bit with all of his heart. He's told her things that he's never heard come back to him. Some things he's never told anyone else. He knows that he may never find another woman that he feels that comfortable with. As he thinks of it, it only makes him miss her even more.

Venom bleeds from Maurice's eyes as Muhsee runs his mouth. "I didn't know," he lies. "She did everything the exact same way it's been done for the past ten years. She wired the money, came here and strapped up. Nothing was different. How was I to know?"

Muhsee is lying through his teeth right now. He isn't lying out of fear of Maurice. He's lying in fear of losing Maurice's business. Losing Maurice as a client will affect him dramatically. Maurice spends a minimum of $600,000 a week. He can't imagine blowing this relationship. Now that it's all blown up he realizes how much of a risk he took. Pussy that he was never going to get and $60,000 a week is nowhere near equivalent to what Maurice brings to the table.

Maurice has informed Muhsee that Lil Bit is pregnant. He can't believe that he didn't notice that. Now he understands why she stopped making the trips herself. He feels betrayed as well. He can't believe he actually got played. Now he realizes her only reason for going out with him was to make him think that he actually had a chance with her. All the while she was only using him.

Maurice feels the ultimate amount of betrayal. He's steaming right now with fury. Never did he imagine that she could be so conniving. It breaks his heart to think that she would actually go through with all of this. He wonders where she got the heart to cross him.

In seconds he comes up with an answer. He assumes that she's done all of this in the name of love. He definitely knows the power of love. He's been using it on and against his women all of his life. Love is the only thing that could make a woman put herself in danger like this. There's no doubt in his mind that her lover has put her up to all of this. But who is he, Maurice asks himself.

"Listen, do not mention any of this to her. When she sends her people over the next time you notify me and I will take everything from there. Do your thing and make the last bit of money that they're ever going to bring to you."

Meanwhile back in the States. Maurice's wife cruises through forbidden land as her sister rides shotgun. The saying 'when the cat is away the mice will play' is a true statement. With Maurice in Jamaica she feels completely safe riding around here in Newark. Being disguised in the rented van makes it all better because no one can spot her and snitch on her to him.

She cruises through the town in awe as she stares like a tourist. She hasn't been in Newark in years. All the changes in the city are unbelievable to her. They've torn down all the historical landmarks of the city and replaced them all with new developments. She feels like a foreigner in the city that she grew up in. If her sister wasn't with her she would be lost. She guides her throughout the city like a tourist guide as she's enroute to her destination.

Meanwhile. It's five minutes before closing time and the shop is already completely empty which is rare. Normally they're in here to the late hours of the evening. Deja shuts off the radio, the television and all of the lights. As she presses the numbers on the security system her phone rings. She rushes to the door to beat the timer. She makes it there with still five seconds left. She steps out of the door and slams it shut behind her. "Hello?" she says into her phone as she stops at the door. Silence is on the other end of the line. "Hello?" she says but no one says a word in reply. "Stupid ass!" she shouts into the phone before she ends the call.

She stands on her tippy toes to grab hold of the stainless steel gate. She snatches it downward with all of her might. Once the gate slams onto the ground she steps on it and kneels down to put the lock on it. She stands up so quickly that the blood rushes to her head. She turns around and a sudden liquid splash snatches her breath away. She closes her eyes out of pure reflex. Caught by surprise she has no clue what's going on. All of a sudden her face heats up tremendously as well as her eyes. She goes into a frenzy as her face burns like it's on fire. "You home wrecking bitch!" she hears. "Now, bitch," the woman says with rage. Deja screams at the top of her lungs as she peeks through one eye to see who stands before her. As soon as the air hits her eye the heat blazes even more.

She stumbles around blindly while starting to rub her face and eyes. Little does she know the more she rubs her face the more layers of skin is peeling away. She bumps into the wall and falls to the ground. She screams like a baby as her face continues to heat up. The more she rubs to ease the burning sensation, the more damage she's doing to her face. "Help! Help!" she screams.

Maurice's wife watches the entire scene from a half a block away. She can actually hear Deja screaming from there. Finally her sister comes running toward the van. She reaches over and pops the passenger's door open before she gets there. She gets in and plops into the seat. Maurice's wife pulls off immediately. She's as nervous as can be right now. "Did you get her good?" she asks.

"Did I?" she replies with confidence. "I got the bitch good. As soon as she looked up I gave her a face full. I actually saw her skin fading into the white meat," she brags. "Fucking skank. That'll teach her."

"Good," Maurice's wife says with satisfaction.

Her work here is done. There was no way she could go on with her life without getting even. The liquid solution was made up by her sister. It consists of hot lye and a small amount of Vaseline. The purpose of the Vaseline is to make the lye stick to the skin. The more she rubbed the more the Vaseline and lye smeared into her skin.

She promised her she would ruin her life if she didn't stay away from Maurice. She didn't take heed so now she has to deal with the repercussions. It's just too bad that the wrong woman is paying the price while the guilty party is in New York living her life.

Maurice's wife has Deja and Lil Bit mixed up. Years ago she got hold of a Nextel phone number that Lil Bit was calling Maurice from. The phone bill linked back to Deja because the phone was in her name. When Maurice learned that his wife had got hold of the number he instructed Lil Bit to shut the phone off. His wife's detective work led her to another number with the exact same number except for the last digit.

Through that phone bill his wife tracked down Deja. She learned of the Range Rover that is in her name as well. She's been secretly doing her own private eye work on Deja for years. Early off she found bank account transfers from his bank account to Deja's bank account. Lil Bit had also opened up a bank account in Deja's name as well.

All in all she believes that Deja is the biggest competition she's had and also the biggest obstacle in their marriage. Now that she's fulfilled her promise she can go on with her life.

"How did the bitch look? Was she pretty at least?"

"How she look?" the sister asks sarcastically. "I couldn't tell," she laughs. "She was pink."

///// CHAPTER 146 /////

The Next Night

The Jamaica get away ended before Rhonda could even get a tour of the place. After meeting Muhsee, Maurice tried to hang around for a few but his rage made it difficult. He quickly switched their flights and left on the next plane. At least Rhonda got a meal out of the deal before they flew back to the States. She was a little disappointed that her trip was cut short but she's more than sure that there will be plenty more.

Rahiem stands back against the tree in the pitch dark cemetery. He's petrified as Maurice stands face to face with him. Maurice's left hand grips Rahiem's collar while his right hand grips the .40 caliber handgun in which the barrel is shoved up Rahiem's nose.

Maurice used Rock to reel Rahiem in. Rock called to set the meeting up. When Rahiem got to the meeting place, Maurice and Sal were awaiting his arrival. They snatched him off of the street and tossed him in the back of the van. He's still clueless as to what this all is about.

Maurice is steaming with anger as he looks into Rahiem's eyes. "Wh, what's this all about?" Rahiem asks.

"Shut the fuck up," Maurice orders. "I'm the only one asking the questions. "One question, one answer, one life to live," Maurice says as he slides a bullet into the chamber. He rests the barrel of the gun onto Rahiem's forehead. "Who did you get the work from?"

Rahiem doesn't think twice. He gives the information up instantly. "His name is Samad. They call him Smooth. He's from Ninth Street. He drives around in different rent- a -cars every week," he says nervously. "He just copped a brand new Audi R8. He used to buy work from me. I would buy the work from Rock," he says as he points to Rock in the background. "I would front it to him for a few points more than I paid for it. Him and my," he says as he's about to throw his cousin's name in the fire. He quickly changes his mind when he realizes the danger he could put D-Nice in. "A couple of months ago he came to me out of nowhere trying to buy a bird but I didn't trust him. He had just come home with a high ass bail and I didn't trust him. He never had his own money to cop before that so I thought the people was trying to set me up. The next thing I know he came up. He had his own keys for sale. I didn't ask where he got it from. I just been buying the blow from him for about a month now," he says as he's finally emptied all of his data on file.

Maurice unleashes the grip from his collar and removes the gun out of his face. "Get out of here," Maurice whispers.

"I can leave?" Rahiem asks as he looks around with extreme caution.

"Go, but I'm warning you. If one word of this gets back to him, I'm coming for you. Keep your mouth shut and you will live a long time."

Rahiem doesn't wait for another second. He backs away from Maurice before disappearing into the darkness.

///// CHAPTER 147 /////

Lil Bit and Sade have just arrived at the University Hospital. As they step closer to the room both of their hearts beat like drums. They don't know what to expect when they get in here.

Lil Bit takes a deep breath before stepping into the room. The moment they set foot inside the room tears fill their eyes. Deja lies in the bed with her face wrapped up like a mummy. White gauze bandages cover her entire head.

Lil Bit walks over to the side of the bed and puts her hand on Deja's shoulder, while Sade stands by her side. They examine her from head to toe and notice bandages on both of Deja's hands as well.

Deja starts to cry instantly. Underneath the thick gauze the tears burn the thin layer of flesh that she has left. She tries to speak but the open sores that surround her lips burn and ache so much that she's afraid to open her mouth.

Lil Bit doesn't know what to say so she asks the dumbest question that she could ask right now. "You alright?"

Deja shakes her head negatively. "I never been in this much pain in my life," she whispers while barely moving her lips.

"What happened?" Lil Bit asks.

Deja very gently stretches her mouth before speaking. "I was closing the shop," she whispers with agony. "I slammed the gate shut and when I looked up, I saw a quick glimpse of a woman before the splash in my eyes blinded me. My eyes and face were on fire. The more I rubbed the more they burned," she cries.

"Who was the woman? Did you see her face? What did she say?" Lil Bit asks.

"I didn't see her face. All she said was you home wrecking bitch." She cries a little louder. "That had to be that crazy woman. The sad part is I don't even know who her husband is. I don't fuck with nobody now. I cut everybody off for Rick," she cries. "Now look at me. My life is over," she cries. They all cry together. Sade and Lil Bit are both traumatized. They were well aware of the woman's threats but never did they imagine her doing anything like this.

Lil Bit feels great sympathy for Deja. She can't imagine going through this. For a brief minute she wonders what she would do if she were in Deja's shoes but what she doesn't know is that Deja is actually wearing her shoes right now.

Hours Later

Visiting hours are now over and they hate to leave her all alone but they have to. Both Lil Bit and Sade's eyes are puffy from crying. They've been crying together the entire time they've been here.

They step into the hallway and just as they do, the doctor approaches the room. "Excuse me," Lil Bit whispers as he steps toward them.

"Yes," he replies as he steps out of the doorway.

"Are you her doctor?"

"Yes, I am," he replies.

"That's our sister in there. We need to know what's going on with her. What was thrown in her face?"

"Well, apparently it was a lye solution mixed with some type of petroleum. The lye ate through many layers of her skin and the tissues," he says sadly.

They shake their heads with sorrow in their eyes. "So, what's next?" Lil Bit asks.

The doctor sighs. "Well, she's definitely going to need cosmetic surgery for starters. I plan to take skin from other parts of her body and apply it to parts of her face."

Lil Bit gets alarmed. She's heard that many of the doctors here in this hospital are students in training. "No disrespect but are you a student?"

"No," he smiles. "I'm a skilled surgeon with twenty years in the business but if you are not comfortable with me there are many other specialists in this field. I have recommendations for you. It's up to her with who she feels more confidence with. One side of her face is damaged more than the other side. I'm sad to say that even the less damaged side is bad off. My biggest concern is her left eye which at this time, she has very little sight in. From the looks of it, there's a strong possibility that she may lose her sight forever."

Tears now flood their eyes. "Doc be straight up with us," Lil Bit says. "Will she ever look the same?"

He hesitates before replying. His silence is killing the both of them. "That depends on the cosmetic surgery."

A Few Hours Later

Maurice steps into his home and the darkness and silence surprises him. He was expecting his daughters to run and tackle him joyfully as they always do. He looks around with a confused look on his face as he makes his way up the stairs. He doesn't hear a peep throughout the house. The first door at the very top of the staircase belongs to his older daughter. He pushes that door open and finds it empty with the bed still made. He walks to the room of the middle daughter and finds the room the same way. "What the?" he asks himself as he walks further down the hall toward his room. He pushes that door open and to his surprise it's empty as well.

He can't think of where they could be at this hour of the night. His wife is never outside of the house in the late night hours. Furthermore she never leaves the house without calling him and he hasn't received a call from her. He quickly recalls seeing her truck in the yard.

He pulls out his phone to doublecheck. He scrolls through all of his incoming calls and finds not a trace of her number. He then checks his messages. Not one has been left by her. He quickly remembers that he left for Jamaica and his phone wasn't working there. Maybe she knew that which is why she didn't call. "Oh, when the cat is away the mice will play," he whispers with sarcasm. He dials her number with rage. "I'm about to let this slick bitch have it," he says to himself. "She don't leave no fucking house without telling me," he says as he dials the last two numbers. His mouth drops wide open when the operator says that the number has been disconnected. He dials it once again, thinking that maybe he dialed the wrong number by mistake. The operator comes on again. "Inga!" he yells as he leaves out of the bedroom. "Inga!"

In less than thirty seconds the housekeeper comes running up the stairs, holding her robe closed tightly. "Yes Sir?" she asks with a look of concern on her face.

"Where Tammy and the kids?"

"I don't know Sir," she says with confusion on her face.

"What you mean, you don't know?" he asks with rage. "What time did they leave out today?"

"Sir, they were never here today."

Maurice starts to worry that maybe something happened to them. "Huh?"

"They left right after you did, two days ago." He stands there in a blur. This isn't making a bit of sense to him. Where they could be he doesn't know. Where could they be with no car? "They had many suitcases when they left. I helped her to the car with the suitcases, me and another woman, she gave me her goodbyes and left."

"Left? Another woman?" He rushes back inside of the bedroom, leaving the housekeeper standing there. As soon as he enters the room he snatches the closet door open. The empty shoe rack sends a chill up his spine. Not a pair of shoes has been left on the rack. He runs over to her nightstand and snatches it open. He finds it empty with not one bra or thong inside. He quickly runs around the room, snatching all the drawers open like a maniac. Everyone of them is empty. He steps over to her armoire and snatches it so hard that he almost rips the doors off of the hinges. He looks in the spot where her jewelry box used to be but it's not. In the place of it there sits her beautiful 10 karat wedding ring. His search is over. He now realizes what this is all about. "She left me," he says as he stands there in shock. "She really fucking left me."

"Sir?" the housekeeper says while peeking into the room. "Is everything ok?"

"Yeah, yeah," he replies. He's too embarrassed to even look her in the eyes. "Everything is alright. Good night," he says. "Damn, she really fucking left me."

///// CHAPTER 148 /////

Maurice's wife speeds up the highway in the middle lane doing the speed limit. The sunroof is peeled back and all the windows are wide open. They've been on the highway for many hours and have many more to go. She is well aware that Maurice will be expecting her to have fled South which is why she has done the total opposite. She's going North. The funny part is the further she gets away from New Jersey the happier she becomes. Taking this long drive has helped her to clear her head. She didn't believe that she could actually build up the heart to leave but now that she has there is no turning back.

She looks in the rearview mirror and studies the peaceful looks on her daughters' faces. They're clueless to where they're going and what this trip is all about. They may not understand today but one day she hopes that they do.

Meanwhile

Maurice pulls off as soon as the passenger door of his pick up truck closes. He heads into the direction of the Newark Airport exit. In the passenger's seat there sits who else but the Stalker. Maurice didn't waste anytime calling him in for his services and the Stalker didn't waste anytime getting here.

The Stalker sits quietly; staring straight ahead as he patiently awaits the details of his next assignment. Maurice exits the airport. As he's cruising 1 and 9 North several thoughts run through his mind. He can't believe that all of this is happening at once. He's had a beautiful ten year run and now this.

His wife actually left him he says to himself over and over and it still sounds crazy to him. She's threatened him over and over but never did he think she would actually pick up and do it.

The last few sleepless nights he learned a lot about himself that he didn't know. He learned that he's an arrogant asshole the majority of the time. He also learned that he has a problem separating his business life from his personal life and at times he deals with both of them the same way. On the street he's an egotistical, revengeful, power freak and so is he in his home. He handles situations with his wife the exact same way that he handles street matters. War is war to him whether it's on the street or in his home. He feels terrible that his wife has left him but he understands why she did. Now accepting it is something totally different.

He thought he meant it when he would tell her to leave him. Honestly he only thought that because his heart was with Lil Bit at the time. Now that he doesn't have Lil Bit either, he feels like a fool. He thought he would be happier without her in the picture. Deep inside he also knew that she deserved more than he was willing to give her.

He can't imagine not seeing his daughters again. He shakes that thought from his head every time it pops up. That thought brings tears to his eyes. Normally his tears bring out a violent streak that he can't tame. When he feels like he's lost he's willing to do anything to win.

All in all he knows that they're in good hands. They will be well taken care of. The money she's taken from him didn't move him at all. In fact he believes that she should have taken more because she deserves it.

He sits back with sorrow in his heart. It's hard for him to determine if the sorrow comes from his family disappearing on him or Lil Bit getting pregnant on him. It may sound crazy but he's quite torn right now.

He can't believe that his number one girl betrayed him like this. The fact that she's willing to have that man's baby is hard for him to accept. For many years he's begged her to have a baby for him and she denied because of his family. She told him she couldn't have a baby for him and her baby be a secret to his other children. She always knew that situation was wrong and she could never take it to that level. He never wanted to hear that. In his mind, the fact that she's willing to give birth for that man shows him that she loves that man more than she ever loved him.

Up until now they have had a beautiful ten years together. He can't believe that she ended it on such a bad note. He can't believe that she has done the things that she's done. If she ever believes that he's going to allow them to ride off in the sunset happily with their baby after crossing him like that they're both in for a rude awakening.

He cruises a little further in silence while he analyzes all the situations that he has before him. A single tear drips down his face. He quickly wipes any trace of it before turning toward the Stalker to speak. "I got three for you for a hundred stacks."

"A hundred stacks for just three?" he asks with amazement.

"Yeah," he whispers. "It's really worth more than that to me but that's all I'm willing to waste on them."

"No problem, big bruh. Just point me in the right direction. Who are they?"

"A pregnant bitch and her boyfriend."

The Stalker looks at him waiting to hear who the third party is but Maurice says nothing. "You said three right?"

"Yeah, a pregnant bitch and her boyfriend," he repeats. "The bitch worth almost sixty-seven thousand."

"Say no more. She's a dead bitch."

///// CHAPTER 149 /////

The black Toyota Camry sits parked in the middle of the busy block. It blends in like a chameleon in between the black van and the black SUV. The driver of the Camry sits back in full concentration as he studies the activity which is taking place before him. His photographic memory snaps a shot of all the key players' faces.

The man sitting in this car is none then less than the Stalker. He's been sitting out here for an hour and a half without anyone recognizing his presence. Maurice has given up a bunch of scattered details but the Stalker knows just how to organize them. He knows very little about Samad except for his description. Once he has a face to match he can start putting the pieces of this puzzle together. The sooner that he's able to put the pieces of this jigsaw puzzle together the sooner he can carry out his hundred thousand dollar mission.

One thing that he knows for sure is this block is Samad's main source of income. With that in mind one thing he can count on is Samad eventually coming through sooner or later. When he does, the Stalker will be right here.

Meanwhile

Lil Bit and Samad have been lounging around in the bed all morning and part of the afternoon. Neither one of them really wants to be here at this time. They both could find something better to do with their time. Lil Bit let Samad talk her into them staying together last night. She felt so uncomfortable being here that she couldn't sleep a wink. She tossed and turned with Maurice on her mind all night.

All she visions is Maurice staking her out in front of the building waiting for them to come out. In no way does she take his threats lightly. That threat alone is why she's still lying in bed. She's afraid to leave out and find Maurice awaiting her exit and because of that she has Samad trapped in here as well.

Samad sits up in the bed while Lil Bit sits in between his legs. Her head rests on his frail chest as he rubs her belly. "You felt that?" she asks with great joy.

"Yeah," he replies rather blandly. His mind isn't on the baby at this moment. The only thing he's thinking about is money and how to obtain more of it. He's been thinking of stretching out lately. Now that he understands the whole concept of wholesaling, he realizes that it makes more sense to sell a kilo for a couple of points and take very little risk as opposed to breaking a kilo down, doubling your money and quadrupling your risks. He realizes that although he makes more money breaking it down, he can sell enough kilos in that time where his profit would still end equally; especially being that he's thousands of dollars cheaper than all of his competitors.

Suddenly a rotten odor rips through Samad's nostrils, interrupting his thoughts. The heat that accompanies the foul odor is boiling. He looks at Lil Bit with his face frowned up. He's scared to take another breath. "Excuse me," she says as she pats her stomach. "The baby makes me so gassy," she says with an innocent smile as if she finds it to be cute. He rolls his eyes with disgust. "I said excuse me."

He says not a word in fear of breathing in the gas. Finally when he thinks it's safe, he speaks. "Damn Ma, you killing me." This is just another one of his many turn offs about her. Lately he's found so many.

Back on the Block

The Stalker pays close attention to the tinted-out black Dodge Charger that has just hit the corner. It cruises through the block less than five miles an hour before it slows down in the middle of the block. The Stalker leans his seat back so that he can't be seen. He watches as a string of vehicles form a line. Behind the Charger there sits a Magnum, a Grand Prix and a Honda Odyssey mini-van.

The Stalker watches as the four vehicles stop short in the middle of the block as well. Everything on the block freezes as the tinted-out vehicles just sit there in the middle of the street. No one has a clue of who is behind the tints. If they only knew they would take off for their lives.

In each car there sits four men. The van has seven men squeezed into it. That's a total of 19 soldiers who are all ready for war against Samad. This is nothing though. There's a pack of at least fifty more on call. These men are here seeking revenge for the Homie Bullet's murder. Bullet told the details of his meeting with Samad shortly afterwards. When he was found dead his murder was no mystery. They knew who had to be behind it.

After looking high and low they realize that he's not present. They all pull off slowly. The Stalker watches as the cars bend the right at the corner. He gets the feeling that he's not the only one in search of someone out here.

////// CHAPTER 150 //////

The black Chevy Impala with the deep tinted windows cruises up the quiet street. Not even a half a block behind, the black Toyota Camry trails it. The Stalker has been carefully tailing this car for over an hour now. Coincidentally as he was driving through the town he happened to spot an Impala that fit the description that Maurice gave him. He claimed that this is the last vehicle that he was seen driving.

After a drive through visit at McDonald's the Stalker tailed the Impala as it cruised through Samad's stomping grounds on Ninth Street. Never did he get out though. He double parked while two of the men ran over and passed money off to him. Immediately after that he sped off and so did the Stalker.

The Stalker can taste success as he watches the brake lights of the Impala brighten up. As the car is being parked, the Stalker inches up a few feet behind. Just as the driver steps out onto the street, the Stalker pulls up closer. He rolls his window down and he has his gun prepared to fire. Suddenly he realizes that this man's description is the total opposite of how Maurice has described him to be. His prey is supposed to be short, frail and light skinned. This man is tall, medium built and his skin is pitch black. Who the fuck is this, the Stalker asks himself.

This in no way is Samad. It's Mike the rent-a-car dude. He traded cars with Samad hours ago. He drove through the block only to get the money that the young boys owed him for renting his cars.

Here the Stalker sits face to face with the wrong man. Mike is petrified as he looks into the unfamiliar man's face. "Uh, excuse me," the Stalker says. "Do you know how to get to Broad and Market?" he asks off of the top of his head. He knows that he can't go wrong with that. Every ghetto has a Broad and Market Street intersection.

Mike swallows the lump of fear in his throat as he catches a glimpse of the stainless steel gun that the Stalker tries to hide on the side of his seat. "Th, that way," he stutters.

"Alright thanks. Have a good day," the Stalker says as he pulls off and cruises down the hill while Mike stands there in awe. Something tells him that the man asking him for directions was the 52 fake out. He believes that he must have been expecting someone else to get out of the car instead of him. But who, he asks himself. That he may never know until he gets another call from Robbery and Homicide telling him that another person was found dead in one of his cars. "Phew," he sighs at the thought of that. He has a total of forty cars floating through Newark alone and the driver that man was in search of could be in any one of them.

Meanwhile

The silence inside the huge empty house is driving Maurice crazy. Never before has he been totally alone in here. Not even Inga the housekeeper is present today. Today is her day off. It's so quiet in here that he wishes she were here so he could at least get a conversation out of her.

Days have passed and the reality that his family is gone has now set in. Each day he misses them more and more. When he told her to leave him, he never thought she actually would and he never thought it would affect him like this if she did. He imagined life without her but he never considered the fact that if she left the girls would leave with her. For some reason he never looked into it that deep. He misses those girls dearly. More surprisingly to him, he misses his wife equally.

He lays back on the couch, just staring at the ceiling. Never before has he felt this empty in his life. He never knew the meaning of lovesick until Lil Bit told him she no longer wanted to be bothered. Before that he never understood what the phrase meant and looked at it as a figment of a person's imagination. Now after going through this with her and his wife, he bears witness that there is true meaning to the phrase. He can't even imagine living life without his family. He realizes now that he's taken her for granted.

He dials away on his phone. "Hello?" the woman says in a sweet voice.

"Ay, Ma," he says with a false sense of joy in his voice.

"Oh, hello Maurice," she replies.

Hearing those words reassures him just how far this thing has gotten. She never calls him Maurice. Ever since he married her daughter she's been calling him Son. "Ma, have you heard from them?" he asks with desperation.

"No, I haven't heard from her."

He can sense a little agitation in her voice. He assumes that it comes from the fact that he's called her five times in the past two hours. Up until now he's been able to hold up his tough guy image. The tears drip down his face slowly. "Ma, please. I know you know where she is with those girls of mine. You're her mother. She doesn't make a move without you knowing about it. I know I wasn't the best husband but I loved her. I provided for them the best I could. Ma, it's killing me over here. Please Ma, tell me where they are so I can go and get my family back?"

Hearing him beg like this breaks her heart. It hurts her so bad that she's almost ready to give up the information. "Maurice, please don't put me in this position," she pleads. She holds the phone as she replays his words to her. She loves him dearly. He may not have been the best husband to her daughter but she couldn't dream of having a better son-in-law. In fact he treats her better than her own sons do. Maurice takes care of her just as he takes care of his own mother. "Maurice, you hurt that girl. I talked to you time after time about the pain that you were putting her through. I even broke my promise to her when I told you that she was even considering leaving you before. Still you didn't take heed. Now look, it's beyond my control. There's nothing I can do about it. I can't lie to you. Yes, I did talk to her today. She's fine. I told her everything you asked me to tell her too."

"What did she say?" he eagerly interrupts.

"She said that there's nothing that she wants to talk to you about. Her days of talking are over. She also said if I tell you where she is she will cut ties off with me as well. Maurice baby, I know her better than you do. That's my daughter. I hate to tell you this but she's done. Once she makes up her mind no one can change it. Don't blame me. Blame her father. That's where she gets her stubbornness from."

"Who is that, Maurice again?" the loud woman shouts in the background. "If he would have put this much energy into his marriage in the beginning he wouldn't be crying the blues now," she says as she rudely snatches the phone from her mother.

"Tanya!" Maurice's mother-in-law shouts.

"No Ma, ain't no need for him to call now stressing you out about it. He messed that relationship up," she says. "Why are you calling here now? You wasn't calling when you was out there destroying your marriage. Don't call now."

"Tanya," the mother says again as Maurice sits there enraged about the way she's talking to him. "Why are you always in our business? Why don't you go to one of your husband's support meetings at the Narcotics Anonymous," he says with sarcasm. "He's still fighting that battle with dope isn't he? Help him overcome that and stay out my business. Ya'll got ya'll own problems. Why you always up in my business?"

"That's my sister. She is my business. It ain't my fault that you a piece of shit of a husband. You a disrespectful, lying, cheating ass nigga, that's all. Live with it."

He's more than furious now. "Listen bitch, I done took all the disrespect that I'm gone take from your ugly ass."

"Bitch? Ugly?" she repeats.

"Maurice!" the mother shouts in the background.

"Yeah, ugly bitch," he revises. "You better recognize strength. You gone learn how to fucking talk to me. You been saying whatever the fuck you want to say to me for years now and I been letting it slide because of Tammy. Now because of you she ain't here no more and I ain't letting it slide no more. You better learn some fucking manners before I teach you some."

"What? Are you threatening me Maurice?" she says loud enough for her mother to hear.

"Maurice," the woman interrupts again.

"Ooh, I'm scared," the woman says with sarcasm. "What you gone do, beat me? This my mouth. I can say whatever I want to say. Who is you?"

"Beat you? Nah, I don't beat bitches. Yeah, it's your mouth and you can say whatever you want to say. But whatever you say to me, your dopefeign ass husband gone pay for it."

"So, now you threatening my husband," she says as she looks at her mother.

"No, I'm promising you, the very next time you come out of your mouth to me, I'm gone track whatever garbage truck his dopehead ass is working on. When I track his ass down, I'm gone make you wish you never opened your mouth up to me. That's not a threat. That's a fucking promise. She sits there quietly. She doesn't fear him doing anything to her but she does fear for her husband though. One thing that she does respect about Maurice is he's definitely about his business. "I love your mother and I love your sister. So I would never do anything to you to hurt them but I'll do everything in my power to hurt you. You talked the love of my life into leaving me. You tried to finish me. Now, I can easily finish you as well. I have no problem taking the love out of your life. Misery loves company." Silence fills the air. "You got anything else you wanna say out of your mouth?" She says not a word in reply. "I didn't think so. Now get the fuck off of my line."

///// CHAPTER 151 /////

Later that Day. The triple Black Beauty cruises up Lyons Avenue. Rapper, Young Jeezy's voice spills from the speakers. "Bitch I'm amazing! Look what I'm blazing. Eyes so low, yeah, I look like an Asian."

Samad takes one long drag before passing the blunt over to his beautiful female passenger. This woman is the latest edition to his exotic collection. As they sit at the traffic light he takes a long stare at her. There she sits sucking the weed up like a Hoover vacuum cleaner. Greedy bitch, he thinks to himself.

She feels him staring at him and turns to him slowly. Her eyes are extremely low, making her look even sexier to him. "What?" she whispers from her sticky and sparkling lips.

"Damn Ma, I'm sorry. What a terrible new boyfriend I am. Today is such a special day that I don't know how I forgot. I been ripping and running so much that I lost track of what today is," he says as she looks at him wondering what he's talking about. "Happy one day anniversary," he says with charm. She turns away with bashfulness as she blushes brightly.

The light changes and Samad pulls off slowly. "Why are you driving so slow?" she asks. "Speed makes my pussy wet," she says seductively.

"Oh yeah?" he asks with surprise of her boldness. "Is that all it takes?" he asks as he looks into her eyes.

"That and a nice stick," she says as she slowly strokes the gear shift.

"Well, I got both of them, speed and a nice stick for you," he says as he switches the gear shift and mashes the gas pedal. The take-off throws her back into the seat. He zooms up the block and just as she said, her pussy gets wetter and wetter and wetter.

A half a block away. "What the fuck?" the Stalker says as he watches the Audi rip up the block. Don't tell me this mufucker seen me, he says to himself. He's been trailing Samad for blocks. He thought he was being discreet but now he realizes that he must not have been. The Stalker mashes his gas pedal but it seems as if he's sitting in place compared to the speed of the Audi.

The Audi bends the right onto Route 78 East, leaving the Stalker far behind.

Samad mashes the gas pedal as soon as he gets onto the ramp. In seconds he reaches the speed of 90 miles an hour. In another two seconds he's already at 120 miles an hour. She sits back with a look of appreciation on her face as her pussy is now as wet as a swimming pool.

The Stalker finally makes it to the ramp of the highway. He looks for as far as he can see and still he sees no sign of the Audi. "Damn, I lost this motherfucker!"

Hours Later

The Stalker realized that he was letting the hundred thousand dollar reward cloud up his mind. It was causing him to do something that he never does which is rush. On top of that he didn't want to take as long as he did with the last assignment that Maurice gave him. He values Maurice's business and would hate to mess up his chances of working with him in the future but from here on out he plans to handle this business the way he knows best and that's take his time. That is how he earned the name the Stalker in the first place.

The details Maurice gave were all over the place and because of that so was the Stalker. That was until he sat back and took a look at what and how he was moving. He was bouncing around from lead to lead without making a bit of progress along the way.

He's now figured out a way to make some progress. He plans to make the score one person at a time. In one case, there's a two in one bonus package.

At the present time he sits in the garage laid back in the driver's seat. Directly across from him sits the snow white Range Rover that belongs to Lil Bit.

He waited around until he found the perfect opportunity to slide into the garage behind one of the residents. It's only 10 P.M. and he's already been here for two hours already. Something tells him that this is going to be a long night. He kicks his shoes off and leans his seat back as he falls into relaxation mode. He plans to make not a move until his victim attempts to get into her truck. Whether it's tonight, tomorrow night, or next year he plans to be right here.

18 Floors Up. Lil Bit lays back in her comfortable bed. She calls herself watching television but the television is actually watching her. She dozes off back and forth every couple of minutes.

She really shouldn't be tired when all she's done all day is lay around the bed the whole day. Samad managed to escape her trap early this afternoon as he claimed he had so much work to do. Still she laid around stuffing her face the rest of the afternoon and evening.

Samad made it out of the house safe and sound which tells her that either Maurice wasn't out there or he doesn't know what Samad looks like. She begged and begged Samad to stay until she ran out of excuses and he was no longer willing to stay in another moment. The streets were calling him or either the newest member of his stable blowing his phone up.

She, on the other hand, was too afraid to gamble like that. Instead she stayed trapped in her home like a prisoner of war. She promises herself that this will never happen again though. Tomorrow she plans to get up bright and early and exit the building during the morning rush hour, when the garage is packed with people. She promises herself that tonight will be the last time that she's trapped here.

///// CHAPTER 152 /////

The Next Morning at 5 A.M.

Samad lays flat on his back snoring as loud as he's ever snored. He's completely exhausted. Yesterday he broke a record for himself. Yesterday was the first time ever in his life that he had a 'three-peat' as he calls it. He slept with three different women back to back yesterday and that's not even counting the little tease he gave Lil Bit before he left her house yesterday morning.

As soon as he left Lil Bit he immediately went to scoop up his latest edition. Less then four hours later, he took another date of his to him and Lil Bit's favorite spot, the Short Hills Hilton. They didn't even stay the entire night. They swam in the pool for a few hours, and rolled around in the bed for another hour before he sent her on her merry way back home to her boyfriend.

His third victim lies curled up next to him. Her head is on his chest, her thighs are wrapped around his and her hands are stuffed down his boxers. They both collapsed here in his apartment after the long night.

Samad picked this woman up from Club Mood in Union. After the club let out he sat out front inside his car. He watched as two women admired his ride from afar. He used that as an invitation to get at them. He pulled up on them in the Black Beauty and invited them to come and take a test ride with him and they accepted.

The only thing on his mind at that time was a Menage'A 'Trois. That would have been the perfect way to end such an awesome day that he had already had. He was hoping to break two records with them. A Menage'A Trois with the women would have taken him to an all time high where he had sex with four women in one day. Also that would have been his very first Menage'A' Trois.

That was Samad's dream but Mike the rent-a-car dude had a dream of his very own. They both came into the club together but they rode in separate cars. When he saw the women getting into the car with Samad instead of just going on about his way in his own car, he followed Samad and refused to leave. He rudely forced himself into their potential threesome situation.

Eventually Samad got so tired of his begging that he sent the friend to Mike's car, while he continued the test ride with the other woman. The test ride led them right to his apartment. That's when she took over. The moment they got into the apartment, she didn't waste a second before she slammed him onto the bed, hopped on top of him and showed him how to really ride.

The Black Beauty never ceases to amaze him. Each time that he brings it out his game rises to a higher level. Not until recently did he begin to understand the importance of driving the right vehicle.

Snoring from both Samad and the woman gets louder and louder. Samad wheezes as she whistles. Suddenly a loud Boom sounds off as the front door is knocked off of the hinges.

Samad sits up with fear, damn near throwing the woman onto the floor. He sits there in suspense, wondering what has happened, when he hears another loud crash. "Oww!" the sharp scream sounds off from D-Nice's room. Samad reaches underneath his pillow and retrieves his nine millimeter. He stands up with a fearful look on his face. The nude woman rolls over onto the floor and slides under the bed for cover.

Footsteps sound off coming toward the door. Fuck that, I'm going out in a blaze, Samad tells himself, believing that a home invasion is in progress. He lifts the gun and aims at the door. A loud crash sounds off as the door swings off of the hinges and slams onto the floor.

"Oww!" the woman screams from under the bed.

Just as he's about to mash the trigger he hears, "Freeze, FBI!" the man says as he ducks for cover. Before Samad knows it at least five FBI Agents are standing at his door high and low. Each one of them has a gun aimed at his head. He stands there frozen, not knowing what to do. "Drop the gun on the bed!" Samad immediately does as he's told. "Now step out with your hands in the air," the agent says slowly.

"You crawl slowly from under the bed," another agent demands as he aims his gun underneath the bed. She crawls like a baby with tears dripping down her face. "Now stand up slowly!" he demands. She stands up just as Samad is baby stepping around the bed.

The both of them meet at the foot of the bed. At this point the agents are paying more attention to the beautiful nude woman than they're paying to Samad. "Now both of you turn around slowly." This move is highly anticipated. They all gawk with pleasure as she gives them the mooning of a lifetime. For a second they lose sight of the fact that they're working. "Now both of you bend over," the lead agent says as he seeks more eye candy.

Both Samad and the woman are in a doggystyle position, side by side. They wish Samad would make a move so they can have a reason to blow his brains out of his head. They pray that the woman moves so they can be pleasured even more. Only seven agents but a total of 14 fully loaded pistols are ready for action and not just gun play.

Thirty Minutes Later

The search is finally over. Samad, Mike the rent-a-car dude and the two nude women lay on their stomachs, ass up in the air. All of their hands are cuffed behind their backs.

Samad feels like the biggest idiot in the world as he looks at all the evidence that he has against him. On the coffee table there lies over two hundred thousand dollars in cash and three semi-automatic weapons. Last but not least, one kilo lies there as well.

It feels like Deja Vue. He's been here before. The only difference is he's on the inside this time and also the stakes are higher this time. Everything is magnified to the tenth power.

As he lays there on the floor something comes to his mind that hasn't in a long time. He thinks of Lil Bit and his baby. That's something that he hasn't thought of since he was broke. Now all of a sudden it has a place in his mind. He shakes his head with disbelief as his life flashes before his eyes. He sees his starting point, and his middle. The finish line creeps up slowly. Now the game is over.

Meanwhile a few Miles Away

Samad's man Dee sits quietly in the back of the unmarked van. Feds raided his home at the exact same time as they were raiding Samad's apartment. He watches closely as they chauffeur him down Market Street enroute to the Federal Holding.

How he's gotten into this position he doesn't know. He's nervous but not fearful because of the fact that they found nothing in his home but less than two thousand dollars in cash. He's thankful that not a gram of coke was anywhere near his apartment. In his mind he foolishly believes that he has nothing to worry about.

A mile and a half away

Dee's man and business partner, Flip is being dragged by his handcuffs up the long corridor. He can't believe that this is happening. Right in the middle of a half a kilo sale, the transaction was interrupted. He looked up and to his surprise seven unmarked cars had them surrounded.

Flip watches his co-defendant-to-be with disgust as he's being dragged as well. "Snitch ass nigga," he mumbles to himself. "I don't believe this nigga."

Little does he know, this man is as stand up as they come. In no way does he play a part in this disaster. He was caught by total surprise just as Flip was. Neither of them can understand how the Feds knew to find them there, which makes both of them look at each other as the culprit.

If everyone here is in total darkness then how did they get here? It's evident that there's a leak somewhere in the crew but who?

///// CHAPTER 153 /////

Four Hours Later

Lil Bit steps hurriedly out of her apartment. She's leaving a few hours later than she really wanted to leave out. The busiest time of this building is normally around 7 A.M. and she wanted to be in the midst of that crowd. She figured that would be perfect just in case Maurice is out there waiting for her, he couldn't do anything to her. That is if he actually cares if someone sees him or not.

As the elevator is approaching her floor, she prays that some of the work crowd is still rushing out. The doors open and she realizes that yet another one of her prayers has not been answered. Not a single person is on the elevator. Her heart immediately starts to beat with fear. She steps onto the elevator and watches the numbers as they go down. Today of all days the elevator speeds through with no stops.

In the Parking Garage

The Stalker sits low in the backseat. He watches the elevator doors closely. Each time the elevator stops and the buzzer sounds off he prays that Lil Bit comes stepping through the doors.

On the seat next to him there lies the .40 caliber. It's fully loaded with 16 rounds but he plans to leave with 15 of them left. He's sure one single shot close range is all it's going to take.

The opening of the elevator doors lifts him up to the edge of his seat. He grabs the gun, preparing himself to go to work. He sighs with frustration when he sees a man stepping out of the elevator instead of Lil Bit. He watches closely as the man steps in his direction. He leans back in the seat to avoid being seen by the man. The man passes Lil Bit's Rover, where the Stalker is sitting. He turns around in the seat, looking behind as the man passes his own vehicle. The man stops short in between the Stalker's car and the small compact car which is parked right next to it.

The Stalker watches from the backseat of the Range Rover as the man gets into the car and pulls off speedily. Once the car is out of his sight he then directs his attention back to the elevator.

The Stalker has been camping out in the back of Lil Bit's truck since the wee hours of the night. He didn't even need his faithful 'slim jim' to get him into this situation. The doors of the Rover were left unlocked just as the majority of these vehicles in the garage are. What a terrible mistake.

Lil Bit manueavers the small car like a professional race car driver as she approaches the fourth floor. She zooms throughout the garage at top speed, causing the tires to screech eardrum piercingly. She gets to the first floor in no time at all. As she approaches the garage gate she slows down before making her exit. She peeks to the left, then the right, then the left again just to be sure. Once she sees no sign of Maurice or any of his vehicles, she steps on the gas pedal and peels out of the garage.

She mashes the gas pedal of Deja's Audi and zips up the street. The speed of the small car surprises her. She accelerates even more and speeds up the block like she's in a high speed car chase.

Without even knowing it, she leaves the Stalker in the garage in the backseat of her Range Rover. Right after her and Sade left the hospital they went to the beauty parlor and picked up the Audi. Deja feared that something would happen to it if it was left there unattended. Lil Bit fell so in love with the car and has been driving it ever since. The Audi was parked on the sixth floor in the designated visitor's section.

If only she knew what was waiting for her on the 20th floor in her own vehicle. In this case what she doesn't know can hurt her.

///// CHAPTER 154 /////

Later that Day. Sade lays back in her recliner with her eyes glued onto the television set as they always are. She's watching one of her favorite shows when suddenly a commercial comes on. She instantly starts flicking through channels looking for something else to watch in the meantime.

As she gets to channel 12, her attention is caught by a familiar location. The area they're showing is not too far away from her house which makes it all the more interesting. She watches attentively as two men and two women are being dragged out of a building in the Seven Oaks section of West Orange.

The four of them have their faces covered from the camera crew. She listens as the reporter states the details. "Early this morning a Federal Investigation ended here in West Orange New Jersey when FBI and Drug Enforcement Agents captured a Newark drug Kingpin. Twenty-seven year old, Newark man, Samad Brown," he says as a mugshot appears on the screen. "Was captured in his suburban apartment, which is also known to be the storage house for his million dollar operation." Sade watches with awe as she sets eyes on Samad's picture. She fumbles for her phone. She hits redial and Lil Bit's number is dialed instantly.

In the Big Apple. Lil Bit is in the bathroom taking her twentieth twinkle for the hour, when she hears her phone ringing back to back. She finishes up and hurries out of the bathroom to catch it. By the tenth ring, she answers. "What now, Sade?" she says in a jokingly manner. "Bitch can't even take a piss," she adds.

"Girl, turn to channel 12!" Sade shouts frantically. "Hurry, hurry!"

Lil Bit waddles as fast as she can to her television. She quickly thinks of what channel that is for her here in New York. She presses the numbers on the box and in seconds she's watching a room full of agents crowded around a table full of guns and money. "What about it?" she asks with no concern. Her eyes are then drawn to the bottom of the screen where she reads 'Newark Drug Kingpin taken into custody.' Maurice comes to mind immediately. Her heart skips a beat. She's taken by total surprise when Samad's picture pops up on the screen. "Kingpin," she says to herself. "Million dollar operation?" Her heart has now stopped beating. She stands there scared stiff as the phone falls from her hand.

"Lil Bit! Lil Bit!" Sade shouts on the line.

Lil Bit can't believe the words that they're saying. Her heart has not ticked since his face popped up on the screen. Suddenly it starts beating a million times a minute. She starts to hyperventilate and her muscles tighten up on her. A series of hot flashes has heated up her entire body. An unexpected pain in her stomach snaps her out of the daze. "Aghh," she gasps as the impact of a mule's kick crashes through the walls of her stomach. A second but more intensified one follws shortly after. "Aghh!" she screams even louder. A third one comes one second behind that one. "Aghh!" she screams with suffering. She collapses onto the floor while holding her stomach. The series of kicks come back to back, getting more and more severe. "Help!"

"Lil Bit!" Sade shouts into the phone.

"Call an ambulance," she manages to utter as she rolls around on the floor in horrendous pain. She clutches her stomach as she screams at the top of her lungs.

///// CHAPTER 155 /////

Hours Later. Samad is in a tremendous state of shock. He still can't belive that this has happened. He's been sitting here alone just dreaming of the worse case scenarios of this matter. For the life of him he doesn't understand how or why the Feds have jumped onto him. For some reason he believes that he's not a big enough deal for the Feds to even waste their time with.

In the beginning he assumed that only him and Mike were caught up in this situation. After eavesdropping and hearing the agents speak in plural terms about they, and them, he assumes that there are others involved. But who, he wonders. If he knew the answer to that question he could start to figure out where all this may have stemmed from.

He feels bad that he got Mike and the girls involved in this mess with him. The selfish part of him makes him able to bare with it. They were dragged in it the same way someone dragged him into it. Just as they don't want to be here neither does he. He just charges it to the game.

His thoughts are interrupted when two agents step into the holding cell that he's in. The moment he sets eyes on them he becomes more terrified than he already was. "Ay Smooth," the black agent says upon his entrance. Can I get something for you? Water, tea, Gatorade, perhaps?"

"Nah," he says as he shakes his head from side to side. The look on his face is as if he's seen a ghost.

"You sure? We all know how much you love Gatorade. That's your favorite beverage, right?" he asks with sarcasm. Samad keeps his mouth shut. "You got anything that you would like to talk to us about? If so, now would be the perfect time." Samad shakes his head negatively. "Come on Smooth, think hard. I'm sure you can come up with something to say. All your co-defendants have. As we speak, they're in there running their mouths non-stop. And guess what the topic is?" he asks with a smile. "You!"

Meanwhile

Lil Bit paces slowly back and forth in the hallway of Beth Israel Hospital in Manhattan. She's in immense pain. Right by her side there stands her devoted friend. Sade walks shoulder to shoulder with her.

The Ambulance came to Lil Bit's house and rushed her here. Sade got here less than an hour later. The shocking news sent Lil Bit into labor. The moment of truth is approaching quickly.

The pain she feels at this point can't be compared to any pain that she's ever felt in her life. She's already promised herself that she will never put herself through this again. Her dreams of having four children have vanished. In fact she's regretting this one more and more with each contraction. During the latter months of her pregnancy she started to get scared whenever she thought of giving birth. She's heard so much about the painful experience that she wasn't looking forward to it in the least bit. The pain that she's feeling now has washed out her fear of delivering. She's ready to get it over with.

Her doctor has instructed her to walk to induce the labor. He told her this two hours ago. Initially she started walking as he instructed. Now two hours later the pain has increased dramatically. She's now damn near crawling.

Another painful contraction rips through her abdomen. "Aghh," she cries from her dry and chapped lips. She clenches her stomach with desperation. Another contraction rips and knocks her to the floor. She falls onto one knee. She gasps for air. "Oh my God," she cries.

"Come on. Get up," Sade coaches. "You gotta walk."

"I can't," she cries.

"Come on, baby. Walk it out," she sings in a teasing manner.

///// CHAPTER 156 /////

Samad makes another phone call with hopes that it will be answered. He's starting to believe that everyone he knows must have gotten nabbed with him. A few on his list are D-Nice, Off the Chain, his girl Shakirah, and of course Lil Bit. Not getting an answer from them makes him more nervous. If all of his outside connections are on the inside with him, he realizes he hasn't a chance of ever getting out.

The phone rings and rings just as it's been doing for days. Suddenly on the fifth ring someone picks up. Yes, he says to himself. "Hello, hello?"

"Hello," Sade replies.

Hearing this voice on Lil Bit's phone alarms Samad. "Yeah. Who this?"

"Ay Samad. This is Sade."

"Ay. Where Lil Bit?"

"She's in the Nursery," she replies.

"Nursery?"

"Yeah, with your beautiful baby girl."

"Baby girl?" he asks in shock. A baby girl, he says to himself. "I'm a father?" he asks with disbelief. "I got a daughter?" A huge smile pops up on his face. As soon as it sets a frown of sadness replaces it. He's regretting the fact that he missed the birth of his baby girl. He also thinks of the possibilities of missing everything else in her life like, her first words, her first steps, her first day of pre-school, her graduation and her wedding day. The thought of that breaks his heart. "Damn," he utters.

"Congratulations!" Sade shouts.

"Thanks," he replies sadly.

"Hold on, here comes the new mommy now."

Lil Bit walks slowly into the room. Her body is badly beaten and so is her face. The delivery took everything out of her but once she laid eyes on the beautiful baby it was worth every bit of the pain that she went through.

"Hello?" she whispers.

"What's up mommy? How you feel?"

"How you think I feel?" she asks with bitterness in her voice.

Her attitude doesn't come as a surprise to him. He was very well expecting her to be salty with him. He desperately thinks of something to say to soothe her bitterness. "So, tell me who do she look like?"

"She's the spitting image of my big sister. We're going to name her after her. Baby Ashley is what we're going to call her. She's high yellow with emerald green eyes," she says as she pictures the baby in her mind. "She's as bald as an eagle though," she smiles. "Not a single strand of hair on her head."

Samad tries to visualize her as well. "Yeah?"

"Yep," she says with a bright glow covering her face. "She's a little ol thing too. Just barely six pounds. She's a few weeks premature thanks to you but the doctor said she will be fine." The glow vanishes from her face. "Samad, I don't know what I'm gone do with you. I don't even know what to say about all of this. In jail on the day your daughter is born?"

"I know, I know. Dig, you heard from anybody? You seen D-Nice?"

"Seen him where?" she asks sarcastically. "How did I see him? I been in here since I seen you on the news. "Psst, two little bitches in your apartment, huh? Who does that?" she asks with sarcasm.

"Listen, that ain't bout nothing. It's not how it looked. You know how the media be blowing shit up. I will explain everything when I get out."

"When you get out? When is that gone be? Maybe you know something that I don't know."

Oh, I will be out," he says with determination. "Don't worry."

"Don't worry? Samad you don't have a clue do you? Have you read the newspaper?"

"Nah, why? What's up?"

"This whole thing is blown up. You've been on every news channel and in the Star Ledger, front page of the Essex section. A Federal investigation, a multi-million dollar operation, murders, and everything, they claim. They even got recordings of you saying some of the stupidest shit I ever heard you say. They quoted you saying some shit about you ain't never gone stop. You gone ride this thing until the wheels fall off."

"What?" he asks as that entire conversation plays in his ears. He remembers word for word what he said and who he said it to. It's all starting to come together now. He's found the answer to all of this. He only made that statement to one person. "What other names were in the paper?"

"You, a Michael Stafford. I think a Demetrius something and a Anthony something. Oh and the two bitches that were in the house with you. Whoever they were," she says with cynicism.

He totally disregards her last statement. The only thing he's thinking about is the one name that she didn't mention. "That's it? You sure?"

"Ain't that enough?"

Now he knows one thing for sure. With him and D-Nice being together day in and day out and his name not mentioned makes D-Nice a suspect. The conversation they've quoted makes him know that his assumption is correct. He doesn't want to belive this but the evidence is right there. His main man has spilled the beans. Damn, he thinks to himself. How could he? If he's told that,

Samad can only imagine what else he may have told them. He thinks of all the valuable information that only D-Nice knows. He's an asset to the Feds which will be a problem for him. It takes him no time at all to come up with a solution to that problem.

///// CHAPTER 157 /////

Maurice sits in the livingroom of the Bat Cave. Across from him sits the Stalker. Both of them wear sadness on their faces as Maurice reads the last words of the newspaper article.

Damn, the Stalker says to himself as he thinks of the thirty-three thousand that he's not going to get now. He just wishes he could have gotten Samad the day he was cruising through in his Audi. That was the Stalker's first and last chance that he could have scored his reward.

"Look at the dumb mufucker now," Maurice says. Seeing Samad in this situation gives him no satisfaction at all. He would rather be reading his name in the obituary section instead. "See, you can lead a horse to the water but you can't make him drink it," he smiles. "Look, he had the connect of a lifetime and what he do with it? Nothing! All he got out of it is a Fed case. That's what the fuck he gets. They crossed me! Now look. Suddenly he gets nervous as he thinks of how much Samad may really know. He wonders if he knows enough to finish him off. Muhsee told him that Lil Bit came alone but he wonders if she's told him every step. Maurice realizes that this could easily drag him into the same situation. If Lil Bit is dragged into it, he's sure he will follow.

Maurice stares the Stalker in the eyes. "Don't worry about the pay cut. The bitch value just went up. The whole hundred is on her face now."

Deja lays back in the hospital bed weeping silently as her visitor sits beside her. He holds her hand to comfort her. His tight reassuring grip gives her a sense of consolation that she hasn't felt in days.

The moment that Rick heard what happened to her he flew straight here from Miami to her rescue her. "Stop crying," he says. "It's gone be alright. We got money," he says arrogantly as he looks into her eyes through the small slit in the thick gauze. "We gone get the best doctors money can buy. After that I'm taking you away from all this madness. You're coming back to Miami with me whether you like it or not. I'm not taking no for an answer."

Lil Bit is up and running. After two short days of hospitalization she was released this morning. Unfortunately Baby Ashley had to remain behind. The doctor said she will be released in a few weeks, permitting all goes well with her.

Lil Bit is already busy on her job. Her and Sade sit in the P.F. Chang Restaurant in Edgewater. They're awaiting the presence of attorney, Tony Austin. She called him hours ago to set up a meeting with him.

He wanted to meet a little closer to his office but she refused. She's promised herself that she is never going in that direction again if she doesn't have to. Edgewater is the furthest that she is willing to go into Jersey. She has one more time to go there and that is to clean out her apartment over there. After that it's a wrap. Jersey will never see her again.

Not only is she worried about Maurice, now she has another problem to add to her troubled life. She worries that the Feds may be onto her as well. Because of his recklessness, she was careful about the way she interacted with him when it came to doing business. She never talked business over the phone and they hardly went out in public together so she's not worrying about that. Her biggest fear is getting a conspiracy charge just for being his girlfriend. She's heard of many cases like that.

As Lil Bit and Sade are sitting at the table, the attractive, smooth attorney stands at the door peeking around, trying to locate them. His arrogance can be sensed from across the room. They both stare at him in admiration as they check his attire. They're shocked at what they see. He looks nothing like the typical stuffy attorney. His puffy Montcler goosedown vest, True Religion Jeans and Nike ACG boots makes him look like the typical hood nigga. The way his hat is propped and tilted on top of his head makes it all flow so naturally, not like he's trying to be cool at all. The only thing that separates him from the average hood nigga is the $125,000, leather band Panerai watch that he sports on his wrist.

"Mr. Austin," Lil Bit shouts to get his attention.

He looks in their direction before diddy bopping over toward their table.

Minutes later, they've all ordered their meals and now Lil Bit is ready to go over the details of their meeting. "Mr. Austin, I know you said that you're done but we're here again in need. As I told you over the phone, this meeting is strictly confidential. Between us and you," she adds. "My mouth to your ears."

"Listen maam," he interrupts. I already promised you over the phone that everything you say to me is confidential. I gave you my word and that's all I have.

"Well last time you didn't keep it confidential. You called Maurice as soon as we left."

"Last time I didn't give you my word. And anyway blame yourself for that because you used his name as a reference. So I referred to him. Trust me, what you say here stays here with us. My word is my bond. My bond is my life. If by chance my word fails then I shall give my life," he says with sincerity in his eyes. "That's how much my word means to me."

"I respect that. Ok, here it is. My girlfriend here," she says as she points to Sade. "Her boyfriend just got jammed up with the Feds. We want to hire you for his defense."

"Not this again. Ladies, come on?"

"No, hear us out, please?"

He smiles. "Now here comes your persistence right? Listen to this. I don't want any parts to any defending in the state of New Jersey. I'm done with these cats," he says with determination. "I will tell you what I can do for ya'll though. I got a girl down in D.C. that I can refer ya'll to. She's one of the best criminal attorney's in the business. I will put ya'll together. That's the best that I can do."

"Is she any good?"

"She learned from the best," he says with an arrogant smile as he taps his chest. "Listen, quiet as kept, we have worked together on every case that we both have had. At this point I don't want to show my face in a Jersey courtroom. Any client of mine I direct to her and she represents them. If need be I will coach her in the case. That way I'm still on the case without even showing my face. You follow me?"

"I follow you."

"Ok, this is what you do. Give me his name and all and I will forward everything over to her. From there she will see what can be done. Oh, and whatever you do do not call my office at any cost. You have my cell number. Just like ya'll don't want Slow Moe to find out, I don't want my wife, I mean my secretary to find out either. Deal?"

"Deal," Lil Bit agrees.

Later that Night

D-Nice sits in the driver's seat of the rented Nissan Murano while Off the Chain sits in the passenger's seat. They're parked on the far end of the block as they supervise the activity.

"Yo, I know Big Bruh sick!" Off the Chain shouts.

"Word up," D-Nice whispers.

"Yo, somebody ain't real right. I'm telling you. I already felt it. I been knew something was fishy about this whole shit. Then Big Bruh called and confirmed it for me," he says as he sneakily grabs hold of his gun. He quickly draws it and points it at D-Nice's dome.

"Yo," D-Nice shouts with fear.

"Yo what?" he asks with fume in his eyes. "You like running your mouth? Huh?"

"Yo, what you talking about?"

"Nigga, you already know what it is. Empty your pockets," he says as he starts to dig in them for him. In seconds he retrieves money from every pocket.

"Come on man," D-Nice pleads. "Run my mouth to who?"

"Why you ignoring Big Bruh's calls? He said he been calling you off the hook."

"I swear it ain't like that. I didn't answer his calls because I didn't want the Feds to drag me into this mess."

"You already in it. I don't call the shots. I just answer the call. Big Bruh pressed the button so I gotta go."

"Yo, I swear to," he manages to say before the Boom goes off. The gunshot sounds off loudly, causing their ears to go deaf. D-Nice's head bangs into the steering wheel. Boom! Boom! Boom! Each shot lands accurately in the back of his head.

Off the Chain watches with great appreciation. He gets out of the car and trots away casually. In seconds he makes it to the corner where his getaway car awaits him. All the valuable information D-Nice had is now useless.

///// CHAPTER 158 /////

Days Later

Samad stands in front of the phone dialing away. As he's listening to the phone ring he prays that Shakirah picks up this time. He can't understand why she hasn't been answering his calls. He's called her everyday since he's been here. He's starting to believe that she must have gotten caught up as well.

Normally he would stash a kilo or two at her house but luckily when they nabbed him he was at the very end of his flip. The one bird that he got caught with happened to be the last one in the flock.

The only thing that Shakirah had in her house is seventy thousand dollars that he left there. That seventy grand is the reason for his persistence. That money is the last money that he has to his name. Without it he can kiss his chances of making bail goodbye. That scares him to death. His back is against the wall. She's forcing him to think of doing something that he never wants to do to her. If he doesn't get through to her he will have no other choice but to let his dog off the chain.

He loves Shakirah dearly but if he feels like she's putting his freedom on the line his love for her will not stop him from doing what has to be done. If he could have his very best friend in the world murdered it's a proven fact that he will never let love get in the way. The phone stops ringing and the answering machine comes on. He dials once more to give her the benefit of the doubt. The answering machine comes on again. "Ok," he mumbles to himself. He hangs the phone up and quickly starts to dial again.

"Hello?" Lil Bit whispers into the phone.

"What's up, Ma?"

"Nothing, I'm here with the lawyer now," she says as she stares into Tony's eyes. "Babe, it doesn't look good for you at all," she says as she steps away from the table. She leaves Tony and Sade behind as she steps toward the bathroom inside the small restaurant here in Hoboken. "The lawyer says he's never seen a case so messy in all of his years of practicing law. He said there's almost nothing that he can do for you. They have everything on their side to finish you off for the rest of your life. He's willing to work on the case to get you the best plea bargain that you can possibly get. He's going to need fifty grand to get started."

"Fifty?" he asks. In no way was he expecting to hear that. There goes his bail money that he was counting on. He sits back and suddenly Lil Bit's words to him play in his ear. 'You started from nothing and you're going to end with nothing.' He feels like a fool right now. He's too ashamed to admit to her that he has no money to go toward the fee.

"Yeah, that's just to get started. This ain't no regular state charge. As soon as you get the money over to him, they will get to work on the case." Silence fills the air. His lack of words strikes her curiosity. "So, what you gone do?" Still he says nothing. "Tell me that wasn't everything?"

"Damn near," he shamefully admits.

"Psst," she sighs. "I don't belive you."

"Just hold tight for a second. Tell him we gone get with him in a day or two. I got a couple of dollars out there. I just gotta catch up with it. Let me get on it. I'll call you later. Love you!" he says as he waits for her reply.

She ends the call with no response. He stands there holding the phone with a bitter taste in his mouth. He quickly dials another phone number and listens impatiently as it rings.

"Yeah?" the man says on the other end.

"Yo!" Samad shouts.

"Big Bruh, what's the deal?" Off the Chain shouts in reply.

"You already know. Yo, dig this. You know where my kennel at off of 15th Avenue?" he says as he talks in code language. "Where I keep that bitch puppy at?"

Off the Chain quickly thinks of 15th Avenue. The only place that he knows about that street is Shakirah's house. "Y, yeah," he stutters.

Samad gets the thought that maybe she's avoiding his calls so that she can keep his money. At this point nothing can be done without it. In order to get it he will do whatever he has to. For her sake, she better hope that she's nabbed and not just ignoring his calls. "Well, I been calling there and the nigga ain't answering the phone. I had a few puppies there. I need you to go by there and see why they ain't answering. They probably trying to keep my shit. If that's the case, take my big Pit there and let him off the chain and let him eat all the puppies over there, you heard?"

"I heard!"

////// CHAPTER 159 //////

2:30 A.M. The jet black customized van rolls down Central Avenue in Newark. At the corner of 12th Street the van makes a right turn. It creeps up the dark block slowly. There's no sign of life on the entire block. It's as dead as all the people are who occupy the huge cemetery to the right.

Just as the van passes 12th Avenue it's steered to the right in a parking position. Both back passengers' doors bust open outwardly before Smurf hops out. He peeks around cautiously to make sure the coast is clear. He then grabs the collar of the man who is lying on his back on the floor of the van. Smurf tugs and tugs but the dead man's body won't budge a bit. On the inside of the van, Rock helps by attempting to roll the body out.

"Hurry up!" Maurice says from the front passneger's seat.

"This mufucker heavy," Rock grunts. Maurice rushes to the back and the three of them struggle to move the body. Finally Smurf steps back as the body rolls out of the van and lands on the curb. Smurf hops back into the van and Sal pulls off immediately, leaving Rahiem's corpse on the side of the road.

After thinking all this over, Maurice recalled that Rahiem could easily link the Federation with Samad. Rahiem was purchasing kilos from Samad which means they may have had his phone tapped as well. The phone could have been the phone that Rock contacted him through when they bought the work from him.

All of this is just an assumption but Maurice would rather be safe than sorry. He would hate to take the risk of being mixed up in any of this if the Feds come for Rahiem. Now that he's dead, the bridge that connects them has been burned down.

Hours Later in Hillside, New Jersey
A loud boom sounds off followed by the door crashing onto the kitchen floor. "FBI!" Not even seconds later the back door is knocked off the hinges as well. The sound of many footsteps echo throughout the empty apartment.

Off the Chain jumps out of his bed and attempts to make a break for it. Just as he grabs hold of the window, he hears. "Freeze!" He turns around with his hands in the air. Standing before him are more than ten FBI agents all dressed in SWAT gear. Each one of them has a machine gun pointed at his head. "Away from the window and on the floor! Now!"

Thirty Minutes Later
The entire house has been ransacked. Off the Chain is being dragged out of his apartment barefoot and in his boxers. The Feds found no money or drugs in his apartment but what they found is far more valuable. They found the murder weapons that were used for each murder that he's committed for Samad.

Just when they think it can't get any worse it does.

///// CHAPTER 160 /////

Days Later
After carefully observing the area, Lil Bit and Sade park in front of the Jersey City apartment building and get out. Lil Bit has come here to pick up her belongings. After that she will be saying farewell to the apartment forever.

They step into the lobby. "Hey Ben," Lil Bit greets with a smile. Ben looks up and his eyes stretch wide open as if he's just seen a ghost. His reaction to her presence confuses her but she doesn't give it much thought. She continues on her way toward the elevator.

Ben looks over at her. "Ay, one second," he says as he peeks back and forth into the management office. He steps over to her and when he gets there he leads her to the corner of the lobby. There they stand hiding behind the huge waterfall. He's being careful not to be seen by management but Lil Bit wonders why. His eyes are shifting all over the place, making her quite nervous. "Listen Dear, I don't know what's going on and I don't care to know but the FBI has been here looking for you. They said they want you for questioning. I don't know what it's about. I'm just warning you."

"The FBI?" she asks with fear. "When?"

"The last time I saw them was two days ago. Altogether I've seen them three times already. Management gave them the key to your apartment. They still have it. My advice to you is to not even go into the apartment. They may have left someone behind, waiting for you."

Lil Bit stands there with terror filled in her heart. She watches his mouth closely but can't believe the words that are coming out of it. "Thank you Ben."

"Baby, go," he says as he peeks into the management office. "They're working with them."

Lil Bit digs into her pocketbook quickly. She extends her hand to Ben. "Here." The two, crisp, one hundred dollar bills tremble in her fingertips.

"No," he says as he shakes his head negatively. "I don't need it. You my girl. You've always taken care of me. Just go away and fast," he says with a look of genuine concern on his face.

That she does. She takes off with lightening speed, leaving Sade standing in the lobby. Sade quickly follows Lil Bit's lead. They hop into the car and Lil Bit peels off before Sade can get fully seated.

"What's going on?" Sade asks.

Lil Bit stares straight ahead in a daze. "The FBI been here looking for me," she says with no emotion at all. She's in a state of shock.

"What?"

"I'm finished."

////// CHAPTER 161 //////

Two Days later. Dee sits in the interrogation room. One agent sits on the edge of the table as the other one sits directly across from him. "So, how long would you say this has been going on?" the agent asks.

"I don't know," Dee replies nervously. "Less than a month, I guess."

"Uhmm, your buddy Flip said close to two months."

"A month, two months…I'm really not sure."

"So, ya'll came into contact with Samad how? Flip says that you introduced them."

Dee sits back in a state of shock. Judging by the sound of things, Flip has been saying a lot. He's thrown him under the bus several times already. "I mean, I don't know him like that. I just knew him from the neighborhood."

"Oh yeah? Flip says ya'll are childhood friends. Listen, I'm gone be completely honest with you. We got everything we need to finish all of ya'll off. No question about that," he says with determination. "We already know what role everybody played in ya'll organization."

"Our organization?" Dee asks in a high pitch voice. "I ain't a part of no organization."

"Oh yes, you are," the agent says with an evil grin on his face. "The only thing left for you to do is admit to the part you played in this and hope for the best plea or you can deny all of this and go to trial. Flip already told us that you only made one thousand dollars profit apiece per kilo. Your attorney fee can start at one hundred thousand dollars. I know you can't afford that because our records don't show you selling a hundred kilos. You're not snitching on him. You're just admitting to the part that you played in all of this, so you can avoid being dragged into all the mess that he's created that you had nothing to do with. Understand?"

Dee sits back thinking it all over before replying. "Yeah, I understand," he says with sadness in his eyes. He's never imagined being in this type of situation.

"It all benefits you in the long run. I'm going home to my wife and children regardless of what decision you make. Your future is in your hands. I just don't want to see you jam yourself up for life when you could have helped yourself. It's on you though," he says as if he has no concern at all. The agent can look in Dee's eyes and tell that he's ready to cooperate. "So, if you had to put a number on the amount of kilos that you purchased from Samad, how many would you say? I tell you what. Just own up to the ten kilos ya'll purchased and ya'll will be charged accordingly for only your actions and not his. Ten kilos can get you about seventy years." The agent is now playing mind games with Dee. He knows he never purchased ten kilos but by throwing the high number out there Dee will have no problem admitting to what he really did purchase.

"Ten kilos? I ain't never had ten kilos! I ain't never seen ten kilos. The most I seen was one and he fronted that to us on consignment." The agent sits back laughing to himself as Dee does just what he hoped he would do. "That only happened once. The other few times he only gave us a half a kilo at a time."

"Oh, ok. So about how many times did ya'll get half a kilos from him?"

"Only like four times."

"Ok," the agent says. "Four half a kilos equals two kilos. And the one whole kilo, equals three kilos altogether, right? Ok, so," he says as he starts writing. "Let's just say guilty of purchasing kilos in the quantity of no less then three but amount not exceeding five. Fair? That's a lot better than ten right?" he asks as he hands the paper over to Dee. "Put your signature on the bottom." Dee reads it carefully and signs his name on the line. He passes the paper back to the agent. "See, that wasn't that bad now was it? I'm not against you. I'm here to help you."

▰▰▰▰▰ CHAPTER 162 ▰▰▰▰▰

Later that Day. Off the Chain sits in the interrogation room. He's bitten all his fingernails and now he's biting the cuticles. The pressure he feels right now, he's never felt in all of his years of doing crime. Throughout his many run ins with the law he's never bumped heads with the Feds. The majority of his cases were petty robberies. With his criminal jacket he's sure anything that they charge him with can finish him off for life.

The agent slams a photo on the table. Off the Chain recognizes the woman immediately. "Attempted murder and tampering of a witness," the agent says. "That's a minimum of fifteen years for the attempted murder and another twenty years for tampering with the witness." He slams another photo face up. Off the Chain recognizes this face as well. It's the Blood Homie, Bullet. "Murder," the agent says. "Another thirty years to life.," he says before he slams another photo down. This photo is of D-Nice. "Murder!" he shouts. "Another thirty to life," he says before slamming another photo onto the table.

Off the Chain sits there in confusion as he thinks of who this photo can be. He's guilty of everything the agent has said so far but that's where it stops. He hasn't done anything outside of that. He stares at the photo of a man that he has never seen in his life. This photo is of Rahiem. After finding Rahiem's body, they automatically suspected Off the Chain for this murder as well.

The agent finally speaks. "Ya'll must have known that we were coming for him next, huh? Ya'll are a lot sharper than we figured. I must admit," he says with a smile. "Murder!" he says as he taps the photo. "That's another thirty to life," he says as he pulls out a calculator and starts punching numbers into it. "Whoa, unless you're a cat with nine lives, you can't do enough living to finish all this time off. You're looking at a minimum of 135 years to life. How old are you?"

"Twenty-seven."

"Let's say that you're lucky enough to make it to ninety. Nah, that will never happen. You don't take care of yourself. You been drinking and drugging all of your life. So, let's say you live to be sixty. You can do your thirty-three years. You have a daughter, right? She can do seventy-five years. Then there will still be twenty-seven years left for your grandchild to do before they're eligible for parole. Wow! That's a lot of time, right? You're going to die in prison."

Off the Chain sits there in shock at the numbers that play in his mind.

"We have evidence proving that you're guilty of all the murders and shootings. There's no getting around that. Ya'll will never be able to beat this. Trust me when I tell you. Don't even consider trial because you don't have the money that it will take to get legal representation. Even if you did, all the money in the world can't save you right now. Only one thing can save you right now. You know what that is?"

Off the Chain opens his eyes wide. "What?" he whispers.

"You," the agent says as he points to Off the Chain. "Only you can save you at this point. You're guilty of the murders. You know it and we know it. We have all the proof too. 'You ready? I was born ready,' the agent says mimicking Off the Chain. "Sound familiar to you?"

Off the Chain knows exactly what he's talking about. Samad asked him that question right before he hopped out and shot the woman that night. He now realizes that they do know what they say they know. Suddenly he gets the feeling that Samad may be trying to flip on him. Motherfucker," he mumbles to himself. "Oh this mufucker trying to put it all on me?" he whispers to himself.

"Cooperation is the key to your success. If you don't cooperate that will be the key to your demise. Admit to the murders that we already know you did and state that Samad ordered and paid you to commit them. You help us and we will help you. That 135 years will be reduced drastically. Less than sixty years old and you will be a free man again. You will be an old man but at least you will be free," he says with a smile. "That's better than dying in prison. It's up to you," he says as he hands the ball point pen over to Off the Chain. "You gonna sign?"

Off the Chain stares at the pen as his mind runs wild. He would hate to do another day in jail. He's been going back and forth to prison all of his life. The reason he even hooked up with Samad was because he hoped the position he was given would keep him out of the spotlight while also keeping food on his table. The sad part is, dealing with Samad is the biggest mistake he could have ever made. If he knew this would be a part of his job he would have continued on with the petty crime that he's always committed. Just to think he was in jail with such a low bail and couldn't make it. Now he realizes that everything happens for a reason. For the first time in his life he wishes he was still in jail. This wouldn't be happening to him. This mufucker done got me in some bullshit, he thinks to himself. He dragged me right into a Fed beef. I ain't have nothing to do with this shit. I can't take the weight for the shit he had going on before me. "Psst," he sighs. Thoughts of cooperating fill his mind but he quickly erases them. "If you already know everything why you need me?"

"We're just trying to save you by giving you the chance to save yourself. Everyone else is saving themselves."

"That's why they're them and I'm me," Off the Chain replies arrogantly.

"So, what are you saying?" the agent asks.

"I'm saying I ain't built like that," he says while staring the agent directly in the eyes. He realizes that this statement is going to cost him dearly but he has no alternative. If he rolls over he will never be able to live with himself. "I take mines on the chin."

"Ok, have it your way," the agent says sarcastically. "I hope you have a strong chin."

///// CHAPTER 163 /////

One Hour Later

Samad sits before the agents once again in the interrogation room. They both sit in front of him side by side like a tag team. Neither of them have said a word in the ten minutes that they've been sitting in here. They both stare at the many papers that are stacked up in their files.

The black agent looks into Samad's eyes without blinking. "Samad Brown," he sings. "What a messy situation you've gotten yourself into. The walls have caved in on you. As ya'll kids say, 'It's a wrap!' he says with a smile. "I see you hired Angelique Reed as your attorney," he says nodding his head up and down. "She's definitely one of the best in the business but even she can't help you. My advice to you is to not even spend a dime on attorney's fees. It can't do you any good. There's not a single crack or crevice for you to crawl through. If I was you I would request death by lethal injection," he teases. "Let me ask you what is it that you hope to get out of all of this? You can't possibly believe that you will ever see the streets again, do you? Huh? Well, let me clear up any doubt that you may have in your mind. You will never see the streets again! You're finished, you heard?" he says in mockery of Samad. "We have informants that have signed statements admitting the purchase of kilos from you. They are now Federal witnesses. Not like Deborah Miles was on the state beef you caught. You know, the murder of the two men on the block?" he asks. "Well, who are you going to call now? Your man

Off the Chain is here with you. He can't answer the call. He's been such a help to us," he lies. "And because of that we plan to take special care of him. He's such a gentleman. He's admitted to us that you paid him for the attempted murder of Deborah Miles, the murder of Bullet and the murder of your good friend D-Nice. Damn Samad...D-Nice? How could you? Ya'll were closer than brothers. Oh and last but not least, Rahiem, D-nice's cousin. We found his dead body laying in the middle of the street. You get more and more treacherous each time," he smiles.

Samad sits back without a clue of what the agent is talking about. He didn't even know that Rahiem had been murdered. Damn, how could Off the Chain say he ordered him to do that when he didn't know anything about the murder.

"And poor Shakirah over there on 15th Avenue. Luckily we got hold of Off the Chain before he made it over to the kennel," he says in mockery to the nonsense code that Samad thought he was talking in. "Had we not got hold of him she would have been dead as well," he says while shaking his head from side to side. "Poor girl. Ya'll been together for so long, she says. She can't believe that you would have her murdered. When we told her that she had no problem telling us everything we needed to know. Oh that sixty thousand that she was holding for you, don't worry about it. It's in good hands now...our hands," he smiles. "You were right when thinking that she was avoiding your calls. She admitted that she had seventy thousand but she blew through ten thousand of it. She figured you didn't need it because you were never coming home. Damn, Shakirah...a thief? Hard to believe that after all these years that she held drugs, guns and money for you, right?" he says in a teasing manner. He looks into Samad's eyes as Samad sits there stunned. "Yeah, she told us everything. Who can you trust in a situation like this? Let me answer that question for you. No one," he says. "Absolutely no one. It's now every man and woman for themselves. Right here, right now, I'm going to give you the chance to play hero. Rescue yourself just like all your co-defendants have rescued themselves. Everybody gave you up. Now you have the chance to give somebody up."

"Ain't nobody to give up," he mumbles.

"Not true, Samad. There's always someone to give up. Do yourself a favor. Give up the coach." Samad sits there in awe. He's shocked to hear that come out of the agent's mouth. "Who is he? Where is he?" Samad realizes that they have no idea who the coach is. They're just familiar with the term. "Samad, I'm not bluffing you. The last money you had is now in our possession. You're dead broke which means you can't afford to even pay your attorney. So, if you're smart, you will take a plea and don't even consider trial. You have three murders that you committed with your own hands. You paid for three more. That's six murders and one attempt. The murders alone will send you away forever. Let's not even talk about the drug charges, the guns and the money. You know?" he asks as he gets up from the table. He snatches his files and his partner gets up as well, following his lead. "You're in way too deep," he says as he walks away from the table. "There's really nothing that we can do to save you or nothing that you can do to save yourself. It's a wrap for you," he says as he grabs hold of the door. "Good day, Samad. See you in court."

"Hold up, hold up!" Samad shouts. Man fuck that, he says to himself. Everybody ain't just gone put everything on me. "Come on man, you gave everybody else a shot to help themselves. Let me get my shot?"

"It's senseless Samad, even if you gave us the big man it wouldn't do you that much good. I mean it could save you a couple of decades," he says as he reels Samad right into his trap.

Samad hesitates before replying. For once in his life his pride is nowhere to be found. The only thing on his mind right now is saving himself. "The big man?" he asks with sarcasm. "What makes you so sure it's a man?" he asks. He now has their full attention. "They say behind every strong man there stands a strong woman," he says with a smile. "Let's make a deal?"

///// CHAPTER 165 /////

Days Later. Deja sits back in the hospital bed. Her face is bare with not a single piece of gauze on it. It's been like this for the past three days now. She has not a clue of what her face looks like because she hasn't had the heart to look into the mirror.

Three days ago her Miami man, Rick sat here and stared into her bare face. The sadness in his eyes told her that it must be an awful sight. The words that came out of his mouth were quite comforting. She can still hear what he said to her. 'Aw Ma, I was expecting it to be far worse off than that.' He downplayed it as if it was nothing but obviously it is something because he hasn't visited her since that day. Nor has he answered any of her calls.

Each and every time that she thinks of the fact that she lost the love of her life it breaks her heart. For the very first time she learned what it felt like to be in love. Just to think that this situation chased him away hurts her dearly.

Suddenly she gets the urge to see what exactly he ran away from. She reaches for the mirror which is in the nightstand. She slowly raises it up to her face as her heart thumps with fear. As she gets it halfway there, she stops. She's scared to go through with it. She gets the heart to do so and begins lifting it again. She closes her eyes before the mirror gets there.

Slowly she opens her better eye and when she does she wishes she was dead. What is before her eyes is the most hideous sight that she has ever seen. The pink transparent skin has patchy sores surrounding it. The left side of her face has been eaten away so badly that the bone structure protrudes boldly. The skin on her face is pink and scaly like the skin of a fish right now but the doctor says eventually it will regain some color back. The scaliness will eventually dry out but it will never go back to normal. At best her face will look like the face of a burn victim.

Her bad eye twitches consistently as the tears drip from it. She drops the mirror onto the floor, shattering it into tiny pieces. At this point she promises herself that she will never look in a mirror ever again. She sobs away like a baby. She can't believe that this has happened to her. She realizes that all the cosmetic surgery in the world will never get her face back to normal. For the rest of her life she will have to live with this face.

An hour later

After crying non stop Deja's tear well eventually went dry. It was then that she sat back and some real thoughts came into her mind. She wonders if this is God's way of punishing her. She promised him that she would never alter her body again after that bootleg booty job. He answered her prayers and brought her back to her original form and still she broke her promise to him. What did she do? She went to the Dominican Republic and got more work done. She's shown her ungratefulness over and over by altering the body that God loaned her to live this life with.

She's made so many changes that it's nothing like the original form that it was loaned to her in. She now regrets it more than ever and wishes she could turn back the hands of time. If she could she would still be the stick boney, flat chested, no booty having, buck tooth woman that she was meant to be.

At this time she would do anything to go back to looking like that woman but she can't so now she's forced to look like this. Her face is always going to be a reminder of her ungratefulness. Whether she likes it or not she knows that she has to accept it.

///// CHAPTER 165 /////

Days Later. Tony called Lil Bit hours ago, stating that it's urgent that they meet. The tone of his voice has her alarmed. She wonders what the emergency meeting is all about. She hopes for the best but she tries to prepare herself for the worst.

This is her first time in Jersey since the apartment situation. Hearing that the Feds want her for questioning has her worried out of her mind. She's been so nervous that she's been staying home. The only time she comes out is to visit Baby Ashley in the hospital. The Fed scare has her considering moving away from here as soon as the baby is released from the hospital.

The moment of truth is here. As Lil Bit sits inside the small booth in Johnny Rockets in Hoboken, Tony Austin rushes inside. He storms directly over to her booth. "Hey," she says.

With no verbal reply, he hands her an envelope. "Inside there's s a check for the fifty grand that you gave me. My partner and I are resigning from this job."

"Huh?" she asks with surprise. "What's the problem?"

"The problem is your girlfriend's dude. My reason for leaving the state of New Jersey is because the business is all screwed up. Nobody is playing fair anymore. Prosecutors are playing dirty, judges playing dirty and the niggas playing dirty. Nobody is standing up anymore. They get caught and they tell on everybody. It's like a game of tag to them. They get caught and automatically they tag someone else. You it!" he says mimicking a child. "I never represented a snitch and my partner doesn't either. Because I refuse to represent snitches my work here is limited. Everybody is telling. That's why I'm leaving from here to open up somewhere else where the epidemic hasn't taken over yet. Someplace where niggas are still standing up for themselves. It's all fucked up here in this town. I swear."

"So, what are you saying?"

"I'm saying that her guy is a rat...a snitch...a stool pidgeon. I want no parts of him. I refuse to defend him. You have your retainer back. Use it to hire another attorney who has no problem with that. There are so many who don't care. I'm out."

A snitch, she repeats to herself. Snitch on who. He doesn't know anyone to snitch on, she believes. She was careful to keep him in the dark totally. She finally speaks. "Who did he snitch on?" Before he answers her, she gets an answer of her own. Now she understands why the Feds came to her apartment. Not once did that come into her mind. She was under the assumption that they must have tapped his phone and found out that she was his girlfriend. She figured they wanted to come to her home to see what he had laying around and maybe question her about some things. It's all coming together now.

"Her name is Latoya Baker?"

Lil Bit hears her name and she damn near faints in front of him. "Latoya Baker? Who is she?" Lil Bit asks as she attempts to throw him off.

"I don't know but she's in deep trouble. The rat bastard claims that she's the supplier of the organization. He's given detail after detail. He's cooperating to the fullest."

Lil Bit can not belive what she's hearing. A rat, she says to herself. And he's ratting on me, his daughter's mother. How could he? I'm the only person that was there for him when he was down. I took his broke ass in and took him to the next level and this is how he repays me? Suddenly Deja's words play in her ears. 'You need to leave that broke motherfucker right there on the street corner that you met him on. He's not on your level.' Lil Bit always knew that he wasn't a born hustler but she felt like he could be groomed. She always felt like he was a kindergarten kid in this game. She doesn't realize that all of this is her fault. Knowledge of this game comes in phases and it can't be learned in a few months. Samad was a kid in this game put in to a grown man's position. She skipped him to the top level so fast that she never got the chance to see what he was really made of. Now look, she's found out what he's made of; nothing but pure jelly. "A snitch?" she says with disgust.

"Yeah, a snitch. "Whoever Latoya Baker is she better get away from here. The Feds are coming for her, if they haven't already gotten hold of her."

Oh, they ain't got her yet, she says to herself. But she's about to get far away though. As soon as Ashley is out of the hospital we're out of here, she tells herself. Trust and believe that!

///// CHAPTER 166 /////

Two Months Later. Lil Bit steps out of Deja's Audi looking tremendously fashionable. She hasn't felt this beautiful in so long. Her weight has dropped back to the normal 120 pounds that she weighed most of her life. The baby hasn't left any unwanted weight but it left Lil Bit with just the right amount of butt and hips that she always wanted.

She lifts the seat up and grabs hold of the babyseat that sits in the back. Baby Ashley has been out of the hospital for a few weeks now and she's doing just fine. It feels good to actually be traveling around with her pride and joy. Too bad she can't travel the land freely as she would like to. The Fed scare has her walking on pins and needles.

The only time she comes to Jersey is to see Deja who is in a state of serious depression right now. At times they fear that she may even commit suicide. She can't live with what her face has become. Lil Bit tries her hardest to be supportive of Deja but right now she has her own dilemma going on and she can barely think straight.

Lil Bit's only reason for coming here today is because Deja needed her to come and pick up the rent money from the girls. They've been working rent free ever since her accident. Lil Bit hated to do it but still she accepted the chore. If she hadn't the girls would have worked rent free for much longer because Deja has no plans of coming out of her home anytime soon. She's too embarrassed to face the world like that so she just stays trapped up in the house drowning in her sorrows. Lil Bit realizes how much of a gamble she's taking by coming here. Samad is well aware of the location of the beauty parlor. She wonders if he told them that too. She hasn't heard from him since Tony broke the news to her. He has no way to contact her because she changed phone numbers. She considers him dead.

Before Lil Bit backs out of the car, she pulls her dark colored wig snug over her head. She then fixes her enormous sunglasses before backing out of the car. She slams the door with one hand as she carries Baby Ashley's car seat in the other hand. She peeks around cautiously as she steps toward the beauty parlor. She hopes her disguise throws them off just in case they are watching.

Lil Bit steps foot into the beauty parlor for the first time in a long time. What she sees before her eyes frustrates her to no end. The music is blasting louder than it's ever been blasted in here. Also the type of music has changed. Hip hop was never allowed to be played in the shop and today they're playing it. Not only is hip hop pouring out of the speakers, they're breaking another golden rule as well. Hip hop videos are being shown on each flat screen in the room.

Lil Bit looks around and notices another big no, no. Three toddlers run back and forth up the aisle and behind the stations as if they're in a park. She then looks to her right, where three young men lay back with their feet on the waiting chairs as if they're in the comfort of their own home.

The lack of Deja's presence has caused this shop to go out of control. It's obvious that the girls have lost their mind. Lil Bit looks at Rhonda who has taken over Deja's chair as if it belongs to her. This takes Lil Bit by total surprise. She stands there fuming. The room becomes tense as all the attention is now on her and Baby Ashley. "Ay, Lil Bit," Rhonda says with joy. She's hoping to break the ice. "Ooh, let me see your baby," she says as she snatches the baby out of Lil Bit's arms. "Ooh, she's so adorable. She quickly gets out of the way of the hurricane that is approaching. She carries the baby a few steps away. As she hides behind the baby she gives the rest of the people in the shop the signal to straighten up but they don't catch it.

Lil Bit snatches the remotes off of the first work station. First she shuts off the music and then the television.

"Yo!" one man has the audacity to yell to her.

Rhonda shakes her head negatively but he isn't paying the least bit of attention to her. She sees the look on Lil Bit's face and can tell that all hell is about to break loose.

"Yo, what?" Lil Bit barks.

"Turn that back on!" he demands.

"Make me turn it back on."

He looks at the girl in the middle station who is giving him the sign to stop while he's ahead. "Psst," he says. "Somebody better tell her something."

"No, I'm about to tell you something. Get the fuck out!" she shouts while looking around the room. "You, you and you, let's go," she says pointing to all the men in the room. "Out! Go." They get up and drag along slowly toward the door while staring into her eyes viciously.

The three toddlers circle her. One of them grabs hold of her legs. She looks down with signs of agitation. "Who kids are these?"

One girl bashfully raises her hand. "Mines," she whispers.

Another girl stands up. Instead of owning up to her child, she shouts. "Justin, come here," she says as if Lil Bit is in the wrong.

"Uh, who customers are those?" Lil Bit asks. No one owns up to them. All the girls watch in suspense of what is about to happen. "Ya'll getting ya'll hair done?" They both shake their heads negatively with nasty looks on their faces. "No babies are allowed in here and no hanging around if you're not getting your hair done. Leave please," she says as politely as she possibly can at this point. They both get up in a hasty manner. They grab hold of their children and step up the aisle.

"No babies allowed and she walked in with a fucking baby," one girl whispers.

"Excuse me?" Lil Bit says.

"I said you walked in with a baby," she says as she grabs hold of the door.

"That's my business and this is my business. That fucking baby owns this shop," she says as she presses the buzzer. "Bye, go!"

All the unwanted visitors are now on the outside of the shop looking inside with rage. Lil Bit feels slightly uncomfortable with them out there but still she keeps her game face on. "And ya'll," she says to the girls who work in the shop. "What the hell ya'll doing in here? Ya'll done bumped ya'll heads? This is a place of business. Not no fucking club."

Twenty Minutes Later. The shop is back in working order. Lil Bit has given them a big speech and she hopes that they're back on track. She's also collected the rent that Deja sent her to collect.

Lil Bit takes a quick peek outside of the shop. Everyone that she's kicked out is still standing out there in the parking lot. She feels quite uneasy about their presence which is why she's called Sade to come just in case things get out of hand. Sade isn't much of a fighter but all Lil Bit needs is for her to hold the baby for her if she has to scrap. She doesn't trust not one of these girls in this shop to watch her back.

Her phone rings. When she looks down at her phone and sees Sade's number that's her cue to leave. "Rhonda!" she shouts. "Hello?" Sade on the other end of the phone tells Lil Bit that she's right around the corner.

Rhonda comes running out of the office with the baby still glued to her chest. She passes Baby Ashley off to her carefully. "Lil Bit, can I keep her? Please?" she begs with a smile. "I have fallen in love with her already. She's so adorable."

"Yeah, come get her adorable ass when she crying all damn night and I can't get no damn sleep," she says with humor. She quickly sits the baby into the car seat and buckles her down. "Alright ya'll, I will be back tomorrow and I expect to see business as usual," she bluffs them knowing damn well that she's not coming anywhere near here. She steps toward the door.

"Lil Bit, here," Rhonda says. "I didn't give you my money." Lil Bit stands at the door as she trots over to her. She passes the money over to her. Bye, Ashley," she waves as she's backpedaling up the aisle.

"Somebody buzz me out." The buzzer sounds off and Lil Bit steps out of the shop. They all watch with satisfaction as she steps toward Deja's car.

"Bitch!" the girl on the end says.

"You can say that again," Rhonda confirms as she waves to Lil Bit one more time. The smile that is glued to her face is of pure phoniness.

The girl does just as Rhonda has told her to do. She says it once again but with more meaning this time. "Bitch!"

Lil Bit places the car seat on the roof of the car. The baby is screaming her head off. "Ok, ok girl, shhhh. I ain't gone be carrying your little spoiled butt all the time," she says as she snatches the passenger's side door open. As she lifts the seat up, the baby's pacifier falls onto the ground. She quickly bends over to pick it up. As she's down there she sees another set of feet directly behind hers. The Nike ACG Boots alarm her. She quickly stands up. She turns around totally on guard for anything that is about to happen. As she's turning her head, she catches a glimpse of the one thing that she is not on gaurd for. There she stands face to face with who but the Stalker. A bright orange glare blinds her before she hears, Boc! The loud sound rings in her ear, somewhat deafening her. A big gust of wind blows in her face before the slug crashes into her cheekbone. She stumbles backwards until her head slams into the roof of the car. Her body drops limply onto the ground. Boc! Boc! She lays there motionless. He kicks her up the ass to check for any sign of resistance but there is none.

The Stalker looks to the crying baby and he immediately thinks of the $33,000 reward that the baby has on her head. He peeks around cautiously as he lifts his gun in the air. The baby is now shouting louder than ever. He aims the gun as he stares into her eyes. The beautiful set of emerald green eyes hypnotizes him, causing him to melt into a trance. He tries to pull the trigger but he can't do it.

Right now he finds out that he's not as cold as he always thought he was. He was totally prepared to kill her, knowing that she was pregnant but he never expected to have to actually shoot the baby. He takes off into flight and almost disappears into thin air like a magician.

The girls all stand in the shop watching in shock; all except Rhonda. She watches with joy as Lil Bit lies on the ground leaking like an old faucet, while her baby screams terribly. "Call the ambulance!" the middle girl screams with terror.

Rhonda's satisfaction comes from the fact that she's just orchestrated this entire episode. Job well done, she tells herself. She's sure the top spot belongs to her now. While in the office she deviously called Maurice who immediately called the Stalker.

Sirens sound off from every direction. Rhonda watches as the police and ambulances zip into the parking lot. She cracks a devilish smile. "Too late."

///// CHAPTER 167 /////

One Week Later. Maurice and the Stalker are sitting in Maurice's pick up truck. On Maurice's lap there sits the Newark Star Ledger. He's been reading this newspaper faithfully everyday in search of valuable information. To date he hasn't seen a word in reference to it.

He sat there and witnessed what he thought was Lil Bit's murder. He was there parked on the side street and saw with his own two eyes the Stalker stand over her emptying shots into her. It broke his heart to watch it but it was something that had to be done.

He looks through the newspaper everyday in search of details of the homicide or her obituary or something but nothing has been in the paper yet. He's starting to wonder why.

"It's in there?" the Stalker asks desperately. He's been here on hold for way too long now. He's ready to get back home but Maurice refuses to break him off a dime until he finds out what is exactly going on.

"Nah, nothing. I can't figure this shit out for nothing."

Meanwhile

Sade sits on the edge of the bed as Lil Bit suddenly makes a move for the first time since she laid splattered on the pavement in the parking lot. Sade's eyes light up with joy.

The ventilator mask is snuggled over Lil Bit's mouth and nose to help her breathe. She's been hooked to the life support machine ever since she's been in here. Sade watches with happiness as Lil Bit's swollen, blackened eyes crack open slightly.

Through the cloudy vision Lil Bit spots Sade standing there. Sade grabs her hand and squeezes it tightly. "I knew you would pull through it, baby. I knew it. You're a fighter. You been fighting all of your life," she says as the tears fall from her eyes. "Baby, I knew it."

Lil Bit would love to say something but she can't muster up the strength to do so. Everything is groggy to her right now. She sees Sade standing here and she realizes that she's laying in a hospital bed hooked up to machines but her memory is not serving her properly. She has no clue of why she's here or how long she's been here. It's all so unclear right now.

She closes her eyes and suddenly a vision of the Stalker's face flashes through her mind. She now stares down the barrel of a gun before the loud boom sounds off in her ears. A bright amber flash blows up in her face before everything goes blank. She can still smell the fragrance of the burning gunsmoke. Everything goes into a blur once again until she remembers a short ambulance ride. The paramedics stand around her. "She's back," the paramedic says. We got a pulse. Hurry, Johnny, hurry." Lil Bit can hear her clearly. The noise in the ambulance is chaotic. The paramedics are shouting at the top of their lungs. The sound of two different people crying makes her look to her left. There she sees Sade sitting, while crying louder than the newborn baby is that she holds in her arms. It's all coming back to her. "My baby," she utters undernerath the ventilator. "Where is my baby?" she asks as she squeezes Sade's hand to get her attention. "Where's Baby Ashley?"

"Don't worry. My mother has her. She's good. We gone take care of her. You just get yourself together so we can get you out of this hospital," she says as she leans over and hugs Lil Bit.

"I Love you," Lil Bit grunts.

"I love you too."

///// CHAPTER 168 /////

Two Months Later. Lil Bit has been out of the hospital for over six weeks. She laid up in the comfort of her own home until she was completely healed. She thanks God everyday that he brought her back to life. Three shots close range and miraculously she's lived to talk about it. The bullet holes that sit on her chest a few inches away from her heart are a constant reminder of how grateful she should be. The most noticeable wound by far is the deep, nickel sized dimple that sets in her left cheek. The dimple gives her a permanent smirk. The dimple and the constant blinking of her left eye, she considers minute. The worst result of the shooting is the constant ringing in her ears that she hears from time to time and the loss of partial hearing in her left ear. Outside of that she's good and now is the perfect time to make her move.

Lil Bit is in full disguise with her blonde wig, red lipstick and big baggy clothes. She steps nervously throughout Newark Airport as Sade follows a few feet behind. Lil Bit holds Baby Ashley in one arm and the baby bag in the other. After struggling through the crowds of people she finally makes it to her departing airline.

She steps up to the counter where she hands two tickets over to the woman.

"Beautiful Hawaii, huh?" the woman asks.

"Yep," she replies. Finally she's making her trip to Hawaii. These were never the terms that she wanted to go under though.

"Boy, do I envy you right now," she says with a smile. Lil Bit smiles back at her in return. "That's such a beautiful baby," she says. "What's her name," she asks as she reads from the ticket. "Let me guess. Hey, Ashley. Can I get your ID please?"

Lil Bit digs ino the baby bag and retrieves her ID. She hands it to the woman as requested. As she lays it down, she realizes that she's laid down the wrong ID. This one says Latoya Baker. Her heart beats like a drum. She quickly snatches the ID just as the woman is reaching for it. "I'm sorry that one is expired," she lies as she digs into the bag once again. She quickly locates the right one this time. "Phew," she sighs as she puts the other ID back into her wallet.

"Thank you, Miss Jones. Ok, Flight 347, to your right, straight ahead. It's the first ramp," she says as she hands the tickets and identification back to Lil Bit.

Lil Bit steps away from the counter and Sade catches up with her. Tears are already building in Sade's eyes. It feels as if she's losing her best friend. She hates to see her leave but she understands that this is best for her. She can either love her from afar, or she can visit her in jail for the rest of their lives, or even worse, visit her grave on her birthday and holidays. Hands down, going away to Hawaii is the best possible answer. "I'm gone miss you, girl," Sade says.

"We gone miss each other," she replies with tears in her eyes. "It's not forever though. As soon as the coast is clear, I'm coming back. I promise you we will be back. Just not no time soon," she whispers as the tears fall from her eyes.

"Just know that I'm always here for you," Sade says. "As soon as you get there, you call me, ok? You know you can count on me. I will wire you your money on every first of the month just as you said. You know your money is good with me. I will not touch a dime of it."

"Girl, you know I'm not worried about that. It's only money. I trust you with my life. And if you need something feel free to use what you need. Your problems are my problems. You've always been there for me when no one else has been."

"That's what real friendship is all about," Sade says as they reach the gate. As soon as Lil Bit stops Sade bear hugs her and the baby as tight as she can. They hug each other until their shoulders are soaked with tears. "I love you," Lil Bit says.

"I love you too," Sade replies as she backs away from them.

Lil Bit quickly looks away to prevent from backing out of this flight. She spins around without looking in Sade's direction. Sade watches as Lil Bit steps down the corridor. As she's walking she fumbles through the baby bag and grabs hold of her wallet. As she flings it open, on both sides there sits an ID with a picture of herself staring up at her. One reads Latoya Baker and the other reads Amber Jones. She grabs the one that belongs to Latoya Baker and snatches it from the wallet.

Four steps away there lies a huge garbage can. As she steps closer, she peeks around with caution. As she's passing the garbage, she sneakily drops the ID into the can. She turns around where she sees Sade watching her closely. She raises her hand high in the air, waving slowly. "Farewell."

//// CHAPTER 169 ////

In Philadelphia. A group of Federal Agents stand in a huge warehouse. The warehouse is filled with nothing but cars. A loud buzzer sounds off and one of the agents hits a button on the remote garage door opener. The huge steel gate opens slowly. They all watch as the unmarked car cruises into the warehouse. The agent quickly hits the remote and the gate starts to close.

The driver of the unmarked car pulls up close to them, where he parks. Two men hop out and step toward the huddle of men. "Everything ready to go?" the lead agent asks as the men step into the huddle.

"Yes Sir," he replies.

"Good. Okay here it is," he says as he hands a small stack of paperwork over to the passenger of the vehicle. "There's a group of about thirty men. All of their photos are in that file you're holding. They call themselves 'The Cocaine Cowboys' emulating an organization that controlled the cocaine market many years ago. These men control the entire North Side of Philly but they trickle out into every other part. They even have small branches in Delaware and Baltimore. Together they make up over seventy five percent of the murder rate on the North Side. Their drug trade consists of cocaine and heroin. The leader, right here," he says as points to a photo. They all stare at the paper. "Shawn Bennett, has been leading this crime family for five years. He first started the organization when he was in jail serving a six year term. In 2005, he gained control by murdering one of the biggest suppliers," he says as he shows them the photo of the man who was in control. Their operation is estimated at more than a million dollars a week. Needless to say that it's up to us to bust this operation up," he says as he stares at them.

"Lance, it's all on you. You are our in," he says as hands the next stack of papers over to him. "Tomorrow is our day. I expect you all up bright and early in the morning. So until then, good night men. Lance come with me," he says as he leads him to the far end of the garage.

He hits the remote and the alarm sounds off. They keep walking until they reach the beautitiful black on black Audi R8. "Here are the keys," he says as he tosses them to him. "The tape has been reset and ready to roll all over again," he says as he snatches the passenger's door open. He grabs hold of a small bag. "Here," he says as he hands the bag over. "Here are the keys to every vehicle in the warehouse. I don't have to tell you to use your discretion unless I tell you otherwise. "The tracking systems have been set on all of them. All the recording devices are ready for taping as well. Tomorrow morning we meet at the Dunkin Donuts, we wire you up and start our day. With all that said, the city is yours!"

The man nods his head up and down without uttering a word. He makes his way around to the the driver's seat of the Audi. "Hold up," the agent says. "I almost forgot," he says as he digs into his front pocket. "Give me that old ID." The man digs into his wallet and he passes his ID to the man. The agent looks at the ID momentarily. "Michael Stafford," he smiles. "A.K.A Mike the rent-a-car dude," he says mimicking the nickname Samad gave him. "No more Mike. Now you're

Richard Jennings," he says with a smile. The man smiles as he grabs hold of the new ID.

He hops into the driver's seat. As soon as he starts the car up, Samad's favorite Young Jeezy song 'Crazy World' plays at top volume. "You're going back to jail that's what my conscience keeps on telling me. I really ain't buying the bullshit they selling me when the government throwing more curves then the letter C," the man sings along as he bops his head to the beat. "They trying to box me in, sit me still like a vegetable. Got damn another trap! I think Bush is trying to punish us, send a message to each and every one of us! Real Gee shit, that's really unheard of when you get more time for selling dope than you get for murder! In this crazy world!" he sings as he pulls off slowly.

The agent watches as Black Beauty cruises out of the garage. Yes, the same Black Beauty that Samad spent close to $115,000 for, another $25,000 for Mike to put it in his company's name, and an additional $20,000 to get his name added onto the top of the list. The only difference is when Samad had it there were Pennsylvania license plates on it. It now has Florida plates.

Samad may not have gotten his full money's worth out of it but the Feds will work it to the best of their benefit. It's the perfect vehicle for 'Richard Jennings' to make his introduction into the city of Philadelphia. They just hope that the vehicle is enticing enough to cause people to gravitate to him.

Whoever the car doesn't bring in, his female accomplice will. Michelle Barnes at one time was a Real Estate Broker who really made her living off of fraudulent house deals. When the Feds finally caught up with her a few months ago she offered them something that she claimed was bigger. In exchange for her freedom she told them that she's willing to give up her biggest client who happens to be Kingpin, Shawn Bennett.

She's known Shawn Bennett for years and they have done a great deal of property business together. She says he trusts her wholeheartedly which makes it all the easier. She's already planted the seeds to this operation by telling Shawn Bennett about her boyfriend from Miami who has kilos for a low price. With the cocaine drought going on it was easy to get him to bite onto the bait. At this very moment, he's waiting for her boyfriend to get into town.

Mike the rent-a-car dude, now Richard Jennings was born as Lance Carter. Last year Lance Carter was caught up in a drug trafficking ring investigation. In the end he was recorded on over one thousand phone conversations, wire taps and all. Twenty other men were indicted with him. After being offered a plea of twenty years he was more than willing to cooperate. He started off by testifying against his own supplier and other dealers that he had formed a business alliance with. In exchange for the destruction of over twenty men's lives, his reward was the deduction of seventeen years off of his time. He traded in seventeen years of his own life for hundreds of years of other men's lives.

He did his job and thought it was all over but the Feds had something else in mind. They came up with a way that they can get the maximum benefit out of Lance Carter. Needless to say they have been getting that ever since. He travels from place to place disguising himself as whatever the Feds need him to be.

The last job was a little more difficult. The nerdy white collar rent a car employee was so out of his character and hard for him to play but he managed to pull it off. Throughout his short term there he managed to be responsible for the arrests of over two hundred men. Their charges range from drug and weapons charges to murder.

Samad was the biggest fish of them all. The sad part is the fact that he made it that way. The Feds sent their paid informant to Enterprise and disguised him as a regional employee because the insurance company made a complaint about all the accidents, murder and mayhem that was going on in their cars. The Feds looked at that like the opportunity to get in and get a grip of what was going on in the streets of Newark. They expected to land a few minor cases here and there that would lead to a bigger fish. Samad just happened to step in the way.

It's almost impossible for anyone of these men to fight their charges due to the tracking systems and tape recorders that each of his rental cars were equipped with. The recordings made it so sweet that they didn't need anybody to snitch. They all told on themselves as they ran their mouths in the rental cars.

Deep down inside, Mike a.ka. Lance, a.k.a. Richard Jennings is looking forward to his new assignment. Now he will be totally in character as he plays a cocaine dealer from Miami. After all, cocaine has always been his passion. He never gave it up because he wanted to. He gave it up because he was forced to. The love of the game still exists in his heart and if this is how he has to play it, he plans to make the best of it.

To remain a free man he will do whatever the Feds need him to do. He will play as a decoy on any assignment, in any city, in any state.

Be on the lookout because your hood could be next!

THE END

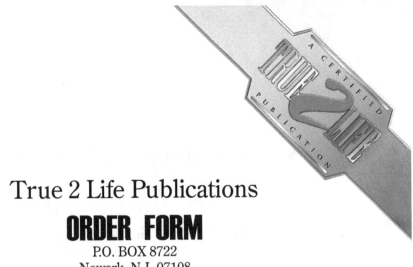

True 2 Life Publications

ORDER FORM

P.O. BOX 8722
Newark, N.J. 07108

www.True2LifeProductions.com
Also by the Author:

No Exit
ISBN # 0-974-0610-0-X $13.95
Sales Tax (6% NJ)   .83
Total $18.63

Caught 'Em Slippin'
ISBN # 0-974-0610-3-4 $14.95
Sales Tax (6% NJ)   .89
Total $19.69

Block Party
ISBN # 0-974-0610-1-8 $14.95
Sales Tax (6% NJ)   .89
Total $19.69

Block Party 2: The Afterparty
ISBN # 0-974-0610-4-2 $14.95
Sales Tax (6% NJ)   .89
Total $19.69

Sincerely Yours
ISBN # 0-974-0610-2-6 $13.95
Sales Tax (6% NJ)   .83
Total $18.63

Block Party 3: Brick City Massacre
ISBN: 0-974-0610-5-0 $14.95
Sales Tax (6% NJ)   .89
Total $19.69

Strapped
ISBN: 0-974-0610-6-1 $14.95
Sales Tax (6% NJ)   .89
Total $19.69

Shipping/ Handling for 1 -3 books
Via U.S. Priority Mail $ 3.85

Each additional book is $1.00

Buy 6 or More Books and Shipping is Free.

True 2 Life Publications

P.O. BOX 8722
Newark, N.J. 07108

www.True2LifeProductions.com

PURCHASER INFORMATION

Name:_____

Address:_____

City:_____

State:_____

Zip Code:_____

Books

No Exit:_____

Block Party: _____

Sincerely Yours: _____

Caught 'Em Slippin': _____

Block Party 2
The Afterparty:_____

Block Party 3
Brick City Massacre: _____

HOW MANY BOOKS?_____

Strapped: _____

Make checks/money orders payable to:

True 2 Life Publications

Printed in the USA
CPSIA information can be obtained
at www.ICGtesting.com
LVHW051115070324
773826LV00020B/200